SLAVE

—— TO ——

ICE & SHADOWS

I'd like to dedicate this book to myself, and to my inner Odele. Who no one really likes, but who is a wonderful snack, anyway.

This book is a slow burn why choose/polyamorous story where the harem is slowly, **emphasis on slowly**, introduced to the FMC.

P.S. Story may contain content unsuitable for readers under the age of 18.

Pronunciation Guide

Thalassar: Tal-uh-sahr

Kappur: Kay-purr

Draconi: Dray-cone-e

Iol: Yo-l

Ventlair: Vent-lair

Gvulis: Vool-liss

Brague: Bra-aag

Eramaea: Era-may-uh

Malabella: Mahl-ah-beh-yaw

Oriana: Or-ee-ah-nuh
Ytgar: Eet-gahrr
Valmundur: Val-mone-doorrr (heavy R roll)
Odalaea: O-dah-lay-uh
Anneli: A-nah-lee
Neves: Nev-ehs
Isolde: Ee-zohl-day
Ingen: In-ehn
Aelfrost: Ale-frost
Amelia: Uh-mail-yuh
Cerul: See-role
Ysengart: I-sin-guart
Ezarah: Ee-zarr-ah
Evander: Evan-derr

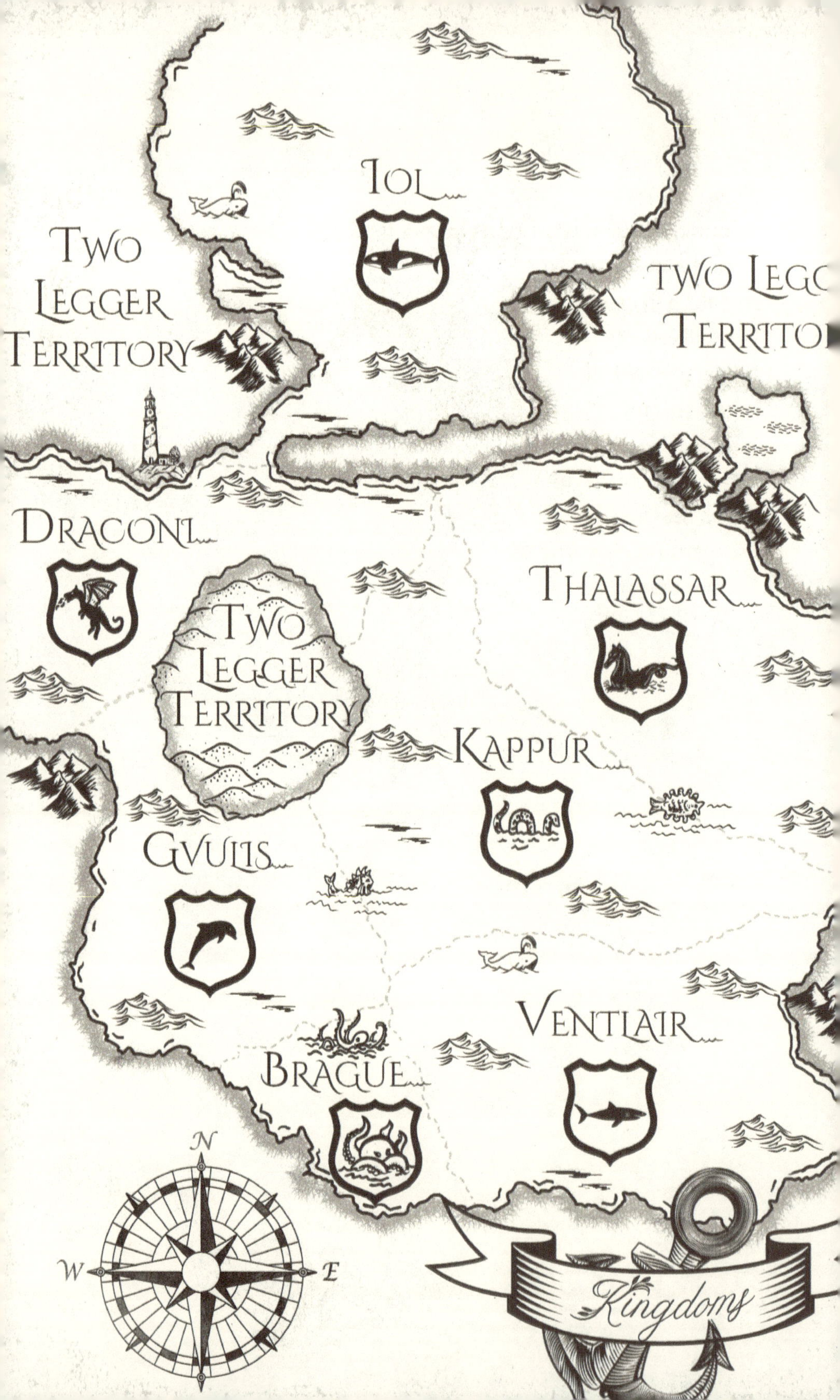

IOL
TWO LEGGER TERRITORY
TWO LEGGER TERRITORY
DRACONI
TWO LEGGER TERRITORY
THALASSAR
KAPPUR
GVULIS
VENTLAIR
BRAGUE
N
W
E
Kingdoms

"My life is over. Positively, dreadfully, and irrevocably *over*." I sniffled, dabbing at my eyes before I continued. "If you find this, remember me. Think of me. For I travel to waters unknown, where I am to be a slave, nothing more than a vessel between one kingdom and another. Though, I confess, I would rather throw myself into the mouth of Prince Kai's dragon than set out on this current forced before me. What an appealing thought. Yes. I have decided. I cannot continue to live in this cruel, cruel world. So by the time you find this, know that I will be long gone—"

"Odele!"

I was startled by the sound of my chamber door opening and closing loudly. I nearly dropped the recording conch I was holding up to my face to capture my disquisition. I gripped it tightly in my trembling fingers, taking a deep, settling breath. This was to be my last conch ever recorded, the final evidence of my unhappiness. It was supposed to be grand, and dramatic, but someone had *interrupted*.

Not *just* someone.

My cousin.

"What are you doing?" Odalaea asked with curious amusement, plopping herself on the bed next to me. In fact, her name was Maisie. Well, it wasn't her *given* name. The name given to her at birth had been Odalaea Malabella Knoll, but then her mother, my aunt, had been murdered and she'd been given to an old mermaid with a horrible taste in names, if she'd baptized my cousin with the name 'Maisie'. Alas, it was what she called herself, a name she had carried her entire life.

"Recording my death conch," I replied absentmindedly. I wondered if I could crash this conch to the ground and record another. Conches were the equivalent to what two-legger called cameras. They were devices used by the mer to record their voices and even moving images inside. Once a conch was smashed, it eliminated the inside message entirely.

Perhaps I could write out my dialogue on a piece of kelp parchment and memorize it beforehand, I mused. It would need extra drama and flourish, of course. Something that would cause my barracuda of a stepmother to shed a tear or two. As the conch I held was *still* recording this unfortunate turn of events, all it would accomplish would be to provide my stepmother some amusement, perhaps a twitch of her lips, for I had never seen her laugh.

Odalaea—*Maisie*—reached over me and plucked the conch from my hands and looked straight into it. "Why must you be so dramatic?" she asked, sufferingly, sounding more like a sardonic sister rather than a cousin.

With annoyance, I reached over and yanked my conch back. "You wouldn't be saying the same thing, cousin, if it was *you* being forced into marriage."

Ugh, just saying it aloud made me want to gag. Somehow, the thought of marrying was even more nauseating than the time my cousin's husband had kissed me.

Not that he'd *meant* to kiss me. Really, I couldn't very well fault him for that mistake. Not when Maisie and I were nearly identical. Our mothers had been twins, and we had inherited their innate beauty. There were few differences between my cousin and I. Our eyes, for one. Hers were as black as stones and mine, though dark, were not *as* dark. I was more rounded than she was, and my sense of style was infinitely better.

I mean, for a princess who had recently found herself bathing in riches, it was baffling why she dressed like a groomsmer when she could wear vivacious dresses in tulle and silk, or any other jeweled accoutrements, instead of that chunk of black obsidian against her collarbone.

"A few weeks ago, I recall *you* trying to force a marriage with Kai on *me*."

I rolled my eyes. Gods, my cousin could hold grudges. "Yeah, but that was different."

Her own eyebrows rose mockingly. Okay, *really*, we had the same hair, a blue-purple, more purple than blue, and a matching tail with aquamarine fins, but how couldn't the mer tell us apart?

"Different how?" she asked with amusement.

"Well, you love Kai. Whereas I feel nothing but disdain for my be-troth—" I broke off on a gag.

Our contract had been signed, and the plans formally announced to the whole of Thalassar, my home kingdom. By this time tomorrow, I would be traveling with the Iolish, the Draconians, and the Kappurins across the seas where I'd be taken to Iol and forced to marry a prince I did not care for.

"I'm sure if you get to know Ytgar, you'll like him…"

I pointed an accusing finger at her. "See? Even you sound uncertain!"

Maisie sighed and shrugged. "Well, it's different, because he propositioned me when I was pretending to be you, knowing that I—or you—was to marry Kai."

I groaned. "And that's the merman they want me to marry!" He was arrogant and loud. *And charming.* Disgusting and smelly. *Attractive.* I shoved aside the complimentary thoughts and frowned. "Really, what benefits could Iol bring Thalassar, anyway? They're so closed off…"

Maisie shrugged again. *Ugh, she was no help.* "I'm not sure, but the queen is angry. You shouldn't do anything to make it worse. Thalassar can't afford another war. Not even with the mysterious Iolish."

There she went, proving to me once again that she was one hundred times a better ruler than I. It hadn't really been a secret. Maisie cared about Thalassar. She cared about the mer. I cared about myself. And I'd rather kill myself than be *that* self-sacrificing. Nevermind the irony.

But she was right. Thalassar had just gotten out of war with Kappur. To plunge us into another one with Iol? A kingdom who had orcas? Did I really want to risk it?

What if I accepted my fate and traveled with the Iolish to marry Prince Ytgar? A part of me would get the wish I'd always wanted; to travel beyond the waters of Thalassar. But wouldn't I just be trading in one prison for another? The Iolish were secretive mer who kept their borders closed off to other kingdoms, even allies. Was that to be my fate as well? Even if Ytgar was charmingly handsome, made me smile, and kissed like a…

I halted my thoughts, refusing to think about the kiss he'd given me weeks ago in the halls of the palace. It had been him trying to prove a point, and I'd nearly succumbed to his charm.

No, I decided vehemently. I would *not* marry Prince Ytgar Neves Isolde. Ever.

Thalassar be damned.

Maisie reached across the space that separated us to grip my hand fiercely in her own. I stared down, startled at the sudden gesture, and oddly touched. Maisie did not trust easily, and she had made no secret of how much she despised me. Not only because of the differences in our personalities, an awning chasm between us, but also because of what she saw as a difference in station as well. I had been raised a proper princess, and she'd been raised a waitress. Touching someone who, until recently, she thought of as so far above her could not have been easy. But she was my cousin, and she was finally starting to accept that.

"I don't think I'm the right person to be givin' you any advice," she said, her Lagoona accent slipping into her words, mingling with her newly acquired Eramaean one. The result was a slew of funny sounding words. "The last thing I want to tell you is that you have to marry someone you don't know or love…" She gave me a bashful smile. "But perhaps you can give Ytgar a chance? Don't do it for your stepmother, do it for Thalassar. You owe your kingdom that much, at least."

A sense of dread ventured through my stomach, piercing my gut uncomfortably. I wanted to lash out with familiar frivolity, to yell and make Maisie feel inferior in every sense of the word. It was how I coped, after all. For as long as I could remember, those reactions had been a part of me, of my very self. I wasn't self sacrificing like my cousin. I'd not do for Thalassar what she had. I'd not save criminals or help mer escape from the gallows. I'd gladly watch the axe come down on the backs of treacherous necks because I *didn't care.* I didn't owe anyone a damn thing. *I* was the princess. *I* was their ruler. *They* had to bow down to *me.*

And I'd not give my freedom up for them.

Or for anyone else.

Not for Thalassar. Not for Maisie. And most certainly not for my stepmother, the shark.

I couldn't very well say this, however. If I knew Maisie, which I did, the moment I gave away the sudden plan forming in my mind, she would alert someone to stop me. She'd chain me to the frozen altar in Iol if it meant benefitting her precious Thalassar.

So I smiled and gave the top of her hand a small pat. "Alright," I agreed, leaving no room for her to doubt me. "I suppose I can try."

Maisie looked me over and smiled before pulling away. "I'm glad." She got up and looked around the room, eyebrows furrowing. "You should pack," she suggested. "We leave tomorrow. You'll need to take warm clothes. Kai tells me Iol is very, very cold."

I bet it was.

I smiled and nodded.

When Maisie finally left my room, I let my facade fall and frowned. Yeah, right. She was insane if she thought I'd listen to her. I had no intention of packing for Iol, nor to travel to any northern waters. Because tonight, I would escape.

I'd escape this kingdom…

…and the Prince of Iol.

Thalassar was a mighty kingdom of old, a traditional place snuggled safely on the edge of two-legger lands. It was composed mostly of small pond villages, with the once-enemy now-ally kingdom of Kappur to the south of it and the dragon infested waters of Draconi to the west.

To me, both kingdoms were nothing but gilded prisons, but I'd still need the help of one to safely escape Iol. That meant I'd travel south through Kappur until I could make it to Ventlair. I had a handful of coins and rubies to hire a hippocampus and shell carriage, and enough to buy a home if I needed so I could continue the life of lavish I desired.

Without a husband.

The coins in my pack weighed my shoulders down, but I'd had to fill it to the rim until the whole thing bulged. I threw another bag over my shoulder containing simple traveling clothes. I wished I could have packed the remaining of my favorite dresses, but there was only so much I could carry. With the riches tucked into my black bag, I would be able to buy new clothes by the dozens, so it didn't matter.

All that mattered was that I leave. Immediately.

So I recorded a quick goodbye to my cousin, for she'd likely be the only one to miss me, and slipped through a secret passageway in the hallway near my room.

The palace had been reconstructed, or at least a part of it, anyway. I'd found the old blueprints to it and had discovered amazing—yet dark and moldy—hiding places and means of escape. I would have preferred to leave through the secret passageway behind the tapestry in my old rooms, but that place had been taken over by Maisie and her harem of filthy lovers. So that was out of the question.

I was stuck swimming through this unfamiliar path, with nothing but the simple glow of a lava globe as my only illumination. The small orb was bigger than my closed fist and rested coldly in my palm. The glass was thick and protective, used to store lava inside.

Sometimes the lava could be transferred out safely from one place to another, if one had the right tools, but they made this one for petty illumination. It barely lit up the path in front of me. In fact, all it did was give off a light around my hand and my face. But it was better than nothing, and I couldn't afford to carry anything else with me.

So I was stuck in the darkness. It wasn't so bad. Not at first. Not until I *didn't* notice the staunching figure floating at the end of the secret hallway until he was right in front of me.

I yelped embarrassingly and jumped back. My heart pounded, breaths coming out in short pants. And when I held the globe up to spotlight the figure before me, I cursed aloud, for I knew my plans had been thwarted.

The merman was encased in darkness, wisps of shadows slanted across his light brown skin. The only thing about him that glowed were the twin orbs of silver eyes glaring at me beneath an expression that was somehow both furious and bland at once.

The merman was a conundrum.

He was a hulking figure, built like a boulder, or more accurately, like a block of ice. He was as frigid and as cold, chiseled like a sculpture of dark glass in his perfection. Silver-white wisps of hair were loose around his cheeks, some of it he kept tied at the back of his neck. He had the muscles of an orca, hidden only behind the thick polar bear pelt he wore around his shoulders, the length of it more astonishing than any of my dresses, hiding his tail entirely. It made me wonder if, like Maisie, he had some strange deformity marring his scales. The merman had the prominent cheekbones of a royal, sharp at the edges, like the steel of a blade.

But I knew better.

This merman wasn't a royal at all, even *if* he was as beautiful as one. He was nothing more than a filthy whale trainer, and Prince Ytgar's lackey.

"You're blocking my exit, you big brute," I snapped impatiently. What was he doing down here? No one but me knew the location to the secret passageways.

His thin lips pursed tightly before twitching. If I didn't know better, I'd say he was smiling, but a moment later he wore the same stoic expression he always sported.

"Move!" I ordered. It was rare that I had to repeat myself. I was the *Princess* of Thalassar, future queen of the realm. Whatever I desired, the mer scrambled over each other to make me happy, to impress. If not, then they'd face the entirety of my wrath and cruelty. This whale trainer scum was beneath me and should have hurried to move his bulky body aside to let me through.

But he didn't.

I wondered if it would hurt him if I threw the lava globe at his face. I supposed there were a few disadvantages to that. One, it'd likely just bounce off his massive muscled body like a pebble against a wall, and two, I'd lose my only source of illumination. Not exactly a well thought-out plan.

I was so distracted with my contemplations on how to get this rock aside that when he finally deigned to speak, the deep rumble of his voice made my entire body vibrate.

"Where are you going, Princess?"

I fought off the effect the tone of his voice had on me. Gods, no. What was it with these Iolish bastards? Did they drink magic tea? Suck on magical ice cubes? Why was it they seemed so enchanting? It was infuriating.

"None of your business," I snapped impatiently, gesturing with the hand holding the lava globe. "Get out of my way, brute."

An eyebrow rose in what was clearly amusement. The bastard was making fun of me! Mermen had been whipped for less. He could have lost his head for that slight once upon a time. Before my own fate had escaped from my fingers. Before my plan crumbled into silt. Before I was sold to the Iolish Prince.

"Why?" he rumbled.

My palms suddenly heated, and the globe almost slipped from my fingers at his questioning. It was just one word, and yet the weight of it was like a thousand pounds.

"Shouldn't you be somewhere polishing Ytgar's belt buckles?"

Both of his beautifully trimmed eyebrows rose. "I am right where I'm supposed to be, Princess."

"In… my way?"

"You don't actually think I will move aside and let you flee from your responsibilities." It wasn't phrased like a question. Something in my gut curdled.

"Who said anything about fleeing?"

He gave me a pointed look that almost made me shiver. *Almost.* "You cannot think me to be *that* daft, Princess."

"Well, I mean, I *could* and I *do*. Orca inbreeding makes the mer as stupid as dragon inbreeding, I hear."

He frowned and, suddenly, the waters became heavy, hot with the intensity of the murderous gleam in those silver eyes that shone in the surrounding darkness. I felt as though my body had been dipped into molten lava and I was suffocating, the gleam in his eyes pervasive. I felt something akin to death balancing on the precipice of these next few moments.

I regretted my words immediately.

Val pried the globe from my tightened fingers and chucked it over my head until we were shrouded in darkness, with nothing but the glow of his abnormal eyes in our company. They gleamed closer and closer still, until I felt the weight of his heavy hands encircle my upper arms and squeeze.

I was suddenly all too aware of the closeness of his body, of the way the ice hard ridges of his front pressed up against me. The thick pelt of fur contrasted his body. Soft on hard. It sent a shiver slicing down my body, made my fins curl. There was imminent danger here, creeping up on me, on us.

Then he was closer, his lips warm near the lobe of my ear. I tried not to flinch. I tried not to move or breathe or remember the sharp lines and angles of his beautiful face.

"You mistake me for Ytgar, Princess." His words were a dangerous warning. "You mistake me for the weak, broken mer at your beck and call." His lips moved up the side of my ear, to my cheek. The graze of them finally made me shiver, despite my resolve to be strong, to not be intimidated. I despised him for what he was doing to my body. "You cannot break me, Princess." Then those silver eyes were right in front of mine, and even in the darkness I saw the promise of danger in those depths. "No one can."

Before I knew what was happening, his strong arms encircled me, causing the breath to whoosh out of me in surprise, and he lifted me up as though I weighed nothing more than a knapsack of crumbled conches. I still had the bag of jewels strapped to my back, and when he flicked me over his shoulder, the straps came undone and gold and rubies drifted along the floor of the little cave.

A groan pushed past my lips, followed by a cry of indignation when I felt his hand settle warmly over the backside of my tail. My *ass*, as two-leggers were prone to call that part of their anatomy. His hand was on *mine*, firm and strong as he held me in place and began swimming. Rubies and coins fell and floated behind him as he carried me back towards the palace. All of my hard work undone within a matter of moments thanks to a disgusting whale trainer.

"You Iolish bastard!" I shrieked, pounding on his backside. He didn't even grunt, and all I managed to do was hurt my own fists against his muscled body. The jerking movements of my arms only jostled the bag on my back. "How *dare* you?" I raged. "Put me down this instant!"

"I think not."

He navigated his way through the secret passageway in the dark, ignoring my shrieks of indignation and anger until we were slipping past the opening. It scraped away, the harsh sound echoing along the halls of the palace. When he stepped fin in the hallway, it was empty, save for the occasional servant hiding behind vases, watching us with wary eyes.

"Find the Captain of my Royal Guard and bring him here at once!" I shrieked to the servant.

A deep rumble resonated down my chest. I realized it was a laugh. This filthy whale trainer was *laughing* at me. Then he did something that froze me cold.

He patted my rear.

"No one is going to save you, Princess," he promised darkly. "They know you have a penchant for disobeying and have been commanded by your queen and king to give you no aid."

I scoffed. The treachery! The audacity! How *dare* they treat me like some common criminal filth in my own home?! There was a real criminal lurking through the palace and it wasn't I, but one by the name of the

Black Blade. How demeaning that I was now being hauled around like a sack of vegetables? Where was the respect? I was royalty. I was his superior!

"Put. Me. Down." I punched my fist straight into his spine. Gods, was the merman made of ice and steel? He hadn't even flinched. "Now!"

I gasped as he jostled me above his shoulder and I bobbed up and down. The sharp jab of his shoulder in my stomach brought little bubbles of tears to my eyes.

On two-legger lands, it was said they cried tears as salty as the waters I lived in. Yet here, mer cried tears of air, the evidence lifting from my eyes in an annoying swarm that frustrated me. It was a weakness, and I prayed he'd not turn around and see.

His grip was adamant, and I knew he wouldn't put me down like I commanded, so I dangled at his back, letting my hands press down the length of him for support. His muscles seemed to tense under me the more my hands explored. And, because I wanted to catch him off guard, perhaps enough so he'd drop me despite the indignity it would cause, I let my hands clamp over his own rear end.

He stopped mid-stroke. "Careful." It came out as both a growl and a warning.

"It's only fair you suffer the same embarrassing indignities, whale train-er." I groped him. By gods, he was hard and firm all over. It was hard not to notice such a thing. Alas, my hands *noticed* and explored by their on volition. Blast my curious body and untameable fingers. They traced over the material of his thick fur pelt. Curiosity had my fingers bunching up into it and as slowly as I possibly could, I began to hike it up.

The slap on my rear came so suddenly, I dropped his cloak and gasped as the pain brought fresh tears to my eyes. "Wh—you—the *audacity*!"

"Do not meddle where you are unwelcome, Princess."

I growled, and because I'd not risk such an indignity again in this defenseless position, I propped my elbows up onto his back and rested my chin in my palm. The only benefit I could find in this was that I *was* being carried. I'd not tire, and this surely was a form of pampering. "I don't see why you cover your tail so secretively," I commented.

"Well it's not as though you are the brightest…"

I froze. Was this whale trainer jesting? Did he *want* to lose his head?

"Tread carefully, whale trainer. I've punished mer for less displays of insolence than yours." And had enjoyed every moment of making them suffer.

"And I've brought many a wild orca to submit. I am not afraid of your tantrums."

Tantrums!

If I wasn't so indisposed at the moment, I'd challenge him to a duel and skewer my sword through his thick, brawny neck. What insolence, coming from a servant! My reputation was surely in tatters because of this encounter alone.

"If you think I fear you because you whip your beasts into submission, you have another thing coming, whale trainer."

"Unlike you, I don't require the use of violence to make my prey submit."

"Unlike me?" I guffawed with indignation. "Well, what's that supposed to mean?" I could practically *feel* the slow curl of the whale trainer's smile, as if that was something one could literally *feel* down to the marrow of their bones. I did. I imagined it perfectly, and so I dug my elbow into his spine, however ineffectual my attempts at hurting him were.

"You know very well what it means." In response to my actions, he jostled me again. This time, I was prepared for the blow and didn't gasp against the onslaught.

"Iolish bastard," I growled.

He chuckled. "Violent and rude. I expected nothing less from you." He gave a sharp turn down a hallway that almost had me sliding off his shoulder. Unfazed, he adjusted me once more and kept on his way as if this were a pleasure stroll.

"Disrespectful and a brute. I expected nothing less of *you*."

"I'll not deny what I am, Princess, but I will say that if you want this Iolish bastard to grovel at your fins because you are the Princess of Thalassar, your wait will be eternal and exhausting."

Suddenly he stopped, and a gasp tore from my lips as he tossed me from over his shoulder and deposited me unkindly to the ground. I fell, my spine hitting a door, and my backside ramming against the floor. I winced against the pain and glared up at the whale trainer. Not a hair of his was out of place. Somehow he managed to look regal and formidable as he loomed menacingly over me. Then he bent down so that we were eye to eye. The fact that he was suddenly at my level didn't make his presence any less imposing.

"You expect blind loyalty from subjects you treat like silt, and when you aren't met with obedience, you lash out with violence and rudeness." His voice held an undercurrent of a vehemence that frightened me despite myself. The flesh on my arms prickled, the back of my neck grew hot and unpleasant. His silver eyes were glowing in the near darkness of the hallway. They looked like shooting stars in the sky, like white two-legger fire that threatened to burn down the very foundations of my soul. "You are a spoiled brat, Princess Odele. But I will tell you this…" He leaned forward, so close that the tips of our noses touched and I felt heat sear through me. When his breath blew against my mouth, I shivered. "…You cannot escape this marriage. You cannot escape Iol."

Anger nearly cleaved my chest in two. "I can," I replied, glad that my voice didn't shake but carried with it the anger that writhed inside me. "And I will."

He was silent for a long time, until the side of his lip lifted up into the smallest of mocking smiles. "You can try," he challenged, "and you will fail."

"Why?" I demanded with frustration. "If you hate me so much, then *why* does your prince want me at all?" Perhaps Iol could break off the engagement and I wouldn't need to flee from my home at all. Maybe I could convince him he didn't need me.

"Make no mistake about it, little Princess, you do not deserve the Prince of Iol." The words were a knife that cut me in half. "But he needs you." He leaned forward until his lips grazed the lobe of my ear. The action had my nerves spiraling inside my chest. "And he *will* have you." He got up and turned, leaving me deposited right where I was.

As if I was nothing more than garbage in the silt, with his words echoing in my mind.

You do not deserve the Prince of Iol.

I spat ineffectually at where he had floated. If anyone didn't deserve someone, it was the Prince of Iol who didn't deserve *me*. I was greater than the most fabulous confection. I was a moon pastry laced with gold trimming. I was the *best* princess in all the kingdoms. He'd be lucky to lick the currents I swam on, to worship me at my fins.

Lucky for him and his Iolish ilk, I had no need for his worship. I had no need for him at all. What I wanted was my freedom. And I meant to have it.

I got up in the most dignified move I could muster and tore the bag from my shoulders. There was nothing left but a coin or two inside. I'd not stoop so low as to go back in that secret passageway and scrape up the money like a common beggar. With a frustrated cry, I threw the bag to the floor and straightened, smoothing out the tail of my dress. This outfit along with my plans, had been thoroughly ruined. I'd toss it into a lava seam the first chance I got.

I turned to face the door he'd dropped me in front of. It was of my rooms. Not the room I'd had all my life, but the new one. For the first time, I cursed my cousin and her lovers. A criminal to my crown forgiven for his crimes ever since the Selection had been abolished; my old Captain of the Royal Guard who had quit his post to follow my cousin; and Prince Kai Li of Draconi, my ex betrothed who was now her husband… It was really a long tedious story I did not wish to repeat ever again.

I truly wanted my old rooms back, but I couldn't fathom sleeping in that bed again after imagining all the unholy things my cousin did in it with her scraps of filth. So I was trapped in inadequate rooms, never mind that it had been my mother's before she'd died. I loathed the lack of passageways.

Speaking of passageways, how had Val known where I'd be? I pondered as I went inside. The room was no less lavish than the previous one I'd stayed in. It had the same basic layout and decor. A massive opened clamshell bed sat in the center of the room, inlaid with plump purple cushioning and a floating canopy of jellyfish above it, casting a luminescent blue spotlight down on it. Pearls in pink, silver, and white bordered the shell around the outer edges. There was a gilded vanity mirror made of two-legger materials, rusted away and opaque from the sea, a writing desk of the same sturdy coral structure as the shelves, and a swim-in closet that held most of my clothes that hadn't been mysteriously shredded by my cousin.

I stopped shy of the threshold, the same question tantalizing my thoughts. How had he known? How could he have possibly known where the passage was?

The answer was in this room, sitting on the beautiful, plump bed in the form of Odalaea—Maisie—Malabella Knoll Li.

My cousin.

"I'm sorry," were the first words out of her mouth.

It was how I knew, though even if she hadn't uttered her guilty apology, I would have known regardless by the look on her face and the fact that she'd been the only one I'd ever told about the passageways. The only one I'd ever shown the blueprints to.

I slammed the door behind me. "You!" I accused vehemently. My cousin flinched. "Why?"

She sat demurely at the end of the bed, her tail curled under her in a position I was very well versed in. It was a tense posture, preparing to flee at the first sign of violence, but the angle was not quite right, perhaps on account of the limp my cousin suffered. When she was younger, she'd been attacked by a gator in the nasty backwater town she'd grown up in. It had left her deformed and with an ugly scar on her aquamarine fin.

Her fingers made a nervous flittering movement in her lap, the only sign of what she truly felt, for her voice was firm, her neck elongated and decisive, like a queen, when she replied, "I had to."

I narrowed my eyes. "You *had* to," I echoed.

She gave me a firm nod. "I knew you would try to escape when we spoke earlier. I knew you wouldn't care about Thalassar's fate and would abandon it to yet another war. So I stopped you."

The relationship we'd so precariously built over the last few weeks suddenly crumbled like the dusty remnants of an old, rusted conch. In her, I had found not just a cousin, but a *sister*. Someone who could share her pains with me, someone I could share my pains with. Yet she betrayed me. The one mer I thought I could trust above all others in this entire wretched kingdom. It had been her.

She'd betrayed me.

"How could you?" The words came out as broken as I felt inside. "You betrayed me to the Iolish! To that smug, rock-like bastard and his master. *How could you?*" I pressed a hand to my chest, as if the action might settle its pounding. As if the action might stop it from breaking.

Maisie didn't flinch. If there was one thing she was now, it was ruthless. Gone was her shy uncertainty. "I care about Thalassar," she explained. "I'll not see it fall to ruin again."

"How could you do that to me?!" I declared on a shout. "Do you know what you've done? Do you know what this marriage will do to me?"

It will kill me slowly, painfully. It will take away everything that I am. It will enslave me to a kingdom of ice. It will be the end to my freedom.

"I'm sorry, but I *had* to." There was a pleading sound to her voice. "Besides, you're strong. You'll survive."

I'd survive, but I wouldn't live, like I only ever desired to live. I'd be shackled to a husband, forced to have half-breed orca children, forced to live in a block of ice for a home. Confined inside a palace and a kingdom like I had been my entire life. I'd see nothing. I'd visit nothing.

I'd die without having first lived.

And that, I feared more than anything else.

Those words were stuck at the back of my throat, clustering together to form the tightest of lumps I couldn't choke past. Words I'd rather choke down than say aloud were there. Words I thought I'd someday be brave enough to share with her. Now I knew it wasn't a question of bravery, of putting my heart out on the silk sleeve of my dress for my cousin to see, but of whether I could confide it to anyone at all.

The answer was no.

There was no one I could trust with these dreams, with my heart. So I locked it all up behind a solidly built wall that I'd so foolishly dared to chip apart in cracks and slivers for her. A cousin who wouldn't have understood why these layered walls were there. A cousin so different from me. She was someone who had longed for home and family, while I'd longed for the world.

Why had I ever thought she could understand me?

I forced the words down and brought up the ones I *knew* would slip from my tongue as easily as a knife slipping through flesh.

"I hate you."

Maisie winced and closed her eyes, as if creating an internal barrier to block out my vehement words.

"You don't mean that," she demurred breathlessly.

How *dare* she presume to know what I felt? "I do." I spun and yanked the door open, an order to leave, and to never come back. "Get out," I commanded. "I don't ever want to see you again."

Maisie got up and limped over to the door. I tried to avoid her black eyes, but it was hard to do when she stopped right beside me, and placed a hand on my shoulder. "I'm sorry, cousin. I don't want to see you, or Thalassar, get hurt."

If you didn't want me hurt, you should have let me leave.

I grit my teeth together. "Get. Out."

She pulled her hand away as if it had burned. A moment later she was gone, and I was slamming the door at her fins. As soon as we had a barrier between us, I let my body slump against the surface. I slid down, buried my hands in my palms…

…and cried.

I HATED THE SOUTH. I hated the stifling weather, the array of colors, and most of all, I hated the mer. Perhaps not *all* mer, but there was one in particular that held my ire. One with infuriatingly pretty brown-black eyes—though they appeared to have flecks of gold in the correct lighting—framed by dark purple lashes, a cute, round nose and a stubborn tilt of her chin.

Odele Malabella Oriana, Princess of the mer kingdom of Thalassar, was grating on my every nerve. She was the hint of frostbite in the dead of winter, painful, infuriating, and to a point… deadly.

I had hoped to be free of this kingdom the moment we'd arrived, but it had been impossible to hurry through the negotiations. The kingdom of Iol in the north, my home kingdom, needed allies. As a kingdom who set ourselves apart from the rest and relied on nearly no one but ourselves, we needed to change that. Lately, things in Iol had not been the same. It wasn't just the newfound poverty, a disparage that could be blamed on the selfish Prime Minister and his tyrannic way of ruling, but the raids as well.

Further north, in the freezing ice waters that extended Iolish territory, things were coming through. Creatures slipping beyond the interconnecting waters of the west that were as deadly as they were mysterious. Food was becoming scarce, and the mer needed to be fed.

Which meant that Iol needed trade.

That had been the plan, anyway. Until my best friend had got the insane notion in his mind that there was no better way to secure an alliance than by marriage to the Thalassarin princess? An impossibility, as she had been engaged to the Dragon Prince Kai Li of Draconi—Iol's oldest enemy.

That was before the truth had come out, and we had arrived in Thalassar just in time to watch the drama of royal secrets unfold. Odele's long-lost cousin and heir of the Kappurin throne had wed the Draconian Prince instead, despite what the contracts had dictated. In bringing the truth of her heritage to light, Odalaea—daughter of the King of Kappur and deceased Princess of Thalassar—had ended the Selection in the kingdom, as well as a war, and managed to secure alliances with Kappur and Draconi.

Why couldn't that have been the mer for Iol? Someone selfless and caring, someone who protected and swam up for what she believed in?

Instead, my best friend got the strange notion that Odele was the one; that with her, Iol would be allied forever with Thalassar through marriage.

While I was certain a marriage alliance would help, Odele was not the princess Iol needed. And if her escape attempt told me anything, it was that she didn't want the alliance any more than I did.

I sent up another silent curse towards my best friend as I made my way down the hallways of the pink quartz castle.

The colors made me sick. I longed to be back at home, where I wouldn't have to hide myself from the truth, where the waters were cold and it magically snowed just as furiously beneath the sea as it did on two-legger lands.

I turned sharply around the corner and came to a stop at my chamber door. Sighing, I opened it and pushed through, already sensing my friend before I even swam inside and closed the door behind me.

He was on the bed, laying across it leisurely and without a care in the world. His white-blond tendrils of hair floated over his forehead and kissed his light brown skin. Frosty blue eyes turned to look at me with careless amusement, as if he knew exactly where I'd been and what I'd been doing. His next words confirmed my thoughts.

"Have fun fetching the princess?" he asked.

I scowled at the note of humor in his words. "Why do you look so satisfied?" I demanded in our native tongue, moving across the room to remove the ties holding together my fur-lined cloak. I felt a sudden surge of rage as I did, knowing that Princess Odele had come painstakingly close to discovering the truth by unveiling me. It only made me more determined to leave this place and get home to Iol as soon as possible.

He turned on the bed and propped his head up onto his hand. The anemones lined up along the edges of the bed swayed towards him, almost as if they couldn't quite get enough of his charm. "I don't see why you're upset, my friend. She's fantastic."

I snorted. As fantastic as a pile of orca silt, but whatever.

He raised an eyebrow. "Don't tell me you don't like her…"

I folded my cloak neatly and set it down on one of the coral shelves of the room. It felt good to finally be rid of the thing. The southern waters were stifling compared to Iol, and wearing it made me feel like I was sitting directly on top of a lava seam. Regardless of my discomfort—of *our* discomfort—it was necessary to wear them, to keep up with our facade, with our lies.

I stretched out my shoulders, deliberately taking a long time to answer the question. He was daft if he thought this would work. "Weren't there any other princesses available for our kingdom?" Someone… less… well, *less.*

"I like her. She's a challenge. She'll be great for us."

Us.

I couldn't help but feel my lip quirk to the side at that. It had always been that way, as we'd known each other since we were children. Since I'd been thrown off the back of a rearing orca and landed in silt and snow, the sound of unabashed laughter echoing through my eardrums. No one ever dared laugh at me. Ever. But he had and still did.

We'd been together ever since.

"I suppose…"

Truth be told, I didn't know what to feel besides this bitterness that arose whenever I saw her. Bitterness and passion in equal measure. As much as I despised her and wanted to bend her over my tail and show her a lesson in manners, there was the vicious heat of desire kindling, urging my every sense to dominate, to control… to kiss… though I'd never admit it aloud.

Even *if* my best friend saw right through me.

"Trust me, *Valmundur.*" He got up, his eyes shining with equal parts innocence and mischief. How he was so good at that, I'd never know.

My expression tightened, eyebrows furrowing into displeasure. I'd gone along with his plan because it was something we did whenever we had the rare opportunity to leave Iol, but taking a betrothed had been a different sort of mischief altogether. I should have said no, but the gods knew we needed Odele just as much as we needed Thalassar. It shouldn't feel like such a burden when I was doing this for the good of my kingdom. For the lives of my mer.

"I trust you with my life," I told him firmly. He was, perhaps, the only one in the seas I could trust to be loyal. To lie for me. To *die* for me. That was, after all, why we kept up with this ruse.

"Then trust me. Get to know the princess, stop brooding so much. Maybe smile at her a bit."

My eyes narrowed. "Are *you* trying to give me relationship advice?"

He barked out sarcastic laughter. "Someone has to. You look like you want to kill her every time you set eyes on her. Mermaids don't like that type of thing. At least, not Thalassarin ones."

I sat on the edge of the bed, quirking a brow. "And what do you know of Thalassarin mermaids?"

Almost unconsciously, his fingers went over his lips, tracing the skin there. As if he were remembering something pleasant. Or rather, someone he'd kissed. "I know this one won't be wooed so easily." He dropped his hand, a smile touching his face. He hardly ever frowned, hardly ever angered. He was my opposite in every way. The better part of myself that I selfishly kept close, even when everyone else around me was cursed with such short lives.

"I don't have to woo her," I murmured with sudden irritation. "I just have to marry her."

Silence followed, a silence that weighed nothing on the length of my broad shoulders, and yet I couldn't bring myself to look into Valmundur's eyes. Into the eyes of my oldest friend, Iol's whale trainer, and the merman pretending to be me.

My hands rested on the curved edge of my black and white tail, the tail of my forefathers, sleek and shining, it resembled the mottled colors of a killer whale; my family's emblem. Like every other kingdom in the seas, our house had a sigil. Draconi's was a fierce dragon, Thalassar's was a hippocampus, Kappur's was a sea snake, Ventlair's a shark, Brague's a sea kraken, Gvulis a dolphin, and we the Iolish were the mighty orcas.

It was perhaps the only part of our ruse that was difficult to hide, as Val's tail differed from my own. His was the color of blue ice, of frost; a blue so light it was almost white, a white so dark it could only be blue. There was no in between, and if the mer saw it, they would automatically know that Prince Ytgar Neves Isolde wasn't who he claimed to be, and that his 'bodyguard' was actually royalty.

"You sound like a martyr," Val groaned, sitting up on the bed. "It's very depressing, and I'm tired of looking at your brooding face. If you'll excuse me…" He hopped off the bed with as much flourish as a royal. He didn't move with the same elegance they taught me since I was old enough to swim in a straight line, but he swam with a swaggering arrogance fit for any royal. It was why it was so easy for him to pretend to be something he was not. "You won't woo her, but I will."

He grabbed his cloak, which he'd laid carelessly across the desk chair, and wrapped it around his shoulders. He turned to the mirror and adjusted every bit of it so it hid the tail that would deem him an imposter. At least, in the eyes of Thalassar, it would be so.

My Iolish mer knew my real identity, they knew that Val pretended to be me for my protection. A necessary lie, in case there was ever an assassination attempt.

Val turned with a pompous twirl of his—my—robes and made his way over to the door. "Be careful, my Prince," I warned as he set his hand against the knob. "It's dangerous to lurk around these halls without a bodyguard."

Val looked over his shoulder and gifted me with his infamous half smirk. "Worry not, *Valmundur.*" He put a little too much emphasis on the name—his own name. "I'll be careful." And then he opened the door and left the room, leaving me to worry—as always—about whether we were both making a huge mistake.

IT'S NOT LIKE I hated my life, hated who I was. But I had to admit, there was something absolutely satisfying about pretending to be royalty. I wonder if this was what Princess Odalaea—Maisie—had felt when she swam around in Odele's silks while thinking she was nothing more than a waitress.

There was a thrill about commanding mer to do what I willed, though I wouldn't call myself demanding. It was the respect I harbored when I disguised myself as Ytgar. Respect I'd never received even as the royal whale trainer. It was a nice change, to be called 'Majesty' and 'Your Highness' instead of 'bastard' and 'servant.' Perhaps I was too arrogant in my role, but I was arrogant anyway. I had to be, if I wanted to survive the harsh life Iol offered.

And I was nothing if not a survivor.

I swam about the palace halls, nodding toward the pretty servant mer, winking as I glided by. They blushed and hid behind vases and their cleaning sponges, as if they couldn't quite believe that a Iolish Prince was paying them any mind.

If only they knew the truth.

Anyway, it didn't matter what I'd been disguised as. I would've winked at them regardless. There was nothing I appreciated more than a beautiful mer. Though there was only one mer in particular I thought of right now. Only one mer I wanted to woo. One mer I wanted to spar with. One mer I wanted to kiss.

I stopped in front of Odele's door and rapped my knuckles against it three times. I waited a couple of heartbeats, a smile on my face. When she finally opened the door, it was with the cutest glare marring her features. I'd expected nothing less.

She scoffed at the sight of me. "What do you want, Iolish?" she demanded unpleasantly.

I hadn't seen her for weeks. Not since we'd met in the hallway and parried with words, trading sarcasm for brittle sarcasm, when I'd first made the proposal of marriage and she'd promptly shot me down.

Luckily, my ego hadn't bruised. Her rejection only made the chase far more fun.

I pressed a hand to my chest as if she'd wounded me. "Can't a mer come and say hello to his betrothed?" *Not your betrothed,* I reminded myself. *She belongs to Ytgar. The real Ytgar. You cannot touch, you can only play.*

I didn't deserve her, anyway.

"If we were truly betrothed, then maybe. But as I have no intention of marrying you, you can say your goodbye to my door's face." She started to slam the door on me, but instinctively, my hand shot out to stop her. She gave a shove, but her door didn't budge. The princess glared at me.

Even the sight of her anger was enough to steal the water from my lungs. She was so beautiful, it was almost painful to look at her when I knew I could never compare. But I threw away those doubts and mustered as much royal confidence as I could.

"We have a contract that says otherwise, Odele." I smiled, knowing it would irritate her.

She glowered. "I did not give you leave to use my name, Iolish."

"I don't need your permission…"

Trading insults with her was fun, and quickly becoming a favorite pastime.

The princess growled, a sound that heated my blood in ways it probably shouldn't have. *She belongs to Ytgar. She belongs to Ytgar…* Damn it all to ice. My body didn't care that she belonged to my best friend, and obviously neither did my heart, if the incessant thumping of it against my ribcage was of any indication. I loved the prospect of the challenge she represented. That's what I told myself this was.

I couldn't possibly be falling for her when we were leagues apart. I may as well have been a scrap of kelp on the hoof of a hippocampus. I was born a bastard, with no money and no prospects. I had nothing to offer her but my pretty face and a heated kiss to prove a point.

And yet…

Princess Odele called to me, like the beckoning song of a siren luring me closer and closer still, until I could do nothing but watch the inevitability of my own demise. Against jagged rocks, in a storm, at night. And even as she lured me to my death, I wanted her just the same.

Why wouldn't I? She was beautiful. Her body hinted at the promise of plump curves, the figure of a mer who had never known hunger. Her hair was long and perfect, a purple-blue that enticed mermen into their wildest fantasies. Her lips were plump, the bottom one bigger than the top, with the smallest of indents in the middle. A mouth meant for sin or salvation, I wasn't sure. The line between the two was blurred when I remembered what it felt like to have her mouth on mine. And her eyes… a mer could get lost in those brown-gold depths. It was impossible to discern the color of them. Were they more black or brown? Were they brown with a hint of gold? All I knew was that they were dark and glaring and beckoning…

And rimmed with red.

As if she had been crying.

I frowned. "What's wrong, Princess?"

Her body stilled for one electrifying moment, as if surprised I'd noticed at all. I noticed everything about her. And Ytgar did too, no matter how badly he wanted to deny it.

"Did someone hurt you?" The hand gripping her door tightened painfully until my knuckles went white. Just the thought of someone hurting her, of doing *anything* to her, made my blood boil.

It took me back to that moment, the moment that should have been her wedding. When Percival Pike, the queen's former advisor, pointed his speargun at her. We didn't think. We reacted. Ytgar and I moved to protect her even though we could've died. My body had known then what I knew now. I wanted her. And I would protect her from all harm. So killing the vicious bastard had been nothing, not even a taint on my soul.

Anyone who harmed her deserved death, or at the very least, excruciating torture.

I pushed the door. It banged back, and I closed the space between us. I couldn't help but take the liberty of grabbing her chin in my fingers and lifting her head up for examination. Yes, her eyes were rimmed red from crying and a bit startled at my sudden movements.

I had a sudden vision of her features softening, of her laying her head on my chest and confessing everything between quiet sobs as I comforted her just before I went and tore apart whoever had done this.

Things weren't so simple with Odele.

She jerked away with a glare. "Get your filthy hands off me, you Iolish bastard."

She'd never know how much the insult stung. Even if I'd heard it all my life, it never got easier to hear.

"Touch me again and lose your fingers," she threatened. "And get this straight, I don't need your help or want it. Whatever that stupid contract says, I'll never be yours. *Never.*" And then she took a stroke back and promptly slammed the door in my face, almost breaking my nose.

Damn it to ice, I cursed aloud in Iolish. Perhaps it was not princely, but I couldn't help the slip up. She'd startled me, though I shouldn't have been surprised.

Odele was vicious and as prickly as a pufferfish. She did not trust easily, and she hated more than she loved. Getting her to trust me, to trust us, would be difficult. But it needed to happen. I wanted her to *want* to be with us, with Ytgar most of all. Because he needed her as much as Iol did, and because I wanted her, even though I shouldn't.

Her love wouldn't be given easily, or freely. Ytgar and I would have to work to earn it, and to do that I needed a solidly built plan. We needed a plan, because I'd freeze in ice if Ytgar let me do all the work alone. Even if I could, it was he who was meant to woo her, not I. And this mermaid needed wooing.

By the gods, I would make it happen. Whether she wanted it or not, expected it or not, by the time I was finished with Odele, she would want to go to Iol of her own free will.

And she would damn well like it.

I SPENT THE ENTIRE night in a gloom, as if a dark and vicious current had swept through me and left me hollow with despair. I had nothing to live for. I'd see no hint of my dowry or my treasure unless I married the Iolish, and though I'd spent my life in riches and wanted nothing more than a lavish life of travel, I couldn't bring myself to go through with it.

So I plotted and decided I would make another attempt at swimming away.

It was obvious I would get nowhere while locked in the palace. The trick was to get those Iolish bastards to trust me on the way to their ice cold kingdom and, when they least suspected it, I would swim away. Perhaps I wouldn't even have to work at getting them to trust me. I wasn't *that* good of an actress. All I had to do was slip away while Val wasn't looking. Or Maisie… or Ytgar… or anyone else that could turn against me.

I was on my own, and I had to make my escape count. That meant I couldn't take jewels with me that would draw attention to myself. Or bags. Or anything. I'd take nothing but the clothes on my back, and maybe I could make a detour to the palace, stock up on supplies and then leave afterwards.

It wasn't much of a plan, but it was the only one I had.

So the morning I was set to depart for Iol, I started packing.

Jessinda, Scarlet, and Silviya were in my room. Distant cousins of mine who shared in my hatred for all things Iolish and Draconian, though today, our mutual dislike didn't bring a smile to my face.

"Life is so unfair," Jessinda complained, quite loudly. "I don't want to go to Iol!"

All three of them were to accompany me to the kingdom of ice as my chaperones and ladies-in-waiting. I couldn't even tell her that complaining was for naught when my escape was imminent. I trusted them all about as far as I could throw them and, given their round figures, it wasn't very far.

"You and me both, Jess," I murmured, throwing a dress from my closet into the open two-legger trunk at the fin of the bed.

"Tragic! O, *tragic.*" She flopped herself onto my bed, jostling Silviya and Scarlet.

Scarlet eyed the selection of dresses I was throwing into the chest at random. "Perhaps," she began timidly, "you should pack warmer clothes, cousin. I hear Iol is very cold."

It honestly didn't matter what I packed, as I had no plan to set fin in Iol at all.

"It's summer," I grumbled, throwing in a short-sleeved dress with a low neckline. "How cold could their kingdom possibly be?"

None of them replied, though I hadn't particularly expected them to. A few more dresses were thrown carelessly in before someone finally spoke again. It was Silviya this time, her chatter lost in the haze of my anger. If she asked me a question, I didn't hear it, much less answer it. I was too busy fuming at Ytgar.

This was all his fault. If he hadn't proposed this stupid marriage to my stepmother, we wouldn't be in this situation at all. But he had to go and ruin the plans for my future. Him and Maisie both.

As if my thoughts had summoned her from whatever hole she'd been hiding in, the door to my rooms opened without a knock, and Maisie was there, framed in the entrance.

All talking ceased.

Behind her, the former captain to my Royal Guard floated, eyes alert on all of us, as if we were a threat to my cousin. My cousin who floated there, frozen and a little uncertain as she took all of us in.

"What do *you* want?" Jessinda asked, not bothering to hide the contempt in her voice or expression. The other mer did the same, looking down at Maisie with disapproving sneers.

I would have brought myself to care about their disdain and defended her, had she not betrayed me. So I let her feel the full force of their unacceptance, for even if we were all distantly related, it was obvious that Jessinda, Silviya, and Scarlet did not accept Maisie into the family.

And why would they? She was raised a waitress, not a royal. She despised royals herself, so how could they bring themselves to like someone who looked down on them? As if this waitress-turned-royal was bred of better stuff than them.

Discrimination went both ways.

Maisie ignored Jessinda, her eyes piercing mine directly. "I need to talk to you."

I steeled myself against those eyes, eyes that were like my own, preparing to fortify my walls against the onslaught of emotion I was sure would come from speaking with her. I had fought for her, fin and scale. I'd given her everything, had suffered near death to bring the truth to light and give her back her rightful place in our royal world. And she repaid me by betraying me.

"We have nothing to talk about," I said firmly, staring at her with just as much vehemence as she did with me. She could not betray me and then come making demands. I was not some servant she could order about. I was her cousin, not her slave.

Her eyes flicked over the mer on my bed and then back to me. "Please," she said breathlessly. I almost believed she was about to cry.

Damn it.

"She said she doesn't want to speak with you," Silviya admonished. "Go away."

"Yeah" Scarlet leaned forward with a wicked gleam in her eyes.

"Leave, bottom feeder," Jessinda added cruelly, obviously relishing in the chance to rip Maisie apart.

And I just sat there while they did it. A part of me—the bigger part of me—laughed with vicious delight at seeing Maisie squirm with discomfort. No matter how proud she professed to be, I still knew there was one aspect of herself that would always make her feel inferior to the rest of us, and that was the fact that she'd been raised in Lagoona. No matter how confident she'd become these past few months she'd been pretending to be me, inside she was still the same unsure, intimidated mer I'd spied on from within secret passageways.

Another part of me, the smaller part, felt a rising defensiveness on her behalf. She was my cousin, betrayal or not, she was still closer to me in blood than any of the mer at my side were. Our mothers had been twins, which meant Maisie and I were interconnected irrevocably. Different halves of a coin. She didn't deserve this treatment...

Whatever. Not my problem. I tried to drown out my sympathy behind my rebuilt walls, solidly reconstructed precisely to keep those feelings at bay. Whatever sentiments I lay at Maisie's fins, she'd only crush with the weight of her expectations. Just like everybody else.

And still…

I sighed.

"Jessinda, Scarlet, Silviya…" My voice cracked like a whip. Commanding. Queenly. It had them quieting instantaneously and turning to look at me with uncertainty. "Leave us for a moment. I'll call you if I have need of you."

Jessinda looked inclined to argue, but after I pierced her with a look, she clamped her lips closed and scrambled off the bed, giving me a proper curtsey before exiting with the others. I didn't miss the look she gave Maisie and Captain Saber as she left, but I didn't pay it much mind. A scalding look was the least Maisie deserved right now.

"Close the door. Tiberius, you can wait in the hallway."

The captain stilled, as if nervous I would do or say something to my cousin. My cousin tensed at my familiar usage of the captain's first name. Oh, but it was so easy to tease her.

Obediently, she closed the door in the captain's face and turned to me. She looked uncertain, and I relished in it, taking a seat at the end of my bed and leaning back with leisure.

"Say what you wish," I commanded. "And then leave."

"They don't like me, do they?"

That obvious, huh? I waved her words away with an annoyed flicker of my fingers. "Jessinda likes kissing her own cousins." The male ones. "I wouldn't worry overmuch about what she does or does not like."

Maisie snorted a laugh before covering the noise with her hand. She took a stroke forward and shrugged. "Well, I didn't really expect them to like me after I told Scarlet that Jessinda was kissing her merfriend behind her back." Another shrug and then another stroke forward. "Odele, I want to apologize."

I blinked at her. "Apologize."

She nodded almost vigorously. "I know it wasn't my business to interfere, but I'm worried about you…"

It was my turn to snort unkindly. "Don't pretend like you ratted me out for my own good. You did it purely out of your own selfishness. Because you care more about Thalassar than you do my feelings."

My cousin had the good grace to look chagrined. Good. She should. She'd ruined my greatest chance at escape and almost ruined my life. Good thing I had a newly formed backup plan. Not that she needed to know anything about that.

"What you call selfishness, I call selflessness." She folded her hands across the flat of her stomach, tilted her chin up a fraction higher. Ever the princess she was becoming, and it was starting to show in fractions. "And I'll admit, you're right, but that wasn't my only reason for stopping you…" She gave pause, took a breath. I watched her fingers stiffen against her stomach, and I wondered if she was steeling herself against her next words. "I don't trust the queen," she admitted, almost reluctantly. "Even if she turned out to not be our mothers' murderer, it doesn't mean she won't do something to you if you disobey."

My eyes narrowed. "Like what?"

Maisie sighed and dropped her hands to her sides. "Like name you an outlaw. Like put a warrant out for your arrest if you flee. Like hiring someone to kill you before you can escape and embarrass her again."

My heart raced a few leagues in my chest before nearly stopping entirely. I straightened in my seat, gauging Maisie's expression.

My cousin had good reason to be wary of my stepmother. The queen wasn't known for her leniency. In fact, the only time I'd seen her show such a thing was a few weeks ago, when she'd let Maisie go unscathed despite the broken contract between Thalassar and Draconi. Though I think she did that to avoid further bloodshed, this time with Kappur *and* Draconi—and the wrath of the Dragon Prince.

We'd all thought the queen was a murderer, that she'd been the one to order the deaths of our mothers. It was a shock to me when the culprit turned out to be Percival instead.

Still, it didn't take away the sinister aura around my stepmother. Or her viciousness and cunning. I wouldn't doubt that she'd do anything in her power to protect her seat on the Thalassarin throne, and I wouldn't put murder past her just yet.

Still, maybe being murdered would be better than being married. The end result would be the same wouldn't it?

"You think she would harm me if I disobeyed again." It wasn't a question, but Maisie answered as if it had been one.

"I do," she said. "She's angry, Odele, and we don't know how she will lash out at you if you don't do what you're told. I—" She stopped, swallowed, looking uncomfortable. "I don't want anything to happen to you. I'm worried about you."

"Fine," I conceded. My head was reeling, but I didn't show my emotions. My confidence was my primary skin, and I exuded it in waves. "I believe you."

And I did. I could tell she was being honest; Maisie was the type of mer who was easily read. If she said she was worried and thought my stepmother would try to do something to me if I didn't obey, I would believe her.

Mainly because, duh, my stepmother was an evil shark.

Relief was evident on her features. Her shoulders slumped forward, as if she'd been truly worried I'd never forgive her.

I could hold a grudge better than anyone I knew, but I couldn't hold one against her.

Not long, anyway.

"Did you really tell Scarlet that Jessinda kissed her merfriend?" I asked, a smile tilting my mouth.

Maisie groaned and dropped her head back. "I'm so ashamed of it."

I giggled. "I'm not. I would have done it myself, eventually. Or at least blackmailed her with that information."

Maisie shrugged. "I'm not a fan of blackmail."

I leaned back on the bed, holding my body up with the palms of my hands as I lifted my tail and dropped it. Lifted, dropped. Lifted, dropped. "You *are* the boring one," I teased.

My cousin laughed, and I did too, but all the while I couldn't help but wonder if what she said was true. Was I in danger again? If I tried to escape, would my stepmother take advantage of that to have me killed so she wouldn't have to abdicate her throne?

It seemed it was time to pay the Queen of Thalassar one final visit.

The queen, like always, sat on her throne. On the throne that had been my mother's. On the throne that was rightfully mine.

The moment my eyes caught hers, there was a glimmer of defiance in my own and the promise of retribution in hers, I knew my cousin's fears were justifiable. Even so, I couldn't find *true* malice in her eyes. All I saw was the desire for power, for control.

Besides, if she'd wanted me dead, wouldn't she have killed me already? It wasn't as if I had any real power anyway. I was the princess of my kingdom, and though the throne should have been mine to inherit weeks ago, there she sat, smug and proud as she took me in at the fin of her throne.

At the fin of it, not sitting upon it.

She'd prevented me from inheriting, had told me I wasn't ready.

It was the truth, but that didn't make it sting any less.

No, I didn't think my stepmother would kill me. Which meant my plan of escape could still work.

"What do you want?" she asked unkindly.

My own eyes narrowed on her a brief moment before finding my father's. His blue eyes regarded me a little sadly, if I dared think it.

He was usually a handsome merman, but he looked a bit unkempt. His long, dark beard was usually studded with jewels and diamonds, or braided down his chest. Today it was bare of frivolity, like his hair that swept down the length of his broad back.

He wore blue robes, a color as rich as his eyes. Eyes that I looked into and sent out the force of my every impossible desire and wish.

"I leave tomorrow," I murmured, my voice cracking around the edges, echoing across the chasm that separated us in more ways than one. He said nothing, so I pressed on, willing my voice not to shake. "You can still change your mind, you know."

His body tensed, fingers digging into the arm of his throne. His lips pressed into a thin line. As his eyes narrowed, the crinkles appeared around the outer edges of them, and it reminded me of the merman he once was.

Of the merman who had picked me up when I cried. The merman who held me tightly in the circle of his arms, crushing me between his body and my mother's. I remembered their kisses, stolen when they thought I wasn't looking. I remembered a love that burned so bright, it rivaled the heat of the sun. I remembered the hand that seemed so big and vast, holding my smaller one. I remembered the tears we both wept when she died, and how he was there to pick up the pieces even when he had nothing left for himself. I remembered him piecing me back together with dresses and jewelry instead of with words and kisses, as if he had no more of them to spare for the daughter his wife had left behind for him to raise.

And he'd had no idea how to raise me, so he wrapped me up in linen and lace, gossamer and silk, diamonds and tiaras, as if that could somehow replace the love that both of us had lost, the mother I longed for, and the wife he could still not get over.

I remembered who he'd been in bits and pieces sometimes, a merman so grand and magnificent, one couldn't help but to love him when he spoke. But that merman wasn't in there any longer. He'd been replaced with something bitter and cold, a shell of the father that had once loved me as fiercely as he had loved my mother.

The love he had for me died when she had.

Still, I looked into his eyes. Into the sad eyes of a broken merman, and willed the fight back into them.

Fight, I begged. *Fight for me.*

It took everything I had to open the doors of my heart for the one simple request. The one thing I'd always wanted. A father who would bleed and die for me. A father who would wage a war for me, like Maisie's father did for her.

But he didn't fight. He didn't wage wars. My father merely looked at me like he would a stranger, and said in a cold, dead voice, "There will be no escaping this, Odele. The contracts have been signed. Tomorrow, you leave Thalassar for Iol and you *will* marry Prince Ytgar whether you like it or not."

My heart almost shattered into small fragments, then dust. Despite the walls I'd erected, his words still managed to pierce through me.

I wanted to cry, to scream. I wanted to *rage*. But I'd expected this, even if that made hearing those words no easier to bear.

As I took my final look at my father, the final time I'd ever see him after this, I couldn't help the treacherous thoughts that spun through my mind.

I just couldn't help but pause and wonder, did he not fight for me because he didn't like what he'd made me? Had I been more like my mother, like Maisie, kind and virtuous, would he have fought for me then? Would he have torn kingdoms apart, even his own, to keep me by his side?

I supposed I'd never know.

I pushed open the doors of the library, keeping my tears at bay. I'd shed them for Maisie, and that was the extent of my sadness, as it had been so obviously depleted.

Now nothing but hollowness remained.

I couldn't go back to the solitude of my new room when there was nothing there for me any longer. So I'd decided to come *here*, to the one place that had always felt like home. The place that filled me with the stories my father wouldn't, the place that held laughter, the place where I'd first discovered kingdoms and oceans that were not like my own. The one place where I'd desired something so desperately, I hadn't quite realized what it was at first. A life that wasn't my own.

I came into the library and was filled with a whole new type of sensation. One that tightened my throat and made me want to weep anew.

This room, no matter how small compared to the grandeur I'd read and listened about, never ceased to amaze me.

The shelves ranged from floor to ceiling, as did the ornate sea glass mirrors that brightened the room, along with the glow of lava globes positioned on every shelf. Each one held row upon row of conches,—some chipped with age, others shining and new—and kelp parchments rolled and tied with seaweed as string.

There were tables of stone, and chairs of coral meant for studying. It had been here that Percival Pike slapped the end of his whip down on the backs of my fingers and hands, making me lose sensation in that area altogether. Yet even his abuse could not make me hate this place.

Here, I was taught of new worlds. This was where I'd learned and studied, where I stayed up late and memorized every word spoken on every conch and written on every kelp parchment.

There had been days where the loneliness had been overwhelming, when even I, with all the love I had for diamonds and silk, had felt the suffocating confines of my golden gilded bedroom and had secretly sought solace between the shelves.

"Princess Odele!"

The merman who called my name with honest excitement was old and wrinkled, and his skin glowed like the light of a lantern. He often radiated the colors of his moods, and his skin currently gave off a bright yellow-white shade of happiness.

He floated behind the front desk where I usually found him, scratching away in his ledger, dipping a quill into squid ink and humming a soft tune to the rhythm of his jangling keys.

"Signing in one last time?" he asked, pushing the 'sign in, sign out' book to the edge of his desk.

I smiled instinctively and swam up to the desk. The ledger was bound with some type of seal leather, the pages thin and made of kelp. The entire book bulged, and on it awaited a quill already dipped in ink and a fresh spot for my name.

I picked up the quill and signed my name with a flourish. When I finished, it was to find the old merman chuckling. My eyebrows rose. "What's so funny?"

He pulled the book back towards himself before answering. "I just wonder how it's possible that your cousin kept up with the facade so long," he mused.

So far, he was the first to comment as much. Ever since mine and Maisie's ruse came to light, we had both been bombarded with astonishment. All anyone could say was that they didn't know how we'd been able to pull that off, that we looked exactly alike, that they couldn't tell us apart… The list went on.

"What do you mean?" I inquired cautiously.

The old merman shrugged. "It was obvious to me from the beginning who she was, and who she was not."

I blinked, not sure I truly believed him. "Hardly anyone can tell us apart."

"Those who don't look closely, perhaps. Maybe if they'd paid the slightest bit of attention to you beyond the tiara and the dresses, they would have noticed that *you*, my dearest Odele, are left handed. And Maisie is not."

My breath caught. One miniscule detail, *one thing* that no one had noticed, yet he *had*. One thing that could have ruined our ruse forever.

I had to teach myself to become ambidextrous now.

I winked at him. "Don't give away our secret."

He winked back. "I wouldn't dare, Princess."

I knew he wouldn't. Of everyone I knew, it was a shame that the palace librarian was the least likely to betray me.

"I'm going to take one last look around before I leave tomorrow," I informed him.

He gestured with his hand. "Of course, Your Majesty. And if there is anything you wish to take with you, take it. This is your library, after all."

After today, it wouldn't be. I didn't voice that aloud, though. I couldn't possibly tell him I'd never see it again, because once I swam away from my fate, for good, I wouldn't be welcome in Thalassar ever again.

I kept silent and swam through the familiar shelves, letting my fingers run delicately across their edges of coral, conch, and kelp. I let my fingertips memorize the textures and temperatures, and I committed every detail to memory. So that when I felt myself drowning in loneliness, I could think back on this moment and remember that the conches felt smooth as they kissed my fingertips, that the edges of my favorite conch on modern warfare was jagged and cut into my skin and onto my cheek from listening to it so often. Or that the conch on kingdoms in the seas had holes right where it curved, not big enough to fit my pinky through.

I knew every bit of this library as much as I knew myself. Maybe more.

I picked up the conch on kingdoms in the seas and pressed it to my ear. It didn't matter where the voice had stopped at—conches always started where the listener stopped listening—I knew the words, had them memorized.

"Iol was founded before the arrival of civilization in the south. It was a kingdom ruled by Vikings, both in the cold seas and on the continental two-legger lands. Iol refused to be colonized. They defended themselves with brute strength and cunning. War raged until after the death of gods' waning moon in the twentieth year. The United Kingdoms of Great Braugish sent their first born princess, Amelia Cerul, and sparked a compromise with Iol.

"Records and history are unclear, yet what we have surmised from the princess was that Iol relinquished some of their brutish ways and established both a monarchy and political justice figure in the form of a Prime Minister. This, of course, took many years.

"Even as Iol began opening the ice gates to their kingdom, they just as easily closed them. Years later, it is still difficult to obtain information on the secretive kingdom unless released directly by the royal family or Prime Minister..."

I stopped mouthing the words and set the conch back on the shelf. Iol had always been a mysterious kingdom, and though I'd studied every single conch we had on them, there was nothing of importance, and most of it was the same.

The United Kingdoms of Great Braguish no longer called itself that; in fact, it had been a century since they were the United Kingdoms. Now they were separate entities, Brague and Ventlair, forced apart by feuds and tyrannic laws.

I'd even tried looking up information on the aforementioned princess and had found very little, except that she'd been promised to the Viking king Torrent Snjor—who was later baptised as Neves in a new, modern language, instead of in the common tongue spoken back then. After her death, her body had been sent back to her royal family in the United Kingdoms. They'd never known if she'd had children, or how she had died. But it was rumored in many sources that in her dead hands, she held a necklace made of the same ice and diamond as the fabled royal Iolish sword.

The sword that Prince Ytgar carried with him.

I couldn't believe they'd promised me to the Iolish. A brutish race descended from savages, *Vikings*, and worse even, the fact that no one knew much about them. There weren't even portraits of the royal family on any records, nothing except the vague mention of their orca-like tails.

I supposed every royal family had some strange characteristic.

For Thalassarin royalty, it was the bright purple-blue tails. For the Iolish, it was the orca. Draconian royalty either had the features of Koi fish or dragons, or both. Braugish had the lower bodies of octopi; Ventlair of sharks, and I wasn't entirely sure what Kappurin royalty had. Perhaps I would ask Maisie about it later.

Then there were the Uncharted Waters to the west of the seven sea kingdoms that the brave dare not venture for fear that they'd never return. Occasionally, an immigrant or two found their way into Thalassar, but how were we to know anything about their home when immigrants were very good at hiding?

I'd dug up conches on the Uncharted Waters, and in all of the vast library, there had been only one. I still remembered the words. Every single one.

Do not venture into the Uncharted Waters.

Of course, that just made me even more curious. I hoped I could visit it one day. Perhaps when I made my escape, it would be to the western waters.

I was still undecided on my destination.

I continued my final trek through the library, weaving my way through shelves, touching my favorite conches, listening to bits and pieces of some of them, as if I didn't already have them memorized from start to finish.

By the time I finished, it was dark out and my fingers had started to cramp up, my arms and ears had started to hurt. So I made my way back to the front of the library. Before I signed out, I turned and breathed the library in one last time.

I missed it already, and I hadn't even left yet. My only solace was knowing that wherever else I'd go, I'd make sure there was a library there. But perhaps I wouldn't even need the adventures and knowledge of others, whispered to me from the confines of old chipped conches. Perhaps I'd be out there in the world finding adventures of my own.

I turned away from the shelves and stained sea glass windows, as if I could also turn away from my heartbreak as well.

It was time to leave.

I swam up to the desk, pulling the ledger towards me without a word. I signed my name slowly, relishing in the finality of it. One last time, the last I'd ever sign my name in this book. The last I'd ever see this glowing merman looking up and smiling at me. Genuinely smiling, like he was truly happy to see me.

No one else looked at me that way.

"You leave tomorrow," he commented, and I swore he sounded sad.

"To the waters of ice and snow." I pushed the ledger back towards him. Slowly.

"I hope you do not take offense, Princess…" He bent below the desk and rummaged around. When he came back up, it was with a woven knapsack, the contents inside rattled. "I took the liberty of selecting those I knew were your favorites." He thrust the bag towards me and when I took it, he bent again and emerged once more with a similar bag. "I also took the liberty of filling this one with empty recording conches." I arched a brow in question and he answered without me having to ask aloud. "In case you want to document your own adventures for future generations."

I took the second bag from his hands. They both carried hefty weight, but this was a labor I didn't mind. I'd never minded the long hours in the library, never minded the bruises I hid behind lavish long sleeves because I hauled sacks similar to these around day after day.

"I don't know if I can accept these." I gestured to the bag that was filled with my favorite conches. He must have been paying very close attention to me, to know which ones I loved.

"You are the princess. You can do what you please."

True. I had merely declined because when I made my escape, I would take nothing with me. I didn't want this parting gift to be in vain.

"I'll miss this place." My confession was little more than a whisper.

"And it won't be the same without you." He reached across the space that separated us and pressed a hand against my shoulder. It was the comforting gesture of a parting touch. It was a goodbye. And it was the regret I had so yearned to see. "A part of me wishes that you didn't have to go, Majesty." He pulled his hand away reluctantly, like he realized a moment too late he shouldn't be placing his hands on the kingdom's princess. But as soon as he took his hand away, I wanted it back where it had been.

"And the other part?" Despite my resolve to stay strong, my voice cracked.

He smiled. "The other part just wants you to be happy."

I smiled sadly, if only to keep myself from crying. I cherished this moment and knew I would keep the secret of it with me always.

I hadn't had my stepmother's regret, or even my father's, yet as far as goodbyes went, this was the one I would treasure the most. It was the most perfect goodbye I could have ever asked for.

"Don't you think it's better to wear something more… practical?" Maisie eyed my fabulous traveling attire distastefully.

Clad in a purple brocade with a thread of silver and gold flowers, the dress was cinched tightly at my waist, made to highlight the finer points of my luscious figure. It had a heart-shaped neckline, giving a teasing hint at the pearl-pink skin of my generous breasts. The sleeves were short, rounded puffs, and the skirts were wide and heavy. My neck was adorned with diamonds and sapphires, as were my ears, wrists, and the ornate headpiece sitting just above my brow inlaid with my glittering tiara.

If perfection had a definition, it would be me.

"Don't you think it's better to wear something more… princess-like?" I countered, eyeing her own simple outfit.

Maisie wore a traveling tunic of white, belted at the waist, a black seal leather overcoat with the spikes of some disgusting creature on the shoulders and breast pockets. She wore a scabbard and her black blade at her hip, the whole thing made entirely of polished obsidian, with a single sapphire jewel studded on the hilt. It was a twin to the one carried by Elias Blackfin—the Black Blade—formerly known as the most wanted criminal in all of Thalassar, and one of my cousin's lovers. Except, his was longer, and studded with black diamonds at the hilt.

My cousin's little entourage surrounded her, each of them forming a protective wall at her back.

Prince Kai, as her husband, was at her left, his soft features set warily on me. He had all the features of a true Draconian, slanted dark eyes, long luxurious hair—not that I'd ever admit that aloud—that he'd tied with a red ribbon away from his face, high cheekbones, and soft lips. He was tall and lithe, with the orange, white, and black spottings on his tail like that of a koi fish.

To her right was the Black Blade. True to his namesake, he was clad in all black, and instead of glaring, he stared at me with never-ending mischief and humor. As if life were just one big joke to him. His skin was brown, his hair curly and black, floating in tendrils around his cheeks.

Behind her was Captain Tiberius Saber, no longer captain. At least, not for Thalassar. His bright aquamarine eyes darted nearly everywhere at once, gauging for possible threats. He was broader than the other two at her sides, more muscular. His skin appeared as though golden rays had trapped behind the surface, tanned and almost bulging, and his hair was bright yellow.

Somewhere behind him there was a procession of Draconian soldiers, advisors, and fearsome dragons as well as Kappurin soldiers.

Even the might of that ensemble would never shy me away from insulting that perfect atrocity of an outfit.

Maisie merely shrugged. "It's rather ostentatious…"

"Oh, as opposed to Lizard Prince's dragon back there?" I snorted. "I am Princess of Thalassar and I will dress as I please."

My cousin blew out an exasperated breath. "I'm just sayin', it might not be exactly comfortable for ridin' a hippocampus, is all."

Again, I snorted. The poor gel had no idea what she was talking about. I didn't want to hold it against her, though, as she was fairly new to Thalassar, to *me*, and didn't know the full extent of my abilities.

Because I wanted to prove my point, and show off for her procession as well as the Iolish bastards and Thalassarin traitors framed around *me*, I gripped the reins of my hippocampus, who I'd been about to mount before Maisie had rudely interrupted, and started to swing myself over her back.

But then someone was behind me, hands gripping at my waist. The action was so startling, I lost my balance and fell forward, upper body sprawling across the saddle in an undignified manner. My tail shot up, and I felt the heavy weight of my dress descend around my waist, and I knew, without a doubt, that everyone had an exceptional view of my entire tail. Scales and all.

Bursts of laughter made me want to bury myself in the silt and never emerge. This type of embarrassing stuff wasn't supposed to happen to me. This was supposed to happen to Maisie or Jessinda. Not me. Never me.

With as much dignity as I could muster, I righted myself, letting my skirts fall into place as I sat up straight on the saddle. I looked down to pierce whoever had dared touch me with a glare.

Of course it was Prince Ytgar. The crownless Iolish bastard was staring at me, a blush dusting his light brown cheekbones as he stared at me with obvious shock.

I gripped the reins tightly in my gloved hands, grinding my teeth together. I managed to spit out, "Foolish Iolish bastard."

"I—I—" He swallowed, and I watched the bob of his throat. Really, did he have to be so attractive? It only made me hate him so much more. And now that he'd thoroughly embarrassed me in front of everyone, I was more determined than ever to get away from him.

"Are you alright?" Maisie asked, chewing on her lip in a serious attempt to keep her laughter at bay.

The Black Blade wasn't so discreet.

I was utterly humiliated. Right in the front gates of the palace of Eramaea, where mer had gathered to watch us depart, in front of my father and my stepmother, in front of news conches, my cousins, and the Iolish. Soon the whole world would be making fun of the situation.

I was always so careful about my appearance, always so careful about my hair and makeup, what I wore and what jewels adorned my body. Never before had anything been out of place. Until now.

"Let's just get on with it," I snapped impatiently. The sooner we left, the sooner I could make my grand escape.

"Aren't you going to say goodbye first?" Maisie asked, suddenly serious.

I looked up to the entrance of the palace, where the queen and king floated. They were both rigid, staring like we were a spectacle entirely beneath them. I glared at the queen first, and she glared right back. There hadn't been any goodbyes inside, and there would be none here. She would not take me in her arms and wish me well. And even if she would have, I'd not welcome the hypocrisy. She wanted me gone and gone was what I'd be.

I couldn't even bring myself to look at my father, so instead I turned away.

"Let's go," I ordered, before snapping the reins and turning away from my home.

Forever.

Valmundur

I'D ONLY MEANT TO help her onto her hippocampus. It was in the plan I'd formulated with Ytgar. It was about wooing her, and mermaids loved to be helped onto their hippocampi—and orcas. There was something intimate about hands on a waist, of feeling the delicate feminine weight, of eyes meeting and holding, of lips parting in a silent invitation for a kiss.

But the moment my hands had encircled her waist, she'd startled and tensed, and everything else had been a silt storm after that.

I was supposed to be wooing her. Not making her hate me.

I chastised and cursed myself to the ice and back as our party marched forward.

I was sure we made a frightening sight to onlookers. The small Iolish party mingling with the Thalassarin Princess and her ladies-in-waiting, the Dragon Prince and his wife, a criminal, the Kappurin King and his guards. Behind us, hippocampi pulled shell carriages with chests of tents, food, clothes, and jewels. Everything except the princess' dowry, which would be received upon marriage. Behind the hippocampi were the Draconian soldiers and their dragons.

"If that's how you woo, then I am not surprised you are alone." Ytgar suddenly appeared beside me, regal atop his white hippocampus, white like the color of his hair and eyes. He was every bit the royal I could never hope to be.

I wasn't one to fall into self-consciousness, that was for mermaids and children, but I couldn't help the newly formed doubt now in my mind. That hadn't gone the way I wanted it to, and Ytgar laughing made everything worse somehow. I was the one to laugh *at*, not to *be* laughed at.

"Shove off," I muttered in our mother tongue. "If you think you can do better, then do it."

Ytgar's lips pressed together with amusement. He was usually so controlled in public, these small displays were a rarity. "It is not a competition," he said. "And I have no interest in wooing her. My only interest is in getting her to Iol and seeing her at the altar."

"That's cold, even for you."

He shrugged. "Such is the way of royal life."

There was a moment of silence that stretched out almost painfully, filling up with words neither of us would say. Things like, be grateful for what you have, and the ice is bluer on the other side. Nonsense that neither of us would ever believe.

"Perhaps I should go speak with her," I finally said, and threw a glance over my shoulder to catch her eye. When I did, I regretted it immediately, and turned back around, a shiver slicing through my spine. The gleam in her brown eyes had been murderous. "Nevermind." I shuddered. "Silt, I really mucked things up." I gripped the reins of my hippocampus to steady myself.

These beasts were rather tame compared to orcas, and the pace we swam at felt rather slow. I had the sudden urge to tear through the water at breakneck speed, but knew that if I pushed the animal too hard, it would be the one to break its neck first, and I'd still have all this pent up frustration inside.

"There's nothing to be done about that, I'm afraid." Ytgar tried to sound reassuring, though his voice was more condescending than anything.

I shot him a glare. "Then you go speak with her." Ytgar's entire body tensed up within seconds after the words left my lips. A mischievous smile curled my lips. "Don't tell me you're afraid of your betrothed?" I jabbed my elbow into his side, and he swatted it away with a grunt.

Echoing my earlier words, he practically growled, "Shove off."

"Just go," I ordered more sternly. "You're the one who should be wooing her anyway, not me." Even if I wanted her, I had to take a stroke aside, eventually. There was absolutely no point in tying myself to her, of answering the seductive call she didn't even know she was singing. She wasn't mine, and I should remember that.

But I didn't want to.

"Go," I urged again, tightly this time. "Just… see if she's alright. Pretend like you're guarding her or something."

Ytgar let his gaze settle over me, long and hard, and for the first time, that stare made me uncomfortable. It was like he was tearing invisible claws through the entirety of my being and ripping out the truth with just a look. It was all it took, the silver-white of his eyes on mine to bring the truth to the light. I knew, and he knew, even if he didn't speak that truth aloud or make me face it myself.

"Fine," he agreed with a sigh. "I will see to your precious princess."

I didn't watch as he steered the hippocampus around to make his way towards her. I didn't want to bring myself to turn around and stare at them together, to see what a beautiful couple the two would make.

She's not yours.
She's not yours.
She's his.
And you'd do well to remember.

Ytgar

VAL WANTED ODELE. THAT truth hit me the moment I looked into his pleading, eager blue eyes. It hit me like an ice spear to the chest in a way that was surprising. Surprising because of the vicious jealousy that seared through me as hot as lava. Jealousy I never knew existed within my own body. A jealousy that, strangely, went both ways.

I had thought Val's insistence had been on account of Iol, of our kingdom's future. Not because he wanted my betrothed.

For a brief moment, I hated him for wanting her, just as much as I hated Odele for inspiring it in him.

I couldn't explain the fierce possessiveness that rose inside me. The need to keep them apart. To stake my claim on her with my lips, my body.

As soon as those savage impulses arose, I shoved them vehemently away. It didn't matter what Val felt, what Odele felt, what *I* felt. It didn't matter what we wanted or how badly or hotly our bodies burned for the impossible.

We had a duty.

A duty I meant to fulfill once we were safely in Iol. But to do that, we had to get there first. All of us.

I knew Odele wouldn't come to Iol quietly, despite what Val thought. For however short our stay had been in Thalassar, I knew her. I recognized her independence, her determination. We were cut from the same iceberg, alike in that regard.

She wanted to be free of responsibility, and I craved responsibility with every fiber of my being.

And I needed her for that.

So, the harder she tested the limits of my patience, as hard as she pushed, I would push back harder.

And I'd secretly enjoy every second of it.

Like I'd told her just the night before, I'd brought many a wild beast to heel.

As I approached her and her ladies-in-waiting, I could feel her anger pulsating like a living, breathing thing in my direction. I nodded to her ladies first, ignoring their disdainful looks, and finally turned to Odele.

Her gaze was piercing and would have withered a lesser merman.

I wasn't a lesser merman.

"Princess," I greeted with a nod of my head.

Her pretty brown eyes narrowed. I couldn't help but feel amused.

"What do *you* want?" she demanded. She said the word 'you' with the same disdain as someone would when using the words 'famine' or 'plague'.

I owed her no explanations; in fact, I should have kept quiet about it entirely. Yet she pushed me.

"Prince Ytgar has commanded me to watch over you for the rest of the journey."

She bristled and shot a glance at her ladies that could only be construed as conspiratorial. When she turned back to me, her eyes were mutinous.

"I don't need a sitter," she replied haughtily. "Tell your *prince,*" she sneered the word, "that I need nothing from him."

I pierced her with a withering glare of my own. She was a formidable opponent, a challenge that warranted a vicious and violent response.

"Perhaps we would be inclined to believe that," I mused, "if you didn't wander about the waters like some type of petulant child."

Her ladies, having heard me, gasped. "The *audacity*!" one of them exclaimed, the red-haired one in an outfit as equally ridiculous as Odele's.

Odele didn't seem scandalized at all by my daring words. Perhaps, if she knew who I truly was, she wouldn't find them daring at all, but rather rightfully spoken.

"How cute," she muttered, pursing her lips. "I suppose in the northern waters, whale trainers can speak to royalty however they please." She sniffed, looking down her nose at me, though I was taller than her. "Where I come from, whale trainers know their place."

My temper flared at the implication in her words, the haughty arrogance to them. Not on my behalf, for she could say what she would about Prince Ytgar all she wanted and I'd not bat an eye. But to speak ill of Val...

"Well, my prince says my place is with you. Like it or not..." I paused and let my gaze rack over every inch of her body, and I felt something flare to life between us. A kernel sparking into something more that hadn't seemed banked in the first place. Desire and passion in equal measure, hidden beneath words meant to spar and harm. It was like swordplay, the mere act of it heating my blood to impossible temperatures. And I knew she felt it, too. "...I will *stay* by your side."

I meant it as both a threat and a promise, as a merciless seduction meant to incite fear and desire to the very core of her being. And judging by the way her body shivered, it worked.

Odele

I WAS TOO AWARE of the big hulking figure riding beside me, sometimes behind me. I was aware of his heat, and the potency of his silver-white eyes, eyes that seemed to dig into the center of my soul and search, despite the walls I had built around myself, the piercing weight of his gaze eradicated them entirely.

The sensations he caused to build inside of me were unnerving. His proximity made my chest pound so loudly, I was sure he could hear it. My palms heated, and my fingers fidgeted against the reins.

It was embarrassing.

Why did my body quake with awareness? Why did I want to turn and lash out at him and bring him lower than he already was? He was a *whale trainer,* for tides' sakes. I shouldn't want to know if his lips were as soft as they looked, or wonder what the hard ridges of his ab muscles would feel like against my palms.

I shouldn't want any of that.

And yet… I did. I couldn't explain it, except to claim madness. The heat of being out in the open waters for hours now was blinding me, clouding my common sense. He was a commoner. He was beneath me. He was everything I loathed and despised. He was Iolish. A bastard. And I was betrothed to his prince.

Ugh.

I could still feel him staring, could see the exact angle of his body in my peripheral vision.

It didn't help that he was attractive. This entire ordeal would have been so much easier had he been ugly. Him and Ytgar both. But of course, they were blessed by the tides with freakish good looks. And Val was blessed with the body of a sea god, all massive shoulders and arms that weren't at all as well hidden beneath the thick fur coat as he thought.

Really, wasn't he hot in that thing?

His lips seemed to quirk up with something akin to amusement. I glared and couldn't help myself from snapping, "What's so funny?"

His silver-white eyes pierced the deepest depths of my soul with their intensity. I fought back the instantaneous reaction to that stare, the shiver and goosebumps that threatened to overwhelm me. His eyes held secrets, and answers. They held questions, passions, hatred, and desire. And they were focused solely on me. I knew then, despite myself, that whatever mermaid dominated his heart would be *his.* Wholly, irrevocably, and entirely.

"Your grumblings," he answered, the side of his mouth twitching. "They're quite amusing."

I scoffed with indignation. "I do *not* grumble."

He turned away, as if the discussion were beneath him, as if it were promptly over.

The conversation was over when I said it was over. "I *don't*," I argued.

He turned back to me with raised eyebrows.

"Well, I *don't*."

He shrugged and turned back to the waters ahead. Silence pulsed between us after that. A silence in which I was all too aware of him. It was uncomfortable, it made me want to fill the spaces of it. What was wrong with me? I was acting like a barnacle.

And it was all his fault.

It made me hate him all the more.

"Iolish bastard," I grumbled. Then he chuckled, the sound grating down my spine, and I found I couldn't ignore him at all. I turned sharply. *"What?"* I demanded.

He gripped the reins with a new carelessness, not the kind that Ytgar displayed. It was still contained, yet on him, it seemed almost rare and out of place. "You complain greatly for a mer bathed in diamonds, silk, hippocampi, and now a handsome betrothed."

I glared haughtily at him. "You find Prince Ytgar handsome."

He froze a brief moment and when he looked at me again, there was something in his expression I'd never seen before. Something akin to mischief. "I *know* he's handsome."

I snorted. "I've seen better."

I really hadn't. I mean, I'd seen my fair share of attractive mermen. Prince Kai was pretty, if one enjoyed mermen who looked more like delicate mermaids. Captain Saber had an attractive sort of face… if one liked depressing mermen suffering from platonic love for the better part of a few years.

Okay, well, I'd been locked in the palace the better part of my life. And yes, I found Ytgar attractive, against my own better judgment. And I couldn't help but compare the two mermen in appearance once again.

Val had the more traditionally handsome features of a royal than Ytgar did, and yet…

What in the tides' was I doing?

These two merman had been so deeply embedded into me already that I was thinking about them in a positive light. I shouldn't have even been worrying about them at all. I should have been plotting my escape. I couldn't let Val distract me from my purpose any longer, my plan.

So with a final eye roll in his direction, I tugged the reins to the side and my hippocampus followed, putting distance between the two of us, wedging myself between Jessinda and Silviya. I kept my eyes ahead the entire time, avoiding Val's gaze, which I felt heavily on me, following me the entire way.

We finally stopped for the night, but instead of stopping at some inn, we were going to be *camping.* I didn't manage to hold back my disgust as I dismounted.

"Camping?" I demanded.

"Couldn't they have found an inn?" Jessinda echoed my thoughts as she dismounted.

Silviya and Scarlet followed, and it was Silviya who crinkled her nose as she did a sweep around the open space that was meant to be our camp. Already the soldiers were unloading the tents from the carriages and erecting them in the silt.

Dragons settled in with their Draconian riders, the massively scaled creatures as majestic as they were dangerous. I gave them a wide berth; the spikes running from their foreheads down to their long barbed tails looked like they could take me out with very little effort.

Kai, being the inbred that he was, went up to his own pet dragon, which was as beautiful and elegant as he was. It was as large as a whale with glittering scales that looked as hard as sapphires. Its long neck stretched out leisurely as Kai smoothed his hand beneath the length of its throat. The dragon's barbed tail curled around its body, vicious, leathery wings tucked around itself against the sudden cold of the night.

"Perhaps the Iolish cannot afford an inn," Silviya scrutinized.

"That wouldn't surprise me," Scarlet added.

I looked around at the terrain. Nothing but open ocean and a few coral reefs around us, not to mention the underpopulated school of fish and other creatures. We weren't far from the city, but we were far enough. From here on out, we would swim into the country folk of Thalassar. The ocean around here was plain, flat.

In other words, not good conditions in which to escape. Not yet, at least.

"It's full of silt." Jessinda lifted her skirts a fraction and shook them, sending silt flying around in a cloud. She coughed daintily into her closed fist and batted her eyelashes a couple of times. "This is despicable. These are no conditions for us."

Indeed, I mused internally. I lifted my own skirts and shook them. Silt flew and when the cloud of it cleared, I found Maisie floating among us, glancing with a rather amused expression at our cousins.

"You are all acting like babies," she commented with a smile. Nothing about her tone spoke of judgement, but it was there in the teasing glint in her eyes and the tilt of her smile. Only I knew it was there, because only I knew her.

"Well, unlike *you,* we weren't raised in the boondocks," Jessinda snapped. Maisie raised a brow. "I was hardly raised in the boondocks."

Jessinda's eyes slid down the atrocity of her traveling outfit. Really, I had tried to tell her. Even so, that didn't give Jessinda the right to insult her. That duty was mine alone. Sure, her outfit was disgusting, an eyesore, and anyone could see the truth in it.

"Jessinda doesn't know basic geography," I told Maisie, earning myself a glare from Jessinda. "Don't bother explaining silt to her."

Maisie snorted and turned sharply towards me. "While they're setting up camp, I'm going to help set up a lava seam." Lava seams were thick globes filled with lava, attached to which was a metal tube that was used to safely release small quantities of the molten liquid. It was used to heat pots of food, or even sand so we could sit around it for warmth. I supposed it resembled what two-leggers would call a bonfire. "Want to help?" she asked, cocking her head to the side.

I blinked. "Why would I want to do that?"

My other cousins snickered in response.

Maisie shrugged. "So we can spend more time together?" she offered.

I'd accept if it didn't involve physical peasant labor.

"You're a princess," I reminded her. "You have mer to help you build sand volcanoes for lava seams."

Her eyebrows rose. "So you know a mountain of silt has to be formed before we use the seam?" She sounded surprised, as I'm sure many were when they realized I wasn't just a pretty face, though my face was rather dazzling. It was a common misconception.

"I have no desire to shove my hands in silt. You have no idea what's crawling in there, cousin."

She shrugged again, as if to say she couldn't care less what she found in the silt. When I made it clear I wasn't going to help her with servant's labor, she left to do it herself.

I tossed the reins of my hippocampus to an awaiting Thalassarin servant and my cousins did the same. Then we floated, waited, and watched them put up our tents. Well, while they watched the labor, I watched Maisie. She bent low in the sand, pulling handfuls of sand towards herself until she formed a small volcano. Elias sidled up to her and bent down to help. They laughed together and exchanged heated stares. Stares that passed off as a silent conversation between the two.

I marveled at it for but a moment. The mer called me spoiled because I liked to surround myself in luxuries and riches. But Maisie was just as spoiled as I. Not with jewels or clothes, but with the mermen she surrounded herself with. She had her own harem, for tides' sakes. She hoarded mermen like a dragon hoarded jewels and was proud of it.

I wondered what it would be like to divide a heart so thoroughly that love was scintillatingly palpable. Like an invisible thread interconnected and wove through their spirits, their fates, making them different, individual, yet one just the same. They shared her, and they loved her, and she loved them each in turn. Equally, yet for different reasons, innately their own.

I never imagined myself in love, but for a moment, watching Maisie, I could see myself clearly. I would wear that same expression on my own face. The expression of a complete and utter fool.

I tore my gaze away and glared when I found Val's and Ytgar's eyes on my form.

The bastards.

At least Ytgar looked away, a flush on his cheeks. Val stared… and stared… Almost as if he knew where my errant thoughts had headed. I didn't like that one bit.

I swam up to the soldiers and servants in charge of my tent and found myself shrieking at them. "Will you hurry up before I have you whipped? I must freshen up before dinner and I wish to retire early!"

Their bodies tensed, but my words had the desired effect. They hurried through the task at a much faster rate now that I was there issuing out orders I shouldn't have been doing in the first place. Really, it was so hard to find reliable help these days.

When they finished, they rushed to fill the inside with lava globes and my chests with my clothes. Once they were done, I pushed my way inside, closing the flaps of my tent behind me. I tried not to shiver at the conditions. Did mer really camp for fun? What a frightening thought. A tent was no place for a princess. Though the cot laid against the floor was plush with pillows and blankets. At the foot of the makeshift bed were three of my chests. Two with my clothes—though I still had a few more chests with clothes somewhere—and the other with my conches.

I bent down to the chest with my conches and flicked it open. I'd divided up the conches into two different chests. There was one that contained stories of adventure and history, and the other contained the blank ones meant for my own.

I picked up a blank conch. Recording conches looked like any normal shell that could be found on the ocean floor. The chamber inside any number of them were meant specifically for messages as long as they were infused with science and magic, they could record anything, trap voices inside or even images in the floating forms of bubbles.

Most times, to record a conch or watch it, you needed a specially made device for it. A recorder, much like the one I'd used back at the palace. To watch the images, all that had to be done was to place the conch face down on a disc—a disc that resembled what two-leggers called a 'record player', which was a remarkably strange name—that twirled and projected the images inside. To record, the conch had to be connected to an equally tedious device, like a stick that went inside the chamber at one end while the other end captured the recording.

The fascinating thing about magic and science was that the two were always evolving, and one couldn't exist without the other. The librarian had given me the newest model conches. These didn't need a recording stick or a disc. All I had to do was aim the chamber at what I wanted captured, and it would capture it. Of course, every conch had a limit as to what would fit inside it. Sometimes the smaller conches held merely a few minutes of conversation or blurry images. The benefit of the newer models was that it could hold up to an hour's worth of clear images.

I aimed the chamber entrance at myself and the inside of it began to glow. It was how I knew it was recording.

"It's me," I whispered. "Princess Odele Malabella Oriana." I paused, not knowing how to continue. I chewed on my bottom lip. "And this is the story of how I was ripped from my home kingdom of Thalassar and thrust on a journey to violent winters and inbred merfreaks."

If there was one thing I learned, it was that every conch was a stage, and I was a performer. The more dramatic the performance, the better. Not that I was exaggerating on any account. The Iolish *were* inbred merfreaks, and it was said that Iolish winters *were* violent.

"I thought that once I turned eighteen, I'd be free from the confines of royal life. My cousin Odalaea—or Maisie, as she prefers to be called—would take the Thalassarin throne, and I'd be free to roam the waters of the world with a sack of coins and a heart full of adventure. Instead, I am forced to be a slave in a kingdom of ice and shadow, and suffer in a way no other princess has ever suffered before.

"I suppose the one good thing to come out of my eighteenth birthday was that my mother's murderer was executed. I only wish he could have died by my own hand."

I stopped talking then, my eyes and mind distancing myself from the reality of where I was as I went back to what had happened weeks before. When Percival Pike, my stepmother's former advisor, had confessed to murdering both my mother and my aunt in his attempt to cleanse our bloodline.

Maisie and I had been so sure my stepmother was guilty that we'd overlooked him entirely. If I hated him for his incessant beatings and lessons, for the feel of a whip crashing against the backs of my hands for *years,* then I utterly loathed him for what he'd done to my mother.

I could still see the tip of the poisoned arrow on his speargun, a speargun we believed he'd hidden beneath his robes at the wedding ceremony of Kai and Maisie. He'd pointed it at me, right after he'd shot my cousin. At that moment, I hadn't thought about the imminence of my death. It hadn't mattered if he'd gotten a clear shot at me. All that mattered was that I reach him in time before he did.

That I kill him in cold blood, the way he'd killed my mother.

I'd wanted to. I'd wanted to run him through. It wasn't like I was new to killing. I'd killed once before. The merman who had forced the poison down my mother's throat, Percival's lackey and mercenary. He'd been trying to kill Maisie, and the rest had been instinct. I hadn't planned it. All I'd thought about was protecting my cousin, the one final link I had that connected me to my mom. It felt like we were connected on some ephemeral level that couldn't be explained even within the bounds of magic or science.

And so I'd shoved the tip of my sword through his chest.

I'd practiced fencing my whole life. I studied warfare. I knew what it all meant, and yet it had always been a game. A vicious game I was good at. I hadn't quite thought of the implications it meant to take someone's life, even someone as disgusting as that mercenary. I hadn't seen his face when he'd died, the moment my sword pierced his heart. Still, I could tell the precise moment when the life left his body. Almost as if I could see it, the phantasmic shadow of his soul slipping from his corporeal self.

That shadow tainted my own soul.

I still had nightmares about him sometimes. Because I'd killed him. I woke in the middle of the night feeling cold all over, disgusted with myself. Not because of what I'd done, but because my mind and body had the audacity to feel *guilty* about it. He'd deserved his death tenfold. I should have made him suffer more.

So why was I losing sleep over it?

And that brought on the awning question that loomed over my head like some two-legger umbrella. What would have happened, had I killed Percival too?

Ytgar and Val had taken that option from me. I should have been grateful. *Should have been.* I was merely irritated. Irritated because of my relief that it hadn't been me. Irritated because I'd wanted it to be me.

My mind was a treacherous pit filled with a myriad of confusing emotions.

I blinked, realizing that the conch was still recording me. I flashed it a dazzling smile as if I were in court in the presence of dozens of my royal admirers.

"I digress, perhaps I'll document this misadventure of mine and introduce you all to the conspirators responsible for my misfortunes. One by the name of Ytgar Neves Isolde, another by the name of Valmundur, though I am unsure of his surname. And my cousin, Odalaea—Maisie—Malabella Knoll Li. Perhaps, by the end of this adventure, they'll find themselves wishing they had never crossed paths with me, for I shall be a fearsome and formidable opponent." With that, I turned the conch facing down, and the light dimmed, indicating that it had stopped recording. Placing it back inside the chest, I closed the lid carefully and then got up and stretched.

Whew, but I was famished and hadn't quite realized it before now. I hoped they had food prepared, for if I was forced to be kept waiting, someone might lose their head.

With a smile on my face, I began undressing. It was at times like this, when I couldn't quite reach the back ribbons of my dress, that I wished for a gaggle of servants to wait hand and fin on me. Yet, I couldn't bring myself to keep them. Even I valued a bit of privacy, and like I'd told Maisie, there was no one who dressed me better than myself. What would a lowly servant know about fashion?

With a yank, I loosened the ribbons holding the dress up in the back. The material loosened around my bodice and I tugged, pulling my arms out of the sleeves and shimmying out of the heavy dress. It pooled down at my fins, and with a kick of my tail, it flew across the tent and landed in a heap on the silt. Whatever. A servant could pick it up later.

I was down to my corset and thin shift. I contemplated my state of dress for a moment. It would be a simple dinner before retiring for bed. There was no need for the same extravagance as when we'd been on the waters, but how could I look anything less than perfect? A simple but beautiful dress would do, and perhaps I'd go free of jewelry except for a golden circlet or tiara, lest these peasants forget I was their superior.

I would need my shift, but perhaps I could take my corset off. It was blasted uncomfortable to eat with the thing on and I'd be retiring soon anyway. My figure was still impeccable without it. I had the curves of a merwoman beyond her years, that was for sure.

I pulled the shift over my shoulders and dropped it to the ground as well. I was left floating in nothing more than a tight corset that pushed my breasts up—a long scrap of lace stitched at the hem of it to float down my tail—when suddenly the tent flaps parted and a figure floated in the entrance.

My breath caught, and heat rose up my neck and crawled to my cheeks.

Val froze, the most still I'd ever seen him. His eyes grazed over my every inch, silver-white eyes touching my skin as warmly as if it had been his own hands. They danced over the edge of my collarbone, my shoulders, to the tops of my swollen breasts.

I should have covered myself. Who did this whale trainer think he was, barging into my tent as if he had the right? A vicious cold rage rose in me, and I readied myself to berate him until he died of shame, yet something stopped me.

It was a heady awareness. A tumultuous sensation that had me floating as still as a fish would when it found itself before a shark. That's what he looked like: predatory. And I was his prey. And for some insane, primitive reason, a treacherous part of me wanted to be.

I let him take in his fill, let his eyes flare silver with the obvious appreciation over my curves, and when his eyes finally found my own once more, I forced a frown to my face.

"What are you doing in here?" I demanded angrily.

He wasn't reacting to my body at all. His lips didn't twitch, and a quick glance lower showed no evidence of a hard ridge of arousal that should be there, though would I even tell with that ridiculous cloak he wore?

"I am to fetch you for dinner."

I crossed my arms against my chest, the action pushing my breasts up higher. It had been a purposeful move, to get a rouse out of him just so I could shoot him back down with equal vehemence. Whale trainers weren't meant to ogle princesses, even if I was tantalizing him purposefully.

His eyes didn't even lower.

Iolish bastard.

"You couldn't knock first? Or are there no doors in Iol?"

The side of his mouth twitched. Finally. A reaction. "Next time I'll make sure to knock on the tent flaps."

Was that sarcasm? Yes, it was, and he was making fun of me! As if he could knock on cloth and it would even make a sound! Did he think I was stupid? Perhaps that wasn't my brightest moment, but good gods, he'd caught me off guard, and his lack of a reaction was damn lowering.

"See to it that you do." I uncrossed my arms. "As you can see, I am in the middle of changing and you have invaded my privacy entirely."

Finally, his eyes flicked over my figure, and a slow smile crept across his face. *Finally.* I prepared a tongue lashing, prepared to shoot down his hopes that he would *ever* have any opportunity to touch me, or to even look at me, or to breathe the same waters as me.

Then he spoke. "Don't worry, Princess," he practically sneered. "Whatever you might have isn't enough to entice me in the least." His eyes flared, and I stiffened defensively at the raw honesty and teasing in his eyes.

"Well, what's that supposed to mean?" I demanded.

He shrugged one massive shoulder. "Only that I can see why you go to such great lengths to wear such ostentatious clothing. You'd be ordinary otherwise."

My face heated, and I was sure the pearly pinkness of my skin was blazing red. "Listen here, you big brute..." I took a couple of strokes forward until we were face to face and pressed an accusing finger against his chest, poking him. "I am a gods' damned *confection,* do you hear me?"

He blinked down at me, unfazed. "Pardon?"

I growled with frustration. "I'm *delicious! Delicious!*"

His silver eyebrows rose. "If you say so, Your Majesty. Dinner is ready." And then he turned and exited the tent, leaving me fuming and staring after him, seeing red. I wished my hands were big enough to fit around his thick, massive neck, if only so I could choke the life right out of him.

How dare he? *How dare he?*

Everyone loved me, even those who didn't deserve me. And my body was perfection. I had curves, generous breasts and wide hips, a flat stomach, and muscled arms and a toned back from all the exercise. I was tall, granted a few inches shorter than my cousin, but at least I wasn't miniscule. I had a pretty face, rather extraordinary if I said so myself. Long beautiful hair, pretty eyes. My nose wasn't as pointed as Maisie's, but it was round, a perfect fit for my face.

I had the ability to rock his gods' damned waters until he forgot his own name.

The bastard.

And I most certainly didn't need jewelry and silk to *make* me beautiful. I was just as dazzling without it, and I'd not sink to his silty level just to prove it. Just because I looked good without it didn't mean I had to go without it. I was a princess, and rich; what would be the point of having such lavishness in my hands if I did not use it?

I ripped the corset from my body and tossed it to the ground and whirled to the trunk where I opened it and whipped out a fantastic dress in lilac. It was less flashy than the other one, but I would look fabulous in it anyway, like I *always* did.

I pulled it on and arranged my hair into small braids before setting a gold crown in the form of interconnecting coral onto my brow. A necklace of pink diamonds followed, as well as golden bracelets on my wrists. Only then did I exit the tent, head held high.

I refused to let his words get to me and make a mockery of who I was.

I was princess of the realm...

...and he'd damn well better remember it.

Ytgar

Damn all the gods to ice and back and to the ice again.

I muttered every curse I could think of in my mind. Anything to push away the sight branded into the roots of my soul of Princess Odele's curvy, luscious, delicious, enticing, fantasy-inducing body.

Damn the gods to *ice*.

Val had sent me to retrieve her from her tent and invite her to dine with us for the night's meal. I hadn't bothered calling my presence, as she would have turned me away, anyway. It wasn't exactly proper to barge into a princess' tent, especially when said princess thought me to be nothing more than a whale trainer, a servant in her eyes.

I was starting to wonder whether my friend had sent me there on purpose. He was so determined on pushing us together, but I saw through his ploy as easily as he'd concocted it. He was trying to get me to feel something for her, trying to make her aware of me. As if her feeling anything for me was within the realm of possibilities. As if that would somehow lessen the blow when we arrived at Iol and she learned the truth about who we really were.

I knew what he thought. That maybe, if she fell for me now, it'd be easier for her to love me once we were wed and she knew the truth.

Love had little to do with it, and his churlish games wouldn't work.

But gods damn it to ice, her body flashed in my mind again.

Mermaids hid all sorts of secrets beneath their gowns. I'd bedded enough to know to never expect the architecture of their flesh, for I'd either be disappointed or thoroughly aroused.

Odele had aroused me, and I could only be glad for the thick cloak around my shoulders that hid the length of my erection the moment I'd seen her.

So much flesh had been a shock at first, I didn't know where to look or if I should avert my eyes. So I simply stared. I took her in like a starving mer desperate for a meal. I wanted to touch her, to possess her, but merely settled for the imprint of her flesh in my mind.

The tantalizing dip of curves inspired fantasies I never knew were possible to have with her of all mer. I wanted to run my fingers down the bare flesh of her shoulders, to slide them across the sharp ridge of her collarbone. I imagined her shivering beneath my touch as my fingers undid the buttons of that blasted corset, not all the way, but just enough to release her breasts to allow me to cup them in my hands. Her nipples would press against the palms of my hands and send awareness straight to my spine.

I would have kissed her then. I would have tasted her tongue, I would have punished and worshipped her in equal measure, putting passion and hatred hand in hand because that's what she inspired in me, and she deserved to feel every tantalizing ounce of it herself.

I pushed those thoughts away and evened out my breaths. Self control. I had to have it at every moment. Self control would get me a say in my kingdom. It would grant me a wife. It would build a political alliance. Even if I had to lock up every single emotion behind thick walls of ice, I'd do it.

I sat next to Val around the pit that radiated warmth. Several had been built around the camp to heat the chilly night. If the Thalassarins thought this was cold, they'd never survive the north.

"So?" he demanded, shoving an elbow into my side that did little more than tickle me. "Is she sitting with us?"

In answer, Princess Odele emerged from her tent, looking regal and angry. She looked straight at me and glared, then wove her way around the camp and went and sat right next to the criminal known as the Black Blade, at an entirely different pit circle.

"She is otherwise engaged," I muttered, unable to help the vicious sensation of jealousy pulsating through my every nerve. I shoved it away, knowing I shouldn't be feeling it in the first place.

"Gods of ice, she looks pissed," Val said in Iolish. It was easy to switch languages off and on. Easy when we wanted to speak freely and no one around us spoke in our tongue. "What did you do to her?" Val pierced me with a glare.

I didn't take my eyes off Odele. She was turned haughtily away from the criminal, though it appeared he was using every effort in his mischievous body to get a rise out of her. It had been more preferable to sit next to him rather than us? She was more stubborn than I thought, and would obviously fight this engagement—this *attraction,* a small voice whispered—every stroke of the way.

"Don't pretend like you don't know," I answered in our language. "You sent me in there on purpose, didn't you?" It didn't matter what he said; as I already knew the answer.

He didn't even have the good grace to look chagrined. "Yes, but it was supposed to inspire passion, not hostility."

"Stop," I ordered vehemently.

"Stop what?"

I glared. "Stop with the matchmaking. It doesn't suit you, and you're acting like an old mermaid. I don't need you setting up trysts for me. I can damn well take care of it myself. You do your part and I'll do mine."

The words came out a bit harsher than I'd intended, but I couldn't help it. He was meddling in things he shouldn't be. Odele would discover the truth soon enough, but for now, we had to keep it a secret, lest any lurking enemies discover anything. His matchmaking wasn't helping. And the sight of her little ways across from me wasn't either.

Gods' ice, I wanted her. With every kindling fiber in my body, I wanted to bend her body over mine and claim her for my own. Really, nothing should be holding me back on claiming what was mine... except for Odele herself, and that attitude of hers. I despised it with as much fervency as I wanted her.

Kingdoms fell when their leaders acted like she did. I wanted to believe that she wasn't this brainless and flippant; I wanted to believe that there was something salvageable in that heart of hers. But that hope was reserved for Val, not me. I didn't have time to search for it, to slowly draw it out of her, to seduce her, hoping for the best.

"I'm just trying to help," Val grumbled, settling into his seat and taking the meal a servant offered. He smiled at the mer and she stared at him, abashed.

"Just stay out of it." I took my plate from the servant but didn't offer up a smile. That was the difference between Val and I. He found the good in mer when it wasn't even there. He fabricated it, spun stories and histories and looked at things through distorted ice. I was practical and saw the raw honesty where he could not. He was a dreamer. An honest dreamer, but a dreamer just the same. He knew perfectly well what she was; he wasn't blind to that much, but he still hoped for more.

"Where is my cousin?" I demanded, crossing my arms against my chest. Perhaps I'd closed my heart off for all possibilities of heartbreak, but that didn't mean I couldn't take comfort in Maisie's presence.

The Black Blade sneered rather distastefully at me. Gods, how I hated that look. I wanted to punch his teeth down his throat. The only thing stopping me was that I knew he was a cheat, and would use whatever means necessary to best me.

"Let me just check my pockets…" He pretended to rummage around his jacket pockets and did so with a smile on his face. I scoffed, and he laughed. "I'm not her keeper, little Princess. Maisie goes where Maisie pleases."

And she did so without an entourage escorting her, a privilege I never had the pleasure of having. I hoped she enjoyed it while it lasted. Being the daughter of such an important mer wouldn't give her much freedom.

"Why are you here?" I asked.

He raised dark eyebrows. "Well, I was sitting here first. If you expect me to get up and leave just because your Royal Highness came to sit next to me, you'll be waiting for an eternity."

I growled with irritation. "I don't mean here in this spot, you foolish scrap of kelp. I mean here. On this journey. Don't you have pockets to pick in the city or something?"

Truthfully, I didn't care why he was here. I was just irritated with Val, and taking it out on anyone within berating distance, which happened to be him. Really, it seemed every mer around me had been sent by the tides to irritate the life out of me. If the gods wanted me dead, they should have done so the moment Percival pointed that speargun at me.

He chuckled. "Where Maisie goes, I go."

"So she swims all over you. At least she's doing something right."

"Get one thing straight now, *Odele,*" he admonished. "No one swims over me. Not her, and most certainly not you. Got that?" There was murder and darkness in his voice that explained just how he'd gotten his nickname, and his reputation for being the most vicious criminal in Thalassar.

But after living my entire life at court, he was foolish if he thought he frightened me.

I snorted.

Then Maisie finally swam up to us with Captain Saber in tow. Though she tried to hold herself tall, I could tell immediately something was wrong. Even the Black Blade could tell, because all humor fell from his face and was replaced with deadly seriousness.

"What's wrong, little fish?" He got up and cradled her arms in his hands. The distance between them was intimate, and though she was recently married to Prince Kai of Draconi, there was no hiding that there was something between her and Elias as well. Something between her and all three of those mermen, for that matter. It was plain to see in the way they looked at her, in the way they touched her.

She tried giving him a smile, but it wavered and her body suddenly wracked with shivers. Her teeth clattered together. "I d-d-d-don't-t-t f-f-f-eel s-s-o good."

Instant worry washed over me and I got up from where I sat, pushing Elias aside, though the criminal wouldn't budge.

"Did you eat anything?" I demanded quietly, gripping her shoulders before pressing a hand to her forehead. "Do you feel the effects of poison?"

The word instantly made Elias and Captain Saber tense. A moment later, as if he'd been in tune with the situation, or listening with his freakish dragon hearing, Kai was there as well.

I could feel the power of his dragon ancestors radiating from him. His eyes glowed blue around the edges, and his nails lengthened into talons.

"What is going on?" He looked back and forth between us all. "My gem?"

She shook her head. "It's not poison, don't worry. It's—" She broke off as another shiver overtook her body. "I j-j-j-just…" She gave out a cry and bent over, clutching her stomach. When her pain subsided, she got back up. "A cramp," she explained almost cheekily. I could just make out the blush rising on her cheekbones. "I think it's… I think it's *time.*"

I suddenly knew what she meant.

"Oooh… ew…" I cringed away from the implications of her words.

For a week, once every year when a mermaid reached her maturity at the *terrific* age of eighteen, she became *fertile.* Which meant that her body would crave a merman's touch and his seed as she became ready to procreate.

Really, I didn't need to know all that.

"Time for what, my gem? Are you sure you're alright?"

Really, mermen were incredibly stupid. I backed away slowly.

"F-f-fine." Maisie shivered. "I need…" She gasped and doubled over as if in pain. "I need…"

"What?" Tiberius demanded worriedly. "Do you need medicine? What is it you need?"

Oh, she needed medicine alright, but more in the form of merdick and less in the form of a poultice.

"Take me to our tent," she almost cried out.

The three mermen shared looks between them but all at once they ushered her towards their tent, which was conveniently placed near Prince Kai's guard dragon. Poor creature would have to listen to the sound of their depravity for the next few hours.

I pitied it and the nightmares it would suffer for weeks.

With them gone, I was completely and utterly alone. A servant came by and offered me a bowl of nourishment and a cup of frothy tea. Finally. Eating would distract me from the disastrous scene I just witnessed. I shuddered as I thought of what was going on in that tent… ew…

Of course, I wasn't exactly virtuous myself… Okay, perhaps that was a lie. But I'd read enough kelp books and listened to enough conches to know how the mechanisms of the mer body worked. I knew how babies were made, what went where and the how and why's. Really, I wasn't an idiot.

I just… couldn't imagine myself doing what Maisie so obviously took joy in.

At least I could promise myself that if I ever took a mer to my bed, it would damn well be in better taste than my cousin's, that was for sure.

The merman I took to my bed would be strong and reliable, he wouldn't be irritating and wouldn't talk overly much. He would do what I said and care more about my pleasure than his own. He would smile in kindness, and keep secrets, and if he could do that, then perhaps I could trust him with my heart.

If such a merman even existed.

"Princess…"

I jolted at the sound of his voice, nearly dropping both my bowl and my cup. Stew sloshed over the bowl and spilled onto the skirts of my dress.

I glared at Prince Ytgar. "Really?" I demanded with heavy irritation. "This is the second time today you've been more disappointing than usual. It's like you're trying to purposely ruin me."

He didn't lose that charming, enigmatic—frustrating—smile of his. But despite the darkness, the glow of the lava globes displayed the flush rising to darken his cheeks.

"Forgive me. On both accounts, Odele."

My eyes narrowed. "I never gave you leave to be so informal." He waved my words off and helped himself to a seat next to me. "I didn't ask you to accompany me, either."

"And yet here I am." He moved his hands around with exaggerated flourish, leaning back on the coral seat with haughty arrogance. Really, his personality rivaled my own, yet his was much more irritating somehow. "And here you are. Alone."

"Yes, well, my companions became otherwise occupied."

"Yes, so I surmised." There was clearly a smile in his voice and when I turned to look at him, sure enough, it was there. As if he knew exactly what was about to occupy their time and he found it all rather amusing.

"Disgusting," I murmured into my bowl.

"You don't like the stew?"

I hadn't meant the stew. I'd meant my cousin's depravity. I shrugged delicately then forced myself to balance both the cup, the bowl and my spoon as I dipped the spoon in it and brought a bite up to my lips.

A burst of blandness assaulted my tongue.

I promptly spit the food back out.

"Disgusting," I muttered again and turned to shove the bowl, spoon, and cup into Ytgar's arms. The prince's frosty blue eyes appeared to be nothing but amused, though I'd caught sight of something else before he shuttered it completely and entirely… Disappointment.

I couldn't explain why that simple flash of a look suddenly withered something inside me. Well, whatever. He could be disappointed in me all he wanted. It wasn't entirely a new sensation, and by now I was immune to the scrutiny. I disappointed everyone around me. My father, my stepmother, Maisie… I was the princess who made mistakes. I was the one who cared only for myself and my own life rather than those around me.

What did I care if I hurt some lowly peasant's feelings? Perhaps they should make better soups.

"I find I am not hungry." I got up and gave Prince Ytgar the cut direct, turning from his painfully pretty form and swam back inside my tent to prepare for bed.

I couldn't wait until we reached denser terrain so I could finally make my grand escape.

Because I honestly didn't think I could take much more of this.

Valmundur

HER MOODS WERE AS interchangeable and as erratic as the tides. She was
a snowstorm, holding the promise of peace and death. Her reaction had
startled me, the sudden brusqueness with which she'd gotten up and left.

Perhaps I shouldn't have cared. Sometimes, I couldn't help but feel that
Ytgar was right. That she was too spoiled, too hateful. It had been there
in the way she'd spat out the bite of food as if it had been poison on her
tongue. I knew what it was, as I'd seen it many times myself on the faces
of other royals.

Once we arrived at Iol, she would know the truth of who I was, so why was I even trying when, to her, I was nothing more than a servant? I mean, I knew what I was, knew I scraped silt and brushed down orcas for a living. The only reason I was still alive was because of Ytgar's generosity and his friendship.

I was nothing compared to her, and I'd be nothing *to* her.

But my heart was such a foolish, susceptible thing. It looked for hope and found it in the most unlikely of mer. I was like a child looking for the beauty in the unknown, looking to play in the danger that was the Princess of Thalassar.

I'd always been this way. No matter what hardships had befallen me, I looked for the good within the bad. I'd been gifted as a servant to the royal household as an orphan with no memory of his mother or father? Well, I had a new life and lived at the palace. I had bruises and scars from trying to handle wild beasts? Each one was a lesson learned and could only make me better. The princess I had foolishly come to care about would despise me once she discovered our difference in rank? At least I could hold dear the memories of when she despised me less.

I always found the good in the bad, and I was determined to find the good in her, too.

Whether Ytgar wanted me to or not.

THEY PACKED UP THE camp early the next morning and we moved out.

Cranky and looking for a fight, I decided to ride alone, a little ways away from my cousins, *all* of them.

Maisie had emerged from her tent looking bedridden and sickly with messy hair and clothes askew, leaving no room to doubt what she had been doing. Just the sight of her in heat like an animal made me sick. She was gasping as if in great pain as she rode in front of Tiberius on his hippocampus, and all three of her mermen were riding close with their nostrils flaring as if they wanted to take her right there on top of the beast with the whole procession watching.

Really, it was revolting and messed with any desire I had to eat breakfast.

The waters were still open and empty, and the fact of it was that it was grating on my nerves. I didn't exactly recognize where we were, not that I would have from experience or anything, as I'd never left Eramaea in my life. I should have recognized the place from my studies. Next time we stopped to make camp, I would pull out some of the conches I'd packed and listen to the one on geography. Perhaps I'd look over a map and decide where it would be best to leave at. Once we reached the small edge of Kappur, we had to travel through to cross into Draconi. Kappur was dense with underwater forestation. It could provide the cover I needed to escape.

It would also provide wild animals if I wanted to get eaten.

Perhaps leaving here on a hippocampus was my best bet.

The troubles of plotting a victorious escape. It was all nice and exciting to hear about in conches, but actually doing it myself? I'd need to listen to a few more. They would at least give me the security I needed to map out a perfect plan.

We rode for hours, and in those hours I did nothing but fume. Those around me spoke and laughed to pass the time, and every second of it just made me more irritable. I was miserable, so I wanted them to be miserable as well.

As nightfall started to approach, Prince Ytgar finally sidled up next to me. By the time he did, I was itching for a fight.

"How are you faring, Princess?" he asked, and I would have thought he seemed genuinely concerned, but I didn't care.

"You could have asked me hours ago," I complained. "I'm starving, saddle sore and have a blistering headache. I need a sand bath and a change of clothes."

He smiled at me. "We'll be stopping soon, and I'll have Val draw up your bath immediately." He winked.

I hadn't realized how close my cousins had gotten to us, or that they'd been straining to hear every single word.

Jessinda snorted unkindly. "If I were you, cousin, I'd not let that whale trainer anywhere near your bath. He'd only soil it with the aroma of a peasant." She laughed and my cousins followed. I let out a small chuckle myself and turned to gauge Prince Ytgar's reaction.

Other than the slight tightening of his hold on the reins, I would have thought the comment hadn't bothered him at all. He was quick to laugh at the joke, like it hadn't bothered him in the least.

"How you can trust he'll know how to draw a bath, I cannot fathom," Silviya stupidly added.

"Come, cousin, it does not require massive talent. Have you seen the bulk of him? It's all he's good for, I reckon. It's not as if they're making him read a missive."

"I've never seen a servant read. Do you think he knows how?"

Oh, how I'd been looking for a distraction such as this. Someone to lash out at, someone to be on the receiving end of my ire, and it would not be Prince Ytgar, but his friend instead. I relished in the cruel words, laughed right along with them.

What did it matter that I quipped and insulted? I was sure he, being a servant and all, would be used to it by now. But he wasn't even near us, couldn't hear the things we were saying. It would have been so much more fun if he had.

I confess, I'd expected Ytgar to defend him, had hoped he would, and yet the blond prince laughed right alongside us and threw in a few cruel barbs of his own as if he insulted his best friend and servant every day.

Which made it all rather boring in the end.

"Commoners," Prince Ytgar scoffed. "Good for one thing only..." He gave a small pause for suspense. "Wiping the silt off our fins."

My cousins burst out into raucous laughter.

"This subject bores me." I yawned. Translation: subject change, please. Really, my cousins were *soooo* predictable. Not that Ytgar was any better, obviously. I'd been hoping to spar, to get rid of my pent-up frustrations with words, sharing them with someone as equally—if not more—facetious as myself.

"What is Iol really like, Your Majesty?" Jessinda batted her eyes in my betrothed's direction.

My reaction was instantaneous. It flared to life inside of me, burning and searing hot. Jealousy, as unexpected as it had been, had me clenching tightly at the reins. I wanted to shoot a glare at her, and the wilder part of me had a weird desire to stake my claim on a merman who could never be mine, as I had no intention of wedding him in the first place.

Besides, I knew Jessinda was only flirting shamelessly with him to spite me, and because she'd caught a side of him we hadn't seen before. As if him insulting his best friend and trainer warranted special attention on her behalf. Really, she was just acting like a home wrecking harlot.

"Iol is…" He paused as he thought his answer over. I wondered what he would say. "Iol is not so cold as you may think, for the mer are warm and welcoming, and enjoy a good party. It's vibrant. It's life. And it may scandalize you to hear this part, but it is savage and magic, and so completely beautiful." As he said this last part, so poetically charming, he stared right at me. My heart gave a stutter despite itself. Even my cousins sighed dreamily.

"How romantic," Jessinda commented, batting her eyelashes once again. Really, a few hours ago she was insulting Iol and the savagery of their kingdom. Now it was romantic? *What a meddling harlot.* She had a thing for her cousins' merfriends and obviously their betrothed as well. I wouldn't be surprised if she tried to corner him for a kiss.

Not that I cared.

His kisses aren't that great, I wanted to snap at her.

It wasn't like they'd completely curled my fins. It's not like I remembered the exact taste and texture of his lips and tongue against mine. It's not like I craved the bite of frost on his lips, or had laid awake days after he kissed me, dreaming of him doing it again.

Nope. Not me. Not at all.

Anyway, I was still reacting to his words, to his description of his home kingdom. I knew there were many mer so deeply rooted to their homes, that they saw its perfections, that they smiled when they spoke about it much like Maisie did when she spoke of Lagoona. Much like Ytgar had just now.

What would I say if someone asked me what I loved about Eramaea? Nothing. The answer was nothing. My home had been a prison. It had taken my mother and lost me my father. It had gained me a cruel stepmother and unfeeling skin on the backs of my hands. It held heartbreak and confinement, and I'd not miss it. I'd not mourn the loss of the Thalassarin throne and didn't care if the queen ever deemed me worthy of it at all. She could keep it. Good riddance.

"Sounds boring," I replied, shrugging.

He laughed idyllically and gave me a shrug of his own. "Once you see it, you'll want nothing else but to get lost in the magic of the frost." He said the words like a promise that curled around my body and tugged, making me tremble almost treacherously.

"I don't doubt it, Your Majesty." Ugh. Jessinda. She'd pulled her hippocampus closer to Ytgar's until they were practically touching. She was so obvious, it was pathetic. "I can't wait to see it."

Annoyed, I leveled my voice into the sweetest sound I could muster. "Weren't you saying moments before Prince Ytgar showed up that you had no interest in—how did you put it?—letting your tits freeze like icicles in savage waters? Or maybe I misheard…"

Jessinda enjoyed using two-legger slang sometimes. She thought it made her sound more edgy. It made her sound ridiculous. Me repeating it to her just made her realize that. Her face shaded red with obvious embarrassment as she looked at Ytgar.

The prince, thankfully, avoided looking at her altogether, and I could tell he was trying to hold in a laugh. I didn't know why that pleased me immensely.

"Odele," Jessinda sneered viciously. "What I said was no worse than what you've said about it." She turned to Ytgar like a petulant child tattling. "The prince would be offended to hear you call it the northern ice cube and even more so if he knew you thought he was inbred with orcas."

Oh, poor Jessinda. Little did she know I'd said all of that to his face.

Ytgar threw his head back and laughed so hard, a stray tear lifted from the corner of his eye. He reached a hand up to swipe it away. "I'm well aware of what my betrothed thinks of me, ladies. It's no secret, and I can tell you how greatly amusing I find her."

I'd been going for the offensive when I'd uttered the words. I frowned.

Even Jessinda seemed taken aback. "Amusing?" she asked.

He nodded. "She's a breath of fresh water. I adore her wit and good humor."

He wasn't supposed to adore my wit and good humor—though I had both in dazzling abundance. He was supposed to dislike me enough that escape would be easy. Though I enjoyed flattery and relished in the vitalization it brought me, he wasn't supposed to say these things.

And blast my heart for giving more incessant lurches.

"Well, I abhor you," I countered.

He laughed good-naturedly. "See?" He pointed. "That sense of humor is marvelous."

"I'm not joking."

He turned and nudged Jessinda as if they were long-lost friends. "A riot, I tell you." And then he sauntered away on his hippocampus without even a goodbye.

"He's very…"

Strange. Abnormal. Weird. Crazy. Not from this world.

"…handsome."

Annoyed, I flicked the reins and my hippocampus shot in front of Jessinda's, startling her own so badly it almost careened her off the side of her saddle. She glared at me as if it were my fault she wasn't a better rider.

"I know what you're doing," I accused quietly.

She tried to look innocent. "What do you mean?"

"Really, Jessi. Kissing Silviya's merfriend behind her back is one thing, but shamelessly flirting with my betrothed in front of me is a new low." My gaze traveled down her frame. "If you think he'd ever be interested in you, you're as daft as a barnacle."

Her face flamed once again, but with anger rather than embarrassment. "What do you care?" she snapped. "You obviously don't want him."

I didn't. So why *did* it matter?

Because it was damned lowering, that's why, to have a cousin who flirted shamelessly with the merman who was supposed to be mine in front of me. Maisie would never have done that.

"You don't want him for yourself, but you don't want anyone else to have him either. Or maybe you desire the ice prince more than you let on."

"You're full of sand if you think that's true." I turned abruptly from her, if only so she couldn't see the expression on my face.

She was right, gods damn it. I was starting to care, and caring was dangerous. The Iolish bastard had careened his way through the walls around my heart; the first layer of it, anyway. I'd not deny he made me smile, or that watching his mouth made me crave another kiss.

But I couldn't.

I wouldn't.

I had to get away before he embedded himself any deeper into my soul than he already had. Which meant I had to move my plan up.

I had to escape.

And soon.

We were reaching the edges of Kappur. We'd traveled for days now, days in which I'd felt more alone and anxious to leave than ever. My cousins weren't speaking to me, which wasn't such a grand loss. And Maisie was so preoccupied with her recent bout of fertility that she was in her tent with Kai, Elias, and Tiberius as much as possible. (I was sure I caught the embarrassment of it on her father's face more than once). Ytgar tried to speak to me many times, to which I straight up ignored him out of fear, and for my own protection. Val merely glared, and no one else save the servants spoke to me for days.

I was ready to leave.

Every night in the solitude of my tent, I plotted. I kept track of the leagues we traveled, marked them every night on the map and listened to every conch on geography I had packed—and there were many—until I finally had a plan and was ready.

Tonight would be the night.

We couldn't stop fast enough. Once night fell, I acted as though nothing was wrong. I took my dinner alone despite the atrocious, bland taste, and then retired to my tent.

I changed into something simple that wouldn't garner much attention. A dress with no jewelry or crowns on me—those I stuffed into a knap-sack—and a dark cloak around my shoulders. I had a map in my bag, and I could sell the jewelry to find an inn once I was far enough away.

I decided to go without a hippocampus. It would slow me down, but with it I'd be easily spotted and recognizable.

Once everything was packed, I laid down on my cot and waited a few hours.

When the camp quieted down, I ventured out discreetly. My heart pounded, but the adrenaline was worth it. I was close to freedom, and I could practically taste it on my lips. The flavor of it on the back of my throat nearly made me weep.

I glanced around the camp. There were guards posted, of course, but most of them were Draconian, and wouldn't question me. Even if they did, well, it was a good thing I spoke Dracon and could bullshark my way out of an uncomfortable situation.

It was a benefit of being a princess. Aside from speaking many languages—Thalassarin, Dracon, and Braugish—I would be excellent at diplomacy.

Though, of course, no one knew this about me.

How could someone who cared so much about her looks and the latest fashions know a lick of Dracon? As for Iolish, I knew a little to gauge conversation, though not enough to speak it fluently.

I hid in the shadows, glad I'd decided so long ago to escape the confines of the palace in Eramaea and explore the streets of the city. It helped me blend in with the shadows. I wasn't as well versed in the secrets of the night as the Black Blade, but I did decently. Decently enough to escape camp and make it a few yards into the vast underwater forestation that would serve as my cover.

Coral reefs, seaweed, grass, and bushes of greenery crowded this area. I wasn't entirely too fearful of what was hiding here. I'd studied up on all manner of creatures that could be creeping through the shadows and was well prepared for any eventuality.

I made it just past the first hedge of coral reef when I was grabbed from behind. Before I could react to the violent onslaught upon me, I was whipped around, and the breath was promptly knocked out of me as I was slammed against a reef. I felt coral crack against my spine and crumble down my back.

Once I regained my breath, I opened my mouth to scream, but a massive hand went over my mouth, muffling the sound entirely.

And then twin orbs of glowing silver shone in the darkness.

"Going somewhere, Princess?" Valmundur asked, his voice tantalizingly dark and low.

I screamed my disbelief into the warmth of his palm.

"You've been acting strangely for days," he explained, as if he thought he was somehow answering a question I didn't ask. "I knew it wouldn't be long."

He went silent, and it was then, after a few minutes of seething, that I saw past my rage and noticed exactly how close he was to me. How his body was angled, hovering just over mine. I could feel the hard press of his muscles through my clothes and my body warmed at his nearness.

There was a heightened sense of awareness, and I knew the moment he felt it too. He didn't give me space, made no move to take a stroke back for decorum's sake. Even with our stations so far apart, even if he was so vilely beneath me, he pressed closer.

And the crazy part was, I welcomed every bit of it.

I LET GO OF that tether I had on my control and let all the rage I felt shine in the look in my eyes. It was a look that would have sent other mer quivering, swimming away from the force of what I could do. Not Odele. She met my look of rage with one of her own, like she had every right to be dignified and upset that I'd foiled her plans.

The good thing about being a silent observer was that it gave me time to notice things, things that others overlooked. Like the fact that she'd been too quiet as of late. That she'd shut herself off from nearly everything and everyone. She'd stopped insulting, had stopped speaking, and I knew she'd been absorbed in thoughts of getting away. Why else would she keep track of the leagues we'd traveled? Why else did she studiously gaze at our every surrounding?

She had been waiting for the perfect moment to escape. To escape Iol. To escape Val. To escape *me*.

It offended me more than it should have. It snapped the tethers I'd tried so hard to hold back.

A temper wouldn't help Iol.

It didn't very well matter now, did it? She was trying to escape, anyway.

Up until now, I'd been nothing but the quiet, brooding bodyguard of Prince Ytgar. I was slightly unconventional, a bit on the daring side, but I always had my self control.

It went away from me now. I wanted to scream at her, shake sense into her. Mostly, I wanted to drive my body into her own and make her beg for forgiveness until I sent her over the edge of unrivaled pleasure.

"You are selfish, Odele. You don't deserve the Prince of Iol." Because maybe if I said those words often enough, it could suck in the torrent of vexing feelings straight out of me. Maybe then the expanse of my confusing lust towards the Princess of Thalassar would diminish into something tamer, something *civil*. Something where this primal need and hatred didn't quite occupy the same space.

But I wanted her. Desperately. Deserving or not, whatever she was, I *desired* her in a way I didn't understand. I wanted to see her punished; I wanted to see her head foggy with need so she could understand just what she was trying to swim away from.

Then maybe she'd think twice about it.

"Where are you going so desperately, Odele?" I whispered against her cheek. And because I was so good with the details, I felt the instantaneous change slice through her body. She shivered in my grasp.

Her reply was muffled by my palm.

"If you scream, no one will help you," I warned just before I slowly slid my hand from her mouth.

"You bastard!" she cried out. I hadn't expected the sudden swing she sent careening towards my face. I didn't have time to dodge as her fist connected to my cheek. I staggered back a fraction and blinked away the tears that emerged from the left eye. A moment later, she was on me again. She struck her fists out like a wild orca bucking a rider off its back.

She was daft if she thought I'd not defend myself.

I shoved her by the shoulders to get her away but, somehow, she grabbed the collar to my cloak, tangled her tail around mine, and together we fell.

I used my arm to cushion the back of her head from the fall, though I shouldn't have been so chivalrous when this was her fault in the first place. Still, my weight collided against her body almost painfully. The breath left her; she gasped for it.

I had the urge to cradle her head in my hand but pushed it away with a reminder of my fury.

When she finally caught water into her lungs, she glared at me. Odele was always so strong, always so determined, so it surprised me entirely to see her on the verge of tears, holding them back, yet she couldn't hide the truth of her despair from me. I heard it in her words as they cracked while she cursed me.

"You've ruined everything," she accused.

"I'm stopping you from something foolish."

"You're ruining my life!" she shouted.

I fought back an eye roll. From what little I'd gauged of her, she thought everyone was out to ruin her life. The line did not faze me.

"You have a duty," I reminded her.

"You don't *understand*…" She broke then, her face contorting into grief and anger, both sentiments clashing over her beautiful features. She was always so strong, so confident, this took me aback. If the tether on my own rage had snapped, then what tether had kept her together?

"Then tell me…"

They were the wrong words to say. Her expression shuttered once again, glare back in place. "Get off of me you filthy, lowly, whale trainer servant!"

I stiffened, then whipped my arm out from beneath her head, letting her head bang into the silt. For a moment, it seemed like she didn't breathe and my mind spun with an indescribable rage. I grabbed her wrists and held them tightly above her body, pinning her down.

"What…" I bent low so that our noses touched, so that she could glimpse the cold fury in my eyes. She wanted ice, I would give it to her. I'd give her the vicious savagery of a snowstorm. I'd become the terror she thought me to be. "…did you call me?"

A shiver tore through her, not from desire, but from fear. She'd do well to fear me, my wrath. She could insult me all she wanted. She could despise me, rage at me, hit me if she wanted, but I'd be damned to the ice if she spoke ill of Val ever again.

"Get off me!" She struggled ineffectually.

"Don't you *ever* speak of me that way again, or it'll be the last thing you ever do. Marriage contract with Iol be damned." I pressed close to her, accentuating my threat. I didn't care that she was the princess, I'd not tolerate it.

She stilled, cocked her head to the side as if studying a particularly fascinating subject. "If you don't care about me, why won't you let me go?" Her voice was almost pleading.

The thought of her leaving was crippling, lowering. It filled me with rage and despair and all the emotions swirling through me were unfathomable. I didn't understand them, wasn't sure if I even wanted to.

"I'll be damned to the ice before I *ever* let you go, do you hear me, Odele?" It was a threat and a promise, both of which I intended to keep. "Iol needs you."

Her breathing grew ragged in the past few moments. She was no longer desperate to wriggle out from beneath me, but formidable as she lifted her chin to become a worthy opponent despite her position.

"I am not Maisie," she said.

My eyebrows rose. "I am aware." Maisie was nowhere near this frustrating.

"I am not noble or self sacrificing. When I want something, I will take it, regardless of the cost."

I pressed my lower body onto hers. "And what is it you want, Odele?"

The moment the words were out of my mouth, something jolted between us. A hyperawareness. The knowledge that we were pressed close together. Chest to chest, navel to navel, tail to tail. The earlier vision of her in nothing but her corset choked the water from my lungs.

I recalled the contours of her body, wondering if she'd be as soft as she looked. Her display of skin had been torturously tantalizing, had stirred desires in me I wasn't sure I could ever feel for her. And the agonizing display of flesh was pressed up against me; I could feel it through my cloak, through her dress. I could feel her heart thumping rapidly against mine as if they could somehow merge together.

I was aware of the space that separated us, and it felt like it would somehow never be small enough, even if she was right in my arms, it would never be enough.

"Nothing you can give me," she whispered breathlessly, and I knew she was just as affected as I.

I bent down so my lips were close enough to touch her own, so my breath fanned against her skin. "Are you sure about that?" I asked.

Her glare told me all I needed to know.

"Damn you," she hissed just before she leaned up and kissed me.

It was like the storm in a bottle unleashed between us with the touch of our lips. Something that should have been simple exploded into a myriad of things. Eruptions, tornadoes, tsunamis… nothing could ever compare to this kiss.

One minute our lips were touching and the next, her tongue was in my mouth, taking aggressively, as if she blamed me for the desires coursing through her body. So I took back just as fervently. Tongue and teeth collided, and there was nothing gentle about it. It was the punishment I'd longed for, but I was no longer sure who was imparting it. Me or Odele? Or perhaps it was the both of us, clashing violently with something better than angry words. Hatred, packed up in the heady press of passion and desire.

Sounds emanated from deep in her throat, sounds of raw, primal pleasure that caused erupting sensations to press from the center of my spine throughout the rest of my body. It was an inexplicable need coming hard and fast.

I let go of her wrists, only to have her nails dig deeply into the cloak at my back. I could feel them pierce into my skin, could feel her desperation in every touch, in the way her hands went up and down the length of my back.

My hands moved of their own desperate volition. I cupped her chin with one, lifting her face up so I could delve deeper into her mouth, devour her, *consume* her. The other slid over her collarbone, down the soft curve to cup her breast.

Gods of ice.

She tore her mouth from mine to gasp at the contact, her body arched up to lean into the touch. I gripped her, squeezed and kneaded the way I'd wanted to the moment I saw her in that corset. She filled my hand, the point of her nipple hard against my palm, even through the material of her dress. But it wasn't enough just to touch. I wanted more, needed it.

I slipped my fingers inside the edge of her bodice, eyes searching hers. Her lids were lowered with desire, and I was struck by how beautiful she was, even when her eyebrows pulled together with anger. It was a mix that was uniquely her own.

I was almost too afraid to speak, afraid that the spell of anger that had settled over us would fragment apart. "Let me give you pleasure." It was more an order than a request, but I wanted her permission. I wanted her to think about what this implied; I didn't want her mind completely clouded by anger and passion. I didn't want this to be something she would regret.

"If you rip my dress…" she rasped between heavy pants. "…I'll shove a knife into your thick neck."

A smile found its way to the edges of my mouth. "Fair enough."

I tugged down the bodice of her dress to reveal her breasts to the waters. They were so, so full, nipples erect and ready for my ministrations, pointing upward in delicious invitation. One I was too inclined to accept. My mouth enclosed over the pearly bud.

Gods, to taste her, to swirl my tongue around her sweet flesh…

Odele cried out loudly and I smiled around her nipple before letting my lips and tongue trail across her skin. I traveled an imaginary path between the valley of her breasts, giving equal attention to her other side.

She made mewling sounds of contentment, gripped me and pulled me close, eager for contact, for the touch of our joined skin, for the flush of heated bodies, of her heat enclosed around me, of thrusts that would take her to the heightened waters of pure and utter bliss.

I wanted that too.

I wanted to explore every inch of her, but not now, not yet. Not until the right time came.

For now this was enough, this anger as a mask to hide the fact that, despite herself, she wanted me. She wanted a commoner, a whale trainer, someone so 'vilely' beneath her that she would do anything she could to deny it. She would lash out, curse me to the ice and back again, push me away, despise me, if only so she'd never realize the inevitable truth.

She *wanted* me.

So I'd damn well give myself to her.

"Lift your skirts." I pulled her into a sitting position. Our bodies floated above the silt, and I kept her upright and steady with one hand against her waist and the other against her lower back.

She frowned down at me, but in the end, the desire won over. One hand gripped her skirts, and she hiked them up slowly.

"You will stay," I ordered, as if she'd ever obey me. I'd make it so. I'd bring her to the heights of pleasure she'd never before felt and make her crave my touch so badly, she could never bear to leave.

"No," she gasped, even as my tongue slid up her scales and to her center, where her body had opened for me. The evidence of her desire.

"Stop swimming away. Stay. *Stay*." I whispered it like a plea and a command just before I pressed my tongue into her center.

She cried out as I tasted her, jerking in my arms. I held her tighter, keeping her pressed firmly against me as I worked my tongue against the soft folds of her inner flesh. She tasted like sin and salvation. Like every dream unfulfilled and every screaming desire balancing on the edge of that drop into the abyss.

I wanted her. Gods, I wanted every bit of her.

"Val…" Her whole body trembled and I could only hold her tighter, as if I wasn't holding her close enough. As if the space that separated us was too vast, too wide, even when it was mere centimeters.

It should have bothered me that she called me by a name that wasn't my own. A darker part of me wanted to say, *'I am Ytgar'* but I held the urge back. Because it was in her pleading cries that I heard it, heard what it was that the real Val saw in her, what he hoped she held in her heart beneath the diamonds, silk, and dresses.

And if this was what it took to bring that side out of her, I'd do it gladly. I'd pull her to the brink of madness and greatness until she was unable to define one or the other. Until she lost her own name within the fray of our passion.

I knew she was close, so close to that edge, and I wanted to bring her there. I wanted her to fall, wanted her to scream. She was at the precipice of it, so close…

I pulled away just before she could shatter, leaving her dangling alone at the edge of that chasm.

Her body trembled even as I dropped her skirts and smoothed them out over her tail. I steeled my spine against weakness and got up, floating in front of her. Her eyes were heavily lidded, but the moment I pressed my palms against her shoulders, they shot open, her purple brows furrowing.

"W-wha—"

I'd rendered her nearly speechless. I could feel her shoulders shaking beneath my palms. My own body was wound tight with need, but I pushed it away, kept my face as impassive as I could muster.

"We should go back." My voice was heavy with a need unfulfilled.

She blinked and even in the darkness, I could make out the flush against her cheeks. "What?" The word was a harsh demand leaving her lips. Like she couldn't quite believe I would make her *feel* such scandalous things and leave her on the brink of release. I couldn't believe it myself. I ached everywhere, and was quite certain she did, too.

I brought my fingers up to her cheek, swiping my thumb against the curve of it. Her eyes widened at the gentleness of the contact. I dropped my hand back to her shoulder. "Stop trying to flee," I whispered firmly. A command and a plea, though in the edge of my voice, it was almost impossible to discern which.

Before giving her a chance to reply, though I saw the answering confusion and underlying anger in her eyes, I grabbed her hand, fingers encircling her delicate wrist.

"Let's go."

And I tugged her back towards the camp.

I COULDN'T SLEEP. AFTER Valmundur deposited me back in the confines of my tent with little more than a grunt I had interpreted as 'good night', I dropped onto my cot and mounds of pillows unceremoniously, feeling… Well, I couldn't quite describe how I felt. Frustrated, that was for sure, and more than a little ashamed.

I knew it was common to be filled with the desires that had earlier overpowered my senses. I knew it was possible to find pleasure in the act as I'd explored my body on more than one occasion. I just hadn't known it'd be possible to find someone who could bring me to such heights of bliss, who could push my body to its limit and had me craving the darkness beneath the edge of that drop…

And then he'd left me suspended, wanting… aching.

I hated him for it. And a shameful part of me craved more of it, of him.

I shouldn't even want it. First of all, he was a lowly commoner, not worth my time, effort, or body. He didn't deserve me or what I had to offer, no matter what he thought. Second, if I had a moral compass at all—which I didn't, but still a bit of guilt nagged at me for it—I was engaged to wed Prince Ytgar, his best friend. Not that I planned to go through with the engagement, but still. I was sure there was a special place in the abyss for these kinds of infractions.

Gods.

I tossed and turned on the cot, aching everywhere. I could still feel the heated burn of his touch, as if his fingertips had branded me irrevocably. There'd be no going back from this. I'd carry the mark of his prints against my skin forever. I'd ache for his touch as much as I'd ached for another kiss from Prince Ytgar.

It was like tasting that first sip of sin; it made me an addict, and all I could think of, imagine and dream, was the scent, touch, and taste of his body.

I wanted it.

I wanted him.

I wanted *more.*

I shot up in bed and glared into the darkness, part of it illuminated only by the floating specks of phytoplankton floating through the waters. How dare he, I demanded silently. How dare he bring me to the brink of what I'd desperately wanted only to take it away from me entirely? Who did that lowly trainer think he was? He was *nothing* compared to me, even if he brought my body to tingling sensations and unimaginable cravings. It was something he was good at, at least, and I demanded to have whatever else he had to offer. I wanted more. I'd make him give me more. I'd bend that scum to my will and then give him a coin for his trouble like a common harlot. When I finished with him, I'd leave and not look back. Then he'd know how little he meant to me. Him, his prince, and his whole kingdom.

I dropped back to my cot with a smile on my face and a newfound vengeance in my heart.

The next morning we packed up and left the camp behind. I held the reins to my hippocampus lightly, tail floating off to the side of the saddle, hugged against the creature's body. Today I wore a dress in pink, with diamonds dangling from the hems of my skirts and sleeves. An ornate crown decorated around my hair, which I'd combed until it shone and trailed behind me like a curtain of enticement.

My cousins swam around me chattering excitedly because Prince Ytgar had joined our little group. He flirted occasionally with Jessinda—which she ate up like the barracuda she was—but only I noticed the way his gaze kept traveling to me, the blue of the icy depths of his eyes burning like molten lava.

After a while, Jessinda noticed, too. "So, cousin," she purred in her sweet-as-candy voice that I knew was laced with poison. "Last night I noticed you emerging from the woods with the prince's whale trainer friend. What was his name again? Val-something?"

I gripped the reins and gritted my teeth. Just my luck that she'd seen me, but I'd refuse to fall to her bait. "Valmundur," I supplied with my own vicious smile. "It's okay, I don't really expect someone with low intelligence as yours to remember such a simple name."

She glared, but didn't drop the sweet facade from her tone. "It's strange that a princess finds herself in the coral forest with a lowly whale trainer. What of your reputation? Surely they'll think you were engaging in a tryst."

My skin prickled at the word 'tryst'. I knew what she was doing. I knew she was saying these things in front of Ytgar because she thought it could get me in trouble somehow. As if I cared what she or anyone else thought of me. Why would I, when I knew exactly what I was? A princess in my gilded perfection.

And because I was perfection, I knew not to rise to that bait. I knew not to answer, not to defend myself because she would see the truth behind my objections. No, it was better not to object at all, but reply with surety and sarcasm.

"I can assure you my reputation has taken its fair share of trysts in the past. As has yours, and yet I cannot seem to find a single someone who gives a damn." I shrugged nonchalantly while her own face heated at the reminder of her own reputation.

Ytgar snorted, the sound not exactly princely, though I welcomed it with the tiniest of smiles in his direction.

"Besides," I added, "Prince Ytgar does not seem the type to bother with petty rumors and lies." Another jab in her direction.

"Quite right," Ytgar said enigmatically. "Besides, I trust Val with my life and as such, with the life—and reputation—of my betrothed as well."

Jessinda made a haughty sound deep in the back of her throat. "I can't see why," she commented arrogantly. "He's merely a whale trainer. Can't see that he's good for much else."

Oh, he was good alright. Very good for other things. But I couldn't say that aloud.

"Well, you're a royal, Jessinda, and I can't seem to figure out what good you are, either."

She cawed indignantly, a sound which I ignored, instead I turned to Ytgar and found surprise on his features that he quickly masked behind an arrogant sort of smile. I turned away from him. I hadn't meant to seek out Val, but he was suddenly there in my line of vision. As if he could sense my gaze on the strength of his back, he turned over his shoulder, silver eyes finding mine. They flared knowingly, causing my face to heat.

I looked away first, and when I looked back, he was already turned around.

Iolish bastard.

Why had I even bothered to defend him? I told myself it was mostly to irritate Jessinda and insult her in the process. He certainly didn't deserve my kind words, so why had I offered them up on his behalf? Simple, because I was planning on using him for my own benefit. To have him give me what he'd selfishly denied the night before, and I didn't want Jessinda reminding me what he was, or of his station. It was embarrassing to know that I was dreaming about fraternizing with a servant.

Gods, what was happening to me?

Being out in the wilds of Thalassar was affecting my better judgement. I needed to see just a small hint of civilization, somehow I needed to reintegrate myself into society and leave behind this savagery before it all became worse.

I needed the comfort of my conches. I needed to listen to them, needed them to remind me of my plan, remind me that I needed to escape before I fell deeper under the spell of his seduction. I was thinking with my body and not my head. I couldn't push aside my goals, what I'd always strived and fought so hard to achieve just because Val had pushed me to the brink of pleasure.

What a confusing mess I'd landed myself in.

It was an easy fix, though. All I had to do was listen to my conches. They were my reminder, my tether on my sanity. They would speak the words of adventure, and the longing for a vast world that would push away the longing of Val's lips and mouth, of silver eyes and heated touches, of the promises of what could never be.

When we stopped to feed and rest the hippocampi that evening, I forced a servant to help me locate the chest filled with my conches. Once she did, I grabbed a few of my favorites as well as a blank one and stuffed them into a knapsack. With that done, I managed to find a quiet, shadowy corner where I knew no one would see me.

Once there, I sat in the silt and pulled out my favorite conch, one that spoke about the history of the seven sea kingdoms, and pressed it to my ear. The voice inside picked up from where it had left off, a deep baritone, soothing and familiar.

I immersed myself in the sound of the history of Kappur, of the mermen explaining the wonders each of the seven sea kingdoms had to offer. As I listened, I felt that familiar tug at my chest, the longing. Vividly, I could picture each and every place. The sea snake sanctuary, the Great Dragon statue, the dragon breeding waters. I could see it all as if I was there, and still knew that my imagination could never, ever, compare to the real thing.

Conches took me to places I couldn't go but wanted to. It was the conches that fed this desire inside of me. It was them who introduced me to worlds and waters besides my own.

The first time I'd ever imagined a life away from Thalassar, from the confines of Eramaea, had been years ago. I'd craved the outside world more than I craved breathing. I was suffocating where I was at, staring at the same thing day after day.

I hated to admit it, but when Prince Kai had arrived from Draconi to formally announce our engagement to all of Thalassar, I had been ecstatic. I'd wanted a little piece of the outside world for myself, and he was swimming into the palace, a descendent of dragons, with the blood of beasts coursing through his veins. When I'd seen him, I'd felt the thrill, the same thrill I had when I'd listened to conches on the kingdom he hailed from.

The reality of him had left me disappointed, and yet I still craved the place of his birth. I craved it like I'd never craved anything before. To travel. To see things beyond a quartz palace and a kingdom that bred hippocampi.

I wanted freedom.

Listening to the conches reminded me of that. I wanted to see more than just open waters and coral reefs. I wanted life. I wanted adventure.

I set the conch down momentarily to pick up a blank one. I trained the open chamber at me, and when it glowed, I began to speak.

"I want adventure," I confessed quietly to it.

It was a dangerous thing, to voice desires out loud. It felt strange doing it now, when I'd never done it before. I kept what I wanted so tightly locked up within me, surrounded by those steel walls I kept around the frantic beating of my heart. Yet for some reason, I had strength anew. I could confess it here when no one was around to listen to the adventurous desires a princess shouldn't have.

"I want to see the things I've only heard about in conches. They claim the Great Dragon statue is made up of a material similar to obsidian, a shining rare marble carved to resemble the Draconian god in all his glory. I can picture it, and still I want to see it. I want to be able to press my hand against the smooth structure and record it. I want to be able to say *'I've been there'*. I want an adventure. I *need* it." I paused, my breathing had grown erratic as I spoke, heavy with the weight of my passion. And now that I had my most treasured secret out, I felt lighter somehow.

Slowly, I put the conch down and started to lift the previous one, when a voice startled me into dropping it into the silt.

"May I sit next to you?"

I jumped and let out a squeal. When I turned, it was to find that infuriating face and body, already helping himself into the silt next to me, smile on his face and blue eyes shining with mischief.

Prince Ytgar.

Valmundur

SHE JUMPED FEARFULLY AND then scrambled to pick up her discarded conches and shove them back into the knapsack at her fins.

"What are you listening to?" I asked quickly.

I didn't want her to hide part of herself away. Perhaps it was selfish of me, since she couldn't be mine anyway, but I wanted to know her like no one else did. Since I'd arrived as she was recording herself, I could hear the last of her whispered words, spoken like a secret, forbidden desire that she forced herself to tear out from within the very recesses of her soul.

That was the Odele I knew was trapped inside her all along. The one Ytgar didn't believe was there. But I caught glimpses of her when she thought no one else was looking or paying attention. I'd seen it when I'd kissed her, when Percival had pointed that speargun at her chest. The kind and caring mer had been there when Maisie had fallen unconscious with a poisoned arrow to her collarbone. It was in the weeks afterwards when her cousin didn't wake up and she swam worriedly through the palace, trying to keep everyone together.

She'd never admit it, but I knew it was there. A part of her that was as essential as the bossiness and the anger, both of which I knew she wore as a shield.

We wore shields to protect ourselves from things that might harm us. What was Odele so afraid of?

"Nothing," she answered, dropping a conch into the bag.

It would take more than me asking a simple question to get her to tell me the truth. Without waiting for permission, I reached for a discarded conch and pressed it to my ear. The inside was filled with a low baritone voice explaining the history of Draconi. I pulled it away.

"I didn't know you liked to listen to conches." Iol didn't have them; we barely had tellies. Not because we couldn't afford them, but because the harsh northern waters couldn't sustain them. The cold was too pressing for that type of technology, and it caused conches to shatter like ice. It was how our kingdom had lived so secretive for so long. We had conches translated onto kelp parchment and books, but they were all in Iolish.

"Yeah, well, there's a lot you don't know about me, Prince." She reached over and snatched it from my hands. "And you'd better not tell anyone you caught me listening to it."

I lifted an eyebrow. What an interesting comment. "Why wouldn't you want anyone to know?"

She shrugged absentmindedly and started packing her stuff away. I felt a moment's worth of panic. I didn't want her to leave. I wanted her to stay,

I wanted us to talk. I wanted to peel back the layers of herself she kept so tightly hidden, and I knew that this was just the beginning.

"Does it matter?" She started to swim up, but I couldn't let her leave. I grabbed her wrist and tugged gently, pulling her back into the silt next to me.

"Please don't leave." I wasn't above begging. Not when I really wanted something. "I don't mean to pry, it's just…" I bit my bottom lip, searching for the correct words. Why was I suddenly nervous? "You like to listen to conches about the world, you're smart, that much is obvious no matter how hard you try to hide it. *Why* do you hide it, Odele?"

She huffed impatiently. "Of course I'm smart. I am the Princess of Thalassar and I've had an extensive education. I am not some lowly, uneducated fool."

Her words stung, but I ignored them to focus instead on the way her hands tightened briefly into fists as she spoke. The movement was almost absent, as if she'd been bracing herself for something unpleasant.

"I know you're smart, but I think you're smarter than what you let on."

She tensed, and flicked her hair from her shoulder, batting her purple lashes at me. "Is that a compliment, Prince?"

I had the sudden urge to tweak her nose; she was so adorable. "I know you speak Dracon."

She blinked, taken off guard. "How do you know?" she demanded.

If her words hadn't been a confession all on its own, I would have been able to tell by her horrified expression. Like she wasn't that good at keeping secrets as she thought.

"When the Draconian party came to Thalassar weeks ago, I watched you. You didn't look like someone who was confused when a native language is spoken around you. I've seen the look many times, but your eyes darted from mouth to mouth as if grasping for every scrap of information you could."

She let out a soft curse, and that's when I knew I was right. She glared at me, though. "Are you going to tell anyone?"

I stared at her. I was no stranger to the beauty of royals. It was like they were born with it, like it was a requirement. Ytgar and his grandmother were both beautiful, formidable. Even Kai had pretty features and Maisie… well, she looked so much like Odele they could have practically been twins. But there was something different about the Princess of Thalassar that wasn't there in the Princess of Kappur. I'd noticed it before, but couldn't quite place my fin on what it was…

"I won't," I found myself promising. "But why hide it?"

She shrugged and her gaze suddenly looked very far away. "Sometimes it's better to hide things…"

I think I understood. "Like… because the world expects you to act and be something you are not, so you give them what they want to see?"

She was a princess. She was selfish and spoiled and that's all anyone bothered to see. They didn't look past that, so they didn't really see her. But I did. I did, and I understood. It was why I'd wanted her. I knew who she was, what she hid.

Odele looked at me as if she were absolutely surprised I'd guessed it. And because I had, I knew she'd try to push me away with rudeness and sarcasm, anything to keep me away from her truth.

I grabbed her bag and pulled out a conch again. This one was blank, if its weight had been of any indication. We may not have had conches in Iol, but I knew how to mark the differences between one that was recorded and one that wasn't.

"Have you traveled to any of those places you're listening about?" I asked, pointing the chamber of the conch in her direction. It glowed as it recorded her frowning form.

"I haven't," she nearly snarled.

I knew she hadn't been. I'd heard her record herself, after all.

"Would you like to?" Again, I knew the answer but wanted to hear her say it.

"Perhaps." She made a swing for the conch I held, but I jerked back out of her reach.

"C'mon, Princess," I teased. "If you could go anywhere in the seas, where would you go right now?"

She frowned at the recording, then chewed at her bottom lip as if contemplating just how much of herself she should share. "The afterlife, so I wouldn't have to continue this absurd conversation. Give me my conch back."

I jerked away from her again. "Ah, ah, ah," I admonished. "That's not an acceptable answer. Come on, beauty mine, where would you go? Or, are you too scared to answer?"

The challenge was well received. She glared, and I knew I'd won. "Fine." She crossed her arms against her chest, the action causing her breasts to lift enticingly. I felt my body react instantaneously. "Right now, I'd really like to see the Great Library of Draconi. I hear they keep their recording inside of discarded dragon eggs instead of conches, and I'm curious. Though I'm more curious to see the library of Brague. I hear it's the best in the seas."

I didn't doubt it.

"And what else would you like to see?"

She rolled her eyes. "The Great Dragon statue of Draconi, if you must know. Now give me back my conch!"

She was like a child stomping her fins. It made me smile. "Draconi is nothing compared to Iol," I told her. "At home, we have statues as big as ice giants, carved to look like trolls. And you should see the capital."

"Trying to sell your kingdom to me on a silver platter, Prince? It won't work."

"You know…" A sudden idea began forming in my mind. A way to convince her to stay. I knew the only reason she'd been in the coral forest with Ytgar was because she'd tried to swim away again. It just made us both want to redouble our efforts to make her stay. "If travel is what you want, what better opportunity than to do it now?"

"What do you mean?"

"I mean, we are on our way to Draconi. I'm sure we'll stop for a few days." I wasn't, but I didn't think it'd be too difficult to secure an invitation from Prince Kai. "While we're there, we can enjoy the sights, see what you've always wanted to see. I mean, we're traveling. It would be a shame not to take advantage of it." I was dangling a bit of raw meat in front of a shark, I knew. It was low to manipulate her like this, but if I was honest with myself, I wanted to see her happy. And I was curious about our enemy kingdom as well.

She contemplated this. "And then what?" she asked.

"What do you mean?"

She gestured with her well-manicured fingers. "What comes after Draconi? I see a few things and then you take me to Iol and I get locked in your ice castle like a slave?"

Was that what she was so afraid of? Being a slave in an ice castle? I supposed, in a way, all royals were slaves to one thing or another.

"You can tour Iol afterwards. You can't tell me it's not on your list of places to visit? You wound me…"

"This conversation bores me."

"Fine. How about after things settle down, we visit some other kingdom? Kappur, or if you want to be especially daring, we can venture to the Uncharted Waters."

She snorted. "Right, because you'd take me there."

"I would." I was surprised I meant the words. I would take her there. I'd take her anywhere she asked of me, if only to see her smile, and I didn't doubt once she saw the beauty of the world, she *would* smile. The problem was, could I? She was meant to marry Ytgar, not me. When she found out the truth, she'd likely want nothing to do with this lowly whale trainer.

"Your kingdom is impoverished. How would you even afford to take me anywhere?"

I had no idea. "Well, Iol is looking to expand its horizons. Why do you think we wanted this marriage in the first place? We need kingdoms to trade with, we need allies. Perhaps while we search for them, you could come with us to help secure them? We'd go all over and we could document our adventure!"

"Whatever." She made the final swipe towards me that wrenched the conch from my hand. With a huff, she shoved it into her knapsack.

I knew her brusque movements resulted from her thinking over my proposition and denying the desire that coursed through her. She wanted to accept, but she didn't want to seem eager.

"I mean it, you know," I whispered the same way I whispered to frightened and particularly violent orcas. "We could document our way to Draconi. There's no need for you to swim away. Why not take advantage of the journey, Odele?"

She froze mid-action, the strap of the bag halfway over her head. Then she shook her head, shaking away the implications of my words, and dropped the strap over her head securely. She didn't answer as she ignored me and began to stroll away, but then again, she didn't need to.

I knew what her answer would be.

Odele

EVER SINCE OUR SECRET little chat, Ytgar stuck by me. As if we shared some sort of camaraderie because I'd confessed all I'd wanted to see in the world. It was infuriating that he took such liberties, the bastard, but I couldn't help but mull his words over and over again.

Until I finally decided that he was right.

I gained nothing from trying to swim away from this, not when Val just hauled me back every time. I could sit back on this hippocampus and enjoy the journey, the first time I'd ever been this far from Eramaea. And he was right, we would make a pit stop in Draconi and I'd see all the curiosities I'd only ever heard about in conches.

I hadn't admitted it to him, but I was curious to see Iol as well. The way he spoke of giant statues had intrigued me, and I knew so little about Iol, I wanted to get my hands on more information. I wanted to see their secretive kingdom, speak their language… I wanted it all. It wouldn't hurt to go along with it, would it?

No, I decided. It wouldn't hurt at all.

I pulled out one of my empty conches to document the journey. Out of the corner of my eye, I saw Ytgar smile that charming smile of his. He was lucky I didn't claw it off of his face, arrogant Iolish bastard.

I trained the conch on myself and smiled as it recorded. "Princess Odele here," I said flippantly. "And I am here ready to document my newest adventure."

"*Our* newest adventure." Ytgar suddenly appeared beside me, looking into the conch.

I frowned and elbowed him in the side. "Get away, Iolish. This is my story."

He gave me a pout. "Come on, *Princessssss…*"

The way he said 'princess' in his Iolish accent sounded a lot like 'prrreen-sess'. His words were harshly spoken because of his accent. I glared at him, an idea forming in my mind.

"I'll let you document this with me *if* you teach me to speak Iolish fluently."

He blinked, surprised by the request. "To learn to speak my language fluently could take years…"

I pierced him with a look and lowered my voice. "Really? I learned to speak Dracon in a month with nothing but a few conches. Do not presume to doubt my abilities to learn."

He blinked. "Right. But I think Val should help me. Two teachers makes the learning easier." I started to protest, but he was already lifting his hand and gesturing to the whale trainer.

Val steered his hippocampus over towards us and fell into flow on my other side so I was between the two. His presence suddenly made me uncomfortable. We hadn't really interacted for days after the 'incident'. That's what I was choosing to call what had happened between us. An unfortunate incident, a temporary lapse in judgment.

I could feel his smugness even though I wasn't looking at him.

Ytgar said something to Val in Iolish. I caught nothing except the word 'Iolish'. When I turned to look at Val, his silver brows were high on his forehead, and his lips seemed to twitch with amusement. The expression made my hands tighten against the reins.

He didn't think I was capable. He thought me as daft as everyone else. Everyone except Ytgar, who had somehow known.

"Languages aren't that difficult if you learn the basic root of them."

Why did I feel this burning need to defend myself from Val's scorn? He was a whale trainer, what did it matter what he thought? I doubted he spoke as many languages as I.

"All languages come from somewhere. If they share the same root, they are considered sister languages because they descend from the 'mother'. If you know the root word and basic meaning, the rest can pretty much string itself together—especially when you combine them with different prefixes or suffixes. I'm not that familiar with Iolish, but from what I've heard, it can be traced back to *Proto-Nordic* times, but that seems a rather broad description of Iolish. I suppose it could be compared to two-legger Icelandic dialect, which I also happen to understand."

There was a silence that seemed to stretch on for leagues. Both mermen were blinking at me, at each other, then back at me again. I could feel my face suddenly flush. I'd forgotten myself. That had never happened before. It was all Ytgar's fault. He had made me feel too comfortable in my skin, had gotten me to open up about my secrets and now Val knew, too.

Damn the Iolish.

"Well then," Val supplied, clearly impressed. "We shall teach you."

For the next few days, we fell into a routine, and I no longer thought of escaping. Despite my resolve to keep them both at bay, I was having fun learning Iolish. They were both surprisingly good teachers, patient yet demanding, and not once did I feel the need to close my hands into fists, to wince at the imaginary pain of a whip slashing across the backs of my hands. Not that I needed it.

I craved this knowledge desperately. Knowledge I couldn't find anywhere else but with the two mermen I'd been so eager to get away from. If I hadn't been so stubborn, this idea would have come to me ages ago. I could have been taking advantage of what they knew.

Iolish was a harsh language, it was guttural and deep, but beautiful. I loved the harsh pronunciation of words, the way it sounded like they were always cursing at one another.

The first thing they taught me were the basic words, the orthography, alphabet, numbers, and simple things. After that, they spoke to each other and to me in Iolish, leaving me to decipher and reply on my own, correcting me when I pronounced or translated something wrong.

Really, by the end of the journey I'd likely be speaking it fluently.

"You're a fast learner," Ytgar praised with a smile.

I gave him an 'I told you so' look. I wasn't some daft harlot. I knew mathematics as well, but that wasn't something I tended to show off, either.

Hours later, we stopped. Not for camp or to take a break, but because we had just reached the outer edges of Kappur, and our party was dispersing.

I guided my hippocampus towards the front where Maisie, Elias, Tiberius, and Kai were saying goodbye to the King of Kappur. I supposed I should get used to thinking of him as my uncle. He had married my aunt, after all.

Maisie and her weirdly formed harem dismounted. She floated in front of her father, and bubble tears were rising from her eyes.

"I just found you," the king was saying, trailing his thumb beneath her eyes to wipe away the tears. "I do not wish to leave you again."

"Me neither," she confessed.

It was an intimate scene, but I couldn't look away. Something about it drew me in. The unknown. And there was a vicious longing in my chest as I looked at father and daughter go in for an embrace. It should have reminded me of my father, of hugs and kisses and tears, but all it did was show me once more what my own father lacked. Courage and affection. The ability to wage war and do whatever it took to find the daughter he had lost.

Those months when I had gone missing, he had sent Captain Saber after me while he fumed from the comforts of his throne. He hadn't cared enough to search.

King Dorian didn't even know Maisie, not really, and he still loved her. It was obvious in the way they embraced.

As if it was their final goodbye and their first.

But Kappur and Draconi were neighboring kingdoms. Even if they had to separate and King Dorian had to return to Kappur's capital, Maisie wasn't far away. Not anymore. Now he knew the truth of her survival. Knew that she was alive. That was as good a gift as any, I supposed.

"I'll miss you, dad," Maisie said.

I had to tear my gaze away and ignore that frantic, erratic beating of my heart. How was it possible that it could break all over again? That it could long for what it would never in a million years have?

I was starting to think I was a masochistic fool.

"Odele."

I turned back to see the King of Kappur gesturing at me to come forward. With my eyes a little wide, I dismounted my hippocampus, tossing my reins to Val absentmindedly, and started forward. Once I was in front of the king—my uncle—he smiled and enveloped me in a warm hug.

Awkward, I did nothing but float there as he squeezed me. I wasn't even sure how to reply. Should I hold him back? How much pressure should I put into the hug? Should I hold him close, keep him at length? What was I supposed to do?

All too soon, it ended, and I didn't get to hold him back.

"Thank you." He placed his hands on my shoulders and squeezed.

"For what?"

He smiled. He was quite a handsome king, though the years had obviously been a little hard on him. At least he hadn't lost his love in that time. At least he wasn't a shell of a merman.

"Because of you, I have my daughter back. If it hadn't been for you, I never would have found her again."

A lump caught in my throat. I supposed he was right. I'd been the one to find the evidence of Maisie's existence. If I hadn't disappeared, then Captain Saber wouldn't have traveled throughout all of Thalassar. He wouldn't have gone to Lagoona and wouldn't have found her and brought her back.

But I supposed, none of this would have happened if he hadn't broken contract and caused a giant mess in the first place. Then again, if he hadn't, I wouldn't exist, and neither would Maisie.

"Well," I said around the tightness of my throat. "I do enjoy happy endings."

He laughed and pulled me into another hug. This time, I hugged him back, unsure if I was doing it right. It didn't seem to matter either way, because his arms still spoke of warmth and protection. Of gratitude and familial love. Once again, it ended all too soon.

We waved goodbye and watched the king and his party turn on their hippocampi and ride away. We watched them until they became silhouettes in the distance. The whole while, Maisie had tears in her eyes and clutched a hand to her heart.

Almost as if hers were breaking, too.

We made it to Draconi a few days after we left Kappur.

The waters here were different. They were darker, brightened by reefs of water lilies and greenery rare to Thalassar.

I was anxious the further we traveled. Perhaps because I was finally close to seeing a kingdom I'd always wanted to. Perhaps because I was afraid they let dragons swim rampant through the waters.

Either way, I had my conch out and was recording every moment of it.

"We're close to the Lizard Prince's home," I told the conch before swivelling it towards said prince.

We rode closer to him up near the front now. Just for the occasion, he sat atop his magnificent beast of a dragon. The thing was majestic and proud; its neck stretched out like royalty in front of it, barbed tail swishing left and right, and leathery wings gliding and pushing itself through the water at a very steady pace.

"How does it feel to be home at last, Lizard Prince?"

Kai didn't bother with a rejoinder. He merely shot me a look of impatience before turning back to the front.

"So this is Draconi?" Ytgar mused, his eyes darting everywhere at once. I could hardly blame him.

Draconi was surprisingly pretty, and we hadn't neared the capital. It was swathed in an array of pinks and oranges. Not as obnoxious as Eramaea, but better somehow. I was surprised to find trees here. They had the same shape and form as two-legger trees, but the trunks were made entirely of corroded coral, entwining and wrapped in a strange, gnarled way. From the tops burst blooms of beautiful pink and red flowers that swayed with the current and broke off and flowed with it.

Ytgar stopped to pick up a discarded flower and turned to offer it to me. It was a gift I was too excited to reject. I placed it behind my ear.

The houses here were different in structure than they were in Thalassar. Every single one of them were rectangular with strangely pointed roofs that curved at each of its four points. On some houses, parts of the roofs were held up by thick pillars, though those appeared to be more richly made in reds, blacks, and golds. The poorer homes still had its own magic to them, though I'd never lived in a home that small…

Bright blooms of flowers surrounded every house. The whole of Draconi smelt like water lilies. It was pleasant.

As we came closer and closer to the capital, to the palace that was Prince Kai's home and the place that housed Draconi's Emperor, the more populated the streets grew. We were greeted with cheers and waterworks—similar to two-legger fireworks—their bright colors bursting in loud pops of green, blue, yellow, orange, and red.

It was almost as if they'd known we'd be arriving.

Prince Kai looked stoically ahead, though he acknowledged his mer with graceful nods. I wondered if he was nervous because Maisie didn't sit atop his dragon with him. From what I knew of Draconian custom, it was that when a new bride arrived, she should be atop the prince's dragon with him.

But Maisie was deathly afraid of riding anything. She had to sit securely in front of Captain Saber on his hippocampus.

The mer of Draconi seemed exotic to me. Maybe it was their tails. Their tails were the bright colors of goldfish and beta fish, flowing and elegant. Slanted eyes regarded me and Prince Ytgar as we pointed our recording conches from one spot to another with unabashed awe.

We made it through the city slowly, and when we finally arrived at the emperor's palace, I swore my jaw unhinged.

"Oh my gods…" It was breathtaking. It was beautiful. It was massive.

"Iol's is better," Ytgar muttered under his breath.

His comment went ignored.

The emperor's home was built with the same structure as the other homes we'd passed. Rectangular, with pillars and gates, pointed roofs… But this was… palatial in its entirety. It was massively built, bigger than our palace in Eramaea. Painted entirely in bright red, with gold and black trimming, banners—with the stamped golden images of a great clawed dragon—hung from the outer gates that flapped with the currents. Along the top walls, mer in armor were positioned with spearguns and arrows.

And hovering just above the palace like a dark cloud was an enormous dragon.

It was black everywhere, so dark it appeared as nothing more than a shadow at first. A massive shadow with long flapping wings and hooked claws. It was as big as a blue whale and looked every bit the formidable and dangerous beast I'd heard about in conches. Its neck stretched out, the top of it jutted with spikes as thick and as sharp as steel. Long twin whiskers flowed from an upper lip that was curled back to reveal sharp and jagged rows of teeth, and a forked tongue inside. It had four legs that curled against its muscular body and a long, twining tail, with barbs at the end that were likely poisonous.

"What is *that?*" Maisie demanded from her position, a little fearfully.

It was I who answered. "The guardian of the palace." I made sure the conch recorded every aspect of its vicious looking body. "It's the emperor's dragon."

"I—I didn't know they grew that big…"

"They grow bigger," Kai supplied gravely.

No one replied because at that moment, the palace gates opened and we were allowed inside.

A long time ago, I dreamt I'd met the emperor. A nightmare, really. I tossed and turned as images filled my mind of my marrying Kai and meeting his thousands of sisters and the ruthless Jiang Li of Draconi.

My dreams had vastly exaggerated.

He was formidable, of course, and the spitting image of Kai. He was taller and broader, with muscles that strained against his black and gold kimono. His tail was much like Kai's with the mottled spots of a koi fish, except his was black and white to Kai's orange, white, and black. They had the same high cheekbones and pretty, slanted, brown eyes. His black hair was tied with a gold slip of ribbon down his back, and the shadow of a beard covered the tip of his pointed chin. The emperor appeared more grave than his son. And angry.

We'd been escorted to see him and the empress by Kai's advisors, Ichiro and Lee. Kai, Maisie, Tiberius, Elias, Ytgar, Val, and I. The rest of our procession had been escorted elsewhere, to guest rooms or straight into the mouths of their dragons, I didn't really care.

Maisie and I curtsied to the emperor and empress. The others bowed. But Kai dropped low to the ground, his forehead touching it. It was the respectful way for Draconians to greet their royalty.

"Hello, father," Kai greeted in Dracon.

The emperor glared down at his son. "Rise, boy."

His tone sent a shiver of foreboding down my spine. Because Maisie was next to me, I noticed her whole body seemed to flinch. Comfortingly, I reached out and brushed her fingers with my own. It seemed to relax her, however slightly.

Kai stared back at his father, and I wondered how he did it. I had thought my stepmother to be a formidable, vicious opponent. She was nothing next to Jiang Li.

When he spoke, he spoke in their own language. But I understood every vicious word. Words he probably assumed none of us would understand. Words he wasn't likely to utter in our own common tongue, because of how cruel they were.

"You deign to show your face after you so thoroughly disappointed me in Thalassar?"

Kai tensed. "Father…"

"Interrupt me again, and it'll be the last thing you ever do, boy." Kai lapsed into silence. "I'd expect an alliance with Thalassar and Princess Odele Malabella. Not with Kappur and the bastard child of Dorian."

His hands closed into fists. "She's not a bastard."

The emperor's eyes narrowed.

His empress let out a bitter laugh. "She's as much a bastard as you."

The emperor cut his wife a scalding look. "Be silent or you'll lose your tongue."

This was an uncomfortable situation. It was then that I remembered that Prince Kai wasn't technically legitimate, although Draconi was much more liberal with bastard children than Thalassar. He was the emperor's only son—he had, like, a thousand daughters—with one of his concubines. Still, bastard or not, he was heir to the throne.

The empress despised him for it.

"I should whip you for your transgression."

Kai's voice was tight when he replied. "We received the secret magic we need to save Draconi, father."

"It means nothing to me now, boy. I should banish you from the kingdom and have you whipped for your insolence and disobedience. Worse, you were tricked by two stupid mermaids."

As much as I enjoyed watching Kai squirm, I couldn't hear this any longer. I would not listen to him speak ill of me or my beloved cousin. I took a stroke forward, putting on the waters of a demure yet clueless mermaid. "Your Royal Majesty," I greeted in Thalassar's common tongue so they could all understand. "Forgive my daring interruption." His gaze slashed towards me. "I wished to formally introduce myself. My name is Odele Malabella Oriana, Princess of Thalassar. We are all most thankful for your generous welcome into such a beautiful kingdom."

His eyes narrowed suspiciously on my tone. I knew he understood me, but I cocked my head to the side and mustered a confused look.

"Oh dear." I turned to Kai. "Forgive me, but I'm not sure how to say that in Dracon. Could you perhaps translate for me?"

"I understand Thalassarin," the emperor interrupted with obvious irritation.

I clapped my hands together. "Excellent. Your kingdom is beautiful. But where are my manners? Let me formally introduce our companions. This is Prince Ytgar Neves Isolde of Iol and his royal bodyguard." I didn't bother saying Val's name, as servants and bodyguards were rarely introduced as anyone of importance. "Captain of the Royal Guard..." I gestured at Tiberius, then at the Black Blade. "...and company. And this is my cousin, and Prince Kai's bride, Odalaea Malabella Knoll Li, Princess of Kappur."

Maisie dipped into a proper curtsey. I wanted to applaud when she didn't even fall over because of her limp.

The emperor didn't look impressed. His gaze flicked judgingly over Maisie's form, then found mine again. They were angry. Not just angry, but furious.

"It was my understanding," he began, his accent thick and deep, "that my son was to wed the Thalassarin Princess. Not the Kappurin Princess. We had a contract."

Well, silt. Draconians and their stupid honor. He probably saw it as a slight to his kingdom, even though my stepmother had given them what they'd desperately wanted anyway.

"Oh, but sire, I thought this change of plans would please you." I managed to look just the right amount of contrite.

"Please me?" His eyes narrowed.

"Well, because of the new alliances, of course. See, had Prince Kai married me, you'd have gained but one ally in Thalassar and an enemy in Kappur. Now, you've not only gained one alliance but more. An alliance with Kappur, obviously, and because Odalaea is my dearest cousin and her mother was from Thalassar—and she was raised there—you have your peace with my kingdom as well. And thanks to my upcoming nuptials to Prince Ytgar, there will be peace between Draconi and Iol. I'm sure of it." I smiled widely at him. "We are making history. Draconi, Iol, Thalassar, and Kappur, all on the same side. It's miraculous!"

The emperor grew silent for a long moment.

"Don't listen to that foolish child," his empress spat in Dracon. I pretended not to understand.

"Be silent," he hissed. Then he smiled widely at me. "I believe, young Princess, that you are correct. This is beneficial to all." He clapped his hands together. "Please, I shall have my servants escort you to your rooms at once. Your hippocampi will be well taken care of. Oh, Odalaea?"

Maisie took a stroke forward. Her head was held high, but I could see the tremble in her fingers. "Yes, Your Majesty?"

He smiled. "Welcome to the family."

I DID NOT WANT to be impressed with Odele's little display, but I was. I didn't speak a lick of Dracon, but I was almost positive that conversation was unpleasant, and Odele had understood every word while giving the impression that she knew nothing. She had manipulated the Emperor of Draconi to her own will and turned the tide in her favor.

She would make a formidable queen if she lost the spoiled selfishness she was known for, I was sure of it.

We were escorted to our rooms side by side by side. The whole while, the Draconian guards stared distrustfully at Val and I. I could hardly blame them when I was glaring as well. There were years of bad waters between Draconi and Iol. We were two neighboring kingdoms so vastly different; it was little wonder we didn't get along.

Iol was harsh, and living there was even harsher. It was a difficult place to survive when we had creatures such as polar bears and sea lions. Because of our proximity to Draconi, we also got dragons, the most dangerous of them all.

Draconi was said to keep their dragons locked away, but that wasn't the case. They let them swim rampant and refused to stop breeding the beasts to protect Iol and its citizens. Years ago, I'd been a child then, a dragon had gotten loose in Iolish waters and killed dozens of innocents.

Draconi had done nothing, offered no recompense for the damage.

And they called us savages.

"You were brilliant, beauty mine. Take a bow!" Val was holding a conch and recording the princess, speaking to her in our mother tongue.

It was like a little game the two had going on. They had documented everything on our journey here. I'd noticed the shift between them as the game continued. Odele chuckled with him, seemed comfortable around him. They'd become friends of sorts. Meanwhile, she still glared at me, and spoke to me only when necessary.

That didn't mean I couldn't see the underlying flare of desire in her eyes. That I didn't recognize exactly what those heated looks were. She wanted me and hated me in the same expanse of breaths and despised me for what she was feeling. I knew, because I felt the exact same way.

Odele tossed her nose up haughtily. "No. I do not need to prove anything with bows or words, and I do not need you to remind me that I'm brilliant. I already know."

She said it all in Iolish, and just the sound of it made my whole body shudder with desire. She had an accent when she spoke, and hadn't quite mastered the rough edges of our language, but she was a quick learner.

Val leaned closer to her, conch in hand as he invaded her personal space. "Now that we're in Draconi, what's the first thing you want to see?"

Odele chewed on her bottom lip in thought. I wondered if she knew she did that, or if she did it entirely on purpose just to entice me. Ever since our tryst in the coral forest, I did nothing but dream about her. Did nothing but want and desperately crave the heat of her tongue against mine, the taste of her on my lips, embedded in my soul.

"I want to see the dragons." Her response was almost flippant, but I noticed the way she flexed her fingers, the way her eyes widened with an anticipated glee. "But first, I would like a bath and a change of clothes."

I almost groaned at the thought of her in the bath. Maybe she *was* doing this on purpose.

"Of course." Val lowered the conch to stop recording. He was having too much fun with that thing. I could admit to a certain curiosity about the device myself, but watching him have fun with it was enough to satiate any lingering doubts.

The guards stopped in front of thin sliding doors that appeared to be made from the same composition of sea fans. They gestured at the doors, indicating whose room was whose, before they swam back down the hall. I didn't doubt that they'd be back to shadow after us distrustfully.

Val reached for Odele's hand with a flourishing gesture and bowed over her knuckles. "I shall count the minutes away from you with sorrow." He pressed a kiss to the tops of her knuckles. "I will miss you every second."

Odele glared down at him. "Does that line ever work?"

He flashed her an impish sort of side smile. "Always."

She sniffed and tugged her fingers away from his grasp. "Well, you need to work on that, because it's not working on me."

"But you admit that you want it to?" He reached over and slid the screen door open to her room.

She rolled her eyes and swept past him into the darkness of the room beyond. She turned, locked her gaze first with Val and then with me, then back to Val again. A smile curled on those luscious lips of hers. Lips that I vividly remembered touching my own. Lips I wanted to taste again. "You're as stupid as a pile of dead clams if you think anything you say could *ever* convince me to fall in love with you." And then she slid the door closed with a force that rattled it on its hinges.

Val sighed wistfully. "Magnificent."

I snorted and turned to make my way towards our room. Servants had already seen to our luggage, and I had to admit I was looking forward to a bath of my own. And then I wanted to leave this kingdom as soon as possible.

Being in Draconi made my skin itch uncomfortably. My hand stayed at my waist, near the hilt of my sword. It was my body's instinct to reach for it in enemy territory, and despite what Odele had said regarding alliances and truces between the kingdom of Iol and Draconi, it wasn't something I saw happening easily or smoothly.

I was more than willing to negotiate for the better of Iol. But the Emperor of Draconi would not agree to lock up his beasts, to send patrols near our borders to protect my mer from the savage creatures. It would mean swimming through the waters of the Uncharted, to circle around and protect Iol from the northernmost front.

The Uncharted Waters were home to vicious yet mysterious mer. It was said they had creatures more fearsome than dragons. It wasn't the unknown creatures that kept me up at night, but the dragons themselves. More than one had gotten through on both sides of our seas and only chaos had followed.

I opened the door to my assigned room and Val followed me inside. The stench of burning assaulted my nostrils. I knew that on two-legger lands, they thought things couldn't burn beneath the waters, but lava that was hot enough to do that. The scent of the room was overpowering; it smelled like spices, and little bubbles shaped like smoke curled from table, to vanity, to desk. There were red and orange lava globes floating like little lanterns on the ceiling. A vase that held water lilies sat in one corner, a folded floor mattress made of bamboo and kelp laid on the far side of the room, with one soft blanket. The wall decor was painted with the image of a dragon mauling into mer, blood and body parts splattered everywhere.

I turned away from it with disgust to look at Val. "The sooner we're out of here, the better."

He eyed the wall paintings distastefully, his nose scrunching up. Then slowly, he turned to look at me. "I know it's not ideal," he said. "But I think we should stay at least for a few days. Odele is really excited to see the kingdom."

"We don't have *time* to see the kingdom. We have other things that need doing." My temper was rising. It was this place. It was the way the Draconians looked at us as if we were monsters, when they were the ones who bred them and kept them as pets. It was the fact that Val was getting closer to Odele, and I should have been furious about it, but I wasn't. Not anymore.

I loved Val more than I loved myself. He was the brother I never had, so I knew what was happening, even if he didn't. I knew he was falling in love with my betrothed. I should have prohibited it, told him to give up this facade we found ourselves in. She should want me. She should laugh with *me*, not him. But... seeing her smile, seeing her speaking our language, joking, falling into easy banter with my best friend... it brought out an inkling of happiness in me I thought long buried.

I had to admit that I wanted it. Wanted the both of them to get along. Soon, once we were married, she would be the most important thing in my life, like Val was.

"We can't," I argued, broking no room for contradictions.

But Val was Val, and I didn't intimidate him like I did others. He raised an eyebrow. "Trust me. It's the only way we'll win her over. Did you know she wanted to see the world?"

Since she didn't speak to me, no, I did not know she wanted to see the world. I knew nothing about her. Except the exact shade of her lips when she was kissed, the taste of her tongue against my own, the way it felt to have her hips jerking eagerly against my mouth...

"Just a few days. Just so she can see all she wants to see and then we can go back."

I wanted to argue, to urge that we leave tomorrow at the latest but I stopped myself. If staying for a few days made Odele happy, if it made it so she would no longer swim away from us, then what could it hurt?

"Fine," I concurred. "A few days. That's it."

Val did a silent cheer that made me glare.

A few days, I told myself. A few days for the good of Iol.

Who was I kidding?

I'd stay a few days, not only because of my selfless need to help my kingdom, but because I longed to see Odele smile again. And if it took a couple of days in my enemy kingdom to get to know her, I'd suffer it tenfold.

"YOUR FATHER IS UPSET with you," I commented quietly.

We were swimming through the palace at a steady pace, one that wasn't too trying on my torn fins. We'd been in Draconi for a few hours, and already I'd been showered with gifts of clothes,—kimonos, one that I currently wore; a beautiful garment in gold with a stamped dragon and water lilies on the back—food, jewels, and so many other things.

I'd met most of Kai's sisters, and even his mother, the emperor's favorite concubine. She was pretty, with a tail that was identical to Kai's in color, though he favored his father in looks. With long brown hair and dark eyes, she looked rather young. Perhaps it was her pale complexion. Regardless, she was nice, greeted me with a warm hug and a kiss on the cheek.

Emperor Jiang Li was a different story.

I didn't speak Dracon, but I'd understood facial features, and he'd looked furious.

"He'll get over it." He shrugged. While I could tell he was happy to be home, as it was obvious in the constant smiles he displayed around his sisters and his mother, I could also tell there was a tightness in his shoulders while out in public. It was the same way he'd acted when we'd been in Thalassar. Stiff, cautious. As if a heavy weight had been placed over his shoulders.

"It's because of our marriage isn't it?"

I didn't want to care, didn't want to feel the inevitable slash of hurt that clenched at my insides. Alas, there it was.

I wanted the emperor's approval. Not having it made me feel small all over again.

"Worry not, my gem." Kai took my hand in his and brought it up to his lips, pressing a kiss to the backs of my knuckles. The action was affectionate. It brought instant warmth over me. "All will be well."

I stopped mid-stroke and tugged at the front lapels of his kimono. He stopped and turned to face me, expression softening into such tenderness.

"Talk to me, Kai," I pleaded softly. "Don't shut me out."

He sighed and looked over my shoulder to where I knew Tiberius and Elias floated side by side. They'd given us just enough distance for an illusion of privacy for appearance's sake, but we didn't fool ourselves into thinking they couldn't hear us.

Finally, his eyes found mine again, the brown depths of them kind and searching. "I could never shut you out, my gem."

I lifted my palm to cradle his cheek. "Then talk to me." It was a firm command and a plea.

"He was… unhappy… at first. He feels you have slighted my honor, his own, and that of this kingdom by the lies at the wedding…"

The wedding where I'd pretended to be Odele and signed my name on the marriage contract with Kai. It was irreversible. We were husband and wife, before the courts and the gods. And I suspected soon we'd be mother and father as well.

"I think I did you a disservice."

"*No.* Don't think it. I love you, and Odele was right. This marriage, and hers to Ytgar, opens up many new doors of opportunity for all of our kingdoms."

I chewed on my bottom lip. "Still, we offended your father. How do I change his view of me?"

"You don't need his approval or validation, my gem. You are perfect, and he will realize it on his own."

I couldn't quite explain the need burning inside me for that validation. I supposed I felt I had to prove myself harder than Odele would have to. To prove that I wasn't just some flippant, daft mermaid from Lagoona. That I could be so much more than just a waitress, that I could be more than my upbringing. That the royals might actually come to respect me.

"Tell me," I pleaded softly.

Kai sighed and moved aside a stray lock of hair from my cheek. "Perhaps, if you prove strong at the Choosing…"

I gulped, fear slamming into me almost immediately. Kai had explained Draconian marriage customs to me, and the Choosing was one I wasn't looking forward to. The ceremony in which the bride chose a dragon of her own and rode it for the first time. Every Draconian royal went through the ceremony. Even the emperor's concubines had their own dragons.

I didn't want one. I was terrified.

But if that's what it would take to impress him, then I'd do it.

"When is the Choosing?" I asked

His expression hardened. "Tonight."

Well, silt.

Odele

I LOUNGED IN THE tub of black sand from the shores of two-legger islands. It was soft against my skin, the grains a welcome novelty. I'd scrubbed handfuls of it dexterously across my body until all the grime and silt from days of travel cleansed off and I felt re-birthed.

Even after I was finished, skin shining, I lay in the tub, tail hanging off the end leisurely. I was in no rush to get up from my spot, not until the sands went cold at least, and I could call for a servant to come and haul the scrub out and refill it once again.

Ah, but it felt so good to be in civilization again. To have luxuries at my fingertips, ripe for the taking. Now that I was here, my fingers, my whole body, itched for the familiarity of the ostentatious. Of the life I was meant to live. Sleeping in tents was obviously not for me, but this was. The luxuries of Draconi were something I could well and truly accept with open arms.

There was a knock on my door, the frantic pounding of a fist.

I ignored it.

Unfortunately, the knocking continued, each thwack more insistent than the last, and then a voice on the other end.

"Odele! Open up! Now!"

Sighing and with a groan, I got out of the tub, shaking off the grains from my hair and body before reaching for a silk kimono-style robe hanging on a hook. Typical Draconian rooms didn't have built in bathing rooms like in Thalassar. Here, the bathing was done in little hot houses, as they called them. They were public, even for royalty. The good thing about being a guest here was that if I requested a tub and sand, they brought it up, which was precisely what I had done.

I slipped the robe on and swam to the door, sliding it open to let Maisie slip inside. She was frantic; it was obvious in the distressed way she swam back and forth across the room, her limping gait all the more prominent in her rush.

"Um, are you okay?" I closed the door for privacy. "Where's your menagerie of lovers?"

She stopped in the middle of the room and turned to me. Her face was bereft of any humor. There was nothing there but worry, and fear.

"What's wrong?" I took a stroke towards her, placing my palms on her shoulders to steady her. "Talk to me, cousin."

She loosed a shaking breath. "The Choosing… it's tonight."

I blinked, momentarily stunned. "So soon?"

Her body started jittering again. "The emperor is furious with us for tricking Kai into marrying me. To win him over, I must impress him at the Choosing but I… I don't think I can."

The Choosing was what I would have gone through, had I been the one to wed Kai. Maisie would be dropped onto their dragon breeding grounds, and she would have to choose her beast and ride it for the first time. It was a long swimming tradition in this kingdom and could not be avoided.

"It's perfectly safe," I reassured her. "They have soldiers and trainers posted around you for your protection. You just have to find one that will bond with you and mount it." My lips twisted into a wry smile. "Just pretend you're mounting your Lizard Prince, though not in such salacious detail."

She didn't even chuckle. Ugh, and it had been a fabulous joke, too.

"I'm scared, Odele," she whispered.

If my cousin was afraid of riding hippocampi, then of course she'd be terrified of a dragon. They were bigger and meaner. At least a hippocampus didn't have teeth that could sear through bone with just a bite.

"The good thing about living in the seas," I explained calmly, "is that we don't really have to worry about falling and breaking our necks." Of course it was always a possibility that the beast could trample her and break her neck, but I didn't need to burden her with that information, did I? All she needed was the reassurance that if she fell, she could fan her fins out at her sides and swim.

She laughed, though the sound was entirely without humor. "My fin is shredded on one side, Odele. If I fall from the beast's back, I *will* more than likely break my neck."

Okay, she had me there. Most times, it was easy to overlook her disability. Now I couldn't help that my eyes wandered down to her tail, as if I could bring myself to see past the golden-black material of her kimono and see the shredded mass of flesh underneath.

I looked back up into her eyes and saw that raw fear, like a living, breathing thing with a soul coming to life.

"Do you want me to go in your stead?"

It was against some Draconian rule, I was sure, but for Maisie, I would grow legs and walk through two-legger hell fire if need be. She was the only family I loved, and the only one who tolerated me with a smile. I would don her disguise and jump on the back of a dragon and throw it in the Emperor's face with joy.

"You need only ask."

She bit her bottom lip, so alike we were in the simplicity of that gesture. I could tell she was contemplating it. Finally, she blew out another breath. "No," she decided. "This is something I have to do myself. Just..." She reached for me, hand enclosing in my own.

I relished in the gesture, for however short it may have lasted. It was difficult to admit, even to myself, that I craved the touch of her affection as much as I craved breathing, even if I encased my heart in steel and pretended it didn't matter, that I didn't want it.

"Be there with me. I can't explain it, but I draw strength from you."

Blood of my blood, kin of my soul. My cousin, as closely bonded as if she were my twin sister.

I felt my heart clench with affection at her words and I had to blink back my tears. She drew strength from me? Of all the wild impossibilities... What she didn't realize was that I was the dependent one. I needed her more than she could ever need me.

"Of course I'll be there." I squeezed her hands back and smiled. "And if the emperor has something nasty to say about you, I know a few Iolish bastards who would be willing to stick an ice sword through his back."

Finally, she laughed at one of my joke's just before she pulled away. "There's no need for that. Just be there. One hour, in the courtyard. They're going to escort us to the breeding grounds."

"Perfect."

She turned to leave, a little less shaky than when she had arrived.

"Odalaea?"

She froze, her hand placed gently over the door.

"You can do this. I know you can."

I could feel her smile even though she didn't turn around to acknowledge my words. She opened the door and swam out of my room, a newfound determination in her stance.

It was then that I realized she hadn't even admonished me for calling her by her true name.

Ytgar and Val framed me, both of them floating like perfect sentinels on either of my sides. I'd pounded against both of their doors, demanding their assistance.

Usually, I wouldn't have bothered with escorts or companions, but maybe I'd need them to stick a knife through the emperor if he so much as insulted my dearest cousin.

And maybe, a small part of me wanted them to be there, my co-conspirators. It seemed like that's what they'd become in the days we'd been together. We studied and traded smiles, jokes, and insults, however tentative. At least, Ytgar did. I was still unsure what Val was to me, though I admonished myself for the fleeting thought. He was *nothing* to me, *should* be nothing to me but a guard, and a nuisance.

Still, I knocked on their doors and told them they were to come with me to witness my cousin's Choosing. They hadn't argued and, even if they loathed to admit it, I knew they were just as curious about the ceremony as I was.

So they went with me, two mermen of ice at my sides. Val, his silver-white eyes piercing holes through my back, to my left; and Ytgar with his bright blue depths arrogant and sarcastic to my right. Not the only ones on our way to witness the event, my cousins swam behind us as my chaperones with Iolish and Thalassarin guards in their wake.

We were led to the courtyard by Draconian guards in metal scaled armor that gleamed like the hides of dragons. They carried spears and katanas, and war helmets shaped like the heads of their beasts. Glorified nannies with fancy accouterments, in my opinion.

We made it to the front gate where carriages were waiting for us. These weren't the shell kind, shaped like nautilus husks or clam shells. These were glistening, shaped like the bodies of dragons with wings carved out in a wide expanse at the back, with claw pointed tips. Dragons the size of hippocampi were tethered to them and shifting restlessly.

The emperor shifted his impatient, stoic gaze over us before he helped his empress into the gilded carriage. Behind him, Maisie was lifted into a similar carriage by Kai and was followed inside by Tiberius, the Black Blade, and someone who I could only assume was Kai's mother.

Another one was waiting for us behind that one. Ytgar handed me up and our party followed inside.

It took but a few moments for the gates to open and our transport to lurch forward. Then a few more moments after that for us to arrive at our destination. I'd barely gotten a good look around the city when we had stopped and were ushered out again.

It didn't matter, though. Because we were here. We had arrived at the Dragon Breeding Grounds.

It took my breath away. I almost doubled over with the awe of it all. It was overwhelming, and the sensation of euphoria inside me like a volcanic eruption, making me reach for the first hand to come near me, not noticing whose it was.

"Look at it," I whispered, clutching the solid, warm hand. *"Look."*

It was a wide expanse of blue water, and around it, looked like an enormous open walled mausoleum with steel, shining bars erected beneath four thick pillars. And inside the massive forested space, were the dragons.

Dozens—no *hundreds*—of them prowled viciously among their confines. Scales of all sizes and colors battered against cages, teeth in all jagged edges gnawed fiercely. Dragons attacked each other, wings spread wide, some shrieked as they dove through the water.

It was like a sanctuary made just for them. A playground for dragons with their own obstacle courses, trees and food stations. Some lounged, others fought, others played.

The beasts were as majestic as they were deadly.

And my cousin had to swim through that and choose one.

I looked over to her, saw her whole body stiffen as she took the beasts in. Kai was behind her, offering reassurance with his hand against her lower back and his lips whispering in her ear. Tiberius was glaring into the cage while Elias's brown skin suddenly seemed to pale a lighter shade.

Then the emperor came over and handed Maisie a bit of rope, the only thing she would take with her inside. She would use it as the reins when she found her dragon.

"The dragon will choose you," the emperor explained in Thalassarin, his accent rough, his tone even more so. "Do not worry, for you will know which one is yours." Then he moved away from her and she was turning to Kai. The Lizard Prince tried to hide behind a stony expression, but his worry was apparent.

"Be safe, my gem. And don't be nervous."

Masie scoffed shakily.

Then she was being turned by Tiberius, and he was holding her in his arms. I almost wondered if the emperor would rage at the impropriety of it, but was surprised when he wore no expression whatsoever.

"You don't have to do this, Maisie," Tiberius said, pulling her close, so close that their lips were but a whisper apart.

"Yes, I do." Maisie pulled away bravely and forced herself to turn. Our eyes met. I didn't smile encouragingly, but lifted my chin up with all the haughty defiance I was known for.

"You are a Malabella, cousin," I reminded her loudly, confidently. "And you know you can do this."

I could see her physically force back a tremble and replace it with confidence and surety. She tilted her chin up and made her way towards the gates of the grounds. Not once did she limp. Not once did she look back.

I sent her a silent cheer, and then bit my lip as I watched the gates open and she swam in.

I squeezed the hand holding mine tighter. Not once had I let go, and couldn't bring myself to look over for comfort. If Maisie had to brave swimming through them, then I could brave watching them.

She swam into the dragon grounds and it was like something in the waters shifted. A hush descended, and every dragon inside seemed to still, as if aware that something was suddenly amiss. That there was someone there who didn't quite belong.

All at once, they turned to look at Maisie.

My hand tightened against flesh, and a gasp caught in my throat.

The dragons roared.

Maisie flinched, the only sign of fear she had shown until now.

A dragon, a muscular, dangerous looking creature with blue scales and leathery wings perched on the top branch of a coral tree, moved its hide, assuming a predatory stance…

…and then it attacked.

It sprung straight towards my cousin. Its wings spread out wide in the water and glided down at an impossible speed towards her. Maisie shrieked and ducked out of the way. Where she'd been floating, the creature struck with its vicious front claws.

The attack stirred the other creatures into a frenzy. The beasts lifted their wings and swarmed. Amidst the fray, Maisie was lost. It wasn't until a space cleared that I saw the flash of purple, her hair whipping around her neck and arms. She swam as fast as she could through the melee of hard bodies, as teeth and claws gnashed around her.

There were guards inside, trying to keep the chaos to a minimum, but they were nowhere near my cousin, so they didn't see when one dragon suddenly swooped straight for her.

A gasp tore out of me then, and I sank my nails into the palms of the hand I was holding.

The dragon tried to use its back claws to grab at her; it was so close and I knew she wouldn't be fast enough to dodge it. My heart beat frantically as I watched, as I prayed to whatever gods that would listen that she be fast enough.

But the dragon never got to her because a second one reared up suddenly from behind Maisie. It was a big one, as big as Kai's dragon, with sleek black scales and a golden underbelly. Its eyes were huge, bulbous things that jutted out from either side of a too small head. Its back had twin rows of jagged spikes, a barbed tail and flowing leathery wings with the puncture marks of holes in them. It seemed viciously deformed compared to the rest of them, yet when it opened its mouth and roared, the waters trembled.

Then, I knew.

"That's the one," I whispered excitedly. "It chose her."

Overcoming her sudden shock, and realizing just what I had in the same moment, Maisie tossed the rope around the deformed dragon's short neck and hauled herself up. I watched with shaking limbs as she hugged her tail tightly to the side of it and yelled, a battle cry to rival any other.

The dragon tore through the water, straight towards the gate, with Maisie on its back. It screeched its way through the melee and when it was close, the guards opened the gates and they tore out of the grounds.

The dragon hovered above us, circling with a slow flap of its thin wings, then a moment later it descended almost cautiously.

Its wingspan created a current that whipped at us before it tucked its wings in and settled into the silt.

"She did it!" I turned up with excitement. It was then that I realized exactly whose hand I was holding.

Val's blazing silver eyes glanced down at me as shock rippled through my body. It had been his hand in mine this whole time. I tugged away, but he held firm, squeezing once before letting me go.

I tried to shake off the feeling of his skin as I turned away, tried to forget the heat in his gaze, but it remained on me like a brand. It followed me as I went over to Maisie to congratulate her and threatened to eradicate the walls I'd fabricated around my heart.

"A Black Moor Dragon," I commented once again.

We were in the palace library, the day after Maisie's Choosing, and I was still in precedented awe.

It was true. Draconians kept their recordings in dragon eggs rather than in conches. The moment I'd laid eyes on them when Ytgar and Val brought me here, I'd been lost.

I immediately picked up an egg—it looked like a large scarlet stone embedded with scales, a small moveable crack on the top that opened to listen to the inside—on the different species of dragons. It was how I now knew that the dragon who had chosen my cousin was a Black Moor.

They were considered the handicapped of the dragons species, as decades of inbreeding had altered their appearance rather drastically, giving them enormous eyes that did not allow for perfect sight, and a delicateness to their wings that made them rather slow. Not really a surprise it had chosen Maisie, then, I supposed.

Yet Maisie's had been formidable when protecting her while afterwards it just buried itself into the silt and ignored her.

As it turned out, there were many different breeds of dragons, as well as different species of *dracon*—beasts that resembled dragons but weren't, essentially, dragons—such as the wyverns, wyrms, and drakes, among others. Draconi didn't breed anything besides dragons, though, as they were tamer than the other species and wouldn't maul their owner's head off in a rage. That wasn't to say those species didn't exist somewhere out there. And that wasn't to say that dragons couldn't be vicious when they wanted to be.

I'd stayed in the library from morning until night, ignoring everyone that came in my path until Ytgar plopped in front of me and bothered me senseless so I would leave. The next day, I was there again.

The sights of all I'd ever wanted to see weren't making me as discreet as I could have been. I couldn't be bothered to care anymore, until one day Jessinda asked, "Why do you bother? It's not like you speak Dracon anyway, so you're basically listening to gibberish."

I should have been happy that Jessinda wasn't smarter or she would have figured out my secret by now. Still, I avoided the library after that, keeping eggs to myself, smuggled in my rooms by Ytgar, who was my only accomplice in all of this.

It had happened so randomly, but Ytgar had become an easy ally. I still couldn't see us swimming up to the altar together—to be fair, I didn't see that happening with anyone—but we still had a fun camaraderie going on and I was enjoying his company.

He was almost as fun as me, though not quite, and he still irritated me sometimes. Well, most times. Okay, I'd admit, while I didn't see the two of us marrying, I could imagine us doing different things. Things that went beyond the coquettish. It was his fault, really. All because he was so steadily flirtatious. It wasn't the flirtation that got me, exactly, but the nearness of his body. The way his lips hovered too close to my cheeks, to the lobe of my ear, to the side of my mouth.

I think he just liked reminding me of that kiss we shared. As if I needed reminding. As if I didn't imagine his mouth in my dreams plunging into my own, taking and demanding, then suddenly becoming someone else's. And when I opened my eyes, it was no longer the depths of blue eyes I saw, but silver ones instead.

I woke up all sorts of confused.

Iolish bastards. Curse them and the way they were chipping away the walls surrounding my heart. As if its structures were made of melting ice instead of stone or steel.

Like right now. I tried not to glare as Ytgar sauntered up to me, pointing one of my blank conches right at my face as if he were a director from a telly program or something as ridiculous as that.

"Are you ready, beauty mine?" he asked in Iolish, the purr in his voice all too suggestive, seductive.

My eyes narrowed. "For what?"

"For me to take you on what might be the ninth or tenth best day of your life." He flicked his fingers at me, an annoying demand that I come forward. When I made no move to obey like some dogfish, he made an irritated sound in the back of his throat, leaned forward and jerked me towards him by the wrist.

"How *dare*—"

"Yeah, yeah, how dare I and stuff. Whatever." He hauled me through the halls of the palace like a dogfish on a leash. The audacity! I tugged at my arm but he didn't budge. He threw me an impatient look over his shoulder. "Do you want your surprise or not?"

"I don't like surprises."

"You'll like this one."

"I highly doubt that."

He just laughed and resumed pulling me. I didn't go easily, struggling the entire way until we made it to the courtyard where Val was waiting with a gaggle of guards, both Iolish and Draconian, and a tethered carriage.

"What is the meaning of this?" I yanked my hand away and turned to rage at Ytgar. "I don't appreciate being hauled around like some pet!"

His eyes rolled with vexation. "Just get in the cart, Princess." He put the conch down at his side, shoving it into the pocket of his long velvet cloak. He turned away from me and jerked open the door to the carriage impatiently.

"I am not your dogfish."

Ytgar's eyes shot upwards, as if praying to his gods for patience. "If you don't get in this damn carriage at once," he whispered contentiously, "I'll have Val pick you up by that pretty little tail and throw you inside."

My body stilled completely. I could feel Val's presence suddenly behind me, hovering like a phantom threat. The chill of his silver eyes on my backside hurt. I didn't curl in on his formidable gaze. I straightened, tilting my chin up in the water.

"Fine," I conceded. I'd go in with my dignity, at least.

Without taking Ytgar's offered hand, I climbed into the carriage, and they came in after me, shutting the doors firmly and then we were off.

I kept silent the whole ride, a stubborn protest at their barbaric handling of me. They didn't speak either, but I felt their presence all too closely, their tension, as if there was something hovering on the tips of their tongues waiting to be released but was locked up too tightly.

Until it wasn't.

"We leave for Iol tomorrow," Ytgar said firmly, finally.

I felt my heart fragment into pieces, like a conch ripping itself apart. I'd known this was coming, of course, but I hadn't wanted to accept it. I enjoyed Draconi. I enjoyed the threads of knowledge I was weaving into the tapestry of my brain. I wanted to stay longer, to spend more time with the cousin I had just found, and who was slipping from me so fast. I knew this couldn't possibly be the end for us, but I'd hoped for a little more time.

"Will you try to escape?" This question came from Val, and I could hear the dare laced between his words. When I shot a look over at him, his eyes were narrowed, but the silver in them was shining as brightly as diamonds as if to say, *'Escape, Princess. I will find you and enjoy every second of it.'*

I sniffed haughtily, throwing my chin up. "I was promised a tour of the world by Prince Ytgar and I'll get one. Even if I have to suffer through the barbarous waters of Iol to get it." I turned away and resumed ignoring them, though my mind was racing.

Iol.

In a couple of days, we'd be arriving at Iol, the freezing northern waters. I'd be forced to marry Ytgar, and then everything after that was a mystery. I had the sudden urge to plead with him, to say, 'Let's not get married and say we did.' But I knew my stepmother had her spies watching me, and if I didn't go through with this marriage, there would be no dowry for Iol and in turn, there would be no traveling to other kingdoms for alliances. Which meant, I'd not get to see the world.

Escaping seemed like such a vast impossibility now. Logically, I knew I'd not get very far with Val trailing after me like a shark after its prey. The thought of being chased sent a thrill through me that I pushed aside when I looked up at Prince Ytgar.

His eyes were intense, trained on my own. In them, I could tell there was something he wanted to say. I recognized the anguish of unspoken words as his eyes flicked between Val and I.

Almost as if he knew something he shouldn't.

Gods, had Val *told* him what had happened between us?

I clenched my hands into fists for a moment before relaxing. What did I care if he knew? I was a Princess, free to do as I pleased. They were not my keepers, my owners. If I wanted to be as selfish as my cousin and hoard mermen for myself, then it was in my right to do so.

Now that I thought about it, the idea had a certain appeal to it…

No. I shook my head back and forth. Val was a lowly servant, and what had once transpired between us couldn't happen again. Ever.

"Close your eyes," Ytgar urged gleefully.

"I am not closing my eyes."

"Come on, beauty mine. Close your eyes."

"Closing your eyes and letting someone else lead you towards a surprise is the surest way to find yourself falling into the abyss, or the mouth of a dragon, or into a pit of starving sharks. No, Ytgar, I do not think I will close my eyes."

Ytgar scoffed and grumbled in Iolish, "You take the fun out of everything." He switched back to Thalassarin. "Fine. Don't close them. You'll love your surprise either way."

And then he handed me down from the carriage and moved his body aside to reveal my surprise.

My hands flew to my mouth to stifle the gasp that ripped from my throat. My fins moved of their own volition. I pushed past the bodies of guards and commoners alike, not caring that I was mingling with the lowly mer of Draconi, not caring about anything except the sight in front of me. I didn't even register that there were tears in my eyes until the bubbles climbed up in swarms to blur my vision.

I swatted them away, and it didn't matter who saw me break down, that there were mer watching me as I dropped my tail to the silt once I came in front of it.

In front of the Great Dragon statue of Draconi.

It was bigger than the emperor's own dragon, more formidable, more deadly, and so much more beautiful. The long length of the statue's body curled with serpentine grace for what seemed like leagues. It was smooth obsidian, all of it, sleek and shining, but every detail carved so specifically, it looked real. From the steel points of scales, to the curved talons on its legs... The wingspan was tucked against its back instead of fanned out, but its length was nearly as long as its tail. The Great Dragon's head was massive, its mouth was closed, but even then I could make out the imprint of teeth pressed against lips. Barbed whiskers flowed from its upper lip, and red eyes looked down into the depths of my soul.

This was their one true deity. The ruler of all their gods, the father of dragons and perhaps the royal line. It was their religious statue, built upon here so long ago, that no one knew who had constructed it, or why. It was a place where the mer came to pray, to give their offerings and ask for things in return.

There was an engraved plaque in front of it, and I read the words as easily as if I was reading Thalassarin.

"It is often said that the Great Dragon fossilized Himself into this statue, and in times of great peril, when our kingdom or our allies should need Him most, He will revive and be our salvation."

"He's beautiful." I pressed my hand against the Great Dragon's snout.

"Iol is better," a voice said in my ear.

I didn't turn to look at Ytgar, even as he kneeled next to me and placed his hand just over my own. His was cold in contrast to the statue that seemed to breathe warmth inside of it.

"I never imagined—" I broke off, feeling the emotion tight in my voice, threatening to close my throat.

This was everything I'd ever dreamed of it being. It was more. It was my dreams come to life in front of me. Everything I heard, everything I saw from conches and parchments, it was here. I was here. I was watching a dream be fulfilled.

Ytgar's hand closed over mine, pressing my palm harder into the statue.

"Is it everything you ever imagined, beauty mine?"

I turned to him then, tears still in my mind.

I'd dreamt of this moment a thousand times, dreamt when I would finally see the Great Dragon statue for myself. In every single one of my daydreams, I had been alone. It was me escaping from my life to see what I'd always longed for. It was me married to Prince Kai and escaping the palace to see this. It was me traveling here with riches in a golden carriage while Maisie looked after Thalassar.

The reality was, I wasn't alone. I hadn't been the one to fulfill my own dream. I hadn't had to swim away to find it waiting for me. The dream had been handed to me by the most unlikely of companions. And for once in my life, I was glad I wasn't alone.

Because sharing this with him, well, it seemed all the more special somehow.

"No," I whispered, turning back to face my dream. "It's better than I imagined."

THIS WAS A SIDE of her I never thought I'd witness. As if seeing her dreams fulfilled had pulled away her hard layers and left a young and vulnerable mermaid in her place. A mermaid who actually had hopes and dreams that weren't tied to riches and frivolity, but of something grander. Of adventure and knowledge, of the richness of the past colliding with her present.

They were statues and places, but to her they were so much more. They represented everything she loved, the knowledge she'd acquired as salvation in her lonely life. Places that weren't just caught in the drifting words of a conch, but something tangible and real. Attainable.

I understood, because the moment she had smiled up at me and said those words, *It's better than what I imagined,* I felt the exact same way.

Maybe she wasn't so far from me at all. Maybe she could come to feel something for me that was beyond friendship. I had no right to want it when she belonged to my best friend. But I wanted her. I did. With every frozen fiber in my body, she thawed my blood and made it course hotly. She made my heart pound. She made me wish for the impossible.

We sat there like that for what felt like hours. Ytgar joined us on her other side, and after a stiff moment of indecision, he placed his palm against the statue next to hers. She hadn't tensed, hadn't pushed him away. She smiled and relished in the moment of her dream coming true.

When it was over, she had no cruel words. There was merely a smile on her face as I helped her up from the silt and dusted the sand from her skirts. She wore a blissfully happy expression as we led her back to the carriage, and the whole ride back to the palace.

And as we escorted her to the door of her room, she turned, leaned up on her fins, and pressed a kiss to my lips.

"Thank you," she whispered, before she drifted off and closed the doors with a sigh behind her.

I blinked at the spot she'd just vacated, stunned into immobility. She'd kissed me. Princess Odele had kissed me, a common low life whale trainer. Granted, she thought me to be the prince, and we had kissed before, but this was different. She had been willing to press her own lips against mine, and that made all the difference.

It took me a moment to remember that Ytgar was behind me, and he had witnessed the whole exchange.

I whirled, my disbelief turning to panic all at once. "Yt—"

He shook his head. "Not here."

I had no choice but to follow him to his room. He was right. I couldn't slip up in the halls of an enemy kingdom. If anyone knew that our identities were switched, what would they do to my prince? This was for his safety, after all.

When we were secure in his room, and he did a sweep around to make sure there were no listening devices, he turned to me. "You love her," he stated without preamble.

I jolted at the straightforwardness, though I shouldn't have been surprised. He spoke like that always. It was the statement I hadn't expected, or the guilt that flushed over my face. Or the shame.

There was no need for a reply, because Ytgar pressed on. "You've kissed her before, haven't you?" There was no accusation, no anger. He just tilted his head curiously to the side.

I couldn't lie to him any more than I already had. "Yes," I confessed.

"Hmm."

"I shouldn't have," I pressed nervously. "I won't lie and say I regret it, because I don't, but I know she is yours and…" I trailed off, not able to put my thoughts together enough to even finish the sentence.

"It doesn't matter that you tell yourself that. You still want her."

I should have hung my head in shame. Here was the prince of my kingdom, the best friend who had gotten me through a childhood filled with poverty. Someone who smuggled me food when I was hungry, who wrapped my hands when they had bled from the whip at the orphanage, who had forced his grandmother to hire me permanently as the stable hand before I came of age. He had given me everything when I deserved nothing. Yet I could not look away from him.

"I do."

He nodded once.

"I know you do, too."

Ytgar jolted at my sudden declaration. He thought he was being secretive, but he wasn't. I saw the way he looked at her when she wasn't watching; I saw the heated glances they threw at each other. It was part of what gave me hope that when she learned the truth, there would still be affection for me in her heart. After all, if she lusted after Ytgar while she thought he was a whale trainer, would she still think me her friend when she learned the truth?

Or would she hate us both?

Ytgar didn't answer, but he didn't need to. His next question did all the answering for him. "Do you really think your feelings for her and hers for you would come to anything bigger?" The question wasn't meant to be cruel, rather a matter-of-fact, but it still sliced through me just the same.

I shrugged, and refrained from telling him that the princess likely didn't have any feelings for me. Not long-lasting ones anyway. "It doesn't matter, does it? She's yours."

He moved over to a far desk and traced his fingers across the surface. His every movement was languid, calculated… precise. "Pretend she wasn't mine," he began. "Do you think the two of you could be something bigger?"

My heart pounded. "Is it a betrayal to you if I say yes?"

Ytgar smiled. "Not at all. Because I feel the same."

I blinked. "What do you mean?"

"I mean, I think the princess likes us both. Or rather, she actually seems to like you, while she fights her attraction to me. Her feelings are there regardless."

My whole body thrummed with elation at the news, dying too quickly into something else. I was duty bound to him, my prince and my friend. "I will take a stroke aside," I offered, though my gut churned painfully at the words.

Ytgar shook his head. "See, that's the thing. I don't *want* you to take a stroke aside."

"What are you talking about?" I demanded. He sounded like he'd gotten hit on the head with a block of ice and was speaking nonsense. Really.

"You know I consider you my brother, right?"

I started to back away, to shake my head. "I'm not worthy—"

"Shut up," he growled. "Shut up and listen." I clamped my lips closed. "You are my brother. Not a brother of my blood, but my brother just the same, and your happiness matters to me."

My throat tightened with emotion. I nodded, unable to do anything else, unable to speak.

"I am… unsure… about the princess. She is a difficult mer to read, but I do think she is attracted to us both."

"Like I said, it doesn't matter."

"But it does. This may seem a bit selfish, but what if she belonged to the both of us?"

The surprise hit me like a shard of ice to my skin. I threw my head back and bit out harsh laughter. "Now I know you're insane," I admonished.

"I'm being perfectly serious, Val."

I shook my head and waved my hands in front of me frantically. "No, no, no, no, no… You can't be serious. She's a princess and I'm—"

"In love with her. And she might come to feel the same about you. How could she not? You are noble, kind, and intelligent…"

"Careful there," I warned. "It's starting to sound like *you're* in love with me."

He snorted. "Loving you and being in love with you are two entirely different things. The latter I do not feel, sorry to disappoint you, but I do love you like my kin despite your stubbornness to comment on our difference in stations every time the chance arises. What I am saying is that this is inevitable. Odele being a part of our lives is an inevitability. She will be my wife, and she wants me, desires me, that's all I can ask for and be grateful for, really. But the two of you share something special, and I have no plans of coming between it. And I'll not allow you to feel guilty for what you feel. So love her, brother mine, without repercussions or shame. We've shared everything, all of our lives, which means that the princess is as much mine as she is yours, if she'll have either of us, that is."

I floated there in dismay, processing his words, the confidence, this *gift* he was placing in my lap. It was too much to imagine him happily accepting Odele and I as something bigger, as something more. I didn't deserve this, wasn't even sure I could accept it.

"Will it upset you?" I asked.

He sighed, almost as if he was growing frustrated with me already. "I should be. Gods of ice know I should be. I should rip off your hand for touching my betrothed, but I can't seem to find the sentiment." He paused, cocked his head to the side. "You have seen Princess Maisie with Kai and her two bodyguards, have you not? That is how I picture Odele. She is too selfish to be content with one merman, and as long as the other is you, I cannot be angry or jealous. There is no one else I'd rather see her with than you."

I wondered if it was treacherous, that we were speaking of this behind Odele's back. If she would be infuriated to hear about us bartering her around like some harlot. But, wait. That wasn't what this was. She wasn't a harlot, she'd never be that. Not an object we exchanged. It was confidence and trust between friends. This was love in its purest form It was… crazy is what it was.

Whatever Ytgar thought he saw, it was hard for me to believe that once Odele knew the whole truth of our deceit, she'd ever want to willingly speak to me again. I was just a whale trainer, and Ytgar was a prince. I'd not hold my breath waiting for something that would likely never come. Who knew if Odele would even want me?

No, she probably didn't.

I was just the merman who had helped one of her many dreams to come true. Other than that, I had nothing at all to offer.

Soon, she would realize that too.

The next day, we packed up to leave and were in the courtyard to say goodbye.

I was glad that we'd soon be gone, but as much excitement I held for the prospect of seeing Iol again, I dreaded leaving. Because the princess would discover our lie, and I wasn't ready for her to hate me yet.

Ytgar and I bowed as respectfully as we could manage to the emperor, even with hatred mirroring in our eyes, we somehow managed not to speak a word, not even that of farewell. Once that was out of the way, we hung back and watched as Odele and her cousins said goodbye to Maisie.

Jessinda, Scarlet, and Silviya curtsied, though it was obvious the gesture was mocking. Maisie took it with dignity, curtsying back without blinking. When the three mer took a few strokes back, Odele came forward.

They were silent a moment, the two mer staring at each other with the same expression. It was like seeing them look into a mirror. They were the same, yet so vastly different.

Then, they threw their arms around one another at the same time. They hugged like it was the last time they'd ever see each other again.

"Thank you," Maisie cried into Odele's neck.

This seemed like such a private moment, but no one could bring themselves to look away. I knew I couldn't.

"Don't you dare thank me for finding you," Odele replied. "I'd have looked for you in the abyss if Tiberius hadn't beaten me to it."

Maisie squeezed her tighter. "You gave me a family."

"You *are* my family, Odalaea. No matter what, you are like a sister to me, and I love you."

It was rare to watch these small moments of vulnerability between the two mer. At times, they were almost hostile with each other, but looking at them now, it was so obvious, the love they shared was palpable. It was real and pure.

Whatever Odele might be, whatever hardness she projected to the world, however cruelly she treated others, there was one intrinsic fact: she loved her cousin dearly.

"I will miss you, Odele. Truly."

"And I you, cousin." Odele pressed a kiss to Maisie's cheek. "Send conches to Iol. I'll be happy to hear about how you're faring. And if anyone dares harm you… I'll kill them myself."

Masie laughed as she pulled away. "That won't be necessary. After all, I have my own dragon now."

"A semi-blind dragon. Really, cousin, you attract the strangest things." She gave a pointed look over Maisie's shoulder at the mermen there, stopping on Tiberius. "I trust I don't need to tell you to look after her?"

"You know you don't."

Odele nodded. "Well, goodbye then. I'll make sure to send you all invitations to my nuptials, I suppose." And she turned, with her head held high, and swam over to her awaiting hippocampus and what few guards we had left for the rest of our journey.

I started to turn away, too with Ytgar at my side, when Prince Kai stopped us.

I turned fast as I watched his taloned hand clamp down on Ytgar's arm, hand around the hilt of my Prince's sword as I began to unsheathe it.

"Don't," Ytgar barked in Iolish.

His silver eyes met the brown ones of the Draconian Prince. Glare for glare.

I slid the sword back into its sheath.

"You have to tell her the truth," Kai hissed at Ytgar, low enough so no one else would hear. "You have to tell her that you're the real prince."

My eyes widened.

Damn him to the ice and back.

He knew the truth.

NEVER BEFORE HAD I wanted to rip someone apart as much as I wanted to rip apart the Prince of Draconi in that moment. I thought of a thousand and one creative ways in which the task could be done. Perhaps I could rip his spine from his tail and then choke him with the curved edges of his own bones. Or maybe I could shove my sword down his throat and watch it freeze his entrails until he became just another statue in my kingdom.

So many possibilities.

My eyes narrowed on the prince. "It is not your concern," I said icily.

It was weeks ago when I had overheard Prince Kai and Maisie—at the time, I'd thought her to be Odele—speaking of her true identity. Kai had followed me and threatened that I keep her secret.

I would've harmed a lesser merman.

But he knew my secrets, knew that I wasn't really a whale trainer, and that Val wasn't really the prince he pretended to be. I was unsure of how he knew; perhaps he had spies in my court. But I could not let him unravel my facade. So we promised to keep one another's secrets.

Now that his was in the light, he wanted to bring mine forth as well, and that simply would not do.

"Odele is my family now," he replied tightly. "Lying to her means you lie to me."

Beside me, Val did not move his hand from the pommel of his sword—my sword—and he snorted. "You Draconians and your misplaced honor. Don't get your eggs in a bunch, Dragon Prince."

Kai's eyes slashed from brown to blue in an instant, evidence that he had the blood of dragons coursing through his veins.

"I'll not allow you to lie to her." His talons curved, the tips of them piercing my skin.

The thought of him intimidating me was laughable. I was born of ice and steel. I'd survived harsh winters, I'd faced down polar bears, dragons, and seals. He was a mere merman, and no threat to me.

Using my other hand, I grabbed him, wrapping it all the way around his delicate wrist, and I squeezed. Really, his bones were so fragile, I could have cracked them in half. I didn't. But I did pull him away from me.

"Touch me again and you lose your hand," I threatened. "Do not forget that I am a prince, too. The difference between us is that I do not need to hide behind the blood of dragons to win battles."

Val snorted.

Kai looked properly offended. Good.

"Do not pretend to care for Odele, whether you consider her family or not. I know you do not care."

His eyes narrowed. "But Maisie does."

"And yet she does not know of our deception either."

The Dragon Prince's lips tightened into a thin, white line.

"How I deal with my betrothed is my business, not yours. You forfeited any claim you ever had on the Princess of Thalassar the moment you chose Maisie over her."

"If you hurt her…"

"We won't," Val replied vehemently. "Yet he is right. It's not your business."

Kai took a stroke back, hardly a retreat, since his whole body seemed to swell like a beast preparing to attack. "I promised you I'd say nothing and I haven't, but she deserves to know the truth."

"And she will," I said. "Now, we must get going. Thank you for your kingdom's hospitality." I bowed stiffly and turned my back to the Prince of Draconi. Surely if he were worried about his honor, he should be more offended by that slight instead.

I heard Val laugh, imagined him bowing just as mockingly before turning and following me towards our hippocampi.

Odele had already mounted hers, and her eyes narrowed as she took us in. "What was that about?" she demanded, eyeing the sleeve of my arm where his talons had torn through the material.

I gripped the reins and hauled myself up, settling into the saddle. Val did the same, and it was he who answered the princess. "Nothing you need to worry yourself over, beauty mine."

She looked like she wanted to press but couldn't really bring herself to care enough to do so, so instead she made clicking noises and her hippocampus turned away.

At Val's command, we were off.

Odele

We traveled further north, and it seemed like, apart from the barren wasteland the waters were becoming, the temperatures of the waters dropped almost every hour. Not even my thickest shift could keep the cold from seeping into my bones and keep me from shivering.

I hadn't glimpsed snow yet, but it didn't seem to matter. The waters were freezing, and I was miserable. My fingers seemed frozen to the reins, so cramped they were from the drop in temperature. I was from warmer waters, used to short sleeves and low bodices, not pelts and furs. Even my lips were too frozen to muster up the will to complain, so I pushed on until we made it closer and closer still, until the waters began to whiten around me. Until I felt those first flakes of frozen snow fall against my lashes and my teeth started chattering.

I couldn't take it anymore.

"You *fool*."

I would have jolted if my body hadn't been chattering already.

Val had appeared next to me, his expression turned into a perpetual scowl.

"H-h-o-ow d-d-d-aa-r-e y-y-o-o-u—"

"Your face is turning blue. Do you have a death wish, you idiot?" He yanked at the strings near his neck and pulled the fur-lined cloak off, revealing another underneath—really, how many layers was he wearing?—and with a swift throw, tossed it over my shoulders.

Warmth immediately enveloped me, but it didn't stop my shaking. I felt frozen down to the marrow of my bones.

Val let loose a curse in Iolish and then reached across the space that separated us, wrapping his arm around my waist. Before I could muster up a chattered protest, he hauled me off my hippocampus and set me firmly in front of him.

"H-h-o-w d-d-a-a-are—"

"Shut up," he growled in my ear. "You'll die if you ride alone much longer."

And then I felt his arms wrap around my body and pull me close, snuggling me into his warmth. Despite my protests, I sighed into him, relishing in the feel of the heat he offered, of the hardness of his body. His arms offered protection from the ice, and I accepted it gladly.

"You should have packed warmer clothes and put them on the moment we started for colder waters."

"O-on-n-ly p-p-peasants w-wear c-cloaks like y-yours."

He chuckled. his breath warm against my cheek. When had he gotten so close to me? In fact, when had we started to move through the water? I'd been so caught up in my misery I hadn't noticed we were continuing our journey. Really, if I had died, it would have been their fault for not stopping for a break in the first place.

"Then you'd be a dead fool."

I wanted to turn my nose up haughtily at him, but I was still shivering and couldn't manage such a simple task. "I'm-m-m your p-p-princess. You will sp-p-peak to m-me with resp-p-pect."

"I'll speak to my princess any way I please. Especially if she is a fool who travels to northern waters without the protection of a fur cloak."

I shivered. Not because of the cold this time, but because of the way he rumbled *my princess*. As if I truly was *his*.

"Many mer unused to these conditions have died of frostbite journeying to Iol."

"You're t-t-trying to t-t-ell m-me I'm-m lucky, then?"

He pulled me closer, one hand holding at the reins and the other rubbing over my body, causing a friction that both warmed and excited me. Treacherous body of mine, my breathing suddenly went labored. I was aware of his every inch pressing against my backside through those heavy layers of pelts he wore.

I wasn't supposed to be thinking of him like that, I tried to remind myself. I was supposed to keep my distance, encase my heart and not give in to my body's scandalous desires.

Curse it all, but I wanted to.

"I am trying to tell you how stupid you are. Do you despise the prospect of marriage so much that you'd rather see yourself a frozen corpse?"

"N-n-no…"

His lips pressed close to the lobe of my ear, and I swore I felt the warmth of his tongue. "Why don't I believe you?"

I tried to jerk away, but he held me firm. "I'm-m-m not lying."

"You've been trying everything you can to escape us since you learned of the engagement. This type of trick doesn't seem so beneath you."

Anger swelled up inside of me. "Well, I value m-my life."

"Good." His arm encircled my waist, fingers digging into my hip. It wasn't a painful touch, rather it was erotic as his fingers skimmed down the side of my hip then curled to the front, dangerously close to where I felt the embarrassing truth of my desire. "We do, too."

I didn't like the way he said 'we' either. The tone of it implied something I didn't understand, and I didn't like not understanding things. I was almost always the smartest person in a room, which always left me at an advantage. Val was unpredictable. It made me nervous and, for the second time in my life, self-conscious.

I didn't like that feeling at all.

"I'm warm enough now," I whispered. "I'd like to ride on my own the rest of the way."

I waited a couple of heartbeats.

Ba-dump.

Ba-dump.

Ba-dump.

"If at any moment you feel cold again, tell me and I'll see to your comfort." His fingers danced from my waist, across my stomach and to my hip. He leaned closer to me, his lips grazing the lobe of my ear once more. "I'll take care of you…" He pulled back and wrapped his arm around me again. "Because you're obviously too foolish to do it yourself."

Before I could give a reply of indignation, he was hoisting me back over to my hippocampus. I barely had time to grab for the reins. His brusque actions almost caused me to slide from the saddle.

Iolish bastard.

I would have slapped him if I hadn't feared my fingers would fall off. Really, how was he not cold? How was he warm at all? The moment I was on my own, I felt my body shiver again. I didn't want to tell him I still needed his heat, didn't want him to know I longed to be in the space of his arms again.

Being near him was too much. It was too tempting, and he knew it.

So I'd not give him the satisfaction.

I dug my tail into the side of my hippocampus and urged it faster. As if the space she put between Val and me would be enough to steady the rapid pounding of my treacherous heart.

It wasn't.

I feared there never would be.

I GRITTED MY TEETH. Stubborn fool. Her pride meant more to her than her own safety.

Granted, I had baited her purposefully, set out to seduce her, to make her body tremble with something other than the cold. It had worked, but I'd pushed her away in the process.

I knew she was fighting her attraction for me, and I suspected why. Because of what I was, because of my rank. My hands gripped the reins at the thought. I wanted to believe there was good in her like Val believed, but that selfishness, her unwillingness to overlook differences in stations filled me with rage.

Val was my best friend. He was better than what others thought of him. He wasn't just a whale trainer, as if that title was some essential part of his character. As if that title meant so much more than his good deeds or what he held in his heart, the very foundations of his soul.

His position and misfortunes in life did not define him.

And if Odele couldn't see that, then I'd make her see it.

The perfect way to do that was by reaching Iol as quickly as we could. To show her the truth, watch our lies unfold, and watch her whole world shatter.

OUR PACE BEGAN TO quicken, and it was so cold neither I nor my cousins could muster up the will to complain. We huddled close together, but still couldn't find warmth, and the Iolish didn't look like they'd be stopping anytime soon.

The northern waters seemed to invigorate them. Where they'd been stoic and grim before, here they appeared to be in their natural element. They laughed and joked—and the Thalassarin guards brooded—in their native language, and I only halfheartedly followed the gist of their conversations.

While most of the Iolish laughed boisterously, the only ones who wore grim expressions the further we went on were Val and Ytgar. The prince looked ill with dread, an expression he wore rather openly, one I didn't associate at all with the merman I had come to know. Meanwhile, Val's features were hard with a quiet determination.

It was all rather odd.

"This is ridiculous," Jessinda muttered between her chattering teeth. She tucked her hands beneath her armpits for warmth. "We need to stop and get a lava pit going. It's too cold."

A nearby Iolish guard heard and snorted unkindly. "Stop and you die." His voice was rough with an accent. "That has been many a mistake of foreigners. Move and it keeps the blood flowing. Stop and you freeze."

Jessinda sniffed, like how dare this guard have the audacity to speak to her? "That's why we would build a lava pit. For warmth. Idiot Iolish."

He chuckled. "And we aren't even at the capital yet." He shook his head back and forth and rode on.

Jessinda scoffed. "The audacity. Shouldn't these barbarians at least care about our hippocampi, if not for us?"

I agreed with a quiet murmur before I felt a presence at my other side. I turned to Prince Ytgar, facing that stony expression.

"A few leagues away there are stables where we will leave your mounts and switch them for ones better accustomed to the cold," he explained.

"I hope it won't be long." I gave my mount a stiff pat on her elongated neck.

"It won't," he promised. "Soon, we'll be in Aelfrost, the capital city of Iol, and in Isolde Palace. We'll make it there by morning."

I slashed him a glance, noted how tense he was, and it wasn't just from the cold. No, the Iolish were used to these harsh conditions and acted like they didn't feel it at all. Something else was wrong with him.

"You don't seem too eager to arrive at your palace, Prince. Is there something I should be aware of?"

His square jaw tightened so hard, I thought it'd break. His nostrils flared and his eyebrows furrowed. A moment later his body relaxed but a fraction.

"Do not be too disappointed in me, Princess," he said.

I blinked, not liking the way he called me princess. It hadn't been mocking, exactly, but something else. It had been laced with the respect I'd often demanded of him since we'd first met. There was no seductive purr to his voice, no hint of teasing or humor in it.

"What?" I asked warily.

He flashed me a sad sort of smile. "When we arrive at Iol, I hope you will not be too disappointed in me."

Before I could ask him what he was talking about, he was riding away. I stared after him, more confused than ever, and with no answers in my grasp. A sudden dread curled its way through me, and I wasn't sure why.

I could guess at the answers all I wanted. I had the rest of our journey to do so.

Valmundur

THE RAYS OF THE sun didn't illuminate the waters of Iol with shades of yellow or vermillion. Mornings in the north were cold, and they were white with frost and blue with ice. Nights were darker things, the white humps of bergs becoming gray in the shadows, and the currents becoming whispers of cold and death.

We had stopped at a lonely inn to change our mounts before we were off again, swimming through the darker waters of our kingdom. Morning came, and with it the illumination that revealed our home.

Iol was not like the other kingdoms. We did not have an open expanse of space thriving with plants of coral and fauna. Life here was harsh, the waters full of terrors. Two-legger lands made entirely of ice surrounded our waters, enclosing us in the cold. Some of the icebergs were so big and thick, they touched the bottom of the ocean floor and rose leagues past the surface above.

Some homes here had been hollowed out of icebergs, others had been made of steel two-legger overturned boats that split in half against the ice and sunk to our depths.

Unlike other kingdoms, we were slaves of the ice. It surrounded us on nearly every side save two: the entrance that connected Iol and Draconi, and the northernmost side that connected Iol to the vast waters of the Uncharted.

We passed massive adjacent walls of ice when we arrived. It was carved in intricate detail to look like frost giants and trolls, massive creatures from two-legger Viking legends that wielded clubs and were covered in hair all over with the ugly faces of nightmares.

I'd captured the look of wonder in Odele's eyes as we passed it and tucked the memory away for later.

We were nearing the capital now. As we passed the city, mer came out and bowed to us in passing.

Ytgar's guards were glad to be home. I was dreading every moment of it.

In about an hour, Princess Odele would discover the truth of our treachery, and I couldn't help but feel the foreboding in my body. Like this was the last time she'd ever look at me with anything resembling friendship again. How long after she discovered the truth would it take for her to regret our every interaction? Our kisses? Not long, I'd wager.

I feared the moment she'd find out, just like I feared this sudden breaking of my heart when she hadn't yet scorned me. But she would.

And once she did, my heart would never be the same.

"WE'LL BE ARRIVING SOON," Val came up beside me to say. "Prepare yourself, for there are many dangerous things awaiting at the palace." With that ominous threat, him and Ytgar rode ahead, the both of them momentarily disappearing.

They returned minutes later, and when they did, my eyes almost bulged out of my head. Though they rode in front, I noticed it. I think we all did. They had switched clothes and weapons. The thick fur-lined coat that Val wore and the thin sword of ice, he had given to Ytgar; the richer thick blue pelt lined with polar bear fur, the cloak of a royal, had been wrapped around Val's broad shoulders as if it had been made for him, and hanging at the ornate belt around his waist, was the royal Isolde Sword. Its white pommel and engraved orca, with the ice blade that glinted like the hard and sharp ridges of diamonds.

"What is going on?" Jessinda hissed as she took them both in incredulously.

"No idea," I murmured back. Was this some type of Iolish custom? Clothes switching? If it was, I had no plans on switching clothes with some filthy commoner. I wouldn't even switch outfits with Jessinda. Not with that horrendous style of hers, let alone a servant. "But I intend to find out."

I dug the side of my tail into the hippocampus and urged it forward. I wove my way through the guards until I made it to the front of the line beside them and glared.

"What's going on?" I demanded with irritation, giving a pointed look to their outfits.

They didn't reply. I wanted to rage at them for ignoring me. Val spoke, though. "We're here."

I whirled, looking up at Isolde Palace.

Large spikes of steel and ice were jammed into silt and snow, forming a half-fence around the palace. A palace built entirely of ice.

If black was the absence of color, white was a kaleidoscope of it. If I'd thought Iol would be merely white and blue, I was wrong. The palace *was* the blue of frost, but it glistened. It glistened like when light touched the panes of a diamond and sparkled in reds, blues, purples, and yellows. Isolde Palace was a massive structure with towers and opened windows, set just beneath a floating iceberg.

It didn't look like a cage at all.

It looked like home.

"I told you Iol was better," Ytgar commented in a voice devoid of humor.

"Let's go," Val urged, starting forward.

I followed behind Val, staring in awe at the palace. Was it really made of ice? When had it been built? Who built it? So many questions flitted through my mind until we finally made it to the palace doors.

Instead of steps leading up to the platform and front doors, there was a long twisted and curved pathway, like a glistening slide of ice leading down to the silt.

We dismounted, throwing our reins to groomsmer. Val floated beside me. I looked around for Ytgar, but caught no sight of the prince. Really, how typical. He was going to leave me alone with his whale trainer guard to be welcomed into the palace.

I scoffed and turned back up. Val made an impatient gesture with his fingers and I followed him as he swam upwards to the platform.

Floating at the top of the platform was a mermaid. She was old, with wrinkles crinkling across her exposed brown skin. She looked regal, despite her old age, and commanding. On her head she wore a tall crown that appeared to be fabricated of ice, diamonds, and sapphires. She wore a fur dress made entirely of polar bear skin, the head of the dead creature hanging over her shoulder, her arms through the paws like sleeves. The claws of the animal were decorated around her wrist like a bracelet, and around her neck, the teeth were slung through a chain of gold.

The dress flowed over her short tail, a tail I caught the simplest of glimpses of, noting it was as the rumors claimed: the tail of an orca.

Val swam up to the old mer. I almost hissed at him to stay back, for it was obvious that this was the Queen of Iol. But he went up to her, took her hands in his own and pressed kisses to the backs of her knuckles.

"Hello," Val whispered, "grandmother."

My head spun.

I stared between the two mer. *Grandmother?* Yes, the resemblance was there, and I was stupid for not having noticed it immediately. Her eyes were as silver as his own, her features prominent and beautiful, or they were perhaps when she'd been younger.

The old mer smiled at Val before pulling her hands away and turning that silver gaze to me.

"Grandmother, Queen Isadora Isolde of Iol, might I present Princess Odele Malabella Oriana of the merkingdom of Thalassar? My betrothed."

My breath caught in my throat. Betrothed? What was going on?

But then the queen answered the question for me, and I knew suddenly, viciously, that I'd been lied to.

"Oh, Ytgar," she said. "What have you done now?"

Ytgar. Val wasn't Valumundur at all. He was Ytgar Neves Isolde. The gods damned Prince of Iol.

He had tricked me. *Ytgar* had tricked me. Okay, not the real Ytgar, the other one. Why was this so confusing?

So, Valmundur was really Prince Ytgar pretending to be a whale trainer and Prince Ytgar was really Valmundur pretending to be a prince.

They'd lied to me. They'd made me believe they were what they were not. And I was too stunned by the revelation to rage my indignation across his blisteringly cold kingdom. I could only float there, with my mouth agape and stare at the prince I'd thought to be a lowly servant. The merman who was really my betrothed, and who had been this entire time.

"Princess Odele, our Prime Minister, Rollo Ysengart."

I was barely able to tear my gaze away from Val—*Ytgar,* his name was *Ytgar*—to bow appropriately to his grandmother and then acknowledge the merman next to her.

He bowed to me and muttered stiffly, "Your Majesty."

The merman was old, though not as old as the queen. He appeared to be my father's age, with graying sideburns, thick bushy eyebrows and a solidly built body. He wore a coat of blue and silver like a military jacket, with adorning chains and buttons all over the lapels.

I dismissed him by turning back to Ytgar with a glare. He met it with an even stare of his own. The bastard didn't even have the decency to look apologetic.

"Her ladies-in-waiting, Lady Jessinda Malabella, Lady Scarlet Malabella, and Lady Silviya Oriana."

My face heated as my cousins echoed 'Your Majesty's' resonated in my mind. Bad enough I was lied to, but my cousins had to bear witness to my shame as well.

This was unforgivable. I—I hated him. Despised Prince Ytgar with every fiber. He had made it so I would. He had thwarted me at every turn; he had taken liberties and made me wallow in shame because of what we'd done when he'd known it hadn't mattered. We were betrothed anyway.

I'd kill him for this. And the real Val too.

Gods. I almost swayed. I *had* kissed a whale trainer. I'd fallen for the ruse, had let my defenses down around them and they'd both betrayed me in the vilest of ways. No wonder he'd looked so solemn the closer we'd gotten here. Because his lies had been about to unravel.

He was right to fear my wrath.

"Let's adjourn to your rooms and ready you for dinner," the queen's voice broke through my murderous thoughts. "I am sure you are all famished after such a long and cold journey." She turned, and we had no options left but to follow her inside.

The queen, her ladies, and her servants showed us to my rooms. Everyone had dispersed, going their own way—the Prime Minister and Ytgar, at least—while we went up to prepare for dinner.

"This shall be your room," the queen said as a servant opened the doors.

I'd expected a palace made entirely of ice to be cold, and yet they had their abundance of lava globes on the walls and the ceiling, not only to serve as illumination, but for warmth as well.

"Your ladies' rooms will be side-by-side and across the hall, should you need anything."

The queen was imperious in her demeanor and looked down on everyone within seeing distance of her, including me. I was sure what she was doing was considered servant's work, but she did it anyway. Perhaps just to get a feel of who I was, what I was. As if she could gauge my personality by merely showing me where I was to sleep.

"You are a princess, so I am sure you know proper etiquette," the queen commented haughtily. "And I am sure your ladies are not entirely clueless to their duties. If they are, worry not, I shall send you new ones."

I ground my teeth together. This queen, grandmother to my betrothed or not, was *not* the boss of me. This was exactly what I had feared when I arrived here. Becoming their slave. It was what I'd been promised would not happen. More the fool me, as the promise had been made by a whale trainer playing at prince.

"My ladies are well versed in their duties," I ground out sweetly. Whether I tolerated my cousins or not, I'd not have *her* trying to send them away.

The queen's silver eyes narrowed imperceptibly. "Good. Then they shall dress you, tend to your hair, and other needs. They will serve as chaperones before you are to wed my grandson, as it is not proper for the two of you to be seen together alone before the wedding. Speaking of weddings, the ceremony will be chosen at a date of my convenience once I have spoken to Ytgar."

My hands clenched into fists. At *her* convenience? It was *my* wedding, and I'd be the one to choose whatever date I pleased, regardless of what she wanted.

"I will assign my guards to watch over you and your ladies." She gestured at one of my trunks—which had been hauled up by a servant—and her servant obeyed, bending to undo the latches and open it.

I cried out my protest as they did. That was the trunk with my conches! How dare she?! But when the trunk opened and the contents inside were revealed, I wanted to weep.

My conches, every single one of them, had cracked. Their pieces, broken and irreparable, littered the inside of my trunk like garbage. Tears stung at the backs of my eyelids. All of my adventures, all the images recorded, and all the history spoken by those before me had crumbled to piles of frozen dust.

The queen *tsk*ed with disapproval. "No, no, this won't do. Do you always travel carrying garbage? Is that the custom in Thalassar? Well, you are in Iol now and we do things differently here." She gestured at another trunk and the servant opened it to reveal my dresses. She started pulling them out to show to her queen. "Soon you will marry my grandson, and you will become the Duke and Duchess of Frost."

I paused. Duchess? That was a lower rank than princess. I was a princess, and heir to the throne of Thalassar, how dare this mer demean me this way? And how dare she violate my privacy by opening my trunks at her own leisure?

The queen *tsk*ed again. "These dresses simply will not do. I heard that Thalassar is a warm kingdom, but these are indecent. I will send my seamstress up to take your measurements straight away and have a whole new wardrobe prepared for you." She turned, eyed me up and down. "I suppose what you have on now is fine for a simple dinner. Do not forget, you are in Iol now, and we do things very different here."

With a ruffle of her fur skirts, the queen and her maids and ladies left.

Jessinda scoffed at the spot where she'd been floating. "Crazy sea-cow."

My cousins murmured their vehement agreements.

I swam over to my trunk with the conches, flipped open the lid again and stared at the contents inside. My cousins quieted around me, no doubt watching as I dropped my tail down and shoved my hands inside the bits and broken pieces. Perhaps something inside was salvageable. How had they broken? Had the servants handled them too roughly? Had the trunk been dropped when switching cart and hippocampus? It felt like I was shoving my hands into ice.

My palms were cut along the jagged edges as I rummaged through them. I dug to the bottom of the trunk, but it was no use. The conches were broken. Every single one of them.

Tears pricked at the backs of my eyelids and I fought hard to keep them at bay. My chin hung to my chest, the sensation coursing through me akin to defeat. I wanted to cry, wanted to scream and rage. I'd been lied to, made a fool of, embarrassed, and had lost the most precious things I owned.

Damn Iol, and damn Ytgar and Val.

I pushed myself up from the ground and whirled to face my cousins. My glare was in place. I took the one emotion I was familiar with, the one that would push away sadness and tears and replace it with a formidability entirely my own. Rage.

"She is not my queen. She is not *our* queen," I told them. They nodded their agreement. "I will not bow to her whims and traditions when we were brought here under lies." I untied the cloak, and it slid from my body. "The first thing I will demand of you, cousins, is your loyalty. The queen will not give up easily, and we must stick together. I'll not have her infiltrating our circle or spying on us. Is that clear?"

They nodded.

"Good. Now find my most scandalous dress and help me get ready for dinner."

"Your visit to Iol proved quite fortuitous indeed."

"Hmm."

"The princess is lovely."

I glared at Iol's Prime Minister. A big merman, to be sure, but not as big as me. My fist to his face could knock him out. Easily. My fingers twitched with the temptation.

Seeing him infuriated me beyond reason. It was just a cruel reminder that my grandmother and I were little more than decorations in our kingdom with very little political power. All the decisions rested on the

Prime Minister's shoulders and his inner circle, our parliament. They were corrupt old mer, all bought and shoved into Rollo's pocket.

My hope for bringing in this marriage alliance with Thalassar was to convince the mer of Iol, my grandmother, and anyone I could, that our ways needed to change. I wasn't hungry for power. I didn't want to rule all. I just wanted to see my kingdom thrive. I wanted us to have a future.

With Rollo, we would not.

So far, and these were my own suspicions, he had robbed the mer of taxpayer money and instead of putting it to the uses it was promised for, like hospitals and schooling, he kept it for himself and his circle.

I wanted to change that. I wanted to destroy the current political system in Iol and rule justly, firmly, and kindly. And to do that I needed Odele. With her and Thalassar at my side, it was the first swim stroke towards change. Perhaps she could help me speak to King Dorian about an alliance with Kappur as well, and help Iol on the currents towards globalization, instead of the hermit life we lived now.

So, yes. I hated Rollo. I hated when he spoke to me. Most of all, I hated when he spoke about my betrothed.

"I was informed, however, that the princess had been in a long decided engagement with the Prince of Draconi before you, is that correct?"

Informed by Mister Shallows, he meant. The mer was insufferable, and I didn't doubt that he'd told Rollo everything that had transpired in Iol since he'd treacherously arrived before us at the behest of his personal bank, the Prime Minister. Undoubtedly, he'd given out the most scandalous, salacious and over-exaggerated details as he could.

The Prime Minister suspected my intentions, I was sure of it, and would do anything he could to stop my proposal from seeing the light of day.

"Before the Prince of Draconi broke contract by marrying the Princess of Kappur," I supplied coldly.

We were floating around the dining room, waiting for the queen, the princess, and their ladies. Usually dinners here were a quiet affair, or they didn't happen at all. My grandmother was strict about etiquette, she always had been rather suffocating. So when dinner came around, I made my quiet escape to the stables.

That's how I'd met Valmundur in the first place. Escaping royal life.

Today was different. I had to present Odele to my grandmother. A part of me just wished I could whisk her away from all this tediousness; the only thing keeping me from doing just that was the fact that she was a royal, and should be used to this. She was strong, and would survive my grandmother. I was sure of it.

Still, I wanted the dinner over, and it hadn't even started yet.

I'd gone up to my rooms when we'd arrived, bathed and changed into something more simple, but would meet with my grandmother's approval.

The palace wasn't as cold as the outside streets of Iol, though it would still be so for Odele. I was wearing a long-sleeved tunic of white, a frost blue vest with golden embroidery along the edges, and a fur-lined cape in royal blue at my shoulders. I did not bother hiding my tail now that I was home, now that Odele knew the truth.

A part of me wished she didn't. I could recall her face so vividly in my mind, the shock at seeing that I, who she believed to be nothing more than a whale trainer, was the royal prince she was betrothed to.

"Only after both princesses tricked him into doing so…"

I was saved the tediousness of a reply when my grandmother arrived in the dining hall trailed by her ladies. I straightened and bowed when she entered, as did Rollo.

"How is the princess faring?" Rollo asked.

The queen didn't smile, though I couldn't ever recall an instance when she smiled, even when I'd been young and had needed a kind word, or the gentle twist of lips. She went to take her seat at the head of the table, a servant already awaiting her as he pulled it out. "She is a work in progress," she commented unkindly. "Her clothes are far too scandalous for Iol, but I shall have her outfitted in no time."

I tried not to sigh too heavily. "Do not push her, grandmother," I urged gently as I took my seat on her other side, the Prime Minister across from me. "Let her get adjusted to life in Iol before you do anything."

The queen scoffed. "There is no time for adjustments, boy. She is here, and her training will begin."

"Training?"

"Why, to become the Duchess of Frost, of course. She must know everything to run her own castle and all that her duty entails…"

I mustered the patience I didn't have for this conversation. "She's a princess. She is fully aware of what needs to be done."

"Well, she is late for dinner. That does not reflect kindly upon her, now does it?"

Just then, Odele entered the dining hall with her cousins, and my breath caught at the sight of her.

She was beautiful, she always was, but she had changed from her simple travel attire and cloak into something much… more. She had to be cold. That was my first thought as my gaze roamed down so much exposed skin. My second thought was of her spread out on the table and me hiking her skirts up to pleasure her until we both forgot our own names.

Her dress was a thin thing of red silk with a neckline that plunged so low, it dipped all the way down between the valley of her breasts to reveal her belly button and a smattering of purple-blue scales. Her breasts were pressed firmly to the material, the curves and shapes of them revealed tantalizingly in hints and peeks. Her nipples pressed against the material, proving that yes, she was very cold indeed.

Her hair hung over her shoulder in wisps of curls. She wore no makeup, but then again, she didn't need it. She was fierce and bold and perfect.

I got up from my chair and watched as she slowly, proudly, made her way next to me to take the seat a servant held out there. I sat when she and her ladies did.

I wanted to say something to her. To tell her how lovely she looked, to tell her how I wanted to push aside the scrap of material and taste her nipples like a dessert…

"Yes, *Prince?*"

I blinked, not realizing I'd been staring at her. I blinked a second time as my mind registered the sarcastic way in which she called me by my title in Thalassarin.

"Is there something you wished to say to me?" She blinked innocently, but I didn't miss the hint of mischief and raw anger in her gaze.

Gods of ice, she was pissed.

"Nothing, Princess." I tore my gaze from her with great difficulty, though I was still aware of her presence, entirely too aware of it.

I looked over at the Prime Minister and noticed his gaze was glued on her bodice appreciatively.

Gods of ice, I wanted to reach across the table and pound my fist down his throat and kill him. I looked away before I could give in to my baser instincts and saw my grandmother's face. She looked furiously shocked.

Perhaps that had been Odele's purpose in the first place.

The first course came and went, and I barely tasted what I ate, or registered the silence around us. I was too focused on Odele, her body next to mine, remembering the feel of her in my arms, the taste of her on my lips. I was glad when the meal was finally over and Odele got up.

"I shall retire to my rooms now," she said demurely, shooting me an inconspicuous look. "Until tomorrow." She whirled in a breath of silk and skirts, her ladies following behind her.

"Allow me to escort you to your rooms," I offered, or rather, demanded.

She stopped, threw a look over her shoulder.

"Let my guards trail you." My grandmother got up then, looking back and forth between us suspiciously.

"No need to trouble yourself, Your Majesty," Odele said. "My Thalassarin guards are quite capable of looking after me themselves." And before the queen could protest, Odele was turning again, and I was following after her.

Desire burning as cold as ice inside me.

Odele

When we made it to the hallway of our rooms, I cast a look to my cousins. Because they knew exactly what it meant, they smiled conspiratorially at me and dispersed into their own rooms, Jessinda going to wait for me in mine while I spoke with Ytgar alone.

"So, *Prince Ytgar*."

He grunted in response.

The bastard.

"Why did you lie to me?" I demanded.

We stopped just before my door, facing each other. I glared up at his own stony expression to find it softening, silver eyes flaring as they raked over the front of my bodice.

Despite the cold, I felt my body heat at the attention.

His eyes found mine again. "The same reason you and Maisie switched places."

"We switched places to uncover royal secrets." I straightened, floated up, so we were just at eye level. I was tired of him looking down at me. "What royal lies are you telling to make any of this justifiable?"

Ytgar snorted and grabbed me, his hand encircling my bare upper arm. I felt his touch down to my bones. "You are mad at Val and I for telling the same lies you and Maisie told. You are mad that we tricked you the same way you tricked Prince Kai." His thumb trailed circles over my skin, and his nostrils flared. "What makes our facade so different?"

Desire flared to life within me but I tamped it down with my anger. "Because," I spat, jerking away from his touch. "You let me believe a filthy whale trainer was royalty. You floated by and watched as I kissed *him*. A *servant*."

He grabbed me by the arms then and slammed me back against the door. I winced at the pain that haroled up my spine. His features weren't soft any longer. Funny how it could change so suddenly from something attractive to something so vicious.

His silver eyes glowed with the threat of danger.

"Do not speak of Val like that *ever* again, do you hear me?"

I realized then, the vehemence he had displayed anytime someone spoke ill of Val... I had assumed it had been the natural reaction to someone insulting you. That hadn't been it at all. His anger had been on behalf of his friend.

"I'll speak of him any way I please," I spat, echoing the words he once said to me. "You're both bastards. Lying, filthy bastards. At least he has an excuse as a commoner for the way he acted. What's yours?"

"Watch your mouth." He leaned close to me, his lips dangerously tempting and infuriatingly *there*. "What does it matter what his station is, Princess? You know what I think?" His lips grazed against the upper curve of my cheek. "I think the reason you're truly upset is because you enjoyed it, enjoyed him. You enjoyed the touch of a *filthy whale trainer*. You want him to touch you again, and you don't know what that means for you." His tongue slid down my neck. I shivered. "You just don't want to admit that you desire what you were taught you shouldn't."

His mouth was lower now, distracting me to temptation, every word a seductive purr that left goosebumps along the ridges of my skin. His tongue traced the outer edge of my breast just before his mouth enclosed around my nipple through the material.

I jerked against his body, eyes closing, head shaking from side to side.

"You want him as much as you want me, so you lash out as if you can somehow avoid the inevitable." He nipped at me through my clothes. "You're selfish and spoiled, but lashing out at me won't change the facts." He slid up my body again and smiled cruelly. "That you ache for the whale trainer you so despise."

My body froze at those words. Iolish bastard! I pushed him away and slapped him hard across his cheek. The sound resonated across the walls of the ice palace.

"Get this straight, Prince. I don't want you, and I most certainly don't want a merman who shovels silt and likes to play at prince, a merman who is not worthy of scraping the mud from my hem. You're delusional if you think I could ever want Iolish filth."

He leaned closer, pressing his arms on either side of me to cage me in, but I was not intimidated. "I warned you," he whispered darkly. And then he opened the door to my rooms and shoved me roughly inside.

I cried out as I landed on the floor in a cold, angry heap. Ytgar loomed in the doorway, smirking down at me one moment, and then slamming the door closed the next.

Jessinda was helping me up in an instant. "What a brute!" she exclaimed angrily, staring at the spot where he'd been floating. "What kind of a prince is he?"

"A savage one," I grumbled as I got up.

His audacity knew no bounds. How dare he imply such filthy accusations? I was not attracted to him or Val... What a load of lies...

He was right.

Maybe I was.

And that's why the betrayal hurt all the more. I never allowed myself to get close to anyone. The only one who truly knew me was Maisie. And then I'd opened myself up to Val, because he'd wormed his way inside my heart. He'd been relentless in his pursual, and I'd fallen.

Straight into the abyss, hauled below the darkness as if tied by an anchor. I'd been a victim of lies, betrayal, and this aching in my chest could only be translated as one thing.

Heartbreak.

"Help me undress, Jessinda," I ordered. "I'd like to go to bed."

I hadn't had time to appreciate the architecture of my room when I'd been so focused on the queen and her servants rummaging through my things, but there was something pretty about the chambers at night.

A servant had come in to see about my lava seam in the room, a little gated, square nook in the wall as well as the one beneath my bed to heat the cushions.

In the darkness, the yellow-white light of the lava shone to illuminate bits and pieces of the room. The ceiling was domed, and figures of orcas and other creatures were carved on the walls. There were fur tapestries and the skins of beasts as rugs on the floor.

The center of the domed ceiling held glass, and with it a clear view of the waters above. Fish swam by in schools, and I observed it so long that I eventually saw a massive blue whale pass overhead like a cloud.

The room was cast in hues of white and darker shades of blues. Though my surroundings were unfamiliar, the vast expanse of it was just as lonely as it had been in Thalassar. The sadness of it echoed within the hollow confines at the center of my chest. Even surrounded by mer, I was always alone, infinitely so. The only time I hadn't felt that way in recent days had been with Val. Joking and recording conches, it was how he'd crumbled through the structure of walls around my heart. Like he'd known what was in my heart, like it had somehow matched his own. He'd known it and had slowly filled it.

I wondered how much of it had been lies.

The next morning, the queen sent up a dress for me. Probably because I'd scandalized her so thoroughly the night before. This one was more modest, though not atrocious. It could actually be considered rather pretty, I supposed, and I wondered if she'd immediately had a dress altered for me.

It was Iolish fashion, a dress made of soft green velvet with a hood lined with white and gray fur. The sleeves were long and pointed, the bodice circular and modest. The hem of the skirt was also lined with fur, and the waist was belted with chains of gold.

"It's not hideous," Silviya supplied as she held it up.

I should have protested it entirely. Made my statement, let the queen know that she did not own me, and I was not her slave.

But the dress was pretty.

And the palace was cold.

I made my cousins help me put it on, and to prove I was worth more than a mere duchess, I placed a crown of gold over my intricate braids.

We met with the queen, who looked rather smug about the fact that I was wearing her dress, and she showed us around Isolde Palace. The whole time she droned on and on about the history of it. Even I, with my thirst for knowledge, grew bored after a while when she kept repeating herself. She even went over the many rules that were expected of me now that I was living under her roof, and what my duties would be when I became duchess.

"Wouldn't she still be a princess once she marries Ytgar?" Scarlet asked curiously.

"No. She becomes duchess."

"That doesn't make sense, though. They could still be prince and princess."

"That is not the way we do things here in Iol. Ytgar's parents were prince and princess, but since they died, the title of prince passed on to Ytgar, but there are still more ahead of him in line for the throne, like his uncles. Now that he is of age to be wed, he will become a duke like it was meant to be."

Iolish monarchies made no sense to me.

So our tour continued, and throughout it all, I didn't see Ytgar or Val at all. Not that I wanted to see them. Okay, maybe I wanted to see Val and demand an explanation. I wanted to know if he had lied to me the whole time. I wanted to look him in the eyes and rage at his royal lies.

When the tour was over and my head was pounding, I made my stealthy escape, ordering my cousins to distract the queen if the need should rise. I slipped out to the courtyard, a place as spectacular as the palace.

There was an ice sculpture fountain from which warm air bubbles shot out and popped into a shower of slushy snow. There was frozen coral that looked like it would crack if you touched it; icicles hung from them like pretty little knives.

Everything here was a winter wonderland, at first glance. I knew what trickery it truly was. Beneath the sparkly beauty of it lay the hint of frostbite and cold death.

I turned away from it and wandered the waters alone. It was cold out here, and I hadn't had the foresight to bring with me a cloak. I was hardly used to such severe weather, and traveling anywhere in Thalassar with a cloak was a bit of a nuisance. I'd need to demand cloaks of my own, and proper attire not given to me by the queen. Perhaps I could find a modiste and have her alter my own dresses.

I circled around to the back of the palace, passed a few white, dead gardens and beyond, to a hovel that was obviously a stable. There was a large wall facing me, one I had to circle around to find the stalls with slated steel roofs held up by thick steel pillars. Each stall was wide and tall, and there were several of them built side by side so the building formed a U shape around the grounds. Beyond, there was another large room with an open door that held saddles, shovels and various other equipment.

Vast expanse of open waters lay before the stables, beckoning freedom and escape. Perhaps if I could get a hippocampus, I could…

I made my way slowly to the stables. They appeared to be empty, but then I heard bucking and a commotion coming from a stall towards the end. I followed the noise and stopped in front of a fence to peer at the creature inside.

It was most definitely not a hippocampus.

It was an orca.

The creature was bucking and swiveling in rage. I stared at it in wide-eyed shock until it noticed me. When it did, I felt true fear.

The orca roared and charged, battering its head against the fence. The whole cage shook and rattled, and I heard the squeaking of hinges undoing…

Then someone shoved me from the side and I cried out as I fell to the ground. Snow and silt flew up to cloud around me. When it died, so did the orca's irate shrieking. It was replaced with the soft cooing words of an accented feminine voice.

I got up, dusting myself off with indignation. "How *dare*—"

"'Are you stupid?" the mermaid interrupted angrily in Iolish, slashing a glare my way.

"Pardon?"

"Never, *ever* approach an orca you don't know like that, not even one that's caged."

My eyes narrowed on her. She was a tall mermaid, obviously well toned from labor. She wore simple black leathers over a silver tail. Her hair was long and wavy down her shoulders, the color of ashy snow. Her skin was a light brown tone. A singular freckle decorated the top of her full, upper lip. She was pretty, in a commoner's way I supposed. With dark glaring eyes and an arrogant demeanor about her.

"I am inclined to believe you haven't an inkling as to who I am, do you?" I sniffed haughtily in her direction.

The mermaid rose a white-gray brow mockingly, and a smile twitched at the side of her full lips. "And I'm inclined to believe you have no idea who I am, do you?"

"You're a commoner. What else is there to know?" I snapped.

"I'm also the mermaid who saved your tail from a very pissed off orca. Get a clue, Princess." She turned from me arrogantly and produced a tool out of her pocket and began tightening the screws on the orca's cage.

"So you *do* know who I am?"

She bit her bottom lip in concentration, didn't answer until she was finished with the task. When she turned, she twirled the tool through her fingers with surprising dexterity. "Yeah, so? Do you want a pastry or something? I'm fresh out. I do have a bucket of whale feed if you prefer."

I gaped. "How *dare*—"

"Shove it, Princess. The whole 'I'm a royal and you're a peasant, bow to me' routine doesn't work on me." She shoved her tool back into her pocket and turned away.

I couldn't believe it. I'd been dismissed by a commoner. And a female one at that. Usually, mermaids were intimidated by me. They trembled in fear in my presence. Who did this mer think she was? Some lowly peasant challenging me, insulting me and berating me? She had absolutely no right!

I stormed after her. "I don't know who you think you are—"

"Anneli Ingen." She hauled a saddle from a wall and hefted it easily into her arms with little more than a grunt. She turned and glared at me. "You're in my way. Move." I barely had time to jump to the side before she was barraging down on me like some type of beast.

"Listen here—"

"Look, I get it. You're the princess, you want me to lick the dust off your hem and are willing to call it respect, maybe even a gift. Thing is, I'm busy and seeing your stupid face is putting me off. Please leave."

Stupid? Stupid! How dare she speak to me that way! I was her better in every way. I was a princess of a powerful kingdom and she was a sickly servant.

"I've had stablemer whipped for less," I threatened.

She hung the saddle up in an open, empty stall and turned to me, looking rather amused. "Want a pastry?"

"Why do you keep offering me confections?" I growled.

She shrugged and turned, grabbing a rake and began cleaning out the stall. "When orcas do things they think are particularly clever, they demand recompense. So, do you expect me to reward you for whipping stable hands? For being a princess? Is that why you throw that information around?"

I stopped. Why *did* I throw that information around? Wait. I shook my head back and forth. She was manipulating me into questioning myself. I threw that information around because I could. Because I *was* a princess, born to a long line of kings and queens, and better than the likes of her.

"So you know I'm better than you," I answered.

Her eyebrows rose, and she paused, leaning onto the rake's pole with both her hands. "How so?"

"I speak languages—"

"So do I. Anyone can learn."

"I was born and lived in a palace."

"I live in a palace too, sweet cheeks. It's not that impressive."

I pressed my fists against my hips. "My father is a king, my mother a queen."

Anneli feigned a shiver. "I suppose I should tell you my father was a royal as well, and my mother the bastard daughter of a war general to impress you." She laughed and resumed her task.

I stared at her, at the gray-white of her hair, wondered if it could be construed as just a dull silver, but then shook it off. "Is any of that true?" I asked.

She paused, looked up at me. "Does it matter if it was? You'd still think yourself better than me because of your fancy speech and your expensive dress. I've got news for you, Princess; anyone can live in finery. I could wear that exact same dress if I wanted to, but I choose not to. And at the end of the day, I'm still a better mer than you, silt shoveling and all. I know my death will be mourned and I'll be missed. Can you say the same?"

I froze, watching as she finished her tasks, mulling over her words ardently. The loneliness closed in on me all over again.

Would I be mourned, were I to die? I wanted to say yes, everyone loved me. They'd be sad. The reality of it was different. The only one who would miss me would be Maisie because the truth was, I had no one else but her. Had let no one else in but her. The other two I'd let in had lied to me terribly.

"She's to be Princess of Iol soon, Anneli. You shouldn't treat her so." The rumbling, arrogant voice startled me into turning around. I hadn't noticed him at all, hadn't heard him so close.

Ytgar—rather, Valmundur—swam towards the open stall, pulling at his side an orca tethered by a rope. My heart palpitated uncomfortably at the sight of him, emotions raging through my insides. He looked no different from when I'd seen him a day ago. He was still just as beautiful with his yellow hair and frost blue eyes, the lithe, muscular form, and arrogant shine in his eyes. The only difference was that now he wore no finery, no swords. He wore the same black leathers that Anneli did, and a long fur coat over it.

Every interaction suddenly assaulted my memories. How I'd thought the disguised Val had the classic beauty of a royal, how it had been so because he was Ytgar. How he'd not acted the part of a perfect prince, because he hadn't been a prince in the first place. Every laugh, every word exchanged, it was there to taunt and infuriate me.

Val led the orca into the stall Anneli was cleaning, pulled the rope from it, gave the beast's body a pat and they both exited, securing the stall after them.

When Val turned, my tail almost shook, and I nearly fell to the ground at the expression there. He was wary, that much was obvious, but there were traces of sadness there as well.

"Like I've been trying to tell her royal pain-in-the-fin over there, we have work to do, and she's in the way." Anneli crossed her arms over her chest and glared at me.

I glared right back, feeling my courage spark again. "Leave," I ordered her. "I have need to speak with him alone."

Anneli snorted. "Pardon? You are no boss of mine."

Why didn't the Iolish obey me? It made me want to yank my hair out.

"It's okay, Anneli." Val pushed himself off of the stall. His golden hair fell shy just above his lashes, blue eyes regarded me cautiously. "Let her stay."

"We have *things* to do."

"I know." He waved her off. "I'll do them while I speak to the princess. Give us a moment." He turned to look at her then. He was so beautiful, it hurt. "Please?"

"Fine," she grumbled, then she turned to me, lip curled into a sneer. She bowed low, mockingly. "Goodbye. *Princess.*"

And then she left.

As soon as she was gone, I glared accusingly at Val, a glare that he ignored in favor of swimming into another stall to take down the saddle from the hook and take it towards their supply room. I followed.

"I need to speak with you," I said.

"So, speak."

"I am your superior," I snapped. "That means when I speak to you, you drop everything else and stay still."

His whole body froze, muscles tensing. I hadn't meant to use such a superior voice, hadn't even meant to say that. I had just wanted to ask him if he'd meant anything at all, or if it had all been a lie.

Val dropped the saddle into the silt and turned, bowing his head in acquiescence. "Yes, Your Majesty. Forgive me."

I wanted him to look me in the eyes. I wanted to see his expression while I raged. I didn't like this submissive side of him. Didn't like that he was acting as if he were beneath me. He was, but this wasn't the Val I'd come to know.

Then I remembered, when my cousins and I had insulted Val who wasn't really Val and he had chimed in with barbs of his own. I had wondered why he wasn't defending his friend, why he let us speak so ill of him, why he'd chimed in with harsh words of his own.

Because that's how he saw himself.

As someone unworthy, as someone beneath me. Despite the fact that he'd been the only one to see through my walls. Despite the fact that he'd been the one to pour life into me, little by little. Despite the fact that he'd been the one to fulfill one of my dreams.

"Why did you kiss me?" I demanded.

Valmundur

"Why?" she demanded.

I could just make out the trembling of her hands as she closed them into fists. I knew she was angry; I would have been too. We'd so thoroughly lied, had stopped her from swimming away, and now here she was. I knew it would come, but I hadn't been prepared for the impact of it.

I had no answer for her. None that were acceptable, anyway. Because I wanted her since the first moment I saw her. Because I wanted to know what that mouth would taste like against mine. Because I'd wanted to know what it felt like, for the first time in my life, to be desired by someone so wholly above my station, that I'd blinded myself into believing that she could actually look past what I really was.

"Why?" she shouted, shoving her fists against my chest.

I deserved that and so much more.

She hit me until she was gasping, and I took it all in without moving. When she finished, she looked up at me, and I swore I saw the sheen of tears glossing over her eyes. It made me feel like a cad.

"Was any of it true?" she demanded. "Or was that all a lie?" She took a stroke away, not allowing me to answer. "Who are you?"

My throat tightened, but I forced the words out. Now was the time for honesty. The time for her to see who and what I really was. "My name is Valmundur Ingen. My last name means *nothing* because I am *nothing*. I am a bastard, and an orphan. I don't know who I am, Your Majesty, but when I was a child, the mistress at the orphanage brought some of us here to help the palace servants. She was grooming us, preparing us for the day when we would be thrown to the streets. The only reason I am here is because of Prince Ytgar." I stopped, took a breath as I remembered that day. "We switched identities to protect him from enemies who might want to murder him. I've no excuse for the lies we've told and all I can say is that I hope you forgive this filthy whale trainer for tainting you so thoroughly."

Her pink skin seemed to pale. She stammered through syllables. "Those things I said…"

"Were true," I boldly interrupted. "Each and every one of them."

She grew quiet and then whispered, so softly I almost didn't hear her, "I didn't know we were talking about *you*."

She hadn't, but it broke my heart just the same.

"If that will be all Your Majesty requires…" I bent down to pick up the saddle.

"Stop," she commanded.

I froze, straightened to her fury.

"You will listen to me, Valmundur Ingen. Everything I ever said about you, all you did was prove me right." Her voice grew in its vehemence, frightened me, and shattered everything inside. "You are a Iolish bastard not fit to scrub the silt from my hem. You lied to me, made me—" She broke off with disgust. "It's vile. Now I know the truth, that yours and Ytgar's plan was to get me to come here to your stupid kingdom under lies. Whatever you thought, whatever illusions you came up with in your deranged commoner mind, rid yourself of them now because I do not want you, nor will I ever want to meddle with your filth again. Do you understand?"

My heart was thumping wildly in my chest. I had the urge to reach for her, to beg for a change of heart, but I stayed petrifyingly still. "Perfectly, Your Majesty."

"Good. Now get out of my sight, whale trainer."

I bowed low and properly to her, ignoring the pain searing through my chest. I'd known these would be the consequences, I'd known she would hate me for it, but knowing what would happen did not lessen the blow when it came. It did not give me the words I needed to change her mind. It did not give me the strength I needed to apologize for my slight.

And it did not lessen the pain of her loss.

I IGNORED ANNELI'S GLARE as I left. I ignored the guards that followed me back to the palace. I ignored the voices that urged me to see the queen, for there was something urgent she needed to speak to me about.

I ignored everyone but my anger, and my anger I used to lash out at the servants. As if that somehow made it better. As if my lashing out at them, ordering to have them whipped and dismissed were somehow my vengeance towards Val. As if ignoring the queen's summons was somehow my vengeance towards Ytgar.

It was satisfying just the same.

Until the day that it wasn't.

Days later, Ytgar stormed into my room. He hadn't bothered to knock, he just barged in, shocking my cousins' delicate sensibilities.

"Get out," he ordered them.

They looked to me for permission, and I gave it with the smallest dip of my head. As soon as they filed dutifully out of the room, I turned away from the mirror at my vanity table and smiled demurely at my betrothed.

"Is there something you required?"

His eyes could have cut daggers through me. "Stop terrorizing the household, Odele."

I blinked innocently. "Whatever do you mean?"

He growled. "Cut the silt. This isn't Thalassar, and I'll not have you treating everyone here terribly just because you're miserable with your own pathetic life."

I got up with a gasp. "Don't speak to me that way."

He took a stroke forward and grabbed my wrist, squeezing tightly. "Mark my words, Princess, I'll not have you treating my staff badly, and I've instructed them not to serve you if you continue."

I yanked my hand away, rubbing the spot where he'd squeezed. "We aren't married yet. I don't have to do anything you say."

His lips twisted into a mocking smile. "Even if we were married, I doubt you'd listen. Hence why I'm taking precautions."

I threw my arms up with irritation. "What am I supposed to do? You're never around, your kingdom is a prison, and I'm bored!"

I'd been promised a tour of the world. Of course, it had been an imposter prince who had made that promise in the first place.

His lips twitched with what I could have sworn was amusement. "I am not your slave." He leaned forward. "I have a kingdom to help run, and cannot be at your beck and call. If you are restless, find something to do." And then he whirled away and stalked off.

I frowned after him and muttered, loud enough so he could hear, "As if you have any power here."

He froze, and I almost wished he'd turn back and give me a tongue lashing, perhaps something else as well, but he just left the room after a moment, slamming the door behind him.

What a bother. It was no fun teasing someone so unresponsive.

That's how, hours later, I found myself exploring the palace, slipping into rooms and peeking out windows until I found one that overlooked the stables.

I told myself I was just taking a peek to see how badly he was suffering, so I could laugh at his misery. It had absolutely nothing to do with this aching loneliness, this *longing* in my chest. It had nothing to do with him, and everything to do with my own selfish desire to see him suffer.

I saw him out in the open waters with the orca that tried to attack me. He was leading it by a tethered rope, but the beast wasn't cooperating. It bucked so hard, it hauled him up through the water and the tether snapped, causing him to fly and land face first into the silt.

I bit back my cry of dismay when the sound of laughter replaced it. Feminine laughter.

Val let out a curse in Iolish and leaned up on his forearms. When he turned his face, I caught the flash of a smile. A smile he had gifted me with. The smile of a friend, of a lover.

I knew who it was for before she even appeared in my line of vision.

Anneli swam over to him, clutching her stomach, bent over laughing. She pointed at him and spat out a joke at his expense. In retaliation, he scooped up snow and silt and tossed it at her. They both dissolved into laughter before she offered him a hand to pull him up, except when he took his hand in hers, he yanked and she sprawled on top of him in the snow.

I felt like I'd been punched in the chest.

This wasn't the misery I was hoping for. This wasn't misery at all. This was… well, it felt like a betrayal. To me, to us, to what we'd had.

Iolish bastard.

I had to tear my gaze away from the window before I saw them do something disgusting like kiss.

This wouldn't do. It was unacceptable, I thought as I stormed out of the palace. I'd find Valmundur and put him in his place. I'd let him know exactly what I thought of his daytime liaison with that female whale trainer. It had been nothing but a matter of a few days and he had already moved on from me. As if I was so easily forgettable.

She wasn't even pretty! I raged as I rounded the palace and came to the stables. Val was no longer there. But Anneli was. She was leading the animal back to its stall. I knew she noticed me, but she didn't acknowledge me.

"Where is Val?" I demanded, crossing my arms against my chest.

The female whale trainer stopped, the beast halfway into the stall. Her eyebrows rose. "Why do you want to know?"

"That's none of your concern."

"It is if you're here to hurt him again."

Oh, yeah. It was obvious I'd hurt him. Obvious in the way he was quick to fall into her arms. If he wasn't hurting now, then he would be when I was finished with him.

"What exactly is Val to you?"

The two shared a last name. *Ingen.* It was the name gifted to Iolish bastard children. So I knew they weren't related, but if I hadn't been paying attention, I wouldn't have noticed the sudden way Anneli tensed, or the grim set of her features. So it was true. She meant something to him.

"He's my friend," she answered slowly, cautiously.

I doubted they were just friends. She felt something more for him. That wouldn't do.

"Well, he's my…" I paused. "…friend."

"Really? Because the other day it looked like you broke his heart."

I'd believe that the moment the sun fell on top of Iol.

"Like I said, mind your business."

Her hands tightened around the rope a brief second before she was shaking her head back and forth. "You're such a headache."

I'd not have this servant scum insulting me. "And you are a loudmouth. Really, what does Val see in you?"

The comment had clearly caught her off guard. She blinked. "Pardon?"

"You." I gestured at the entirety of her body. At the leathers, the silver and gray hair, the infuriatingly perfectly placed freckle, her curves. "Why would he like someone like you?"

Anneli snorted. "Perhaps because I'm not a spoiled, pretentious, stuck up princess."

My face flamed involuntarily. I was left bereft of words and infuriated. And I really, really wanted to hit her. I contemplated that decision when the beast on her tether started bucking and thrashing.

Anneli tugged at the rope, but the beast didn't budge. It seemed furious for some reason and she didn't seem able to keep it under control.

"Calm your beast," I demanded impatiently.

The mermaid slashed a glare at me. "Good idea, Princess."

"Just trying to be helpful."

In fact, I was sure I was being everything but helpful as I watched her struggle with the thing for a few more minutes at most. The situation went from bad to worse when the orca bucked so hard, Anneli dropped the rope holding it, and it charged.

Straight at me.

Surprised, I shrieked, throwing my hands up to protect my face as it bore down on me too quickly for me to do anything but float there.

The heavyweight of its body threw me straight into the silt, knocking the breath from my body, making me ache all over. I swore I saw the blinking lights of two-legger stars behind my closed eyelids. When I opened them and the haze cleared, it was to see the orca looming over me, its massive face threateningly close, so close I could see the depths of murder in its black eyes and the thickness of its massive teeth.

"Gods," I choked.

The orca roared.

What had I studied about orcas? The beasts liked to assert their dominance when faced with an opponent. Was this what it was doing? Asserting dominance over me? I could either submit or challenge it and earn its respect.

Or be killed in the process.

I was no quitter.

I screamed my rage and pent-up frustrations back at it. All my sorrow and my loss, my anger and violence. Startled, the orca blinked at me. Would this be the moment I died? No. It couldn't be. I still had to give Val a piece of my mind. I still had a world to see and adventures to make.

I lifted my head up and bumped it lightly against the orca's.

"Get away from me this instant," I ordered in my best princess voice.

Surprisingly, the creature obeyed, taking a few strokes back.

When it was a good distance away, I got up and dusted myself off. Anneli quickly wrapped a rope around the beast's neck and led him into his stall, caging him inside.

She let loose a breath and turned to me. There was no mistaking the shock marring her features, the disbelief.

"He could have killed you."

I shrugged. "Orcas are pack creatures. Since he doesn't have a pack of his own, he tried asserting his dominance over me by charging and getting me to submit, but I challenged him and bumped his head to assert my own position."

Anneli blinked at me.

Gods, was it so difficult for mer to believe that I *knew* things? The only one who hadn't been surprised was Val, and I missed that. I missed him not treating me with surprise when I displayed intelligence. Like he couldn't quite believe it. But he did. He knew what I hid. He *knew* me.

"I'm surprised you knew what to do."

I shrugged carelessly. "I know quite a few things, and yet mer are still surprised."

She regarded me curiously for a moment, cocking her head slightly to the side. "Hm," she mumbled. "Interesting." She came closer, circling me like a shark would its prey. Her gaze skimming from my head to my tail fin. She got closer still, holding her chin in her hand, and I floated abnormally still. For some reason.

"Arms out," she ordered.

"Excuse you?"

She rolled her eyes and grabbed both of my arms, pulling them so I was holding them out at my sides. I stayed like that—for some reason—while she felt along the length of my arm and took the liberty of letting her fingers dance down my side, to my hip and down my tail.

"Hey!" I jerked away, glaring down at her.

She hung her head in exasperation then slowly got up. "You have the body of a natural rider."

"Yes, well, I am the greatest rider in all of Thalassar."

Anneli crossed her arms, mockingly. "It's not riding if you haven't ridden on an orca, Princess."

"How different can they be?"

I found out that they could be very different indeed.

Never one to let a challenge go unanswered, I had to take Anneli up on proving that riding an orca was just as easy as riding a hippocampus.

How wrong I was.

She saddled up one of the tamer orcas for me, handed me the reins, wished me good fortune and leaned back against the stalls, watching as I was thrown from it.

Again.

And again.

And again.

The whale trainer dissolved into a fit of hysterical laughter. "That's twenty by my count."

Twenty times the thing knocked me into the silt, and still I got back on. To prove to her and myself that I was still a great rider, even if this orca was proving to be a rather difficult opponent.

"You've given me a defective mount," I complained, not for the first time.

"Nah, she's our gentlest. Aren't you, girl?"

If this was their gentlest, I'd hate to see their most wild. One thing was for certain, orcas were definitely not tame animals like hippocampi. That made this seem all the more dangerous, more adventurous. I wanted nothing if not my own adventure.

"It's your outfit." Anneli came over and held a hand down to help me up. I was surprised at the gesture still. She was rude and arrogant and took no care with how she spoke to me. The mer obviously didn't like me very much, and she still helped me up from the silt.

Was this what friendship was?

"What's wrong with my outfit?" I asked indignantly, dusting the skirts off. I was wearing a pretty silk dress in blue, with lace and ruffles and fur.

"You're kidding me, right?" One of Anneli's eyebrows rose as she took in my clothes.

"What's wrong with it?"

"It's a dress!"

"And it's perfect. Really, you should try one on sometime."

Her eyes narrowed. "I own dresses, okay? I just choose not to wear them."

"And I choose not to look like a stable hand."

She heaved another exasperated sigh. She seemed to do a lot of that in my presence. I should have been annoyed by it, but a smile crept its way to my lips. I couldn't help it. Despite all her faults and her brusque outer exterior, I found myself warming up to this servant. For some reason.

"The right clothes will help make riding flow smoothly," she supplied.

I pulled myself back on top of the beast, holding tightly to the reins. "A true rider learns to do so no matter what he or she is wearing." With a cry, I flicked the reins, hugging my tail tightly to the beast's side. It shot forward, so Anneli's reply was lost out in the cacophony of the water whistling through my ears.

This was freedom, pure and simple. I loved every second, the feeling like I was flying and not by my own volition. I was being taken to distances I never knew, at high speeds, with the current whipping back my hair. The loneliness was suddenly gone, and it was just me and this happiness.

Until I was thrown off once again.

I careened into the ground, face slamming into the silt. Pain spiraled through my every nerve, especially those in my face. Gods, that was going to leave a mark. I pressed my palms into the silt, the grains and ice abrading my palms, and pushed myself up. The first thing I saw was the cloud of blood, and then I felt the warmth of it leave my nose.

Gods on a pastry.

"Princess! Are you alright?" A gentle hand gripped my arm and helped me up. "Damn, that was a hard fall. Look at me." She whirled me around to face her and searched my eyes for a sign of a concussion. "Are you alright?"

I pushed her away and swiped at my nose. "I want to go again."

"I think you've had enough for today, Princess."

"I am your superior, and I'll tell you when I've had enough. I want to go again."

"Stop acting like a petulant child and shut up. We don't always get what we want in life." She threw my arm around her shoulder. "It's time to go back to your pretty little rooms and soak in a bath, I think."

My brain swirled. I was suddenly dizzy and nauseous at the same time. I groaned.

"See?" Anneli admonished before letting out a shrill whistle. It was her call to the orca that had knocked me on my face.

"I want to learn."

"And I'll teach you," she promised. "But first, you need your rest."

I rested and put ice on my face, and the next day I escaped the palace and went out again. It became a routine. I saw very little of Ytgar, and hardly anything of Val—I suspected Anneli sent him away before I arrived—though I swore I felt both of their presence while we worked. I spent most of my days with my new friend.

Funny how it was so easy to call her that now.

She taught me how to ride, how to tame. She taught me how to communicate with the orcas until I was as good as she was. She didn't realize I was good at memorization. This was like study to me, and I absorbed it like a sea sponge. And every night I went back to my rooms and wrote with ink and kelp parchment my learning of the day. There were no conches, but it didn't stop me from recording every detail into a journal.

One day after training, as I leaned against a stall and watched her scrape the silt, she grumbled. "You could help, you know."

"I could."

"But you won't." She stabbed the rake in the sand.

"I won't."

There was a pause, and I chewed my bottom lip, contemplating how much I should ask when I finally couldn't hold my curiosity back any longer. "Is there truly nothing between you and Val?"

She paused. "Well…" Rake. Rake. Rake. "There was, in the past. But we are friends now. Nothing more."

That didn't bring me comfort.

"It doesn't matter anyway," I dismissed. "He's a commoner."

Anneli paused again, and it was a moment before I noticed how curiously she was eyeing me. "For someone who professes to despise commoners so much, you spend a great deal of time either befriending them or asking about them."

I puffed up indignantly. "I do not!"

She stopped raking. "All I'm saying is that you put a lot of emphasis on stations and positions as if it mattered."

I turned, leaning my arms against the cold steel of the fence, steel I felt even through the thick sleeves of the velvet dress I wore. My tail curled behind me. My body was aching all over from the physical strain I'd put it under.

"But it does matter. At least, in my world it does." In my world, the rich rose above the poor. We lived in castles, ate good food, we had money and ruled and looked to further power. Those at the bottom scraped and fought and served us. It was the way of the world.

"Why?" Anneli asked, genuinely curious. As if she couldn't quite fathom the way of the world.

"Because..." How could I explain it so she understood? "It just is. Princesses cannot care for commoners. Can't befriend them, marry them."

"Ah..." She set aside her rake and closed in on me, placing her own bare palms against the fence and leaning into it. "But I'm a commoner. I'm also your friend."

"Tentative friend," I corrected her. "As I still don't know if I like you or not."

With a push against steel, she was off the fence and turning towards the wall where she pulled down a saddle and a sponge to shine it. "I like you well enough sometimes," she said as if whispering a confession. "But answer me this, when Val was pretending to be Prince Ytgar—yes, the whole kingdom knows they switched identities when they left—what did you like the most about him?" She scrubbed the sponge across the leather of the saddle as she waited for me to answer

"So many qualities to choose from, how could I possibly pick one?" I pressed a hand to my chest and fluttered my eyes mockingly.

Anneli shot me a look that said 'be serious.'

I sighed.

What had I liked the most about Val? I chewed at my bottom lip. Perhaps his ability to make me smile, or the way he irritated me and even so, I still couldn't manage to get enough. Or maybe it was the way he kissed, or how when he looked at me, it was like I was the only mer left in the world, or how he made me seem like I was… unattainable… worth *more.*

"He saw me," I whispered, knowing the moment the words left my mouth that they were right. He saw me when no one else did. Everyone looked at me and saw the facade I'd so carefully constructed. They saw a daft princess, because it's what I'd led them to believe I was. He'd known differently from the first moment.

And for that I would always love him.

"He still sees you, Odele. That hasn't changed. Who he was when he became Ytgar is still there. So what should it matter what he wears or what he does for a living? Inside, he's still the same."

I blinked away the tears that threatened to rise.

My emotions were a torrent inside of me. Epiphanies rarely happened, but the one that suddenly crashed over me, like a rogue wave on a shore, sent every fiber and drop of blood inside of me spiraling. She was right. Gods, she was right.

It didn't forgive his betrayal, but he had never hid himself from me, his true self, and I realized with sudden clarity that I missed it. I missed him. It had been the reason I had sought out the stables in the first place, the reason I'd kept coming around. To catch a glimpse of him, to impress him with the adventure I was foraging all on my own.

"Here he comes," Anneli hissed suddenly, her eyes signaling behind me.

I turned and saw the two mermen I hadn't interacted with in what felt like weeks. I felt their presence tremble deep to my core. They both wore grim expressions as they came near and a sliver of foreboding slipped down my spine.

"What's wrong?" Anneli obviously felt it too, for her voice was bereft of all humor.

It was Ytgar who answered, and he stared right at me as he did so. "There's been another attack," he ground out. "The warriors have been called."

Everything after that happened in a flurry of activity. Ytgar ordered me to go inside the palace and bar myself in my room while Anneli hurried to prepare the mounts, strapping saddles across their backs. The prince gave her orders to prepare, to do things.

I felt worthless.

"I can help, too."

Ytgar shot me a glare. "You can help by going to the palace and not get in our way."

He doubted me still. He, like all others, thought me daft and useless. I'd led them to think that, so it shouldn't have hurt, but I'd proved to him I could speak Iolish in a matter of weeks, shouldn't he trust me with this too?

I turned to look at the merman who, above all others, knew exactly what I was capable of. Val was staring at me, but he promptly looked away when I noticed his attention. That rejection stung more than it should have.

I tilted my head up in Ytgar's direction. "I am going to help." Without waiting for permission, I swept past him and reached for a heavy saddle off the side. My muscles screamed in protest but I gritted my teeth and bore through it as I hauled it over towards a mount.

"Gods of ice," Ytgar cursed. "For the last time, get—"

"Let her help," Val interrupted. "We don't have time to float about and argue."

Ytgar conceded, albeit with a glare and a few more curses in Iolish, perhaps some of them aimed my way.

The rest of those moments were spent in silence as Anneli and I readied the mounts as warriors began pouring into the stables, already dressed in neutral colors of white and soft blues and grays, colors to blend in with the ice and furs to keep them warm.

"Time to leave!" Ytgar ordered. The warriors mounted, raged a battle cry and shot off. He turned to me before reaching for the reins. "Get inside, and don't come out," he growled.

Iolish brute.

He hopped onto his mount and sped away, calling after Val.

"Don't worry, Princess," Val said stiffly, respectfully, as he held the reins to his own beast. "Dragons break through our borders quite often."

I blanched. "Dragons?" Someone had left that miniscule detail out.

Val nodded, lips forming a grim line. "It's dangerous work, but we can handle it."

"You're going with them?" I demanded, hands knotting into my skirts with fear.

His expression went from stiff and formal to something else. To anger. "I may be a lowly whale trainer, Princess, but I can assure you that every single Iolish mer is quite capable of defending our kingdom." He started to turn away.

"That's not what I meant!" Frustrated, I made a rush to grab him by the sleeve and turn him to me. I couldn't explain the sudden desperation that gripped me, except to say that I was afraid. I didn't feel fear often, but here I did. As if he would leave and something terrible would happen without me having ever told him…

"You see me," I whispered, almost stupidly.

His blond brows furrowed. "Well, I do have two eyes…"

"No. I mean, ugh, I'm mucking this up like a foolish guppy. I'm trying to—" Apologize. I couldn't say the word. I didn't want to. Not because I was incapable, but because I'd much rather show him.

So I grabbed Val's face in my hands and did what I'd been wanting to do since the first time he'd caught me off guard in the hallways of Eramaea.

I kissed *him.*

Our mouths melded together, and I registered his brief shock before he groaned, a plea, or a curse, I wasn't sure, but a moment later his tongue was pushing past my lips and I let him inside. His arm wrapped around my waist and pulled me closer, so close our bodies fit perfectly. I felt his every hard ridge through his furs, through his leathers, and I welcomed it. I welcomed the rough calluses of his fingers as he palmed my face, thumb swiping over the curve of my cheek.

The shock of his tongue against my own alerted my every sense, it livened me, making a tremble sweep through my body. I pressed closer, as if close could never be close enough. As if he could consume me entirely with the press of his body, the untamed claim of his lips and teeth.

All too soon, it ended.

Our noses touched, lips a whisper away. My eyes fluttered open to find him staring at me with awe and confusion. I knew he was going to ask, but I didn't want him to break this moment. I wanted to kiss him again, wanted to be wrapped up in his arms. But he had to go. He had a kingdom to help defend.

"You are more than that," I assured against his lips. "Be safe, both of you, and come back to me. I'll be angry if you don't."

His lips curled into a slow smile. "We wouldn't want that, would we?"

Then Val turned, mounted, and left.

Odele

DESPITE WANTING TO IGNORE Ytgar's brutish command, I did what he said after Anneli convinced me it was for my safety. Sometimes the dragons that broke through terrorized towns. None of them had breached the capital yet, but everyone was to hide inside until the warriors came back and deemed it safe.

So it was in the palace I waited, pacing through my rooms, the halls, everywhere I could. The queen grumbled at me more than once regarding royal etiquette and the fact that I was an embarrassment with my fluttering about.

Perhaps I was, so I sat demurely next to her and glared at everyone around me. Especially at the Prime Minister.

I hadn't asked, but I suspected he resided here at the palace as well. He was a big merman, though not as big as Ytgar. He had the muscles of a warrior, and it only served to help me wonder why he was being cowardly, locked away with the mermaids of the palace instead of out fighting for his kingdom.

From whisperings and my own observations, I gathered that Ytgar didn't like him very much because he was in a position of power, but did little with it other than steal taxpayer money. I knew Ytgar was hoping to change the monarchy and rule himself, if only to save his mer.

While I didn't feel like leading was the path for me, like I'd never make a good queen, I knew Iol deserved better than this coward.

"Surely we have sufficient guards here at the palace," I commented to everyone present. "Your Iolish personal guard and my Thalassarin guard, well I'd say we are well enough protected."

The queen nodded confidently. "It is merely a precaution. Those beasts have never crossed towards the capital."

I gave the Prime Minister a pointed look. "Tell me, Rollo, do you suffer from a limp?"

My question caught him off guard. "I beg your pardon?"

The queen gaped at me. "Princess, royals do not ask such questions!"

"Forgive me, Your Majesty, I am just trying to discern something. My dearest cousin Odalaea suffers from a limp and it makes doing all sorts of tasks difficult, you see."

Rollo's eyes narrowed. "What has that to do with me?"

I gave him my sweetest smile. "I'm trying to discern if your disabilities prevent you from fighting with the other warriors and volunteers to defend the kingdom you rule."

He nearly choked. He recuperated enough to glare hatefully at me and say, as if speaking to a daft and petulant child, "I am no warrior. I am the leader of this kingdom. Were I to die fighting, it would throw the kingdom in turmoil and leave it vulnerable for all manner of beastly creatures."

I knew what his words really meant. The bloody coward.

I suddenly knew what Maisie must have felt seeing someone on the throne with all the power who was unfit to rule. The sudden sensation of wanting them gone, replaced with someone new and trustworthy. Someone who cared about the mer and the kingdom. Not someone hungry for power, but someone who could actually make a difference.

That wasn't me, but I'd gladly help Ytgar find the one for the position, if only to see this mer thrown in the gallows with his head pinned to a pike.

A commotion at the front of the palace had us jumping up from our seats. The guards were instantly alert and pushed forward to protect us. I didn't like floating idly by, so I pushed my way to the front, despite the queen's vehement protests. I yanked a sword from the sheath at one of the guard's waist and started forward.

The doors burst open and warriors poured through. With them, Val. His eyes sought mine and he came rushing to me quickly.

I started to ask if he was okay, searching for any visible injuries when he interrupted. "It's Ytgar," he rasped. "Ytgar is hurt."

Ytgar

My side screamed in protest, still I sat up against the cushions of my bed, where only moments ago my fellow warriors had gently laid me down. As if I was a damn mermaid in need of coddling.

"We need to hold a council meeting," I declared through gritted teeth to one of them. "Right now. Call the Prime Minister and his circle together."

The warrior looked uncomfortable, inclined to argue with me. "Prince, you are in no condition—"

"Don't tell me what I can and cannot do," I interrupted icily.

This was important. More important than me. We needed to talk about a course of action, something to prevent this from happening again. The dragon had been a massive creature and had gotten too close to escaping towards the palace. We needed to prepare for any eventuality. That meant more guards, more orcas, a change of laws, a truce with Draconi…

Anything.

The village had been thoroughly decimated. I could still picture the crumbling ice structures, their homes, the bodies strewn bloody through the water. We had arrived in time to watch the dragon take a bite out of a few locals.

My stomach twisted at the memory.

Even as I fought for other lives, to prevent what I had witnessed from happening again, the image haunted me with every vicious swipe I aimed at the creature. And when the creature had reached for Val, I hadn't thought. I had reacted, pushing him aside to take the blow that would have ended his life.

I didn't regret it.

But I wouldn't let this injury hinder me useless either.

"I said call the meeting!" I shouted. It was infuriating, having no power in my own kingdom. What good was the title of prince when I could do nothing to help the mer that were suffering? I'd gladly strip myself of title and rank, if it only meant I could be of better use to my kingdom.

"Ytgar! What has happened?"

I turned sharply at the voice of my grandmother as she suddenly barged into my rooms. Great. Now I'd get nowhere.

"Nothing, grandmother."

Another gasp behind her had me cursing silently. Odele floated in the doorway, her ladies maids behind her and Val behind them, looking equal parts sick and guilty.

"You're hurt!" Odele exclaimed, and gods of ice, it almost sounded like she cared.

My betrothed pushed past everyone to swim hurriedly into the room. She was at my side in a flash, pushing down the covers to reveal my bare chest—I noticed her eyes linger over my skin, heating momentarily—and the bandaged wound that was already seeping through with blood.

"What happened?" she demanded angrily, turning to direct the question at one of my warriors. He withered under the force of her glare. "How could you not protect your prince? *How* could you let this happen?"

Gods of ice, she was formidable, and the warrior rightly feared her scorn.

"The dragon—"

"Get out!" she screeched. "All of you, get out!" She got up and whirled to her ladies, who flinched at her seething wrath. "Fetch me lava globes and warm rags to wrap the wound. I'll be needing needle and thread, fermented sea wine and root of leez, if you can find it." She glared. "Make *sure* you find it. And hurry."

Her maids curtsied and left quickly.

My grandmother was glaring at her. "Odele, what in gods' names are you doing? We have doctors for this! You are making an utter fool of yourself!"

Then Odele bravely, shockingly, floated to her full height. She towered over my grandmother a mere few inches and matched her stern stare for one of her own.

"Get. Out." she ordered.

My grandmother blinked. "Pardon?"

"Get out! All of you, except for Val! I'll not have you hovering while he's recovering!"

The queen looked at her indignantly, obviously trying to find out where such audacity had come from. I was still trying to figure that out myself when Odele ushered everyone aggressively out. Every warrior, servant, and lady, and slammed the door in their faces.

She made her way back to me, perching herself at the edge of the bed. She swatted my hands away and grabbed the edge of the bindings around my abdomen.

"I have to see the extent of the damage," she said quietly, firmly, and began unwrapping. Once the wound was revealed, she didn't blanch, but frowned with displeasure. "Do you despise the idea of marriage to me so much that you'd rather see yourself a mauled corpse?"

I couldn't help but chuckle at the words she threw back in my face. Words I had said to her myself. It seemed so long ago now.

"I told you there was no escaping Iol, Princess. There is no escaping *me*." Her eyes heated at the promise of my threat and my desire.

"Ytgar…"

I looked past her shoulder to where Val floated. He'd grown pale as he stared at my wound, his throat bobbed up and down as he swallowed.

"Don't look so grim," I admonished. "I'll always save your life, even if it means forfeiting my own."

"Don't," he snapped. "Don't say that. You are the prince and I—"

"Val," Odele interrupted. She didn't turn towards him, but was examining my wound thoroughly. "Don't start."

"You'd be dead if I hadn't done what I did."

His face went paler, and I knew what he wanted to say before he said it, but it was Odele who interrupted before he could get the words out.

"Will you both stop trying to prove who loves the other more? It's disgusting to listen to. If you're going to get mushy, at least kiss so it'll be more entertaining."

Val and I recoiled at the thought. "Kiss?" he demanded. "What?"

She shrugged. "You act like a couple."

"We do not," I argued, trying to sit up, and regretting it immediately when pain seared straight through me.

Odele pursed her lips. "You do. It's infuriating to listen to the drama without seeing any real action."

"Get this straight!" Val sputtered, and I noticed the color rising back to his cheeks. "I am not attracted to mermen. I am not attracted to Ytgar, nor will I ever be."

"Well, why not? Don't you think he's handsome?"

"Well, yes but—"

She cocked her head to the side. "So it's his personality that you're opposed to?"

"Of course not, Ytgar is great."

"Then—"

"I don't like mermen! Why am I even defending myself?" He threw his hands up and began pacing the room.

"Methinks you doth protest too much, beauty mine."

Val growled. "I'm leaving, wench." But before he did, he looked into my eyes, searching for permission. I knew what he was asking, just like he already knew what my answer would be. Carefully, slowly, he bent towards Odele, took her face in his hands, and firmly kissed her on the mouth.

I looked away as she moaned and only turned back when Val spoke again.

"Was that the kiss of someone attracted to mermen?"

She shrugged. "I'll have to see how you kiss Ytgar in order to—"

"I'm leaving!" he scoffed with disgust. A moment later, he was gone.

Silence enveloped us without him here.

I searched for the words to say, but they never came. A knock on the door did, instead. Odele went to open it and let her ladies march through along with a servant, and started instructing them unkindly on where they should leave everything. When it was all to her liking, she made them leave and slammed the door.

Once settled back to my side, she gripped the bottle of fermented sea wine by the neck and tore the top off with her teeth. Without warning, she bent and poured the dark liquid over my wound. It escaped its glass like tendrils of dark smoke that floated down to my mauled flesh.

I winced.

She spat the cork out and let the bottle of wine sink to the floor. "It had to be cleansed." She then took one of the warm rags and began wiping away whatever grime or silt had accumulated in the wound. I tried to keep very still, but her fingers were tempting me to the point of distraction.

"Perhaps you should call for a medic," I suggested tightly.

She stilled momentarily before resuming cleaning, her movements becoming brusque. "I know you think me incapable of things, but I can assure you, I am able to do the simplest of tasks."

She sounded defensive. Well, what had she expected? It's not as though I thought she was unintelligent, she had proved that she wasn't. She had made it clear time and time again that manual labor and things such as these were beneath her. Also, a part of me worried she was trying to secretly kill me for my lies.

"This is no simple task."

She shot me an exasperated look. "You were clawed by a dragon. Dragon claws can be as poisonous as their teeth. An effective counter to such a wound is a substance with the root of leez, as it kills away whatever bacteria and traces the beast left behind. Draconians have been using it for thousands of years when a mer is attacked by a dragon, though it is not a widely known cure, as dragons are limited only to Draconian breeding grounds and royal stables."

Gods of ice.

"How do you know that?"

She smiled mischievously. "I know a lot of things that would surprise you, Iolish."

I didn't doubt it, and my body ached, not from the wound, but from her words, and I wanted her to show me exactly what it was she knew.

"Is that why you spent so much time at the Royal Library in Draconi?" I asked gently.

This information seemed vital, somehow, and I wanted to know it, was desperate to know her the way Val seemed to know her.

She shrugged as she finished dabbing the last of my wound. Then she grabbed for the needle and thread and pinched my wound closed to begin sewing it. I hissed out a breath.

"Since I was a child," she began softly, as if confiding a secret to me, "I was always good at memorizing things around me. I remembered everything I ever read or heard, word for word. I still can. So studying always came too easy for me, but I pretended otherwise."

I noticed the way her hands twitched almost involuntarily. I wanted to reach out and put my hand over hers but held back.

"Why?" I asked.

She paused briefly.

"I see the way your fingers twitch sometimes when you answer questions. Almost as if you're bracing yourself for the feel of a whip."

Her breath hitched. Was she surprised I'd noticed? I was a royal, and I was familiar with the curse of our punishments.

"Percival liked to punish me." She pulled the last bit of string into place, tying it off. Then she reached for the root of leez she'd sent for, put it in her mouth and chewed it before spitting it back out and covering it over my wound. She was silent for a long moment as she placed the last bit of the strange brown-green plant against my wound.

When she finished, she turned her hand over so she was staring at the backs of her knuckles. "I have no feeling here anymore." With one hand, she slid them across her knuckles, tracing the contours there. "He always hit me so hard, I'd end up bleeding."

I growled, the sound ripped from somewhere primitive inside me. A part I hadn't known existed. If I could bring that merman back to life, it'd be so I could help kill him all over again. Slowly and torturously.

"Why go through with it, if you knew the answers?"

"At first it was rebellion. Then I realized it granted me an audience with my stepmother and my father. It was the only time I ever saw him, even if it was just so he could lecture me and stare at me with disappointment in his eyes."

Her eyes had gone far away, back to that memory, the image of her father's disappointed eyes. I knew the look well, knew what it could do to a fragile heart. What it had done to my own.

I pressed my palm to her cheek. For a moment, she leaned into my touch gladly, sighing contentedly, before pulling away and grabbing for the new, fresh bindings. She pressed the end just below my wound and leaned over, starting to wrap it around and around.

I inhaled the scent of her, feeling my desire strike me like two-legger lightning.

She spoke as she worked. "I'm used to his disappointment. The only time he never had that look was when he was looking at Maisie—" She broke off and I heard her swallow, as if she were forcing away a tightness in her throat. "And my mother. I knew he wanted me to be like her so desperately, but I wanted him to love me for me, not for her. She was beautiful, kind, and generous. I knew I'd never amount to her greatness, and I didn't want to, so I settled for something different."

"Your father put too much pressure on your shoulders," I said, knowing that I'd thought the same of my own grandmother. "When my father had died, the queen tried to thrust me into his role of greatness. The only difference was that I built myself up to it, only to realize I could do nothing with my own gifts."

She smiled a little sadly at me. "I swam out of my mother's shadow long ago, but the expectations are still there, and they still haunt me somehow."

She finished placing the last of the binding in place and sat back, clearly finished. But I wasn't finished, and I didn't want this to be over. I grabbed her wrist to keep her here.

"I am finished, Prince," she said. "Despite the fact you think me stupid and incapable and prefer to have me locked in an ice palace rather than be of use…"

I reeled back as if she'd slapped me. Honestly, her fist to my jaw would have hurt less. My mouth dropped open, closed again.

"Is that why you think I ordered you to the palace earlier?"

She lifted her chin. "Isn't it? You've made it very clear you think very little of me."

Anger rose, fierce and hot. I couldn't help the feelings she inspired deep in my chest. She made me lose my carefully constructed control, made me feel a torrent of emotions I knew I shouldn't, but still did.

I gripped her by the chin tightly and pulled her close. She struggled, and my wound felt like it was burning, but I wanted to look into the depths of her dark eyes, wanted her to see the sincerity in mine.

"I told you to come back to the palace, you fool, because I wanted you to be *safe*."

She blinked rapidly, and I wondered if she was willing away tears. "Truly?" she asked quietly.

"Regardless that you've proven time and time again that you despise me and think my mer beneath you, I still care for you."

"I don't think your mer are beneath me."

I pierced her with a look and she sighed.

"Fine, but I am a princess. I like nice things and to be cared for. There should be no crime in that. Besides..." She chewed on her bottom lip and I wanted to take her mouth in my own. "I like Val well enough."

I'd been waiting for the moment she would be willing to admit it. I knew she had feelings for him, knew she was changing her closed minded view regarding 'servants'. I'd seen her with Anneli enough to know that the whale trainer was changing her mind where we had failed.

"You love him," I murmured.

Her whole body tensed.

"And he loves you." There was no accusation in my tone, just cold, hard fact.

She shifted almost uncomfortably. "That... that doesn't bother you?" Her head cocked to the side as she studied me like I was some fascinating new species of creature.

My hand slipped to her waist and slid down to the curve of her tail. "Why would it bother me? You are my betrothed, he is my best friend." Then I leaned forward despite my body's protests, just so I could whisper against the lobe of her ear. "I don't mind sharing."

When I pulled back, I had the satisfaction of watching her face flush brightly.

She tried to regain her composure, but her voice was hoarse when she said, "You must trust him a great deal if you're willing to share me with him."

I could tell she was inquiring, curious about our relationship. Most mer were.

"We were short on servants," I explained. "So my grandmother likes to do charity work and called for help from a local orphanage. We were children, perhaps seven or eight. He'd been sent to work in the stables, and I was escaping my grandmother's lessons." I smiled a bit at the memory. "One of the orcas got out of control and charged straight for me. I hadn't yet mastered my riding, so I just floated there as it came towards me. Then someone was pushing me out of the way of danger. I remember seeing Val's face, and I was so frightened, I got up and left without saying anything. The next day, I went back for my riding lessons. The orca bucked me off, and I fell to the silt. I heard laughter and when I looked up, he was making fun of me. No one had ever made fun of me before."

"There's just something about commoners making fun of royalty that bonds us." Odele smiled, and I knew she was speaking of Anneli. I'd heard that the female trainer had shoved Odele and promptly called her stupid.

"We've been friends ever since. I made my grandmother hire him when he left the orphanage."

"You're not as stiff as I thought you were," she teased.

"Stiff? Me?" I was offended. I wasn't stiff. Was I? I was serious, but I had to be, or else I'd never be taken seriously. I frowned and reached for the bodice of her velvet dress, tugging at the material so she fell over me. "I'll show you stiff," I grumbled, and kissed her.

She tasted like I remembered, but sweeter somehow. I was crippled with my desire for her, with my need for more. I kissed her, mouths opening together, tongues dancing and mating. I suddenly cursed my injury, knowing I'd not be able to take this all the way, but I could make it as pleasurable as possible for her.

I tore my mouth from her and kissed my way down her neck. She arched into me, groaning, her fingers digging into my shoulder, the other threading through the strands of my hair. Her nails scraping against my scalp urged me on. I wanted fast and fierce I wanted to…

I gripped her by the waist and flipped her so she was beneath me.

Gods of ice, what a stupid idea.

The pain at the brusque action suddenly had me wheezing.

"See what you've done? Iolish brute!"

She slipped from beneath me and turned me back onto the bed, pushing me gently to the cushions. White spots danced behind my closed eyelids, and the strain of the day suddenly weighed on me too heavily. I started to drift off into unconsciousness but before I succumbed completely, I felt the press of her lips against my own.

"Sleep," she urged.

And I found myself obeying.

Odele

Ytgar healed in no time, with no signs of dragon poison coursing through his veins. Soon, he was out of bed and training, and all too soon his grandmother was announcing the date she had decided for our wedding.

"Your wedding shall take place two days before our Saint Valence festival," the queen announced over breakfast.

I nearly choked on my food.

In all the commotion of the past few days, I'd forgotten all about the queen's wedding plans.

I looked over at Ytgar from across the table where he was seated. His silver eyes were shining with the heated promise of unfinished business.

"Good," he replied, tearing his gaze from mine. "I want to be wed as soon as possible."

A shiver sliced down my body.

"Great," the queen exclaimed. "We have five days to prepare!"

Five days.

The next five days were spent in a flurry of activity. Activity that I was all too used to. It reminded me of being in Thalassar, and for a second, I was pierced with guilt, as I hadn't thought of home since I'd left, hadn't missed it. I guess it had never been a true home to begin with. While in Iol, I was feeling true happiness finally and I had to admit, excitement over the wedding.

It took a few days to get my dress made, a few to practice our vows and sort out the menu. When everything was done and ready and the day arrived, I woke up feeling nervous.

My cousins came into the room hours later, along with servants and the seamstress. After I was barely able to fill my belly with the food they offered, I was bathed and scrubbed, then the seamstress began corseting me with white ribbons.

The dress was slipped over my body, a beauty of a thing that sparkled with every movement as if it had been made entirely with ice and diamonds. They'd been sewed onto sparkling white velvet and dangled like icicles swaying with the current. The bodice was decent, modest and circular, the waist cinched and the skirts heavy. She attached a long fur cloak from clips on my shoulders, letting it trail behind me tantalizingly.

My cousins helped do my hair, twisting strands of it to showcase the beauty of my face, pressing clips all around the crown of my head so it looked like I was actually wearing one. The rest of the strands were curled over my shoulder, bright against my white and blue.

"Makeup?" Jessinda asked, rummaging through the cosmetics on the vanity.

"Perhaps a little."

I was pampered, a shadow of ground mother-of-pearl brushed slightly along my eyelids to give the illusion that I sparkled as well. When they finished, they took a stroke back, and I was left staring at my lone reflection in the mirror.

I always knew I was beautiful, there was no denying it, not when I resembled my mother so greatly. But there was something different about seeing me now. Moments away from being wed to the Prince of Iol.

"You look beautiful," the seamstress offered.

I smiled ruefully. "I know." The words weren't conceited, but were said softly, confidently.

I hadn't wanted this so long ago. I would have done anything to avoid this moment. Now, everything was different. I was changed. Everything had changed.

And I was ready.

I got up.

"Let's go."

The Iolish celebrated their gods unlike Thalassarins. They had a temple dedicated to them, where the wedding ceremony would be held. I was taken there in a carriage and when I arrived at the temple, it was to find a crowd already there.

I swam out of the carriage and into the temple. There would be no father to swim me up the aisle, no one to shed tears as I tied myself to this merman forever. There had been no time to send an invitation to Maisie, and I wished I had conches left over to record this moment so she could relive it with me.

But I was alone, like I was always alone. The only difference was, I didn't feel the suffocating loneliness.

I felt ready.

When Ytgar turned and watched me swim down the aisle, my breath caught. He was decked out in a jacket of white and silver, with hints of blue embroidery here or there. He wore immaculate white gloves, and a belt over his tunic with the sheathed sword of the Isolde line at his waist. He looked like a military merman, a warrior, and at his shoulders was a long fur cloak that matched my own.

His hair was slicked away from his face and tied at the back of his neck, a single strand stubbornly clinging to the side of his cheek.

He'd never looked more beautiful.

I stopped at his side and we turned to each other, marking the beginning of the ceremony.

An hour later, we were wed, letting the strips of cloth representing the colors of our two nations slip from our grasp before he bent down and took my lips in his. I sighed against his mouth, but he pulled away too quickly, the silver in his eyes a promise of more, of much, much more later.

Later couldn't come soon enough.

Ytgar

"CONGRATULATIONS."

I didn't need to turn, but a smile touched my lips. "Thank you."

Val clapped my shoulder, and we stood like that, watching as the mer took part in the revelry that was my wedding party.

Personally, I wanted it all over. I wanted to finally have Odele alone, to finally claim her in the way we both so desperately wanted.

She'd been sending me heated glances ever since we'd left the Temple of Gods, and I could feel the need rising hotly inside of me with each passing moment.

"With all the festivities and prep, I never got to thank you for what you did for me with that dragon."

I cut him a glare. "Call us even for the many times you have risked your own life for mine. Now forget it."

He heaved a breath. "That's the thing, I can't. I owe you my life. I owe you everything. You've given me more than I deserve, and more still." His eyes went to Odele where she was seated with Anneli—who wore a pretty dress in silver-gray to match her hair and tail—laughing over a cup of frothy Iolish ale.

"I'm not giving her to you," I reminded him gently. "It's her decision. She loves you. She confessed as much."

I could almost feel his lips quirk up into a smile. "Did she?"

"In her way, yes. She is as willing to be with us as we are with her."

His body seemed to tense at the revelation, as if it hadn't been all but obvious since the first moment, since he was pretending to be me.

I sighed and turned to my friend. To the one mer in the whole kingdom who had dared to laugh at me when no one else would. The one who saw me, who kept me from drowning on air when the pressure and helplessness became too much. He was so good at seeing the good in others.

I just wished he saw the good in himself.

"I wonder when you'll finally realize how worthy you truly are of her," I murmured, squeezing his shoulder tightly. As if the simplicity of that action could convey everything I was feeling. Could convey the truth through my eyes, so that he would finally see. "When you'll finally see how much you are worth."

I clapped him once on the back and turned, making my way over to my wife.

Wife. So strange that I could now call her that, stranger still, she hadn't tried to swim away at all. It still brought an annoyed twitch to my lips to think of all those times she'd tried to flee before. I'd bring her back each time, no matter what, I'd always bring her back. From the dead if I had to. I'd knock on the god of death's door and barrel through just to find her.

"Princess," I greeted with a half smile. I let my gaze rake over her body, stopping at the swells of her bodice, up the arch of her neck, to the flush on her cheeks. Her dark eyes heated when they met mine. We stared, and my own eyes pierced hers, asking that silent question I didn't need to voice aloud. *Are you ready?*

She gave me a small, almost imperceptible nod.

"*Aaand,* that's my cue to leave." Anneli squeezed my shoulder as she swept past me in a tuft of velvet and fur.

I held my hand out to my wife and counted the heartbeats.

One.

Two.

She placed her palm on mine and I closed my fingers around it.

I smiled. "Let's go home."

Valmundur

She was finally happy.

The knowledge made my chest ache, not with sorrow, but with happiness. I knew she had something in her all along. I'd caught glimpses of it, hidden behind that mask of frivolity, anger and overlaying hurt. It had taken that small nudge to bring out what I knew she was capable of. What I'd known all along.

She was worthy, she always had been.

I watched as Ytgar swept her up gallantly into his arms, the action surprising and almost out of character for him. But she made him happy as well, whether or not he denied it. I knew the truth. I was good at catching the truth.

Except maybe when it really mattered.

I looked down at my hands once they disappeared. They were the calloused hands of a workmer's. There was nothing gentle about them. They were hands that had seen hardships, that had shoveled silt and tamed orcas. There was an invisible trace of blood here, of enemies I had killed in the name of my prince, of our kingdom. I had killed dragons, creatures, and mer. These were the hands of an orphan, of a bastard with no name.

Ingen.

No one.

The name orphans are given when they're dumped on doorsteps, with no clue who sired them. And I must have had a sire, a father, a mother. I hadn't been birthed magically from nothing. And my identity had been stripped from me—if I'd ever had an identity at all—and I'd been given one anew.

Valmundur Ignen.

No one of importance.

And yet, I had scraped my way to the top to prove myself worthy, to the prince, my friend. And it was thanks to him I was still alive and not begging for scraps of raw fish in a gutter somewhere. He didn't realize what a gift this life was, what it meant to me, and all that he was offering to a poor mer who only wanted better.

I was unworthy of such riches and kindness, wasn't I? Was I? *Am I?*

The princess had fallen in love with me, and I with her. That had to mean something, right? Sometimes you could scrape the grime off your body to reveal the clean layers underneath. I saw it often enough in others, but it was harder to see it in myself.

There had to be someone worthwhile beneath the silt, the hardships, the blood.

I just needed to peel back the layers to find it.

"The waters are filled with love and it's sickening."

Anneli came up beside me and took a swig of her ale before slamming the cup back down on the tray of a passing waiter.

If there was anyone who understood what it meant to be a bastard, it was her. The difference was that Anneli knew who her parents were, and didn't care. She was wholly herself and didn't apologize for it. She didn't feel unclean, didn't see herself as any less.

Not that she ever could be when she was the bastard daughter of the former Prince Lohki Neves Isolde of Iol, and Ytgar's elder sister. It was a carefully kept secret, one that no one was to know, not even Ytgar. If the truth came out, the queen would likely see her murdered to keep an immaculate image on the Isolde family name.

But a bastard was still a bastard, and no one understood me more than she.

"The bride and groom will be occupied for a while," she commented.

"Yup."

She cast me a long side look. "Does that bother you?"

I knew she was curious about the state of our relationship, knew she wondered if Ytgar and I were going to share the princess. It was a slightly unconventional situation, but did it matter? When Odele loved, she loved fiercely, with her entire soul, and whoever was lucky enough to be on the receiving end of that… well…

"Not at all." I smiled widely.

Because Odele loved me, too. And I loved her, and I loved Ytgar. We loved each other.

And as long as I had that, the most precious gift, then, gods of ice, I might be worthy after all.

My things had been moved from my room and into a new one along with Ytgar's. It was a temporary wedding suite until the queen officially gifted us our own palace, apparently. I didn't complain.

Not when Ytgar swept me through the doors, closing them with a kick of his tail behind him, and made his way to the bed.

He dropped me onto the edge of the bed with a smirk, his big frame looming over me. It should have been menacing, I should have been frightened, nervous, but all I felt was anticipation. I'd been waiting for the heated glances he'd sent me all day to become something more. To become physical instead of fantasy.

I wanted him to touch me like he had so many nights ago when I'd thought him to be Val and he'd caught me fleeing.

I wanted the heights of that pleasure. And I wanted to give it to him in turn.

My fingertips itched to reach for him, to run my palms down his chest. They said that foreplay was the best way to build up that anticipation, but we were already there, had arrived with nothing more than exchanged looks throughout the day, with a promise of what was to come right here. Right now.

"You look beautiful," he whispered, expression serious. I couldn't recall a time I ever saw him genuinely smile or laugh. His face was always etched in the gravest of lines, like he had burdens hovering on his wide shoulders that even with his massive build, he couldn't carry. I was never one to take on other mer's problems or responsibilities. But he was mine now, and I was his. I might not know a way to mention it, perhaps we didn't know how to talk to each other yet, but I could unburden him with this.

I placed my palm over his chest, feeling the beating of his heart. It was a steady pounding, so different from my own. Solid, reliable. My fingers closed around the material of his jacket.

His hand came down over mine, pressing my palm deeper into his chest like he wanted to consume every aspect of me with his touch and with his silver-white eyes.

"You aren't nervous," I commented, feeling my tongue thick with emotion. I swallowed and tried to control my trembling to match his stillness.

His silver brows rose. "Are you?"

Was I? My heart was beating rather fast, but…

"No," I replied honestly.

His lips curled sensually, and his hand went from grabbing my wrist to sliding down the length of my arm. He was a prince of an ice kingdom, and yet he trailed nothing but heat in his wake. His fingers met my shoulders, slid over to my neck where his thumb caressed my throat in slow, gentle movements. He pushed aside a lock of my purple hair and stared at the spot where my pulse beat, at the purple gills hidden below my ears.

He moved to my shoulders once more and, in one deft movement, he was undoing the clips that tethered the long fur cloak to my dress. It slid sinuously down my back. I felt lighter without it, but still too heavy. I wanted him to divest me of everything, but he seemed bent on a slow seduction. As if he had all the time in the world for this.

For me.

"When I saw you swim down that aisle…" He paused, breath catching as his fingers roved over the flesh of my exposed skin, my collarbone and lower down, to the top of my bodice.

"Yes?" The word came out a breathless rasp.

He looked me in the eyes, his white eyes flaring dark silver with desire and honesty in equal measure. "My heart almost stopped."

His hands cupped my sides, dangerously close to my breasts. They felt full with the need for his touch, but he didn't give me my request, even as I arched back so he could. His palms slid down my sides to my waist where he slowly began unhooking small button after small button, following the trail around my hips and up my back where his hands stayed.

"You looked so beautiful." The top loosened a fraction. He paused. "But you know that, don't you?" He eased forward then, so close that our mouths were centimeters apart, so I could see his every fine, elegant angle, the high cheekbones, each individual lash framing bright eyes and lips, that were tantalizingly close to kissing me. "You know you're beautiful."

"Yes," I gasped, leaning forward, silently begging him to take my mouth.

He leaned back, though, and pulled at the sleeves of the dress, letting it slip over my body and fall to my waist.

His eyes flared as he took in my corset. A tight thing with an abundance of white ribbons laced all around.

I hated the seamstress for this frivolity so much right now.

Ytgar knelt before me, holding me by the waist. "Lift your hips for me, love," he growled, his voice a delicious purr. I braced my hands on the cushions and obeyed, as he hooked his fingers into the dress and pulled it from me until it was a sparkling heap on the floor.

Until I was clad in nothing but my corset, a taffeta of lace attached at the waist, trailing down to cover my tail.

His hands slid up my body. It was amazing what he could accomplish with nothing but the warm feel of his palms through thin material. His fingers dug into my waist and he caught me entirely off guard as he suddenly flipped me so my front side pressed into the cushions.

I gasped at the suddenness of it and shivered when his body covered mine from behind. He pressed against me, chest to back, every button and scrape of material from his jacket abrading my skin in the best of ways. He leaned over me. I felt the fan of his breath against the back of my neck and then closer to my ear.

"Feel what you do to me," he urged, pressing his hips into me. "Feel what you've always done to me, love." He ground into me harder, and I felt it, felt the length of his arousal through his tunic, pressing up against my lower back, causing my whole body to shudder.

His lips went to my neck, pressing a kiss there that nearly caused me to collapse on the spot. Then his hands were at the edges of lace ribbons and he began pulling through the maze of them with practiced ease. He had to lean back to do it, and when he finished, he pushed the material aside to expose my back to the cold. I was instantly warmed when his lips found my spine, gliding a pathway from the waist up with kisses, the feel of his tongue.

His kisses continued, to the back of my neck, along the sharp edge of my jaw. His arm snaked around me to grip my chin and turn my face.

"I want you," he whispered against my mouth. He seemed to be searching for permission.

Gladly, I gave it.

"Then take me."

His mouth came over mine. That first taste of his lips was an aphrodisiac, and I was drunk on him. My mouth opened and his tongue thrust inside, devouring, claiming. I let him take the lead. For now, I would let him guide me to the heights of pleasure.

While his mouth plundered, his hips thrust against me, desperate and ready. I wanted him, hard and fast. I wasn't afraid, but eager. I twisted against his heavy weight, tearing my mouth from his reluctantly.

"Now," I commanded. "I need you now."

"So demanding," he muttered and then turned me once again. "But I rule here, Princess." He yanked the corset from me, throwing it over his shoulder in a heap of tattered material. I gasped as he bent and took a taut nipple in his mouth. The feel of the warmth of his mouth around my skin nearly lifted me off the bed in ecstasy.

"Gods," I cried out, gripping his shoulders. Too much, he was wearing too much. It wasn't fair. I clawed at his clothes even as his ministrations continued and then traveled down... down...

His lips were on my stomach, fingers touching the scattering of purple scales.

"I want to taste you again." His tongue dipped into my belly button and then went lower to where the V of my hips met my scales, to that sweet spot in the center of me that opened and was ready for our joining.

My hips jerked against him. "Take me," I cried. I wanted him, needed him with a desperation that was unlike me. I didn't care. He was making me feel, and that was all that mattered.

Then his tongue dipped inside of me and I lost all thoughts completely. I screamed, hips coming off the cushions. He held me steady by the hips, diving in and out, tongue licking and swirling, bringing me back to that familiar edge with the promise of a fall. I was panting and heaving, desperate for it. My whole body was wound tight, I was crying his name, cursing him in Thalassarin and Iolish, wanting what he had selfishly denied me last time…

And I fell.

I spiraled out of control down that abyss and screamed. I came off of the bed, gripping him tightly by the shoulders as a torrent of emotions raged a maelstrom inside me. When the feelings ebbed, I dropped to the bed again, my limbs weak, body tingling, wanting more.

Ytgar leaned up, a triumphant smile on his face.

I frowned at it just before a smile of my own curled my lips.

"It's my turn now." I grabbed him by the shoulders and, with all the strength I possessed, flipped him—though I was sure he let me do it—so that I was on top.

"I am not one of your beasts," I told him menacingly, fingers tearing at the lapels of his jacket, sending buttons swirling through the water around us. I pushed the material from his shoulders and he lifted up to hurry it along, pulling it from his arms until he was clad in nothing but his tunic. "You cannot tame me and you are not my keeper." I lifted the hem of his tunic up, pulling it over his shoulders until he was as naked as I.

My gaze roamed over the lines and shadows of his body, dark muscles that rippled down his chest and abdomen. Proof of his prowess, of his strength. He was so massively built, I should have been intimidated.

I felt empowered.

My gaze went lower, caught on the length of his erection waiting for me. I knew I could bring him pleasure with my mouth just as he brought me to that peak, but then the game would be over all too soon. I wanted him to suffer. I wanted him to be brought to heel. I wanted to dominate him like he'd tried to dominate me.

Only, I'd succeed.

I let my finger drop to his length and slowly, sensuously, I trailed the tip of my nail up the side of him, stopping at the tip, feeling his heat, relishing in the shudder his powerful body gave.

I'd never done this before, any of this, but my imagination was a vast, vast place, and I could only imagine. I knew what I wanted to do to him, and his body's reactions would guide me in the right direction.

I wrapped my tail around his, keeping him pinned to the bed. I knew he could easily overpower me, but he was letting me take the lead. He was letting me dominate him.

"Do you want me?" I asked, sinking myself into him, letting the very tip of him touch my entrance. He groaned, head falling to the cushions.

I'd never seen him look so discomposed. I had the power here. I was the boss. I was the *queen.*

"Every inch," he rasped, his fingers scraping up my sides. "Come to me and let me show you paradise."

My palms braced over his chest as I slowly sunk into him, inch by beautiful inch, I let him fill me and gasped at the penetrating sensation. It felt… it felt like paradise.

My fingers dug into his skin, raking across his chest, traveling down to the flesh of his scar. I was careful to avoid it, but the sight of it gave me pause, a brief pause that to him must have felt like an hour.

His hands grasped my hips, and he slid me up and down his length, causing a delightful friction between us. I threw my head back and gasped.

"Let me teach you," he urged, moving our bodies together. Our hips met, flesh for flesh, as we moved in a synchronized rhythm. He touched something inside me, pressed against it with every slow, gentle stroke. His every muscle was taut with strain, the cords on his neck standing out against his skin. Like this pained him as much as it did me.

So I moved faster with my hands braced against his skin. I moved, finding my own rhythm until I felt it, felt that sensation building up inside of me once more, climbing higher and higher…

I ground down against him and spiraled, letting myself go to the shuddering exploding inside me. Two-legger stars danced behind my eyes as it overwhelmed me.

Ytgar cried out at the same moment I did, gripping me tighter, grinding me up and down, up and down at a faster pace. His touch was rough and so, so welcome.

I fell into a boneless heap against his chest, nose buried into the crook where his neck met his shoulder. Our breaths mingled, and I felt the frantic pounding of my heart. Wait, that was his, mingling with my own, pressing against each other in a battle for dominance.

I pressed a tentative kiss to his collarbone.

In a movement that was so tender, he pushed aside the hair from my shoulder, wrapping an arm around me to pull me close, fingers trailing patterns and drawings against my shoulder.

I placed my palm against his chest and propped my chin up on it to look at him, finding him observing me with a smile on his face.

"Don't look so smug." I frowned.

He chuckled and leaned up to press a kiss against my nose.

"Don't look so grumpy. It's not exactly confidence inspiring."

I snorted. "As if you have a problem with confidence."

His expression seemed to shutter before he tried to mask it behind stoic lines. But I saw it and wondered.

He merely said, "Everyone has insecurities, Princess."

"And what are yours?"

He was quiet, as if contemplating what exactly he should tell me. I tried not to let it bother me, when I'd been the same way before. But I wanted to know. Genuinely, truly.

"Helplessness," he replied. At my inquiring look, he elaborated. "I have no power and I want it. Not for myself, but to help the mer of my kingdom. They need someone who is willing to stick up for them, to help them. I want to be that mer, and if not me, then I will find someone else, because the Iolish deserve better lives, and I am helpless to give them what they deserve."

That was Maisie's fear as well, when she'd been pretending to be me. A fear I couldn't relate to, but could now somehow understand. I traced a pattern with my nail against his skin. I didn't know what to say, didn't believe I had the ability to help him change anything. I was as useless as he was. As useless here as I was in Thalassar. Like him, I was not respected, not cared for, and had little power to help.

"For what it's worth," I murmured, pressing a kiss just over the rapid beating of his heart. "I think you'd make a great ruler."

His smile was genuine and nearly heart stopping. His fingers slid down to my waist and adjusted me comfortably. I realized we were still joined together, as close as any two mer could ever be. His hips lifted a fraction, and I smiled.

I could not unburden his troubles, his worries, but at least I could gift him with this.

"Enough talking." I pressed a finger to his lips. "I want to know what other things you can show me." I ground against him and he laughed, grabbing me and flipping me so I was beneath him.

And we made love and forgot our troubles.

Again.

And again.

And again.

"What is a Saint Valence day festival?" I asked.

"Don't you celebrate your gods in Thalassar?" Anneli replied.

I shrugged. "My kingdom isn't exactly religious…"

"Valence day is a celebration of the ice god of love. The stories go that the God Valence fell in love with the goddess of the moon, but he was stuck in the icy seas and she in the sky. He made a deal with the God of gods and beseeched that he open a bridge between worlds so they could meet and he could profess his love. The God of gods does not give in to demands, but he felt sorry for Valence, and so he gave him one day only. On this day, Valence fashioned a beautiful gift of ice for the goddess of the moon and met her on the bridge, where he gave her his gift and declared his love, and she promptly rejected him."

"Well, that sounds depressing."

Anneli shrugged. "It's a celebration of honesty. It's for mer to be honest with themselves and their feelings of love and friendships. There's a festival and a gift exchange. You can profess your love to whoever you want and if they give you a gift, it is in acceptance. If they don't, it's a rejection. Some mer probably end up heartbroken at the end of the night, but it's better than bottling up their feelings forever."

I contemplated this. I supposed she was right. It didn't really matter what Valence day was; I was just excited to celebrate a Iolish holiday, to learn more about the place I now called my home.

"Are you going to give a gift?" I asked curiously, pressing my fist into my chin as I leaned over the stable fence.

She shook her head. "Nah, there's no one in my life I love like that. Probably just give some gifts to friends."

A gift exchange festival… I enjoyed the fancy and the frivolous, and the festival was tomorrow.

I got up. "I'm going to go prepare my gifts," I said by way of goodbye. I barely caught sight of her smirk and her wave before I was turning around and rushing to the palace.

The day of the festival arrived and my cousins came in to dress me. I usually enjoyed dressing myself, but I allowed it. They filled the silence with excited chatter about the festival. They'd been about as delighted as I was when we first came here, which was not a lot, but now we were all excited about our new lives. There was just something about the ice kingdom that drew a mer in, if you were willing to look past the bitter cold. At least they made up for that in style.

Today I wore a dress of frost blue, the same color as Val's eyes, the upper bodice and sleeves made of a slick, soft velvet, embroidered with the images of silver snowflakes and winter animals, like polar bears, penguins, foxes, and orcas. The neckline was high, it surrounded my neck with silver-gray fur, the same stitched fur at the ends of both of my sleeves and at the waist, a fur that spread down my tail to keep me warm. A silver and gold belt tightened at my waist, highlighting the soft dip of my curves, even through the material.

Jessinda, Scarlet, and Silviya all exchanged conspiratorial glances. I frowned at them in the reflection of the mirror.

"What's going on?" I demanded.

Jessinda bobbed up and down in the water giddily. "We have gifts for you."

They seemed to produce said gifts from nowhere. One by one, they gave them to me.

Jessinda handed me a pair of soft silk gloves with pearl buttons at the wrists. I smiled as I slipped them on, wishing with everything I had that I could feel them over the entirety of my hands, instead of just my palms.

Silviya went next, placing a crown on my head. A dainty little thing made of wire and glass and blue gems that sparkled and matched my dress. I knew without asking that she'd made it herself.

Finally Scarlet gave me her gift. A pair of earrings, one silver and one blue. Shades that matched the exact color of Ytgar and Val's eyes.

I slipped them on.

My eyes filled with tears I didn't shed. Instead, I lifted my arms, and they flocked to me, enveloping me in a group hug.

"I do love you mers," I whispered through the tightness in my throat.

"Aww, and we love you, too."

Even though we fought, argued, backstabbed, and overall seemed like we despised each other, I knew it was just a part of our royal lives. In reality, I'd never trade these mer. For anyone, or anything.

Even for all the diamonds in the world.

Iol was alive with the festivities, I had never seen a kingdom so excited to celebrate love before. Even the queen was smiling and in a good mood.

The palace gates were open to all, though most of the mer went out to celebrate on the streets. There were parades, dancing and music, and today everyone was a friendly face. There was a theatre production telling the story of the god Valence, and mer handed out masquerade masks with the faces of their gods. The mer accepted them, and soon everywhere you turned, there were beautiful masks staring back at you.

I swam through the streets with my cousins, as it was the first time I'd actually been anywhere other than the palace or the stables. We looped arms, passing vendors in their little stalls, observing and laughing.

This place breathed life and color, fun and adventure. It was home.

Two figures floated in our path, stopping us. They both wore masks. The bigger merman of the two wore the mask of the God of gods, while the other wore the tragic face of the god Valence.

"Princess," the Valence masked merman bowed with a flourish.

They both wore rich clothes and furs, and though they were devoid of the extravagant weaponry that identified them, I'd recognize Ytgar and Val anywhere.

Ytgar did the same, though his bow was much more elegant. He took my outstretched hand, but instead of pressing a kiss to the backs of my knuckles, he turned my hand over and kissed the center of my palm.

I felt the warmth of his lips down to my fins.

My cousins dispersed discreetly and, as soon as they were gone, Ytgar and Val straightened, pulling their masks off in synchronized movements.

"You chased off my companions with your innuendos," I admonished my husband, though I did so with a smile on my face.

"The prince is a brute," Val chuckled. "But I shall make it up to you with better company and by buying you a *rakaouris.*" He placed his hand on my lower back and guided me towards one of the vendors.

"What's a *rakaouris?*"

"Only the most delicious dessert known to mer." We stopped and Val ordered three.

Rakaouris were shaved ice in a cup, topped with a liquid flavoring of your choice. I chose a creamy one that tasted like vanilla seeds, with sprinkled jelly bubbles on top that burst in my mouth with each bite. I groaned at the explosion of flavors on my tongue.

"I *looove* dessert," I moaned.

When I looked up, it was to find both Val and Ytgar ignoring their own *rakaouris* and staring at me, more specifically, my mouth. To tease, I let my tongue dart across my lower lip. Their eyes flared with twin desire.

"Really, the two of you are so easily readable."

"Hey, we aren't the ones orgasming over shaved ice." Val scooped up some with his spoon and shoved it into his mouth. He obviously didn't appreciate the finer tastes in life or, at least, he didn't show it.

We finished our *rakaouris* and deposited the trash in nearby fishnets and wandered around a bit more. Val gave me my promised tour of the city and when we reached their plaza, I couldn't help but gape.

We hadn't passed through here when we came from Draconi. I would have remembered it. I would have remembered the statues.

Row upon row of them, adjacent to each other to frame a path that mer could swim through. I stopped in front of every single one.

The statues were carved of ice as thick and as clear as glass, and in such intricate detail, it all looked so real. We passed the likeness of a polar bear raising its paw to attack, of a mother and her cub, a school of penguins, orcas, blue whales, foxes, and wolves. There were creatures, both two-legger and mer alike, in all sorts of positions, there were even some of the more mythical ones like frost giants and ice trolls, sea goblins and creatures with the upper body of unicorns and the lower bodies of fish.

I was staring at a particularly nice statue of a baby orca when Val came up close behind me, his chest brushing against my back. He bent down, lips grazing the lobe of my ear. "I told you Iol was better."

I turned slowly, letting my gloved hands slide up his chest to hook around the back of his neck. "You did, didn't you? I've never known a mer more full of himself than you."

His arms encircled my waist, and he pulled me up so our faces were level with each other, the tips of our noses touching, our mouths close enough for a kiss.

"I have a present for you," he whispered against my cheek. "One I'd like to give you in private." The purred words curled down the length of my spine, making my fins stand on edge. I liked what he implied very much.

"I have a gift for you, too," I whispered, equally seductively.

He nodded, nostrils flaring. He set me back to rights and grabbed my wrist, tugging me alongside him.

"Wait!" I stopped, turning to Ytgar. He was watching us with a smile pulling at his lips.

"Go," he urged. "I'll be here when you get back."

I shook Val's hold on me lightly and went over to my husband. I stood up on my fins and pressed a kiss to his lips. "I have a gift for you as well," I said.

His eyebrows rose. "Oh?"

I reached into the pocket of my fur skirts—they were big pockets—and pulled out a gift that Silviya helped me make.

"Bend down," I ordered. He obeyed and slowly, ritualistically, I placed a crown of ice and steel upon my husband's head. "Rise," I told him. He did, and I saw the emotions fracture across his face. "You are royalty," I said. "And you have the power, if you're brave enough to take it."

I swore the big warrior's eyes glossed over with tears. He said nothing, but I could make out the thumping of his heart, and knew words were unnecessary when he bent down and pressed a fast, yet fierce kiss to my mouth.

"I have a gift for you too." He reached into his own pocket and pulled out a small closed clam shell made of ice. His fingers pried it open and revealed a ring inside. I stared at it, a simple gold band with a stone made of ice in its center, and stamped inside, the Isolde crest of an orca. "I never proposed properly, and this is a family heirloom. It belongs to you now." He took it out and placed it on my finger. It was a perfect fit. "Go," he urged, pushing me gently by the shoulders. "Valmundur awaits."

Nothing else, no other words, mattered. They weren't necessary at all. This meant so much more. It was acceptance, wholly and absolutely. Symbols. Of what he was to me and what I was to him.

It was love.

Plain and simple.

Love.

My palms felt warm with nervousness as I led Odele away from the busier parts of the city, away from the music of revelry and into the quiet solitude of ice caves. They were a little hollow near the walls that surrounded the kingdom that you could swim up to. Inside there was a cove that led up to two-legger land, with a warm waterfall that rushed into the small pool and heated the waters.

We breached the surface, holding our breath against the onslaught of warm air. She smiled mischievously at me and swam to the edge of the cove and slid up onto the surface of ice.

Mer could withstand a few breaths of air, but after a while, it would make us lightheaded. I was starting to feel the effects. Or maybe that was just because of Odele. Because her hair clung to her skin and droplets of water slid down her body.

She looked around the cove. Sound echoed strangely in two-legger air, so I heard the repetitive, sonopherous *drip drip drip* of the water slipping from her body onto ice and the quiet, slow rush of the waterfall.

"This is amazing," she whispered. The words even came out strange, harsh and clipped, instead of musical, like a song.

We stayed like that for a few more moments before neither of us could stand the air anymore and dove back under the waters.

"I promised you a tour, didn't I?" I grinned, taking in her joyous expression.

"You promised me we could document our adventure together…" Her voice grew slightly sad. "But every single conch broke."

My heart plummeted. This hadn't been the turn I wanted the conversation to take. The space between us suddenly seemed so vast, and I closed it with a few strokes of my tail, reaching for her hand, tilting her chin up so she could meet my eyes.

"I should have told you," I whispered, emotion catching in the lilt of my voice. "I should have told you that the conches break in icy waters."

Her lip trembled, but she put up a brave facade. It hurt her more than she'd show, and it made me feel guilty. I didn't want that expression on her face at all.

I reached into the pocket of my cloak. "I know you've received a lot of jewelry today." I pulled out her gift. I hadn't wrapped it or placed it in a fancy shell, but my gift was genuine just the same. "Would you care for one more piece?"

I had worked on it for hours, scraping away at the ice, smoothing out every curve, hollowing it so it looked perfect. It was small and less ostentatious. No jewels decorated it, save for the silver chain wrapped around a small loop.

She took the glass conch shell from my hands, fingers sliding over it. She looked up at me, and a tear fell from the corner of her eye. "You made this?"

Heat rose to my cheeks. "I just wanted you to have a conch that wouldn't fall apart. It's made from magical Iolish ice, so it will never melt, no matter how far south you go."

She held it up with her thumb and forefinger, peeking into the hole. "Does it record?"

My heart plummeted at the question. "No," I replied tensely. "I didn't know how to get it to do that."

She stared at it a moment longer before handing it back to me by the chain. My heart nearly stopped. Was this my rejection? I held it close as she began digging into her own pocket.

"I have a gift for you, too." She pulled out rolled up kelp parchments and outstretched her arm, handing them to me. I took them, unrolled them, and looked at the neat scrawl there in Iolish. It was an outline, detailed, of our adventures together.

"Just because the conches broke, didn't mean the adventures had to stop. I want you to add your version to this Iolish copy."

I let out a breath of laughter and tucked the parchments into my cloak. "I love it."

She pursed her lips. "You better." Then she was swiping at her long hair, pulling it over one shoulder and turning around, exposing the back of her neck. "Put it on me," she commanded.

My hands trembled slightly as I undid the clasp and wrapped it gently around her throat, securing it. My hands paused where they were, fingertips hovering near her fur collar. I longed to see skin, wanted to feel her warmth, touch her, kiss her.

Slowly, she turned around, pressing herself closer to me. I blinked, once, twice, and then she was leaning up and capturing my mouth in hers.

"I love it," she whispered against my lips.

And just like that, it was like a current swept me up in the maelstrom. I pulled her close, lifting her by the waist so her breasts crushed against my chest. I recaptured her mouth. It was a vicious storm. It was flirtation and dreams accomplished. It was desire incarnate. It was the fragmentation of every single doubt falling into an abyss, replaced with one thing only. Hope.

I remembered the taste of her mouth so vividly, remembered what it felt like to tease and to explore. But this time, she gripped for me with equal fervor, her nails pushing impatiently at my cloak until it fell from my shoulders and sunk to the ground below.

I nipped and sucked, my teeth gripping at her lower lip, causing a groan to emanate from deep in her throat, a sound that caused pleasure to ripple through my entire body.

I tore away from her long enough to ask, "Are you sure you want this, beauty mine?" I was breathless, and so was she. "Because once I start, I won't stop until I make you mine."

Her reply was quick and full of surety. "I want you," she said. "I want this."

It was all I needed to hear.

I kissed her again, slowly, desperately, roughly. My hands moved across the expanse of her curves, pulling hooks and tugging strings until her bodice loosened. With a quick tug, the dress slid over her skin and into a heap with my cloak. I left her in nothing but her corset with the stitched skirt.

I groaned as I began tugging at the strings from behind. "Stop wearing these," I pleaded, getting the last of it undone and tearing it from her body until she was naked before me.

I began quick work of divesting myself of my own clothing until we were both exposed, bare, nearly as close as two mer could ever be. We reached for one another at the same time. I grabbed her hips as she grabbed my shoulders.

This was rushed, it was desperation, primal need in its rawest form. There was no going slow with us, no time for steady seduction. It was rough, our need for each other, as if we'd sampled the other before and were desperate for that fix. She was an addiction. A drug. She was an impossibility, as impossible as the secrets whispered by tides, or heat in the northern waters, and I had to do all I could to keep her in my grasp, lest I find her a shadow, a phantom of my own fantasies.

But she was here. She was real, and her mouth was pressing kisses to my neck, her tongue was trailing against my skin. Too hot, my blood boiled. I wanted her, desperately.

"Now," I growled. She gasped as I thrust inside her to the hilt. Groaning, she dropped her head to my shoulder, pressing tighter against me.

I thrust up, her body slick and rising against mine. It was savage. In this moment, I became the beast she always believed me to be. Each thrust of my hips against her body was accompanied by a rasping gasp escaping her lips, followed by her nails raking against my shoulders, and the begging words I longed to hear.

"Don't stop, don't stop."

I didn't, couldn't. She unleashed something inside of me. Some primal instinct that wanted to dominate and take everything she was offering. So I took, and I took, hands and body rough against her until she reached the point of no return. Until she fragmented like ice in my arms and fell apart. Even then, I moved harder. I cried her name, bit the crook of her neck and moved until she shattered all over again and I followed her into the depths.

We sank slowly to the seafloor onto the same heap as our clothes. I held her close, pressing her face into the crook of my shoulder. Our breaths mingled, the beating of our hearts a singular rhythm in tune, one with the other.

I pressed a kiss to her temple and dared to say the words I'd wanted to since I first met the real her.

"I love you."

Her breath hitched and her reply echoed in the waters around me. "And I, you."

And we clung to each other, body against body, heartbeat against heartbeat.

And the singular truth that united us like the invisible threads of fate.

Love.

Odele

WE DRESSED SLOWLY. I almost didn't want to leave, not when this place was so peaceful, so warm even without the heavy outfits we wore. When everything was secured and in place, I smiled at Val, still feeling the heated pressure of his touch against my skin like phantasm hands of a memory.

A very delicious memory.

"We should go," Val suggested with a bit of reluctance in his voice, too.

"I want to look once more." This place would forever be branded into my memories. In my mind, it became our place. Something that would stay with us forever.

He smiled, and I gave a kick of my tail, going all the way to the top to that little cove that led to two-legger land. Of warm hot springs and icy surfaces. My head breached the surface.

And I came face to face with a polar bear.

I froze, fear rooting me right where I was.

The beast blinked at me, taking me in. Then in one moment, its lip curled away to reveal sharp, vicious teeth. It roared, blowing, hot wet breath against my face. I screamed as a massive paw reached out to swipe at me.

I ducked, but the claw still snagged against my hair and yanked. I screamed, pulling myself away with as much strength I could muster, tearing hairs from my scalp in the process.

I swam down, tears blinding my vision and collided with Val's body. He tugged me to him and the roar of the creature followed us as we tried to make our escape. But the bear followed. Its powerful white body pushed through the water with a vengeance, matching our own speed. It tore after us even as we left the cove and tore through Iolish waters.

There were no guards here; everyone was at the festivities and we were a ways away from them. Too far to be saved, left in open waters with nothing but silt and snow.

Fear, blood curdling and vicious, ripped through me like a blade of ice. We would die here, and there was nothing I could do about it. We had no weapons, were free of them on this day that was supposed to be about love and joy. I squeezed Val's hand in my own, projecting my fear, my final goodbye.

And then he let go and shoved me. "Go!" he urged. "Save yourself!"

My heart tore into pieces. "I—I can't leave you."

He growled at me, every bit the vicious Iolish warrior he professed to be. I saw regret there, but there was no fear at all. Just the desire to protect. To make this sacrifice.

Val shouted one last time before he whirled and let out a battle cry that shook the foundation of the waters. He came face to face with the bear, raising his fists as if ready for battle.

He'd told me to leave, but how could I? How could I leave him there to face this danger all alone? I couldn't. I was selfish, I was spoiled, and cared more for myself than others most times. But at this moment, I saw him lift his sword in the halls of Thalassar, the sword of Iolish royalty, and stab it through the monster who had murdered my family.

For me.

I was many things, but a coward was not one of them. And I'd not leave Val to face this alone.

In a split second, I made my choice. I tore the crown from my head and threw it with all of my might, distracting the beast as it bounded against its nose. The bear blinked and turned to me, raging, it screeched, causing a swarm of bubbles to escape in front of it.

It gave Val just enough time to locate a weapon on the ground and get up, preparing for a vicious swing to its jaw…

The polar bear turned and darted away.

My breaths came out in heaves as I blinked at the spot it had just vacated.

Val cursed and dropped the makeshift weapon and whirled, rushing to me. He pulled me against him, anger palpitating off of him in waves.

He grabbed my face in his hands and shouted. "I told you to leave!"

I grasped for him, I'd fall apart otherwise. "I couldn't leave you," I gasped, and then the tears poured. They swarmed out of me as the fear finally registered. I'd been close to losing him, too close, and it hit me like the impact of an orca's body. Like for a moment, I imagined what it would have been like if things had gone differently. What it would have been like to watch someone else in my life that I loved ripped away from me? "You could've died." I gripped him by the cloak, feeling that he was real, that he wasn't hurt.

Val let out a string of curses and pulled me to his chest. "It was my fault," he hissed. "I should've known better. I shouldn't have taken you there. I—I can't lose you."

"And I can't lose you, either." I sniffled, pulled away. "Why did it leave?"

Val shrugged. "Something must have scared it off."

I nodded. "We should hurry back, before something worse comes after us."

"I don't know if there's anything worse than a polar bear, honestly."

We turned and saw for ourselves just how wrong that statement was.

It was the movement of silt and snow rising and falling in crisp clumps and grains. Rising to take on the form of something much, much worse.

A scaled body loomed over us, long neck curved down, obsidian eyes glaring, lips pulled back into a snarl. Massive leathery wings spread out behind it and the dragon stretched out its neck, and it screeched.

Val grabbed my hand and pulled me aside just as the dragon struck.

"Swim!" he screamed.

I didn't need to be told twice.

We swam a fast as our fins could carry us, even as the shadow of the beast loomed behind us and swooped low in the water, taking a swipe that Val dodged, pulling me with him. We fell into the silt, Val cradling me in his arms to take most of the blow.

I squeezed my eyes shut and waited for the end.

But it never came.

The dragon swooped over us and shot ahead with blinding speed.

Straight to the capital of Iol.

We swam as fast as we could to the city. To warn them. But fast wasn't fast enough, and we were too late. As we neared, the sounds of music and revelry quickly became the sounds of screams and death.

"We're too late," I gasped as we neared. Thunderous shrieks, the sound of cries and glass shattering, of buildings of ice and steel crumbling into skeletal structures. Terror and violence as the dragon tore through the city with a vengeance no one could fathom.

"I have to go and help," Val said breathlessly. "The warriors will be gathering and preparing the orcas and their weapons. I have to help."

I tugged at his sleeve. "Let me go with you."

He looked torn between telling me to hide and wanting to keep me close. If he told me to hide, I'd follow. I'd always follow.

"Stay close to me."

And then he took my hand.

The city was in a chaos of destruction and blood. Of crumbling ice and protruding steel. It was a cacophony of cries and screams of terror and pain. Wherever we turned, children cried for their mothers, mer cried for their friends and loved ones.

We passed through the plaza. We'd been here an hour ago, and the statues were crumbled stumps in the silt. I shrieked at children as we passed, grabbing for their hands, making them swim after Val and I. I wanted to help, wanted to fight, but I was useless without a weapon, without means to protect them. But I had to try, had to help get them to safety. So I grabbed for hands, called to children and mer as we passed.

The dragon raged overhead, making its way to the more crowded parts of the city. Warriors had already gathered, riding their orcas to meet the dragon in high waters. I was transfixed as the warriors gave out blood curdling cries and urged their mounts towards the beast. Orcas rammed into its sides, vicious and strong, they knocked it sideways while the warriors pierced it with spears and axes.

The dragon shrieked its rage and retaliated, twisting its long neck around, biting sharp claws down on the closest orca and warrior.

Blood burst in the water, a scream caught in my throat. The death of their comrade didn't stop the warriors from attacking. It gave them greater strength. They surrounded it, poked, stabbed, and prodded. Its cries filled the water, but it still didn't go down.

And then, right in front of it a lone rider rose, coming face to face before the beast.

I froze in terror, even as small hands tugged at my skirts, forcibly trying to pull me forward.

"No." The word tore from my throat.

Val froze at my side. "The idiot," he cursed.

The lone rider.

It was Ytgar.

In one hand he held the reins to his majestic mount, and in the other a long spear of ice.

He looked like a god ripped straight from the ice to avenge his mer. His face was set in an expression of grim determination and fury. Light gleamed off the crown of ice and steel settled firmly over his brow, like a winking promise of death and retribution.

He had never before looked so formidable.

Upon seeing the Prince of Iol, the dragon attacked, stretching its neck out, opening its jaws. Ytgar and his mount dodged one stroke back, and the beast snapped on empty water. Furious, it opened its gargantuan mouth and roared...

…And Ytgar brought his arm back and forward, letting loose the spear in one vicious throw, straight into the throat of the dragon.

It choked on blood and ice as the spear tore through its flesh, silencing its last shriek. It spiraled dead through the water, landing with a thundering shudder and a boom.

Just like that, the battle ended.

And I sank into the debris and wept.

The city. My beautiful city. My home. It had been thoroughly destroyed.

We picked our way through crumbling structures and dead bodies, searching for survivors. There were hardly any.

What was supposed to be a festival of love had become bathed in blood and terror.

My tears had long since vanished, replaced with steely determination. Warriors were collecting bodies, pulling them from under the ice. I tried not to look at faces. Not yet.

"Odele!" I startled, glancing up as Ytgar rushed towards Val and I. His body slammed into mine, arms wrapping around me. "You're safe, love," he cried against my hair. "I was so worried."

I blinked back new tears that threatened and pulled away, pushing unkindly against his chest. "You could have been killed!"However brave it might have been, it could have killed him.

Ytgar cradled my cheek and smiled sadly down at me. "Better me than my mer."

My hands tightened against his cloak. "Don't say that," I threatened. "Don't you dare say that."

His expression turned grim. "How did it get so close to the capital without anyone noticing?" He turned to look at the dead beast, sprawled across the snowy silt, forcing me to look in the same direction.

My brain absorbed its image and there was something about the dragon, something not quite right. Something I couldn't quite put my fin on. It was strange, but my mind was still in the chaos, too distressed to figure it out, so I turned away.

"We need to call a meeting," Ytgar decided. "Action needs to be taken now. To ensure that this doesn't *ever* happen again."

"We need to take action!" Ytgar shouted, not for the first time, in the face of the Iolish Prime Minister.

The meeting wasn't going as planned. The Prime Minister and his inner circle all wore equally grim expressions, but none of them wanted to listen to Ytgar.

He had pushed and pushed his plans for a better Iol, for a protected Iol but it was like he had no voice. Overlooked. Ignored.

And they were good ideas. Ideas to make peace with their enemies, to build protective walls and magical wards, to make friends with the mer who bred these monsters, to set up warriors at their borders. To make friends.

Mister Shallows said, his ugly wrinkly face pressed close to Ytgar. "Speak to the Prime Minister with respect, boy prince."

The insult had me tightening my hands into fists. For the first time I noticed I was without a glove, having lost it somewhere in the frays of chaos.

We were present, the queen and I, though we'd both been silent while Ytgar argued his case.

"A boy prince I may be," Ytgar began, in a voice like black ice. "But my ideas are good, and you all know it."

Mister Shallows scoffed. "Your ideas are ridiculous. Peace negotiations with Draconi? We have spoken to the emperor before and he cares not for the beasts he sets free into our waters."

Ytgar's fists tightened, and everyone in the inner circle followed the movement with wary eyes. "We haven't spoken to him at all. You hide away behind walls of ice because you think it's what's best for Iol, but it's not. We need allies. We need friends. Do you think anyone will come to our aid should we find more of those creatures at our front door? You've shut the other kingdoms out so long, it's like we no longer exist. Don't you understand?"

"This is how we have lived for centuries, boy prince. Do you think because you give a poorly built plan and wear a pretend crown on your brow, that you rule here?"

I got up then, stretching to my full height, tilting my chin up to glare at Mister Shallows, to glare at all of them. And then I said, in perfect Iolish, "While the boy prince with the pretend crown was out there risking his life for the mer of this kingdom, you were hiding behind the ice walls of the palace like cowards."

Every single one of them blinked rapidly at me. Either because they couldn't believe I'd had the audacity to speak before them, or because I'd spoken their own language, which they hadn't known I could speak. That was the fun part about hiding one's true intelligence. It caught others completely off guard.

"If you do not agree with my husband's proposals, then make a few of your own, although I don't see how you could disagree with his very sound plans."

"Sound?" Mister Shallows almost shrieked. "What would you know about politics and international relations? You're more daft than he is."

Ytgar would have killed him for that slight alone had I not spoken first, my eyes narrowed on the old merman. "I'll speak in terms simple enough for you to understand. It was the twentieth year of the Malabella-Kleitz reign, or two hundred years ago, when the United Republic of Brague attacked Ventlair for riches. They were smaller then, with little to no allies. The troops were at their doorstep. They were with one fin in the grave until the prince of the kingdom slipped from the castle and traveled to Thalassar for days without guards, alone, where he offered his very life to his enemy, in exchange for help for his kingdom. And so the alliance was formed and Thalassar brought their allies to Ventlair and surrounded the Republic of Brague in a battle that ended quickly." Silence followed. "The point," I went on, "Is that pride does not win battles. Allies do. Alliances do. It's making peace with an enemy for the greater good of the mer you're sworn to protect. And if that's not something you can do, then you don't deserve to rule in the first place."

Silence echoed against ice walls, with nothing to calm me from the eruption of anger but Ytgar's hand on the small of my back.

I'd left Mister Shallows speechless. I'd left them all them all speechless.

Rollo was staring intently at me, his hand in his chin. Finally, he said, surprising us all, "The Princess is right."

"Of course I am."

"I am ruler of the mer, and I need to protect them. Like Shallows says, we have spoken over and over again to the Draconian Emperor and he has done nothing to stop the beasts. This cannot go unanswered, and action must be taken."

A feeling of foreboding sliced through me.

"Raise the banners," he ordered. "For the warriors shall march and retaliate."

No. *No.* That's not what I'd meant, not what I'd wanted.

The Prime Minister smiled. "I formally declare war against the merkingdom of Draconi." He turned away from us. "May the gods have mercy on the dragon breeders. Because Iol will not."

PRINCESS
IN
FROST CASTLES

THIS BOOK IS FOR those who cast themselves behind shadows, for those who wear shoes they think they'll never fill. You don't have to fill anyone's shoes but your own.

You are glorious.

Disclaimer: This book is a slow burn why choose story that may contain content unsuitable for readers under the age of 18.

P.S. Remember how I said the mermen are slowly introduced in this series? Well, hold your knickers tight, my readers, because merman number three is in this one.

Odele

FROM THE WALLS OF Isolde Palace, portraits hung. Aligned all along the frozen walls of the hallway, they were like sentinels, the images of Isolde royalty staring down with ice in their eyes.

I swam beside every portrait, giving equal attention to each one, memorizing their every intricate detail. Names were engraved on steel plates beneath each image. A long line of Isoldes, Neves, Frosts, and Snows. Kings and queens, princes and princesses, dukes and duchesses.

Lava globes hung from glass chandeliers above me, the soft yellow glow illuminating each face. The delicate brush strokes were cast in dancing shadows. I was no artist, but I could tell that each painting was done with the careful precision of someone who loved what they did.

Silver and blue eyes ran down the long line of my husband's lineage. The eyes of frost and harsh winters, expressions equally deadly and grave. All these mer had a few things in common besides the twin disapproving orbs on their faces. Tails, long and strong with the sleek black and white coloring like those of orcas; pale shades of skin drawn tightly over elegant and beautiful features.

But then I stopped on *her* portrait.

She looked small and delicate compared to the Viking-like mer that came before her. With dark skin and even darker eyes and hair, she sat regally upon her throne and glared at me with an expression that demanded power and respect, and received them both in equal measure. I could feel the spirit of that glare even in the portrait.

Below, the steel plate was engraved in the language of the cold northern kingdom of Iol: *Amelia Cerul, Princess of Castle Frost.*

I'd heard of her in the few conch shells I'd been able to scrape up on the once foreign kingdom that was now my home. She'd been Princess of the United Kingdoms of Great Braguish, and the first in their history to be sent to the mysterious kingdom of Iol. She'd brought changes with her to the kingdom; among them, a government, a Prime Minister, and a new way of life.

The conch I'd listened to said that when she'd died, the Iolish had sent her body back to the United Kingdoms. There had been no evidence of hardship, and no clue as to what brought on her demise. But in her dead hands, she clutched a necklace of ice with the Isolde family crest.

An ice that didn't melt. An ice made of the same material of the conch I wore on a thin chain around my neck.

I fingered the edges of my necklace softly as I bent closer to the portrait. If I squinted, I could just make out the hint of her own necklace disappearing down her bodice.

Seeing it made me feel closer to her in a way I couldn't quite explain. I felt a kinship as I looked at this portrait of a long since deceased mermaid, the princess of the old Brague, a foreign kingdom, but with ice in her veins.

I took a stroke back and compared once again. Down the line of figures after her, every single mer sported the same orca tail and silver-white eyes, the same elegance and beauty of the Neves Isolde line, but her brown skin left a permanent mark on her descendants. A part of herself that still remained even if she was all but forgotten.

"I expected to find you in the stables, not here."

The voice echoed around me like black ice. I didn't turn to greet him, but physically relaxed when he sidled in beside me.

The silver-white eyes of my husband pierced the painting of his ancestor. I could see bits of her in him. Elegant cheekbones, sharp and cold beauty, dark skin and a gaze that promised the thrill of violence.

But his touch was gentle. His fingers grazed my palms, causing a delicious sensation of protection and promise to slide slowly over me.

"I needed to clear my head." I threaded my fingers through his and held tightly. For a moment, I stared down at our hands so firmly clasped. Weeks ago, I hadn't been able to stand the sight of him. I'd craved his touch secretly, thinking every single bit of the merman next to me was forbidden and dangerous, nothing more than a taint on my soul and body.

That had been before his royal lies had come into the light. Before I'd known that the merman hadn't been a whale trainer, a servant, like he'd led me to believe, but something else.

A prince. A warrior.

Someone I had come to tentatively love.

And even before then, something about him had called to me, like the magic buried deeply within whale song. It was entrancing beauty, and he'd had me captured since that first moment. *Not* that I'd tell him so.

"I confess, I need to do the same." His tone was grave, and when I looked up at him, it was to meet the clenching of his jaw, the rage shining in the silver depths of his eyes.

The anger thrummed steadily, dangerously, from his every pore. He kept it tightly controlled, but I knew he desired to unleash every bit of his fury in violence and death like his Viking forefathers.

He wanted to be better than that.

"What's happening down there?"

I *knew* what was happening, but I couldn't stop myself from asking. I'd witnessed the aftermath of the chaos that had occurred only hours before.

A dragon had broken through Iolish borders. It had forced its way to the capital and had destroyed it. And the truce that Ytgar so desperately wanted with Draconi, the merkingdom of dragons, had been pushed heavily upon the Prime Minister. Instead of heeding wise words, he'd declared war against the neighboring kingdom.

"The warriors are preparing for battle. He wants them to swim straight to Draconi and fight."

A sigh pressed heavily down on my body. Dread curled its way in my gut.

War.

I'd lived through one war already. The war between my home kingdom of Thalassar and the kingdom of Kappur had lasted for years.

I hadn't cared then, because it was others going to war for me while I survived behind the rose quartz walls of my palace. But then I'd discovered so many secrets, and Kappur and Thalassar were now allies, thanks to my cousin and her father.

This was different.

Different because I'd started thinking of Iol as my home. Different because I *loved* it here. Different because my husband was a warrior. Different because my cousin Odalaea now lived in Draconi.

The kingdom that Rollo wanted to attack.

There was something wrong about all of this. Trepidation had sliced a path down my chest from the moment Prime Minister Rollo Ysengart had declared war against Draconi. It wasn't just my former betrothed's kingdom—it was my *cousin's* kingdom.

Something was *wrong.*

I just couldn't place what.

And no matter how vehemently Ytgar and I argued against it, the Prime Minister was adamant in his decision.

This was the last straw.

Draconi would pay.

"Our warriors and our orcas are strong," Ytgar continued, his tone low, dark. "But Draconi has *dragons.*"

Dragons.

Massive beasts. Creatures with barbed tails and venomous teeth and claws. With wings and legs and—

A gasp tore through me as the realization hit me like the blow of an orca to my side.

"Dragons," I whispered.

I could feel Ytgar's eyes on me as I worked out the facts in my mind. Stupid. How could I have been so stupid? The shock of the attack had completely blinded me to something that should have been obvious from the beginning.

"Dragons," I repeated.

"Odele?" Ytgar slipped his fingers from mine and gently turned me, keeping his hands on my shoulders. "Is something wrong?"

I looked up at my husband, at the grave lines that marred the elegant features of his face. He still wore the crown of sapphires and steel I'd made for him. It was a symbol of the king he deserved to be. While his hair seemed wildly askew, the white strands floating and curling over his cheekbones, the crown was straight.

I smiled broadly at him and stood tall on my fins so that our mouths were level, a whisper apart. I pressed a firm kiss to his lips. "I think I may have just figured out how to stop this war from happening."

"I want to see the beast."

The Prime Minister had been meeting with his inner circle of old corrupt mer when I barged in and demanded they follow me. I thought they merely followed to give me the benefit of the doubt.

I wasn't nervous. If there was one thing I could trust, it was my intelligence, my memorization skills. They didn't believe I was good at much, but I'd proved them wrong time and time again. I'd prove them wrong in this, too.

Its body littered the streets of Iol. Sprawled atop an icy mound, it was surrounded by debris and the bodies of its kills.

I didn't fear approaching it, even as Ytgar and Val framed my sides like guards, eyeing the leathery white-gray body of it warily.

It had blended in perfectly with its surroundings, which was why we hadn't seen it coming in the first place.

"What have you brought us out here for, child?" Ytgar's grandmother, Queen Isadora Isolde, demanded regally.

Her words were echoed with angry murmurs from the Prime Minister's inner circle.

I took a breath and pointed at the beast. "Look carefully at the creature." My finger pointed down the length of its body. "Notice anything?"

Citizens, warriors, and royals alike all surrounded me, and they all remained silent.

"What is there to see?" Rollo demanded in a clipped, impatient voice. "It's a dragon."

"And do you *know* how many species of Dracon there are?" At their blank stares, I elaborated. "Dragons, wyrms, drakes, and wyverns are all species of Dracon. Dragon-like creatures. Different species, different characteristics."

"So?" The queen's eyes bore into mine, hardly concealing the contempt that lingered in those depths.

"So… Dragons are defined by specific characteristics. Two wings and hooked claws." I pointed at the wings. "Long tails…" I gestured at the barbed tail. "And four legs." My hands went to my hips in triumph. Surely they saw it now?

"And? Get to the point already." This came from Mister Shallows, his voice a grating annoyance down my spine.

I sighed, throwing my hands up. "This beast has *two* legs. Not four. Really, Mister Shallows, your abilities as a foreign diplomat are deplorable; I thought you'd at least be able to *count* with success."

The wrinkled merman's face reddened.

I went on, "This creature is a wyvern, and Draconians do not and have *never* bred wyverns."

It was like a revelation, one that eased the pain in my chest by astronomical proportions. Draconi was safe. Iol would be safe. Odalaea would be as well.

We didn't need a war.

A war would destroy my cousin completely.

It would destroy us all.

I looked up, my dark eyes darting between Ytgar and Val, two mermen who had stolen my heart completely. Val wore a grim expression, but there was no mistaking the flash of pride in the frosty depths of his eyes. Ytgar was harder to read, his expression solemn. But I knew he was as hopeful as I was that this war could be avoided.

I looked at Rollo. The Prime Minister floated regally, his broad shoulders pushed back as his cruel eyes glared down at the beast and then flicked up to me.

"How do you even know this?" His voice was clipped with impatience.

I fought back the eye-roll that threatened to make me look unattractive. "Because, unlike you, I do not close myself off from the outside world. While we were in Draconi, I visited the palace library. I'm sure even a simpleton like you can guess that Draconi has many eggshells on the subject of dragons."Rollo waved off my words with a dismissive gesture of his hand.

The audacity.

"The words were likely all in Dracon. *I* am sure you were confused, little Princess."

My lips curled into the slowest of mocking smiles. "Dracon is a language I speak fluently, Prime Minister. *And I've never met a ruler more asinine than you.*" I said that last part in Dracon, my words precise, fast. They caused him to blink and then shift uncomfortably. Good. "Will you float there and argue with me the rest of the day? Do you need me to prove my intelligence to you? I can speak Braguish, Iolish, Dracon, and Thalassarin. I can listen to a conch one time and memorize every single word. I could take a moment to show you, but conches can't survive here, and we're a bit pressed on time. So, as princess, I order you to call off your warriors because Draconi didn't do this."

My decree superseded his own, Iolish rules and their hierarchy be *damned.* They wanted to name me Duchess of Frost, but I'd show them. I was Princess of Thalassar. I was power and command. And I *would* be obeyed.

Echoing silence vibrated all around the cold waters. Every single mer took in the sight of me, like I was either a hero, or completely mad for disrespecting their ruler so publicly. Everyone seemed to be holding their breaths waiting for the outcome.

"How can you be so sure it was not Draconi?" he finally asked.

I had the sudden urge to rip my hair out from the roots. Had he not been listening to a word I said? Or was he merely that daft?

"Because they don't breed wyverns."

"Perhaps they secretly do."

"They don't."

"Enough!" He screamed the word out at me. I didn't flinch, but suddenly Val and Ytgar were there, shielding me with their powerful fur-cloaked bodies. The Prime Minister glared, his facade of a tranquil ruler crumbling right before everyone's eyes, and he didn't seem to care at all. "The only reason you defend Draconi is because your cousin now resides there."

I shoved between Val and Ytgar, wedging myself tightly in the middle. "It's precisely because of my cousin and her husband that I know Draconi would never harm Iol."

She was too good, and the Dragon Prince wouldn't spill unnecessary blood. Not when he knew how much Odalaea and I cared for one another.

"And yet it is not the Dragon Prince or his wife who rule."

No.

It was Emperor Jiang Li.

I'd met the vicious merman myself. Cruelty was a living thing inside him. It lurked there alongside the beast that swam through the blood of his entire lineage. But would he be unnecessarily cruel? I couldn't believe it. No matter how many wars the Emperor had won, no matter how heinous or mean, he would not breed wyverns.

Dragons were vicious. They were savage, and they were wild, but they could be tamed to the emperor's will. Wyverns knew only destruction and chaos. And the one dead at our fins had wreaked that exactly.

"It wasn't them," I ground out, but knew my protests only fell on deaf ears.

"Perhaps it was."

I glared at the Prime Minister. Why was he so determined to go to war with Draconi? Did he want to see his mer dead? Because that would be the outcome. Death and blood. Ice and lava. Orca and dragon.

"You are willing to risk the lives of your mer all based on a *perhaps?*"

Before Rollo could reply, Ytgar was speaking. "At least give Draconi a chance to explain themselves. Let us go there and speak to the emperor.

Let us see for ourselves if there are wyverns among the dragons. War is not the only option, Rollo."

Some of the warriors glanced at their prince. He had no say in their kingdom, but he cared about them. And right now they weren't seeing the merman with no power in his own home, but the savage warrior who rode up to the face of a wyvern and threw a spear of ice straight through the beast's throat.

They were seeing a protector.

A warrior.

A king.

Rollo noticed it the same moment I did. He was inclined to argue, desperate to let his pride shroud his good sense—if he had any—and send mer out to their deaths.

"Fine," he conceded. "A small party will travel to Draconi to discover the truth of the Emperor's treachery. Whatever you discover, no matter how harsh the truth, will determine the outcome of this."

And with a final scathing glare my way, the Prime Minister turned and swam away.

"Your wife over-swims her bounds, Ytgar." The queen floated before us, her servants and ladies behind her.

The sight of them made my gut clench.

Hours. It had been hours since I'd last seen anyone. Not Jessinda, Silviya, Scarlet, or even Anneli. And bodies were still being recovered from under the debris, but I was too frightened to look into any of their faces. I fought the urge to finger one gloved hand with the ungloved one—a gift from my cousin. I must have lost it when Val and I had been swimming away from the threat of death. Even my dainty little crown had been lost, and I hadn't even noticed.

"We are on the brink of war, grandmother," Ytgar replied tightly. "Etiquette has no place here." Then he took my hand and tugged me close, whirling us around so we gave our back to the Queen of Iol.

Gasps sounded out at the obvious gesture of disrespect.

"Insolent little mer," she cursed. "If only your father were here…"

"Well, he's not," Ytgar interrupted over his shoulder. "He's dead. And all of us will be too if you don't get the Prime Minister under control."

He didn't wait to listen to her sputtering reply, but pulled me alongside him as we left the scene of chaos behind. We swam with all the straight-backed pride of the royalty that we were, and we didn't look back.

Ytgar

Never before had I challenged my grandmother, let alone publicly. The thoughts swirling through my mind were a maelstrom, and the thundering of my heart was as vicious as the currents of snow and ice.

It was entirely because of Odele.

She was fearless in her defense of Draconi and Iol, fearless in her defense of *me*. Why had I ever thought she would not make a good wife? Why had I ever thought she would not bring good things to my kingdom?

She was vivacious and intelligent and feared nothing.

I admired every single aspect of her right now.

She filled me with the courage to be what I always believed I could be but feared to really become. To confront Rollo and my grandmother without fear of repercussion.

"Can I just say," Val murmured from her other side, "that you are a fantastic mermaid?" We swam through the fray and the destruction that the wyvern had wreaked. It physically hurt to see jagged bits of ice and steel, blood and bodies crumbled into the silt. The death and destruction I had tried so long to avoid was becoming inevitable now.

Her hair had come undone from the beautiful coils it had been in earlier during the festival, tangling against her cheeks, the little silver and blue earrings piercing the lobes of her ears. She tossed some of the strands aside, the action both arrogant and flattered.

"I know," she answered.

If there was one thing she was certain of, it was of her own intelligence and worth. Modesty was not a term she knew.

It seemed so long ago that I'd secretly wished Maisie would be the mer Iol had needed for salvation. She was sweet, gentle, and kind. What a fool I'd been. No one else would have been able to defend me. No one else would have made me feel this savage thing inside my chest right in the spot where my heart beat.

"Rollo is a fool if he thinks we can go to war with Draconi," I said vehemently, gaze sweeping around the aftermath. My kingdom was reduced to rubble and strewn bodies.

Valence Day was a celebration of love and friendship. Now, because of this, there would always be the sharp, brittle reminder of death and travesty.

My mer deserved better. They deserved a better ruler. A better kingdom.

"Our warriors are strong, but Draconi has *dragons*. The emperor's beast alone could decimate half our army. We just don't have the numbers." Val stopped abruptly, his jaw tight as he bent down to smooth his palm down the flank of an injured orca.

The expression of pain climbed over his features with visceral slowness until it matched the pain in the orca's eyes. Tendrils of blood curled up from its body, its breaths heaving painfully. A noise of immense pain ripped from it.

And there was nothing I could do to ease its suffering.

"I need to find Anneli," Val ground out. "She's a better healer than I. She can save him."

It took him a few moments to extricate himself from the orca's side, and he did so with pain and regret marring his every feature.

"I haven't seen her." My gaze scanned the horizon. There were too many mer rushing about. Too many mer helping, lifting bodies, assisting the injured. I tried looking for a flash of silver hair and scales but shook my head when I didn't catch sight of her.

"Go find her," Odele suggested, placing her hand on his arm. "We need to help everyone anyway."

Val nodded and swallowed tightly. His eyes darted around cautiously, and then he put his palm to her cheek. He wanted to kiss her. Kiss her like it could very well be his last moment in these waters. He held himself back, content enough to feel his skin against hers, gazing at her as if she were the only star winking at him from above a two-legger sky and he was desperate for a wish.

"Thank you." He dropped his hand and turned to me. I could see the searching in his gaze, as if he were still asking me for permission. As if he still needed it to love her.

Even after all he'd done today, he still questioned his worth. He had protected her when I couldn't. Saved her, kept her *safe*. Odele had briefed me on what had happened. Valmundur had been willing to lay his life down for hers.

Protecting was second nature for him. Valmundur was *good*. That kindness was so intricately woven into the very fibers of his soul. I just wished he could see it in himself. And not in small bursts. Not occasionally, but *always*.

"Once everything is in order here, we will prepare to depart for Draconi." My words were a firm command, the spaces laced with all the love and words I couldn't say.

He nodded. He understood. He would always understand.

"I'll come find you." And then Val was turning and darting away, his frosty blue tail flicking with urgent movements behind him.

Once he was gone, I turned to Odele. "Will you help?"

Something dangerous flared in the dark depths of her eyes, and I knew the question had offended her. Weeks ago, she never would have lifted a finger to help those in need. She didn't care. That same selfish mer still lived inside her. I saw her emerge in violent wisps of indignation and fury, and yet she was innately different now. Or maybe she had always been this way. Maybe she had always cared and could never bring herself to show it, the same way I could never bring myself to show the wilder, uncontrollable parts of me.

"Why must you always insist on insulting me?" she demanded.

My fingers reached out to trail down her cheek until I gripped her chin in my hand. I forced her to look at me, willing her to see the raging desperation in my eyes. "It is not an insult, my love. I am begging you to help because my mer need you. *I* need you."

She made me stronger, bolder, and I needed her at my side. Needed my mer to see that we cared, the both of us. They'd seen enough for themselves, seen how she defended their lives against the possibility of war. They'd seen the lava of vicious destruction in her eyes, and now they needed to feel the gentle warmth.

Her expression softened and very slowly, her palms pressed against my chest where she felt the steady beating of my heart branding her skin, possessing her every nerve ending, the very veins that coursed through her.

She was *mine.*
"Of course, I'll help," she whispered.
"Good."

Because I couldn't imagine doing this without her by my side.

We worked well into the night, reuniting families. Val found Anneli relatively unharmed. The injured orcas were all rounded up and led to the stables to be tended to, and then came the hard part—identifying the bodies of my dead mer.

We searched tirelessly at the faces of every dead mer, and I knew Odele was looking for her cousins. I saw equal parts despair and relief on her face with each body that turned out to be a stranger instead of her cousins.

Still, she didn't stop. Even when night started to converge into morning and we were exhausted, she helped by making a list of missing mer, of the deceased, of displaced children and parents. And not once did she complain. Even when the shadows spread beneath her eyes, she pushed forward with determination.

The eyes of the Iolish followed the princess about as she flitted from one spot to the next. I could see the admiration there. Perhaps she hadn't had it before, perhaps they'd heard the stories of her selfishness, but none of it was present now.

"Maybe you should take a break," I suggested quietly, pressing my hand against her lower back. I could feel her body trembling with exhaustion that she was fighting with everything she had.

Her tired eyes found mine, gleaming stubbornly in the dull light of lava globes and ice. "Are *you* going to take a break?"

I couldn't. There was still so much to do, things I needed to set right before we left for Draconi.

She read the answer in my eyes and shrugged my hand away from her. "I won't be resting either," she decided firmly and resumed her work.

She only stopped when Jessinda pushed against the crowds and called out her name.

"Odele! Cousin!"

Odele's face transformed into an expression of relief as she dropped everything and swam, as fast as the exhaustion would let her, to meet her cousin halfway.

The two mer embraced, clinging tightly to each other, letting out gasps that could be construed as sobs. When they pulled away, Odele cradled Jessinda's cheeks. It was the closest I'd ever seen them; the closest I'd ever seen palpable affection.

"Are you alright? I've searched everywhere for you." Only Odele could make her worry sound like admonishment. She was glaring at her cousin as if it was all her fault.

A sob ripped from Jessinda's throat, and tears rose from her eyes in tiny little air bubbles. "Odele, come quickly. It's—gods—*Silviya*—"

Odele's skin paled. Her grip on her cousin tightened, nails digging into her arms.

"Take me to her."

Ice seemed to swallow up the sounds. There was nothing but a silence so infinite it broke the barriers of sanity, plunging every little thing into madness. It was the silence Odele emanated that worried me. It was silence that kept her lips firmly pursed, her body and every movement as gentle as the soft falling of snowflakes drifting through water.

She kept her composure even while her cousins fell apart at her sides. They sobbed and cried out with their heads thrown back, as if their cries could pierce past icebergs and water, as if they could beseech the two-legger gods themselves to change this tragedy.

Her body looked so frail. Bent at odd angles, Silviya was pinned to the snowy silt, a jagged chunk of ice jutting out from her abdomen. It was hard to tell what killed her. The ice, or the debris that had crushed the rest of her body. The blood had long since stopped flowing, leaving the once beautiful mermaid nothing more than a pale cadaver.

Her black hair still floated, long straight tendrils that smoked around her white, crushed face. Her silver tail was marred with grotesque scrapes and cuts that bisected across her body in cruel angles.

The wyvern had torn apart buildings, and ice was as painful as steel when it pierced the flesh.

"We were together," Scarlet sobbed. "It happened so fast! I—I couldn't—"

Odele stared down, unmoving, at the body of her cousin. She was preternaturally still. I could barely see the rise and fall of her chest. Her face was expressionless, drawn in calm lines. Nothing to indicate she felt anything at all.

Slowly she pulled her gaze away from the gruesome sight and looked at the Thalassarin guards behind her, mermen who took in the body of their lady with sadness.

"Take her body to Isolde Palace and place her in her room." Her voice was firm. It betrayed nothing, not anger or sadness. She turned to her sobbing cousins hovering over Silviya's body and placed her hands on their shoulders. "Prepare her body for the journey home."

They obeyed her with a slowness that spoke of a deep sadness. The guards went forward and, as carefully as they could, pried the shard of ice from her, lifting her body between them. When they took her away, Jessinda and Scarlet's sobs followed behind, leaving a swarming trail of tears behind.

Only when they were gone did I swim up to Odele and place my hands on her shoulders.

She jerked away from my touch.

"Do not touch me, Iolish," she spat unkindly.

I took a stroke away from her and the venom in her words. She sounded precisely like the same pretentious princess I'd despised before.

She whirled around, shoulders straight, chin tilted. I looked for the tremble of a chin, or tears rising from her eyes. But her eyes were as piercing as glaciers. Her fingers flexed at her sides, a telling gesture I knew she did when she believed she'd failed. Like she was bracing herself for the whack of a whip down on her knuckles.

"Odele… this isn't your fault."

There it was, the slightest tremble in her facade, one she reconstructed within seconds behind steel walls. Even if I battered against her structures, she'd never let me in. She wasn't used to it. Neither was I.

I had no idea how to take away her pain, no idea what I should do to help her.

"Of course, it isn't. Now get out of my way, *Prince.* Your mer need you, and I have important matters to tend to."

She shoved past me and I turned to watch her go. Her pace was steady as she picked her way past the rubble and made her way towards the palace.

"Prince Ytgar, forgive the interruption…"

I turned to face the timid servant floating before me. She was a frail looking thing with hunched shoulders and a light, darting gaze. Another orphan, hired to tend to the palace.

"Yes?" I asked, trying to remember her name but unable to summon it up.

"I know you're busy, Your Highness, but you told me to find you in case the princess… Ah… Well, in case she became… *difficult.*"

I sighed, a feeling of foreboding traipsing through me. Weariness was already weighing down on me. It had been an hour since Odele had left me, an hour where I'd done nothing but worry for her well-being as I finished my duties around the streets.

"What's going on now?" I reached up to run my hand through my hair but stopped when my fingertips touched the steel crown. It seemed so long ago now that she'd given this to me, placed it over my brow as if I were truly a king and not just a singular form of decoration to my own kingdom.

"I… I think it would be best if you came and saw for yourself, Your Highness."

That's how I found myself following the servant through the halls of Isolde Palace, all the way up to the rooms I shared with Odele. I saw the problem as soon as we came near the open doorway. A servant came barreling out, a look of pure terror on her face. Following her was a glass teacup that promptly shattered against the hall wall.

"Get out!" Odele's shriek followed. "All of you get out! You worthless pile of guppies! I'll have you whipped for this!"

More servants swarmed out, some of them in sobs. Once they were out of the way, the shattering force of more teacups and trays followed.

"Worthless! All of you!"

I turned to the line of servants, especially the sobbing ones. "I will handle my wife. Thank you for your assistance."

They curtsied and hurried away.

Sighing, I swam into the room, dodging a spoon that suddenly came hurtling my way.

"Get out, Iolish bastard!" she shrieked.

I glared, closing the doors to our rooms behind me.

Odele floated in the center of the room before a small coral table that held the remnants of a tea set. She still wore her dress from earlier, now a tattered scrap of a thing. Her hair was wild around her face, and there was something feral in her eyes. Her chest rose and fell with furious gasps.

"Get. Out."

I swam further into the room cautiously, like I would approach a violent, unpredictable orca.

"I ordered you not to terrorize the staff." I stopped on the other side of the little coral table. It was the only thing that separated us. I wanted to pick it up and toss it across the room, take her in my arms and hold her.

But I had ironclad self control.

I crossed my arms against my chest, narrowing my eyes at her.

"Perhaps I'd not terrorize your staff if they weren't entirely *useless*." The final word fell off into a broken, fragmented sound. She took in a shuddering breath, held it.

In that moment, I saw everything she was feeling. Every single piece of her shattering at her fins. The sorrow, the loss, so many chaotic emotions warring inside her without a release.

And this was her release. This was her way of letting loose the rage, every small bit of her fury.

Not with hand holding. Not with tears. That wasn't Odele. She would not lay down and weep.

She wanted fury. She wanted sparring. She wanted violence.

She wanted *war*.

And I'd very well give it to her.

"You're a spoiled brat, Princess," I sneered. "That's all this is. It's not about their work, about what they do right or wrong. It's about you. You want them to fear you." I placed my palms against the table and leaned forward, so close that the tips of our noses touched. I could feel my blood coursing through my veins, flaring with the rapid rush of violence and desire. "But I am not them, Odele. And I do not fear you."

Her breath caught in her throat, eyes darting down to capture attention on my mouth.

I wanted to kiss her.

"Then you're a bastard *and* a fool." Her hand came up so fast, I barely saw the knife until the cold bite of metal kissed my throat.

I swallowed, the workings of my throat scraping across the blade so it pressed deeper into my skin, cutting a thin line across my flesh. Her hand didn't tremble once.

"You won't hurt me, Odele." My lips twisted into a cruel smirk.

"I will."

"You can try." But I didn't let her. My hand shot out quickly, grabbing her tightly by the wrist, squeezing until she let out a cry of pain and the weapon clattered from her hand and onto the table between us. "But you will fail."

My free hand gripped the edge of the table and forced it aside as easily as if it were a scrap of cloth. It clattered to the icy floor with a loud bang that resonated in the space between us. A space I closed by pushing her back… back… back until her spine hit the far wall, and she gasped.

Our bodies kissed intimately, pressing together chest to chest, navel to navel, tail to tail. I pinned her wrist to the wall at her side and grabbed the other one even as she swung it out to punch me, doing the same to that side.

She struggled. "Let go of me, Iolish bastard."

I bent so my lips were hovering a kiss away from her own. "I'll never let you go, Princess. No matter how cruel you think you can be, I can be a thousand times crueler. Every time you try to escape me, I will find you and bring you back. I'll tie you to my bed, enslave you in my ice castle. Every. Single. Time." I accentuated my point, pressing gentle, promising kisses to her cheek, her jaw, her neck.

Her body shuddered in my hold.

"I despise you." Her breath was a rasp of anger and desire.

A smile twisted my lips. "Good," I breathed.

And then I kissed her.

It was a torrent of wild, angry desire. I released her wrists to grab her hips and pulled her closer, if only so she could feel the hard press of my shaft against her. She responded with equal angry fervor, digging her nails tightly into my shoulders.

Her kisses were violent, teeth biting at my lip with aggressive force, tongue thrusting in languid strokes. Her tail wrapped slowly around my waist and I held her still against me as I whirled and let ourselves fall to the ground.

The pain was jarring, but the passion didn't dim in the least. I fell across her body and she gasped at the stinging sensation against my mouth, groaning and clawing at my clothes.

She pressed her hips up against mine and in one sudden, forceful move, she had me flipped on my back, pressing me down with her body.

Odele leaned up, slowly, sinuously, and I felt the sting of her slap on my face before my mind registered she'd even raised her hand. Spots danced behind my closed lids, and when I opened them, her hands were curled into fists that she began slamming relentlessly into me.

And I took it because I could. She could push me, and I'd push back. I'd meet her violence for violence, passion for passion.

My fingers rammed into the roots of her hair and tugged. She cried out as I yanked her back mercilessly. It was a fierce dance for dominance between us, one I'd gladly accept. There were no words, just war. Our bodies were swords and shields, pushing and pulling against each other, and we spilled kisses like blood.

Because it was the only relief we could find.

I flipped her again, slamming her to the ground. She gasped, tears flowing from her eyes, but I didn't stop. I lifted her, our bodies melding. She punched me, and blood lifted from the corner of my mouth. I barely felt it. I felt only this savage, vicious need for violence and thrill, for *her*.

Unspoken frustrations pulsed like hushed words spoken across a quiet room. I pressed her against the wall once more and gripped the bodice of her dress. I pulled it, and the material tore right down the middle, opening up like a robe.

It bared her entirely to me.

Glorious.

She was glorious.

I molded my hand to her breast, feeling the hard peak of her nipple pressing tightly to my palm. She groaned, jerking her body into me even as her own fingers went to my tunic and ripped through the buttons. Each one flew, and her warm hands slipped to touch my bare skin beneath the material, pushing everything off of me. My clothes slid down my tail, and then I was bare before her.

The ferocity of her movements was exotic. Every feral cry of rage that she exclaimed against my skin was sensual in a way that shouldn't have been possible.

And yet there was pleasure in the pain, in every rough touch.

My hands slid down the skin at her waist, caressing the smattering of scales along her abdomen. I found the opening at the V of her hips, right at the center of her desire.

I touched her.

She cried out against my mouth.

"Iolish… bastard…" she panted.

I took it as a compliment.

Her hips thrusted against my ministrations, and she bit down against my chin, up to my lips. She grabbed my face, nails raking across my cheeks until she drew blood.

"Now," she ordered. "Now."

My hands pulled away, and in one quick, violent thrust, I sheathed myself fully into her.

We gasped against each other and I stilled. For one torturously slow second, I stilled inside her.

And then I began to move.

My hips slammed against hers, my movements rougher with each passing thrust. Each slamming movement of my body sent her higher and higher up the wall.

I felt the pleasure building to painful proportions, felt it down to the base of my spine.

"Faster…" she groaned against the curve of my neck.

When she bit down at my collarbone, I obliged, pumping in and out of her with the urgency that wired every single nerve in my body. And when she exploded, falling apart in the space of my arms, I followed.

Sparks danced behind my eyelids as we gently fell back to the floor, me on my back and Odele sprawled above me. Her cheek rested against my chest, and I held her close, the rapid rise and fall of our breathing mingling was the only sound around us.

And then Odele began to sob.

My throat closed tightly at the sound, and I pulled her closer, my hand holding the back of her head to me.

"She's dead," she cried, her voice breaking in agonized gasps. "She's d-d-dead."

"I'm sorry, my love."

I wished I could take her pain in myself, suffer it so she wouldn't have to.

"It's my f—"

"Don't say it." I gripped her cheeks and lifted her face so that our eyes met. "Do not even think it, Odele. It's not your fault."

Her breaths shuddered and minutes passed, but she finally nodded and dropped her head back to my chest. Her tears still came, but they were quieter now. Silent things that floated above us, forming soft air clouds that burst into tiny snowflakes.

Eventually, her sobs quieted.

Eventually, the tears stopped.

Eventually, Odele gave into her exhaustion and fell into the darkness of sleep.

Valmundur

I looked up from the orca I was currently tending to. Its fin was broken, the bones shattered from the fight with the wyvern. The poor creature was in terrible pain, and I was doing my best to treat it. I'd wrapped its fin in rolls of silk and kelp and was merely waiting on a servant to arrive with a tonic that would ease its suffering.

Anneli hovered above me, a glare drawing expressive lines over her pretty features, her arms crossed against her chest.

The mermaid looked as exhausted as I felt, though I couldn't blame her. Every single mer was working furiously to clean up the mess that had been made. Whether it was disposing of bodies, healing the injured mer or orca, or feeding lost children and parents, everyone had a task.

She'd been swimming frenziedly from orca to orca, binding wounds, distributing tonics, setting bones, or mourning the ones she couldn't save.

The fatigue showed. Shadows were prominent beneath her eyes, her long silver colored hair was in tangles and knots. Her leathers were tattered where debris had fallen on her. There were a few scrapes and bruises over her cheeks and neck, but she looked otherwise fine.

"I'm going with you to Draconi," she announced again, firmly and slowly, as if I was an idiot who didn't speak Iolish.

I sighed as I finished wrapping the last bit of binding on the orca and patted her rear. "Good girl," I murmured before stretching up to my full height. "Are you sure that's a good idea?"

She glowered, and I knew danger was coming. It was flashing like thunder clouds in the depths of her eyes. Black and silver and gray. Skies and lightning and clouds. That's what Anneli was, what she'd always been. As wild and as free as the tempest of a storm.

"You can't stop me."

My relationship with Anneli ran deep into the roots of our pasts. It was delicate yet strong, honest yet forged in lies. We were both orphans, raised in the same cruel building under the same watchful eye of a cold and angry merwoman.

Ingen.

No one.

That's what they called us, what we'd grown up thinking we were. Except, Anneli wasn't no one at all. She was someone. She knew where she came from even if I didn't.

A bastard princess.

She liked to joke about it when we were younger, lying on cold floors of ice with itchy furs weighing us down. We slept close together then, her hand in mine, the relationship between two children a precarious, trustful, *ignorant* thing.

"Can you imagine me in a palace?" she'd joke in the whispering darkness. "Wearing dresses and dancing with my father?"

I'd snort right alongside her because the very notion was ridiculous. Anneli, a *princess*? She was too adventurous for that, too daring for the constricting binds of royal life. We'd known that even then.

The king sometimes visited her in the dead of the night, bestowing gifts upon her because she was his most precious secret. She shared those gifts with me and no one else.

It wasn't until later that we realized she was his most shameful secret.

One she kept to this day.

I only knew the truth of it because when we were young, we had confided in each other in more ways than one. With our secrets, our hearts, and our bodies.

But we both longed for more. And I could see the *more* in her eyes as she glared at me now. The pillars of our relationship were firmly rooted in glares like that. We were honest with one another, even while we lied to everyone else, even if I lied to Ytgar about the fact that he had a half sister.

It just wasn't my secret to tell.

"How do you know we're even going?" I crossed my arms against my chest, the gesture mocking hers.

One gray-white eyebrow rose. "Everyone is talking about it." She sounded exasperated, like she couldn't believe how stupid I was. "I'm going with you."

It was an order, not a request.

She'd been wrong so long ago. Anneli *would* make a good princess. As formidable as Odele, and just as stubborn when she wanted something.

But that wasn't the life for her, and I didn't bring it up. I didn't even dare joke about it. The last time we'd spoken of her father had been when he'd died. And the last time I'd told her to tell Ytgar who she was, she'd promptly given me a black eye and told me to keep my mouth shut.

I hated lying to my best friend. I knew he was lonely, desperate for family. Him and Odele were alike in that regard. They both desperately needed someone they could confide in, someone who shared their blood. Maisie was that for Odele, and I knew Anneli would be that for Ytgar if she gave him the chance.

"Why do you want to go?"

"Because I want to get a closer look at the dragons. If we go to war, I want to see what our orcas will be up against. It's my duty to train them, to protect them."

Her love for the animals swam deep inside her. She cared for them like she hadn't cared for anyone else in her life. Because when you grew up feeling worthless and alone, it was the animals who could make you feel alive again. Like you had someone looking forward to your arrival, someone who didn't judge or toss you to the side because they were ashamed of your existence.

Animals were faithful.

"Then you should start packing," I suggested with resignation. There was no turning her back from this. She'd obviously made up her mind. "We'll probably be leaving soon."

It was only then that the expression on her face changed entirely. One moment it held the violence and promise of destruction, and the next it held a brief flash of uncertainty.

"Will you ask Prince Ytgar if he will allow me to go?"

I stared at her, took in her every detail. I didn't understand why she was so averse to speaking with him, to confessing.

I was Ingen.

I was *no one* to demand an explanation from her.

So I merely nodded and murmured, "Alright."

Odele

Our bags were packed, the orcas had been readied, and Silviya's body had been prepared.

I'd sent her off first. Thalassarin guards and two Iolish escorts were accompanying Silviya home, and they would deliver a message I'd written on kelp parchment. It held an explanation for my stepmother and father, for Silviya's family. My cousins huddled around her body, and we said our quiet, solemn goodbyes.

When they'd gone, I ushered my cousins into my chambers and sat them down while I paced before them. Back and forth, back and forth.

I stopped, turned to them, and kept my voice low. "You will not be accompanying me to Draconi this time."

Surprise mixed with the grief on their expressions. It was Jessinda who asked, her voice breaking apart on the word, "Why?"

I set about pacing again.

I always prided myself in being the smartest in the room. There was hardly a puzzle I couldn't solve, or a conch I couldn't memorize. But this was a mystery I didn't understand.

"Rollo is adamant that there will be a war while the queen does nothing to stop or contradict him. I want you to find out *why*."

This had been a little game of ours, fabricated when we were younger and we wanted to learn things. It was how I'd collected so many secrets sometimes. I used my cousins, setting them free about the palace. We all had our little talents. They weren't really so incredibly daft, but rather were all too good at pretending to be.

It was how they could extricate secrets.

Simple things like who was kissing who, or who was seen where.

This was the same thing.

Just a bit more deadly and dangerous.

"You will be my eyes and ears here. Your targets? Prime Minister Rollo and the queen."

They sat up straighter, taking in my every word eagerly and seriously.

"Be careful. This isn't Thalassar, and I won't be here to protect you. Trust no one, not even the servants. Only each other. Do you understand?"

They nodded, and I sighed my relief.

Rollo was planning something. I didn't know what or why, but I was going to find out.

Cries and the song of orcas rang out from outside the palace. My call to leave.

"Stay safe, my cousins," I ordered, "and help me find out what that bastard is up to."

This would not be a personal visit, so we took very little with us. Food, furs, and small packs of clothes for each of us. Our riding party was small, too. Ytgar, Val, Mister Shallows, Anneli, and myself. A few guards would escort us there and back, but this procession was so miniscule compared to the one we had when we first got to Iol.

When I made my way out of the palace, it was to find my mount already saddled, and Anneli perched atop her own next to mine.

She was dressed in her typical black riding leathers and gloves, and a massive fur cloak. It wasn't as ostentatious as mine, nor as pretty. It didn't have the same silver and blue gilded thread with stitched snowflakes and storms. It wasn't made of soft velvet, but a rougher material meant more for practicality rather than fashion. The fur's cloak was raised over her head. A polar bear skin, the jaw wide open so it looked like it would swallow her head whole. The teeth of the beast rested just over her forehead, and the sight of it suddenly unnerved me.

She looked like a warrior, all silver and white with hints of black like night.

I hopped on, gripping the reins tightly in my gloved hands, and raised my brows in her direction. "You're coming too?"

Her lips pulled back in a sarcastic sneer, the silence answering for her. *Isn't it obvious?*

I sniffed haughtily in her direction. "Don't know how much use you'll be to us, whale trainer."

Anneli rolled her eyes until the whites of them were visible. "Back to that then, Princess? Fine. When your mount keels over from exhaustion, know that I am one of the few who knows what remedies are best for their speedy recovery. Do you know how to tend to scrapes on orca flesh, pretentious princess?"

I did not, but I wouldn't admit that to her.

"I suppose you can come along." I pretended like it mattered if she did or didn't. The truth was, I didn't care. I couldn't bring myself to care about anything other than the impending war. And my cousin's death.

My relationship with my cousins was strange. More often than naught, we were enemies, battling to be the prettiest, the most fashionable, the one with the most power. We fought more than we laughed, and we hated each other more than we liked each other.

But she had been family.

And she'd been brutally killed.

When I closed my eyes, I could picture her mangled body, bones smashed from the brutal force of ice and steel, face scraped and swollen with bruises. And that enormous shard of ice jammed into her flesh, pinning her to the sea floor.

And now Rollo wanted a war with Draconi?

I couldn't help but feel like everyone I loved was meant to die. My grandparents, my mother, my aunt, my sister, my cousin…

And the one family member that mattered to me more than any other, more than Jessinda and Scarlet—however cruel that may sound—was a whole enemy kingdom away.

I couldn't keep Silviya safe. I couldn't keep my mother or aunt alive. I couldn't keep my father's love.

But, by the gods, I swore I would keep Maisie safe.

If it was the last thing I did.

I pulled my rage close to me, let it wrap around me like a blanket of biting ice, and the only thing that could bring solace was the warmth of revenge. But revenge against who? Where had the wyvern come from? Certainly not Draconi, so *where*?

"Odele…" Anneli's soft voice cut through my thoughts and had me snapping my attention to her. Her gray-silver eyes flared, so similar to Ytgar's that I had to blink and stare at her again. "I'm sorry," she whispered. "About your cousin."

The words were like shoving a knife into an already bleeding wound. They threatened to cripple me, but I straightened my shoulders, letting a glare settle over my features.

"I have no need of your condolences," I nearly snapped.

Anneli's expression didn't change. Even while my eyes begged, *fight with me, fight with me,* she didn't fall into it. She looked at me like I was everything I felt inside. Sad and broken.

Weak.

I was not weak.

I would not be.

"Why are you coming, anyway?" I sniffed, desperate for a subject change. I couldn't stand the inquiring, sympathetic gaze. I'd break if she looked at me that way.

"Because you'll need all the help you can get, *Princess.*"

"We do, beauty mine." Val was suddenly there, pulling his mount to a stop beside Anneli. He carelessly leaned his elbows on his mount.

He already wore his facade like a comfortable second skin. The one that had me fooled into believing he was truly a prince. The crown I'd given Ytgar rested over Val's own brow, a pale gray against his yellow hair. It was the piercing beauty of his eyes that drew me in. They danced with mischief. He didn't bother with sorrow or empty words of comfort.

"The Prime Minister's spy is coming with us, and we need mer we can trust in our inner circle." His eyes trailed over to said spy. Mister Shallows was a few swim strokes away, though not close enough to hear this exchange. He was lifting his thin, wrinkled body onto his mount.

I despised the mer, and seeing the glinting malice of his expression only made me hate him more.

"We can't afford to turn on each other, beauty mine." Val's words had me drawing my gaze back to him. His expression had softened, though his eyes remained hard and focused on Mister Shallows. When those frosty eyes flicked back to me, I could read the emotions in them so clearly. "We have to stick together."

My fingers tightened against the reins. I was so used to being alone, to keeping others at bay. Even my cousins I kept at arm's length. Never really feeling, never truly trusting.

Not until I'd found Maisie, had I brought someone a bit closer.

Not until I'd come to Iol had I allowed myself to open up to the mer that now surrounded me, and my world felt infinitely changed somehow.

"Fine," I ground out, though I felt like, with this one word, I was giving away so much more than my agreement.

It felt like I was giving away the entirety of my heart.

The frosty currents whipped daggers at my face, but we didn't slow down.

Even as my nose and lips grew numb with the burning sense of pain and my fingers shook within my gloves, we didn't stop. I didn't beg for rest. We rode through the snowstorm as fast as the orcas could travel, but it didn't feel fast enough.

I didn't remember falling asleep, couldn't remember anything beyond the blur of ice and my own exhaustion. My fingers felt frozen to the reins, and the orca was strong beneath me. It felt like we went for days without food, without speaking. Nothing was more important than getting to Draconi.

Nothing.

Soon, the harsh waters began clearing, drifting away to a quiet snowfall in the water. The blow of the current ceased its violence and made way for a clear path nearing the border. It was only then that we slowed.

Ytgar fell back beside me, his steady silver gaze roaming over my every inch. He saw more than he let on. And whatever he saw, he wouldn't comment on. I could trust him to keep whatever sorrow he dug from the expression on my face to himself.

I wasn't like other mer. My feelings… they were complicated things I liked to lock away, and when they threatened to emerge, I constructed walls and vaulted ceilings that I dared not let anyone get through. And he threatened the foundations of it, made me vulnerable. So I lashed out in the only way I knew how. With violence, with passion. We mingled the two like they belonged together. It was only then that I felt everything inside me shatter into a thousand irreparable pieces.

He didn't try to piece me back together, as if he knew more than anyone that this loss was impossible to fix. He didn't need to say anything when the gentle caress of his fingers against my skin, the distraction he offered, was more than enough.

"Ride with me." His voice carried to me like a whistle along the current. Soft, musical. Seductive.

I didn't nod, and he didn't wait for permission as he reached across the space that separated us and wrapped a strong arm around my waist, only to hoist me off and settle me in front of him.

Immediately enveloped in his warmth, I sighed and snuggled against him. I hadn't realized how cold I was until this moment. His arms wrapped around me to grip the reins and we continued on.

"You should rest," he suggested. "The journey is still long."

I wanted to. In fact, sleep beckoned the closing of my eyelids invitingly. I kept them open, staring at his face. The light reflected off of the ice and brushed across his face, making the silver rings around his eyes glow like crystalline sparks of recently fallen snow.

"Tell me a story," I whispered.

He was silent for so long, I thought he wouldn't oblige my request. When he finally did, his voice was a rumbling rasp of seduction, and I relished in every bit.

"Once, many years ago, there lived a kingdom of ice. A desolate, harsh place where creatures ventured to die, for this kingdom scarcely had food. All they knew was blood, violence, and death. And while the kingdoms around them thrived and evolved, they were slower to do so. They knew nothing beyond their little lives. Their rulers were chosen based on who was the strongest, on who could keep the mer alive.

"One day, their world changed when a faraway kingdom dared to visit. They were mer with weak bodies, but strong minds. Strong minds that allowed them to venture into the harsh Iolish waters without death falling upon them. These strangers were an oddity, welcomed as curious guests in ice huts. It was then that a deal was made.

"This kingdom wanted new warriors, see. They wanted treasures that the icebergs sunk; they wanted furs and rare two-legger metals. So the bargain was struck.

"The Iolish would gift this kingdom with what they needed in exchange for one thing. A princess for their king. Amelia Cerul was given to Iol, and with her, she brought in the foreign knowledge of governments, things the Iolish knew not of.

"They were married and they fell in love, and their love brought changes among the kingdom. It brought possibilities, a thirst for life and knowledge beyond the icy walls and waters of a cold and harsh kingdom. And so they planned to change the kingdom, but…"

He paused then, and I opened my eyes—when had I closed them?—and stared at him. His brows were furrowed into grave lines.

"And then what?" I prompted, nudging him softly with my shoulder.

"And because someone didn't want her to change more than she already had, the Princess of Castle Frost died, and her body sent back to her home kingdom."

My heart lurched at the words.

"That's a terrible story."

"But it's a story just the same, my love."

Besides a bastard, he was also a cynic.

"How did the princess die?" The conch I'd listened to had little information about her, except to say they could find no visible signs of death.

"She killed herself."

I blinked at the words; they were so surprising they left me speechless.

I pictured her. That beautiful mer with dark skin and eyes, a stare stubborn and strong. I couldn't imagine her being so weak as to kill herself.

"W—wha—"

"She was cornered by the Prime Minister under a governmental regime she created. The mer felt threatened by her rule and wanted to kill her. Instead of giving him the satisfaction, she took a vial of poison that she kept within a carved conch of ice the king had given her."

I knew that throughout history, some royals were known to keep poison close in case they were ever caught by an enemy. Rather than to allow themselves to be taken as hostages, brutalized, or worse, they killed themselves in a single act of valor.

"The king never knew. Not until later, but by then it was too late, and he'd been killed as well.

"It was the start of a brutal regime. The children were allowed to live, but under rules and a strict agreement. No power, just decorative figures with wealth. They took what Amelia brought to the kingdom and twisted it irrevocably and made a mess of Iol."

"And this is basic Iolish history?"

"Yes."

A gift he'd given me, one I craved more than any fairytale, more than any happily ever after, because he knew *me*.

"If I learn enough about your mer, maybe I could find a solution to your problem." My nails traced lightly over his furs, as if he could feel the sensation of my hand scraping down skin even through gloves and cloaks. "Maybe I can help you get your kingdom back, give back the power that belongs to you."

Ytgar smiled, but he didn't respond. His lack of response made me want to argue. He didn't believe I could do it. No matter how much we advanced with whatever lay between us, we always seemed to take a few strokes back.

He pressed a kiss to my forehead, the movement gentle, his lips warm as he murmured against my skin, "Get some sleep, my love." He pulled back and flicked the reins, urging the mount to go faster. "You can't change Iol if you're exhausted."

Draconi was as pretty as I remembered. And just as pretentious.

The scent of lilies was carried by the soft swaying currents, and everything was swathed in peaceful colors of pinks, blues, and golds. The closer to the capital we made it, the bolder the colors of the waters grew. Blue, black, and red.

"Pretty," Anneli murmured, her eyes darting around her surroundings. A pink water lily drifted off the coral bark of a sea tree and drifted by us.

This was the first time she'd ever left Iol. She wasn't staring at it the same way Odele had the first time we'd come here. There was no adoration or complete fascination in her gaze, just cold calculation. She scanned the waters above as if she expected a dragon to come down and swoop out at us at any moment.

Everything was calm, steady.

Treacherous.

"Seems suspicious."

Ytgar sidled up beside me. Out of Iol, our facade was already in place. The Isolde sword bumped against my hip with foreign comfort. A sword was just a sword, but the symbology of this one made me feel a worthy protector. It was a reminder of who I owed, and who I would give my life for.

"It's too quiet," he agreed, piercing silver eyes roaming the waters around us, above us. Suspicion pulsed off him in intense waves. He turned, half-facing the warriors at our backs. "Prepare your weapons." The scrape of swords of steel and ice slipping from scabbards followed the order. "Eyes above, below, and behind."

As a unit, the Iolish warriors snapped into formation, raising shields in a protective circle and sealing around both Odele and I.

I wanted to shove them aside. I wanted to be at the front, protecting Ytgar from whatever it was he sensed was out there. He was the prince, and he was on the front lines. If he died, what would be the point of me pretending to be him? Even Anneli was holding up a shield and sword, looking every bit the warrior as the rest.

I tightened my fist around the Isolde sword and ripped it from its sheath, brandishing it and angling my body in front of Odele's.

The princess didn't flinch; rather, she looked annoyed. "Give me a weapon," she hissed.

Because I knew she would argue her case relentlessly, I grabbed for a spare dagger at my waist and handed it over to her. She held it with the ease of someone who knew how to use it. Sometimes it was easy to forget that she'd had extensive fencing training in Thalassar.

"Forward!" Ytgar commanded.

We were corralled in the center of the group, swimming further into Draconi. Our fin strokes echoed as loudly as the clanking of steel and shields.

Eerie. This whole damn situation was eerie.

"Stop!"

The procession froze, and my eyes scanned the waters above in the silence. I angled myself closer to Odele. "Stay close to me, beauty mine."

She didn't respond, but her dark eyes gave acquiescence with a single glaring look.

Minutes ticked by. Minutes where there was nothing but silence, our battle-ready breathing, and the drifting blow of the current.

Odele's eyebrows furrowed. "I don't see any—"

Her words were cut off with the sharp echoing screech of a sound we recognized all too well. It was the sound of terror. The sound of destruction.

The sound of a dragon.

The hairs at the back of my neck rose as my body tensed. The orcas beneath us bucked in wild fear before settling calmly with a soft word from their riders.

"Ready your weapons!" Ytgar commanded harshly.

The warriors let out ferocious battle cries, banging swords against shields before pointing them upwards.

And there, in the distance, shadows formed high in the waters. A swarm of darkness, a darkness that parted into a dozen hovering figures. The closer they got, the more massive they seemed, until we could see every single detail. From the gleaming of dark scales, to the thickly pleated armor of the riders.

The dragons cried out, the sound reverberating and shaking the waters. Necks elongated, wings pushing them through the water, their mouths opened to reveal hundreds of sharp teeth that snapped down upon us.

The orcas reared as the dragons swiped, sending orcas and warriors flying back.

The protective circle broke, bodies clashed, and I fought to steady my mount even while I reached for Odele to pull her closer into the space of my protection, but we were blasted apart by the vicious force of a dragon's tail.

I careened to the side, heard the princess cry out as she toppled off her orca and grunted as she hit the silt next to a fallen Mister Shallows. My own body fell, my mount nearly crushing me into the silt. I rolled on the ground and shot back up, brandishing the Isolde sword.

The dragons swarmed us. They swooped low, their riders jumping from their backs to meet katana against swords and engage in battle against the Iolish.

We were spread apart now, and there was no protection. Not for Ytgar, not for me, and not for Odele.

A Draconian in dragon leathers made his way towards the princess, katana threateningly in front of him. He raised it over his head.

I cried out and made a mad dash for her, but Odele was quick and vicious. She met his sword with her dagger, pushing it back. She parried with the much smaller weapon like it was a dance that came naturally in every sinuous movement of her twisting body. She dodged and whirled, bringing her arm up and down against the warrior's head until he crumpled to the silt.

I made it there as he fell, kicking his sword away with my fins, even as my long furs got in the way of the action.

I reached for her, pulling her into my arm to keep her safe while brandishing the sword with the other hand.

Mister Shallows' distressed cries were mere background noise; I wouldn't care if he died here. But Odele… I needed to get Odele to safety, away from the cacophony of the surrounding battle, but even as the enormity of the task dawned on me, my eyes searched for Ytgar in the fray.

He was engaged in a battle of his own against an obviously formidable opponent. The Draconian warrior was strong, his face concealed behind a helmet shaped like the head of a dragon. The steel of his katana glinted as it clashed against Ytgar's sword of ice. Ephemeral sparks seemed to shower over them both.

They clashed and fought, pushed and danced around each other, neither tiring nor giving in. It seemed everyone had stopped to stare at this battle, so enthralled they were by it. Their every movement was hypnotizing, equal parts savage and skilled.

And then the Draconian warrior shot forward, feinted left and went right just as Ytgar lifted his sword. The Draconian took advantage of his exposed side.

I barely had time to cry out a warning before he was slicing through furs.

Ytgar twisted and fell into the silt, panting. He raised his sword, but the Draconian knocked it from his hands. The katana raised, ready to deliver that final blow…

But then a blur of flesh and fur was suddenly there, dropping from the waters just above the Draconian from her orca. Steel clashed against steel and Anneli pushed the warrior back with a battle cry screaming from her lips.

The sudden appearance and her aggression startled the warrior. She didn't give him a moment to breathe.

She pushed her sword against his with punishing force, jerking it up so the tip neared his mask. The Draconian jerked back, and the helmet was yanked from his face to reveal a merman with long black hair and one lone strip of white, dark slanted eyes, and a scar slashing across the bridge of his nose.

He pushed Anneli back, swiping out at her silver tail with his own purple-black one. She fell through the water and onto the silt. Just as his katana came swinging down towards her, she rolled away from it. But the Draconian was fast. Before she could get up, he had her by her hair and was yanking her body against his and sliding his forearm around her throat, keeping her pinned to him.

She struggled, and he tightened his hold, bending low to whisper something in her ear that caused her to freeze.

Her eyes flashed with all the dangers of a storm and in one quick, deft move, Anneli grabbed the Draconian by the arm and flipped him over her shoulder, slamming him into the silt. The merman gasped, even as she dove for her sword and pressed the tip of it against his throat.

The merman smiled and called out loud words in Draconian.

Beside me, Odele translated, loud enough for all to hear. "Cease the fight."

Everyone, even the Draconian warriors, obeyed the command.

Anneli's chest rose up and down with the force of her breathing. She glared down at the warrior who merely smiled up at her with mischief gleaming in his dark eyes. And then he kicked out his tail, swiping hers right from under her. As she started to fall into the silt, the warrior shot up and grabbed her waist, pulling her against his body before she could fall.

Then he was whirling and pushing her away, floating tall once more and taking to the Iolish warriors.

"Emperor Jiang Li welcomes you to Draconi," he said in Thalassarin common tongue, his deep accent curling around his every word.

His dark eyes gleamed as he took in Anneli, who took a few strokes back to her half-brother's side. She eyed the warrior with the same cold calculation she had his kingdom, like she didn't trust him. And she shouldn't. The bastard had almost killed Ytgar, though my prince now appeared to be unharmed besides the torn furs.

The warrior bowed low in my direction. His stance was dangerous, his eyes holding the slightest hint of a threat. "The Dragon Emperor wishes us to escort you to the palace." His attention turned to Anneli once more, gleaming with something akin to malice. "And it will be my greatest pleasure to do so."

"THIS IS THE SILTIEST welcome I've ever received." I pushed my way through bodies of Iolish guards, all but shoving Val into the silt in my furious pathway towards the Draconian warriors. I came face to face with the merman who had nearly skewered my husband with his sword.

My hands balled into fists but instead of swinging and breaking his jaw like I really wanted to, I pressed them into my stomach. My chin tilted up haughtily.

The Draconian warrior merely stared, his expression smoothed into impassivity. His slender features and slanted eyes regarding me with cool indifference. As if he wasn't before royalty. The bastard didn't even bow. His audacity was baffling.

"How dare you attack the Iolish royal party?"

I felt a tug at my arm and a moment later I was pulled away from the warrior, the view of him blocked by both Anneli and Ytgar, brandishing their swords protectively.

The warrior looked at him as if he were bored. "Please put your swords away or we will be forced to disarm you." His tone was insolent.

"There is no need for more violence." Val swam up to the front, placing a hand on Ytgar's arm so he lowered the weapon. Warily, the Iolish did as Val bade, the sliding of crackling ice sounded as they sheathed their swords. "Escort us to your emperor."

The Dragon Emperor Jiang Li sat upon his throne, a massive scaled structure carved of obsidian shaped in the wings of a dragon. As he sat upon it, the wings seemed to spread wide from his back. He looked like a real dragon, exactly like his namesake claimed him to be.

He was leaning forward, his elbow on his lap and his chin rested on his palm. His long hair was braided back with a golden ribbon, and he wore black robes that flowed around his beautiful tail.

He exuded danger and violence in tidal waves.

The Draconian throne room stank of the burning stench of spice and lava. Slow curling tendrils of the incense rose in the little air bubbles through the water. The lava globes were dimmed so the room was cast in an ominous glow.

Beside him sat the empress, and at their sides were Prince Kai and my dearest cousin. Behind her, like an ever-present sentinel, Tiberius floated.

Maisie wore Draconian robes stitched with flowers and goldfish, her expression carved in grave lines. Prince Kai's was even more serious.

Val and I swam to the front, but we didn't bow. No one did. We didn't even greet each other. Silence surrounded us, as thick as the stench that permeated the water. The echoing chasm of it felt like a play for dominance, like a trial.

I refused to bow down to the emperor's methods, refused to look weak.

"Never have I been so disrespected by another monarchy in all my life." I made sure he could hear the laced venom between every word.

The emperor's lips curled up into a sneer even while his brows pulled together angrily. "You dare come here and speak to me of disrespect, child?" Slowly, he unfurled himself from the throne, rising languidly to his full, formidable height. He took a stroke forward, the thrust of his strength stirring the waters. When he loomed over me, I felt a trickle of fear slide down my spine but steeled myself against it. "The last time you were here…" His finger came out to caress my cheek. "…you promised me a friendship with Iol. And yet the currents carry the news that Iol has declared war against Draconi."

Silt. How had he found out so fast? What spies did Iol house? My eyes wanted to stray to Mister Shallows behind us, but I resisted the urge.

"Perhaps Draconi's hospitality never mattered to you at all. Perhaps you do not truly care that your *dearest cousin* resides here at the palace…"

The heavy weight of his words struck me like a threat. The breath caught in my throat, and I could feel the thunderous treachery of my heart. The emperor could hear it too. He smiled and dropped his hand, taking a firm stroke back.

"You bring soldiers to my home." He took a seat, his tail curling around the fin of his throne, elbow propping up against the armrest.

He was the epitome of careless, but I knew better than to trust the stance when the truth of his rabid violence was in his dark, slanted eyes. This was the Dragon Emperor. He was the greatest Draconian warrior to ever live.

Stories were whispered in the depths of conches of his greatness. I was right to fear him and stupid not to show it.

"With whispers of war against my mer, what other welcome had you expected, little Princess?"

Everything about him was condescending.

"Your Majesty, we have come, not to bring war, but to ask questions and hopefully to receive answers." Val, ever the portrait of a perfect prince, bowed low and respectfully, even while his eyes were as hard as chips of ice.

"Answers…" the emperor echoed. "Your kingdom threatens war upon my kingdom, and you have the audacity to demand *answers.*" The last word was said on a breath of a whisper, and yet it held all the command as if he'd shouted it. The effect of it was instantaneous, violent. His sentinels floating guard slid their katanas from their sheaths.

The Iolish pulled out their own weapons.

The tension in the room was a tightening whip ready to snap down at any moment.

Prince Kai shifted. "Father, we must hear what they have to say."

It took a moment for me to recognize the words in Dracon.

The emperor glared at his son. "You are too soft," he admonished in their language. "What happened to the brutal Dragon Prince who led us to many victories?"

Kai didn't look offended, but his lips tightened painfully. "Father, I must insist. She is family now. It is not honorable to slaughter family or visitors in the royal throne room."

There was a pause. A firm nod from the emperor had his guards putting their weapons away once more.

I shifted restlessly.

This was going nowhere. The emperor wanted us dead. If I didn't find a way to appeal to him, he would surely try to slaughter us all, and I'd not let that happen.

"Emperor, I must beg your forgiveness." The entire room silenced instantaneously at the slew of perfect Dracon I spoke. Some blinked in surprise, even Emperor Jiang himself. "We have caused great offense to your household and your kingdom, but I swear to you on the life of my cousin that we come in peace."

Emperor Jiang stared, and his searing gaze made me feel like he could see straight into my soul. Or maybe he was putting the puzzle pieces of me together. As if with a few sentences my entire persona was suddenly distorted, and he didn't quite know what to make of me.

"You speak Dracon," he mused.

I inclined my head, though the familiar rush of pride wasn't there, or if it was, I couldn't feel it past my nerves and the frantic pounding of my heart.

"How?"

His gaze was an almost painful thing. So painful, I could swear he would be able to tell a lie from the truth.

"I taught myself."

He waved a hand at me like he was dismissing my words. "Impossible."

Everyone doubted me. Like all the others, I'd just have to prove him wrong.

"The library in Thalassar offers an extensive conch collection on Dracon. It took me but a month to learn to speak and understand it, another half month to learn to write it." I cocked my head to the side. "Besides, wasn't it the great warrior Aki Watase and Emperor in Draconi's Red Oranda Dragon dynasty who said, 'There are no such things as impossibilities, rather fools without faith, love, and a solution'?"

The fun thing about proving to everyone that you were the smartest in the room was the joy at seeing their blank stares, the surprise, even the embarrassment. I could summon none of that now. Not when there were things even more urgent than my own egotistical feelings.

"Very well," Emperor Jiang finally said. "What are your questions?"

I didn't let my relief show. "The kingdom of Iol was attacked by a wyvern in the heart of its capital. Many were killed. Among them… my cousin, Silviya…" My eyes strayed to Maisie where I briefly registered the shock on her face before turning back to the Emperor. "The Prime Minister is a fool and a sad excuse for a Iolish ruler. The declarations of war… they're true…" Anger flashed in his eyes, so I pushed on. "We have delayed them because we do not want a war. We've been sent to prove to the Prime Minister that Draconi does not house wyverns."

"Of course, Draconi doesn't house wyverns," Kai replied. "Those beasts are the most violent of the Drakes—" He broke off when the emperor held his hand up for silence.

Emperor Jiang regarded me, stroking his chin like every telly villain to ever exist. "You wish to search my breeding grounds." It wasn't a question.

"Any evidence you are able to provide…"

He nodded and got up again. "While war brings honor, I will not risk lives on the paranoia of a mad merman. Be warned, though I give you permission to find what evidence you need, do not think this threat will go unforgiven." He glared, and his next words sent a sliver of trepidation down my spine. "If Iol officially declares war, Draconi *will* respond, and the banners of blood will be raised."

Ytgar

FANCY PRISONERS. THAT'S ALL we were. It's what we'd been reduced to as we were escorted from the burning stench of the emperor's throne room by a dozen guards, including the bastard who had bested me.

I tried to ignore him, but I kept throwing surreptitious glances his way, and then glared when I noticed the way he was looking at Anneli.

Like he wanted to spar with her all over again. And not exactly in the violent way.

I owed the whale trainer my life now, and I'd be damned before I allowed some Draconian to go near her.

"Anneli," I snapped. Slowly, she turned to me, raising her gray eyebrows in what could very well be both curiosity and defiance. "Follow the princess."

Mainly because Odele was swimming ways ahead of us, arm in arm with Maisie while Val, Prince Kai, and Tiberius were trailing a few strokes behind them. She needed protection, someone who was alert to any threat that might befall.

With languid slowness, she obeyed my command and went over to her. Once gone, the Draconian sidled up to me and chuckled.

"Iol breeds merwomen as fiercely as Draconians do." It sounded like a strange sort of compliment. His dark eyes settled over me mockingly. "At least *they'll* put up a fight if our kingdoms go to war."

My nails dug into my palms as I fisted my hands. The urge to slam my knuckles into his face was there, but that seemed to be precisely what he wanted. I'd not give him the satisfaction of seeing me lose control. He'd bested me in combat; I'd not let him best me in this, too.

"There will be no war," I said tightly.

"That's not for us to decide, Iolish."

The mer at my side had no idea who he was talking to. That I was really the prince. Even if he had known, his words would still ring there between us. Because they were true. It wasn't for us to decide. It wasn't for *me* to decide.

The frustration those words brought shouldn't have hurt, they shouldn't have brought rage. I should be used to them, but the truth of the matter was that I wasn't used to them. I couldn't bear the truth behind them, that I was nothing.

But if I wanted to make a change, I needed to *be* something. If I wanted to save thousands of lives, then I would throw away the facade I drowned myself in and fix the problem.

That's exactly what I meant to do.

I made my excuses in half mumbled apologies and wound my way up to Odele's side. Kai's narrowed eyes trained on me, while Maisie looked curious.

"We need to talk. All of us. Now."

"We can speak freely in our room." Kai steered us down the hall and took a right, stopping at the end of the hall before an enormous sliding screen door. He took the handle and opened it. Maisie and Odele swam through first, then Val and Tiberius. Before Anneli could go through, I grabbed her arm and pulled her back.

"Wait." I didn't let go. I could see her curiosity etched on her elegant features, on the high cheekbones and thin lips. She was very pretty; then again, Iol had its abundance of pretty mermaids. She was just prettier than most, even if she tried to hide that beauty behind drab clothing. She wasn't like Odele, who knew she was beautiful and reveled in it, or even like Maisie who shied away from it. Anneli knew she was beautiful, and to her it was nothing more than a hindrance.

I'd grown up alongside the mermaid. Albeit, not in the same way Val had. Those two shared a bond that swam deeper than blood. It was a bond based on shared poverty and the last name Ingen. So deep, in fact, that when I'd forced my grandmother to hire him as our stablemer, he had asked if she could be hired as well.

While I'd spoken to her often enough, I didn't know her. She was distant, colder than even me. Not many would have been brave enough to do what she had. To drop from her orca in front of a swinging blade.

"Thank you." I squeezed once, let go. "For what you did…"

"There is nothing to thank me for, my—" She broke off abruptly, aware that we still floated out in the hall. "I was doing my duty."

"Duty or not, I am in your debt."

If I hadn't been watching her closely, I wouldn't have noticed the sudden tightening of her expression, the look on her face was almost indecipherable, gone so quickly that for a moment I thought it hadn't been there at all. But I saw it. Anger. It was an anger that I couldn't really fathom.

But then she was smiling and gesturing to the entrance. "After you."

As I swam inside with them, everything else was forgotten. Her expression, my own unease, everything was lost as soon as I entered the room to tell them my plan.

"Anneli, this is my cousin Odalaea—sorry, Maisie—Maisie, this is Anneli."

This was a strange introduction. Being used to bows and curtsies, proper titles and surnames, the words tasted odd as they left my lips. That was all my world revolved around. Propriety. But even if I addressed my cousin by her royal title, as Princes Odalaea of Kappur, she would have waved the words off as little more than courtesy.

My friend had no title to speak of, and if Anneli wasn't impressed with mine, she wouldn't be impressed with Maisie's either.

What did Anneli have against royal titles, anyway?

"You made a friend." Maisie smiled widely as she took Anneli's hand in her own and gave it a firm shake.

"Why do you sound so surprised by that?" I demanded.

"Tentative friend," Anneli interjected. "I still haven't decided if I like her or not."

"My guess is *not*."

I turned sharply at that other voice inside the room. I hadn't paid much attention to my surroundings when I'd been so wrapped in Maisie and the safety her presence provided. She was comfort. She was more my home than Thalassar had ever been, and with her I could share the sorrow of the loss of Silviya. They were cousins too, after all.

I was looking at my surroundings *now*. The room was massive, the stench of incense clinging to the sea silk curtains hanging by the open window to reveal the Draconian waters beyond. Water lilies and fish drifted in from the currents and sea flowers of all colors burst in bright blooms near the windowsill.

There was an enormous mound of pillows shoved into one corner. Atop them sat the Black Blade, the one who'd spoken.

With languid, almost sensual movements, he got up from where he sat and prowled over to us. He came up behind Maisie, wrapping his arms around her, palms resting lightly over her stomach. He bent and pressed a kiss to her cheek.

He was as vomit-inducing as I remembered. He still had that sly grin and mischievous eyes, but his hair had grown out over the past month.

"Odele…" he greeted.

My eyes rolled nearly to the back of my head. "That's 'Princess Odele' to you, filthy criminal."

He laughed with genuine happiness, the sound foreign on his lips. What was going on? I observed him, observed the way he pressed so close and protectively against my cousin. This wasn't exactly *normal*. They were always so sickeningly in love, but it was never… *obvious*. Even Kai was pressing closer to her, and Tiberius hovered even more than usual.

I blinked.

"You—" I broke off as the realization hit me, as the hands of the Black Blade, a notoriously dangerous criminal to Thalassar, settled gently over her stomach.

The journey, her yearly heat…

"You're with child."

Maisie's pink skin tone flushed brightly, the color rising up her neck and staining her cheeks. It was only then I noticed how different she looked. Her face was rounder, and her complexion matched mine perfectly. I'd always been a bit wider than her, where she'd been leaner and muscular. Now we were identical in our bodies.

But she—

"Oh my gods, you *are*."

Her silence was answer enough.

"Congratulations…"

"You don't sound too excited," she pointed out shyly.

"No, no. I'm happy for you. This is the most wonderful news! I'm going to be an aunt! Wait…" I paused, just as I was about to launch myself into her arms. "Who's the father?" The heavy weight of their silence—all *three* of their silences—made my stomach churn. "Oh gods, you're going to have mutant salamander babies with the Lizard Prince." I glared accusingly at the Draconian. "You defiled my cousin with your seed."

He sighed, a long-suffering sound that I chose to ignore.

"Does it matter?" Tiberius cut through my accusations, his own voice clipped and irritated.

To think, he once spoke to me respectfully, once looked at me like he'd steal every treasure from the depths of the abyss, collect every conch from every library that existed in the ocean for me. His love had been a superficial thing. He hadn't truly loved *me*, but rather the *idea* of me. He saw something that hadn't been there and had placed me on a pedestal, swam carefully around me like I was a fragile broken mermaid he didn't wish to disturb.

That wasn't love.

Love was the violent kiss of passion. It was indescribable and unexpected.

"If any of you sullied her with illegitimate children, do you know what harm it could do to her rule?" I didn't want to say it, but I had to. I knew what the rules were in Draconi. The emperor had a harem, had so many children, I honestly lost count. He legitimized every single one. But Maisie was a foreigner. She wasn't an empress, didn't belong to a harem. Would the emperor see it as a slight on his honor? To his son's? Were mermaids held in the same standards as mermen?

"Royals are allowed harems in Draconi." Kai's fingers closed over Maisie's shoulder, as if his touch was meant to bring her comfort or protection.

As if she needed it from me.

Or my words.

I was protecting her, being honest. Nothing more. They liked to tread gently through the truth. I gave it to her in all its brunt force. She deserved that much after living a lie for nineteen years.

"She'll be fine." Tiberius smoothed a hand over his short hair.

"Are you all finished with your bickering?" Ytgar pushed his way to the front, his impatience evident in his posture.

Tiberius angled himself so his body was in front of Maisie's, shielding her from Ytgar's striking distance.

"We have important things to discuss." Ytgar barely glanced at my old guard.

"What could a whale trainer possibly have to talk about?" Elias asked, his eyes gleaming with malice.

"Perhaps the impending war? And I'm not a whale trainer, criminal. I am Prince Ytgar Neves Isolde."

The silence following his confession was so profound, I could hear the thumping of every nervous heartbeat. Or maybe that was my own. Maybe it was Val's. I had no clue. I almost choked on breaths of water with his admission.

"Are you *insane*?" The vestiges of Val's carefully constructed control and charm snapped. He whirled on his prince with an accusing glare.

Ytgar merely crossed his arms against his massive chest. How had I ever believed this merman was a whale trainer? He exuded power and dominance, even in his stance. Even if it weren't for his innate, elegant beauty, I should have known from his posture. He had all the bearing of a powerful royal, of a king waiting to be obeyed.

They registered it like a smack to the face, soaking up the truth. I sensed their anger keenly, because I'd been on the receiving end of those lies at one point.

Maisie jerked away from the Black Blade and stared between the two mermen before looking at me, her black eyes searching for confirmation.

"It's true," I confessed quietly, though I wasn't sure exactly what Ytgar's angle was here, or why he had confessed to the prince of his enemy kingdom present.

"It was a *secret*," Val snapped. "For his protection against his enemies." His blue eyes went straight to Prince Kai when he said 'enemies'.

Enemy, the Lizard Prince? Despite his reputation as a ruthless warrior, he seemed harmless enough to me. But if I had to look at it from the point of view of an actual royal, of a queen, from the art of war I studiously poured over for hours and hours in Thalassar, I would say that everyone was an enemy, even when they were your friends.

Nothing could guarantee our protection from Draconi. Not even Prince Kai. Not even Maisie. I realized that now. They didn't rule here. It was easy to forget that when we were far away in Iol. Being here reminded me that Emperor Jiang was the one in charge.

And he'd respond to Iol's call of war with one of his own. He'd bring the wrath of his gargantuan dragon down upon the Iolish, and blood would taint the waters when it slaughtered the mer.

I tried not to let my errant thoughts settle over me like a bad premonition.

"You forget, Prince Ytgar, I have known your secret for a while." Maisie snapped her attention to her husband. More specifically, to his words.

I did, too.

"Wait. What?"

"How could you have known?" Maisie and I shouted at the same time.

Kai's eyes softened on Maisie in a look of such tenderness, it was disgusting. "Spies, my gem. Draconi has its share of spies everywhere. That, and there are rumors that the Iolish monarchy have silver hair and eyes." His gaze flicked over to Anneli for a split second, so quick I swore I almost imagined it, and then to Ytgar where it stayed.

"Congratulations are in order for your intellect, I suppose." Ytgar's tone held no amusement whatsoever. "You figured it out in Thalassar, blackmailed me once, and threatened me twice. You're the paragon of an excellent ruler."

"Blackmail?"

"Threatened?"

Maisie and I turned to Kai at the same time

"You blackmailed my husband?"

Kai glanced at me, unapologetic. "Of course, I did. He overheard something he shouldn't have. I was protecting your secret."

"You mean Maisie's secret."

He waved my words off with a flick of his long fingers. I wanted to break one. "Your secrets were one and the same. There was no difference."

I threw my hands up. "Of course, there was a difference! Stupid Draconian."

"Why didn't you tell me?" Maisie cut in, trying to calm the argument that was obviously attempting to brew between us. Too late. I was already angry.

"I promised I'd keep his secrets, so I did. You did not need to know."

"No," Captain Saber replied smoothly. "But perhaps *I* needed to know in order to protect her."

"The threat had been dealt with." Kai's hands drew up into fists. The animosity between them was startling. And here I'd assumed everything was a perfect harmony between them all.

"And what about you?" Tiberius demanded, turning to Elias. "You collect secrets. Did you know about this, too?"

The dark-haired mermaid shrugged his shoulders nonchalantly, though his eyes were alight with mischief, with all the secrets in this room he was collecting. "I didn't," he confessed. "But I do now. But that's besides the point. Why confess your identity now?"

It looked like Ytgar wasn't going to say anything. After a few moments, he spoke. "Because I want my kingdom to change. But how can I bring about change, how can I preach it and expect to find allies if I'm living a royal lie?" His fingers slowly worked at the tie of his heavy cloak and undid it. With visceral slowness, he let it slip from his shoulders to the ground until he was before them in his tunic and fur vest, the fins of his orca-like tail visible to all. "I want this to be a new regime. I want to make friends. I want to end this war before it even begins. And I will start with you."

He held his hand out, and beats of silence passed between them.

Ba-dump.

Ba-dump.

My heart felt like it would explode from my chest.

And then Prince Kai smiled, a small tilt of his lips. He clasped his hand on Ytgar's forearm and my husband did the same. They shook on it, and I loosed a slow breath.

This... This was history in the making.

It was erasing years of unease between two princes. It was the start of an alliance.

It was the start of a friendship.

The next day the emperor led us to the Dragon Breeding Grounds. We were to search through them, to look for wyverns. We didn't find any anywhere, in fact. Most mer in Draconi had dragons. The royals' beasts were massive creatures meant for riding while the citizens had smaller dragons the sizes of hippocampi or catfish. Meant to keep as pets.

No wyverns roamed the waters. In fact, they kept dragons very tightly leashed. While they were easily controlled in comparison to the other species of drakes, they were still wild, savage animals. They still had the reckless ability to pillage through Draconi and tear down its foundations. Their precautions against this were superb.

"I knew we wouldn't find anything here!" I exclaimed with equal parts relief and dread. I glared at Mister Shallows. "The wyvern threat is coming from somewhere else. Likely further north, from the Uncharted Waters. A war with Draconi is unnecessary. You can swim along and tell Prime Minister Rollo that." I snapped the end bit like I would at a dogfish who needed to follow orders.

Because that's all Mister Shallows was: a dogfish sniffing out information and secrets to take back to the Prime Minister. This was information I'd gladly let him take back to his boss if it meant stopping a war.

"Perhaps I will take it back." Mister Shallows sniffed in my direction, face scrunching up as if I were as odorous as he. The bastard. "He will want to know everything that transpired here." His tone was ominous, but I shook it off. He was just a creepy merman. I didn't think there was any way to salvage him from that.

Besides, with no evidence, we couldn't possibly go to war.

I made Ytgar and Val brush me up on every Iolish law they could remember. What I really needed was to read old Iolish documents. While kings and queens could declare war at their leisure, I wondered if a Prime Minister could do so as well. Monarchs were more, 'do as I please'. But the Prime Minister had a council, upon which the queen and Ytgar both sat. Perhaps before declaring such a thing, he'd need their permission first or at least a majority vote. Although he had most of the council in his gilded pocket, it wouldn't be difficult to declare war on Draconi just because.

If we wanted to fight him, we needed a solid argument, a defense.

"Tell him to cease all action until we arrive there," I ordered.

Mister Shallows blinked. "You are not returning to Iol?"

I smiled sweetly at the merman. "I would like to stay and enjoy my cousin's company. She was not able to attend my wedding, and I have so much to catch her up on. Please, take two of our guards and have a safe journey back." I was excellent at faking pleasantries. It took Mister Shallows off guard, but he eventually nodded and left for the palace to pack.

"We aren't leaving with him?" Val asked, his eyebrows raised.

We had just made it back to the palace after visiting several homes and the Dragon Breeding Grounds. I made sure the emperor heard me while I'd ordered Mister Shallows around just before he swam away with his son, my cousin, and his guards. We stayed behind.

"Rollo will want more proof than this. We have to give it to him. We can't leave yet." I turned to Ytgar. "Send out guards, your most discreet ones, to comb through Draconian waters. If they *are* housing wyverns, which is unlikely, we have to find them and be sure they aren't hiding any."

"Yes," Ytgar agreed. "We cannot afford to have Rollo call us fools for trusting the Draconians. While I do trust their honesty, he will not and will want proof."

"Record it with dragon eggs," I said. "Perhaps the images in harder materials can survive the waters of Iol."

The soldiers around us listened with rapt attention.

"I will help too."

I nearly jumped out of my skin at the merman's sudden appearance. It was the warrior who had almost killed Ytgar. No longer clad in fierce pleated armor, he looked friendlier, even with the angry scar bisecting his face. I glared at him. The others weren't as friendly. Their swords were out in an instant.

"There's no need for that." He waved away their weapons. "I wish to help you."

"Really?" My eyes narrowed on him. "I'm not sure I can believe that. Why would you, a Draconian warrior, wish to help the Iolish?"

The moment his eyes settled on Anneli, I knew the answer. It was in the heated flare of desire there, the longing and curiosity he quickly hid behind an intense and mischievous smile. "I've come to desire the taste for the Iolish, as surprising as that might be." Ytgar angled his body so that he was in front of my friend, cutting off her expression from my view. The warrior glared. "And I have as little desire to go to war as you do. I do not wish to kill innocents based on a foolish merman's paranoia. Let me help you."

"How do we know you won't try to lead my own guards astray or straight into the mouth of a dragon?" Ytgar demanded.

He had a point.

"We don't even know your name," I added.

"Forgive me, Princess." He took my stiff fingers in his own leather-gloved hand and bowed low over mine, ever the portrait of a proper mer. "I am Kane Feng Han." He released my fingers and turned his attention to Anneli, who peeked at the scene from around Ytgar's body. Kane smiled and bowed in her direction, and I watched the flex of his fingers. Maybe he desired to grab her hand, too. "I am a warrior of the Black Ryukin Dynasty, protector of Draconi and Emperor Jiang Li. I offer my services to you gladly, and if it pleases you, I will allow your warriors to lead the way. I'll not speak or give advice. I will merely observe along with them."

I looked for a spark of malice within him but could find none.

"This is a bad idea," Val hissed quietly in Ytgar's ear. If I could hear it, surely Kane could hear it as well. "We don't know him. He could lead our mer into a trap."

"I'll go with him," Anneli offered, taking a stroke forward.

Ytgar and Val stilled, turning silently to her. But she wasn't looking at them at all. She was looking at Kane.

The protectiveness rose from both Val and my husband. She was like a sister to them, and I could tell they didn't want to sacrifice her safety at all.

I'd like to see them try to stop her.

"Absolutely not," Ytgar said at the same time I exclaimed,

"Let her go."

He slashed a glare my way before turning back to Anneli. "We need you here."

She kept her temper in check. This was her prince, after all, though her words were still hard and frustrated. "Need me to do what, exactly? Sit around and play monarchy? I am Ingen, do not forget. My talents will be better suited elsewhere."

They both looked inclined to argue, but we didn't have time for that. "Go with him. Make sure everyone separates into groups; you'll cover more water that way. Document everything and return by nightfall. Understood?"

She nodded and didn't wait for Val or Ytgar to stop her. She swam forward in front of Kane. He bowed low, giving her the same respect he'd offered me. "Tell me, Lady Anneli, have you ever mounted a dragon before?"

Holy silt.

I could hear all the insinuation beneath that question.

Anneli smirked. "No."

"Do you want to?"

"Orcas are infinitely better mounts."

Gods damn.

She was almost as clever as me.

Almost.

"You're acting like an overprotective brother. She knows what she's doing. Besides, she saved your sorry tail against him. I'm sure she will be fine."

The two brutes hadn't stopped grumbling since she'd left. Even as we started swimming back to the palace and the waters started to darken, they hadn't shut up about it.

It was all rather irritating.

We were alone, the three of us, with two singular guards. It felt good to not have a whole procession following us around, especially the Draconians. It felt like no matter where I turned, eyes were on me, on us, regarding us with suspicion. Or perhaps they were contemplating murder.

With the guards, I felt safe, but I felt safer not having them near. I knew if it came down to it, the best warriors to protect me were Ytgar and Val. Of course, I wasn't exactly hopeless myself. I knew how to wield a blade, a sword.

"This is dangerous." Val stopped and turned to look behind us. "Sending away all our guards? Anyone could easily sneak up on—" He broke off abruptly as a figure swam from the shadows, startling us completely.

We drew our swords immediately and pointed them at the ominous stranger who was so obviously not Draconian.

"There is no need for violence, Prince Ytgar." The stranger bowed low in Ytgar's direction then turned to me and did the same, "Princess Odele." Finally, he turned to Val. "And Valmundur. Good evening."

"Who in the ice are you?" Val demanded, pointing the tip of his sword under the stranger's chin. "And how do you know our names?"

The stranger held very still. The merman was older, with graying slips of hair in the blond. Wrinkles pulling tightly at his skin, which was *green*. Not a soft sea-foam green, but a darker, violent green. Every inch of his visible body was scaled, his forearms, his neck, and his face. His face was as reptilian as a dragon, and yet his every aspect was wholly mer.

How did this stranger know our names? More specifically, how did he know who Ytgar truly was? The only ones we told were Maisie and her harem of filth. They wouldn't have betrayed us, couldn't have.

"Forgive me, my lord," the merman apologized, his lips tilting into a tense smile. "I should have introduced myself before appearing from the shadows."

"Yeah, you should have. Who the hell are you?" Val dug the tip of the sword in slightly deeper.

"Forgive me. I am Ric Saentin, and I was sent to find you and extend an invitation."

"An invitation to what?" Ytgar demanded coldly.

"Prince, the sword, if you please…" His whole body trembled.

He wore strange, tattered brown robes with stitches that spoke of a desperate attempt to be sewn together. He looked homeless, and I wondered how he even made it past the gates of the palace.

"Put the sword down, Val."

He obeyed, and the merman visibly relaxed.

"Now we can begin again." He straightened his robes and bowed with exuberant flourish. "Good evening Princess, Prince. I was sent to extend an invitation to you on behalf of King Adrian Ezarah Evander. He wishes to have an audience with you."

I tried to bring forth the faces of all the royals I'd ever heard of but came up blank.

"The king of *what*?" Ytgar demanded. He hadn't heard of him, either.

Ric blinked. "Why, the King of the Uncharted Waters, of course."

The King of the Uncharted Waters requested an audience with us.

The king.

The Uncharted.

The words in the conch I'd listened to so long ago rang through my mind.

Never visit the Uncharted Waters.

But I was never one for following orders. My sense of adventure, the sense of *more* was stronger than any doubts. The curiosity burned as hot as a lava globe inside me. The Uncharted Waters had a king, and he went by the name of Adrian.

"You expect us to swim all the way to the Uncharted Waters to meet your king alone?" Val demanded, lifting his sword once more.

Ric held his hands up and took a small stroke back. "Oh, no, no, no. You misunderstand me. You need not travel into the Uncharted when my king is here in Draconi."

I blanched at that. How had the king snuck into Draconi without the emperor noticing?

"Absolutely not," Valmundur argued. "We cannot leave on such short notice. And how do we know you speak the truth? The Uncharted Waters are rumored to be dangerous, and you plan on taking us to its king?" He scoffed. "I don't think so."

"If it pleases you, my king can be more accommodating and meet you on the outskirts of the Draconian capital so you're closer to your allies. If it will bring you more comfort."

"No." Ytgar crossed his arms across his chest, the gesture one of finality.

Ric looked to me, a pleading look in his eyes as if he wanted my help to make them see reason. The thing was, no matter how great my curiosity, I could not swim into an enemy encampment blindly.

"Why does he wish to see us?" I asked.

He began flittering nervously. "I'm afraid it is a sensitive matter that only my king himself—"

"Either you tell us what he wants, or you can go to your king empty-handed," I interrupted haughtily, lifting my chin up.

My response very well depended on his next answer.

He looked between Prince Ytgar and myself before sighing. "Word on the currents is that you are searching for allies in the kingdom of Iol for the upcoming war…" He dropped his voice to a whisper. "That is why he would like to speak to you. To propose an alliance between Iol and the Uncharted."

Everything within me stilled.

An alliance. An alliance between two mysterious kingdoms. It was unheard of. The Uncharted was unheard of, as mysterious as it was untouchable.

What seemed like a vast, far away and unknown place was suddenly in front of me. So clear. So touchable.

"Odele…" My attention snapped to Ytgar. His silver eyes glowed in the darkness as they regarded me. "It's too dangerous."

I could hear the words he wasn't saying; they were all too obvious in the dangerous gleam of his eyes.

But we needed an alliance.

"You will not leave me behind, Ytgar." I crossed my arms against my chest.

"You can't possibly be considering this?" Val demanded.

"I am," Ytgar replied. "The truth is, we cannot take any chances. We do not know if Rollo will declare war or not. If it comes to that, we need alliances. Yes, I will speak to King Adrian if he is offering what we need."

Val shook his head furiously. "We don't know if it's a trap!"

"Which is precisely why Odele must stay here."

"You are *not* leaving me behind like some old rag." I shoved my hands against his chest, but it was like pushing a solid block of ice. He didn't budge. "I am your wife, not some harlot you can order about."

"I'm trying to protect you."

"I can protect myself, you bastard." My chest heaved with fury. "When will you stop treating me like an incompetent fool and as a valuable asset?"

He sighed and looked over to Val. "Don't look at me," Val growled. "I agree with her. She's smart and capable. You don't have to protect everyone around you from everything all the time."

"Yes, I do!" he shouted.

His carefully constructed composure shattered in one shouting instant. He gripped my upper arms and shook me in one forceful jerk. I gasped as I looked up at him.

We'd been violent before, shared it like a passion. It united us like the intricate woven thread in a tapestry or the components that made up our souls. It was our push and pull when things became too much, when we couldn't form the words to describe what we really felt inside but our bodies could all too well.

This was different.

It frightened me.

It broke my heart.

"I've lost everyone I've ever loved, Odele. My mother, my father. It's like everyone around me is doomed for death. I cannot let that happen to you. I cannot lose anyone else that I love."

Our hearts thumped together, making me realize how close we truly were. Our bodies meshed together.

Chest to chest.

Heart to heart.

In every gods damned possible way.

The rhythm of his frantic beating told the rest of the story that his mouth couldn't.

"I—I—"

I reached a hand up to cradle his cheek. Here was my heart given form. The same fears that thrummed through him like living, breathing slivers also pulsated through me, in every thumping beating of my heart. And I hadn't quite realized it before now; that like me, he had no one.

"You won't lose me," I whispered. "Because I have plans for our future, and death is not one of them." I lifted myself on the tips of my fins and pressed a kiss to his firm lips. "Trust me. Trust Val. All will be well."

It took a moment. A long torturous moment before he dropped his forehead to mine. "I love you, Odele."

"I know."

"I cannot lose you."

"You won't."

He sighed. "Fine." He pulled away from me and turned to Ric. I'd almost forgotten the mer was there. He took the scene in with quiet, curious eyes. "Take us to your king."

It took all night of riding the orcas at an almost impossible speed, but we eventually made it to the King of the Uncharted Waters' encampment.

Draconi was a small kingdom, though the open space of the waters made it seem so vast. It was an excellent space for meeting with an enormous party in secret.

And they *were* a rather large party. Their camp bustled with activity; it looked like a small village rather than an actual camp. Tents rose through the water, thick pelts tied together with thick ropes of seaweed.

Ric led us straight through the camp, the three of us alone with our two guards amidst hundreds of Uncharted savages.

Except they didn't exactly look at all like the savages the stories had told us about. They were simply mer. Mer with odd features; dozens of eyes and limbs, sharp teeth and distorted bodies. With tails and sea legs, webbed fingers, chests, and torsos.

Mer that looked more animal than anything, but still mer nonetheless. They stopped to stare as we zipped by. Like we were the oddities among them. Perhaps we were. But when they began whispering to each other as we passed, I held my head up high. Even when I was nervous, I tried not to show it.

What would King Adrian look like? What did he want? Why was his entire camp on the outskirts of the Draconian capital? I had so many questions and was soon about to get answers.

Past the tents and little volcanoes of lava pits, Ric led us to the centermost part of the camp. The crowd was thicker here, the crush of it surrounding a dais like an audience. When we dismounted, mer came to take our mounts away without a word. And when Ric led us towards the dais, the crowds parted down the middle to let us through.

When we were at the front, we didn't bow. At least, I didn't. Perhaps it was because the image before me was captivating in every single way.

It was the throne that captured my attention first. The throne sat on the silt, like it'd been born there—though it was obvious they'd traveled with it from the Uncharted. Thrones didn't just sit in the middle of desolate Draconian waters.

It was an ivory thing made entirely of bones. The bones welded together naturally with coral and barnacles, with twisting curves and spikes. Ribs and the skulls of mer and fish adorned it, with the massive jaws of a dragon skull framed the top. Or was it a wyvern? I couldn't tell.

The center of the crudely erected bones held an ivory cushion.

Atop it sat a merman.

Not a merman with dozens of eyes or tentacle ears, but a merman with a tail the dark color of umber and copper. A color as dark as my eyes.

His tail curled leisurely around the drowned skeleton of a two-legger at his side. My gaze slowly slid up. Up the clean white and red robes and jacket, higher still to those hands resting on the armrest, up the wide chest that captivated my attention before finally landing on his face.

Two-leggers had stories of pirates and swashbucklers. Criminals who traveled and thrived on adventure, who wore eyepatches and sunk to the depths with their ships and their treasures.

This merman… he had an eyepatch just over his left eye. A black circular thing made of leather, held together by an elastic string. It covered his eye entirely, but I could make out the sliver of scars rising over his eyebrow and down his cheekbone.

His other eye was uncovered, a bright yellow-gold. And his hair? It was the color of two-legger fire, wisps and flickers of it dancing around his shoulders. He wore no crown, but he didn't need one to appear kingly. It was in his posture, in the lazy way he leaned against the throne, one fist cradling his chin and the other tightened around the armrest.

Our eyes met, and I felt a jolt slide down my spine. Bumps rose all along my flesh at the dangerous gleam on the handsome merman's face.

He smiled and straightened. "Welcome Prince Ytgar, Princess Odele…" His voice was smoky sin, and he spoke Thalassarin with the curling tendrils of an accent. "I am Adrian Ezarah Evander, King of the Uncharted Waters."

THERE WERE MOMENTS IN one's history that forged the push of the currents towards the future of greatness. An intricate moment of my life had been the blade that had sliced down the skin at my face, but the most vital moment was now, having Princess Odele Malabella Oriana floating before me.

I'd heard many rumors whispered of the Thalassarin Princess, had seen her through many conches brought to me by my spies. But nothing in my imagination or in a blurry silvery image could compare to the royal before me.

"Your messenger led us to believe you traveled here specifically for us." The princess did not acknowledge me, my title, or my greeting. I was beneath her, that much was made clear as she looked around the camp with disdain, her nose sniffing through the stench of poverty that was my mer. "Though it appears you've been here for a while." Her dark eyes settled accusingly over my messenger, who swallowed nervously upon her formidability.

"Given the circumstances…" I drew her attention back to me with the cool flick of my words, "I assumed meeting in familiar surroundings would bring more comfort to you and your companions." A smirk pulled at my lips. "As well as make the journey less arduous."

Her eyes slowly narrowed into disapproval. "How kind of you to look after our welfare."

A game had sprouted between us, one I knew very well. She wanted to gauge my reaction, understand me. To do that, she would sling barbed words in my direction.

"I am nothing if not accommodating." With a final lingering look in her direction, I managed to tear my eye away from her to look at her companions.

The blond merman was Valmundur Ingen, and the silver-haired one was Prince Ytgar Neves Isolde, the princess' husband.

I greeted them with a slow nod. "I welcome you to our encampment as our honored guests."

"What do you want?" the prince practically growled. I could see his hand flexing near his weapon, a weapon of simple make, not fit for royalty at all, while the merman with ice in his gaze wore the sword of Iolish royalty at his side. A sword with an orca engraved pommel, and a blade made of ice stronger than steel.

I leaned back on my throne then. A structure composed of the bones of my enemies, of every creature I'd killed who had tried to kill me. A symbol of my victory, of the currents of success I'd forged through this life, and the legacy I wished to leave behind. Of violence and winning.

My fingers pressed to the ring on my right-hand finger, where I twisted it round and round. It was polished from smooth obsidian, a dark color that *almost* resembled the princess' eyes. I stared at her eyes now, feeling a jolting sense of *something* squeeze at my chest. I couldn't quite place what it was, though I knew it was something akin to possession. Desire. A need or a thirst unquenched.

She shifted only slightly, her chest rising and falling with sudden labored breathing.

I smiled, the movement almost cruel.

I knew how to be cruel, mainly because circumstances had forced it upon me even when I hadn't wanted it. In the Uncharted, it was the vicious and the strong who thrived, who survived. So I'd adapted cruelty like a third language, and became *very* good at it.

"I want," I answered with deliberate slowness, "to give you the answers to all that you seek." *And more.* I looked at the princess as I thought this, almost willing the silent thought to flicker through her pretty little mind. For a moment, it was like she heard it, and I had the satisfaction of watching a flush bloom across her cheeks.

"What in the name of ice are you talking about?" Valmundur demanded, shifting almost imperceptibly so his body blocked Odele from my view. Even if I couldn't see her, I was aware of her.

My eyes narrowed on Valmundur—Val, my sources said they called him—and I leaned forward, letting my elbows rest on my tail. My posture was full of carelessness and all the stillness of a rockfish.

"Perhaps you've been playing at being prince for so long, little whale trainer, that you've forgotten etiquette when addressing a king."

All three of them visibly stilled. But why would they be so surprised? I'd known their names, my messenger had known their true selves, and still they froze when it was acknowledged aloud.

"How do you know so much about us?" Prince Ytgar reached for his sword then, palm gripping tightly at the hilt; so tightly, it looked like he'd crack it just by the force of his curious anger.

"And what *else* do you know?" Odele lightly pushed Val aside to peer up at me. She stared like I was both a curiosity and a threat. I wanted to be offended but felt more amused than anything. After all, I wasn't a danger to her or to her companions.

I gave her my full attention. "Word on the currents say that a war is bubbling." Her face betrayed no truth of my words, though it didn't need to. I knew what was happening. "We Uncharted may be set apart from the rest of the seven sea kingdoms, but we are as well informed as you, if not more."

The princess shared a look with her companions, a conspiratorial one that set me on edge. I didn't trust those glances. They were the kind of glances mer gave one another just before they stabbed an enemy in the back.

I wasn't an enemy.

They needed to know that.

"I want an alliance," I stated, no preamble, no more beating around the coral.

Ytgar blinked at me. "Alliance?" he echoed the word like it was a foreign concept to him. Perhaps it was. It was known far and wide that the Iolish had no allies. And here I was, offering one up to him.

"I can offer you my soldiers in the upcoming war."

"Hate to tell you this, Your *Majesty*, since you seem so full of illusions, but there won't be a war." Valmundur looked smug as he delivered this news.

My fingers went to the ring once more. Odele noticed the action, her eyes staying on it as I twisted, then snapped back up to my face as I said, "A war is inevitable."

"There won't be a war against Draconi," she spoke confidently. I could smell the uncertainty from where I sat.

"Not with Draconi, no," I agreed as I leaned back. "But with someone far, far worse."

More glances exchanged between the three. "What are you saying?" Ytgar asked.

"I'm saying that I know who released wyverns into your city of ice. And it wasn't Draconi."

A pause pulsed around us. I could tell they were processing this, weighing my words, trying to decide what exactly I knew.

I knew every single detail.

I pushed on, "Even now as we speak, the war against Iol brews. A war that has been plotted and meticulously planned for years, ever since I was a meager immigrant captured in the cages of Thalassar and given this scar." My fingers brushed along the edge of the patch I wore over my bad eye while the good one settled on Princess Odele. Hearing the name of her kingdom made her body give off the slightest of jolts. I wondered what she felt knowing it was her kin who had done this to me.

"If a war has been brewing for so long, why are you only telling us just now?" Valmundur accused. His fingers flexed, and I knew he wanted to reach for the comfort of his sword, wanted to draw it on me and skewer me to my throne of bones.

My fingers flicked against the armrest. "I was nothing back then but an immigrant in a cage with others." Steel bars had been encased around us, and there was nothing quite like the suffocating confines of being a prisoner, a slave. The feeling of starvation and hopelessness, and then the sweet taste of freedom that I couldn't savor beneath the pain of blood and infection.

My fingers flexed as well. I wanted to touch the patch at my eye again, to run my fingers down the ridge of scar tissue that Thalassarin guards had left behind.

Instead, I looked to the princess. The princess who came from the one place I once despised with every fiber of my being so long ago.

"Do you understand hatred?" I asked her. "True hatred is born of mer who have nothing left. It is as slow as it is vicious. It boils inside the soul and overtakes everything else until you are left with one thought and one alone." I leaned closer. Even while a few strokes of space separated us, I felt her proximity as if she were sitting upon my lap. "*Vengeance.*"

Prince Ytgar began to unsheathe his sword, the biting sound of ice sliding against steel meant to be a threat.

I sat back again, smiling in the prince's direction. "Vengeance has been cast upon the seven sea kingdoms. So many kingdoms to conquer would come with such a slow planning process. To answer your question, I did not speak of it, because I did not believe it to be a threat until now. Now that it is, I bring you to my camp, offering you an alliance with the soldiers of the Uncharted Waters, and you *dare* pull a sword upon its king?"

My hand, I realized then, was gripping so tightly at the armrest of my throne that the skull of a mer who dared tried to stab me in the back crushed beneath my grip. Ivory crumbs rained down through the water.

Odele swam forward, closer towards the fin of my throne. "You say vengeance is coming for the sea kingdoms. Why? And why Iol?"

"Because Iol does not have aid. It makes for conquering it that much easier. But I will lend you troops and help your kingdom win against this threat."

Odele's eyes narrowed on my words as did Ytgar's and Val's. It was Ytgar who swam forward first and asked the question they were all thinking. "Why would you help us?"

And what do you want in exchange?

It went unsaid but rang rather loudly around us.

I fingered the obsidian ring as I looked into Odele's eyes and smiled. "Nothing ever comes for free, you're right. What I want is your influence."

"Iol has no influence," Ytgar dismissed with a wave of his hand. "If we did, we would not be meeting in secrecy with you."

"On the contrary." I draped my arm over the back of my throne, gaze lingering over Odele's form. "The princess has great influence. Married to the Iolish Prince, Princess of Thalassar, cousin to the Princess of Kappur and now cousin through marriage with the Prince of Draconi. The whole kingdom is practically in your family's pocket and I want it. I want you to help the other kingdoms recognize our own as legitimate."

Odele scoffed. "And how do you expect my influence to give you all that?"

My fingers raised up to my lips, where my mouth touched the cool obsidian ring. A smile curled at my lips, wide and knowing, and the gesture made them immediately uncomfortable. I dropped my hand. "Simple," I said. "You marry me."

Ytgar

YOU MARRY ME.

Gods in hell and ice. The merman was delusional. He was insane. And he wanted to die.

The hilt of the sword still rested in my hand, half pulled from its sheath. His words make me pull it out completely and, damn the consequences, I pointed it straight at King Adrian.

"No." My answer was a command, tightly spoken.

His eerie yellow eye hardly glanced at me, like I was barely an afterthought, not even a threat. It was a look I was used to. One that said,

'You have no power here.' And all I wanted to do was show him just how powerful I could be.

Odele had been shocked into obvious silence, and yet it was to her he looked. A mermaid who held the key to his maddening idea. Like she had all the answers to every question he'd ever had.

No wonder he had stared at her so passionately when we'd arrived.

The vestiges of my control were snapping, hanging by a simple thread.

"Do you forget she is married to me?"

The bastard flicked his fingers carelessly. "Semantics. The mer of the Uncharted are polygamous. More than one husband or wife is accepted and encouraged." Then his eyes drifted over to me, and the look on his face almost made me shiver. "I do not mind sharing."

As if I'd ever…

"No," I ground out.

His eyes narrowed. "Fortunately," he purred, "it is not your decision to make."

"How do we even know you're telling the truth of who you are? You think that throne makes you a king? It could be a lie."

I could tell I upset him, it was evident in the twitching of his fingers, though his face betrayed no emotion save for contained malice. "The Uncharted divides itself into tribes," he explained with barely concealed irritation. "Each tribe is ruled by a king." He leaned forward. There was something mocking in that gesture every time he made it, every time he lounged and leaned. "An imprisoned immigrant I may have been at one point, but I went back to the Uncharted Waters and I *conquered* and I *took*. And now I am king of half of the waters you and your ilk are so afraid to visit."

Only half. I wondered who ruled over the over half but didn't ask.

"Anarchy existed beyond your borders before I took control and gave it order. We have beasts on the other side that you couldn't even begin to fathom. Beasts as vicious as the wyvern that could make a difference in the war your kingdom wants to fight. The only question is…" He looked from me to Odele. "…will you accept that difference?"

A PRECARIOUS VULNERABILITY SAT firmly in my chest. I used Ytgar's image as a mask I hid behind. Perhaps that's what the promise of his mask had always been. Somewhere I could hide my true nature so other mer would not know the shame of who and what I was.

This stranger had so easily unmasked me, *us*. The action of it left me feeling naked and slightly afraid.

Ytgar continued to question Adrian's legitimacy as ruler in a low, angry voice.

If only my prince could see what I saw.

This merman before us was not just playing at royalty like I was. No, being a royal was much more than having a pretty face. It was in the attitude, in the stance, in the way those around him looked *to* him. And this merman was well and truly a king.

"Will you make a difference?" he asked.

Silence pressed all around us. Odele took a breath, opening her mouth to answer but Ytgar cut in, pulling her back against his chest.

"An alliance," he ground out. "We can sign a contract if you wish, swearing fealty to one another…"

King Adrian *tsk*ed impatiently. "We all know marriage is the most secure way for a true alliance. It ensures loyalty." He sighed, rubbing a hand over his face. "I can see you do not trust me. As a show of faith, I will give you the gift of information." He braced himself against the armrests of his throne. "A secret to prove you can trust me. The one you seek who is responsible for the wyverns in Iol? She is the queen of the other half of the Uncharted Waters." He paused, took a breath. "And she is my sister."

The shock and silence that rippled through the waters was pressing, suffocating.

"Your *sister*?" Odele echoed incredulously. "*That's* supposed to make us trust you?"

His yellow eye hardened, fingers tightening on ivory bone. "Yes. I tell you this because if we ally, I will give you the armies you need to kill her."

"You expect us to trust someone who wants to commit patricide?" I demanded.

Odele snorted a small laugh. "The word is sororicide, Val. He wants to commit sororicide." Her dark gaze pierced him.

King Adrian's shoulder lifted. "I want her stopped. You have no idea what she's capable of."

If what he said was true, if she was the one who sent the wyverns to Iol, then yes, we did know what she was capable of, the destruction a single wyvern could wreak. And we had no idea how many more of those creatures she had.

"Why don't your armies just kill her off?" Ytgar asked suspiciously.

"My sister has the wilder beasts on her side. I need allies as much as your own kingdom. And like I said…" He paused, stroked his chin. "Princess Odele has influence in powerful places."

"And once we help you off your sister you, what, get control over the other half of the Uncharted?" Ytgar gestured with his sword.

The mischievous smile reappeared on his face. "That's just one of the perks that comes with winning."

"Unbelievable."

King Adrian shook his head back and forth, then pushed himself up from his throne. He ignored Ytgar and focused the whole of his intensity on Odele and Odele only. "This is not a decision to be made in a single moment. My camp and mer are at your disposal, should you wish to rest. Please, think on it." He took a few strokes down his dais until he was close to Odele. Not close enough to touch, but close enough for her to be aware of him.

I felt like an outside spectator looking in. Like I didn't belong among them at all.

He leaned forward and smirked. "I know a marriage could be *very* beneficial… for all of us."

The undertone of his words held the promise of something far more sinister than alliances. I doubted he was even talking about alliances at all.

And when he left, Odele floated there staring at the spot he'd vacated, chewing furiously at her bottom lip.

"It's not our decision," I whispered, breaking the silence King Adrian left in his wake. "Whatever you decide, beauty mine, we will support you." It hurt to say the words, but they were so infinitely true.

"This is a bad idea," Ytgar argued.

I pierced him with a glare.

We couldn't control Odele, we never could, and I didn't want to. I didn't think Ytgar really wanted to either. He was worried, wary, but we knew what this alliance could bring.

When Odele turned to face me, it was with a world of questions in her eyes, but she didn't need to ask a single one of them.

We already knew what the outcome would be.

Odele

THE AUDACITY OF THE king was astounding. Though, try as hard as I might, I couldn't find offense when the merman seemed so confident. He was definitely alluring and, gods damn it, I loathed to admit that he was handsome.

In a daring, two-legger pirate type of way.

Like he commanded sin and nightmares, tides and maelstroms.

Something about him was entirely too captivating, and I didn't want to fall prey to it. Polygamy? The very notion was… offensive. Astounding. Incredulous.

I would not be another mermaid in his long stream of conquests. Although I had Ytgar and Val to myself, I wouldn't share them with another.

I was selfish like that.

They had given us a tent to rest in. Their grandest, it seemed, and it was only slightly dusty… which meant it was too dusty.

I coughed delicately into my fist.

Ytgar and Val were arguing quietly in the corner of the tent. They didn't even notice when I grew annoyed with their bickering and got up, slipping out of the tent flaps to take in a breath of fresh water.

Sentinels guarded the outside of the tent with oddly shaped spears and armor, with row upon vicious row of spikes.

The mer had sea legs that swayed back and forth, keeping them hovering a few strokes from the silt. Their eerie eyes regarded me curiously, but they didn't stop me as I swam past them.

It was a bad idea to wander around an unknown camp, surrounded by such strange mer who were ruled by a king of the mysterious waters. And yet I didn't care. Why should I? They wouldn't dare harm me and if they did, well, I'd kill them before they ever got the chance.

With or without a dagger.

I didn't have a dagger or any other form of weaponry with me, to be honest, but it didn't matter.

I knew they wouldn't harm me. I knew it like I knew the sun set on two-legger lands. I knew it like I knew the moon affected the tides or knew there was beauty in the bite of frost.

There was something about King Adrian… something that seemed honest. Malicious, sensual, yes. He didn't have the eyes of a liar. No harm would befall me here.

I wove my way through tents. All the colors here were dull, in murky shades of browns and umber, of dirty whites, and gold with lost glitter.

It was a rather pathetic looking camp. It stunk of poverty and depression.

I wrinkled my nose at it. Perhaps he'd promised an army, but King Adrian had never said what *size* it would be. He never promised numbers.

Clever, clever king.

"Princess Odele…" the merman I was thinking of interrupted.

I didn't flinch as he sidled up to my side from behind. My head tilted higher, and my hands smoothed out the already perfectly straight front of my dress.

"*Majesty,*" I murmured mockingly as I side eyed him.

He was staring at me unabashedly, a smirk tilting up the side of his full lips.

He was alone, with no guards to trail after him, without the comfort of protection they offered. Then again, a merman who conquered half of the Uncharted Waters likely didn't need guards.

Maybe he was a force to be reckoned with.

"You do not believe me."

I snorted. "I believe you well enough, Your Majesty." I looked him up and down. He wore robes far finer than the tents or the mer around him. He had all the bearings of a royal. Then again, Val had, too, and he'd fooled me easily. And yet…

"I believe you are a king, and I believe you want your sister dead."

Pain flared in that oddly colored yellow eye of his, quickly masked behind a hard expression. But a pain like that was so raw, I recognized it instantly for what it truly was. Pain like that couldn't be faked.

"And I believe you have an army." My gaze strayed to our surroundings, to the impoverished state of his camp. "Yet you never specified how many soldiers you *have.*"

He made an amused sound. "Clever mer." His hand settled on my arm.

Had we been in Thalassar, the gesture would have been considered entirely too improper. But we were in Draconi, and this was Uncharted royalty taking liberties in the simplest of gestures with his hand on my arm.

Still, I felt his touch, felt his nearness. Not a subtle thing but like a shock rippling through my every nerve.

And I wondered if he felt it, too.

"Come." He pulled me along. "Let me show you the might of my armies."

The camp may have been a poor thing, but his armies were not. He led me away from the tents, from the hustling sounds of activity, his hand gentle upon my arm.

Ways away from the camp, his army dwelled.

Thousands of mer armed in leathers and spears, hippocampi and beasts without names, none I recognized from any scrolls or conches. Beasts with serpentine tails, beasts with scales and wings, beasts with razor sharp spikes trailing down their spines. Creatures that looked both gentle and vicious.

Creatures that could face wyverns.

I was impressed.

"Do you think you can buy my hand with your pathetic little army?" I asked haughtily, turning from his soldiers to him.

A low rumble of a chuckle emanated from deep within his chest. It sounded as sensual as his voice, irritatingly so.

He grabbed me by the shoulders and slowly steered me away towards a large tent in dyed colors of gold, red, and white.

I held no ounce of fear as he led me past the open tent flaps, sentinels closing them behind him, and into the spacious luxury of what were obviously his quarters.

"I'm not trying to buy you or convince you, Princess." With demanding slowness, he sat me down among a pile of plush pillows with stitched anemones along the sides. He sat next to me, snapping his fingers once.

Servants peeled their camouflaged bodies from the corners of the rooms and bustled around quickly, coming towards the both of us bearing trays laden with foods, rich meats, kelp and greens. They placed two-legger wine glasses with chipped stems and a decanter of frothy, amber liquid in front of us.

King Adrian dismissed them once everything was settled, and we were alone once more.

He pulled the lid from the decanter and poured two cups of the liquid, handing one off to me.

He didn't speak again until I took that first sip, and the liquid burned down my throat like two-legger fire.

"I think you already know what answer you want to give to my proposal, Princess."

"How pretentious of you," I murmured, taking another fiery sip. I swallowed, leveled my eyes with his yellow one. "Very few mermen in the seas exist who would dare to cross me. I cannot decide if you're brave or very foolish."

King Adrian took a sip, his lips grazing carefully over the rim, his hand and head tipping back as he swallowed the liquid. I was captivated by the movements of his throat, by the way the muscles in his arm bunched as he flexed.

Everything about him was alluring. Seductive. Hypnotic.

My face heated, and it had nothing to do with the fermented alcohol in my hands.

He finished the drink off in one swallow and discarded his cup on the tray, hissing as the last of the liquid slipped down his throat.

"I am but an honest merman who has earned his way through the seas." His arms widened at his sides in a grand gesture at the decadence of his tent.

"Yes, you have an army, and you have a particularly average tent. How good for you."

His hands dropped at his sides, his yellow eye twinkling as he laughed. "Many stories were told of you, Princess." That dangerous, predatory eye slashed a single glance over my figure. "I can see they are all true."

I wondered which stories he'd heard but decided it didn't matter.

"I've heard no stories of *you,* however, and I am very curious." I set the cup aside and leaned back against the cushions, my eyebrows raising. "Tell me one."

His fingers went to the ring on his finger, the gesture almost as subconscious as my fingers twitching from the imaginary feel of a whip. Black obsidian, thick and rock-like, he twirled it round and round and round.

I held my hands out, gripping his ringed hand. Warmth radiated onto me, as welcome as frost in the heat. He didn't pull away or tense. His grip in mine was relaxed.

I placed his hand near my lap, fingers grazing over the scars along the skin at his knuckles. His fingers were long, lithe, the ring settled on his middle one. I touched it, a small smile pulling at my lips.

"My cousin wears one around her neck. Very few mer can find pure black obsidian." My words were a request.

Tell me how you got this.

"The reason pure obsidian is so rare is because it can only be found in certain areas. The southernmost part of the Uncharted Waters is one such area. That's where I'm from." He pulled his hand away and pried off the ring, setting the big chunk on his palm. "I brought some of it with me to Thalassar when I migrated into the seven seas with my sister." He placed the ring into my hand.

It was heavy, both the stone and the tone of his voice.

I knew this would not be a nice story. Then again, perhaps I hadn't wanted it to be.

Pain brought mer together. It revealed them in their most honest and true forms, something that couldn't be faked.

"There were soldiers everywhere. I was younger then, hadn't paid much attention to what was going on. All I wanted was a better life." He paused for a moment. "The Selection… it's what got us caught. They questioned us, asked us to prove our identities, our Thalassarin citizenship." He broke off and chuckled, closing his eyes and shaking his head back and forth. "I hadn't even known your mer did things like that. Kelpwork?" He scoffed. "They threw all of us in a cage with the Selects who had tried to flee and were to be executed. That was the kindest thing they did to us."

I—I hadn't known.

Of course I hadn't known, because I hadn't cared. It wasn't my life. It wasn't affecting me. I'd been safe inside the protection of my little quartz palace.

No one else outside of it mattered to me. I never thought about them, never lost sleep over them. After all, there were thousands of orphans out there, mer died every day, fell on hard times. Was I to mourn every single one of them? What would my tears do? What would *mourning* do for them?

Yet *cages?*

I knew what it was to live within confines.

A cage was a cage, no matter its size, no matter how different the bars.

My hand tightened around the ring, fingers pushing it into my palm.

"They beat us first. The immigrants? We had the worst of it. The ones who tried to flee selection, they were beheaded immediately. They broke the law but were still Thalassarin, so it was fine. Us? We were different. Uncharted. No government, we were savage mer and as such, deserved savage punishment.

"They took the mermaids first, among them my sister. The things they did to her… I will not even mention. Yet they made us watch. They made *me* watch."

I didn't want to listen to this story anymore. But to turn away from it would make me a coward. Those had been my mer, my *citizens.* How vile and cruel.

And I'd done nothing to stop it.

Because it hadn't been my fault. It had been King Dorian's, my step-mother's, and my father's. I was always overlooked, never allowed to make any decisions.

Because you led them to believe you were but a fool.

Slowly, King Adrian's hand lifted, fingers gripping the strap of his eyepatch. He swallowed once before he pulled it off to reveal what was underneath.

I'd known he had a scar. I'd seen the tendrils of it bisecting above his eyebrow and down his cheek.

But this was mutilation.

It was ugly. Violent.

Heartbreaking.

His eye looked as though it had been pried straight out of its socket, leaving nothing behind but a permanently closed eyelid with warped silver flesh behind. It ran from his forehead down to the side of his chin. On top, the scars were thinner. It was around the eye where it was mangled.

My mer had done this to him.

I swallowed the lump in my throat and reached for the scar. The scars seemed to abrade my skin, branding me a murderous mer. An ignorant fool that everyone thought me to be.

His hand encircled my wrist gently. Not to stop my explorations as my fingers glided softly over the marred flesh, but to hold me or to steady himself. I wasn't sure.

"They gave me this when I tried to protect my sister, but what they gave her was far, far worse."

I couldn't even imagine…

"There was a merman there. He helped us escape. Eyes like a demon, but a gentle heart. The pure obsidian I meant to sell, to convince the rich mer of the seven seas to mine? It became his that day, my parting gift to him as thanks for saving us from further pain." He chuckled, and I felt the rumble of his breath fan across my wrist. "I wonder what happened to him…"

I released his scar and pressed the ring back into his hand, a tentative smile on my face.

"They say the ocean is a vast place," I whispered. "But I find it to be rather small. Your friend? I think I know who he is. And trust me when I say… he's doing quite well for himself."

The Black Blade was doing well indeed, if the smile on my cousin's face had been any indication.

"I'm glad to hear that."

Silence pressed between us that became almost suffering and unbearable. I cleared my throat. It didn't matter, I shouldn't care, and yet I found myself asking, "Do you despise me for what my mer did to you?"

My gaze kept going to that scar, to all the pain behind it.

"I did at first. Years ago. I hated all the seven sea kingdoms and so I took my mer back to the Uncharted, and hatred was what fueled me to conquer. But then, I forgave." He leaned back, throwing his arm leisurely against one edge of the cushions. He regarded me softly. "I didn't want to live my life full of hatred, because I saw what that path did to my sister. She was never the same. What they did to her that day… It destroyed her completely.

"I just want a better life for my mer. I want us to move freely between kingdoms, to not live in fear of the confines of cages. I thought we could accomplish that peacefully. Cruelty loses its appeal after a while. When our ideas warred, eventually so did we. And now here we are, on opposite sides of the seas."

He looked a little sad, and I couldn't blame him.

"So you want to stop your sister from conquering and spreading hate?" At his nod, I asked my next question. "And do you really think marriage to me will help?"

He smirked, and I felt like I was staring at the devil himself.

"I know it will."

Something in the promise of his gaze made goosebumps rise along my arms. There was something else in that stare, something hidden. I leaned forward. "What do you want from me?"

"I think you know." His eye gleamed dangerously.

I shook my head. "No. I mean, what do you want from me? Are you expecting me to be a savior to your mer? Are you expecting me to ride out into battle? Because I can tell you right now, King Adrian…" I leaned forward, close enough to feel his heat. "I am not self sacrificing. I won't mourn every lost soul. I am cruel and selfish. So, answer me this, *why* do you want me?"

"If you ask me not to expect selflessness from you, do not expect poetry from *me*, Princess." He leaned forward until we were touching, until the panes of his chest were against the soft curves of my own. "I want you for my own gain. I want you because you can help me help my kingdom. I want you because I *do*. I'm just as selfish as you are."

My breathing grew labored at his proximity, at his curling words, at the things he was making me feel with just the warmth of his voice.

"You don't even know me," I whispered against his skin. My lips were close to his scarred cheek, hovering a whisper away. "You've only heard rumors."

And I could imagine what every little rumor said. The things whispered in the spaces between the currents. Daft. Useless. Foolish.

Every little word they imagined me to be in the back of my throat.

"I know what the rumors say. I also know you speak many languages fluently, that you have excellent skills at memorization. I know you aren't what everyone thinks you are."

I leaned away from him, needing the distance to steady the maelstrom of my mind. I blinked, regaining my composure.

"Let's say I accept your proposal, your armies, your war. What would you expect from me as your wife?" I reached for the glass of fermented wine with steady fingers. "My mind? My body?" I took a sip. "Fidelity?"

"*If*," he emphasized, "you agree to my proposal, I will expect *everything.*"

I gave pause at that, eyebrows pulling together tightly. "Everything? Even fidelity?"

"If you're concerned I'll try to prohibit you from being with Prince Ytgar and Valmundur, don't bother. I won't object, as I don't mind sharing."

"Well, I do mind."

He chuckled and leaned close, prying the cup from my hands to set it aside. "Greedy little thing." He murmured the words like a compliment. "Do you want me to put you at ease? I have no wives or husbands, no merfriends waiting for me to claim their hands, nor do I want them. All I want is *you*."

"I haven't said yes yet."

He smiled, and I realized just how dangerously close he was to my mouth. "You haven't said no, either." His fingers were suddenly there, trailing little patterns against the sensitive spots on my flesh.

"We don't even know if we'll be compatible." I shivered.

What had I meant by that? I wasn't sure. Compatible in what way?

"Then maybe…" His lips came closer while one hand gripped my shoulder, thumb moving back and forth against my collarbone. "…we should test the waters?"

And he kissed me.

It was everything I never knew I wanted, *needed.*

His lips devoured my own. This was no slow playful dance. No teasing. This was consumption, plain and simple. This was a taking, a *claiming.* He was taking exactly what he wanted. There was no time to get to know one another slowly.

His tongue tangled against mine, savage and sensual, drawing my pleasure out in languid strokes. Every inch of him pressed against me, his body angling over mine. His fingers dug into my shoulders as he roughly shoved me against the pillows.

My whole body quivered in ecstasy at the very touch of him. This was a violent maelstrom between us. It was the calm of the storm before a wave rushed through land, destroying everything in its wake. I grappled for him, pulling him closer. His body pressed against me, our hips thrusting in desperate movements.

I'd never known pleasure to build this high this fast. Maybe the game of foreplay had been hidden somewhere between our words, pressing and pulsating between us to become this.

His hands skimmed up and down my sides, leaving a trail of heat wherever his palms touched. I felt the heat of him through the thick velvet of my dress. He explored, like it was his right to do so. And I touched him, my fingers tracing the ridges outlining his scar gently, even while the fingers gripping his shoulder were aggressive in their desperation.

He pulled away, his mouth going to my chin, trailing a pathway lower down my throat, teeth grazing across my collarbone. I gasped at the sensation, lifting into him.

"I'll make you feel good, Princess." His palm curved up my breast, kneading it, while the other tugged at the hem of my dress, yanking it up.

His hand went between us, fingers traveling up my scales to my hips, touching the slit of my opening.

I cried out at the pleasure spiraling through my body at the simple contact.

"That's music to my ears, love." His fingers slid in, stroking deep inside me, over and over again. Just the feel of his fingers inside me, bringing out the torturous pleasure slowly, painfully, had me thrusting into him, willing him to go faster, harder.

At some point the line between pleasure and pain blurred in the rough movements of his hand, in the aggressive force of our push and pull. He kissed me and it tasted like sin. And when his fingers pinched the very center of my desire, it felt like both a punishment and a gift.

I screamed, collapsing against the mounds of pillows. My limbs and body were both sated, tingling from the afterglow of my pleasure.

His fingers were still firmly inside me, moving slowly. "Accept my proposal," he whispered between gasping breaths.

My heart thumped.

I wasn't self sacrificing. Everyone knew this. I didn't care what happened to others. Nothing mattered to me but my own pleasure.

And right now, my pleasure was a living thing around us, caressing and urging the desperate breaths from my body.

"I accept."

IF I'D KNOWN A kiss would seal the fate of my mer, I would have kissed her sooner. But I couldn't stop with just a kiss. She deserved more. Much, much more.

She deserved the passionate fury of rogue waves and tides, of silt storms and the dangerous searing of heat. She was passionate enough, a force to be reckoned with. A storm all in herself. It lived within her, threatened destruction.

And it threatened peace.

If there was one thing I knew from our short time together, it was that she would bring peace. To my mer, to our future.

She denied being self sacrificing. She wasn't selfless. No, selfless mer didn't conquer. They didn't win. I needed a ruthless bride, an intelligent bride. If there was one intricate truth the both of us understood, it was that our selfishness and stubbornness would help keep what was ours.

And destroy all those who threatened to take it away.

"I'll send servants in to prepare you immediately." I pulled away from her, drawing her up into a sitting position with one hand, while my other slipped from her heat.

She blinked at me as I smoothed down her dress. I kept my hands lingering near her for longer than necessary before I picked up the eye patch and secured it over my scarred eye once more.

"I'll send them in immediately," I repeated, my eye lingering over her. And because I couldn't help myself, I reached out and took an errant purple-blue strand between my fingers and twisted it round and round. I smiled as I released it and when I started to get up, she stopped me by gripping my wrist.

"Wait."

I raised a brow.

"I have one demand."

Of course, she did.

Greedy, demanding, delicious thing.

I smiled.

"I'm listening."

Odele

Servants came in immediately after he exited the tent and began fussing over me. They brought jars of sand in and they wasted no time, two of them stripping me while the other scrubbed the grains all over my body.

I was used to being waited on hand and fin, though not in this. I enjoyed pampering myself, the ritual of it. I liked to braid my own hair and dress myself because no one could make me look more fabulous than myself.

But I let this happen without complaint. I enjoyed the ceremony of what would be my second wedding ceremony. To a King of the Uncharted.

"King Adrian has instructed us to brief you on Uncharted wedding ceremonies," one of the servants said as she swept my hair over my shoulder to scrub sand along my bare back. "When it is announced, you will choose a Watcher."

I wrinkled my nose at the term. "Watcher? What's that?"

She paused a little hesitant before pushing onward. "It's tradition. After the vows are spoken, the Watcher goes with the bride and groom, or brides and grooms or brides and groom or... well, you understand, I'm sure... and observes while they consummate the marriage."

Wait. What?

That meant someone had to watch while Adrian and I...

"That's weird."

She flicked my long hair back from my shoulder and began running her hands through the strands, dusting out any lingering sand. "It's tradition. It ensures that no lies are told regarding the legitimacy of the union. Don't fret, Your Majesty. The Watcher can be *whoever* you choose."

I wondered if those words were an insinuation of some kind but shook it off when the tent flaps suddenly flew back. Ytgar and Val barreled through the entrance.

They stopped, taking in my naked form.

The servants let out small noises of surprise and rushed to place a robe over me. I waved them away.

"It's true, then," Ytgar all but growled. "You agreed to his proposal."

I tilted my chin up defiantly. "I did."

His hands tightened into fists at his sides, his nostrils flaring. His face tightened into an expression of rage he was trying so hard to conceal.

Val placed a hand on his shoulder. The effect was instantaneous. Ytgar relaxed, eyelids fluttering closed, he let out a breath and slowly nodded.

"It's your decision," he said with a touch of finality. His eyes opened, the silver piercing entirely through my core. "I just hope you know what in gods' ice you are doing."

"I do." The words held so much truth, they felt *right*. The same way I'd felt *right* when I'd swam up the altar to meet with Ytgar, this was that same sensation. Certainty. A smile touched my lips as I turned slowly over to Val. "Valmundur Ingen, I've demanded something from King Adrian." I turned to the servants and inclined my head.

They immediately got to work, pulling Val deeper into the tent. They tugged at his clothes, yanking them from his body in swift, quick-fingered movements.

He protested, but the servants were stronger, relentless, and soon they had him as bare-tailed as me.

"What in the ice—"

"Don't complain, Iolish." I winked. "Let the servants pamper you. It's not every day you get to marry a princess, after all."

Valmundur

"WHAT ARE YOU TALKING about?"

It was hard to wrap my head around everything when the servants were bustling around the tent, draping fabric over me, shoving my arms through tunics and jackets. They moved with surprising speed, blurs in the water as they dressed me fully.

I looked down at what they'd outfitted me in. It was a white jacket with red and gold trimming, and silk spun tassels hanging from the shoulders. The tunic beneath it was long and rich, hanging down halfway to my tail.

It was a uniform meant for a king.

I wasn't used to being so exposed. I had already gotten used to hiding who I was like it was something shameful and now I was on display, wearing riches like *I* was someone to be proud of.

"I'm not just marrying King Adrian today, Val. I'm marrying you as well."

I whirled to gape at Odele who still floated, gloriously naked, and beaming at me with her hands on her scaled hips.

"What do you mean?" I asked slowly.

"It means I'm marrying the both of you today. You won't marry each other, so don't worry about that. You'll be marrying me. If you'll have me, but of course you will." She flicked aside her long hair, eyelashes fluttering with exaggeration. "Why wouldn't you?"

I tried not to feel so dumbfounded but couldn't help the awe, the shock that carved a path through my chest.

"Why would *you* want to marry *me*?" My hands shook from the disbelief. This was… I wasn't sure what it was. I'd given her my body, given her pleasure, but marriage was something else entirely. At least with the former she was receiving something in return. In marriage, I had nothing to offer her other than… me…

And I still wasn't sure I was good enough.

"Why are you hesitating?" Her dark eyes scrutinized me. I was always good at reading her, and in her expression I saw the hurt. I knew then that this was very, very serious. She wasn't just acting frivolous on purpose, but because she was nervous of what I'd say. Of all the crazy notions, that she'd be nervous I'd reject *her*?

The last thing I wanted to do was hurt her.

"Can you all give us a moment alone, please?"

I waited until the servants filed out of the tent, likely waiting on the other side to listen in on every word, but I didn't care.

In here, it was just Ytgar, Odele, and I.

I swam up to her, taking her hands and uncurling her fingers from her palms, threading mine through the spaces between hers. I pulled her close, every naked inch of her.

"Are you sure you want…" I paused, almost afraid to utter the words aloud. I wasn't sure she could ever understand all the reasons I, a nobody without an ounce of royal blood, wasn't good enough for her. "Are you sure you want *me*?"

There was a pause so profound, the fear slipped inside me. I wanted her to be sure, but I was scared she wouldn't be. That this was just a fancy. Why would she love me? Why would she care when I lied to her, tricked her, gave her nothing but heartache?

"I'm not sure," she whispered.

My heart fragmented at the words. I wasn't even aware a heart could break like this between one furious second and the next. But it could. It did.

I started to pull away, but she gripped me tightly.

"It's because you asked me that question that I *know* with every scale on my body and every beat of my heart that I want you, Val. All of you." She slid her hands up my arms to cup my cheeks. "You see me, Val. You saw me when no one else did. And I see you too. Because…" She swallowed, turned to Ytgar, and held out her hand, palm facing up. He took it, and she pulled him close so that she was between us. We were all infinitesimally close. "I love you both. Don't," she cut a warning glance to me, "mock me. I won't say it again."

No. She wouldn't say it again. She wouldn't gift kind words and honesty out or wear them on the lace sleeve of her dress. It's what pain did, it's what a lack of love did, and that truth connected the three of us. It was perhaps one of the few things we had in common. Not blood, not our pasts, but the pain.

And the emptiness in each and every one of our hearts became filled with each other until we were sharing *this*. The love we never had but always desired.

What we couldn't find elsewhere, we found in each other.

And that would always mean something.

It would mean everything.

"I love you, too, beauty mine." I pressed a soft kiss on her forehead and lingered there, smiling against her skin. "Yes. I'll marry you."

My dress was the color of umber, trails of glittering fabric stitched in bits and pieces along the waistline, the same yellow-gold that matched his eye. The servants placed a white sash around me and a delicate dark red cloak around my shoulders.

The waters were filled with Uncharted mer as I was led towards the center of the camp by the servants, where the ceremony would take place.

Floating side by side were Adrian and Val, both wearing similar styled outfits, though Adrian wore a crown made of bone and obsidian upon his head.

Before them floated a very old and hunched mer with many wrinkles slashing across his exposed skin. He wore red robes with a collar of antlers and teeth stitched along the neck. In gnarled, firm fingers, he held a staff like some shaman.

They led me straight towards them, settling me between Adrian and Val.

The silence was a loud cacophony, echoing in my ears, preceded by the shaman waving his staff around. The movement caused a slow, whistling sound. Whatever was inside the bulbous head of it rattled and shook, and the waters vibrated in response.

And the old mer began to speak in a language I didn't understand—the language of the Uncharted was ancient and rough—but the quietly spoken words captivated me all the same.

Adrian leaned close. He appeared to be glowing with sinfully wicked colors, clumps of luminescent phytoplankton dancing around him as he explained, "Mer of the Uncharted are gifted magic wielders. Magic and science go hand in hand, and yet there are very few privileged with the gift of magic song. It's what makes tellies work. It's what gives us protection from the two-leggers who would otherwise hunt us to extinction. Magic is everything."

The old merman spoke again, his voice rising and falling. The waters stirred at the sound of it. Like it was music, and they were the tune, drums clashing and bellowing.

"Magic is in all we do. It is in life and death, in whale song, in emotions. It is an energy within us, it is in happiness and sadness, in giving birth, in sex. It is in the bonds we create. And marriage is a bond."

Adrian went silent and took my hands in his, turning me to face him fully. "I have a gift for you."

A servant swam up, offering up a fancy pillow. On top of it sat a dagger with a brass hilt carved into the image of a fierce wyvern. Adrian picked it up and handed it to me. I grabbed it by the hilt, feeling the perfect balance of it in my palm.

"It's beautiful." I placed it gently back onto the pillow the servant held up. He bowed and swam away with it.

Adrian took my hands in his once again, a satisfied smile pulling at his mouth. "Now, repeat after me, Princess. 'I seal these words with magic and promise as the savage gods of love and death do witness, to bind myself to Princess Odele Malabella Oriana as my bride.'" He nodded his encouragement. "Now you."

"I seal these words with magic and promise as the savage gods of love and death do witness, to bind myself to King Adrian Ezarah Evander as my groom."

The shaman spoke a few firm words and Adrian pulled me close. His hand went up to cup the back of my neck as he leaned towards me. He smirked.

"Trust me, *love*," he murmured, the word both sarcastic and endearing on his lips.

"I do."

And I'd never trusted anyone so intimately, so quickly except for Maisie. Maybe that made me a fool.

But it didn't matter anymore because Adrian was kissing me, devouring my mouth. His tongue slipped past the seams of my lips, tasting, taking.

I sighed, leaning into him; all too soon, the kiss ended.

Then Adrian was turning me, his hands skimming down my sides as he pressed my back up against his chest.

His breath fanned against the lobe of my ear as he whispered lowly, darkly, "Now repeat them to Val."

I fought back a shiver, my voice shaking as I repeated the vows to Val.

When he repeated them to me, I felt something settle over us, tying us together.

And then Val leaned forward and pressed his lips to mine, and I was stuck between the two of them, feeling overwhelmed by every little inch of them.

His tongue flicked across my bottom lip just before he pulled it between his teeth.

My hands slid up his chest where I felt the pounding of his heart against my palm.

It was that rhythmic thumping that measured the next few seconds.

Magic.

It was magic.

When he pulled away, the blue in his eyes sparkled like a fresh coat of frost.

"Wife," he whispered sensually.

The shaman interrupted my reply with deep, curling words.

"'Now you must choose a Watcher,'" Adrian's voice flittered darkly through my ear, translating the old mer's words.

I swallowed. The Watcher would be witness to the consummation of the marriage. He or she would observe everything that transpired between Adrian, Val, and I.

It can be anyone.

My eyes found silver ones in the waters.

"I choose Prince Ytgar Neves Isolde as my Watcher."

Ytgar

A SERVANT EXPLAINED THE duties of Watcher to me quickly and quietly as they ushered me into a tent with Odele. They left shortly after, leaving the two of us alone.

A strange tradition with a total lack of privacy, an opinion I'd voiced aloud.

"In some areas of the Uncharted," they had explained patiently, "the Watcher lies with the bride before the husband does to test her purity."

I stared at Odele now. She bore the waters of confidence but the biting of her bottom lip and the twitching of her fingers were telling gestures. She was nervous.

I swam up to her, letting my hands settle over her shoulders gently. "You don't have to do this, you know."

She smiled. "It's already done. I know you aren't happy with sharing me—"

"I've known Val my entire life," I interrupted. "He's been my best friend for years. I love him, trust him. I don't know Adrian, and now I'm meant to trust him with you?" I grabbed her chin with my index finger and thumb, tilting her face up slightly so she could see the affliction in my eyes. "I don't want to see you hurt."

"He won't hurt me."

"How do you know?"

"I just do."

I sighed, pulling away from her to run a hand through my hair. I felt like I'd already aged a decade in the past few hours. I was resigned to these events, forced to be a bystander as they unfolded.

"You don't love him."

"I didn't love you, either. The truth is, I want his armies. I need his beasts so they can help destroy the ones responsible for all that chaos, for Silviya's death. It's not like I'm not getting anything out of this deal, either. I'm not free or cheap, husband."

How she could still joke now was beyond me.

Fine.

If she wanted to see this through to the end, I'd do my duty as Watcher.

With steady strokes, I circled her and stopped just at her back. My fingers worked deftly to untie the little cloak clipped at her shoulders. Slowly, I began to undress her for Val and Adrian. Each article I pulled off, I let the material slide languidly over her skin before I folded it and placed it in a chest. Continuing, my fingers brushed against her skin in teasing motions until she was clad in nothing but a thin, transparent chemise made entirely of spun silk.

All without looking into her eyes. I feared if I did, I'd lose all semblance of control and re-consummate our own marriage. Briskly striding to the tent flaps, I threw them back. Adrian and Val were waiting on the other side. A crowd had slowly gathered behind them, far enough away to give the illusion of privacy, but I knew they'd be listening to everything that transpired here.

I led them inside, securing the flaps after them and turned, arms crossing against my chest.

Adrian and Val floated there, taking every inch of Odele in. From the tips of her exposed fins up to her wide, dark eyes and floating tendrils of hair.

No one moved.

"Well?" I urged.

Val whirled and glared before turning back. "This all seems so ceremonial and stiff. I need a drink." He made his way over to where the servants had left a tray of food and drink, poured himself a glass of fermented wine, and then downed it all in one swallow.

"I know how tedious traditions can seem…" Adrian joined Val and poured three more glasses of the beverage. He handed one to Odele with a smile and then swam over to hand the other one to me. "But they're the foundation of our mer. They want to make sure their future is secured, and that they'll have a place in this world." He took a slow drink and sat among his enormous mound of pillows. "While it's for them, it is also for us. We don't have to treat it like a chore. We can all enjoy ourselves. After all…" He smiled as he tugged at the hem of Odele's chemise with his free hand, pulling her down almost on his lap. He turned his face, whispering against her cheek. "We have all night."

His hand glided up her side to cup the underside of her breast, the movement so casual it couldn't be anything but sensual.

The merman was gods damned alluring. Like sin and sex given form.

Odele let out the smallest of gasps, her body angling into his touch, fingers grasping her cup.

"Enjoy yourselves," Adrian ordered before taking another sip. "You too, Watcher."

I wanted this over with, but he seemed to want to drag it on so I had no choice but to go along with it or suffer alone.

I downed the contents in one swallow. When I pulled the cup away and licked my lips, Adrian's yellow eye followed the movement with a sort of… malicious glee.

It was unnerving.

His hand roamed over Odele's body like he couldn't go a moment without touching her. All the while, that eye flicked between Val and me knowingly, challengingly.

Val poured himself another drink, tipped the cup back, and drank before discarding the glass and sitting on Odele's other side, throwing his arm leisurely around her shoulders.

"Being married feels different," he commented, pulling her closer to him. His fingers roamed through the tresses of her hair, playing with the strands, curling them around his finger and letting them float. "It's like, within a few words and the next, you suddenly find your entire world changed." His fingers went to her bare shoulder, down the length of her arm. "And nothing more could ever compare. Nothing could ever make you happier."

"Who knew you were such a romantic?" Odele teased, lifting her face up to press a gentle kiss to his chin.

"I've always been a romantic, beauty mine." He leaned back so her lips could press fully to his throat, and down lower to his collarbone.

As she continued kissing Val, she moved her body over his. Adrian slid his palms down her spine and hips, watching me as he touched her.

Daring me.

To do what, I wasn't sure yet.

"Drink, beauty mine," Val urged, gripping the bottom of her glass and pushing it to her lips. She obliged without complaint and when she finished, he took the glass from her and discarded it. "Now can you kiss me? I'd like to know what it feels like to kiss my wife over and over again."

He took her mouth in his like he was desperate and hungry. Her hands went to grab at his shoulders and they fell against the mounds of pillows, Odele on top of Val. He gripped her hips and pulled her down on top of him, his tongue stroking her bottom lip, teeth biting, causing her to groan against him.

Adrian watched, his lips twitching with obvious amusement. His hand stroked almost absentmindedly against her back. He gripped the neck of her chemise and tugged.

A ripping sound resonated around us.

Odele stilled.

Val stilled.

Odele threw a glare over her shoulder. She opened her mouth to berate him for ripping her clothes, but Val flicked his tongue over her lips.

"Don't stop," he demanded.

So she didn't.

Adrian tossed aside his own glass and angled his body behind Odele, aligning his hips with her backside. Slowly, he peeled the tattered chemise from her skin and bent to trail a pathway of kisses down her spine.

She arched, groaning at his touch, and the very sound of her desire seared straight through me like the cleaving of a cold blade.

Adrian dug his fingers into the roots of her hair and tugged so her neck arched, and Val pressed kisses to her throat.

They were so in sync with one another, all three of them equal in their desire.

It was like slowly freezing to death. Torturous.

And Adrian knew it. He turned to look at me, even as his hand slipped to Odele's front, pushing aside the tattered material that still clung there to press his fingers into her opening.

She cried out, bucking against Val, who silenced her cries by devouring her mouth.

Adrian's chest pressed to her back, the flicking movements of his fingers were entirely visible to me. I watched, fascinated, captivated by the aggressive movements, by Odele's own desperation as she rode out the waves of her desire against his touch.

"Care to join us, Watcher?" he asked breathlessly. "I'm sure our wife wouldn't mind having you here." His lips went to her ear and he bit down hard on the tender lobe. "Would you?"

His fingers moved faster and faster until Odele's whole body shuddered in a chasm of intense pleasure that I could feel as if it were my very own.

Gods of ice.

I got up and peeled the clothes from my body and joined them.

Adrian

HE PROWLED TOWARDS US like a great hulking predator. Slowly he shrugged the jacket from his shoulders, letting it drop unceremoniously into the silt. He reached for the hem of his tunic and pulled it over himself, leaving his whole body bare to my hungry gaze.

He was sculpted like an ancient god, all rippling muscles that carved down his abdomen in chiseled perfection. His silver white hair curled against his shoulders, soft licks and kisses against his brown skin.

I took him in, feeling my tongue suddenly heavy in my mouth. Desire was a heady scent around us. My fingers were deep inside Odele's tightness, drawing out her pleasure and gasping cries that were swallowed up by Val's lips and tongue.

I slid up along the warmth of her clit and her hips shuddered, her body trembling

Ytgar watched her. He watched me as I ripped the pleasure from her sinuous body, and he craved it. And in my gaze, I dared him to take, to let go of that control, to turn his anger into pleasure right here with us.

My fingers slipped from her heat but I kept a firm grip on her hips, pushing her body down onto Val's.

"Hike his tunic up," I ordered.

This was easy. Taking control, demanding, *wanting*. Pushing those around me for *more*.

"Don't tell me what to do," Odele growled, even as her fingers steadily gripping the hem of his tunic and lifted to reveal the jutting member aligned at her entrance.

"Touch him." My voice was a growl against the back of her neck. I grabbed her wrist, hand hovering over the back of hers to guide her palm to his erection. I pressed the heel of her hand firmly against the head of his member, and the gasps crying out from both of them hardened me all the more.

Taking her fingers, I closed them around his length and slid them up and down before pulling away.

"Stroke him…"

He groaned as her hand slid up and down and squeezed the length of him. When he couldn't take it anymore, he grabbed her wrist and pushed her away.

"Stop." The word was a breathless plea that tore desperately from his throat. "Let me." He grabbed her hips, palms settling just over mine, and with one slick thrust he was inside her.

And then Ytgar was beside us, bending low, brushing aside her hair with a gentle touch of his fingertips. He turned her face to him and plunged his tongue into her mouth, kissing and devouring her, while his hand slid up to palm her breast. She groaned into him, even while Val pounded into her.

Her back rammed into my chest; I held her steady, pushing her down by the hips to meet Val's thrusts with vicious ones of her own.

I touched and kneaded and kissed my way down her spine, relishing in the sound of her desperate cries and when she finally reached that peak of release, her whole body quivered, and her gasps were the perfect sounds of torture.

THEIR HANDS OVERWHELMED ME, their mouths ignited something within me, and the feel of Val beneath me… His every plunging thrust matched the rhythm of Ytgar's tongue and Adrian's kisses along my skin.

Hitting the height of pleasure, it ripped through me like an unexpected wave. And I rode the aftershocks, sliding up and down Val's length until the pleasure built and built again.

But then he was pulling out of me, and I was lost without the haze of his touch. But his hands were there, turning me so I was now facing Adrian.

The King of the Uncharted looked down on me with menace gleaming in that one yellow eye. The eyepatch covered his scar, but I longed to reach out and touch it, to feel the ridges of pain that wove us together.

He didn't speak, but his eye held the gleaming sin of promise. He hiked his tunic up and for the first time, I caught sight of his length, hard and ready.

"Are you watching, Prince?" he purred darkly in Ytgar's direction, even while that eye never left mine.

In response, Ytgar's hand slid over my chest, up to my throat. The warmth of his palm was scorching, a brand all on its own.

"Good," Adrian smirked.

And when he entered me in one hard thrust, I felt that like a brand, too.

His every movement *was* a brand, a claiming that slid me further and further up Val's chest. And then their hands were on me again, traveling every inch of me at once; I couldn't keep track of anything anymore, other than the pleasure spiraling inside me. It was uncontrollable, building with each drawn thrust of his length.

Ytgar turned my face and kissed me.

It was then that I shattered, screaming out my release into his mouth, biting down on his lip because it was a punishment and I wanted him to suffer, too.

And pain had never felt so good.

It was the one thing uniting us, after all.

HER BODY LAID OVER mine like it belonged. Like we fit together perfectly. Each one of us, side by side by side.

We'd pleasured her into exhaustion, had been pleasured into it. Her screams came one after the other each time an orgasm ripped straight out of her body. And with each one, the glorious sensation at knowing I was part of *this*.

They did not trust me fully. At least, Ytgar and Val were still wary, but all this time, they'd only ever had each other. Val and Ytgar. And then Odele. Now, me.

I knew they didn't know what precisely to make of me or my intentions. Soon, they'd see. They'd *know* that I was exactly what I claimed to be. I wouldn't have to tell them; they were smart and would figure it out on their own.

They lay sleeping, Ytgar and Val turned slightly away from Odele and I.

My eye was closed, my heart beating steadily in my chest, and I relished in the soft, slow ministrations of Odele's fingertips against my skin. She traced her nails absently over my collarbone, up my throat, over my cheek, and stopped shy at the edge of the eyepatch.

I could almost feel her silent hesitation as she debated doing what she wanted to do. She was curious. I didn't blame her. I would have been curious too.

Slowly, I felt her pry the eyepatch off, slipping it from me to bare the marred flesh where my eye used to be. My breath hitched, but I gave no other indication that I was awake.

I was almost too afraid to open my eye. What would I see if I did? I'd showed it to her earlier, and she'd touched it with sadness and pity. Now would she be disgusted? Would she realize she'd married a deformed merman and swim away in fear?

No. She was too strong for that.

Even if she looked at me with disgust, it didn't matter. It would hurt, like it always hurt when mer first glimpsed at my injury and curled away in disgust, but I knew it made me stronger. It was a mark of survival. And anyway, who was the real monster? Me, with mangled scars, or the mer who had created me?

Slowly, I opened my eye and peeked down at her.

Her palm rested against my chest, which her chin rested on top of. The other hand stilled near my scar. She started to pull away, but I stopped her by gripping her wrist.

"It's fine," I assured her, though I wasn't sure why.

Her fingers settled softly against the curve of my cheekbone, and I dropped my hand to her waist. "Does it hurt?" she whispered.

Only in the best of ways…

"Not anymore."

It had been years since it last pained me. Sometimes it brought discomfort, but mostly it was a phantom pain.

"Do you have nightmares about what happened?" Her voice held the slightest tone of haunting in it. It had me looking down at her, but her eyes were far away, even while her fingers traced lightly over my face.

"My sister's nightmares were worse, I think." I cupped her face with my palm, drawing her eyes to me. "Is something troubling you?"

She blew out a breath and tried to force a smile to her face, but it didn't quite reach her eyes. "Do you ever think about killing them for revenge?"

"All the time. Not because of what they did to me, but because of what they did to my sister."

They'd broken her in every way. Her body, her spirit. And it was all my fault.

"I could help you, you know." The words rushed quietly from her mouth. "I could find a list of the soldiers and their stations back in Thalassar. I could easily find out who did this to you and make them pay."

My heart began pounding. There was such vehemence in her voice that I believed every word of it. She would avenge me if she could.

"I wouldn't ask it of you."

"You wouldn't have to." Her fingers slid up to the edges of my scars. "I am not *good* like my cousin. I—" She broke off and swallowed. "I killed a merman because he threatened someone I love. And I'd do it again, even if it means tainting my own soul."

When Odele loved, she loved furiously, without restraint and without apology. For those she loved, she was capable of anything, of everything.

We were alike in that regard.

"I'm not useless." She spat the words as if she were trying to convince herself and not me. "I can protect all of you. Not with goodness, but…" The words trailed off as her fingers continued their exploration.

"I know you can."

I wouldn't have married her otherwise. After I'd come into power, I'd sent spies to research all they could about Thalassar and the royals there. They bought the information from notorious street criminals and brought it back to me. I knew absolutely everything about Odele, even the things she didn't know herself, and I knew I needed to take action when I'd heard of my sister's plot to attack Iol.

I needed to marry her.

"I'm sorry," she whispered. "My mer did this…"

My hands slid up her lower back. "It's not your fault."

"So much pain…"

Pain.

It was something I noticed lay between the three of them, like a magical cord that united three different souls, making them one. And she looked at me like I belonged, like I was a part of that and she was tying me to them in the only way she knew how.

Her fingers settled over the swollen ridges of my scar, and I closed my eye against the pain of her touch, against the scholar's curiosity in her dark eyes. There was no fear or disgust, but an endless fascination. Like the angry mar of flesh was a puzzle she had yet to solve. Fragmented pieces that she just couldn't seem to fit into place.

Little did she know it was because I was broken, with pieces of me lost along the pain. Some fragments were destroyed, but some still clung to the remnants of the gentle merman I used to be, as if that would somehow fix the shattered thing I was now. Little did she know that you couldn't force jagged edges into the spaces where they no longer fit.

"Enough." I grabbed her wrist to stop her exploration and gifted her with a smile.

Slowly, my hand ran up her sides, stopping to thumb the undersides of her full breasts. She sighed and her body curved into mine. "Kiss me, love," I ordered quietly. "We can turn the pain into pleasure, if only for a moment."

A smile curved at the edges of her lips, and she bent down and obliged.

I took her mouth in mine hungrily, stroking tongue against tongue in drawn out movements while my hands slipped between us to tweak her nipples.

Then I flipped her so she was beneath me and kissed my way down her stomach…

…and made her forget everything else entirely.

Odele

With the marriage thoroughly consummated, we decided to march on towards Draconi's capital.

The information that came from Adrian was just too much to keep to ourselves. And if someone was using wyverns and framing Draconi for the destruction they wreaked, Emperor Jiang Li had the right to know what was happening and why.

The camp packed up. Ytgar, Val, and I mounted our orcas while Adrian mounted a vicious looking dragon-hippocampus hybrid. The massive beast had the body of a hippocampus and the razor claws and legs of a dragon, serpentine tail and jagged spikes on the end.

It made the orcas wary; they thrashed about, and I made soothing noises to try to calm them, shooting it wary glances myself.

"She's gentle." Adrian patted her between the eyes.

I wasn't too keen on believing him.

But he did look formidable riding her. In his white jacket with golden lapels, red velvet cloak, and dark buttons, his red hair was loose and tousled beneath the crown of ivory bone.

I wore a matching one, just as heavy but this one was encrusted at the base with a long line of obsidian stones. I used to associate obsidian only with Maisie and the Black Blade, but now… my husband.

The king.

I could still feel the firm set of his fingers as he pushed aside floating tendrils of my hair just before he set the crown on my head.

"My queen," he'd said with a smile.

The words were a jolt through my senses. Queen.

I was a queen now.

In the past, the words would have sent panic searing through my insides at the heavy weight of responsibility the word carried. It didn't now. Because I knew what this really was. A symbol of unity, nothing more. Making those who harmed what was mine suffer. Vengeance in the form of a black and white crown.

I let the thought surround me as we rode, let it consume me so my head was held high as we all rode side by side by side by side, until we made it straight to the Emperor's palace, the army at our backs.

When sentinels swooped down on their dragons to greet us with their spears, I hopped off my orca with Ytgar and Val and approached them with a smile on my face.

"Tell Emperor Jiang Li that *Queen* Odele Malabella Oriana is here to speak with him."

He gave us an immediate audience, mostly to rage with vicious strokes from one side of the room to the other. When we entered his throne room, he whirled, a furious expression on his beautifully elegant features.

"How dare you?" he spat, the jerking movements of his anger billowing the folds of his robes and cloak up like billowing tenebrous shadows behind him. "How dare you insult me upon the gates of my own palace?!"

He screamed the words out in Dracon, coming face to face with me. I didn't recoil in fear, but his proximity was unnerving.

"Emperor Jiang Li?" Adrian's hand shot out, palm pressing against the emperor's chest. The simplicity of the action caused every single Draconian warrior present to pull their katanas from their sheaths and point them in our direction. All Adrian did was smirk at the action. He did not fear them; he didn't seem to fear anything. The scar on his eye was proof enough of all he'd endured, and this was nothing compared to the pain of being locked in a cage, of witnessing the torture of his sister, or the carving of his eye. "Take a stroke away from my wife."

Ytgar and Val came forward on my other side, assuming the same protective stance as Adrian.

The emperor eyed them angrily and, with a cold fury, slowly took a stroke back. He pulled himself together, straightening the disorder of his kimono before he spoke again.

"You come and mock me with a pretend husband, when I know you are already married to Prince Ytgar Neves Isolde. So who is this? And why does he bring his armies like he means to attack the front gates of my palace?"

He spoke only to me, only in Dracon, like I was the only one who could understand the language. I answered him first in his own language, "We bring you no offense, but come bearing the truth." Then, in the common tongue. "This is Prince Ytgar," I said, placing a hand on Ytgar's chest. "This was not done with the intention of disrespecting you, but rather as a precautionary measure. Regardless, I'm married to all three of these mer now, and we have important information to discuss. Will you listen to us?"

At that moment, the doors to the throne room burst open, Prince Kai and Maisie swimming through. Maisie rushed into the room, took one look at the armed guards and frowned, then looked to us.

"Where have you been?" she demanded, swimming in front of me. "I was worried about where you'd gone off to, and then this random army shows up… I thought we were under attack! I thought something had happened to you!"

Her eyes were wide and glossy, and she looked on the verge of bursting into tears. Instead, she choked back a sob and threw her arms around my neck and pulled me close.

"Don't leave without sending me a message, Odele," she admonished.

I was so surprised at the action, but I wrapped my arms around her waist and held her close. She had gained more weight in her midsection. The difference was slight and could only be noted if you pressed close to her.

She pulled away, her eyes going inconspicuously to Adrian. "Who is he?" she whispered.

I pushed her away lightly by the shoulders. "My husband. I'll explain later. Right now, it's urgent I speak with Emperor Jiang Li regarding the upcoming war."

Maisie took a stroke back and revealed the emperor's expression. "The war you assured me would not happen? That war?"

"We discovered who was truly behind the wyvern attacks on Iol, Your Majesty, and we know they wanted Draconi to take the blame for them."

The emperor was quiet a moment; he glared us down before slowly moving backwards and sitting upon his throne. When he did, he stroked his chin thoughtfully. "Go on."

"There is a Queen of the Uncharted Waters. She's using wyverns to attack Iol purposefully so we can blame you for it. She's framing you for these crimes to keep up more conflict between our two kingdoms, hoping we will go to war. It gives her the opportunity to swoop in and take over."

Silence greeted my rushed explanation of the happenings, of Adrian's sister and the threats we were facing.

"If the Uncharted wishes to take Iol by force, I fail to see what problem it is of mine."

My anger flared to life inside. "Weren't you listening to anything I said? They're *framing* you to pit us against each other. She has to be stopped."

The emperor pushed himself off his throne. "When word reached me that Iol wanted a war with Draconi," he began slowly, dangerously, "I accepted it. I may be the Dragon Emperor, but that does not mean I have a desire for bloodshed any more than you do. And yet, when threatened, I will rally my troops to protect my mer. You come to me, with an Uncharted immigrant husband, you bring his armies to my door, and speak of a threat no one has heard of or seen and expect me to rally my troops behind you to Iol?" He snorted. "How foolish do you think me to be, little Princess?"

Never in my life had I wanted to take a swing at someone more than I did right then at the Draconian Emperor. The bastard. He couldn't see the threat when it was right in front of his face.

"Why would I go through such an elaborate plan to trick you into going to Iol? Don't you think I have an infinite amount of better things I could be doing right now?" My arms crossed against my chest and my fins flared angrily.

"The same reason you would hide within the walls of your own palace in Thalassar for months pretending to have disappeared. The same reason you would allow your commoner of a cousin to disguise herself as you and marry a prince. Because you are childish and bored."

The words hit me like little teeth bites sinking into my skin. I felt each one like a carefully placed slap. The Emperor of Draconi, like everyone else, doubted me, doubted my worth.

And when the pain came and rose, threatening to rip out in painful sobs, it wasn't his voice I heard, but my father's, Percival's. It was that phantasmal shadow of my mother looming before me, beckoning me to follow in her strokes, and my own rejection of it as I swam out into the light. It was the showering of gifts bestowed upon a little girl who'd needed love instead.

"Call my wife a liar again, and I will not be so lenient with your mangled corpse," Adrian threatened, taking a stroke forward.

But then Kai was there, intercepting his pathway towards the emperor. "Do not threaten a Draconian warrior, foreigner. It will not end well for you." The prince's brown eyes flashed blue, and the change of his features happened in a blink. His body distorted into the slashing features of a dragon before changing back wholly mer.

"Can we just *stop* arguing? Please?" Maisie placed a hand on Kai's arm, tugging him back. "If there's one thing I know about my cousin, it's that she wouldn't lie. Not about something as serious as this. Please, let's just hear them out—without judgment."

I shot Maisie a grateful look.

"We already heard what they have to say. I do not believe them," the emperor growled, crossing his arms against his chest.

Adrian took a stroke back, so he was at my side. "If it's proof you're after, then I can give you none but my word."

"Your word means as little to me as your false status as king."

I KNEW WHEN THIS started how pretentious the seven kingdoms were, knew how cruel they could be. His words were no surprise. He didn't accept my rule. He called himself the Dragon Emperor, thought himself a ruthless ruler.

This mer had no idea what the definition of ruthless was.

One night in the Uncharted waters would have him rolled in a ball on the silt floor, crying for the mother who would never come.

It was a territory I had survived with the sheer force of my will. It was a territory I had crawled back to, bleeding, without an eye, holding my sister's broken body in my arms. I fought off infection, nearly died, and I had thrived. I'd conquered more tribes and land than this dragonbred could ever imagine.

That didn't matter to him, though. None of it would. Because the rich and powerful always overlooked what wasn't floating at the height of their noses. I, and my mer, would be overlooked. But when they needed us, he would regret every single decision and every single foul word spoken here today.

I'd make sure of it.

"My sister seeks to conquer and conquer she will. She will not stop with Iol, but will continue until she has the seas in her grasp. She despises the seven sea kingdoms and seeks to destroy you all. And she will. Do you know why?" I glared at the emperor, at his son, who held Odele's cousin close, his hand hovering protectively around her abdomen. "She has beasts. Not just wyverns, but creatures you could never imagine exist. And beasts win battles, in the end. Do not underestimate her."

The beating silence pressed in throughout the throne room. The emperor contemplated my every word, and I steeled myself for what I knew the answer would be. Though I wasn't sure why I'd expected anything else from the pretentious and the powerful.

They didn't see what wasn't floating in front of their noses.

So when my sister came and decimated Draconi, left only ruins in her wake, he would see. But by then it would be too late.

"Draconi will not fight Uncharted mer's battles." His eyes strayed to Odele. "Not even with pretty words of alliance. Not even for *you*."

"Then I pray for the gods to have mercy on all of our souls."

Because my sister will not.

Odele

"War is imminent," I argued on a harsh whisper as we swam out of the throne room. "There is no avoiding it. A wyvern already destroyed the capital. *One* wyvern. If she has more beasts at her disposal, think of what it'll do to Iol. And then they'll come for you." We stopped just outside of the hall and I reached for my cousin's hands, cupping them in my own. "I know I haven't given you reason to trust me before, but trust I'm telling the truth now."

Maisie and Kai shared a look, one I couldn't really decipher. Then Kai sighed and nodded. "I'll speak to my father, though I do not think it will do any good." With that, he disappeared back into the throne room, closing the sliding doors behind him.

Maisie eyed Adrian up and down, her dark eyes stopping on the patch over his eye and the hint of scars on his chin and forehead, only to settle on the obsidian ring firmly on his finger. She let out a small noise of surprise. Her hand reached for the matching ring she wore around her throat, and she grasped it in her palm.

If Adrian noticed, he said nothing.

"You really are from the Uncharted." It wasn't a question.

Adrian nodded anyway in Maisie's direction. "I am."

Her grasp on her ring tightened. "And you really are a king?"

He lifted one shoulder in an elegant shrug. "Yes. Self-proclaimed, but isn't that what all kings are? Kill enough mer and they ascend your rank every time."

Maisie shuddered at the word *kill*.

My cousin was such a pure soul. She'd never murdered anyone in her life, and I doubted she'd ever thought about it, either. Not like me. I had the blood of a mercenary on my hands. To save her life, I'd shoved my sword through his chest and watched the life leave his body.

Once you've killed someone, something in you *changed*. Something that should be difficult to do suddenly didn't seem that way anymore. No matter how many stains upon your soul, the word death breathed easier now. The nightmares soon stopped and something you didn't really contemplate before now became such an intricate part of life.

And war and death went hand in hand.

My cousin had seen death, but she'd never taken a life.

If the war came as far as Draconi before we could stop it, I feared she wouldn't have a choice.

And it would destroy her soul.

"I don't want another war," Maisie whispered.

I never understood war before. Not in the way Maisie did. I hadn't witnessed my friends get chosen for Selection. On the contrary, it was my stepmother who'd decreed it. I hadn't cared about deserters, those who swam away from responsibility. They'd mattered little to me.

I could never understand what Maisie was feeling or why she hated war so much.

As someone who had studied the intricacies of royalty her whole life, I knew that sometimes, war was a necessary evil. It was natural, to fight and conquer.

It was easier to think of things like that rather than invest emotions in battles and soldiers, in the poor and homeless.

It was why Maisie's heart broke every time.

It was a weakness I didn't want.

"But there will be one if we can't convince the emperor to help us." I kept my voice low so she could make out the gravity of the situation, if she hadn't already.

"That's just it, right?" Maisie let out a soft laugh, a sound that was entirely without humor. "If Draconi gives you troops, you'll lead them straight to a war we know nothing about. How can you ask us to send mer to their deaths for more than rumors?" She sent a cutting glance towards Adrian. "Forgive me, but it's your sister you want to fight? What's her name?" Her eyes narrowed, as if searching for a lie on his breath, in his posture.

Adrian didn't even falter. "Alexxandrina Ezarah Evander. I—I used to call her Alexx."

There was a world of infinite hurt in his voice.

I couldn't imagine being pitched against your own sister... But coincidentally, that's what this felt like with Maisie. Like we suddenly found ourselves on opposite sides. We were always so different, separate halves of a whole, but together just the same.

"We need your help. If you could help me get other kingdoms to back us up. Your father will listen to you." My throat tightened, but I pushed past the pain. "*My* father will listen to you. We can stop the war before it even begins."

And now she was looking at me, shaking her head softly. "And yet mer will still die."

"Peace always brings the possibility of death, Odalaea."

She flinched at my use of her real name, like I'd chastised her. Perhaps I had.

"I'm sorry, Odele. I can't… I can't send a message to my father asking for troops. Kappur just got out of a war themselves, and I won't be responsible for sending mer to their deaths. You can't know what war is like, what being *Selected* is like."

"Neither do you!" I snapped back, my patience wearing thin. "You've never *been* Selected, cousin. You've never been anything other than a waitress in Lagoona. But you're a princess now. One day you'll be queen. These are the decisions queens make. They're hard and bloody, and you wanted to make a change. Well, not everything is singing and hand holding. Some mer can't be reasoned with and so force is necessary!"

"How do you know?" she demanded, her voice rising. "Have you even seen this Queen Alexxandria? Have you tried to speak with her or are you just trusting the word of your new husband? How do you know you can trust him?"

"I just *do*." I paused, taking in a sharp breath that seared my lungs. "You didn't see the destruction. You didn't hold our cousin's dead body in your arms or send her home with a note to her parents. I want whoever wreaked that havoc to pay for what they did to our family. And I'm asking you to help me."

"What you're asking for is revenge."

"I'm asking you to be a royal for once, to take the role you were meant to play, and help stop that destruction from happening again. I came here to warn you that Iol wanted to attack Draconi for a crime they didn't know you hadn't committed. I came because I love you and didn't want you caught in harm's way. Now I'm asking you to help Iol and the Uncharted fight. The might of all of our armies alone could frighten her into submission, and if not that, they can help bring about her destruction so this never happens again."

Maisie chewed on her bottom lip and I waited, holding my breath. She had to say she would help. Whatever she could, even if it meant trying to convince her father, the King of Kappur, to spare troops, to give aid. To convince anyone she could… it would make a world of difference. To this war.

To me.

But Maisie shook her head. "You don't understand war and death, Odele. You don't understand *Selection*. I can't help you. I'm sorry."

It felt like she'd cleaved my heart herself. Perhaps I didn't understand war the way she did, but I understood death perfectly fine.

"I've killed for you." My voice broke into a thousand fragmented, heart-broken pieces. "I understand death because I stabbed my sword through a mercenary's chest for you. Because I love you. I almost died for you because I love you. Maybe that's what you don't understand. I gave up everything to give you the crown you rightly deserved, the past that was rightfully yours, and you cannot do this for me? Perhaps I don't understand Selection or war, Odalaea." The tears came then even when I tried to force them angrily away. They ripped out of me unbidden, and my voice trembled as I looked into the eyes of the one mer I thought I could count on unconditionally, only to realize that all this time, I may have been wrong.

"But I understand unconditional love, and I don't think *you* do. I'd die for you, that's what that means. I'd kill for you and those I care about. It's nice to know you wouldn't do the same." I turned away from her, and took in a breath, holding my head up high. The weight of the crown on my head suddenly felt heavier, a burden I never wanted but suddenly found thrust upon me, and I meant to see this through, to see my vengeance through.

"Let's go," I told my husbands. "I have conches to send."

Swimming away from my cousin was hard. Trying to keep my emotions together was even harder. But I swam away with sobs stuck in my throat and all the doubt of another family member cleaving through my chest.

I'd wanted so desperately to swim out from behind the shadow of the goodness of my mother. To be loved for me and not her. To be different, no matter what it took, and I'd succeeded. Except I wasn't under the shadow I wanted, even when I'd done everything I could to fling myself into it.

I would forever be the Selfish Princess. The princess who knew nothing. Not how to rule, only how to destroy and to take.

It seemed like it didn't matter how often I begged for my family to love me the way I loved them; it wouldn't happen.

"Odele!"

I looked up and blinked as a blur of white and silver crashed into me, wrapping hands around my arms. When she pulled away, there was worry in that gaze and cold anger as well.

"Where have you been?" Anneli demanded. "I came back with the scouts and we couldn't find you anywhere. We searched and there was no sign of wyverns or wyvern grounds, but we can expand the search and…" She paused, cocked her head to the side. "What are you wearing?"

In all the excitement, I'd completely forgotten that we'd sent Anneli and a few other Iolish guards to search Draconian waters.

"What's going on?" Her gaze slashed to Adrian, to his robes, his crown. "Who's he?"

I sighed, feeling the pain slowly ebb. "It's a long story."

Her hands settled on her hips. "I'm listening…"

WE DIDN'T LEAVE DRACONI right away. We probably should have. A part of me wanted to be in Iol. To prepare my troops, to speak with the Prime Minister, but I knew it was more important to find allies first.

We spent our days recording conch after tedious conch, to send to any of the sea kingdoms who would consider us allies. Kingdoms who owed Thalassar. Odele recorded so many conches and sent them out with the fastest messengers to Brague, Kappur, Ventlair, and even to her own father in Thalassar.

"Dad," she'd whispered in the recording. "We didn't part on the best of terms, but I need you now."

When she'd explained the upcoming war, it had been with a steady, emotionless voice. The whole time, I just wanted to pull her into my arms and hold her as I remembered the look of pure devastation on her face when Maisie had declined her help.

Why I ever thought Maisie could have been the ruler Iol needed was beyond me. She was kind-hearted and endearing, but too afraid to face the harder things. Odele claimed she wasn't made for those things either. She never wanted the responsibilities, but when they were thrust upon her, she bore the weight of the crown on her head like it was meant for her.

She could deny the fit of that crown all she wanted; she could say she wasn't worthy, that she was selfish and didn't care, but I knew the truth. The best rulers were selfish. The best rulers won when they had something to lose. The best rulers pushed on and persevered. The best rulers were the ones who denied their greatness.

"The last my spies claim, my sister was seen here." Adrian leaned over the kelp map spread out on the table, moving figurines into place.

We were in our room in the emperor's palace. Ever since we'd barged in with the Uncharted armies, he'd kept us under the watchful eyes of his armed guards, so our meetings were limited to the bedrooms.

The map before us displayed the seven sea kingdoms, and with Adrian's help, he'd deciphered and marked out the territories beyond, the ones not charted on our maps.

He placed the figurines that represented his sister along the northern-most parts of the uncharted, near the Iolish borders.

"I'll send messengers to Iol immediately," I said, leaning my knuckles against the table as I loomed over the map. "They'll inform the Prime Minister and my grandmother of the threat. I'll have the warriors strengthen the borders just in case. We don't know how close Alexxandria is to Iol."

"We have the benefit of knowing she's coming," Adrian explained. "She won't catch you off guard again."

Val sat down on a chair. His face was haggard from lack of sleep. We all looked like we'd seen better days. War had a way of doing that to a mer. A war where we had friends in abundance and no allies to speak of. "Fortifying our borders won't make much of a difference if she has wyverns. We need beasts to help guard. Orcas alone can't hold those things back."

"I'll send my own beasts with your messengers to help hold the lines." Adrian's yellow eye found mine, and we shared a nod of agreement. "Let's hope we're not too late getting there."

Val sighed with exasperation. "Are we really just going to sit around and do nothing while she marches towards our home? We need to be in Iol. We need to help prepare for battle."

"It's a battle we can't win without more armies," Adrian argued. "I know what it is to want to get a war over with, Val, but we can't. My army is great, but it's only a fraction of what my sister has at her disposal. With Iol, the odds are evened out, but we need Draconi. We need beasts. Numbers don't win battles, but strategy does."

"I *know* that, but this waiting is…"

He didn't need to finish that sentence. We all already knew what it was. It was excruciating. The faster the days went by, the more Iol was in danger. And we had no idea when or if we would get allies.

"Right now, we need to wait for at least a few replies. While we do that, we need to build a strategic defense and plan of attack in case she does penetrate Iol."

On and off the discussion went. We planned with moves and countermoves, moving and removing pieces and figurines from the map. We calculated every possible outcome, every plan we could think of until our heads ached.

Hours later, Odele burst into the room with Anneli, two conches in her hands. "We received conches from Brague and Ventlair!" she announced, placing them down on the table. "Their replies, no doubt. Everyone be quiet so we can listen."

She turned the conch over, and a silver light emanated from it. A second later, bubbles emerged to form one giant one, where the silvery image of the recording played inside.

Though the conch recording bore no solid colors, I could grasp wisps of it here and there, like hair a burning red-black color. Color wasn't needed at all to hide the slow curl of a malicious smile of the royal in the recording.

"Princess Odele, I was surprised to receive your urgent missive and have taken it upon myself to record one and send it speedily back to you…"

"That's the Queen of Brague," Odele explained quietly.

The queen continued, "I will first congratulate you on your marriage to the mysterious Prince of Iol, and I send my condolences on the second matter you addressed. It's most distressing to learn of an imminent war upon your icy kingdom towards the north. I'm afraid my regrets are all I have to offer you at this time. As you know, Brague is the smallest kingdom in the seven seas, and I'm afraid we are not equipped with the soldiers you desire. Best of luck in your endeavors. It would be such a shame if death befell you at such a young age." She smiled. "Goodbye."

The bubbles burst, signaling the end of the conch.

"Venomous bitch," Odele snapped, grabbing the conch and hurling it against the wall. It shattered into dozens of little pieces.

"Let's listen to the one from Ventlair," Anneli suggested, turning that conch around.

The bubbles rose, and another face appeared.

"Congratulations on your marriage to the Prince of Iol. I regret to inform you, however, that we cannot—"

Odele grabbed the conch before he could finish and threw it against the wall as well. "Damn it!" she screamed, kicking a chair with her fins.

While she raged, I turned to Anneli, who was staring at Odele worriedly. "Go send messengers to Iol," I ordered. "Tell them that the threat is coming. They must fortify the borders. King Adrian will send beasts and his own mer to help."

"Find Ric," Adrian added. "He will know who to send."

Anneli nodded and exited the room, closing the doors behind her.

"Beauty mine, you need to calm down." Val reached for her, but Odele jerked away.

"Calm down?" she screamed. "How am I supposed to calm down when no one will take this war seriously?" She turned and with a vicious sweep of her arm, knocked away the map and all its contents to the ground.

Val reached for her then, pulling her close so her face rested on his chest "Shh, beauty mine. All will be well." He didn't sound like he particularly believed that.

"You're a lying bastard, Val." She leaned into him anyway, as if his very touch was calming.

Adrian swam up behind her, pressing his hands to her shoulders to massage them gently. "They're right. War is always a slow building thing. It takes time." He leaned down and pressed a soft kiss to her neck.

She sighed and leaned back into him.

The effect the noise had on my body was instantaneous.

"We've been overworking…" Adrian kissed the spot on her neck I knew was sensitive. "You're exhausted."

"So are you…" she groaned, even as she leaned back into his caresses.

"We should take a break," Adrian suggested, his fingers already sliding to the front of her body so that his hands were between Val and Odele's, where he began working at the buttons on her dress.

"A break sounds nice," she agreed on a breathy sigh.

I almost growled aloud. The sound was everything I needed to hear to prowl closer. I watched as Adrian's fingers flicked button after button. The material parted halfway down and the king, impatient, didn't undo the rest, but slipped his hand beneath her chemise to squeeze her breast.

She gasped, leaning into him while her fingers dug into Val's shoulders.

Adrian was good at that, at taking and distracting. And he wanted Odele distracted, wanted to give her that desperate release, to help her take out her frustrations in better ways so that, just for a moment, she didn't have to think about war, or death, or anything that was coming.

Just this.

This intimacy between the four of us.

Val tilted her head up and bent down to kiss her while Adrian touched her from behind.

I hadn't touched her since the night of their wedding. I'd been the Watcher, forced to see them take the lead. Now, I wanted that initiative.

I prowled closer and closer, nudging Val off to the side so that I was in front of her instead. His body angled to the side, taking her kissing mouth with him.

I had the patience for this. For long, drawn out pleasure that the other two did not.

Slowly, my fingers finished working at the buttons on her dress and I peeled it from her body, along with her chemise. My fingers skimmed across her skin in the lightest of brushes that drew out soft sighs wherever they lingered.

Adrian held one breast in his hand, the sight of him tweaking her nipple, pinching it to a ready peak pained my erection.

I wanted her.

But first…

My fingers brushed the underside of her other breast. I watched as her nipple hardened with each gentle stroke of my fingers, even as they slid down to the soft panes of her stomach, hands gripping her hips, and I bent to trail a pathway of kisses. My tongue dipped into her bellybutton, skimmed across the purple-blue scales of her abdomen and then lower, lower…

Val's mouth stole her gasps, and Adrian heightened her pleasure with sensual kisses to her neck. And I bent lower, just below the V of her waistline to the opening of her desire. I pressed forward and gave one languid stroke of my tongue up her folds.

Her hips pressed against my mouth, and I smiled against the desperation of her movements. She tasted sweet. Like sin and want. Like everything I never should have wanted but had anyway. I plunged, and I took with sweeping, dominant strokes of my tongue. I opened her folds with my fingers, sliding one in, and then two while my tongue drew out her pleasure.

She moaned in pleasure and writhed against me while Adrian held her steady with one hand while the other dug into the roots of my silver hair and pushed my face harder into her heat. Demanding, he was always so demanding. I let him set the pace as I made love to her with my mouth. His hand pushed and controlled the rhythm. First, I sucked her hard, rough, my fingers moving in and out relentlessly. Then he slowed and so did I, pulling my fingers out and letting my tongue do all the work. I swirled the tip right over her pearl.

She tore her mouth from Val's and cried out her pleasure, her hands gripping the side of my face to yank me up.

I went willingly, though I wanted to draw out her pleasure more, bring her to a mind shattering climax.

"My turn," she all but growled, dropping to her fins and yanking my tunic above my waist.

I stared, transfixed, as she leaned forward to my pulsing erection. Her lips pursed just before she pressed one soft kiss to the tip.

That action alone had me groaning, reaching for her head.

She jerked away. "Don't touch me," she commanded. Her dark eyes gleamed with malice. "I want you restrained."

Acting on some silent command, Adrian and Val moved on either side of me, grabbing my arms and pulling them back.

"I want you to feel hopeless," she teased. "I want you to lose all control." She leaned forward and slid her tongue from the base of my erection all the way to the tip, causing pleasure to rivet up my spine.

And then she took me in her mouth.

I gasped, yanking my arms. I wanted to touch her, to feel her, *guide* her, but Val and Adrian held me back. Even while her tongue slid along me, her mouth encircling me, she rode my member like she was punishing me for something, though what it was, I couldn't be sure yet. All I knew was an exquisite pleasure low in my stomach, coursing through my entire body.

My hips moved against the rhythm of her torturous mouth. Her teeth scraped against the base of me, and I cried out as that tightening feeling grew and I exploded in endless seams of pleasure.

Odele took me deeper into her mouth as I found my release, sucking harder, swallowing the very essence of me.

Slowly, her lips slid down, and she released me with a quiet popping sound. I glared down at her and she licked her lips, mischief shining in her eyes.

She looked glorious.

I yanked my arms away from the mermen at my sides and hauled Odele up by the arms. Unceremoniously, unforgivingly, I pulled her to me and punished her with a kiss.

"I wanted to be inside you when I came," I growled against her lips.

She twisted them into a smile. "Too bad."

Two could play at that game. I smiled, and the sight of it made her frown.

"It's alright." My hands slid up her chest, stopping at her throat. My thumb skimmed the ridge of her sharp collarbone. I bent low, breath fanning across her cheek. "The night isn't over yet." I spun her around and pulled her to my chest so her back was to me. Then I whirled, so she was facing a smiling, knowing Adrian and Val.

"What are you doing?" she asked breathlessly.

"Returning the favor, my love." My hand slid down the curve of her hip and then to her center. I inserted one finger and stroked up and down her inner folds, stopping just at the edge of her nub. "Who do you want first? Choose."

"I—I—"

"No?" I smirked against her cheek. "Then I will choose for you. Val… come *thrust* inside her."

Adrian made a small sound of disappointment. My eyes met his gaze, and I smiled. "Don't worry," I told him as I slid my fingers up, rubbing against her clit just as Val came forward, gripping her hips, and thrust to the hilt inside her.

I teased her clit as he thrust.

"There's plenty else for you to do as well."

She gasped, her body trembled, and I beckoned Adrian forward with a dip of my chin. He obliged, coming to one side.

"Kiss her," I ordered.

Adrian took her mouth in his, tongue sliding over her bottom lip before thrusting in her mouth matching the sounds of her every gasp.

"Good," I purred in her ear. "Now lift his tunic up and hold him in your hand."

She tore her lips away and gasped, fingers fumbling for his tunic, her body jerking against mine with every thrust of Val's hips. Adrian helped her along the way, lifting his tunic and holding the hem of it between his teeth.

I relished in the sound of his gasp as she grabbed the base of him.

My finger slid across her nub and her grip on Adrian tightened while Val's thrusts became wilder.

"Stroke him," I ordered, wrapping a free hand over hers to give her the rhythm against his erection. She stroked and squeezed, and his hips jerked against her hand while Val well and thoroughly slammed into her body.

And I controlled them all, her pleasure, theirs. My fingers set the pace against her clit, my tail wrapping around her to keep her steady. I could feel her riding higher and higher on that blissful edge that would lead her plunging to a chasm of maddening desire. I drew it out further and further, balancing on the delicate edge, just before I pulled away and denied her that release.

"Iolish...bastard..." she cursed.

Never before had any other words sounded sweeter.

"Patience, my love." I kissed her delicate throat before turning her head and plunging my mouth into hers. When I pulled away, I stroked her clit once more and inserted another finger inside, stretching her to fullness.

"Do you feel that?" I whispered darkly.

"I—I—"

"I know you do, love. That is what it feels like to lose control."

And then I gave her what she desired, pinching her nub until she screamed with desire. As we rode wave after wave of it, she squeezed Adrian tightly as he continued to pump his hips. A few moments later, Val released inside her and Adrian cried out her name as they came together.

And I watched it all. I was commander of their bodies, the Watcher.

I smiled and pressed a final, demanding kiss to her cheek while she slumped against Val's chest and fell into an exhausted sleep.

We slept side by side. When Odele had fallen asleep, we'd carried her to the bed and let her lie between us. She'd alternated between snuggling me and Val. Even while we were plagued with exhaustion ourselves, we couldn't seem to fall asleep.

Silence permeated around us, full of all the words we didn't say aloud and all the fears we dare not tell anyone, not even each other.

Even a few hours of bliss couldn't wayward our fears or hopes.

A soft knocking at the door disturbed the pathway of my thoughts, and I looked over. I really didn't want to get up, but it could be important.

The sound woke Odele up. She groaned and stretched her arms over her head, fins kicking the blankets down ever so slightly to reveal one curve of her breast and the outline of a pert nipple.

I wanted to take it in my mouth.

Instead, another knock sounded, more urgently this time.

With a groan, I got up, reaching for my tunic and I slipped it on.

"Who is it?" Val complained, pressing the heels of his hands to his eyes. "It's the middle of the night. Tell them to go away."

"I agree." Odele sighed as she snuggled closer to him.

Adrian murmured an agreement.

I rolled my eyes in their direction and went to the door, opening it to reveal Anneli on the other side.

Her face was ashen, nearly pale, and I knew something was wrong.

All the earlier bliss left my body, and I was instantly alert. "What is it?" I demanded. "What's wrong?"

"Your Majesty…" She sounded breathless, and her voice cracked. "The messengers you sent ahead? They came back with news. I'm sorry, Prince Ytgar, but… Iol… it's already fallen."

The words echoed in my mind as we rushed to slip on our clothes and left the room. Emperor Jiang Li was waiting for us in his throne room, expression grave. Kai and Maisie were there as well.

"We told you this would happen!" I swam nose to nose with the emperor, giving him a glimpse of every bit of the rage burning in my depths. My hand fisted at my side, and the urge to bring my fist to his face was a dominant thing inside me. "We told you there was a threat, that we needed *aid*. Now look!"

The emperor looked over my head to whoever was behind me, and I felt a touch on my arm and recognized it as Val's. He pulled me back.

"What's the report?" Ytgar demanded, taking a stroke forward. His Iolish militia were in the room, floating before a map spread out on a table.

"We assume the Uncharte—the queen's half," one of them amended, "circled around the northernmost part to take Iol from the north. They've secured the southern border. We can only assume they've secured the northern one as well."

Ytgar's voice was full of brittle cold, as dangerous as black ice against unsuspecting limbs. It was a sound that wreaked death. "Did anyone make contact?" he asked.

He kept everything from his voice except for that; the threat of vengeance, the promise of death and destruction, battle, taking back what was his.

"No, my Prince. However, as we were leaving, we were stopped by one of the Queen's Uncharted. He gave us a message to bring back to you."

"What message?" Val demanded. His grip was tight around my arm, a painfully steady thing keeping me tethered to the conversation, preventing me from slipping into hopelessness, madness.

The warrior swallowed tightly, a muscle in his jaw twitching. Then, he met Ytgar's gaze. "'Queen Alexxandria sends her regards and is happy for the warm welcome the ice mer have given her. There is one piece of the hospitality missing, however. The prince is nowhere to be found. Tell him to come. Tell him I am waiting. Tell him if he does not arrive soon, I'll send him the head of his grandmother.'"

Something within me cleaved, and I knew Ytgar was feeling the same thing. But if he was going to be strong, so was I. But I couldn't get the image of his grandmother out of my mind. She was old, strong, *stubborn.* I didn't know much about Queen Alexxandria, except for the death and destruction she wreaked upon the seas. And that was enough to know that she would break the queen, and that would break Ytgar.

"You know you can't go, right?" I shook Val's hold off to reach for Ytgar. "She'd kill you both, and it would only make her stronger." I tried to sound reasonable, not cruel. But I knew, deep in my heart, if it was between the queen and Ytgar, I would save Ytgar. Even if I couldn't spare him the pain.

His silver eyes found mine, and there was an infinite world of sadness in his depths. Like the lonely desolate waters with miles and miles of ice. Like he knew where my thoughts had strayed, and I wondered if he'd hate me for the dark turn of them, for being the ruler who would gladly condemn her if it meant saving the merman I loved.

That was precisely *why* I wasn't fit to rule. I was not my mother. I was not Maisie. I couldn't be kind. I couldn't find a solution that wouldn't end in the queen's death or bartering a life for a life. All I saw was the problem, *my* merman being threatened…

And me, refusing to bow down to the whims of a terrorist to save him.

Even at the expense of a monarch's life.

This was precisely why I never wanted to rule. Because this decision was the wrong decision. It was the wrong choice, the bad one. It's not what kind souls did, and I didn't care.

I was selfish.

I always would be.

"I know…" Ytgar sighed, running a hand through his hair. He turned back to the map, glaring at the many pieces that represented Queen Alexxandria and her army. Then, he looked back up at the Emperor. "Iol has fallen. I will take my kingdom back, but I will need your aid. Do we have it, Dragon Emperor?"

Kai's father stroked his chin thoughtfully. "Your words were proven true. Yet… now that we know there is indeed a threat, I still cannot help you."

"Father…" Kai started a stroke forward.

The emperor held up his hand. "Silence, boy. I will explain. The threat is real, and if what you say is true and she seeks to destroy the seven sea kingdoms, I cannot leave my kingdom unprotected. I won't spare even one mer." He then turned to his guards. "Raise the banners of war. Fortify our borders against any threat. If the queen comes, we will know. And we will stop her."

I almost staggered through the water. He wasn't helping; he wasn't going to *help.*

"The queen and my *cousins* are in Iol," I said, looking at Maisie. My cousin met my gaze with sadness in her black eyes. "We need your help to get them *out.*"

The emperor shook his head. "There is no way to safely retrieve them. That is the price of war, child. They'll be caught in the middle of the war and if you go there, you will only be going to your death."

"So, what are we supposed to do? Just stay here?" My voice rose.

"Iol has fallen. Draconi's doors are opened for you to stay if that is what you wish. But we will not help you on a fool's mission to try and take Iol back."

Because that's all the ice kingdom was worth to Draconi. He didn't care, but why would he? They'd been enemies for centuries, hostile neighbors. Not even a common enemy could unite them. Not even my relationship to Maisie could do that.

I looked my cousin in the eye and steeled myself against the heartbreak that followed, the rush of hopelessness I couldn't let show. For Ytgar, I had to be strong. For my cousins, who were locked in a frost castle with a murderous queen, alone.

"Thank you for your hospitality," I spoke through gritted teeth. "My husbands and I will take our leave now." I curtsied to the emperor and turned, gesturing at my whole party to follow me out.

"Odele…"

I ignored her. What could I say to the cousin who refused to swim up for me like I'd done for her time and time again? Not even the sound of her broken voice, the whispered way she uttered her sound of regret, was enough to make me stop and turn around.

Not even when my heart whispered at me to do it; I was too afraid of what I might find there. Regret?

Or perhaps, a cousin who never truly loved me at all.

"We have to go help them," Anneli urged.

We were back in our room trying to decide what our next swim strokes would be.

"We can't just leave them to suffer," Val agreed.

"That would mean giving Ytgar up to my sister. I am sorry your kingdom has fallen, but we knew this was coming. We can't afford to act rashly now. If she gets her hands on Ytgar, she will have the entire Iolish monarchy at her disposal, and any chance we had of making allies, of saving Iol… it'll be gone." Adrian leaned his palms against the surface of the table. His yellow gaze was grave, his cheeks and neck flushed with anger. "My sister thinks all the monarchs are corrupt. She's looking to eradicate them entirely. It'll throw the balance and order off."

"So, what are we supposed to do?" Ytgar argued. He still looked every bit the deadly Iolish warrior, almost as if the rage centered him. He was the calm before the storm, the silence before a volcanic eruption destroyed everything in its pathway. "If we attack, our army will be decimated against hers. If I give myself up, we'll all be dead."

I'd been trained for this, for war and strategy. I couldn't keep track of the number of times I'd stayed up late in the royal library, listening to conches on battles and the games of war. I thought I was so smart, thought that I would have won them if it had been me in those stories. I would have done it better. And yet, now that I was faced with war, and I was as lost as those generals and warriors were. Maybe even more so.

I took a breath, tried to center my breathing while they argued around me. I barely heard their voices, almost as if I didn't even really want to.

Instead, I listened to the one inside my mind. Voices of those generals and warriors, of kings and queens, of conquerors.

"Let's bring out the facts, shall we?" I interrupted them, raising my voice over their shouting just to be heard. "Alexxandria has Iol surrounded. Our family and our loved ones are there." Likely being tortured, I didn't add. "We have no allies." My hand swept across the broken bits of rejection conches. "We are still waiting on replies from Kappur and Thalassar. Our army isn't as grand as hers, so if we march straight on, it'll likely put our loved ones in danger or get us killed in the process. She wants Ytgar, but if we give him to her, it'll be placing more power in her hands. If we do nothing, everyone dies anyway."

My temples started to pound relentlessly. There had to be a way out of this. There *had* to be.

"How long does it take to get from Draconi to Iol?" Adrian asked.

"On orcas, a week or more, depending on the pace. On your beasts, two days probably." Ytgar settled him with a narrowed glare. "Why?"

"We can send a messenger, tell her we agree to my sister's terms but first, we want proof that your grandmother is alive. Once we get that proof, we tell her Prince Ytgar will ride out to Iol on an orca. The lie can buy us some time to make a plan and take action." His yellow eye did a sweep around the room, settling on one of his generals. "Send one of the beasts and a messenger. We don't have time to waste."

The general nodded, bowed, and made his exit.

"So that's it? We're just going to sit around and wait?" Val demanded angrily, slamming his fists onto the table.

"There's nothing else we *can* do except buy time and make a plan."

"We don't even have a plan! We're swimming in circles!"

Adrian opened his mouth to argue, but I couldn't take it anymore. "Stop," I pleaded, interjecting. "Both of you please, just stop." My voice broke with heartbreak and exhaustion despite my resolve to stay strong. I just couldn't… not right now. I couldn't listen to it.

Everything was building up and threatening to shatter what little sanity I had left. All this planning, all this ruling, I had no idea what I was doing. I wasn't good at this. My mother had been. Maisie would be. For all my memorization skills, I had no idea what to do right now.

My cousins were there in that castle. Ytgar's grandmother. I'd not sacrifice him or any of us in this room to get them back, and yet we had to do something. But what? There was nothing I could do. Nothing I knew how to do.

"Everyone get out," Adrian ordered unkindly. "Our wife has had a trying night and needs her rest. We will speak again tomorrow morning."

I didn't watch them leave, but I heard them. It wasn't until a hand touched my shoulder that I realized my face was buried in my hands. I looked up to find three worried faces staring down at me.

Hysteria trickled out of me in the form of soft, humorless laughter.

"My love, are you alright?" Ytgar's soft hands cupped my chin, thumbs swiping across my cheeks tenderly.

A laugh burst past my lips. "No, I'm not alright."

"What can we do to make it better?"

I shook his hand away from my face and glowered. "I should be the one asking that question. I'm the one who should help make this better." The words tasted extremely bitter leaving my mouth. "You all married me for the alliances I could bring. *What* alliances? No kingdom in all the seven seas wants to help me. We are *alone*." I looked at all of them, and just felt my heart break all over again. There was such trust in their gazes. Hope. What fools. "I never wanted to marry princes or kings. I never wanted to marry *anyone*. Do you know why?" I was met with silence. "Because it meant responsibility I didn't want. It meant all of this. I am not made for ruling. What good was all of my studying if I can't even come up with a solution to our problem?"

I wanted to throw something or punch someone. Instead, I felt... dejected. Defeated...

"You think I married you because I wanted an alliance?" Val asked, leveling his eyes with mine. "Because I can tell you for a fact right now, beauty mine, that isn't the case." His smirk made a real laugh escape my throat.

"You're such a Iolish bastard."

Adrian studied me. In one smooth gesture, he pulled the patch from his eye and ran his fingers against the puckered scar. "I'll not lie to you, love," he whispered, his fingers lingering against his marred skin. "I did want your influence. But that wasn't the whole truth. I also wanted you to be mine. Because you are intelligent, and as regal as any queen."

Ytgar cupped my chin once more. "The crown fits you perfectly," he said, his expression set with grim determination. "The only one trying to remold it is you. And you don't need to."

The sob that came after that was unexpected, as were the tears.

"You made her cry. Great going, Prince," Val admonished.

"I hate the three of you," I said half-heartedly. The truth was, I didn't hate them at all. No one had ever accepted me before. I was cast within the shadow of my mother, my cousin. I was always being compared, and yet these three were claiming I had what it took, every broken piece of me.

They believed in me when I couldn't believe in myself.

"Just hold me," I ordered. "I don't want to think about anything else for a while. Please."

It was Ytgar who pulled me into his arms and lifted me, carrying me towards the bed where he gently laid me down. Val followed, and then Adrian, and we all laid together holding each other close until we fell asleep.

In each other's arms.

As if it were the last night we had… before everything else went to silt.

THE WATERS WERE PERFECTLY quiet. It was a night of shadows, meant for stealth and precision.

Meant for sneaking away from the palace. Away from Draconi.

Away from Odele.

It had been torturous, the mere thought of leaving her. I'd lain awake for hours after they'd already fallen asleep staring at her features, calm in sleep. The tips of her purple-blue eyelashes grazed the top of her cheek and the delicate heel of her hand cushioned her face.

I loved her. It hurt to think about leaving the way I was going to, without even a goodbye. But no matter how difficult that was, it was also easier. Easier to get away without her arguing, without her threatening me. If she begged me to stay, then I would.

But I couldn't.

Not when Iol needed me.

So, I'd silently packed a bag and crept from the room. I needed to get there fast; to do so I'd take one of Adrian's beasts instead of an orca. I needed to make it to Iol and put on the facade of my life if I was going to convince Queen Alexxandria that I was Ytgar Neves Isolde, Prince of Iol.

It was madness, this plan. But it was the only one I had. At least if I fooled her, my presence would buy Queen Isadora time. It would buy Odele and the others time to come up with a better plan.

The Iolish were loyal to Ytgar, and they knew I masqueraded as him when we left Iol. They would lie for me. I knew that for a fact deep in my bones.

For Ytgar, I had to do it.

The stables were full of all manner of beasts. The stablemer were lulled to sleep on chairs, so they didn't notice when I went up to one and observed it. I lifted its tail, its wings, gauging the speed it would take to get me to Iol.

I started to saddle it, tying my pack to the side when a bag hitting the silt startled me into whirling around.

"Gods of ice," I cursed lowly as I glared at Anneli.

The sound had been her dropping her own bag to the silt. I took her in; she was dressed in riding leathers and a warm cloak—a cloak meant for Iolish weather.

"I'm coming with you," she announced.

I turned away from her, throwing my cloak around my shoulders. "You can't." And that was that.

A derisive snort came from her. "Funny that you think you can tell me what to do." Without another word, she came on the other side of the beast and began tying her back to the saddle.

I glared at her from over hard, sparkling scales. "I mean it, Anneli. You can't come. This isn't a game. I could be killed."

Her silver-gray eyes rolled with annoyance. "All the more reason for me to go. Someone has to look after your sorry hide."

Gods of ice save me from insufferable, demanding females. "Can you please go back inside and go to bed?" It was a command, leaving no room for her to argue with me.

Her own eyes glared back, but this time the fury of the storm she raged didn't threaten me. "You're like a brother to me. I will not let you go off on a death mission alone. Besides, I hate sitting around here waiting for things to just happen. I want to help."

"If Ytgar knew I was putting his sis—"

"Don't you dare finish that sentence," she interjected coldly. "He doesn't know, and I want to keep it that way. I want to protect him as much as I want to protect you. And I know you're going to go take his place, and you'll need my help in case things go awry."

I tried to steady my breathing. She was right. Of course she was right. I had no idea if my facade would even work against Alexxandria. All I had was this hope, and if things didn't work out, if I was caught? What then?

Anneli smirked knowingly. "You need me."

I scoffed. "Fine. Whatever. But don't slow me down." I swung myself up onto the saddle and gripped the reins.

"The only one slowing anyone down is you, Ingen." She hopped on behind me, wrapping her arms around my waist.

With a soft nudge to the beast's side, it took off slowly. At least that was the pace I'd set for now until we were away from the palace. I didn't want to give anyone a chance to catch up to me, to try and stop me.

We rode in silence, coming to the outskirts of the palace and continuing through the gates. But when the stirrings of the water pulsed and shook, I picked up speed without looking back.

Please don't be Odele, I prayed to the gods.

It wasn't her.

It was Ytgar.

He intercepted us, dropping from his orca in front of us, causing me to yank back on the reins. The beast roared back, pawing at the water.

I dropped from the creature, tossing the reins to Anneli and swimming over to him, a cold look of fury on my face, in my chest.

"What were you thinking, going in front of an animal that big?" I demanded.

Ytgar leveled my stare with an equally angry one of his own. "I could ask you the same question, Valmundur." His arms crossed against his chest. "I know where you're going, and I won't let you."

"You can't make me do anything, so either get out of the way or we'll go around you. Or above you. It doesn't matter, we'll still leave."

Ytgar's eyes sparked in a fury I'd never seen marring his expression before. "I am your prince," he breathed. "And you will obey me."

My temper flared. "You are my prince and I mean to protect you! Don't you understand?" My hands shot out to shove against his shoulders, pushing him back against the waters.

I'd fought with my friend before, it was impossible *not* to when we were so catastrophically different. But this was a different type of fight. This was real. The anger was real, the kind that you couldn't come back from or swim away from.

"I know what this is about, Val. You think I don't?" He didn't have to yell, but the words sliced through me as if he had. They penetrated past delicate flesh and bone. They *hurt.*

"It's about me doing what I have to. It's about me buying you time, saving your family. Your *life.*"

Ytgar snorted. "This isn't about saving my life. This is about ending yours."

I reeled back as if he'd punched me.

He saw my weak spot, and he aimed for it with something far harsher than mere blows. "You always thought you weren't good enough. You always thought you were lesser than me. What will pretending to be me accomplish? Nothing, that's what. She will kill you if she thinks you're me, or worse, when she finds out you lied, she'll torture you. Either way, the results will be the same. You'll wind up dead."

"That's a risk I knew I was taking when I pretended to be you. My life for yours. That was the deal, right?"

"No!" he shouted then, and I flinched back from the force of it. "That was never the deal. How could you think I'd ever want to exchange your life for mine? You're worth more than me, Val. If you leave right now and pretend to be me, you might as well lay the sword in my hand and let me stab you myself. I'll not be the cause of your death."

My hand flittered to the pommel of the Isolde sword. It wasn't mine, had never been mine, but it fit as if it were. I'd been caught up in the facade of royalty so long, I was getting too comfortable with it. I wanted to believe it's what I truly was. And because of that, I was confident I could fool the queen. I could make this work. Why couldn't Ytgar see that?

"You know there's no other way." I swam a stroke forward, gripping his shoulders. I wanted to squeeze them, bring him close in a crushing grip, but there was a finality in that gesture neither of us were ready for.

"What are you trying to prove?" Ytgar whispered, and his words broke into a thousand agonized pieces.

I smiled at him. "Nothing at all. You're my prince. My brother. I will die for you, for Odele, even for Adrian, because I love you. I am the only one who can do this. You have to let me go, Ytgar."

You have to.

For so long I'd been his crutch. The one keeping him grounded in the court of royal lies, of mer who didn't really care about him, who gave him no power, who couldn't see his potential.

It was in this moment I realized that the one who was holding on wasn't me.

It was him.

A single tear rose from his eye.

The sight was so startling, my fingers dug tighter into his shoulders. I'd never seen Ytgar cry before.

Slowly, he lowered his head, defeated. When he looked up again, there was determination in his eyes, and he said one word, only one that mattered. "Survive."

I nodded and pulled him close, gripping him by the back of the neck and leaning my forehead against his. "Tell Odele I said goodbye."

And I pulled away before he could say anything else, mounting back in front of Anneli.

She looked down at Ytgar, and there was something in her eyes, secrets it looked like she wanted to convey.

"Do you want to—"

"No," she snapped. "Let's go."

I snapped the reins, and we were off.

And I didn't look back.

Ytgar

I WATCHED VAL GO, and it felt like I was saying goodbye than more to just a friend. It was as if I was watching a part of me ride off into the darkness, too. Part of my soul that was intricately woven into me. It was like a thread of a different tapestry that didn't quite belong but fit into the spaces between mine anyway.

I missed him.

It would not be an easy journey, not be an easy task.

I didn't know if he'd make it, and a sudden gripping part of me wished I'd held him for just a little bit longer, just a little bit tighter. Wished I'd said words I'd never said before.

That was the tricky thing about goodbyes. You could go over the memory of it time and time again, and wish and hope, but in the end you never got that second chance.

I watched until he disappeared from the horizon. And when he did, I pressed a kiss to my fingers, and touched my fingers to my temple, willing the currents and the gods to watch over him.

"Survive, my brother."

Because I wanted that second chance.

"Where's Val?" Odele's hands slid across the empty space where Val had lain only hours before. Sleep pressed against her beautiful features, giving her a peaceful expression; downturned eyelids, a lazy tilt to her smile. Adrian laid at her side, sprawled across the bed. His eyes peeked open and his hands reached for her to pull her close.

She went to him, letting out a deep contented sigh.

It *hurt.*

Val had left without a proper goodbye because he'd known she would try to stop him, so he'd left the difficult part for me. He'd left me behind to break our wife's heart.

I wanted to hate him for it, wanted to curse him to the ice and back, but I couldn't summon up enough energy to do so.

Adrian's arms wrapped around her waist and pulled her naked body closer, pressing distracted kisses to her lower back and sides.

Odele was staring at me, brows pulling together as her too-keen eyes flicked over my face and noted my expression. "Ytgar?" She pushed Adrian away and got up, dragging the sheets with her, keeping them pressed around her body. "What's wrong?" Her eyes flicked around the room. "Where's Val?"

Maybe if her eyes darted around more, if they darted around faster, he would appear. Maybe my best friend would appear from behind a piece of furniture or open the sliding sea fan doors to our room at any moment, a smile splayed across his face.

Maybe it would all be a dream.

But Val didn't swim through our door, even while Odele asked the question twice more.

Our eyes held, and mine nearly burned with the sting of unshed tears. Odele stopped. Her eyes took in my expression and she sucked in a sharp breath.

"No." She took a stroke back, shaking her head back and forth. "Where is he, Ytgar?" she demanded. I still couldn't speak. She dropped the sheet and lunged for me, gripping the lapels of my coat in her fists to shake me. "Where. Is. Val?"

"Gone." The word tore from me in a broken, fragmented sound.

This was what Val had left for me. To watch the light of her happiness leave her eyes, and the heartbreak shatter across her face. I never thought my friend to be a coward until now, and the sentiment pulsed inside me like a living, breathing thing that I didn't want to, but couldn't help but to believe.

He'd left me to break Odele's heart.

"No." Her fists tightened on the material of my clothes. She dug her fists into my body, gifting me with a hard shove. "You have to go get him. You have to bring him back. She'll kill him." Her thoughts came tumbling from her mouth in a disjointed, angry manner. "Get him back, Ytgar! You have to bring him back!"

"He's not coming back. He's *gone*."

I wished I could unsee the expression on her face, could eliminate it from my mind, but it was branded inside me now. Forever.

"He left me." Her fingers loosened their hold on my shirt front. "He left me." The words echoed angrily throughout the room. Her eyes narrowed as she looked up at me. "You let him leave?"

"I didn't have a choice."

Even to my own ears that sounded like a pathetic excuse. I was Prince of Iol. I could have tied him to the bed and kept him here by force, but I couldn't have taken away his free will. I'd never stoop that low and betray everything we had.

What did that make me?

I'd promised Odele again and again that if she swam away I would find her and bring her back, I'd shackle her to me because I'd wanted her, *needed* her with a desperate ache. I could have done the same thing for Val, but I hadn't.

Because this was different.

It would have broken everything between us, and my brother who I loved more than anything, would have ended up despising me entirely.

"Iolish bastard!" Her fists connected painfully to my chest before I even registered that she'd raised them. Again and again she punched her fists into my chest and I took every bit of it like I deserved it.

Valmundur had left me behind to break her heart for him and this had always been the way we'd cope. In violence and heated passion, only this time, there was no passion to be found.

Just broken piles of heartbreak that we stuck our hands into and sliced at our skin. I took it, because I deserved it. Because if Val was going out there to pretend to be me, then I'd take the punishment meant for him.

"He left me!" Odele repeated those words over and over, striking me each time.

I gasped and my eyes stung.

But then Adrian was behind her, gripping her writs and pulling her to his chest. She turned in his arms and crumpled onto him. They sunk to the floor and he rocked her back and forth while she screamed. She didn't shed a single tear, and that somehow hurt even more.

Odele raged for a mere five minutes before she got up, dressed, and straightened her shoulders regally. She was as vicious as a storm, with moods as sporadic as the sea. It was calm I saw there. Raging, dark calm.

"We cannot waste the time he's given us," she said, her voice scratchy from the screams. "We need to make a plan right away."

For the next few hours, while we waited for any word from Kappur or Thalassar, we poured over a possible plan. Odele listened with rapt attention.

"It makes no sense to place the weakest warriors on the front lines," she said, rearranging the pieces on the map as if it were a chessboard. "We can't afford to lose *anyone*. We need the beasts at a higher altitude with snipers on their backs. There are always archers looking to take down anyone at a higher level, so we need them to be taken out by a separate team."

She spoke as if she'd spent years fighting wars or planning to fight them. Like she lived and breathed the art of war.

For hours we parried ideas back and forth. Hours suddenly became days. We felt Val's loss around us like a phantom. We didn't speak of him except to whisper his name in the darkness of night or in startled cries in our dreams. We weren't sure if he'd made it to Iol, but I had hope.

I knew Odele did too.

Odele shot up in bed, grasping the side that should have been Val's and gripped at empty sheets instead. Her chest heaved with the rapid rise and fall of her breaths. It took her a moment to realize where she was, as if she'd still been caught in the tight grip of her nightmare. Her fingers relaxed against the sheets and her breathing steadied, but her eyes remained fixated on the dimly lit lanterns floating above our heads.

Without a word, I pulled her into my arms, tucking her head beneath my chin. My eyes met Adrian's yellow one and we shared a twin look of worry.

"He left me," she said, her voice neither sad nor angry. It was… empty. That worried more than her raging could have. Odele pulled slightly away from me to look into my eyes. Her expression was solemn. "You helped him leave me."

I wished I had something to say to that, some way to defend myself or explain why I had to let Val go, but the words didn't come. The truth was, I wasn't sure if it had been the right decision at all. It hadn't even been mine to make.

Val wanted to prove something to himself, to others. It was something I didn't understand, perhaps I'd never understand it but I had to respect it.

And pray to the gods I wouldn't live to regret it.

Adrian pressed closer to us on Odele's other side. His fingers slid up her side, cupping her hip. Her eyes closed against his touch and within moments, she fell asleep.

The silence was interrupted by the mingling of Adrian's and my harsh breathing and Odele's steady murmurs.

"She doesn't blame you," Adrian interrupted the sounds on a dark whisper.

"I blame myself." My fingers ran through the tresses of her hair, the action causing her to snuggle closer to me. It hurt my heart to hold her this close, our bodies slightly slanted on Val's side of the bed. Like by laying here we could somehow absorb whatever essence of himself he'd left behind, if he'd left any behind at all.

Val was an extension of myself, my life, my very soul. Without him here I felt that vital piece missing; I knew it was the same for Odele. It was why she'd woken up gasping for two nights in a row since he'd left, and it hurt knowing there was nothing I could do to make it better, that there was a gap between us that wouldn't be filled until Val came back. If he ever came back.

I couldn't think like that.

"You couldn't have stopped him, you know."

My eyes narrowed on Adrian's words. He looked so sure in the dimness of the room that a fierce wave of anger and hatred for the merman rose up inside me.

"What would you know about what I could have or couldn't have done?" I hissed. "You don't know me, and you don't know Val."

One of his thick shoulders lifted in a careless shrug. "I know enough."

"You've been with us for days, not months, not *years*. What could you possibly know?"

That single yellow eye gleamed maliciously in the darkness. I could feel the pulsating energy of danger rolling off of his body, sending slivers of something indescribable down my spine.

"I know that you're holding too tightly to Val, that you'd gladly take the blame for him so she hates you and not him for leaving when we all know it was his decision. You're both so self destructive, you'd jump one in front of the other to save each other from being the target of harm that in the end, the both of you will get hit."

His hand slid across the cushions of the shell bed and grazed the skin of my arm. I flinched, but his fingers clamped down on my shoulder. His arm wrapped around Odele's body to pull me close so the three of us were pressed together tightly.

"Val is your weakness," he whispered. "Weakness will get you killed."

"Are you suggesting I cut Val loose?"

"Not at all. I'm saying not to show weakness or my sister will tear Val apart."

The words were spoken like a promise and a threat I felt down to my bones, and the words he didn't say pressed heavily around us.

If she hasn't already.

The space between us that Val had once occupied suddenly became filled with planning, plotting, and our feeble attempt at organizing our troops. When we weren't in our room with Adrian's generals, we were training them to fight.

Odele had thrown herself into the role with renewed vigor, as if the more she plotted and planned, the greater our chances would be of getting Val back.

We hadn't heard a word from him and terror lived inside me constantly at all the possible things that could have ended in his demise. Had he made it to Iol? Had he killed Queen Alexxandria? Had a beast gotten to him before he even made it to our borders? The questions repeated over and over in my mind to which I had no real answers.

I tried not to let every minute haunt me, but I prayed to the gods he survived and bought us the time we needed to receive the replies from the remaining sea kingdoms.

On the fourth day since Val had left, a knock interrupted our fervent planning.

"Come in," I called out impatiently.

A servant came in and bowed. "Forgive the interruption, Your Majesties. Emperor Jiang Li requests an audience with you. A conch has arrived from Kappur and Thalassar, along with a message from Iol. They are waiting in the throne room for you."

Finally.

Their replies had arrived.

WE RELEASED THE BEAST we rode a few leagues away from Iol. It had taken us two days without rest to get there and when we finally made it, we whispered our thanks, slapped his flank, and watched him disappear the way we came.

I sent a silent prayer up to the gods to watch over him.

And then we swam.

For the most part, we went in silence, weapons drawn, cloaks tight against the harsh cold. Even if I was going in blindly to pretend to be Ytgar, it wouldn't be very wise to alert them of our presence. We quietly swam half a league towards Iol. Then another half a league. Just as we were nearing the borders and the ice troll statues, we slowed, ducking behind white glaciers to peek over the top.

There was something odd about the structures of the ice trolls. The carved faces were… I wasn't sure. I squinted my eyes, trying to make out why they looked so distorted.

I noticed at the same time Anneli did. She made a soft gasping noise.

"Those are… heads…"

She was right.

Nailed to the faces of the trolls, with ice and steel spears, were severed heads. Each stake was perforated with one. The heads of old mer, frosted over with ice and drained of blood.

"The heads of the Prime Minister's inner circle."

I bit down hard at my lip at Anneli's words. I could see that now and bile rose up in the back of my throat.

Adrian had said his sister was ruthless, but to hammer the head of the Iolish government at their borders? It was cruel, and yet it was a message.

She was here to conquer.

To take.

Fear rose in my chest, but I crushed it down, replacing it with whatever scraps of bravery I had left.

For Ytgar. For Odele. For Iol. This was for them, not for me. Not to prove my worth, but to give them a fighting chance.

Two days had passed already since I'd last said goodbye to Ytgar, and I hoped they'd finally come up with a plan. I hoped I could buy them some time.

"Stick to the glaciers," I ordered, releasing the sword from its sheath. The borders were being patrolled, and I'd send any Uncharted scum to the depths of the abyss with the gods of hell.

With a lingering look at Anneli, I started forward, ducking behind glaciers, keeping my attention alert on all my surroundings.

The entrance to Iol was right there, just past the ice trolls. What would be on the other side? Dragons? Wyverns? What other beasts did Alexxandria have at her disposal? I wasn't sure, hadn't thought to ask.

I should have.

I *really* should have.

Holding our breaths, we passed the entrance, eyes alert to every startling sound. But the kingdom was desolate. There was miles and miles of snow and ice, but nothing more.

But then Anneli gripped my arm, and I lifted my sword, turning to look at her. She made wild gestures to stay silent with her sword hand and pointed in front of us. Right before our noses, if we'd gone a few strokes closer, we'd likely be dead.

It blended in with its surroundings, with a white hide and a shining coat of blue along the ridges of its scales. Its wings were tucked tightly against its back, massive head in clawed paws, and the soft snoring coming from its nostrils made a current of bubbles blow hotly.

Wyvern, Anneli mouthed.

The beast was as wide as the walls of glaciers that harrowed the pathway to Iol. The length of its tail and the tip of its nose reached from one end of the entrance to the other.

Anneli made another series of quiet, slow motions so as to not disturb the waters. I looked over at its tail and nodded.

We swam in that direction, rising to higher altitudes to swim softly over it. The waters threatened to stir but our pace was so painstakingly slow, you couldn't really tell. We moved in turns, monitoring the predator as it snored. I wanted to hurry, to put in a burst of speed, but this had to be done with delicacy. No matter how badly I wanted to stab the sword through its eye in vengeance, I knew we wouldn't win against it.

That thing would chew us up and spit us out.

It felt like hours later that we finally made it to the other side and slowly went away from the wyvern. It wasn't until it was ways behind us that I even dared to breathe. Hysteria wanted to push out of me, but I held it in, staring gravely at Anneli.

"Make your way to the stables. Do all you can to blend in. I will go to the palace and meet the queen myself."

We still had a few leagues to make it to the capital, but we had to get the plan out now in case there was anyone patrolling these parts.

It was hours later, but we finally made it, and Anneli gave me a silent nod of goodbye. With her, there would be no kind words or touching scenes. That meant finality, and I knew she'd fight that.

This wasn't final to her.

This was the pathway to victory.

She darted away.

The city wasn't as desolate as the outskirts had been. This was even more dangerous. Uncharted mer and beasts roamed the streets by the dozens, and it was hard to hide from them, hard not to feel intimidated by them. The waters seemed darker now, but when I looked up, it was to realize the lines of beasts and wyverns she had at her disposal, all spread out across the higher waters like sentinels waiting for a scrap of meat to tear through. They swayed and floated, weaved around each other silently, dangerously.

The proof of her grip on Iol was prominent in the dead bodies littered across the city. I wondered about them but didn't stop to stare. Had they defied her and were killed for it? Or had this all been sport to her? The sight of each body I passed had hatred and rage pulsing through me, a desire for vengeance. To protect what was mine.

I wanted to stab my sword through Alexxandria's chest and end it now. But I had no idea where she was. Likely inside the castle, keeping Queen Isadora and other royals hostage. I hoped she was okay, hoped she hadn't pinned her head to a spike somewhere and was now just waiting for Ytgar to off him too.

Over my dead body, I thought savagely as I wove my way around streets and guards.

I wondered if there was some type of curfew, or if the Iolish were merely too afraid to leave their homes. The sight in the altitudes of the water was frightening enough.

I didn't want to think that she'd decimated the entire city.

Cautiously, I neared the palace. The gates were being watched, but I didn't enter through the front. I made my way around the ice gates towards the servant's entrance.

It was empty at first sight, and as I entered, silence greeted me.

I wasn't expecting the sudden body that threw its way towards me, or the pain splintering my hand as the sword flew from my grasp. I cursed and fought blindly at the creature in the dark. I couldn't see it, didn't know what it was. But then I felt the blow to my chest, and pain riveting up through my body, ringing in my skull.

A deep voice chuckled and then came the blow to my temple.

And I met the darkness.

Waking was slow and painful. I didn't want to do it, not with the nausea rolling around in my stomach or the pain dancing around in my head. My temples throbbed, and my body ached painfully. My arms felt weird… I tried to move them but couldn't, and I wondered if they tied me down.

I peeked an eye open and met dancing, flickering lights from within lava globes. It was the first thing I saw.

I rolled slowly, grunting in pain. No, my hands weren't tied, but they'd fallen asleep due to the painful position I lay against the floor.

Ice bit into my cheek and it hurt to peel my face from the floor as I rolled and looked up at the ceiling, at the crystal-clear ceiling overhead where wyverns circled from the outside, their silhouettes passing above me.

I listened for sounds, but there were no sounds. No talking, no screaming sense of torture… There was… silence.

Grunting, I pushed myself up on my elbows and swept my glance around the room then down at myself. My cloak was missing, as was the Isolde sword. Damn it. I'd been caught off guard, disarmed. I was a failure. But another sweep around the room showed me that they hadn't taken the items from me at all, whoever *they* were. The cloak lay around the back of a cushioned chair, and my sword laid against the surface of a table, all within arm's reach.

I shot up despite the pain and felt like my movements were… sluggish… as I jerkily swam towards the table, grasping for the sword.

I yanked it from its sheath and turned.

I knew I was in the palace. The lava globes illuminated as much, and I'd been in here with Ytgar enough to know the place by heart. We were in the Isolde throne room. I recognized the round table they used in the Prime Minister's political meetings and the queen's throne she used for grand events.

The windows all around the spacious room were opened, filtering a cold breeze inside. Not even the heat of the lava seams could keep the cold away.

It was at one of the windows I saw her.

She was half-turned from me so that only the right side of her face was visible.

I almost gasped aloud.

She was blindingly pretty. Beautiful. The light of ice and lava shone in from the window, highlighting every delicate feature of her face. The curve of her soft cheek, the tip of her nose, lush lips that pressed together firmly.

Two-leggers had legends of angels, creatures that were beautiful, godsent.

That's what this mer looked like.

Regal in her bearing, she wore a black velvet dress lined with gold fur along the collar and at the hem, a heavy cloak around her shoulders. Her auburn hair was pulled back into a chignon behind her neck, and golden weaves were threaded through her strands in the front, making it looked like a crown.

If it hadn't been for the color of her hair or the umber color of her tail, I wouldn't have known what she was. But the yellow of her eyes is what gave her away.

Queen Alexxandria.

Adrian's sister.

She didn't seem like she noticed me at all. Her focus was intent on whatever was outside the window. It was like I wasn't even there.

I could end all of this now. Stab the sword through her heart. But how many mer did she have hiding in the room, waiting for me to make that mistake? I turned my gaze through every nook and cranny, but I saw nothing.

This made things easier, then.

I started forward, gripping the sword tightly in my hand.

"Are you really going to try to kill me?" she spoke, and her lilting musical voice had me staggering backwards, freezing.

Her lip tilted up into a smile and slowly, she turned to face me.

And I gasped.

One half of her face was incandescently beautiful. And the other? It was marred with puckered, angry scars that slashed over almost every bit of skin. Angry red lines curved from the corner of the left side of her mouth and rose into festering, angry scars up her temple, down her eye and cheek. It was bright against the paleness of her face, a wound that hadn't seemed to quite heal. It distorted her features, turning them into something grotesque and angry.

I couldn't help but stare at the scarred part of her face with disgusted fascination.

What was it that Adrian had said?

His sister had suffered an attack in Thalassar, and she despised the whole of the seven sea kingdoms because of it. These scars were superficial, and I wondered at the ones she kept close to her heart.

Her delicate head cocked to the side.

Stop looking at her scar, I willed myself, but it was impossible not to. It was hypnotizing.

"My mer found you wandering through the palace servant's entrance," she commented as if I wasn't there staring at her like a fool, as if I hadn't just charged in her direction with a royal sword ready to take her heart out.

I tried to will myself to move. But I couldn't. I mean, how could I harm an unarmed mer? One that looked so… delicate… soft. It felt treacherous.

"And you carry the Isolde sword, yet I do not know you." Her voice held a wistful, amused tone to it.

If evil had a sound, it wasn't her voice. She just looked… like a lost young mer, afraid, alone. I recognized the signs.

I cleared my throat. "I'm Prince Ytgar Neves Isolde."

One eyebrow rose. One, because the other had vanished behind mangled flesh. "Really?" she purred. Her eyes took me in, from the length of my exposed skin down to my frost blue tail.

I was so, so dead.

She saw past me.

I had to put on the facade of my life if I wanted to keep it intact.

I twirled the sword, lowered it and bowed like a proper royal, dazzling her with a smile that didn't even make her blink. "I've no manners. I'm sure you understand. Waking up in such a situation does badly for the orientation. I am Prince Ytgar Neves Isolde. You are Queen Alexxandria Ezarah Evander, I assume?" I straightened, a smile still in place.

She blinked at my mouth, then up at my eyes. "At your service." She curtsied.

It was all so achingly… polite. Almost mundane.

Her eyes roamed over me again. "Forgive me, but are you really the Iolish Prince?" Her head cocked to the side again. "I was under the impression that Iolish royalty inherited certain… features…" A pointed look at my tail. "Features you do not have."

That was the most common misconception about Iolish royalty. Anneli was from royalty, and she had a silver tail. I smiled. "Genes, I'm sure you understand. I'm an embarrassment to my family because of it."

"Right." She turned away from me, gifting me with the right side of her face, the pretty side. "So, *Prince Ytgar*," the words sounded sarcastic, knowing, "you have honored my message and have decided to turn yourself in to save the life of your grandmother."

"Of course."

She turned back to me and in an instant, her entire expression changed. Like she'd been wearing a mask, covering up the poison behind the sweetness. Like lacing sea wasp venom within a candy or a *rakarouris*, and you couldn't taste it until it was too late.

"You look nothing like her."

I swallowed, my neck prickling with sudden unease. "Like I said, I'm an embarrassment to my family."

Her head cocked once more, but instead of the gesture looking delicate now, it was like a predator observing their prey right before it pounced. Like a dragon seeing a morsel it meant to devour.

It was frightening.

"Why do I not believe you?"

I should have charged then. I wanted to, but the double doors to the throne room flew open, startling me to turn my gaze away from her.

Mistake.

Luckily, she didn't attack, didn't pounce. She was as entranced with who came through as I was.

Uncharted guards held between them Jessinda, gripping tightly at her upper arms. She didn't struggle, didn't quake with fear though I saw the trembling of her jaw, like it hurt keeping herself put together.

A knot formed in my stomach.

What was Alexxandria on about?

The guards stopped and waited a beat. A moment later they gripped Jessinda by the back of her neck, causing her to cry out. With a hard shove they pushed her into a low bow before the queen. When they pulled her up, Jessinda's eyes were full of defiance.

"Thank you for bringing her in," Alexxandria said, smoothing out her already straight velvet dress.

The guards bowed and took a single stroke back.

Jessinda glared at the queen before turning to me. Her eyes spoke of relief and sadness. I hadn't exactly been close to Odele's cousins. They insulted anyone below their station, but while I'd pretended to be Ytgar, they'd flirted, *she'd* flirted, in a rather charming way. And… well, she was Odele's cousin. And my wife cared for her.

When Alexxandria spoke again, she drew our attention to her, and the knot in my stomach grew more painful. "Because I would like a second opinion, I have brought in a witness." Her long fingers gestured at Jessinda.

"A witness for what?" the young mer demanded.

I willed her to be quiet.

The queen was more vicious than she appeared, delicacy be damned. We didn't know what all she was capable of. To what scale she would take her rage out. I mean, the heads of government officials on spikes was one thing, but there were worse things, more dangerous things that could be done to get someone to suffer.

And the queen seemed well versed in all of them.

"This young mer claims to be the Prince of Iol. I am not inclined to believe him." She'd somehow gotten closer to me, so close I could lift the sword and ram it straight through her stomach, but she barely looked at it. Like it was no threat to her, a toothpick instead of a sword.

That's how I knew how dangerous she was.

Her fingers reached out and gripped my chin. She jerked it up and looked deep into my eyes, and I found myself staring back into hers.

One was yellow, a sinister color that matched her brother's. The other was dull, almost white. As if the knife that had slashed her pretty features had dimmed the color there, had stolen part of her soul as well.

"I want you to be honest, young Jessinda." She shoved my face away and took a stroke back. "Is he really Prince Ytgar Neves Isolde?"

Silt.

Siltsiltsiltsiltsiltsilt—

I wanted to turn and look at her, to send her signals, but I kept my gaze fixated on the queen's cruel eyes.

I didn't expect Jessinda to lie for me. Not when her life was on the line. She needed to save herself, so I wouldn't blame her for telling the truth.

I wouldn't blame her if it killed me.

I closed my eyes, waited for the words that would condemn me, and thought of everything I never said, and all the love I should have professed to Odele before I came to my death.

And yet…

"He speaks true. He is Ytgar Neves Isolde, the Prince of Iol."

My eyes shot open, but I didn't turn to look at her, didn't let my expression change or shift at all. It would condemn her, hurt her.

I breathed.

In.

Out.

Repeat.

The queen stared and stared at Jessinda. Her own expression didn't shift. But then she smiled. "Really," she mused. "We shall see." She nodded to one of the guards. He bowed and exited.

It was only a few minutes before he came back, and when he did, he wasn't alone.

Along with him swam Rollo. The Iolish Prime Minister.

He wasn't hauled in like Jessinda had been, but the old mer swam in with pride in his stride, his head tilted up, his back straight. He stopped before the queen and bowed low and properly. "Your Majesty," he greeted tightly.

When he straightened, the queen was smiling widely at him. One side of her mouth beautiful, the other down-turned to look more like a frown. "Prime Minister Rollo, thank you for joining us. I need your assistance."

His gaze never even flicked to me. "Anything, Your Majesty."

"I merely need confirmation. I need you to identify this merman for me. He claims he is the prince you see, as does Lady Jessinda. I'd like the truth from you."

I held my breath once more.

I never liked Rollo. The kingdom never really liked Rollo, but he was loyal to Queen Isadora. He would lie for me, too. This just might work. Hope started to bloom in my chest but after a second of silence, I turned and met Rollo's eyes.

"This merman is not the prince," he said simply, cruelly. "He is but a mere whale trainer who likes to play at royalty. A local orphan named Valmundur Ingen, and the prince's best friend."

My heart dropped to the pit of my stomach like an anchor. Painfully, cruelly, it left me gasping for breath and words, for thoughts.

"How interesting, indeed," the queen smiled, turning to Jessinda again. "So, you've lied."

Jessinda turned to Rollo and spat, "Traitor!" She made a lunge for him, but the guards shot forward and hauled her backwards even as she strained against them, even as she fought.

I started forward to protect her, but the second guard and Rollo were on me, fast in their maneuvers, they flicked the sword from my hand and restrained my hands behind my back.

Traitor. Rollo was a traitor. He was working with Alexxandria and had given away my identity.

And now we would die for the deceit.

"Let her go!" I shouted, fighting against their hold.

The hilt of a sword came banging against the back of my head, nearly blinding me with pain. I gasped, falling over at my tail. They held me, gripping my hair with their nails and forcing my gaze up on Jessinda.

More guards had come through the door and forced her down. She screamed in earnest now, crying out her rage and fear as they shoved her against the ground and bared the back of her neck.

All the while, Alexxandria watched with a cruel twisted smile on her face.

"Please!" I shouted at her. "Leave her alone!"

The queen turned to me then, her smile fading, expression growing serious, malicious. "You have no power to give me orders, Valmundur. Besides," she turned back to Jessinda, "I do not tolerate liars." With a signal of her hand, one of the guards procured a large, sharp axe.

Jessinda screamed and bucked.

"Let me go! Let me up! You bitch! My cousin will kill you for this!"

They smoothed out her wild tresses of hair, placed the tip of the axe on the back of her neck.

My heart thumped. "Jessinda!" I croaked. "I'm so sorry, Jessinda!" I struggled, but their hold was adamant.

Jessinda turned her face to me. "Val, I'm sorry, I'm so sorry, tell Odele… tell her—"

"It'll be okay, Jess. Just look at me, okay, you'll be fine!" I let out a curse, struggled, and Rollo growled in my ears. "You traitor," I snarled. "I'll kill you for this!"

"Val—" Jessinda gasped as the axe arced up.

"Jessinda look at me, it'll be okay…"

She sobbed. "Tell Odele that I'm sorry. Tell Odele that I tried."

"Jessinda, just look at me alright… it's okay. It's okay."

The words were a lie.

We all knew it.

Alexxandria's voice was cruel. "Let this be a lesson to all."

And then the axe came swinging down.

Blood.

Bursting and bright red, it rose in violent blooms around the water. Her head separated from her neck and swirled, going round and round, rising.

I couldn't look away from the horror of it.

You did this, a voice in my head whispered the accusation. If I hadn't come here, if I hadn't lied. Jessinda would be alive.

The pain Odele had suffered with Silviya's death had been heartbreaking; this would break her soul completely.

It was my fault.

A guard ripped her floating head by the hair, and they yanked her stiff body away by the tail. Disrespectfully, they pulled her away, dragging her limp body across the ice.

Leaving a trail of smoking blood behind.

"What about this one Your Majesty?" Rollo asked, pushing at my head aggressively. I limply let him, my eyes drifting up to find Alexxandria glaring down at me.

She contemplated me with cruel eyes. "Throw him in the dungeons," she finally commanded.

Rollo hesitated. "Are you sure that's wise?"

Her glare was a blade searing through flesh. A violent riptide pulling bodies beneath the waves. It was death. Destruction.

It was fear.

"Question me again, Prime Minister, and you'll find your head on a pike alongside the brethren you betrayed. Do not think for a moment that just because you helped me gain entry into this kingdom or betrayed your own for months to get my wyverns through, that you are irreplaceable. Do you understand?"

The bastard.

He'd been betraying Iol this entire time. That's why he never listened to Ytgar's proposals. It's why he had pushed so hard for a war with Draconi. He'd known it hadn't been them at all. He'd wanted us gone, wanted us out of the way so he could let these treacherous mer into our home.

"I understand. Forgive me, Your Majesty."

"I owe you no explanations, but if this one truly is good friends with the prince, we can use him as a hostage. If the old crone didn't motivate him to come to me, then maybe this one might." She started to turn away.

"And what of the Princess of Thalassar?"

She stopped, turned with annoyance. "What of her?"

I stiffened, looked up.

"She is insignificant. I want to destroy Iol. From what I hear, the Thalassarin Princess is a spoiled brat, not worthy of notice."

Good. Let her think that. Let her overlook my wife. Let Odele be safe. Please gods, let her be safe.

"I do not wish to contradict you, but she's not what she seems. She's resourceful, and she has the might of many kingdoms behind her. Thalassar, Draconi, Kappur…"

The queen shrugged. "She has allies, but none that will come to her aid." She stopped, stroking her chin thoughtfully. "But we cannot let her be a nuisance, either. Let's send the princess a message." She smiled, and it curdled my blood. "Send the head by wyvern. It's faster." Then she looked at me and frowned. "Get this one out of my sight."

A blinding burst of pain followed her words.

I welcomed the darkness this time, easily succumbing to its sweet embrace.

Odele

I PRACTICALLY RUSHED INTO the emperor's throne room, pushing ahead of everyone there. Maisie and Kai were at the front, but I ignored them. If there was a message from Kappur and Thalassar, I wanted to hear them immediately. But the message from Iol? That was far more urgent, far more important than anything else.

The emperor was before me, across from me in front of his table. On it sat two conches, side by side, and a kelp and rope woven knapsack, weighed down with blocks of stone.

Iol's waters couldn't sustain conches, so I knew the knapsack was from them. I frowned at it, curious as to what might be inside.

I reached for it, yanked it towards me across the surface of the table.

A hand went to my shoulder, another one to my waist. I recognized the touches, my shoulder was Ytgar, at my waist was Adrian. Their hands brought me comfort while Val's absence brought me heartache.

It had been four days since I'd last seen him. I missed him so much it almost crippled me. Any news from Iol, if it was news from him, came first.

My hands shook as I went to the mouth of the knapsack and started untying it.

"A messenger gave this to my guards," the emperor explained in a dark voice. "We think he was one of your Uncharted." He directed that to Adrian.

His fingers tightened along my waist.

I took in a shaking breath. Ytgar squeezing my shoulder.

I pulled the strings, and the sack fell open to reveal...

Oh gods.

I jerked back, falling against Adrian's chest. "No..." I tried to avert my eyes to the horror within the sack but couldn't. It was grotesque, brutal. It was heartbreaking. "No, no, no..." I denied it, sealing my eyes closed and shaking my head back and forth.

This couldn't be happening.

It *couldn't*.

I whirled away, pushing at the arms that tried to grab me and fell to the ground, heaving onto the floor.

Gasps rang around, and the emperor's voice speaking in Dracon, "Get that out of here!"

"No!" I got up on shaking fins and turned. Tears were pouring around my face without me even realizing it. My chest pressurized.

I should be used to death.

I should have known...

Everyone I loved died after all…

A sob cleaved out of my chest, and I gasped and gasped, as my trembling hands reached inside the sack to pull out Jessinda's severed head.

"No… No…" I cried again, smoothing out the stiff tendrils of her hair from a pale, cold cheek. Her eyes were wide with terror, a permanence of the emotion etched onto her face in death.

My cousin had suffered. She had been killed.

"Jess…" I shook the head, a part of me hoping this was an illusion, magic, something… a lie… anything. I shook her. "Wake up, this can't be true… You're fine. You're okay…"

The head didn't move. Didn't blink.

Didn't speak.

It was Jessinda.

And she was dead.

"No…" I touched my forehead to her cold one. "I'm sorry. I'm so sorry…" The sobs came harder then, and I gripped her close to me. The last bit of my cousin. Another of my cousins, dead. "Odele…" Maisie's hand clamped over my shoulder and I could feel her physically trying to pry me away from Jessinda.

"Get off of me!" I screamed, shoving her aside.

Everyone was staring at me. I was falling apart in front of them. I couldn't… I couldn't.

Carefully, I placed her head back into the sack and tied it with precise fingers. Then I reached for the first conch, a message from Kappur, I turned it over and played it for all to see.

The Kappurin King appeared in wisps of silver threads. His expression was grave. "Princess Odele, Prince Ytgar, I've received your conch and have replied as swiftly as I possibly could. Though I regret to inform you that with Kappur recently coming out of war with Thalassar, we have no supplies or warriors to spare. I send my greatest condolences and wish you the best of luck in this difficult time. War is no easy thing, niece, and I know the costs of one. Good luck."

His image burst into thousands of little bubbles.

My heart fell.

I reached for the one from Thalassar and brought it close to the erratic pounding of my heart. If I expected to feel closer to home, I didn't. If anything, I felt further away. Like an outsider looking in. My fingers shook as I turned it over.

Silver bubbles rose up near my face. Close, the image that appeared near my face was close. I held the conch out away from me and watched the image of my father form. The surprise of seeing him almost startled me into dropping the conch, but I held it firmly as he opened his mouth and began speaking.

"Daughter, I was surprised to receive your conch, and even more surprised at the contents within." He paused, taking a breath. I could almost feel the piercing of his blue eyes against mine, cleaving my heart, my soul. "If it is warriors you are after, I have spoken with your mother—"

"Stepmother," I numbly corrected.

"—and we have come to the agreement that we cannot be privy to a war against the mythical Uncharted. As you should be aware, Thalassar has recently come out of a war with Kappur and Selection has been abolished. Due to the nature of the contract and bill of the abolishment, we cannot spare any soldiers for you at this time, as they are all needed for more important tasks. Before you curse me and display your anger, I'd like to remind you that you cleansed your hands of us, and the alliance with Iol can only extend so far. However, I am glad to see you are taking your new duties as princess seriously, though saddened that you have driven your new home to war. Best wishes, your father."

The bubble burst, and the disappointment of his words rained down in the silence around us.

I stared, blinking at it.

I thought I couldn't be broken any further.

Clearly, I'd been wrong.

I could.

My father… I thought at least he'd fight for me, the way that the King of Kappur had raged war for Maisie. This had been his last chance, his last chance to win back my heart, and he'd failed.

We both had.

Perhaps he hadn't tried because I hadn't been the best daughter. I was selfish. I was mean. He'd been the one to create me. Perhaps, it wasn't me he hated at all, but himself. Because in me he saw his own failures.

And I'd pushed him away and tried to bring him closer but all it served was to drift us apart. Because I was the daughter of the wife he'd never again see, the daughter he didn't really want.

And I'd put him upon a pedestal, had desired his love like a starving shark. I'd taken all the gifts he'd given me as if it were his love instead of demanding what I should have in the first place.

It all made sense now.

I should have demanded.

For so long, I'd placed responsibility on the shoulders of others. On the shoulders of my father, my mother, my cousins… I'd lived in the shadows of others for so long because my father had cast one over me. I'd cast myself beneath it and had tried so hard to remove myself from it that I became something everyone hated. Something no one wanted to ally themselves with.

But I was more than that.

I was more than a selfish princess. Val had seen that in me.

I just hardly ever saw it in myself.

And for once that shadow looming over me didn't seem quite as intimidating. Perhaps I didn't even have to measure up to it. Or perhaps I already had.

I'd known all along what I was. All the words hurled at me like insults, everything I shamefully hid. They weren't flaws at all. They were my intricate truths, parts of me that had gotten me this far. That had kept me alive. That had given me three husbands. That had given me the strength and the love I needed to protect my family.

Even if they wouldn't do the same for me.

"I am Princess Odele Malabella Oriana," I whispered firmly to every single person within the room. "Daughter to Queen Odette Malabella Sanitorum. My mother was a gentle, peaceful ruler. The mer loved her and for too long, I've lived in the shadows of her good deeds. But I am not my mother." I looked up at them with the rage of burning lava. "I am a survivor. I am brutal. Honest. And I am not self-sacrificing. But I am smart. I have the will of iron, and I will do anything for the ones I love." My eyes went over to Maisie, glared, then darted away. "I will take what armies I have, and I will march into Iol. I will save Val, I will save my remaining cousin, and I will kill anyone that gets in my way."

Then I dropped the conch and turned from them to swim away.

"Gather your armies, King Adrian," I ordered, holding my head up high. "Tonight, we ride to Iol. To war. And let nothing get in our way."

Tonight, we march on.

And tomorrow?

I would take back what was mine.

For I was a Duchess of Frost. Princess of Thalassar. Queen of the Uncharted.

And vengeance, in violence and in blood, would be mine.

QUEEN

OF

FROZEN WAR

Para Victor Hugo.
Te amo de aquí al poste.

FEW DRAGONS WERE HARMED within the contents of this book.

Because I'm as extra as Odele, I'm adding a second dedication in this book. To Lidiya Foxglove, who unknowingly helped inspire the Royal mer world. The first time I read Kingdoms of Sky and Shadow, I thought, huh, her characters remind me of anime. I wanna write anime main characters, too. And so the mer were born.

DEEP IN THE NORTHERN waters, the currents stirred along the border where Draconi met Iol. The frigid bite of rushing bubbles had become a familiarity, and though I felt the ice seep deep into my bones, the joy and comfort Iol had once brought eluded me.

Another blast of cold bubbles shot through the open tent flaps. I tightened my fur cloak around my shoulders, tucking my neck into the collar.

"Estimated number of enemy troops?" I spread my gloved hands across the bottom edge of the kelp map. It lay across the makeshift table in our camp. It depicted the seven sea kingdoms, from the warmer kingdom of

Ventlair in the south, and the ice cap waters of Iol in the north, even the waters to the west. The Uncharted Waters had been carefully scribbled and added in by Adrian's careful hand.

Finally, everything I cared to know was there. According to Adrian, the Uncharted Waters didn't have cities. They had tribes, ruled over by mages, kings, and queens. The waters were filled with magic and hybrid creatures, strange mer and mysteries that made fear tremble through the hearts of those east of them.

Never venture to the Uncharted Waters.

I almost snorted at that singular voice I'd listened to so long ago within a conch and the advice he'd tried to impart. Little did he know a Princess of Thalassar would marry the king of such a frightening place.

Little did he know the queen of the other half would plan on invading *us.*

"My scouts have been passing messages." Adrian slid small figurines across the map towards the northernmost part of Iol borders. "They have around five thousand more troops than us."

A shiver went through me that had nothing to do with the cold and everything to do with that number. My lips threatened to tremble, but I kept determination in my voice as I asked, "What about beasts?"

That was the important question. It was the beasts that would win battles. It was the beasts that would make or break us.

Adrian's lips pressed together in a grave line. His fingers reached for a figurine made of steel, and he played with the sharp edges before wrapping it around his palm and squeezing. Blood plumed from his fist and he pulled it close to his chest as if he didn't feel the pain, as if he didn't feel anything at all. "Hundreds."

I rubbed at my temples with my hand. A headache was pounding there, but not matter how much I tried to soothe the throbbing ache, it would not be abated. It had been a week since I'd decided to accept my status as queen and to help the mer of Iol and the Uncharted.

I was no closer to saving them today than I had been yesterday. Or the week before. Or the month before.

Hearing about ruling in conches was vastly different than actually ruling, than *actually* plotting a war.

A week felt like a lifetime. We could have gotten to Iol sooner on our own, but with a whole army to transport, things were slow, and we still didn't have a plan. Not one that would be effective at any rate. Not when we had so much to lose.

I stared down at the map and the figures that separated our armies from the enemy's, at the figures that represented the troops of allies we didn't have.

My heart ached at the sight of dragons scattered over Draconi, at the hippocampi scattered over Thalassar, and even the sea snakes over Kappur. How was it possible to have roots in all these waters and have no one come to our aid?

What hurt the most wasn't the lack of support from my father or my stepmother, as I'd expected nothing less from them, but the lack of support from Maisie.

I knew she dreaded war, knew she held little power, but to have her blatantly deny help had cleaved my chest into dusty ruins. Ruins which I rose up from anew, a crown perched over my brow and the weight of two kingdoms on my shoulders.

With or without her, I'd save the kingdom I'd come to love and think of as my home.

Feeling renewed, and the headache abated, I tapped my gloved fingers against the map. "Numbers don't win battles," I said, making sure to look into every worried face floating around the table. Adrian and Ytgar, generals and soldiers, leaders of their ranks and the fiercest of their tribes.

"They help, though," a general pointed out nervously.

"Cunning and skill win battles," I reminded them. Then I smiled, a half twist of my lips that was arrogant and sure, even if I didn't exactly feel it inside. "Do not forget, you have the smartest mer in the seven sea kingdoms on your side. If anyone can find out how to win this battle, I can."

It wasn't met with laughs. Not this time. Not with the vast difference between our armies blinking at them from the map.

"Hey!" I snapped and their eyes shot up to me. "We will figure it out. I promise you that. Now, tell everyone to pack up. We march on tomorrow."

They saluted at my obvious dismissal and exited the war tent, leaving me alone with both Adrian and Ytgar. With the warriors gone, I placed my palms against the surface of the table and leaned over the map, head hanging. The pulsing headache was back at full force. Doubts crept in at the most inopportune moments, within seconds after feeling put together.

"Can we really do this?" I whispered, despair threatening to choke me. "Can we really beat her on our own?"

I felt strong arms wrap around my midsection and pull me back against a hard chest. I knew the contours of his body, memorized them the way I would the words in a conch. His chin rested against the top of my head, and in his arms, I felt a little lighter, knowing he shared bits of my pain eased the ache inside, however slightly.

"I don't know," Ytgar said from above me, tightening his arms around my stomach. "But we will figure it out."

"We have to figure it out soon," Adrian cut in, knocking over the figurines on the map with a single swipe of his hand. "It's been weeks since…" He trailed off, eyes taking me in worriedly like I'd fall apart.

I didn't need him finishing that sentence to know what he meant. It had been a week since we left Draconi in a rush. A week since I'd received the severed head of my cousin as a gift from Queen Alexxandria, my husband's tyrannical sister.

But it'd been *weeks* since Val had left us.

It was a loss I felt keenly down to the depths of my soul. Like every strand inside me was cutting itself apart, destroying me from the inside out.

Ytgar must have known what I was thinking, because he pulled me closer to share in my sadness.

"Surely we would have heard something from him by now?" Adrian's voice was gentle but firm. I knew he was somehow preparing me for the worst.

I didn't want to believe the worst.

If something happened to Val, surely I would feel it in my soul, in my heart.

"She has our families captive." My voice shook. "If we attack, then she could kill them."

"If we don't attack, they'll die anyway, love." Adrian's hand came over my own. His was gloved in black leather, and even through the material I felt the warmth of his palm searing me. "We have to march on and attack."

Anxiety hummed a tune in my chest. I knew Adrian was anxious himself. He wanted to get going, to get this over with. He wanted to see his sister dead. *Get in line,* I wanted to sneer. She'd taken my kingdom for herself, and for that slight alone I would make her pay.

Ytgar's arms slipped from my body so he could float beside me and brush his fingers along the space on the map that dominated Iol. Though the kingdom bordered near two-legger lands of ice and was a vast expanse of water, you could swim through the cold for weeks without having reached civilization or the capital of Aelfrost. The cold made everything slower, and the ice wall passage that led into the kingdom still seemed so far away. After passing that, it was a two-day slow swim to make it to the capital. A week or so with the army.

"We can't blindly swim in," Ytgar murmured gravely.

Adrian frowned in the prince's direction. "You're stalling. Both of you." There was a hint of accusation in his voice.

Ytgar leveled his silver eyed gaze at my second husband. Tension beat between them. It was the same battle every day for the past week. The same hot and cold intensity with me between them, forced to choose sides. "We have more to lose than you," Ytgar practically growled.

Violence sprang through the water, a painful energy that had me closing my eyes in both annoyance and heartbreak. I couldn't stand war, couldn't stand ruling. I'd always shied away from it because I knew somewhere inside myself that I was not meant for it. I'd finally silenced that voice, but the pressure of the decision felt like it was too much.

"If you think that, then you're a fool. I have just as much to lose in this war as you do. What of my army? My tribes?"

"What of *my* grandmother? My best friend?"

"You think their lives are more important than others? If so, then turn in your crown now, for the needs of the few never outweigh the needs of the many."

"Would you two care to whip out your merdicks now to compare sizes?" I cut through icily before they could argue any further. "Or will you both shut your mouths and let me *think*?"

Ytgar wisely shut his mouth, but it didn't steal the glare away from his elegant features. He was beautiful even when he was angry. Wisps of silver-white hair clung to his cheeks like snow pressed to his brown skin. He was regal in his bearing, back straight, and a white, blue, and golden cloak around his shoulders with thick fur stitched around the edges.

Adrian's single yellow eye narrowed on me. A black eye patch covered his other eye, or lack of one. It had been cut out years ago by Thalassarin soldiers, by my mer, when he'd migrated to the seven seas with his sister. The evidence of that cruel day peeked out from behind the patch in silver scars that bisected down his cheek, to his chin, and over the top of his brow.

He wore his own fur cloak in black, red, and gold. Colors of his own home, of the kingdom he wanted legitimized through marriage to me.

"You've been thinking for weeks now, love." His accent and the way he spoke Thalassarin common tongue made the words sound angrier, harsher. "We need to stop thinking and make a plan."

"You don't think I know that?!" In a blinding flash of anger, I grabbed the edge of the map and yanked it straight off the table, scattering the pieces off and watching them slowly sink into the cold silt. I gripped the edge of the table, heaving in painful breaths. "I don't know what I'm doing..." I admitted on a low whisper, and it hurt to even say the words.

I'd been so confident when we started that I'd make Alexxandria pay for the wyvern that wreaked havoc on Iol, for taking my kingdom, and for killing my cousins. The rage fueled me to take my revenge, to take back what was mine in destruction and blood. Yet when this all started, when the numbers of the troops rolled in, maps were drawn, the enemy pinpointed, no amount of conches or kelp books I'd read could help me win this war.

I was always the smartest in a room, it was a fact I prided myself on, but I didn't know what I was doing. I couldn't blindly lead them into slaughter, not because I was afraid of the lives that would be lost; this was war, I *knew* the consequences, but because I couldn't afford us to lose.

"I have mulled over every plan, analyzed every angle. We cannot afford delays, we do not have the numbers, and we have everything to lose while she has everything to gain." A sob rose in my chest and lodged tightly in my throat. I didn't dare unleash it; I spoke through it and gritted teeth. "I am waiting because I need to form a plan that will *win.*"

Silence followed my words, but I didn't look up. I couldn't bear to see the look I knew would be in their eyes. Pity, worry. I didn't want it. I wanted ideas, I wanted victory.

And I meant to have it.

All I needed was a little more time.

"Love..." Adrian reached a hand out to me.

I looked up then, glaring, before I slapped his arm away. "Do not condescend to me," I growled. "Don't you dare."

Adrian reached for me, gripping me tightly by the waist and whipping me around to lift me up and sit me atop the table. He loomed above me, pressing terribly close into my personal space, a look of bright anger in his eye. "I am not *condescending* to you." He flashed his teeth, and then he pressed the tip of his nose against my own. "I am trying to *comfort* you."

"I don't want your comfort."

"Fine," he hissed, pulling away slightly. "Then I won't comfort you."

My hand pressed against the velvet of his cloak, where I felt the steady pounding of his heartbeat against my palm. My fingers closed against the material and I tugged him close. "Good," I whispered just before my mouth closed over his.

I had no room for gentle lies in my heart. I despised them. They were falsehoods meant to reassure and give a blind sense of hope. I wanted honesty, raw and primitive honesty. And this was how I would get it.

There was no love between King Adrian and me. Not the same way it pulsed angrily between Ytgar and I, or the way it hummed between Valmundur and I. The way I felt for Adrian was… inexplicable. It was an ache building up in my gut, spreading like a vicious venom towards my heart. It was a curiosity for broken things, and lust and power. It was anger and pain in equal measure, and a deep longing for something more.

Even if I didn't love him, even if he didn't love *me,* this kiss spoke of the violent emotions exploding into shards of glass that pierced deep into my heart and stayed. It was dominant and commanding, a brand on my very soul.

His lips claimed, quickly taking over the kiss with his mouth and tongue. He growled against me, a sound of rapidly building desire that zinged straight down to my core. His tongue tangled against mine in stroke after stroke.

A moan tore from my throat. This… this was what I needed. Not comfort, but desperate release.

Adrian's fingers slid into the roots of my hair, gripping tightly at the purple strands to angle my head back so he could delve in deeper. My own fingers began fumbling with the strings of his thick cloak, tugging to pull them apart.

"There's no time for that…" Adrian pulled away to admonish, a sly grin curving the edges of his mouth. That single yellow eye flashed dangerously, desperately, while his fingers reached for the hem of the front of my dress and slowly pulled it up.

A sigh echoed around us, and in a single, distracted moment, I turned to see Ytgar's grim expression as he started to leave. My heart thumped a heavy rhythm, and my hand shot out to grab him by the cloak.

"Wait," I demanded.

Ytgar stopped, his shoulders rigid, his whole posture tense. He turned his head slightly to the side to regard me with a menacing sort of expression.

It had been this way since Val had left.

Angry bouts of sex and Valmundur were what kept us tightly tethered. His absence left a vast chasm of empty space between us. Like Ytgar could never fathom *how* to move on without him.

At night he held me close, and yet it was the only intimacy he allowed between us besides comforting kisses or strong arms wrapped around me from behind. When it came to sex, he'd turn the other way. I wondered if it was because he'd grown used to sharing me with Val, and since his best friend wasn't here it was somehow a betrayal to him, to the three of us and the delicately woven strands of trust and union between us.

I'd given him his space. He'd coped in his way, and I'd coped in mine. He'd thrown himself into battle plans with us, and I used Adrian for pleasure.

"Stay," I whispered. It was both a command and a plea. We'd been physically apart for far too long, and I could no longer stand it. "I need you." My fingers tightened on his cloak, and I took in a shuddering breath. "We need each other."

Val was like a ghost between us. There'd been absolutely no word from him, from anyone in Iol. Queen Alexxandria had given us her demands. Surrender Prince Ytgar Neves Isolde or die. Valmundur had disguised himself as the prince to take his place. We hadn't heard a word since.

Ytgar and I... we loved each other, but we also loved Val. We'd been together—Adrian, Ytgar, Val, and I, *all of us*—and now we were missing *one* piece in our group. It was almost enough to topple our foundation down.

I didn't want to let it.

I *couldn't* allow it.

"Stay," I pleaded again. "Please."

Ytgar's eyes closed like he was attempting to find the willpower to fight me off but couldn't quite seem to muster it up. I could see his resolve hanging on by a thread.

"It's not a betrayal." I pried my fingers from his cloak, pulling my hand back to set my palm on Adrian's arm. I'd not force him, not if he didn't want to. But I couldn't float by and watch him fade away from my grasp.

He sighed and ran a hand over his face, then turned to face us. The past few weeks had taken their toll on all of us, and it was prominent on Ytgar's features.

His eyes were bloodshot, and shadows seemed to take up permanent residence beneath them. His sharp cheekbones appeared to be even sharper, and while he was still beautiful, still fierce, he looked *tired*.

We needed to be connected now more than ever.

He reached a hand out and trailed his fingers down the side of my face. The movements were gentle.

A small smile twisted his mouth before he leaned forward and pressed a tender kiss against my temple. "I can deny you nothing right now," he whispered against my skin.

"I've missed you," I confessed.

"And I, you."

And then he kissed me, and it was like we'd never been apart. His mouth consumed, as desperately and as violently as Adrian's had. With his tongue lashing against mine, he projected his fears, his wants, and he gave and I took, grabbing the back of his neck to pull him closer.

Adrian's hands slid up my sides, stopping so his thumbs grazed the undersides of my breasts. His fingers danced across my chest and tweaked my nipples through the velvet material.

I gasped against Ytgar's mouth at the sudden action from Adrian, and Ytgar swallowed the sound with his tongue and teeth. He bit down on my bottom lip, taking it between his lips to suck. I groaned, leaning into Adrian while being completely consumed by Ytgar.

It was an onslaught of sensation that had my core quivering immediately. My fingers slipped between the silver-white strands of Ytgar's hair and tugged, pulling him closer to me, while my body arched into Adrian's ministrations.

Hands molded against my chest and slipped over my stomach, back to the hem of my dress before the prince had interrupted. The hem slid up the length of my scales and bunched up near my stomach, baring me to the cold chill of the water. A moment later, my body was warmed with the press of his leather clad fingers sliding up the slit of my opening.

My hips rolled against the movement of deft fingers penetrating me; in and out they slid, pressing against the walls of my core. I cried out, tearing my mouth from Ytgar's while Adrian slid a finger up to my most sensitive spot and pressed down.

Pleasure rolled through my entire body at the contact. My body took in the length of his fingers as he stretched me; he leaned forward to kiss the rapid thumping of the pulse at my throat.

I sighed against Adrian, and Ytgar tossed aside errant tendrils of hair from my neck to kiss my other side, tongue sliding down the skin of my throat. Hands, I wasn't sure whose, tugged at the drawstrings on my cloak and pulled, tossing the cloak from my shoulders.

A shudder went through me at the blast of cold, but I was once again enveloped in the warmth of their bodies.

"You're so warm," Adrian rasped against my body. His movements were relentless, drawing out the pleasure with every delicious stroke. "Feel how warm she is."

A deep growl rumbled through Ytgar's chest, and his teeth grazed across my collarbone with sensual slowness. "Yes." He licked a line up my throat just before I felt a second pair of gloveless fingers joining the others, expanding me from the inside.

"Oh, Gods…" My hands dropped to the tabletop as my body arched, hips lifting against their sliding movements. "More…" I demanded. *"More."*

They both moved at their own pace, Adrian with deep, demanding thrusts while Ytgar moved slowly, drawing out the anticipation. The mix of the two paces was so overwhelming, my head spun in a torrent of violent circles.

"Come for us." Adrian's thumb circled the sensitive nub of my desire, and I fell against the table, sprawling my arms at my sides. Their movements were languid, and they brought me higher, higher to the edge of the cliff…

My desire came. It fragmented in quick bursts that expanded throughout my entire body, from the tips of my hair to the ends of my tailfin. They drew out my cries, and my hips rode out the sensations, and my mouth opened to scream out my pleasure.

As my limbs shook with a mixture of weakness and pleasure, I sighed. Their fingers were still hard inside me, but Adrian wiggled, causing me to gasp before he pulled out. There was a strange emptiness without him there, but that hand he slid up my abdomen, between my breasts, up my neck and settled over my lips.

His finger traced over my mouth. "Taste yourself," he whispered, pressing the leather-clad digit into my mouth. I sucked him in, tasting ecstasy. I kept him in my mouth, biting down against the underside of his finger. "Do you want to do the honors, Prince?" A sly grin spread across his mouth.

"I do." He slipped away from me but didn't give me time to miss his warmth because his hands gripped my hips and yanked me close. His black and white tail wrapped around my purple-blue one, keeping me steadily pinned against him.

His nails dug into my hips, the violent pressure of it heightening the sensation of desire through me all over again. The material of his clothes pressed against my naked tail then the hem of his tunic slid up between us, scraping sensually over my scales. A moment later, I felt the warm press of his member, the tip sliding up my tail and pressing against my opening.

He entered me, inch by slow inch until he filled me completely to the hilt. He paused, pulsing inside me, throbbing and demanding.

The lack of movement only made my body thrum and crave more. I jerked my hips up to demand it, but his hands pressed me down, keeping me still.

"Slow," he rasped.

I groaned, eyes fluttering open. I wanted to frown at him, but Adrian pulled my attention away from Ytgar by gripping me by the back of the head and pulling my gaze to the side. My throat tightened as I looked up into that flashing eye, then my gaze lowered to where his other hand was hiking up his clothes.

When he bared himself before me, my tongue darted across my lower lip at the sight of his long, rigid member. The tip glistened, holding the promise of pleasure and bliss. He palmed the underside of it, holding it in his fist. His hand slid down his length, then back up again. Down... up... down... My eyes were hypnotized by the erotic movements, of the slow jerks of his wrists as he pleasured himself.

Then he leaned forward, and the tip of his member was centimeters away from my lips. If I leaned over just a bit more, I could take him in my mouth.

"Do it," he ordered.

I slid my tongue over his smooth head, twirling it in lazy, sensual circles that caused his breath to hitch. I wrapped my lips around the head of him, then slowly sucked him into my mouth, inch by inch, until the tip of his member touched the back of my throat.

He groaned, hips angling deeper into my mouth while his hand pulled the back of my head closer. He filled my mouth completely, and I was forced to relax my jaw to take in the heavy length of him. I slid my tongue against the underside of him, sucked him deeper.

And then Ytgar slid in and out of me.

My hips bucked against the pressure of him inside me, and I gasped around Adrian's member, taking him in even deeper with the action.

Adrian hissed out a breath. "Use your teeth."

Ytgar slid, in and out, angling his hips so every time he slid back into me, I felt it against the cleft of my desire.

I slid down Adrian's length, putting the slightest bit of pressure with my teeth, scraping against him. His hips jerked against my mouth, while Ytgar's pressed deeply into me.

Soon, my mouth mimicked the movements of Ytgar's hips. Slow and deep, the pleasure was drawn out in rolling waves, in slow curls of my tongue, in deep rolls of hips, in the panting gasps of our mingled breathing.

"Yes…" Adrian hissed the word through his teeth, bracing one hand against the edge of the table while the other demanded a faster pacing at the back of my neck. Fingers slipped through the strands of my hair and curled, tightening in their desperation.

They both filled me to the brink, their bodies demanding every inch of me firmly, deliciously.

Adrian muttered something in his language, something I didn't quite understand but could have very well been a curse or a plea.

His hand left the back of my head and slid down my body. His fingers shoved into my opening, stretching me further. The two of them invading me… it was tight… it was…

"Come for us, love," Adrian demanded.

Ytgar thrust, and Adrian touched the nub of my desire.

I fell hard and fast into the chasm of pleasure, my orgasm spiraling throughout all my nerve endings. I screamed against Adrian's softness, working my head back and forth as the two of them rode out the sensations of my body. Adrian pinched and tweaked my nub, and my whole body quivered as another orgasm followed that one, slower yet no less intense.

Ytgar grunted and moved faster inside me, against my inner walls, against Adrian's fingers. Together, they rode me to the brink of madness, and I'd be damned if I went there alone.

I sucked harder, putting pressure onto his member before scraping my teeth along the underside of him. I reached a hand out to grip the base of him, to move up and down, squeezing, tightening my grip against him while my hips rose up to met their rapidly increasing thrusts.

"Gods…" Adrian let out a slew of harsh words in the language of the Uncharted.

He slid in and out of my mouth, faster and faster, while Ytgar pulled my hips up, yanking my lower body towards him. That single action sent my pleasure spiraling.

Mine, and theirs.

We exploded together. Adrian pumped inside my mouth, rasping out breathless words, while Ytgar pulled me up, my lips slipping away from Adrian, so our chests kissed intimately. He growled something in Iolish I didn't quite catch before plunging his tongue into my mouth.

He kissed the same way he fought. Fiercely and with his whole attention as he spent himself inside me.

As the last of his shudders wracked through his powerful body, he pulled away from my mouth, pressing his forehead against my own.

At our sides, Adrian closed in on us and gripped Ytgar by the chin with his leather-clad hand, bringing his face a scant few inches from his. A sly, mischievous smile pressed on his beautiful lips. "How do I taste inside your mouth, Prince?" His tongue flicked out over the seams of Ytgar's, causing the prince to jerk back a surprised fraction. "Hmm…" Adrian's tongue ran against his bottom lip. "Delicious."

My heart thumped at the action, and I could feel the beat mirrored in Ytgar's own chest. The Prince of Iol blinked with quiet confusion at the

King of the Uncharted Waters. Tension pulsed between them, an erotic tension that permeated the water with sexual desire.

"I—I—" Ytgar stammered for words.

"Will the two of you kiss again?" It was a demand, rather than a request, even while the words left me breathlessly.

There'd been something innately erotic about the way Adrian's tongue slid over Ytgar's mouth, and I wondered what it would be like to see their tongues clash, to see these two dominant men in my life battle mouth against mouth.

"While I'm not keen on sharing," I continued, "I wouldn't mind *this*." My fingers slipped into the roots of their hair, the texture of the soft strands sliding between the spaces of them. I pressed, moving their faces a few inches closer.

Ytgar's member was still hard inside me, and twitched at the action.

"Only if it pleases my Queen." Adrian smirked.

"There are an infinite number of things that please me." I leaned forward and licked a line down Ytgar's cheek, to the edge of his jaw. "Kissing pleases me." I rolled against Ytgar, feeling the long length of him press sensually against my nub. A soft sigh pushed from my throat. "Coming against you pleases me." My fingers slid down to the nape of their necks, and I pressed them closer still. "And seeing the two of you kiss would *definitely* please me."

"Do you want to?" Adrian was a whisper away from Ytgar's mouth.

Ytgar's lips pressed together as he mulled over the question. "I've never…"

Adrian's hand went to his chin, gripping him firmly. "I'll guide you."

I wasn't sure who met who first. Or maybe they met somewhere in the middle. All I knew was that, between one blink and the next, their mouths were pressed together, and Adrian was taking, devouring. His mouth opened over Ytgar's, tongue sliding over his in languid strokes.

It awoke something within the Iolish Prince. He groaned, a sound born deep within his throat, before his hand went to the back of Adrian's head and pulled him close. He plundered, fighting for dominance of the kiss. Their mouths molded together in perfect form and synchronization.

It was like watching a battle, like listening to one embedded deep in the bowels of an old conch. A clash of swords was the tangling of tongues, the cries of the fallen echoed deep within their throats. And I was merely a spectator to this erotic, violent display.

I groaned as I watched it unfold, rolling my hips against Ytgar's hard length still deeply buried within me. His member twitched, one hand reaching out to palm my hip and keep me steady. I moved against him, driven entirely by what I witnessed.

Adrian kept one hand firmly pressed to the back of Ytgar's head, while the other pressed against my lower back. He pushed, almost like he was guiding the movements of my hip rolls. He was controlling even in that.

Ytgar finally tore from Adrian's mouth, and he seemed to do it with a bit of agonizing reluctance.

He growled, digging his nails into my waist, and he *moved*. His thrusts were as deep as before, but quicker now. He grinded into me with punishing force. Like he could somehow bury himself deep inside me and find the beginnings of my soul.

Perhaps I wanted him to find it. Perhaps I wanted my soul to weave around his like a claiming, if it hadn't happened already.

We rode together, our breaths rising in harsh pants that echoed along the waters of the war tent. This was merely a battle between us all. A fight to claim, to remember what we had lost, what we would lose, and the pain that still connected us like a thread.

Adrian's lips went to my neck, his tongue and teeth grazing my sensitive flesh. He didn't interrupt, didn't interfere as Ytgar's movements became a bit rougher, and I relished in the very feel of it. I needed this. *He* needed this. And Adrian was aware that this was our moment, and he seemed glad to stick to the sidelines. His hand slipped down the bodice of my dress where he grasped at my breast, squeezing and tweaking my nipple.

I arched into the touch, hips pressing tighter against Ytgar's body. The action caused him to groan, and I knew he was close; so, so close. I grinded against him, slamming with a hard thrust of my hips just as he cried out his release and took my lip into his mouth, biting down until I saw two-legger stars sear across my closed eyelids.

I collapsed against him, heaving in breaths in the aftermath of our connection.

He slowly slipped from me, and I felt the loss of him like the loss of a limb. It was empty without him inside me, and it seemed like he was disconnecting when he pulled away from me, taking a stroke back.

This was supposed to have brought us together.

Not tear us apart.

He took a deep, steadying breath that rumbled in his chest, then ran his hands through his hair. He looked over at me, still sitting at the edge of the table, Adrian pressed close to my side with his hand down my bodice, and my dress bunched up near my lap.

He looked at me with an infinite amount of love and an equal amount of sadness.

It cleaved my heart in two.

But then he swam back in my direction and cupped my face in his hands. The tips of our noses pressed together, as intimate as a kiss. "I love you," he whispered, his voice hoarse. He dropped his forehead to mine. "So much."

A smile touched my mouth. I slid my hands up his muscular arms and squeezed, the action conveying everything I was feeling.

His fingers trailed a pathway down my skin, stopping at the edges of my exposed collarbone. His eyes locked between my breasts, just above Adrian's hand, a necklace of ice sat against my skin.

Sorrow overwhelmed his features, and I felt the echoes of it deep in my own heart.

"I miss him," he choked out.

Adrian's hand slipped from my bodice and gripped my upper arm for support.

I looked down at the necklace. It had been a gift from Val, so long ago now, it seemed. On Saint Valence Day in Iol, a celebration of friendship and of love, he'd carved the little conch shell necklace from a special, magical Iolish ice. An ice that would never melt.

"I just wish I knew he was okay." He voiced the fears we hadn't really spoken since he'd gone. "I just wish…"

"…there was a way to get him a message?" I asked, my eyes glued fiercely to my bodice.

I looked up and smiled.

Already, a plan was forming in my mind.

"What?" Ytgar's silver brows pulled together in a frown as he noted my expression.

I slid from the table, straightening out my clothes. My mind spun in a hurricane as my thoughts and ideas began piecing themselves together for the first time in a long time. I moved down to my discarded cloak and threw it around my shoulders, tying the strings together with excited fingers.

"Odele…" Ytgar started to reach for me, but I dodged and stared at Adrian.

"I need your mage," I told him.

His eyebrow rose, but he didn't question me. He merely nodded, righted his clothing, pulled on his cloak, and went in search of the old merman, ducking beyond the tent flaps.

I turned to Ytgar then, hope shining, for the first time in weeks, in my eyes. "I think we can get a message to Val," I told him.

His eyes sparked, and the same sensation I felt, suddenly filled him.

I explained my thoughts, the choppy bits, while my mind smoothed out the rough edges of a maddening plan that I wasn't entirely sure would even work.

But I had to try.

And I willed Val to hold on just a little longer.

I'D LOST TRACK OF the days. It was hard to count them in the cold dungeons without the help of light, voices, or any mer contact at all.

Darkness and cold pressed around me, and within the cold metal bars and steel ceiling, the currents drifted in ice and snow. I kept the one cloak I had wrapped tightly around my body. I was used to this weather, but my fins were still freezing; and I was used to the hunger, but my stomach still coiled in pain.

The moment after they'd dragged Jessinda's body away, Queen Alexxandria had ordered them to lock me up. Her guards had none too kindly dragged my fighting body away from her. They beat me along the way before they'd shoved me face first into an empty dungeon cell.

No one had come for me. Not the guards, not the queen, not Anneli, and not Odele, Ytgar, or Adrian.

I knew they would come. I knew Odele and Ytgar would pull the earth of two-legger lands straight into the sea if it meant my freedom. And yet the fact that they hadn't yet… well, I couldn't help but feel a swarm of overwhelming sorrow drown my soul. Sorrow and pain.

I was alone in my cage, and I couldn't help but wonder if this was some poetic sense of justice for the queen. She'd been in a cage, had been tortured by Thalassarin soldiers. When would my torment come?

And what exactly would it entail?

My fingers reached up to trace over my temple, my eyelid. I tried to imagine a festering wound there, one similar to the queen's. She'd poked at it until the infection spread on her skin, in her heart, and never let it fully heal.

I could not judge what I didn't understand, and while her anger was warranted, *this* was not. To avenge herself, she was willing to let all the mer in the seven sea kingdoms suffer for things they had no control over.

I kept picturing the white wyvern that had torn through Iol so many weeks ago. The chaos it caused, and the destruction it left in its wake. Every time I closed my eyes to sleep on the icy ground, my cheek abrading against the grains of silt and snow, I saw the image of Jessinda's head, of the blade against her neck, of the smoking plumes of blood as they dragged her away.

The sight invaded my nightmares until it was hard for me to even fall asleep. The loneliness of the cell was crueler somehow. Maybe that was Alexxandria's plan. To drive me to madness before she broke my body.

My body she could break if she wished, but my mind would remain my own. Whatever games the queen was playing, I'd win, that I vowed.

I tucked the cloak tighter around my shoulders and stared into the darkness.

Queen Alexxandria would *not* break me.

My fingers were steady as I undid the clasp of my necklace and gripped the golden chain, holding it out before me at arm's length.

Mer had gathered around to hear what I had to say, and what should have been a nervous moment, was anything but. I was confident, sure in my decision. I knew my plan would work, because I refused for it to fail.

The little conch shell made of ice swung back and forth like a pendulum, the movements slow and hypnotizing. And very promising.

The mer surrounding me. Ytgar, Adrian, their generals, and the mage all stared at it with furrowed brows. One of them cleared his throat. "What is it?"

A smile touched my lips. "This, my subject, is the answer to all our problems."

His eyes were piercing and confused. "Which would be…?"

I set the necklace down gently on the table in front of me. The same table where Adrian and Ytgar had pleasured me immensely. The map was intact, as were all the figurines representing the troops of the seven sea kingdoms, as Ytgar had fixed them before I called the meeting.

I placed the shell right over the marking of Aelfrost, just past the twin walls of ice trolls that marked the borders of Iol, a few days travel from where Draconi met the ice kingdom. The landmarks were well drawn on the map. I studied them with a smile on my face.

The borders.

The ice troll sculptures.

A dozen little towns.

Aelfrost.

Even more little towns.

The northernmost part of the kingdom.

"What is the biggest problem we have right now?" I asked, sweeping my hand over the map in a confident gesture.

"The lack of troops?" Adrian's general supplied.

"The lack of a plan?" another added.

I shook my head and answered my own question aloud. "The lack of communication." I looked over to Adrian as I tapped a fingernail against the northernmost part of Iol, where their borders connected to the Uncharted. "How many troops does your sister have here, according to your spies?"

His muscular arms were crossed against his chest. He answered without hesitation. "Five thousand."

"And how many does she have total in her army?"

"Ten thousand."

"And how many are in Iol?"

He paused, and a slow, knowing smile spread across his face. "I don't know."

"Exactly. We don't *know*." I took a few of the wyvern figurines that represented his sister and spread them out down near Draconi, where their western borders met the Uncharted. "We know they took troops and invaded, but we don't know how many because we lack the proper communication with Iol. What if her troops are in Draconi, lying in secret and waiting to attack with their beasts?"

"They couldn't," a general argued. "The Dragon Emperor knows of the threat."

I shook my head again. "What he knows is what we told him. He thinks the might of her whole army is in Iol. Maybe it is, maybe it isn't. What we can be sure of is that the emperor is likely gathering his own troops and will do a sweep of his waters. *If*," I emphasized, "she does have troops near Draconi, then that's one less problem for us."

"But we don't know if they are there or not," the general pointed out.

"Which is precisely why we need to communicate with someone in Iol. We need to know how many soldiers she has there and plan our attack around that."

Adrian, who I hadn't yet told of the plan, smiled as the realization dawned on him. He was quick to catch on, my husband.

"Everyone knows that conches break in Iol. It's likely another reason why Alexxandria attacked Iol. We are vulnerable." Ytgar pressed his knuckles onto the table to lean over the map. I could hear the disdain in his voice, the disgust with his kingdom, and the searing desire to fix what was so terribly broken. "She wanted us closed off. No communication, no messages… nothing."

"Since conches break in Iolish waters, how are we going to get word out? Kelp parchments?"

I looked at the general who suggested it and dazzled him with a smile. "With conches." He looked at me like I was a rather slow, pathetic life form. The barracuda. "A conch made of ice that doesn't melt or break." I picked up the necklace again and turned to the mage. He'd been quiet, and no one had addressed him or his presence up until now. His eyes were hidden behind saggy eyelids and wrinkles, but I knew his gaze was fixated intently on me, on my words. "This is where you come in. Recording conches are fueled with both magic and science. I need *you* to use your magic for this."

His old body seemed to stir to life. The necklace made of antlers hanging around his neck clanked with his every swaying movement. He spoke low, softly, and in the language of the Uncharted. I didn't understand the words, but Adrian did, and my king leaned his ear close to the mage and listened.

"'Magic is sacred,'" he translated. "'It is a gift from our gods. It is what tethers the mages to the sacrament of our creators. It cannot be used laxly.'"

I fought back the gritting of my teeth. I'd never punched an old merman, but I could be forced to reconsider.

"'However,'" Adrian continued, his voice smooth and enchanting, "'the gods have spoken to me, and with this, I shall help you and my King.'"

I slowly loosed the breath I had inadvertently caught in my throat and nodded.

"What about the science of it?" the same general asked.

I was getting pretty annoyed with his damn interrogation.

"I will take care of that part myself."

He didn't question me, but his expression didn't change. He placed a fist over his heart and bowed. "Yes, my Queen."

I nodded at the respect and looked around the room. "The first step is to create it, and then we send the message out to those in Iol. We may not be able to fight her from the outside, but perhaps we can from within."

Ytgar leaned over the map, his eyes shining with vengeance. "If we can infiltrate Iol right under Alexxandria's fins, then perhaps we can defeat her. With the right messages in the right hands, the Iolish will rise up."

And so together, we began to plot.

THROWING MYSELF INTO PLANNING gave me the purpose my life in Iol never had. In camp, the mer listened to my rule, my opinions. Even the mer of the Uncharted respected me. Despite the fact I was a foreign prince, they treated me the same way they treated Adrian and Odele.

It gave me a renewed sense of purpose. But even with the busy days and nights now occupying my time, Valmundur still filled my mind.

I'd let him go, and maybe I should have yanked him off the beast he escaped on so many nights ago and tied him to me. But he'd made his choice without thinking the consequences through, and now I had to live in the aftermath of his decisions. With the uncertainty.

Was he dead, alive?

I prayed to the gods every spare minute I got that he be alive.

Because if he wasn't… it would be like losing another part of me. The same way Maisie was Odele's other half, Val was mine.

Without him I was empty.

I plotted and planned alongside Odele, Adrian, and the Uncharted to take Iol back. Not only for the mer, but for Val, for my grandmother. For everyone I ever professed to fight for. I now had that chance.

It was just heartbreaking that things had to come to this for it to happen.

I helped train the warriors of the Uncharted, who were from the southern waters of their home and weren't used to the cold. I taught them how to find warmth in the ice, how to protect themselves from frostbite, how to hold their weapons in gloved hands and maneuver them through snowy waters.

The Uncharted mer were quick learners, with the fierce determination to survive and fight like any Iolish. I was instructing Adrian's generals first, so they could then instruct their ranks.

I held my spear tightly in one hand, a shield in the other. The mer before me charged, quick push of his sea legs, and he was in front of me. I dodged the thrust of his weapon and he barreled past me. A quick turn, and I brought my shield crashing against his back.

He sprawled into the cold silt, sputtering curses in his language I was sure were at my expense.

"You're too quick to attack without looking for weakness first."

He pushed himself up from the ground, bringing with him his weapon and shield, turning to glare at me. "Battle is quick," he spat almost angrily. "It gives you no room to float there and think, just waiting for your opponent to attack you."

If Odele could hear him, she would snort and make a retort that his body couldn't keep up with his little brain, or that it was too arduous of a task for him. I didn't say any of these things.

"You're right," I agreed.

He blinked, obviously not expecting that answer.

"Battle is quick, it's bloody, and in the midst of the fray, your opponents won't be looking for weak spots. They will swing to kill and move on to the next."

I lifted my spear and whacked him straight against his unprotected shoulder. He cried out and jerked to the side with the action.

"Which is why you need to be smarter than them if you want to live."

I'd been in battles before. In battles with beasts that have broken through our borders, and a battle of beasts was fiercer than the battle of mer. I wanted them to live, and to do that, we needed strategy.

"Fight me," I taunted, banging my spear down against his shield. "Knock me into the silt. Find my weak point. Be quick and be smart, because on the battlefield it'll be the difference between life and death."

I brought the spear arching over my shoulder and slamming down towards him. This time, he dodged, twirling through the water to my left, my shield arm.

A smirk touched my lips as I followed on quick fin. I whirled and our weapons clashed against each other, but I was bigger, stronger, more skilled than him. I pushed him back easily.

"You're small," I said between hits, "which means you need to rely on speed." I aimed for the right side of his body, which he left exposed. "Shield up!" He obeyed just as my spear swung down and clamored against the surface of steel. I took a stroke back, a smirk pulling at the side of my mouth. "I am being kind to you." His eyes found mine from over his shield. "But your enemies will not be." And I struck.

The force of my blow shattered his weapon into shards of ice and remnants of steel. It rained over him and with a final, forceful kick of my tail against his shield, he fell to the silt, panting.

I turned in a slow circle to meet the eyes of every mer assembled around me. "The cold waters make you slower, but you must learn to live with the pain of frost. This will be a frozen war; we are vastly outnumbered in mer and in beasts, so fight with skill and cunning." My eyes stopped on King Adrian's. I hadn't noticed him among the warriors. He was at the front of the party in his umber and black fur cloak and black leather gloves, arms crossed against the bulk of his chest. "Even treachery if you have to."

His yellow eye glowed with mischief, and a slow, curling smile spread across his mouth. A mouth my eyes dropped to. I remembered the feel of his tongue clashing against mine as he plundered my mouth the same way pirates plundered for treasure.

Heat climbed my cheeks and I swallowed, eyes finding his yellow one again. He knew what I was thinking, I could tell, and it just made me even more nervous.

I suddenly found myself in tumultuous waters. It was unfamiliar, the sensation inside me, and I didn't know what to make of it. I honestly didn't want to make anything of it at all. It had been a one-time thing, a piece of myself given to Adrian in a moment of extreme vulnerability.

I was feeling that quite a lot these days.

Vulnerable.

It made me feel weak, like the same pitiful merman who had no power or say. Yet that wasn't quite true, either, was it? It had been as much an invigorating experience as it had been shaky.

"I want to fight you," Adrian announced, his voice like the sharp slap of a whip against water.

My fist tightened around my spear and I inclined my head, nodding to the empty spot his comrade had just vacated. "By all means."

With his smile still in place, he prowled forward like a hulking predator. It was odd to see myself so deeply reflected in him. Yet Adrian had a confidence, a surety that I did not.

His mer swarmed him, bringing forth a spear and a shield. He strapped the shield on first, slipping the leather ties onto his arms and tightening them against him. Then he gripped the spear and twirled his wrist in a warming up motion.

"Do you know how I won my half of the Uncharted Waters, Prince?" he asked, his voice a dangerous, seductive drawl.

I didn't rise to his bait.

"I conquered because my obsidian blade enjoyed the taste of flesh and bone." He pointed his spear out in my direction. A promise and a threat.

The hairs on the back of my neck prickled. This merman… this merman was dangerous. If it hadn't been evident before, it certainly was now.

He prowled from one side to the other, sizing me up like a morsel. It was both threatening and promising. It was like he meant to kill as much as he meant to seduce, and I steeled myself against the onslaught of emotions that simple action caused.

I was no fool, and I'd not be tricked by such a display.

The waters were suddenly permeated with a foreign emotion, one I couldn't quite comprehend or discern. It wasn't a fight for dominance over Odele. No, she was dominant, a force to be reckoned with all on her own. This was a challenge. Pure and simple. To accept, to give in, to him? To me? To break apart my vulnerability piece by brittle piece and make me stronger?

Perhaps.

I hefted my shield and arched back my spear.

Challenge accepted.

Adrian smiled.

Our spears met in the middle.

THE FORCE OF OUR collision rang down to my very bones. The way my muscles trembled as our spears pressed against one another in an effort to push the other back could have been considered erotic.

Heat rippled over my skin. He was strong; then again, I hadn't expected him to be weak.

I respected Prince Ytgar Neves Isolde the same way I respected opponents worthy enough to cross me. But all those opponents had lost, and their heads had been added as nothing more than adornments to my ivory throne.

Ytgar would not be another one. But I did want to conquer the prince. I wanted him to let loose those chains he tightly kept around himself. He'd been caged too long, and once released, would be a force to be reckoned with.

And I meant to unleash every savage bit of him.

We pushed against each other's spears, grunts tearing through the backs of our throats. I couldn't help the smile that curled my mouth. "Can you still taste me in your mouth, Ice Prince?" I taunted. "Because I can taste you."

He reacted exactly as I wanted him to. Not by faltering, but by steeling himself in the haze of anger that curtained his vulnerability.

What he didn't understand was that the vulnerabilities made us stronger. That the more we had to lose, the more we would fight to keep them. That the things he saw as weaknesses, in the end, would be his greatest strengths.

He pushed me back, and I jerked away from him, but we met again with quick dexterity. Our weapons clashed as we parried. Dodged. Parried. Dodged. Parried. He whirled, taking advantage of my sightless left eye and swung his spear down. But I'd trained my other eye to move fast, trained my body to anticipate things based on the stirring of water, on gut instinct. I may have been missing an eye, but I wasn't blind, and I wasn't a fool.

I lifted my shield and his spear clamored against it, reverberating through my entire body.

Silt, he was *strong.*

He didn't give me a moment to recuperate. He was on me again, in movements that spoke of blood and battle. He was no stranger to war.

But I was its incarnate.

I rolled onto the silt, using the shield against the ground to give me leverage, I pushed myself off of the silt and shot up. The spear in my hand thrust towards him, tearing through the vulnerable part of his side. It snagged against his fur cloak, and with a hard yank, a piece of the material drifted down.

I brought the spear crashing sideways, the side of it hitting against Ytgar. He grunted in a brief flash of pain, but took a stroke to the side, and our spears met once more.

We parried together, tiring each other out. He was skillful and found my weaknesses with ease. He hit me, and I fell flat on my back and blinked just as his spear came crashing towards me. I rolled and felt a blinding flash of pain against my back. I gasped for a breath, and he kicked me with his tail fins so I was looking up at him as he loomed over me.

I tasted the coppery tang of blood in my mouth and smiled a wide tooth grin at him, watching plumes of blood rise above my face.

"Do you like it rough, Prince?"

In response, his fin slammed down onto my shield arm and pain ricocheted up my nerve endings.

I laughed. "Are you punishing me because you didn't like the kiss?" I said this loud enough for everyone to hear. His whole body stiffened. "Or are you punishing me because you enjoyed it too much?"

I wanted him to fight back. To turn that weakness into strength. And this was his weakness. Being judged by the mer he helped rule over. Their eyes were on us, soaking up every bit of this information like sea sponges. I knew it. Ytgar knew it.

Now what are you going to do about it?

He pressed the tip of his blunted spear into my neck. I swallowed, feeling the dull scrape of it like teeth bent on seduction.

And I relished in the very feel of it.

In my life, I'd enjoyed relationships with mermaids and mermen alike. There was something pleasurable about the softness of a mermaid, all lush curves and sensual skin. There was also something immensely satisfying about the rougher edges of a merman.

Traditionally, there were polyamorous relationships, and I'd had a few in the past, but Odele was my future now. I was satisfied with her. Only her.

And if it pleased her to watch me seduce her first husband, I'd gladly do it. Beyond her wishes, and his, I wouldn't touch him.

But this game was too much fun.

Besides, the Prince of Iol was too attractive, with his silver-white eyes and hair curling around his brown cheeks, he looked every bit the prince he was.

No…

Every bit a king.

"If you think…" He dug the tip of the spear in just a little deeper. "…that your little display would distract me, it didn't."

"What a shame…"

"Do you know why it doesn't matter what you say?"

I attempted a shrug, but he kept me pressed to the silt, so I couldn't do much but open my palms out at my sides.

He smirked down at me. A hulking beast with vulnerability shining in the depths of his eyes. A vulnerability he molded into strength and cunning.

"Because it's the truth."

A wave of murmurs whispered all around us, but Ytgar did not falter. His smirk still in place, he bent down closer to me, his hair falling over his forehead.

"Why should I fear the truth, when I am here, and you are there?"

Why, indeed.

"Perhaps," I began steadily, "you should have realized this long ago." I gripped the end of the spear and pushed it, closing my fist around it. My hand trembled as I pushed it away. "Your biggest weakness is your greatest strength." My other hand went up to caress my eyepatch and the scars that decorated my skin. "Let Val be your strength. Let me. Let Odele."

His spear didn't waver, but he did pull it back, out of my grip, slamming it deep into the silt so it stood on its own. Then, he held his hand out to me and I took it. We squeezed just before he hauled me up and our chests collided.

My body ached and my muscles screamed, but something between us had changed. A fragile trust suddenly forged itself into something new, something strong and reliable.

Something with the strength to win this war.

Odele

CREATING A MAGICAL RECORDING conch was a delicate matter. It required a great deal of concentration, tools, and a whole lot of patience.

I wore coral framed glasses, with lenses made from clear sea glass. They enhanced the sight so I could see inside the little shell. I used tweezers and a thin needle to arrange the bands and cogs inside. The magic of the mage would activate it so it could record.

Because I'd studied the mechanics of the devices, I told the mage it was the magic of communication, of light and sound. He'd seemed to understand me just fine. From what I'd learned, the cogs and gears within the conch pushed at the magic and molded the light and sound to grab images and hold them within or project them out.

While I busied myself with readying the inside of it, he meditated, chanted, and hummed. Instead of it being distracting, it filled me with a steady sense of calmness. I felt invigorated with purpose. Despite my confidence, I was still a little apprehensive about this invention.

If we successfully melded this science and magic, it would be an enormous revolution for Iol. Not only make a giant difference in the war, but also afterwards, when I helped Ytgar take the throne that was rightfully his and build alliances between kingdoms.

I wasn't getting ahead of myself. We *had* to win. I refused to lose, refused to bow down to Queen Alexxandria and her violent whims.

The chanting stopped and was replaced with heavy breathing. I paused what I was doing to listen intently to the sound. I set my tools down and turned slightly to face him in my chair.

His wrinkled eyelids were closed. Honestly, he looked half dead.

"How does one become a mage?" I asked. Partly out of curiosity but mostly to assure myself that he wasn't going to keel over before he got the recorder finished.

His eyes opened and settled on me. It was a bit unnerving. The color of his eyes wasn't anything ethereal, but he had a piercing gaze that made me feel like he was looking inside my soul.

"One does not become a mage," he responded in a thick accent. His Thalassarin was rather good, and I hadn't even been aware that he could speak it. Was that magic? "One is born a mage. It is a gift from the gods."

I rested my arm across the back of the chair I sat in, curling my fin around the legs of it. "So you were born with magic in your veins?"

"The gods gift the magic when the time is right. Only they know who is worthy of the gift."

Oookay.

"So, basically you are born with magic or not, and the gods give it to you when they want?"

A deep sigh exhaled from his nose, causing a swarm of bubbles to rise around his face. "In simpler terms, yes. So even if a mage does not receive his gift until years later, it matters not. He was born to be mage."

"Is the magic taught or do you just... know?"

"It cannot be taught to those without the gift in their blood. Magic, *all* magic, is taught by the gods. They speak to us through this..." He opened his palms and balls of light swirled between his fingertips.

I was enraptured by the sight, my breath catching in the back of my throat. I'd never seen a mage before. Sure, I'd read about them, listened to conches on them, but they were *rare*. And I had one in front of me using magic, overwhelming me entirely.

His palms closed and the light disappeared. "Their voices speak within our blood. With so few of us in the sea, we cannot teach one another, so it is our gods who give us their knowledge, and it is in them who we trust." He closed his eyes again and resumed his series of *oms* and *noms*.

"And do your gods have anything to say about the upcoming war?"

His eyes didn't open, but I could see his entire body still. He took a deep, centering breath. "The gods cannot help us in this war."

And he went silent once more.

I stared at the old merman a long time, feeling a heaviness settle in my chest, right over my heart.

Eventually, I turned back to my work with firm, steady hands.

No. The gods could not help us in this war.

But I could.

The last gear had been set into place, the necklace placed into the mage's opened palms. He clasped his hands around it and began chanting, humming, and I was the sole witness within the tent. A current that hadn't been there suddenly stirred, whipping around at the flaps of my cloak and velvet skirt, yet the merman did not appear to feel it.

Light and shadows danced around the tent, and the energy in the waters changed. I felt it. I felt the embodiment of magic come to life in colors and wisps, in bubbles and torrents of emotions and storms that became tangible around us.

My eyes widened as I took it all in. As the colors, light, and shadows swirled together in a maelstrom of sensation, in a hurricane around the old merman. It twirled and twirled, and his chants grew louder and louder. And then the magic was suctioned straight into the conch.

And all was still once more.

He opened his hands and the conch made of ice sat in the center of his wrinkled palm, glowing blue and red from within.

After a moment, I dared move closer to him, bending at the tail in front of him. His eyes found mine and held before he held his hands out.

This time, my fingers did shake as I took the necklace by the chain and held it up, watching it sway softly back and forth. The chamber glowed and then settled. I stared it, almost too afraid to do anything, almost too afraid to breathe.

I took the little shell between my thumb and forefinger, letting the chain drift down. I took a breath, looked to the mage for encouragement. He gave me a slow nod.

So I looked into the chamber, and I started to record.

I pushed aside the tent flaps and emerged on the other side to find Ytgar and Adrian assembled.

The mer of the camp hadn't been informed what we were trying to do, save for the generals, who were sworn to secrecy. We hadn't wanted to get their hopes up in case it didn't work. But now my husbands were in front of me, waiting to see if it had.

If the merge of science and magic had worked.

Ytgar and Adrian were polar opposites of one another. The sun and the moon. Two-legger flames and ice. But both had their arms crossed tightly across their chests, Ytgar's expression set in grave, elegant lines, while Adrian's lips quirked up into a smile.

"Well?" Adrian asked.

I took a stroke forward, expression grave. The shell was tight in my fist, the chain dangling from between my fingers.

A slow smile curled my lips as I held it up.

"It worked!"

Adrian was there first, wrapping his strong arms around my waist and twirling with me through the water. I was passed off to Ytgar, who grabbed me by the back of the head and crushed me to him in a mind-numbing kiss.

He pulled away, touching his forehead to mine. "You did it," he whispered breathlessly.

"You doubted me," I whispered back.

He shook his head. "Never, my love. *Never.*"

He set me back on my fins. "You know what this means?"

"It means," Adrian drawled, "that we can march on."

Ytgar

IT FELT GOOD TO finally be able to move forward. Every second in this war was crucial to Val's survival, to my grandmother's.

I was taking Adrian's words to heart. I hadn't kept Val or my grandmother from my mind, but I stopped letting the uncertainty torture me. It was a weakness, he was right, and I planned on turning them into my greatest strength.

Besides Odele and Adrian, they were the only family I had left. And because of that, I *would* save them from Queen Alexxandria. My love for them was my strength.

We were mounted on our beasts, Odele, Adrian, and I leading the procession of warriors. Adrian had positioned everyone in battle ready positions, as we were traveling straight into Iol, and were unsure about who or what awaited us in my kingdom.

Two beasts followed us from higher waters with snipers atop them, watching over us. He separated the procession into sections, each section with one of his generals commanding them. Behind us were more beasts. It had been Odele's idea to keep them behind. She hadn't wanted the weakest fighters in front, but it was also a bad idea to keep the strongest beasts up here. Especially when we had no notion on how many of the queen's beasts waited for us there.

"I'd almost forgotten how blasted cold it was here." Odele emitted a shiver to accentuate her words. She burrowed herself deeper into her furs.

Adrian was from the southwestern waters of the Uncharted, and he'd described the heat he was used to, yet he appeared completely at ease. He always looked cool and put together before any situation. His black furs were wrapped tightly around him, and his black leather-clad fingers gripped steadily at the reins. His red hair flicked against his face like the curling fingers of two-legger fire.

The mer of Iol were used to blending into our surroundings. It made the difference between life and death. We preferred tones of white, varying shades of blue, and gray. The Uncharted stuck out like sore thumbs in bright colors of yellow, red, and umber.

I supposed it didn't matter what they wore.

Alexxandria knew we were coming anyway.

I reached my arm out, wrapping it around Odele's waist and hauled her off her mount to place her in front of me.

It had become a sort of tradition between us now, to hold her close as we traveled through the coldness of Iol. She pressed her back against my chest with a contented sigh.

It felt good to fall into this routine amidst all the chaos that had become our lives.

"After this is all over, I want to travel somewhere warmer," Odele announced, her voice holding certainty.

No one wanted to voice the unfathomable. That this wouldn't be over. That we wouldn't win. That we would all die and there would be nowhere warmer if we were buried ten strokes beneath a snowy grave.

"I'll take you to Saavaj'i," Adrian whispered, a smile on his lips. His voice, too, was full of hope.

Odele angled her body to the side to stare at him. "Saavaj'i?"

His eyebrow lifted and his smile turned slightly mocking. "You didn't think we called ourselves the 'Uncharted' all the time, did you? It was a name given to us by the seven sea kingdoms who were too afraid to venture into our waters. We have tribes, traditions, and societies just like you. Even if we don't have buildings or advanced technology doesn't make us uncivilized."

Odele leaned forward, eager for this information. Adrian wasn't exactly secretive regarding his past or his waters, or what he'd done to become king, but he hadn't spoken very freely about it since that first meeting.

Perhaps his past and the stories of it had been swallowed up by the chaos of war planning. We hadn't known him long, but King Adrian had proven himself worthy of Odele; reliable, intelligent, and strong.

I caught those thoughts and almost jolted. They'd sounded admiring, lying on the borders of attraction. But I wasn't attracted to Adrian. We'd kissed once in a moment of vulnerability. It wouldn't happen again. Because I wasn't attracted to mermen, not in the way Adrian obviously seemed to be, but Adrian was... he was seductive. Plainly and simply seductive.

I'd always been considered predatory. *A hulking brute,* Odele had called me so long ago. I knew I was serious. I'd always kept a mask in place because I was royalty without power, and I needed power to rule. So I'd molded my image into something different, and it was who I'd become. It's what I *was.* But if I was a silent and brooding predator, he was the slithering sensuality of a sea snake, with bright colors that seduced and entranced, just before he went in for the venomous kill.

"Teach me to speak your language," Odele demanded.

A smirk touched my lips. She was always so eager to learn new things.

"It might take some time," Adrian replied, echoing words Val and I had once said to her.

He should know by now that she was smarter than others, and what took one years, would take her mere months or less.

"I'm a fast learner." She leaned back against me, resting her head against my chin. My arm tightened around her. "You'd do well to remember that, King."

We traveled a few more minutes in silence. Already we crested the hill that led to the wall of troll sentinels. This was where we had to be ready. My grip tightened around my wife, and I steadied my mount's pace. With a nod at Adrian, the king gave a hand signal. Everyone readied themselves as we swam over that snowy hill and came before the ice troll carvings.

I yanked my mount to a halt, my next breath catching in the back of my throat.

"Is that..." Odele leaned forward to get a better look at what we were seeing.

My heart pounded a new beat of fury, because pinned to the faces of the ice trolls by spikes of steel, were the severed heads of the Prime Minister's inner circle.

I held Odele closer and urged my mount forward cautiously. Adrian followed at my side, the procession at our backs. I couldn't tear my eyes away from the heads. Steel spikes stuck out of their foreheads. Their faces were pale, their mouths opened, eyes rolled to the back of their heads in obvious terror.

"Alexxandria..." Adrian whispered. There was a tight fury packed into that single word. "This is her doing."

Odele's gaze swept over each face, stopping on one in particular. "Mister Shallows was a barracuda," she whispered, studying his face. "He deserved to get punched repeatedly and kicked out of the inner circle, but…" She trailed off, shaking her head. A couple of purple tendrils came loose from her chignon and rose up to tickle my nose.

"Let's go forward," I ordered. "Cautiously. Eyes open." I made a clicking noise and my mount went onward. I tried not to look at the heads of Iol's government. Whatever they'd been, they'd still been Iolish, and a fierce wave of protectiveness washed over my body.

I'd noticed the Prime Minister's head missing from that little collection and wondered if she was keeping him because he was the ruler of my kingdom, if she'd killed him a different way, or, like my grandmother, she had him held hostage.

We passed by the sculptures and came into a vast clearing with lumps and valleys of frozen silt and snow. A few more miles and we'd arrive to the first Iolish town. What waited for us there? Who else had the queen killed? Had my mer's numbers been decimated to but a heartbreaking fraction?

I looked up to the higher waters when a screech from one of the beasts rang out. They circled frantically over one another, their wings long and gliding.

Adrian held up a hand and we stopped. "Something's wrong." His yellow eye squinted up at the brightness of the waters above us and the frantic wing beats of the hybrid beasts. He gave out a shrill whistle, waited a moment, and the snipers above whistled back. He turned to us, shaking his head. "They don't see anything."

"It's probably nothing…" I murmured, though I didn't quite believe the words. Animals were always more intuitive than mer. If they were working themselves up into a frenzy, it was for a reason. Something was bothering them. A threat. "We should push on. Stay on high alert."

We started forward, ready to crest over another valley of snow when suddenly, the snow started to move. It rose in lumps and jagged edges, higher and higher within a few, split seconds. Our mounts reared with fear, and Odele cried out as she toppled to the side and fell into the snow.

What we'd thought to be snow rose higher, and higher still, until the light of the waters shone off its fearsome face and revealed the form of a stark white wyvern looming above us.

Its massive wings spread from one long end of the water to another, sharply tipped talons curving and dangerous. Its neck elongated, and its massive jaws opened and let out a roar that shook the icebergs.

It was gargantuan, bigger than even the beasts above us and set to guard the entrance of Iol.

A second was all it took for the creature to strike.

Its head shot down towards the snow.

Straight towards the direction where Odele had fallen.

THE WYVERN'S GAPING JAWS went straight to Odele.

A cry sprang from my lips even as I pulled my sword from its sheath and urged my mount towards her.

But the creature was faster. It jammed down towards the snow. With a cry, Odele rolled in the snow and the water, pushing herself away. It nearly snagged her fins as its snout slammed into the ground.

A shower of silt and snow rained around us in a cloud that blocked Odele from my view.

"Odele!" I screamed her name, heard Ytgar do the same.

She didn't reply.

I looked above and whistled out my orders to attack. In response, the beasts dove down as the snipers trained their arrows on the wyvern, shooting at his scaled hide. The arrows embedded into its scales, and it shrieked its rage as plumes of blood drifted from it.

The warriors at our backs charged, pulling out swords and shields as they came towards the creature, demanding blood and death.

The creature flapped its massive wings, tail swiping at the warriors. The barbed end of its tail smacked against some of my mer, and they flew across the water with agonizing cries.

The cloud of snow cleared, and my eye frantically searched for Odele.

When my eye captured sight of her, she was buried in the silt, lifting herself up and coughing.

My heart seized at the sight behind her. She was unsuspecting, disoriented, it seemed, and the tail of the creature was swinging towards her with deadly force.

I kicked my fin against the side of my mount and urged it forward, screaming her name, ripping it from the depths of my soul.

The tail was closer now and getting closer still.

I can't lose her. I can't.

At this moment, alliances didn't matter. My mer didn't matter. The Uncharted Waters didn't matter. The only thing I lived and breathed for was her, her safety.

I couldn't fail to protect her. I needed to get to her, needed to save her.

I'd be damned if I let Alexxandria take Odele from me.

If she did, I'd kill her myself. I'd show her no mercy.

But I didn't even want to contemplate losing Odele. I couldn't. We'd known each other little time, knew little about one another except for the intimate press of body against body, of the delicate sighs of pleasure. And yet she was already intricately woven into my every fiber in a way I hadn't allowed myself to realize before this very moment.

I couldn't be a mer who realized what he had when he lost it.

For her, I'd rip hell up from the abyss. For her, I'd barrel through the doors of the gods themselves. Strong emotions I had never known I'd been able to feel were overpowering my every sense.

Was it love?

Yes.

The answer burned viciously at the back of my throat.

This was love.

And I'd rather throw myself to the mercy of my cruelest gods if it meant saving Odele's life and forfeiting mine in the process.

I heard Adrian's scream before I heard the whistling approach of *something*. I turned just in time to see the barbed tail of the wyvern come flying towards me.

My head spun with pain and dizziness from my fall, but I managed to shoot myself up through the water just as it came crashing towards me and grazed against my body. I gasped, the pain pushing me up further. My eyes blinked away bubbles of tears at the sudden sensation as the water left my lungs, but I swam quickly away from it.

I barely caught the look of relief on Adrian's features before he schooled his expression once again. The black sword in his hand seemed to gleam beneath the light of the ice, and already my mind was racing continuous laps.

Time seemed to slow down; sound seemed to fade. I looked around, my hand reaching up to my neck to clutch at the conch of ice hanging there. The action gave me strength. It gave me a plan. Mer were screaming in pain and in raging battle cries as they fought the wyvern. The snipers shot from above, and beasts came forth to attack, but the creature was too big…

It would kill us all unless…

Unless we weakened it first.

"A distraction!" I screamed at Adrian. "I need a distraction!"

My words registered, and he gave a tight nod before whistling out his commands. He had a whole secret language with his warriors established that consisted entirely of sounds; whistles and animal cries. They followed his command immediately. The snipers circled around the beast with careful precision, while I unsheathed the wyvern knife Adrian had gifted me at our wedding.

I hadn't used it before now, but it seemed fitting somehow.

I wove my way around the thrashing body of the creature. The others kept it distracted enough that it didn't feel me grip a hand along one of its jagged, icy-looking spikes to pull myself closer to it. I placed the sharp blade in my mouth, gripping it between my teeth, and used my hands to yank myself up, up its neck and further still. My every muscle screamed a violent protest.

I held on because it was so strong, too strong, and it almost knocked me off its back.

I took a breath and pushed myself off from its neck and whirled up… up… down… until I came face to face with the beast.

Its eyes were the blue of frost with a violent tinge of red inside. Its nostrils flared as it took me in. All it had to do was open its mouth, widen its jaws and take me in with a violent snap and I'd be done for.

But I was Duchess of Castle Frost, Princess Odele Malabella Oriana of Thalassar, and Queen of the Uncharted Waters. I was selfish, hated, intelligent. I wasn't my mother or my cousin. I wasn't soft or kind-hearted. I had so many faults.

But a coward, I was not.

With a fierce cry, I slashed the dagger forward, running it in a swift line across the wyvern's eyes. Rendering it blind. It roared and snapped, but I was quick on my fins and with the blade, because a moment later, I slashed the blade through its nostrils. Rendering it senseless.

"Now!" I shouted, darting away from the creature.

Our beasts swooped in on it. Without its eyes, without its sense of smell, a wyvern was weak, defenseless.

The beasts tore through the wyvern's neck. It thrashed and tried to fight back with its claws, but it couldn't. It had been caught off guard.

And now it would die.

Gripping the handle of the dagger tightly in my fist, I watched as teeth gnashed at its neck and blood burst in violent torrents. The harder our beasts fought, the more the wyvern was weakened, until the fight left it entirely.

Until, with a final jerk of its flesh from bone, it dropped into a heap on the snow.

Dead.

My breath didn't ease from my mouth until our beasts stood atop it with their sharp claws and roared to the waters in triumph.

Thank the gods. I dropped my hand at my side, easing my grip slightly on the wyvern-hilt dagger. My heart was pounding against my chest in demanding, angry beats. I took a deep breath in, willing away the sudden fear in the aftermath of the chaos.

"Odele!" I turned just as strong arms wrapped around me, and winced at the pull of pain through my body. Gods, the creature had hit me harder than I thought, and I was likely bruised on my side. Adrian pulled away, framing my face in his hands. He leaned in for a kiss. Not a tentative one, but one that bared his entire soul. His tongue flicked across mine in demanding strokes, like he could somehow reach deep in my soul and pour all his love into me.

Because that's what the kiss was.

Love. Unbridled, raw, and passionate love.

He pulled away reluctantly and whispered something in his language against my lips. Something I didn't understand but could feel down to the recesses of my heart.

Before I could ask for a translation, I was pulled around and into Ytgar's arms. "My love," he whispered as he pressed his lips to my face. He kept repeating those words over and over again. "My love."

My love.

My love.

I pulled away. "I'm fine," I assured them.

"Thank the gods."

We all seemed to bask in one another for a split second before we started to move. There was a lot to do in the aftermath of this.

We split into groups as we separated the dead—two—and the injured—twelve. After we saw the bodies of the dead and injured and they were tended to, we gathered with the generals to plan our next move of attack.

"We need to move on," one of the general's urged.

"We can't," Ytgar shot back. "First we need to send Valmundur the message."

"Besides," another general added, "we aren't sure what else is waiting for us. We need to be better prepared. We cannot afford to lose soldiers. We are outnumbered as is."

Adrian cut in before an argument could break out. "We continue with the plan as before. Give ourselves a day of rest while we send the message out to Valmundur. Aelfrost is still a few days away. We just send scouts ahead before we take the whole procession goes forward."

They all seemed to agree with this, because they murmured softly, nodding their heads.

I was distracted, gripping the conch tightly in the palm of my hand. My side... it hurt, and I tried to ignore it to pay attention to the words being said, but it was suddenly too hard to breathe.

"Odele?"

I blinked up at Ytgar. His palm was out.

"The conch?" he asked slowly, as if it hadn't been the first time he'd asked.

"Oh." I swallowed and with shaking fingers, unhooked the chain from around my neck, slipped the conch off, and dropped it onto his hand. His palm closed around it.

"I'm going to send it off now." Ytgar looked around at all the generals. Just that chilling look in his eyes had them all bowing before he exited the tent.

I didn't watch him go.

Pain...

Pain...

A hand pressed against my lower back. "My love..."

I took in a shuddering breath and looked over at Adrian. Even moving my head was an effort.

His eyebrow furrowed. "Are you alright?"

I forced a smile and took a stroke forward. "I'm fi—" Before I could get the words out, my tail gave out beneath me and I crashed into him, gasping for breath.

"Odele!"

I tried to take in a rasping breath, but I felt like my throat was closing and I was gasping, writhing in pain.

"I—it hurts..."

My vision started blurring, but I felt his hands against my cloak, tugging off my clothes, and then his shocked gasp. "The wyvern… it cut you!"

The pain, its tail… it had hit me, but I hadn't thought…

"Odele, you're bleeding. Stay with me."

But I couldn't, I was fading fast. But if the barbed tail had gotten me, it had likely been poisonous. "Root of leez," I gasped.

My throat closed and I gripped at skin, my nails weakly raking across it. Strong arms held me, a voice called out to me, but I couldn't hear anything.

Because the darkness claimed me.

Valmundur

For the first time in days—weeks?—I heard voices. They approached my cell, growing louder with each stroke closer. I looked up, flakes of snow frozen against my eyelashes, as shadows flicked along the ice and steel walls of the prison.

Slowly, I forced myself to sit up. Hunger was claiming me for its own, and my stomach recoiled at the movement. I leaned against the cold wall, pulling my furs tighter around myself. The furs no longer brought me warmth. It was like the cold, the snow, and the ice had seeped through the material and taken permanent residence up in my bones. It was all I knew. That and the hunger.

The voices grew louder, and they spoke in a language I didn't understand. The language of the Uncharted, of one of the many tribes of those treacherous waters.

Three guards came up to my current prison, looking at me with malicious grins through the bars. One of them procured a key from the pockets of his furs and slipped it into the lock, turning. The squeak as the doors to my prison opened for the first time in forever.

I didn't bother to fight back as they hauled me to my fins with aggressive force. They yanked me out of the cell without a word, but they didn't speak for me to know what was happening.

Queen Alexxandria was demanding an audience with me.

Light hit me as they hauled me out of the prison I'd known as home. It was white and blue, a kaleidoscope of color, as the light hit the ice palace and shone a rainbow across the waters of the kingdom. It was the same, and yet everything was different. Where life had once bustled, the streets of Iol were now dead.

No children sang or swam around, but wyverns circled overhead, monitoring, waiting for someone they could feast on. They hauled me along the edges of the palace, in the shadows, before shoving me through the servant's entry.

They practically dragged me all the way up to where Queen Alexxandria waited. I caught no sights of servants, heard no whispers of gossips. Everything was... silent. Dead.

They brought me to the throne room and tossed me to the cold ground almost angrily.

I pushed myself up on my palms, lifting my head up. I saw Queen Alexxandria through the blond wisps of my hair and sucked in a breath.

She was turned from me so that only one half of her face was visible. She was still as beautiful as the first time I'd seen her. Sharp features, plump lips, and a singular glowing yellow eye. When she turned, though, which she did at that moment, I could see the other half of her face. The half distorted by violence, by tragedy. The left half of her face was slashed in a red scar that puckered with age-old infection, making her look beastly.

Her voice, though, when she spoke, was melodic. "Hello, Valmundur. How are you?" She said it conversationally, like we were friends. As if she hadn't ordered me beaten and locked up. The strange thing about the question was that she appeared to genuinely want to know the answer.

"Fine," I rasped, feeling the pain that word caused in the back of my throat.

She nodded, as if the answer pleased her immensely. "You may rise, Valmundur."

The guards holding me down hauled me up, keeping me grasped in their tight grip with their swords against my lower back. I didn't bother to struggle. I knew how futile it would be.

She stared at me, her mismatched eyes flicking over my no doubt haggard form. She studied me in a scholarly type of way, like I was a puzzle she was trying to solve. I wondered briefly what she saw when she looked at me. If she saw someone she wanted to thoroughly destroy, the same way she wanted to destroy the seven sea kingdoms or if she saw... something else?

"It seems our war plans have taken an... unexpected twist." She drew those last two words out with slow, flicking curls of her tongue, said almost in an angry sneer. "I have offered your friends many chances at surrender, yet my spies in their camp tell me that they are marching on. Already, they've defeated the white wyvern guardian of the border."

Yes! I gave a silent cheer yet schooled my expression into one of neutrality. I knew Ytgar, Adrian, and Odele would come. They would destroy this queen and take back what was ours.

Her next words had the hope freezing in my chest.

"Now I have no choice but to send an assassin to murder the Princess of Thalassar."

I jerked forward, ready to lunge for her throat. To grasp her delicate neck beneath my hands and kill her. The guards yanked me back. I struggled against them, fighting, kicking with my tail, but I was weak and malnourished, and their swords dug through my clothes and into my flesh.

I fell back to the ground, gasping in pain as blood rushed warmly out of my body. It was a mere flesh wound, yet it still hurt like a brand.

"You can't!" I shouted, struggling on the ground. They pressed their swords into my back, preventing me from moving or struggling too much.

Her gaze seemed disinterested as it stared down at me like I was a pathetic life form. "I can, and I will." Her hand rose to hover centimeters from the scarred side of her face. It was a movement that was heartbreaking and tragic, and in both her eyes, rage shone an ephemeral light that pierced me straight down to my soul. "You've seen this scar." Her hand lowered. "Thalassar did it." She turned abruptly, so I could only see her scars, only see the rise of red flesh curving down her cheek, where she once would have been beautiful. "They did this and much more to me."

I knew the story. Adrian had told us. "That wasn't Thalassar." I tried to get up, but the points of their swords pressed me down to the cold floor. "It was a few wayward soldiers! You cannot blame the entire kingdom for a few mermen's actions!"

She turned to me, slashing all of her fury in a single cutting glance. "'Wayward soldiers'?" She tossed her head back and let out the cruel sound of her bitter laughter. "Thalassar and the rest of the seven sea kingdoms treat the immigrants of the Uncharted Waters like we're nothing more than slaves. Tell me, Valmundur Ingen, do you know how many of the Uncharted mer venture into the seven sea kingdoms, only to disappear and never be seen again?"

A lump formed in my throat. "No," I replied tightly.

She sneered down at me with disgust. "Of course, you don't. You live comfortably in this precious little palace. You do not lack for warmth or a meal. You lack for nothing!"

If only she knew what I truly was, where I was raised. Perhaps I'd had a roof over my head, but growing up in a Iolish orphanage, I lacked warmth and food plenty.

"Those who do not die on the way here are taken as slaves," the queen went on in a much gentler voice, no trace of emotion in it. "As sex slaves, as laborers to the kingdoms here. Did you know that?"

I released a breath through my nostrils. "I didn't." Surely it would've been heard of by now, right? If one of the kingdoms was keeping slaves? Slavery had been abolished centuries ago. It was forbidden… Or it should have been.

If they were Uncharted mer, mer without documents, mer without homes or someone to rage a complaint with the authorities over them then… perhaps it was possible.

"This war is just the beginning, Valmundur. I had meant to leave the princess alone for now. I've heard the rumors about her. So many rumors, how could I ever believe even one of them? But even if she is not completely daft and selfish, she is still the princess of the kingdom that did this to me." She gestured wildly at her face. "And for that she will pay."

"She was just a child! You cannot hold her accountable for something that happened when she was young, something she had no power over at the time!"

She bent down at my level, the dark fur of her skirts pooling around her tail as her fingers firmly gripped my chin to hold my gaze in place. "I was a child, too," she whispered, as if the words were a confession to the gods. "And still I suffered." She smiled, one half of her lips curling widely, the other downturned grotesquely. "But being Princess of Thalassar is not her only offense. You see, my spies gifted me with a bit of information, and it appears my brother has tainted our lineage by marrying her before the gods."

No. No! They had a spy in their midst who was feeding everything to her. I wished I wasn't so worthless right now. I wished I could kill her and end this all. I should have done it before when I'd first woken in this room with sword in hand. I should have ended her then.

Now she was threatening to destroy everything I cared about. Ytgar, Odele, even *Adrian…* My life, my *love*, the only mer I'd ever truly cared about. The one I'd seen, the one who had seen me. And she was threatening to take it all away and smiling while she did it.

My hands fisted against the cold floor.

"Let her death be a lesson to my baby brother." She pulled her hand away and got up, backing up a few strokes.

I had to ask, because I couldn't be thrown into that dungeon again without knowing. "A lesson in what?"

"A lesson that he should never, *ever* try to cross me. Because I will take everything he loves away." She turned away from me and started swimming away. "His incessant questions have annoyed me," she called out to her guards. "See to it that he, too, is punished."

I growled after her, cursing her life, her rule, wishing like I'd never wished before, that I ended her life that day.

But my words of fury were drowned away as I felt that first blow to my temple, as fist after fist crashed against my body…

…and all I could feel was the pain.

Anneli

Growing up in an orphanage, I had no real concept of home, of family. It was one thing to share blood with a king, a long line of a royal family, and another entirely to actually feel like I truly belonged with them.

I never felt like I belonged anywhere until the day Valmundur managed to get the both of us jobs at the palace I'd only ever glimpsed at from the outside. A place where my blood relatives lived, a place I had grown to call home, even while the family that should have been mine had no idea who I was.

The Isoldes were born with the tails of orcas. It was in their genetics, frosty, elegant features and brown skin, silver-white hair, and regal bearing.

I was none of these things. My tail was the color of ash, and my hair a dull silver. My skin was a tone of brown lighter than my half-brother's.

Even thinking that in my mind sounded foreign.

Half-brother.

Anyway, my home. It wasn't home any longer. It had been taken over by hundreds of Uncharted scum. It was easy to set them apart from the Iolish. We Iolish wore colors that blended into the ice; they wore bright colors in tones of yellow and brown, but also black.

They were mer with cruel features, who carried weapons around to intimidate the ice mer, to control us and take over our kingdom.

Since I'd arrived, I'd already witnessed four public beatings and seven executions of mer as young as twelve for throwing rocks at a guard.

They were fueled by chaos and followed no order except their own and their queen's.

Wyverns were their sentinels; massive creatures that circled the waters above, shrouding Iol in shadows of fear, causing the mer to lock themselves within the confines of their homes. If they had a home to go to. Most of the buildings here at the capital had been destroyed in the wyvern attack. So many children, families, had created makeshift tents of steel and ice to huddle within, away from the watchful eyes of those beasts.

They chased away the humpback whales, and they made the orcas nervous. When Val and I had separated, I'd gone straight to the stables only to discover that some of the orcas I'd cared for since their birth had died. I'd stayed to care for the others, to blend in, and to wait for instruction.

I knew from over talkative guards that Val had been taken that first day, thrown straight into the dungeons alone. I wanted to visit him, to let him know I would be getting him out of his prison, but he was guarded around the clock. Sentinels floated outside of the dungeons, making sure no one went in or out.

I'd observed; I was good at that. It would be impossible to go in and save him, when their way of rotation didn't allow me any blind spots, any time to slip past them. It was guarded *at all times.*

I hated waiting, hated having nothing to do, so I busied myself with caring for my orcas. The poor traumatized animals leaned to me for comfort, and I leaned to them.

I kept my eyes warily on the guards.

They were everywhere, taking over the palace and the stables. They treated the animals roughly. That first day when I'd dared defend an orca being whipped, I'd received a black eye. That guard hadn't taken his eyes off me since.

He stared at me now. I felt his gaze boring between my shoulder blades as I sponged down an orca carefully, methodically.

The Uncharted guards were vicious, especially when it came to mermaids. I could hear them crying in the night sometimes, but when I'd get up to help the mermaids, the sound would quickly cut off. The next morning, I'd find them dead and wyvern's swooping down to feast on their bodies.

My home had become a kingdom of horrors.

Rage had begun to consume me because of it.

After sponging down the orca and putting away the supplies, I exited his stall, locking it back up. The palace staff had been kept on to cater to the guards' every whims. It helped us survive, swim without being noticed too much.

As I started to turn, I felt rough hands press against my sides and slam me into the bars of the stall. The orca inside bucked in rage as I was attacked. A body loomed over me, a face pressed close to my cheek. I didn't struggle. It was a consumption of energy, and I'd need to save all I had if I wanted to get out of this alive. I pressed my hands against the bars and made a series of motions with my fingers that the orca saw. Saw, and understood.

The voice in my ear growled words in a language I didn't understand but knew were lewd. I didn't give the bile a chance to rise to my throat, but slowly eased my wrist between the spaces of the bars. The orca pressed close, dropping a cold steel item in my hand.

"Good boy," I whispered my praise.

I had them so well trained.

His palm pressed to the back of my head, digging me into the cold steel while another hand went to the back of my training leathers.

His first mistake was leaving my hands free. I wondered how many mermaids he'd done this to. How many he'd let their hands free so they could fight him because he enjoyed the violence?

This was a mistake.

And it would be his last.

My hand closed around the hilt of the small dagger the orca had given me, I turned my arm and slammed the blade straight into his throat, hitting vital arteries. He gasped and jerked away from me. I whirled around. Luckily, he was the only guard on duty.

Taking the knife, I rushed forward and jammed it into his throat again, sawing back and forth in quick movements. His unsuspecting death and pain reflected in his eyes, and the last thing he saw before he fell back was my face, smiling at him.

He'd messed with the wrong mermaid.

And I hoped he suffered in his afterlife.

I tore the knife from his neck, watching the plumes of blood rise from it. Now, I had to move quickly. I tossed the dagger back inside the orca's stall and bent to lift the merman by the shoulders. With quick, darting eyes, I made sure no one was there to see me as I drug his body past the opening of the training field and into the frozen forestation of Iol.

Above me, the wyverns roared. They smelled his blood.

I left him there and darted away quickly, just in time as a wyvern swooped down and swallowed the merman whole.

The good thing about those beasts was that they could hide evidence, and they didn't discriminate.

Heart pounding in my chest, I made my way back to the stables, where I gripped the bars and pressed my forehead to them, struggling to steady my breathing.

And then I felt a pinch against my tail fin and cried out. That had hurt! I looked down, lifting my tail to find a small crab tethering a pincer to my fins. I glared at it and tried to shake it off. It wouldn't budge.

"Get off!" I grabbed it by the shell and tugged it away from me, setting it on my palm and bringing it up to my face. "What do you want?" The poor thing was probably scared. It snapped a pincer near my nose and I jerked back. "What?" It waved its second pincer near my face and I noticed it was carrying something with it.

A small conch shell carved from ice.

I frowned, prying it from its grip. "Where did you get this?" I recognized it.

Val had carved this. I'd watch him slave over it during work hours while he'd left me with the heavy loads, the bastard. The last time I'd seen it, it'd been around Odele's neck.

"What in the seas—"

The crab knocked its pincers against the side of his face and pointed at me, gesturing that I press it to my ear.

"Conches don't work here—ow!" It pinched my nose and held. "Alright, alright." I pressed the chamber of the ice conch to my ear. "See? Nothi—" My breath caught in my throat as a voice flittered through my ear.

Holy silt.

Odele

"WE NEED TO MOVE out already!" I shouted, tossing aside the furs from my tail and getting up. I only felt the slightest tug of pain, but even then, that wasn't enough to stop me from doing what needed to be done. We were in the middle of a war. I'd been scratched by the barbed tail of a wyvern, not crippled.

Adrian and Ytgar floated before the makeshift bed in our shared tent, both of them brooding with their arms crossed against their chests.

"We're taking a night to rest, so get back beneath those covers before I tie you down myself." Adrian's yellow eye glowed with the hint of a dangerous promise. "Now."

I scoffed at him. He may have been king, and my husband, but that didn't give him the right to tell me what I could and couldn't do.

Uncharted bastard.

And Ytgar? My gaze slashed to his angrily. Really, he should know better than to pull this silt with me. Once I set my mind to something, there was hardly anything anyone could do to change it.

"We're at war," I argued, moving to grab my clothes. They'd divested me of them when I'd fainted from the poison in order to heal me. I'd woken up only moments ago to find out that they'd used root of leez, like I had on Ytgar so long ago now it seemed, and magic to heal me. "I've rested long enough. Let's go."

I grabbed for a velvet dress and brought it up. Before I could even think about putting it on, Adrian was there, yanking the material from my grip and tossing it back to the silt. He gripped my upper arms in tight hands and shook me once.

"Gods damn it, Odele, you almost *died*!" he shouted, and the raw agony in his voice gave me pause. It gave us all pause. Adrian took in a shuddering breath and shook his head, dropping his forehead to mine. Our skin kissed, and it felt more intimate than the press of our bodies. "Can you please take a moment to *rest*?" The plea tore out of his mouth in a rippling sound of agony that had my body submitting to his wishes as he gently pushed me back down onto the cot and pulled the covers around my body.

"Careful, King Adrian," I warned, my voice heavy with emotion. "It almost sounds like you care."

That yellow eye pierced into me, nearly to my soul, and I had to swallow back the lump that rose in my throat. I wouldn't get emotional. I refused to.

"I do care." His fingers feathered across my collarbone. "You are my wife."

"But you don't love me."

His eye narrowed on my words and he flicked the loose strands of hair from my neck. He leaned forward and pressed his lips to the pulse at my throat. It beat steadily against his mouth. "You're going to make me say it, aren't you?" he asked.

My eyes closed at the feel of him against my skin. Just the slightest touch from him, and my mind was a pool of desire and wanton thoughts. "Say what?" I arched into him, and the words sounded more like a moan, a demand than anything else.

His tongue flicked over my pulse, then traveled higher, up to my chin and to my mouth. He pulled away, his hand curving up my cheek. Adrian looked me in the eye as he confessed, "I love you, Odele."

Something in my heart lurched.

I'd married this merman for what he could provide; his armies, a fighting chance, and information. And because I'd wanted him from that first moment I saw him lounging regally on his ivory throne. He was power, and he thrived on winning. The compatibility had been palpable between us, like we'd been made for one another.

Even while we'd promised each other no words of love, we had the respect and pleasure that came with being husband and wife. Love, it was supposed to build up slowly, right? It had certainly been that way for Ytgar, Val, and I. The desire with my two Iolish, it had been there from the start; a forbidden, shameful thing it seemed. Love had come throughout the long cold days of travel. It had come in the halls of Draconi and the palace of Iol.

What I had with Adrian was eruptive. It was quick, a feeling that we might have already had buried deep within us, like a dragon within its egg, hiding, only to tear its way out once we finally did meet.

He loved me.

And I—I loved him.

"Kiss me," I ordered. "I want to feel you."

He dropped his head and pressed the chastest of kisses against my mouth, and I groaned in frustration, reaching for his shoulders just as he started to pull away. "We can't." He tried to gently push me back against the pillows. "You're hurt."

My eyes narrowed. "I'm well enough for this. You healed me with medicine and magic. I almost *died*." Perhaps I was laying it on too thick, but I knew just what to say to crack through his barriers. "I want to feel alive again." I slipped my fingers through his black fur cloak, pushing it off his shoulders. "Help me feel alive again."

His eye closed, a look of pain tightening at his beautiful features. Finally, he gave in, helping me by shrugging the clothes from his body. He tugged off his gloves with his teeth, the sight erotic, just before he reached for the hem of his dark tunic and pulled it over his body.

I glanced over his shoulder in time to see Ytgar exit the tent. I was tempted to tell him to join us, but this moment? It was intimate. It was necessary between Adrian and me.

We'd enjoyed each other plenty of times before, but this was different now. Now, he'd said the words. Now, the feelings were delicately placed between us for the both of us to explore in a riptide of claiming desire.

I focused my attention back on Adrian as the flaps to our tent closed. He braced his arms on either side of my head and leaned over me. The only thing separating us now was the material of the blanket. I wanted that gone. I wanted to feel the heat of his skin searing me down to the bone.

I wanted everything he had to offer and more.

I wanted to take and claim, to fall into bliss with him and not emerge from it.

Finally, finally, he leaned down and took my mouth in his in a possessive kiss to rival all others. His tongue delved in to take in languid, deep strokes. Our tongues tangled together, and the groan rose high in the back of my throat. I could tell by the taste of his tongue and the sudden demanding press of his hands against my blanket-clad waist that this would be no slow joining. It would be fast, and desperate.

And full of love.

One hand holding his body above mine, the other he used to yank the blanket out of our way. When his lower body pressed down on me and I felt the slick slide of his member against my stomach, I arched into him. He pinned my tail down with his, wrapping the length of it around mine to keep me steady.

Our kiss ended, and his tongue went to the pulse at my neck. I felt the bite of his teeth send ripples of heady desire pounding through my body. Everywhere he touched, he left an ache, a need that seemed would never be quenched.

His hands gripped my hips and pulled me up. The folds of my opening touched the smooth head of his member, and he slid up and down slowly against me. It was the only moment of slowness he would allow himself, because a moment later, he pushed inside me, filling me inch by quick inch, settling himself deep within my body. And then he began to move.

His hips jerked, pounded, while his hands pulled my body up to meet him, thrust for thrust. The roll of his hips caused his member to slide against my nub of desire, and each time, I saw the shine of two-legger stars dance behind my eyelids.

I groaned as he picked up the pace, moving faster, and faster. I could do nothing but hold on for the ride, lift my hips to meet his. It was raw, nothing expert about the way our bodies met, but it was delicious just the same.

I craved the hard push of his member like I did a confection.

It was bliss. Every moment of this was…

I rose higher up, and he sensed my folds closing around him, forcing him deeper inside. He slid up, pressed to me in one slamming finality of his hips…

Together we came.

I screamed, shooting up on the cot and reaching for his shoulders. I was not quiet, nor was he. His pants and groans sounded in my ear as we rode through the aftershocks of our joined pleasure. We rode and rode and rode until the last of our desire had abated, and we fell into a heap atop one another.

Adrian pulled me close, wrapping his arms around my shoulders, tucking my head beneath his chin. "I didn't hurt you?" he rasped.

He was still hard inside me. I could feel the pulse between us, the ache at my entrance. "Only in the best of ways."

His fingers began trailing a small pathway down my arm, tracing over my scales there like he was counting every contour of me. "My sister vowed to defeat me." His voice was dark, tragic. "I cannot lose you, love." He pulled me closer, as if the words themselves brought a chill through his body and he needed to assure himself that I was here, that I was alive.

My hand went to cup his cheek. "I'm not going anywhere, Adrian. That's a promise."

His whole body was still tense, and he didn't let me go. "If anyone tries to take me from you, I will make them suffer my wrath. Every violent bit of it."

He sealed that promise with a kiss. I should have felt the shivers then, but I didn't. I felt safe. Protected. I knew, without a doubt, that if something ever happened to me, if anyone tried to kill me then Adrian would make good on his promise.

He would make them pay.

I promised Adrian I would rest while he went to oversee the packing of the camp. I'd agreed, if only because of his own peace of mind.

Everything had suddenly changed between us. We'd never skirted around our feelings since we met; we were honest in every way, so I would give him this small relief, but I wouldn't stay still on the blasted cot.

I got up and began rummaging through my chest of things in search for something to wear. Tomorrow morning, we would march into battle with the Queen of the Uncharted, and I needed an outfit perfect for my own status as queen.

Anneli complained my dresses weren't meant for riding or fighting. I'd still wear a dress, but it had to be something warm enough for the harsh conditions of Iol, light enough to quickly move around in, tight enough to not slip from my body, and yet loose enough to allow for freedom of movement with a weapon.

Because tomorrow, I planned on fighting. I would not be shoved onto the sidelines. I would not be shoved behind guards while everyone jumped into the fray.

I would be at the front, between Ytgar and Adrian, with sword and shield as my decorations, the blood of my enemies filling the waters. I would kill and fight with the soldiers because I was not afraid of death, of killing or dying.

I would defy all the odds, that I was confident of. We would win. We would take our kingdom back, and I would see Val again.

That, I vowed on my mother's life.

I floated up, clutching the clothes I'd chosen for tomorrow's battle to the thin shift I'd changed into. I turned, setting them over the table to observe them. They were a fashionable clash of colors, something I'd never worn before, sewn up by the battle leather makers just for the occasion.

I'd go to war in style.

The tent flaps opening drew my attention towards the entrance.

I froze, heart slamming up to catch in my throat. I'd expected Adrian, or Ytgar. No one else had the audacity to barge into our tent without announcing themselves first. And this merman wasn't a servant. He was a warrior; his leathers marked him and his rank. His skin was an ashen-looking green, and his gaze looked both nervous and murderous.

It appeared he was here to kill me.

It was obvious from the sword he held in his hand and the nervous shaking of his arm. "Don't scream, Princess." His voice was guttural and angry. He lifted his sword and pointed it at me.

As if that were enough to intimidate me.

This bastard was so, so dead.

And if he thought I was some meek princess who would go down without a fight, he had another thing coming.

"No one will help you. Everyone is busy. This will be easier if you just don't struggle." His accent was rough as he spoke the common tongue of Thalassarin, but I understood his every curling word.

I snorted. "I don't need to scream." By the end of this encounter, it'd be him screaming. My arms crossed against my chest as he slowly moved towards me, even as I discreetly moved back. I just needed my dagger, and a single well-placed blow to his throat would end his sorry little life. "Who sent you?" I demanded.

He didn't answer, but I didn't need him to.

We were in the middle of a war, and an assassin had showed up in my tent, catching me alone? Queen Alexxandria had likely sent him to murder me. And this mer was wearing the colors of Adrian's Uncharted warrriors, which meant we had a spy in our midst.

My heart lurched at that. If there was a spy, how much had he told her of our battle plans? What all did he know? More importantly, had he told her of our contact with Val?

We'd kept that only between the generals and ourselves, but I knew how quickly word could get around…

"Stop right there, Princess."

My eyes narrowed on him. "That's 'Queen' to you, traitor." I eased back. My dagger was on the pile of clothes they'd divested me of when they'd healed me. I could kick the dagger up with my fins, catch it, and throw it at him. It could work… I just needed to get a little closer…

But he lunged forward with the sword, pressing the tip to my neck, even as I tried to dodge. The action only caused the blade to dig into my flesh, nicking the skin and causing blood to flow. The sting of the wound was painful. I jerked back, keeping an eye on the weapon.

That was the trick to fighting. Eye the weapon, not the mer.

But he was a warrior, and he had skill. He jabbed the weapon at me with aggressive force. I whirled away from him and the blade, ramming into a bit of furniture that sent me sprawling to the ground face first. I sensed the stirring in the water and rolled in the silt just as the blade came crashing down where my body had once been.

I dove for the dagger sitting on the pile of my clothes but was yanked back by the hem of my shift.

A tearing sound rang through the tent and I felt the cold press of water against my bare back. I kicked my fin out, hitting the merman in the chest. He grunted, and his hold slackened. I dragged myself away from him, turning. The material slipped from my back. My fingers dug into the silt and I pushed myself away from his sword.

"Stop moving, you little harlot." He dug the tip of the sword into my right shoulder. Malicious glee shone in his eyes as he did it. I bit the inside of my cheek to avoid crying out in pain, but it felt like a brand. The blade pierced past my flesh, it hurt, it—

I cried out, falling, my head hitting the ground. I lifted my left hand up, fingers grazing the material of my discarded clothes. My fist closed around them and I pulled it close, reaching, searching for the touch of steel at my fingertips.

"All hail Queen Alexx—" He broke off as I brought the wyvern handled blade hurtling forward, straight towards his throat. He jerked back with surprise, pulling the sword from my shoulder. I had only one shot and—he ducked, the dagger merely nicking his cheek.

Gods damn it.

I shot up. If he wanted to take me down, he'd do it while I floated, not on the ground like a pathetic little dog fish.

"If you're going to kill me," I taunted, "then you do it now, and you leave. Because when King Adrian and Prince Ytgar find my body, they will kill you, slowly. And they will not be kind."

He growled and lunged forward. I dodged with swiftness, weaving my way around furniture, missing the edge of his sword.

This needed to end. Now.

I dove for my discarded dagger, hands clasping around it just as I turned. Our blades clashed, steel ringing the tune of death around us.

"Now the odds are even," I gritted as I pushed against his much bigger blade. I rolled and jumped up. Our blades clashed again, the edge of his sword slicing across my arm. I retaliated by cutting a slice across his face.

I was panting now. Though I'd been healed with magic, the pain of the wound was still there, and the exertion was slowing me down, making me weak.

He kicked his fins against my chest, and the breath was knocked straight out of me. My back hit the ground, and I heaved. His sword lifted above his head, but he never got the chance to bring it crashing down towards me.

Another body appeared in front of him, tearing the sword from his unsuspecting grip. His eyes widened and words sputtered from his mouth.

Adrian dropped the sword to the side, gripped the merman by the lapels of his coat, and pounded a fist straight into his face.

The merman went down like a sack of rocks. Adrian didn't stop, though. The tent was filled with the sounds of flesh pounding against flesh, of the crunching of bone and the sound of Adrian's unbridled rage.

I got up and looked around, gathering my senses about me. The tent flaps were flung open and servants were rushing away. A moment later, guards poured into our tent along with Ytgar and they watched as Adrian brutalized the merman with his fists. No one made a move to stop him.

"Adrian," my voice came out as a snap.

His fist froze mid-punch, and he turned to focus that one eye on me.

"He's a spy."

Rage flashed in a single cutting moment. "He tried to kill you."

I nodded. "He was sent by Alexxandria."

His whole body seemed to still at that announcement. His fist tightened and he turned, pounding it again once, twice more. He hauled the barely conscious merman up by the jacket, bringing his broken and bloody face close to his. "I'm not going to kill you yet," he promised darkly. "By the time I'm through with you, you'll be begging for death. And even then, I won't grant it." He yanked the merman up and tossed him in the direction of his generals. "Lock this scum up and set guards on him."

They hauled him away, kicking his tail and cursing all the way. As soon as they were gone, Ytgar swam up to me, pulling up the lapels of my tatter chemise. I hadn't realized it had fallen down to my breasts, or that I was still bleeding.

He covered me gently, his fingers brushing aside hair, stopping right near the wound at my neck. "What happened?"

I didn't shake. I wasn't traumatized. I wasn't vulnerable. I was *angry*. Not for myself or the wounds he'd inflicted, which would leave scars over my flesh, but for Val, and what information might have doomed him.

"Odele?" Ytgar's voice pulled me from my thoughts.

"I'm fine." The words came out more vehemently than I'd intended. I turned to Adrian. He hadn't come near me at all since barging into the tent and saving me life. He looked detached, cold, and the leather gloves were tightened into fists in a way that seemed like they'd come apart at the seams. "He's a spy," I repeated. "He's been feeding Alexxandria information. We need to know what he's told her."

If he'd compromised the one thing we had to take Iol back… The conch was our only salvation, and now I feared it could be our doom—and Val's death.

"Whatever information he gave, he will tell us," Adrian said darkly. "If I can promise you nothing else, I can promise you that."

He started to turn away, a rigid set to his shoulders and a finality in the gesture.

Quiet rage thrummed through his body, even through Ytgar beside me. But at least Ytgar was touching me. At least his hands were reassuring in the aftermath of my near death. Adrian was pulling away.

I didn't want him to pull away.

"Wait."

I darted forward and grabbed his arm. He tensed even further. "Let go of my arm, Odele," he ordered, kingly in his manner.

"No."

He tore his arm from my grasp and whirled around to face me. He didn't speak, but he didn't need to. I knew what emotions were tightly wound within him, especially after the intimate confession that had happened only an hour before this situation.

Adrian hauled me forward and I slammed into his chest just before his lips came crashing down against mine.

Adrian

THE PROSPECT OF LOSING had never tasted this agonizing. Especially when the one I'd nearly lost had been Odele. My wife. My *love*.

I should have known there'd be spies in my midst, I should have taken precautions. She should have been better guarded against this. I should have *known* that someone would go after her. Because this was war, and it was as sneaky as it was brutal.

My tongue claimed Odele, as if I could somehow tear a pathway down to her soul or inhale hers into mine somehow. This moment felt raw and vital, because I'd almost lost her not even an hour after I'd confessed my feelings.

It just served to remind me how easily something could be taken away.

But I couldn't let that happen. Not her. I'd rather grow legs and walk straight into two-legger fire if it meant the difference between her life and death.

I pulled away reluctantly, and I knew the emotion reflected in my voice. "I cannot lose you. Do you understand me?"

My fingers went to her neck, to the wound there. She had other bright forming bruises on her and scrapes from the sword along her arm. Just seeing the wounds marring her precious skin brought rage erupting within me all over again. She shouldn't have scars, she shouldn't be hurt at all.

I'll kill him. I'll tear him limb from limb while his heart still beats in his chest. He will wish for death and even then, I'll not grant it.

"Ytgar."

The Iolish prince straightened into a military stance, his shoulders tight. A quiet fury shone in the depths of his silver-white eyes. I could trust no one but him with her life, because like me, he would do whatever it took to protect the mer he loved.

Energy rolled off him in waves, a restlessness. He hadn't really spoken, but he didn't need to for me to understand what he was feeling. Silent communication passed between a single glance.

"Watch over her." I still said it aloud for Odele's benefit.

She blinked, staring between the two of us like we were coconspirators against her. "Wait a tail flipping moment." She yanked on my arm again. "'Watch her'? What am I, a dogfish?" Her voice held the perfect tone of indignation.

Her indignation didn't matter. Not anymore. Not when her life was on the line.

"Where are you going that I can't go with you?"

I tried releasing the tenseness from my body, but I couldn't. I was battle ready. Someone under my protection, my *wife* was threatened. A spy had held her at sword point and nearly killed her in our tent.

"I have an assassin to interrogate."

"Not without me."

I looked to the ceiling of the tent, praying to my gods for the patience to deal with her stubbornness. "No."

"I didn't ask for your permission. I'm going. I have a right to know why he tried to assassinate me and what information your interrogation will provide." She crossed her arms against her chest, and my eyes strayed to the tattered material falling over her shoulders.

Honesty, a voice in my head whispered. What she needed here was honesty; I had to explain why I couldn't let her come watch me interrogate him.

I took a breath. "There is a side of me that you have not yet seen, my love," I began slowly. "It is cruel and unforgiving." *And I don't want you to see me like that.* Those words went unsaid but pulsed in the silence between us.

She uncrossed her arms and took a single stroke towards me so that our chests touched. She lifted an arm up and brushed aside wisps of my hair. "Good," she whispered. "That bastard tried to kill me. Show him no mercy."

My heart clenched and my throat tightened. I swallowed and found a smile curling at my lips. "Ah, my sweet, bloodthirsty wife. What of your soul?"

Her eyes flashed with an emotion I couldn't quite place. She shrugged a shoulder. "I've killed before." The words were a confession that cleaved straight through my chest.

It had me reaching for her hands and bringing them up to my mouth, lips kissing softly at her knuckles. These hands, they were bloodstained. I knew she wasn't pure of soul. She was the very definition of ferocity. She would kill, protect, and for that, I loved her all the more.

"I'll kill again, because if killing, if *destroying* makes any bit of a difference in this war, then what difference does it make how many pieces of
my soul I forfeit?"

Ah, my bloodthirsty, beautiful wife.

"That's music to my ears."

We both knew it wouldn't be a forfeiting of her soul at all. Not when,
deep down, I knew she relished in the violence as much as I did, because
she was a conqueror. She fought, and she took, and she kept.

She could handle the violence.

She could handle every crazed, broken, ugly bit of me.

The assassin had been tied up and confined within a tent. He was bound
and gagged to a chair, held down by the tail and the arms.

A single globe of lava illuminated him in the center of the tent. His eyes
darted up to me as I swam inside. Then they darted behind me to Odele
and Ytgar before straying back to Odele and holding.

That wouldn't do at all.

Slowly, I untied the strings of my cloak and shrugged it off, letting it fall
into the silt. A small blast of cold hit me, but I ignored it. "Let's get one
thing straight right now, assassin." I drew his attention to me with those
dark words. I took one sleeve of my tunic and began rolling it up slowly,
methodically. As if I'd done this a thousand times before.

I had.

"You will not look at my wife. You will not look at the Iolish prince."
I went to the other sleeve, rolling it up to my elbows. "You will look at
no one but me. Is that clear?" He didn't respond. Already we were off to
a terrible start. I pried the leather patch from my face and let it fall. Every
scarred bit of me was visible to him now, and my face was the one he'd

be seeing in his nightmares in hell. "I don't believe I made myself clear." I drove my fist straight into his gut. He doubled over gasping from the force of the blow. "Do. You. Understand?"

Between painful gasps for breath, he nodded.

"Good." I straightened. "I am going to ask you a series of questions, and you're going to answer every single one of them honestly. I have a special skillset, you see. I can *always* tell when someone is lying to me." I bent at the tail so our faces were level. I could smell his fear and the determination to remain strong. "You aren't going to lie to me, are you?"

Slowly, and with hatred in his gaze, he shook his head.

I smirked. "Good. Then let's get started."

It had been too long since I'd last heard the sounds of a screaming victim. There was a moment, after the initial broken ribs and bruised face, when things got *personal*. Like when I shoved a dagger into his eye. It was satisfying; in some sick, paradoxical way it was like making love. Getting to know someone on such an intimate level that his cries of agony became music to my ears, drowning out the memory of Odele's shouts of pain. The sight of his blood was my wife's vengeance, though no matter how many times my knife met his flesh, it would never be enough to make up for the bruises on her skin.

Every crunch of the bones within his fingers brought forth the answers I wanted to hear. He didn't dare lie to me, and soon, I knew all of this mer's secrets. He'd dissolved into uncontrollable sobs by the time my blade had pierced him between the ribs, and I'd been sure he'd told me everything I needed to know, but I couldn't stop and I knew that I was being purposefully cruel. Mercy was not a word I knew.

It had been for my benefit. A warning to all those who would dare try and cross me.

You do not come near the Princess of Thalassar with a knife and come out unscathed.

You do not try to take what was mine.

During those moments where I let the more primitive, savage side of me show, Odele and Ytgar had stayed through it all. Silent spectators to my viciousness. And when the assassin took in his final gasping breaths just before I shoved a blade into his heart and watched him die, I turned to meet their gazes.

I expected disgust, even a sliver of fear. They'd wanted to see the King of the Uncharted unleased, well, here he was. They would finally see what I was capable of, what a true savage I was. That all the stories of the mer of the Uncharted were true. We were cruel, because we needed to be. We had to protect what was ours by any means necessary.

This was how I'd conquered the tribes. This was how I became their king. In violence, in blood, and in death.

But there was no fear to be seen in the faces of my wife or the Iolish prince. His expression was pulled tight, and he barely flicked a glance over the dead body of the mer who had let the final pieces of information fall into place. And Odele… her whole posture held a glowing sort of pride to it, and she was looking at me no differently than she had before. There was still love shining in her depths.

I wondered if that love was stronger than disgust.

Now she knew I carried decades worth of violence on my shoulders and would still carry it even after all of this was over.

"You heard him," I whispered. My voice sounded loud in the silence of the tent. Not louder than his screams had been.

Ytgar gave a tight nod.

Odele bit at her bottom lip.

I unrolled my sleeves and bent to pick up the fur cloak, tossing it over my shoulders. A new energy replaced the old one within my body. This was far from over. Not even close. The hunt was still on.

Because Alexxandria had another spy in our midst.

Odele

I DIDN'T SHIVER AWAY from the violence of Adrian. In fact, I relished in it. The taint on my soul I'd felt after I'd killed the mercenary that had threatened my cousin's life wasn't in me any longer.

First kills were always the hardest, but it had been a necessary evil. That's what ruling was. It was hardening your heart. It was becoming queen instead of a coward, because there were things that had to get done for survival.

And I'd found someone as similar as I in that ideology, someone who was willing to go to any length to protect what he loved.

Ytgar was a gentler ruler, yet he knew the rules of this game as well as we did. He knew this was war, that our lives were on the line, so he didn't oppose to Adrian's beatings. He'd hardened himself as much as I had during the interrogation, and together we'd watched as he'd bared the mer's every single secret.

Now he was dead, the only thing preventing him from floating up and overturning in the tent was the rope that kept him tethered to that chair.

"Someone has betrayed us." Adrian pulled his gloves over his long fingers, securing the buttons before crossing his arms over his chest. There was still a tightness winding through his body, because this wasn't over yet. There was still someone in our camp who was spying for Alexxandria, passing along information about our whereabouts and our plans. And gods, did she know about the conch to Val? How many spies did we have? According to the assassin, it had been only one, though he'd died before he could reveal the identity of the mer, and Adrian said it was the truth. But that was one that the assassin knew of. What if there were more?

Anxiety thrummed through me.

"How do we find the sea scum?" I asked.

Adrian looked at me with that one gleaming eye. He hadn't put his eye patch back on, so the scar that slashed down the entire left side of his face drew my eye. It was an ugly wound, yet he wasn't ugly, and all the scar did was draw to his allure. "We need to flush the spy out."

"We don't know who it is, but I'd bet it was either one of your generals or one of their second hand mer," Ytgar chimed in. "It'd have to be someone well placed to get the insider information. Things others at the camp won't know about."

"Not necessarily," Adrian said. "Spies are good at blending in with the background. It could easily be someone we've overlooked, someone we've spoken freely in front of. A servant or a groomsmer…"

So it could have been anybody.

I pressed my fingers to the wound at my neck. "So how do we proceed?"

Silence followed the question as they thought over all the possibilities. Ytgar cleared his throat. "I suggest a trap." We turned to look at him. He was in planning mode, military mode. His eyes sparked as he spoke. "We plant false information for the spy, lock down the camp, and find out who is sneaking away with that information."

"Catch them in the act." Adrian rubbed his chin, admiration etching over his features, in the curl of his smile. "Brilliant, Prince."

"But what false information can we give?"

Ytgar turned a rare smile at me. "I have the perfect plan."

"What do you mean we aren't attacking her?" the generals demanded.

Adrian crossed his arms against his chest and stared down at his generals, daring them to defy him. He was intimidating, with his bulk. He was the same size as Ytgar, but his scar gave him an edge that the Iolish didn't have.

"There has been a change of plans," Adrian drawled. "In light of the recent events, we are going to do this differently. Instead of facing off with my sister on the battlefield, we're going to be sending an assassin to eliminate her. I've already sent out word to my spies in her ranks."

His generals looked to one another incredulously. Which one of them was the culprit? Was it even one of them? Or was it the servant circling around the table filling up the goblets to the brim with frothy ale? Could it be the right hand mer of the generals? The cadets? The soldiers packed in the tight circle of the war tent?

I tried not to look too suspiciously as Adrian began barking out orders to his mer. He laid out a map and began ordering them to take positions for their night's watch. It was a set up that would allow free movement for the spy to take his sorry tail towards Iol… and towards Queen Alexxandria without getting caught.

Little did the spy know that we'd be there waiting for him, or her.

That night, we waited in the cold waters, camouflaged behind an iceberg, wrapped in our polar bear skins. I tried not to ogle too much at the sight Adrian made in white fur. It was different from his usual black or red. Ytgar, as always, looked incredibly well put together given the circumstances. He always looked perfect. As a prince, I didn't think he could look anything but.

The waters were still and quiet, cast in dull shadows and little illumination. It was bright enough to catch silhouettes of traitors, but dark enough to hide their features.

Our eyes were alert, and our voices silent as we peered past the iceberg in different directions, looking for any sign of the spy. It had been hours, and I was starting to get restless, nervous.

I held the wyvern handled dagger tightly in my grip, unwilling to release it. The traitor *had* to pass through here to get to his queen. It wasn't like there were many places the scum could flee to.

I wasn't going to give up hope. I couldn't…

It felt like hours later when I finally caught a flickering of movement, a shadow darting past bergs at a quick and cautious pace.

My hand shot out to grip Ytgar's arm. His silver eyes met mine in the darkness and I gestured towards that direction. They narrowed when they caught sight of the darting figure. It was definitely a mer.

He pressed a finger to his lips. As if I'd make a sound.

Iolish bastard, I mouthed.

He let out a silent snicker before he signaled to Adrian and the two of them crept around the berg and towards the figure.

I stayed right where I was, watching as they disappeared into darker shadows. I held my breath, waited. The figure darted out again, only this time it was pursued by two more figures. A moment later, he was tackled into the snowy silt, and a grunt sounded as a struggle ensued.

I jumped over the iceberg, kicking my tail and swimming towards the fight. When I approached, it was to find the traitor pinned face first into the silt, with Ytgar's tail digging into his back. The voice and curses in the language of the Uncharted were obviously male, even muffled into the silt.

"Stop struggling or the Iolish prince will shove his sword through your spine," Adrian commanded.

The struggling stopped and Ytgar hauled him up by the back of his cloak then swung his sword around to press it against his neck.

He turned, and up close, I could make out the features of the mer. I narrowed my eyes over him. "I don't know you."

"But I do." Adrian took a stroke forward. "He's attendant to my second general. What's your name again?"

Ytgar dug his sword deeper into his neck. The mer gritted out his answer. "Gillian Jesh."

I looked the treacherous scum in the eyes. "What information have you been taking to Alexxandria?"

My question was met with silence.

"Answer her!" Adrian demanded. Ytgar pressed the blade of his sword in deeper.

He still didn't answer. "It doesn't matter," I dismissed. "Your king will get the truth from you in due time."

Finally, a reaction. His eyes held the briefest sense of panic within them. He was familiar with my husband's methods of extraction. Good.

"Or you can tell me right now and skip all the messy stuff. What did you tell her?"

He was silent.

I sighed. "Really, if you want to do this the hard way, you can. After all, it's not my fingers King Adrian will break one by one. Did you know that when he sticks his knife between the first and second ribs of his victim, it makes this abnormal sloshing sound? Or the crunch of bones shattering in an arm? It's music to my king's ears."

The merman's skin paled. Then, he struggled against Ytgar's firm hold, but the prince held him tightly, digging the blade even tighter against his neck. "Let me go!" he shouted, kicking his fin, nearly grazing me with it.

"If you want leniency, you will tell me what Alexxandria knows!"

"Everything!" he shouted. "She knows everything! How many troops you have, where you plan on attacking, that you two are married, that you have no allies!"

I took a stroke close, so close that my nose nearly slammed into his. Through gritted teeth, I hissed, "Did you tell her anything about Valmundur?"

The vehemence and murder in my voice startled a few blinks from the mer. "J-Just that he left," he stammered.

"What about the conch?"

"Conch?" He looked genuinely confused. "What are you talking about? What conch?"

So that was one secret he hadn't divulged. I turned to Adrian, who'd been observing the interaction. His yellow eye was narrowed on the mer, gauging his every reaction.

"She doesn't know about the message we sent to Iol?" I whispered.

He squirmed, and bubble tears slipped from his eyes. "I told you everything I know! Please! I don't know anything about a conch or a message. I told her what I observed and conversations from the generals! I swear!"

I turned back to Adrian. He gave the subtlest of nods.

He's telling the truth.

I sighed a discreet sound of relief and straightened, taking a stroke back. I hardened my expression, my posture as I looked the traitor in the eyes. "Well, Gillian Jesh. I, Duchess of Castle Frost, Princess Odele Malabella Oriana of Thalassar, Queen of the Uncharted Waters, charge you with treason against the sea kingdoms of Saavaj'i and Iol." I paused, a hard edge dripping into my words. "The sentence is death."

The next morning, the drums sounded. They pounded and pulsed through the water, like the steady heartbeat of a mer charging into bloody battle. They were a call to the camp. Each one a command, an announcement, a *warning*.

A dais had been raised in the middle of the camp, and it was on that dais where the traitor was tied up and surrounded by guards, forced to bend on the surface. He cried loudly, the sounds overshadowed by the beating of the execution drums.

The mer had gathered around the bottom of the structure, and their cries of surprise and outrage were also drowned away.

Adrian, Ytgar, and I swam into the fray, and the crowd parted down the middle for us. I was between the king and the prince, our heads held high, crowns gleaming atop our heads.

Adrian's crown was a heavy obsidian, eroded with ivory bone; Ytgar's was that crown of steel and diamonds I'd helped make for him; I wore the crown of a queen. No tiara decorated my head, but an actual crown, a tall structure, thick and studded with obsidian, ivory, diamonds, and pink quartz.

Together, we looked ruthless and unforgiving as we swam up the structure. Our velvet and fur cloaks billowed around our tails. The drums pushed us, the sounds seeming to guide our movements as we formed a line behind the sniveling traitor.

And then there was silence.

Adrian took a stroke forward, and his voice rang out loud and clear throughout the waters. He commanded respect and fear with the mere power of his voice. "Am I your king?" That one slashing yellow eye roamed over the crowd like the dangerous hint of a promise, of a threat. "*Am* I your king?"

A single roaring shout of "Yes!" rose up around us.

With a single, dexterous movement of his black, leather clad fingers, he pulled at the drawstrings of his cloak. The black fur drifted from his shoulders and slid down his back and onto the surface of the makeshift stage. "Have I not been a fair leader?"

"Yes!"

He moved down the buttons of his long-sleeved tunic. The movements were beautiful, captivating in every way. And each time he spoke, his voice rose higher and higher, his accent gruffer, until the words started slipping deep into the edges of his own language. I understood every word somehow. Perhaps because we'd camped with the Uncharted, and I'd picked up bits and pieces of their language, but I didn't need to be fluent in the savagery of his rage to be captivated, to understand.

He slipped the tunic from his body until he was clad in absolutely nothing but those dark gloves and his eye patch. Even then, he slowly peeled them off. And when he was vulnerable before his mer, scar and all, he spoke again, his voice rising to a shout. "Have I not given you everything? Have I not protected you from harm? Have I not given you glory? Have I not led you into battle to conquer?"

"Yes!"

This seemed intimate in all its viciousness. A ritual of some kind between Adrian and his mer. So different from anything else I'd ever seen or witnessed. It was magic. Somehow, this was magic, and I felt the power thrum around us all.

"Have I not promised you a better future?"

"Yes!"

"Have I not given everything to fulfill that promise?"

"Yes!"

"Have I not ruled justly and cruelly as our gods demand?"

"YES!"

Silence permeated the water, broken through with Adrian's harsh and rapid inhalations. "Then will you tell me, mer of my heart and of my gods, why Gillian Jesh has betrayed us to our enemy?"

Shocked gasps rippled through the crowd. I took them in, every angry expression before turning back to Adrian.

"He has sold information to our enemy and because of him, my *wife,* your *queen,* was nearly assassinated." His head turned, and his eye found mine. It was such a tender expression that vanished within the next moment as he turned around and threw his arms out at his sides. "And what fate befalls those who turn their tails on their king?"

"Death!"

"What end will this mer meet at the tip of a blade?"

"Death!"

"What gift do we give our gods today?"

"DEATH!"

He took a stroke back and turned to me, giving me a single nod.

It's time.

I took a stroke forward. When I spoke, my voice rang clearly. I didn't hide anything; I showed the rage that had been building towards this moment. "On this day, of the forty-sixth year of the Malabella-Isolde Neves-Evander reign, in the names of the mer kingdom of Iol, Saavaj'i, and Thalassar, on the outskirts of the Iolish borders of this Tidesday, first New Moon, I, Duchess of Frost, Princess of Thalassar, and Queen of Saavaj'i and the Uncharted Waters sentence you to die."

The mer cried harder, his shoulders racking up and down in uncontrollable sobs. He didn't try to swim away. Why would he? It would only doom him further. His head was bowed, forehead kissing the stage.

A guard brought forth the executioner's sword. I moved to take it, but Ytgar grabbed my upper arm before I could.

"I'll do it," he stated tightly. His silver eyes shining, glowing like luminescent jellyfish.

"I have to do this." This was war, and he'd compromised us. He would pay for his betrayal, and he would be used as an example to others who wished to betray us.

"This is my war, too." Ytgar yanked me back, tossed aside part of his cloak and pulled out the sword he kept at his hip. It wasn't the Isolde sword with the orca pommel; Val had taken that with him to Aelfrost. This sword was still massive, strong. He looked intimidating with it in his hands. Murderous.

Yes, this was as much Ytgar's war as it was ours. We were all fighting for something, for someone. I'd sentence this sea scum to death, and he would swing the sword, and that was okay. Because as long as one of us did it, that was all that really mattered.

Ytgar swam off to the side of the traitor and lifted the sword. The mer cried and was shoved to the floor, his neck exposed. Ytgar gripped the sword tightly, his gaze intent as he swung the sword down...

...and the waters were filled with blood.

HE'D COMPROMISED OUR MISSION, could have cost us the war, could have cost us Val's *life*. And for that offense alone, I would make him pay.

I swung the sword with all the force my rage would allow me and more. In one swinging, swift cut, the blade sliced through the traitor's neck.

Blood exploded through the water in a dark, cloudy burst. It swept over me, and I tasted his blood. The blood of the treacherous scum who had almost cost me everything. For the briefest, cruelest moment, I relished in it. I let the blood wash over me and enjoyed it.

Because this, this was a battle won. And Adrian's savagery and tradition was so contagious, I felt like I was no longer a part of myself as this unfolded, and yet at the same time, I accepted and embraced it with open arms. Because this was what freedom of control felt like. It was the reality of ruling. Ruling was not sitting impatiently behind a circle of old mer, demanding they listen. It wasn't pushing kelp pages at them and waiting for them to change their minds.

To govern, I had to conquer. I had to change. I had to take the sword and prove myself.

Because what I wanted was not going to fall into my lap. I had to take it. I had to grip the sword and swing. I had to give in to this, whatever it was that Adrian was bringing into our lives.

It was beautiful.

And we would win.

THE HEAD SWIRLED THROUGH the water, floating and bobbing. The blood cleared, floating above us and dissolving into but a mere memory of where his life had once been.

The cold currents pressed against my body. I was cold, and yet I did not feel it beyond the rage thrumming through my blood.

I turned to a guard and gestured at the head. "Bag it," I commanded, "and send it to my sister."

Let her know the truth.

Let her know that I'll wreak havoc upon her and her armies, that I will take my sword and cleave it through her heart myself, if she dared to try and take away what I loved ever again.

Valmundur

THEY'D BEATEN ME UNTIL my ribs had broken and an eye had closed. Pain spiraled through every inch of my body, and had throbbed ever since they finished and tossed me back into my cell. I'd dragged myself into the corner, huddling within my furs. I hadn't moved since.

I was in too much pain, too weak, and my tail didn't seem to be cooperating with me. Maybe it was the lack of hope, rendering me immobile. Maybe it was the nightmares that refused to leave even in my waking moments.

An assassin had been sent to murder Odele. Had he succeeded? Just the thought of it made me ill, sent my heart fragmenting into thousands of pieces. How many times could I experience a sense of loss this profound? This heartbreak just kept repeating over and over again.

That was the hardest part. Not the injuries, the pain, but the not knowing, being locked away without light or contact. They were killing me slowly from the inside.

If the queen wanted to make me go mad, then she was choosing the perfect way to send me off into insanity.

"Val. Psst, Val!"

My eye slowly pried open; my eyelashes had felt like they'd frozen against my cheek bones. I blinked away the bright glow of a lava globe that blinded me from across my dark cell. It was the first light I'd seen in days. I'd already embraced the shadows flickering within shadows, so seeing the steadily held orb surprised me.

Seeing who held it surprised me even more.

I sat up, moving for the first time in what felt like days. The sudden action pulled at my every muscle painfully and I winced.

"Anneli?"

The mermaid floated on the other side of the confines of my prison, holding a small glass globe with bright blue light. It illuminated the expression pulled tightly at her features. She stared at me like she didn't recognize me.

I grunted as I dragged myself towards her. It hurt to move; my tail felt broken, so I dug my nails into the cold ice beneath me and pulled myself to the bars. I wrapped my stiff fingers around them, feeling the cold bite into my skin.

Her face pressed close to the bars. In the light, her eyes looked blue-gray.

"What are you doing here?" I asked, my voice hoarse. I could see her perfectly out of one eye, but the other was swollen shut. "How did you get passed the guards?"

"The queen's messenger came in and they got distracted. I only have a few moments." Her gaze raked over my injuries. "You look like the gods drug you through the ice and slapped you against it repeatedly."

Gods, it felt so good to hear her voice, to hear something that wasn't my own nightmares. A rough laugh scraped from my throat, the sound echoing harshly in the prison. "Yeah," I agreed. "I feel it, too."

"We don't have time. Here." Her hand shoved between the bars. I looked down at her closed fist, and she made a series of annoyed gestures that I held my palm out. She dropped a small conch made of ice in it.

I stared at it, a shiver going through my spine. I'd made this for Odele. I'd gifted it to her on Saint Valence day. A conch of ice because all the ones she'd loved dearly had broken the moment she'd set fin in Iol. I'd just wanted to give a bit of herself back to her.

Why did Anneli have it?

Only one reason came into my mind.

I closed my fist around it, pressing my forehead against the bars, dropping my gaze to the ice. "She's gone, then?" Just saying the words felt raw... *wrong.* She couldn't have been gone. I would have known, somewhere deep in my heart, I would have known my wife had been murdered. I would have felt her loss, wouldn't I have?

Tears pressed to my eyes and sobs clawed their way up my chest and throat. The heartbreak? It *could* get worse, and it did.

Because it felt like I was dead now, too.

And then a sharp tug on my ear had me jerking my head up, my face banging painfully against the bars.

"Focus!" Anneli hissed. "Listen to the conch, Val."

My eyebrows pulled together. She stared at me, completely exasperated.

I knew not to let her order me around twice, so I pinched the thing between my thumb and forefinger and lifted it to my ear and listened.

The voice that spoke had me bracing a hand against the bars, gasping for breath with disbelief. It was...she was...

"Hello Val," Odele's voice whispered, the words spoken with just enough anger and haughtiness for a chuckle to push past my lips. It was so innately her. "Do you like my new invention? How does it feel having the smartest wife to ever swim the seas?" I threw my head back and laughed. Anneli shushed me with annoyance. "Sorry it's taken so long, but we are coming for you. We are coming for Iol. Raise arms from within. Rally the Iolish and give us an in." I listened intently as she began going through the details of her plan in a clipped, hurried voice. When she finished, I was smiling, hope blooming in my chest. "I love you Val," she whispered, the words reflected deeply in her voice. "Don't let it get to your head," she added. "I still plan on slapping you when we see each other again, Iolish bastard."

The recording stopped. I kept it pressed it to my ear, a smile broad on my face. "She's not dead…"

"A dead mer can't send messages now, can they?" Anneli put her hand through the bars and yanked on the lobe of my ear. "Focus, Val, or we'll both be dead!"

I sobered, handing the conch back to her. If I kept it, the guards would find it. "There's nothing I can do from here. The queen takes me to her sometimes and tells me her plans. That's all I can give you from in here. You have to rally everyone. You have to!"

A determined look crossed over her face. She gave me a firm nod. "I will."

A smile touched my mouth. "Be ready, Anneli, because the war is coming to us."

Draconi

A few weeks earlier…

PREGNANCY WAS GROWING TEDIOUS. It seemed to last forever, and while there were no obvious changes in my body save for the slightest bump of my stomach and the bigger breasts,—honestly, I just looked like I'd gained all the weight Lagoona poverty had never given me—but it was there in other ways.

It was the incessant emotions that seemed to overpower all my common sense. All I did was cry, and scream, and most recently, wallow in my own self-piteous thoughts.

At the root of those thoughts was Odele. The crest fallen expression on her face when I'd denied my help.

"I understand unconditional love, and I don't think you do. I'd die for you, that's what that means. I'd kill for you and those I care about. It's nice to know you wouldn't do the same."

Those words had haunted me ever since she'd left.

They filled me with a guilty sense of dread, and a deep dark voice in my mind couldn't help but whisper, "It's true."

For so long, I'd hated Odele for being a terrible ruler, a despicable princess. Then I'd discovered she was my cousin and I wasn't sure exactly what it was I should feel. Relief? No, that wasn't it at all. Sometimes, I still held a bitter resentment towards her because of her lack of ability to swim up and take the crown she was meant to wield. She hadn't wanted it, had acted like it didn't matter. Nothing ever mattered to her except her own obsessive compulsions, and I'd hated her for it. Even while I loved her simply for being family.

How could two emotions live to war so violently inside me?

But then things seemed to change since she'd come back from Iol. She seemed different. She seemed like she actually cared… and I wasn't sure what to make of the new her or of the fierce protectiveness she had over Iol, when she hadn't even felt it for Thalassar.

All I knew was that I couldn't willingly help send mer to their deaths. Not after Thalassar, not after the Selection. I didn't have it in me, and I refused to have deaths on my conscious. That didn't mean I didn't love Odele, did it?

I couldn't be sure.

"My gem?"

At the sound of Kai's voice, I turned away from the window where the bustle of Draconi's streets had captivated me. He was framed in the doorway of our room, an expression of worry pulling at his elegant features.

He was always worrying these days. With the threat of a war looming over the kingdom, he was constantly in war meetings with his father and out scouting the waters in search of the Uncharted threat.

No one was sure it was entirely real yet, but Odele had been adamant that it was.

I'd seen the head of my cousin Jessinda sent to us in a sack. Of course I believed it was real. But it was hard for them to believe in a faceless enemy from waters so far away. From waters no one had ever heard from before. Now they emerged from the darkness, a sister versus brother, and my cousin had been sucked into it all as if she were trapped within a sink hole.

"Yes?" I tucked a lock of hair behind my ear. I was tired, and I was sure it reflected in the shadows beneath my eyes. My hand strayed towards my stomach. It was hard, and with the weight I put on, I knew I looked like Odele now more than ever. I was wider in the hips, and my bust had grown larger. It wasn't obvious with the flowing clothes I wore.

"Are you alright?" He took a stroke into the room and stopped.

I understood his wariness. I was being sensitive lately, perhaps too sensitive. Sometimes I'd crave his touch, Tiberius's and Elias's too, but other days I just didn't want them near me.

Today was the latter.

Pregnancy.

"I'm fine," I responded tightly.

But I wasn't fine. They could all see that. Everything was just heightened, and I missed my cousin. We hadn't parted on the friendliest of terms, and I could the betrayal in her eyes, but beneath that, a never ending well of heartbreak. Like I'd disappointed her somehow, and I didn't even know why.

I understood that she wanted everyone to bow to her whims, but this was war. It was life and death. Those armies she wanted were mer with lives, homes, and families.

"I think I need fresh water." It was suddenly hard to breathe.

I wasn't a traitor to my cousin. Was I?

"I can ask Tiberius to guard you if—"

"No, thank you."

"What about Elias? I can send a servant to get him from the hot house—"

"I want to be alone right now."

A brief look of hurt slashed over his face that he quickly schooled with a smile. "Of course. I understand."

Did he? I doubted it. I doubted anyone understood the turmoil that warred inside me. But I hated feeling like I was hurting him.

So as I swam out, I stopped in front of him and leaned up to press a soft kiss to his lips. He smiled against my mouth and pulled me close, gently, cautiously.

When I pulled away, he was smiling.

"I'll see you in a bit," I promised.

"Of course, my gem."

I left him there, swimming out into the halls of the palace. I'd already memorized every inch of the place, and yet it somehow still didn't feel like home. Not truly. Perhaps it was because everyone was so careful around the emperor—especially Kai—and we couldn't really be ourselves, lest we face his wrath.

I felt like I was suffocating.

I missed Thalassar, I missed Lagoona, my little blue boat in the cattail forest. Most of all, I missed my father. To find him only to say goodbye? It physically hurt when we had so much lost time to make up for.

Sighing and running my fingers through my hair, I rounded the hall and smacked into a warm, muscular body.

I looked up, an apology tumbling from my lips that froze when I realized just who I'd run into.

"Your Majesty!" I bowed quickly, hoping he wouldn't reprimand me for my blundering mistake. I'd seen him reprimand mer for less.

He wasn't cruel, exactly. He was very strict and traditional, with a face that bespoke of perpetual anger. I looked up into that face, straightening.

His dark, unforgiving gaze pierced me. I stared at him a moment and then started to make my escape. The harsh, cutting tone of his voice stopped me. "Are you alright?"

If my father-in-law could tell I was unwell, then maybe I should look into a mirror. "I'm fine, Your Majesty," I ground out. I tried to slip past him, but he intercepted me before I could.

"Come with me." He held out his arm or me to take. I stared at it with distrust. His frown deepened. "That's an order."

Emperor Jiang Li's war office was formidable. Dragons were splashed in angry lines of paint against the walls. Red and yellow lanterns floated around the room, illuminating the weapons hanging on the walls. Katanas, bows and arrows, lances, maces, and so many weapons and leathers made from the scales of dragons.

He swam up to the massive table. "You should sit. It's not good to be on your fins all day in your condition." He pulled out a chair and gestured to it.

Tentatively, I swam to it and sat down. My eyes stayed on him as he swam around the enormous table and took a seat on the opposite side of me. He towered over me, even sitting down. He was intimidating, in every aspect of the word.

"I remember when Yu was pregnant with Kai," he said. The confession startled me, as did the far away look shining in his eyes like he was recalling something pleasant. "She appeared as sickly as you do."

My eyes narrowed.

"We thought the child would not live." His voice went grave. It almost sounded like he cared. "Then again, we also thought the child she carried was female so…"

I didn't know how to reply to him, so I kept silent. We stared at one another. This was… odd. I hadn't really spoken to the emperor beyond our first uncomfortable introduction and his clipped instructions during the Choosing.

He acted like I didn't exist.

I knew he didn't like me because of how Odele and I had tricked Kai during our wedding in Thalassar, when I'd pretended to be her and married him when he'd thought he was marrying Odele. The emperor saw it as a slight on his honor as well as his family's.

I didn't want to care; Kai told me not to care, but I did. I didn't want to be known as merely the daft waitress from Lagoona who'd tricked the Prince of Draconi. I still had this desire to prove myself to the royals around me.

"You're having more than one," he predicted.

"How do you know that?" I finally spoke.

"You were with three mermen during your yearly time, were you not?" He stroked the hairs along his chin, amusement glittering in his dark, slanted eyes.

I felt my face flame at the proclamation. We hadn't really tried very hard to hide the fact that I was intimate with Tiberius, Elias, and Kai. Sometimes all at once. But hearing him say it aloud was odd. It felt like I was being judged somehow, even though the emperor would be the biggest hypocrite to judge me for having three lovers when he had dozens.

His hand waved away my embarrassment. "No need to wear that expression. Harems and concubines are traditional here in Draconi. Though, I had hoped it would be Kai to have concubines."

The thought of him having concubines filled me with a surprising jealous rage that I probably had no right to feel.

"But he is devoted to you entirely. He loves you; I can see that."

"And I love him." My voice was firm, controlled. My back had straightened as I looked him in the eye, daring him to contradict me. If he did, I would not hold my anger back. He'd ignored me enough, had treated me ill enough already, and even if the start of mine and Kai's relationship had been based on lies, we had worked through it. We loved one another, and I wouldn't have anyone, not even the fearsome Dragon Emperor, tell me it wasn't true.

But the emperor regarded me closely, carefully. "I know. And that is why I still allow you to live within my kingdom."

I released a breath, inclining back slightly in my seat.

"I love all of my concubines, and I love all of my children. Just as you will love all three of your children."

If I had a drink, I would have sputtered it out. "Three?" I choked.

"Three mermen, three seeds, three children."

"Surely if it were more than one I'd be larger by now?"

"Not necessarily." He rested his elbows onto the table, interlacing his fingers together. "Males, I think."

I shrugged. "I don't think the gender matters too much."

"Perhaps not. So…" He leaned forward on his elbows, piercing me with that unrelenting stare. "What ails you, daughter?"

A strange tingling sensation rushed through me at that single word. Daughter. My heart clenched. It was a word I didn't hear often. A word I'd never heard growing up in Lagoona, and now I found it pressed upon me by my father, and now by the emperor.

I blinked away the tears that threatened and cleared my throat. The words tumbled out of me in quick honesty. "I keep thinking about Odele and this war. She wanted my help and I denied it, and I can't help feeling like I betrayed her somehow. Did I? Is it a betrayal to her that I didn't even *try*? These are lives we're talking about. How could I knowingly send them out to war knowing they may not return?"

I was panting by the time I finished, and the emperor's eyes had softened considerably.

A few pressing beats of silence pressed between us. "You have a soft heart." He reached a hand out, palm facing up, fingers beckoning. I took it and he clasped his fingers firmly in mine, holding me steady. "A soft heart will allow your mer to love you. But it makes it easy to be conquered."

My eyebrows pulled together.

"Tell me, daughter, is it better to be loved or feared?"

"Loved." The answer came easily. I knew what it was to fear a monarchy and their rules.

"It's a trick question. It's a double-edged sword. If your subjects love you too much, they can easily take advantage of that kindness. If you are too feared, they might rise up against you."

"So royals can't win."

"The trick is to find a perfect balance between the two. Let them love you, and let them fear you." He pulled his fingers away from mine and, using his index fingers, pressed his fingertips together.

"How do you do that?"

He pressed his palms against the surface of the table. "Ruling is very similar to parenting. You must show them love, but you must also be firm for their own wellbeing. If you prohibit a child from swimming into the cage of a dragon and they do so anyway, they must be punished for breaking the rules, rules that allow for a perfectly balanced structure in society."

Right. That made sense. I nodded.

"Leniency can be given, yet in certain instances it should not. Give one mer one second chance, they will all want a second chance, and the balance of the structure will be tipped. Let me ask you this: if there is an enemy pounding at the gates of your kingdom, threatening the lives of the mer you so love, what do you do? How do you protect them if you do not want to fight? Where are the soldiers to protect the mer you love? If you do not protect them, the love they have for you will shatter, because they are the structure of your kingdom. They are what will make you empress, queen… princess. If you do not protect them, then who will?"

If you do not protect them, then who will?

Odele had protected me, had believed in me, had helped find my father and return my birthright to me. She'd protected me when no one else had. She'd lifted her sword and had killed for me. She would have killed Percival—for me. And when she'd asked for my help in return, I'd let my fear hold me back.

"Why won't you help the Iolish and Uncharted armies?" My voice was a weak whisper.

He leaned back in his chair and rubbed his hand across his jaw. "War is complicated. But I cannot move my armies and leave Draconi unprotected. When in war, you must look at every angle of battle." He sighed. "And to answer your previous question, do *you* believe you betrayed your cousin by denying her the help she desperately needs?"

I chewed at my bottom lip. "I—I—" I took a breath. "I do."

"Then you have your answer."

I'd betrayed my cousin. All along I'd had that answer but hadn't wanted to face it. But the emperor was unapologetic, honest, as he stared at me and gifted me with what I should have known all along. The reason I was so unwell.

"Is there a way I can make it up to her?" My fingers gripped at the material of my skirts.

"Perhaps."

There was so much insinuation behind that word. So much underlying that single word that I read all too well.

"Would you reconsider sending troops to Iol?" I asked hopefully.

His arm draped leisurely on the back of his chair. "That depends, daughter."

"Depends on what?"

He smiled. "On whether or not you can convince me."

Ytgar

Everything was silent, still. Soft flakes of snow swirled along with the currents of the water only to drift into the silt. Anyone from Iol would have been able to tell that this stillness was preternatural. Orcas and blue whales should have roamed freely from above; many thought the icier waters were desolate and lacked life, but they should have been bursting with it. With whale song and schools of dolphins, with the groaning of bergs moving through the water, of the cascades of tumbling ice crashing into the silt.

It was eerily silent, because we willed it.

It was silent because our armies were in position, waiting for the signal to attack.

For the start of the war.

We'd snuck in during the night towards Aelfrost; the capital was a mere few leagues away, protected by Uncharted scum and their sleeping, unsuspecting wyverns. To get to Aelfrost, we had to get past them.

I was mounted atop a white beast, camouflaged in the gray ice from above. My eyes scanned across the horizon, catching sight of the positions of my well-hidden unit. Waiting for my command.

I eyed the enemy below, counting heads. They had a small army guarding the small village on the outskirts of the capital. I bore witness to the way the Uncharted treated my mer, the way they enslaved the mermen and abused the mermaids.

I didn't take my eyes off of it for even a second. I took it in with a cold fury that I kept in my heart, saving it for the right moment.

The right moment was now.

Their blood would bloom through the Iolish waters tonight.

And I would relish in every violent bit of it.

Lifting the bow and arrow I held tightly in my hands, I pulled the string back and let my arrow fly straight into the throat of a sniper.

And so the war began.

THE FIRST OF THE snipers fell, a signal that the war had begun from above.

I made a series of clicking noises, digging my tail into the side of my hybrid beast. It shot down with a roar that trembled the waters and awoke the wyverns below.

It was a clash of claws and scales, of screeches and answering cries. I held tightly to the reins of my beast as it charged, and we collided against a wyvern.

My body jostled as the beasts fought. It was strength and blood, pain and a powerful push and pull of creatures stronger than any mer. I held tightly, ducking as claws came slashing towards me. My own beast retaliated, his barbed tail shooting out to pierce the underside of sensitive flesh of the wyvern.

It cried its rage and pain, and I tugged on the reins, giving it my commands in a series of slight pulls. It attacked, teeth searing straight into the wyvern's neck. It bit down and pulled out the flesh, killing it instantaneously.

It moved towards another beast and a battle began anew.

I tasted the blood, took it into my lungs, and laughed in the face of battle.

WE WERE DIVIDED INTO three units. Our plan had changed due to the traitor's oversharing of our every move. Ytgar and his troops took out the snipers from above, while Adrian and his Uncharted mer, riding the backs of their armored hybrid beasts, took out the wyverns.

I led the third unit from the lower waters, closer to the silt. We waited for the thickness of the initial battle to cease. My body thrummed with anticipation, and the slightest bit of fear I'd never admit to. We couldn't go in, not with so many wyverns. We needed to take them out first, or at least the majority of them.

So we waited, and we watched.

I held my breath, too afraid to breathe. But then the first wyverns started falling. It wasn't hard to make out in the chaos of the battle. Such massive beasts weren't difficult to miss. Adrian swooped down on his hybrid beast, cleaving through the enemy lines without fear.

One after another, they fell into piles of snow and blood, the cacophonous sounds of their dying shrieks shrill in the water. The bergs that served as our cover rattled with the force of their cries. Debris rained down around us in terrifying chunks, but we held still as Adrian led the assault against the creatures.

We took our share of death. Every time one of our own fell, my hand gripped my sword tighter. It was easy to distinguish our troops among the fray; white, blue, and gray furs adorned everyone like they were Iolishborn, like they were bred of ice and cold and steel.

The chaos was violent and terrifying, and I tried to mold my senses to every single inch of it. I familiarized myself with the sounds of war, the heart wrenching cries of the dying, and the terror that the beasts induced. I counted wing strokes, felt the stirrings it caused in the water, and felt the abrasions of falling ice against my cheeks with a welcoming heart.

The battle thickened until it was nothing but a blow of flying snow and clouds of dark blood. Steel and shields clashed, and when the blood cleared, I knew it was time.

I tugged at the reins of my hybrid mount and together we rose through the water. One by one, my soldiers flanked around my sides. A cry of fury and motivation kissed my lips and rang across the battle waters.

In one hand I held tightly to my sword of ice and steel, the other strapped with a shield. I rose as their queen, as the one who would help lead them to victory.

My velvet cloak whipped against the slashing of the currents, billowing behind me like a dark blue shadow. Diamonds and steel lined my shoulder plates, twining in a pattern of snowflakes up my neck and down the tops of my breasts. White velvet hugged my body, my diamond and silver breastplate embracing me like a lover.

It was a dress made for battle.

It was a dress to remind them who here was queen.

The dress billowed down my tail. Interloping chains tugged the dress against my hips, and the wyvern dagger was sheathed at my side. Today, we'd be taking back Iol and I'd help do so in style.

We charged into the fray. My sword was just another extension of me that slashed angrily through the bodies of my enemies. It cut through steel, leather, and flesh; blood bloomed in short bursts but dissolved just as quickly.

My body jostled above my mount, and my arm ached from the force with which I swung my sword. The other felt like it'd tear straight out of its socket. Axes flew at me and I lifted my shield to block the jarring blows.

I charged through the lines. Wyverns and beasts battled above us, but I focused, trying not to let anything else distract me from my single mission: break through the lines and lead our warriors to the capital.

We tore past their barriers and kicked our mounts into a swift swim. The taste of victory was sweet on my tongue as we charged forward at full speed. We were close, so close to taking our kingdom back.

A roar reverberated from above, and Adrian came swooping down over our heads. I ducked to avoid getting hit by the barbed end of the hybrid's tail and looked up with narrowed eyes. The beast soared through the water and we followed close behind, determination and the thrill of the battle coursing through us like the very blood in our bodies could hear the song of death and vengeance.

It rose up, thirsting for blood. I felt it like a burning need in my gut, to take, to conquer, to win back what was rightfully ours. To save Val and avenge my cousin.

Adrian's beast cried out in front of us and slammed down into the silt. Its wings spread wide at its sides and we came to a roaring halt behind it.

I steadied my mount's unease, patting it on the side of its flank. The beast's wings tucked into its spine and Adrian hopped off the back of it. Why wasn't he moving forward? Why had he stopped?

Aelfrost was just a few strokes away. From here I could see the rising spikes of the ice palace…

…and the wyverns barricading our entrance to the capital.

Side by side they sat camouflaged in the silt; massive scaled bodies pressed together like vicious looking sentinels that ranged from one side of the ice down, down, down for leagues like a solid wall of ice before us. Pressed together by their scaled bodies, there was hardly any room to slip between them.

Interloping steel chains rattled as they moved, and I followed the long line of it; the swooping chain wrapped around talons and long necks, tying one wyvern to another, and another, and another, leaving only their wings free. Wings that rose through the water, tall and leather, the clawed tips glinted in the glare of the ice that reflected off of them.

There was direct space above them, space we could swim up and over, and they wouldn't reach us if not for the long line of wyverns that hovered closer to the surface like two-legger clouds right above the wall of wyverns.

If we even tried to slip over them, the wyverns above could slam us right back down onto those below, completely and utterly destroying us.

Beyond the guards, I could make out the tall peaks and spires of Isolde Palace, winking at us in a kaleidoscope of shining colors. Close, we were so *close* to taking back what was ours, but we couldn't have predicted this. We should have. Somehow, we should have known that Alexxandria would have done everything in her power, used every weapon in her arsenal, to block us from taking our kingdom back.

And now here we were, on the crosscurrent of our own ignorance and stupidity, staring up at the line of unmoving sentinels, and with one singular thought floating through my mind, over and over again:

Oh, silt.

Valmundur

I SENSED THE CHANGE in the waters immediately. I might not have known how many days have passed since I'd last seen Anneli, since we'd last made those plans that would change everything for the better. I was still locked within the darkness, still starved and aching, my face and body throbbing from the guards' brutal beating, but hope was a living thing inside my chest.

It was the one thing keeping me alive.

I wasn't a warrior, not in the same sense that Ytgar was. But in Iol, every merman and every mermaid are groomed for the art of fighting since birth. Even us Ingen knew the importance of wielding a sword and shield. So while I'd trained whales for more than half of my life, I still knew my way around battlewaters, and that was why I noticed the change settle over Iol.

First came the preternatural stillness, a quieting of everything and everyone. It was like magic, like a sixth sense taking over. It told the mer that something was coming, something on the horizon coming closer and closer. It made us hold our breaths in fear and anticipation just before we would catch sight of the chaos heading straight towards us.

Then came the fray of the battle; a loud cacophonous crash that choked away the silence in a single sweeping move. It was steel sliding from sheathes, the clinking of shields, the slap of leather straps, the soft battle-ready cries of orcas.

And finally, *finally,* came the symphony of the screams of the dying. Of sword piercing past leather, steel, and flesh. Of the roaring battle cries of soldiers swallowed whole by the rushing bodies.

When the sounds came, I shot up despite the pain in my ribs and wrapped my stiff fingers around the bars of my cell. Every single nerve in my body thrummed to life; my heart beat faster and faster and my breathing grew almost labored.

It was time.

The plan had been set in motion. Odele, Ytgar, and Adrian were coming; they'd cut through Alexxandria's soldiers, and they *were coming.* Now it was time for the Iolish to fight back from within.

"Come on," I gritted out, fingers tightening around the bars. "Come on."

I counted the seconds in my mind, dreading and breathing in the stench of my own fear, tasting the headiness of it on my tongue. I tried not to let thoughts of the worst possible scenarios invade my mind, but there they were.

What if Anneli had gotten caught? What if no one wanted to rally? What if the guards didn't leave their posts? What if the plan failed?

Stop thinking, I told myself. *Focus.* It was thoughts like those that could destroy a warrior completely, that could get them killed. I couldn't doubt myself or anyone else. I had to remain tranquil, confident, which meant I couldn't sit here doing *nothing* like I've sat here doing *nothing* since I'd been locked up.

I'd tried to break myself out those first few days, but without rocks, without anything to help pick the lock, all I'd managed was to scream myself hoarse and make my fingers bleed.

Now, though, I had to at least try once again. Not with brute force but in another way. The way Odele would.

I fiddled with a button on my fur cloak, yanking it off. Then I slipped my hand out from the bars, feeling for the lock. My cheeks pressed against the cold steel as I felt my way towards the keyhole and shoved the tip of the button in.

I could almost hear Odele's voice there guiding me to be smart.

Hurry, you Iolish bastard, she'd say with irritation and a little bit of fear.

I bit the inside of my cheek as I moved the button—a shark tooth—around. I twisted and wiggled and when I heard the snap of it breaking in half, I swore and tossed the remnants of it to the side.

Then I heard a clang and pressed closer to the bars, peering down the darkened hallway. There was a rushed stirring in the water, and I held my breath then loosed it just as Anneli barreled down towards me.

She was breathing fiercely, her chest rising heavily up and down. In her hand she gripped a rake, and her small gray-white braids floating against her cheeks. She was in her training leathers and fur cloak, as prepared for battle as she could be, given that Alexxandria had confiscated every Iolish's weapon.

"The war's started," she said by way of greeting. "The chaos drew the guards away, but we don't have much time. Take a stroke back; I need to break the lock."

I did as she bade, pushing myself away from the bars just as she brought the forked end of the rake up and banging down across the lock. She grunted with the force of her hits, banging against it repeatedly. Frustrated cries forced their way past her throat heavily as she tried and tried to break me free of my confines.

"Come. On!" she screamed as the rake came banging uselessly against the lock. "I couldn't grab the damn keys," she panted.

My hopes deflated. Of course she hadn't grabbed the keys. It was a sure way for her to land within the mouth of a damn wyvern.

"I'm not giving up." She lifted her rake higher and banged it once, twice, punctuating each bang with a vicious cry, "I. Am. Not. Leaving. You. Behind!"

"Hey! What are you doing?" We both startled at the voice and the sudden appearance of Uncharted guards. Three of them rushed forward right as Anneli whirled, brandishing her rake just as a guard brought his sword clashing against it.

She met his blow with a cry of strength that surprised the guard, sending him jerking back through the water. The other two guards spread out, flanking at her sides.

"Look out!" I screamed my fingers gripping the bars. Silt. Siltsiltsiltsiltsiltsilt—

I needed to get to her somehow, but I couldn't. I was useless here in my prison.

But Anneli wasn't an untried mermaid. She'd seen her fair share of battles, had fought her fair share of wyverns, and had taken down criminals herself.

The two guards at her sides lunged for her. She kicked her tail, shooting up for higher waters, and they crashed together, swords hitting and showering the dungeon in sparks. They shook their heads to clear the disorientation just as Anneli dropped from above again, parrying with her rake. She sent the forked end through the shoulder of one and yanked it back out, twirling, hitting the handled end against the nose of the other.

She moved effortlessly, like she'd been born and bred in battle. It was the blood of her warrior parents flowing through her veins. Her mother had been a general to King Isolde's legions. One of the best in history, and while she'd never received a single lesson from her parents, she'd honed her skills on her own.

She gave a cry now, though, as one of the guards brought the hilt of his sword slamming down against her temple in a surprised, unguarded move. She stumbled, and that was all they needed to attack.

The rake was slammed from her fingers, and she was kicked to the ground and hauled up by her braids once more. She screamed, not from pain, but from rage as he hauled her against his chest, arching her neck painfully.

"You stupid bitch," he spat against her cheek.

She bucked against him as the other two guards crowded around her.

"No!" she screamed.

I banged my fists against the bars. "Let her go, you bastards!"

I was merely background noise to them, and I'd be forced to watch them harm my best friend, my *sister*, and kill her while I was helpless to do anything about it.

"Let her *go!*" My fists pounded against the bars until my knuckles bled.

My chest compressed with my own terror as they grabbed her, beat her, and she fought against them with all that she had. Her tail kicked against the stomach of one of the guard's and he doubled over gasping.

"I'll kill you all," she threatened, her eyes shining with lightning fury. She was a storm raging across two-legger skies, a force to be reckoned with, and the dark promise of their deaths loomed in her gaze.

"Shut up!" A guard backhanded her and sent her sprawling to the ground. He kicked her ribs with his tail.

She let out a cry of pain.

"Let go of her, you bastards!"

The waters rumbled and a distant cry reached my ears, a cry I knew by heart, echoing throughout the steel dungeon.

A moment later a blur of black and white came barreling into the room, straight towards the unsuspecting guards. Their sudden screams were cut short as the orca tore through their flesh and ripped them apart in vicious, violent pieces.

The orca spit aside their bodies, letting their limbs float through the water unkindly, then it turned and bent gently to nudge Anneli with its nose.

"Anneli, you're okay," I breathed. "You're fine. Get up, you're okay."

Slowly, grunting, she lifted her arm and let her orca help her up. Relief washed over me in a single giant wave as she bent over and took in sharp breaths.

"Damn bastards," she groaned. "Told them… I'd… kill them all."

My fingers didn't slacken from the bars. "Anneli…" My throat was tight with emotion. I felt the sting of tears behind my eyelids at what I was about to say. She looked up at me, trust and love in her eyes, and even the slightest bit of fear.

That's what cleaved my chest in two. The fear. She was a mermaid who feared so little, and to see the expression so prominent on her features hurt.

"Anneli," I repeated. "You have to go right now."

She took in a breath. "I will," she said firmly. "We will. Just… give me a moment." She breathed heavily.

"We don't have a moment. More guards can come back at any minute."

She nodded and bent down through the remains of a guard, rummaging through the pockets of his fur cloak. When she straightened, it was empty handed. "Let me just find the keys."

"No!" I banged my fist against the bars and my skin split opened. She froze. "You have to leave now. You don't know when they'll come back or how many more. Hide the bodies and leave me here."

She shook her head back and forth, a glare slashing over her features. "I'm *not* leaving you. Don't ask it of me." Then she bent and rummaged through cloaks again. She came up empty handed and with a curse springing from her lips.

"How the hell don't they have keys?"

Disappointment pressed on me, but it didn't matter. What mattered was that she needed to get out. Now. "Anneli, you have to go now."

"I can't leave you!"

"You have to!"

She swam up to the bars, gripping them so our hands grazed. Tears glossed over her eyes, but she left them unshed.

I took a breath. "Listen to me. You have to hide the bodies and get out of here. Don't argue with me," I snapped when she opened her mouth to interrupt. "You have to leave me. You *have* to because you are my sister." Not by blood, but in heart; our situations had pushed us to become family, but it was more than that. It was love, wholly and entirely. "If something happened to you, I'd never be able to live with myself again. So do as I say and get the hell out of here, because if things go wrong, you are the *only* one who can get messages to Odele and Ytgar. Do you understand?"

"I—I—"

I reached through the bars and grabbed her by the cloak and pulled her close. "Do you understand?" I demanded.

Slowly, reluctantly, she nodded. "I understand."

My fingers released her furs and pushed her away. "Then go, and don't look back. Besides, if things *do* go wrong, I'm the only one who has contact with Alexxandria." I didn't even want to think about things going wrong, but I had to look at all the possibilities. "I can give you information if needed."

She nodded and turned, gathering up the strewn body parts without flinching. With one last lingering look my way, she and her orca left.

I watched her go, and when she disappeared from my line of vision, I swam backwards and sat down in my cell, listening to the torturous, heart wrenching cries of the battle beyond my prison.

Anneli

IT WAS TORTURE HAVING to leave Val. It was torture being so close to liberating him and then having to turn away and leave him locked in a cage. This whole mess of a situation was complete and utter silt.

With the help of my orca, we dumped the remains of the body. I led him back to the stables and into his stalls. He'd led me to free Val and helped me destroy the scum who'd attacked me, but what came next was too much, too violent. And while orcas were bred for violence and battle here in the harsh waters of Iol, I couldn't bring myself to lead this one to his death.

In the end, though, this was war, and there would always be death.

I just hoped and prayed to the gods that it wouldn't be Val.

Sister, he'd called me.

There had once been a time when I had felt more. When *we* had felt more. In our youth, we'd had nothing and no one but each other. It had been so easy to share everything. From our secrets, to our lives, to our bodies. But he hadn't been what I needed, or wanted, and yet the love was still there. It was alive within me like the burning of molten lava breaking past volcanic rock.

I loved him as a friend, as a lover, as a brother, and always would. He'd saved me, even when I couldn't save him.

But if I couldn't free him from the confines of his cage, then I'd do it in other ways. I'd fight. I'd get to Ytgar and Odele, and together we would win.

All around us, the Iolish were rising up in arms. I'd given them the message, and they'd taken whatever they could find to defend themselves, to kill, while Odele and her armies distracted the soldiers and the wyverns, drawing those eyes away from us as we tore apart the army from within.

I watched as guards who had become our tormentors were beaten into the snowy silt and killed instantly.

It was little more than they deserved.

They couldn't keep control over the Iolish. Even without weapons, even using rakes and jagged bits of ice instead of swords, they were fierce warriors. Their homes had been taken from them. They'd been enslaved, imprisoned, their homes destroyed.

Now, they were out for blood.

An ice shattering shriek rumbled through the water that had my head jerking up to Isolde Palace. A figure clawed its way up the top of it. Fierce and a brownish black, the beast was chained by the neck, broken chains that swung back and forth over the tip of the palace's spires. Its elongated neck was thrown back and it was screeching its rage to the waters.

From a high window of the palace, a figure swam from it, and I didn't need to see her—I'd never seen her before—to know who she was. Queen Alexxandria.

I caught a flash of red hair as she slipped up and mounted the beast. A moment later the beast let out another rumbling roar just before it leapt off the palace and swam west.

I watched it soar, my heart pounding viciously in my chest.

She was heading to the direction of the battle, in the direction of Ytgar and Odele.

"No." The breath whooshed straight out of me. "No."

I kicked my tail into a maddening swim. My whole body ached, my ribs felt like they'd been crushed, but I swam as hard and as fast as my bruised body allowed.

To follow the queen.

THE BEASTS MADE NO move to attack us or swipe at us. For the fiercest of the Drakes, they seemed a bit tame. It was as if they'd been raised in cruelty and chains and were waiting for instructions, though instructions on what, I couldn't be sure. I gazed up at the long line of their scarred, scaled bodies.

It wasn't until I heard it that I understood what they were waiting on, or rather, *who.*

The shrieks came to us first, a shrill sound reverberating through the waters. It sent the wyverns into a frenzy. They bucked against each other, their heads slamming painfully against each other. Their wings flapped up in the water, but the chains kept them pinned to the silt.

They answered the cry with shrill ones of their own, and the mere sound of their voices rising together sent a terrible kiss of fear down my spine.

I gripped my sword tighter, burrowing myself steadily onto the saddle of my mount. My shield weighed my arm down, but I lifted it, a silent command to the soldiers at my back to do the same.

We'd taken down her forces behind us and had all met here at the barricade, hoping sheer numbers alone would frighten the beasts.

But what could frighten a creature that was the most dangerous thing in the waters? Certainly not us.

Together we floated on our mounts before our soldiers, units undivided. Ytgar, Adrian, and I.

"She's here," Adrian said darkly.

I didn't need to ask him who he meant.

We already knew.

A beast as massive as the thing that had destroyed Iol came swooping down from higher waters. As it did, every single wyvern down the line lifted their wings and bowed their necks, submitting to an alpha. I'd listened to a conch on the subject in Draconi. Drakes were pack creatures, and the strongest among them was their leader. The only one they'd ever bow to.

And theirs had just showed up.

It glided and landed carefully along the wings of the other wyverns, lifting its own up in a show of brute force, casting a long shadow against the ice. Its skin was a ruddy brown-black color, with terrible scars marring along its body like it'd been tortured since birth. Interloping circlets of iron wrapped around its collared neck, the end of it swinging back and forth through the water.

It was vicious, with a crown of spikes framing the top of its head and dripping black teeth. Its neck lowered, and on the back of the creature there was a mermaid sitting on a saddle made of bone.

I watched with curiosity as Queen Alexxandria, my sister-in-law, all things considered, slid from her saddle and patiently swam her way next to her creature's face.

She wore a dress of dark velvet, a deep color that offset the paleness of her skin but somehow brightened the red of her hair. Her red strands had been braided back so not a slip was out of place or loose, and on her head, she wore the crown of Isolde royalty.

The crown of Queen Isadora.

Seeing it on her head made a seething rage erupt inside me, but I said nothing as I took the rest of her in. Half of her face was infinitely beautiful. Smooth, unblemished skin with features that were simply perfect, even more perfect than mine, like she was a goddess-born mer blessed with blinding beauty. It was in the curve of her eye, the arch of her brow, the plump pout to her lips.

But the other half of her face… it was covered completely with a half mask of metal and bone that curved over her forehead and down along one half of her face, her jawline, and her chin. The only thing visible to me was her milky white eye, and the scars that bisected down to hide beneath that grotesque, ugly mask.

I didn't want to admit that she looked terrifying, but she did.

And when she spoke, her voice was melodic, and the currents swept the beautiful sound of it towards us and our soldiers, loud and pretty all the same. "Hello, little brother." The visible half of her face twisted up into a smile. "I see you've brought your armies to me." Her eyes flicked over to me. "And your wife."

A soft growl emanated from Adrian's throat. "Sister," he greeted coolly, and there was no disguising the hatred in every curling word of his tone. "I told you we'd meet again."

Her attention shifted back to him. "Yes, I do recall you saying something to that effect. What were the words, exactly?" She tapped a finger against the chin of the mask. "Ah! I remember. 'And the next time we meet, it will end with my sword piercing your heart, and the life leaving your eyes, and

I'll weep, dearest sister, for the mer that was lost to me so long ago.'" Her smile turned cruel, and Adrian didn't react at all to what she'd said.

I wondered what he was feeling, coming face to face with her again.

This was the first time I was meeting her, and while her entrance had been rather impressive, I was getting more annoyed by the moment.

"Here you are," she continued, "yet your sword is not in my heart and I am still very much alive. But you will not be for much longer."

"Threaten me all you like, Alexx." He pointed his sword in her direction. "I *will* have your life. Either right here, right now, or another time. The result will always be the same. You will die."

Soft laughter trickled out of her throat. "Such big words for someone who finds themselves so outmatched, wouldn't you agree? I have an army and you have…" Her gaze slipped to the soldiers now, and I could feel some of them recoiling from that too perfect half of her face and the other grotesque side as well. She sneered. "…nothing. You have nothing compared to what I have. Nothing but a handful of Iolish soldiers and a pretty new bride."

When she turned the force of her full attention to me, I lifted my chin higher, daring her to test me. I was feeling murderous right now. *Test me,* my eyes pleaded. *I'll stab a barracuda.*

"Such a pretty face," she purred, and the words themselves sounded like a threat and a promise rolled into one. "I don't believe we've been properly introduced. I am Alexxandria Ezarah Evander, Queen of the Uncharted and of Iol."

Hearing her give herself the title of my husband's birthright sent rage coiling up and erupting into exploding lava within me. I wanted to arch my sword, throw it like a spear, and watch it slice over the exposed half of her face.

I kept my cool. I wouldn't have any other time, but the mer were depending on me. Lives were at stake. And… and she had Val.

I had to use my intelligence, not sarcasm, not my wit.

"You give yourself the title of a queen when you are nothing but a usurper with a crown, but I'll play. I am Odele Malabella Oriana, Duchess of Castle Frost, Princess and heir to the throne of Thalassar, Queen of the Uncharted Waters." A smirk tilted my mouth. "And unlike you, I don't need beasts to steal kingdoms for me. I have plenty in abundance."

A dangerous game, that's what it was, but she met me power for power.

"Then you don't mind if I keep this one for myself?"

"On the contrary, I'm not very good at sharing my things. Never have been since I was a guppy with a crown and the kingdom I was to inherit resting on my shoulders. Iol is *mine*, Queen Alexxandria, and I will ask you only once to surrender it or face your death."

If she surrendered, I'd kill her anyway, but she didn't need to know that. She didn't need to know anything except my own strength that I felt rising up in me as I faced her.

"Such big threats for mer who haven't the armies to best me." She lifted a finger and stroked it over her wyvern's sharp horn. The creature stirred but didn't make any sudden movements. "You forget that I could decimate all of you right now. I could unleash every single one of these wyverns against your pathetic excuse for an army and watch them die. Then, I would take you back to the palace with me, Odele, and take extra care with your torture for being Thalassarin alone."

She was right. She could decimate us right now. We'd put up a fight, but even I could see the losing odds here. She wasn't attacking, even when she had the advantage, so what did she want?

"You haven't seen the extent of my armies yet, Alexxandria," I bluffed. I had to make her think we had aid coming to us, or she might just rip us apart.

The queen threw her head back and laughed. "Such pretty lies from such an ignorant youth. You think I do not know that no aid is coming? And who could blame the kingdoms? Why would they ever help you? I've heard the rumors about my brother's wife. Selfish and daft, a stupid mermaid who cares only for jewels and finery. That is a trait all those in the seven sea kingdoms share, I think, as not even Prince Ytgar or the other Iolish realized their Prime Minister betrayed them to me since the beginning."

Her voice was taunting, cruel, and the words sent a jolt through me. Bastard. That selfish bastard. I knew he was a worthless sack of filth, knew he'd been a pathetic excuse of a merman. I wished he was in front of me now, so I could shove my sword through his throat and watch him writhe through the water like a fish on a hook.

Bastard. Traitor. Treacherous bastard.

I dared to sneak a peek at Ytgar. He betrayed nothing but the strong workings of his jaw.

"Think what you will," I replied tightly. "But if you do not surrender now, you will feel our might and our rage, and we will take back what is ours in violence and in blood."

Slowly, she pushed her dark coppery tail and swam backwards where she mounted her beast again. As if this conversation was nearing its end.

I reached for the reins of my mount with my shield arm and held them steady. The battle was beginning.

"You are mistaken, Princess. You see, it is you who will feel my might if you do not surrender. It is all over you." Her gaze swept over all three of us, then behind us to our armies, before going back to us. "Bow before me," she commanded. "Bow before the might of my wyverns and the strength of my army. Bow before the Queen of the Uncharted and Conqueror of Iol, and I will be lenient with your souls."

"Lenient with our souls?" Adrian snarled. "You still speak as though you are as untouchable as a goddess, but you are not. You can bleed and die like the rest of us, and it is you who will die here today, because we will not bow down. We will not surrender."

The soft calculation of rage flicked on and off in her eyes. She ignored Adrian and turned to Ytgar. "What about you, Iolish Prince? I have made you many offers of leniency and you have ignored every single one. This is the last. Bow to me as your new queen or suffer my wrath."

Ytgar looked up, looking like an old Viking god of legend himself with battle ripped furs exposing the thickly corded muscles on his arms. His face was etched into many hard lines of fury and a thirst for vengeance that mirrored my own. I heard him take in a single breath and let it loose. He looked the queen straight in the eyes and smiled and said, "I choose your wrath."

Something akin to disappointment seemed to shine in the yellow depth of her eye. "The love I have for my little brother will buy you this day only before we meet tomorrow on the battlewaters. Think of it as my gift to you. As for my wrath, that you will feel now." Though the words were calm, I could feel an undercurrent within them. Something dark and dangerous.

The queen snapped her fingers. A single moment later, two figures appeared from the waters above, one guard escorting someone else.

The sight of her made my breath catch tightly in my throat. I wanted to look at Ytgar, but I couldn't find the will to turn away as Alexxandria escorted Queen Isadora Isolde before us all.

Ytgar

THE SIGHT OF MY grandmother nearly brought me tumbling from my mount and bowing down in the silt. What had once been a mighty queen, someone I'd looked up to in my youth, someone strong and powerful was a fragment of that before my eyes.

Her long white hair had been shorn from her head entirely so that only wisps of hair remained. Her eyes were wide and slightly haunted, but it was her body that worried me the most. Clad in a simple nightshift, I could see the frail body beneath. Not muscular like the Iolish should be, but thin and covered in lacerations. As if she'd been starved and tortured.

Silver eyes met my own. My grandmother looked down on me, and her expression changed. Weakness was gone, like it was something that didn't exist in her vocabulary. And it was then that I knew that she wasn't strong at all but had always pretended for me. So that I could find strength in her.

Seeing her put that strength into place now made every single terrible thing I'd ever said or thought of her vanish within a single instant. She was strong. She was fierce. And she was showing it now as she straightened her posture, even as the guard shoved her forward. Her hands were bound behind her back, so she stumbled but righted herself just as the guard left.

My grandmother floated before the face of Queen Alexxandria's wyvern, looking like the queen that she was.

"I see the fear in your eyes, Ice Prince. Will you surrender to me now? Will you bow?"

I tore my eyes away from my grandmother for a split second to train my glare on Alexxandria. She looked so smug atop her beast, wearing the crown of my family as if it belonged on her filthy head.

The rage inside me was an ice storm looking to kill, but also desperate to survive.

"Well?" she prompted.

I looked to my grandmother again, feeling everything within me weaken, because I knew what was coming, even if I didn't want to accept it. I knew what would happen next, and whose death it would bring.

I looked into those eyes. They were the eyes of my father, they were my eyes, and I'd never realized how alike we were until this moment.

It was those eyes that screamed at me as she stared. *"Do not bow down. Do not surrender."*

My hands trembled and I tightened them on both sword and reins so no one could see the fear that was thrumming so wildly in me, out of me, around me.

"Bow," Alexxandria commanded. "Or your grandmother dies."

My heart skipped beats, and my breath caught painfully. The scales were carefully balanced now. If I bowed to save my grandmother, the symbol of strength and resistance we'd worked so hard to build for our army would crumble. It would make me a traitor to them and our cause. But if I didn't, my grandmother would die.

I couldn't have more family around me dying. I couldn't. It would end me. My mother, my father, and her? It was something I didn't think I'd ever be able to come back from.

My resolve was breaking, and my grandmother could see it. She knew what I was going to say. Somehow, she'd always known my thoughts. She straightened and she spoke, "We come from the first Vikings, from the savage warriors of ice and snow and steel. Our ancestors have gifted us their savage cunning; we take what we want, we survive in the harshest of conditions. We are strong, and we are proud. We are of the Neves Isolde lineage, my dearest grandson, and we *bow to no one*."

Tears stung behind my eyes, and I forced them away to look at her one last time.

One last time.

My grandmother looked forward, tearing her eyes away from me. "I will never bow to you," she said, her voice rising to be heard like the whistling of a snowy current pushing through the water. "I choose death."

And so I would, too.

"I choose death," I echoed the words with a heavy, treacherous heart.

Alexxandria smiled cruelly, though only one half of her face was visible. I waited; waited for the sword to fall, for my grandmother's head to roll. But the swinging axe never came. Instead, Alexxandria chuckled softly and murmured a single, cutting word:

"Feast."

And her wyvern swallowed my grandmother whole.

The sounds of Ytgar's screams were drowned out by the cruel, calculated voice of my twin sister.

"Tomorrow, we'll meet in battle."

Ytgar's voice rose, a single word repeated over and over again.

"No!"

No.

No.

He slid from the side of his mount and lurched forward, making his way up towards Alexxandria.

"Ytgar, no!" I jumped from my own beast and tackled him into the silt. His face shoved into the snow, muffling his terrible cries. He bucked and fought against me and I used all my strength to hold him down. "If you attack her, you'll die." My voice was cool warning in his ear. He sobbed into the snow but stopped moving. When I was sure he wouldn't slip from my grasp, I looked up.

I watched with a detached sort of clarity as my sister nudged the beast beneath her and it turned to swim away. With it gone, every single wyvern that formed a wall, barricading us out, snapped up tall to keep us from swimming after her. To keep from even a single archer's arrow from hitting her through the back of the head.

In her wake, she'd left a rippling shock through the soldiers, and a heartbreak I could feel curl around me in a phantom grip emanating from Ytgar.

His whole body slackened, but his shoulders were tense, his fingers digging into the silt. The sobs racked through his whole body, and the force of his sobs cleaved my soul in two.

My sister had done this; my flesh and *blood* had cruelly, unflinchingly commanded her wyvern to swallow the Queen of Iol whole. There was nothing I could have done to stop it, logically I knew that, but the guilt consumed me like the gargantuan mouth of her beast.

Beside that, a pit of rage carved a hollow path through my gut. It tore through me like talon curved claws until my body shook as hard as Ytgar's; but instead of heartbreak, it was a thirst and a single consuming thought that nearly pushed me over the edge.

Revenge.

Odele slipped from her mount. Gone were her sword and shield as she bent to place her hands against Ytgar's back. Her face had paled, but her words were soothing as she murmured into his ears, urging him to please get up.

He didn't move.

He wouldn't.

My sister had a terrible way of rendering a mer dead while living.

So I leaned down, my lips grazing the soft lobe of his ear. Not in a sensual way, but in a dangerous one, holding all the thrilling promise of murder and blood. "She will pay," I vowed low so only he could hear. "Together, we will make her pay for this."

And she would. I'd let her go once before, a shameful secret I'd kept from Odele and the others. So long ago we'd faced one another in battle, and I'd looked into her face and seen the broken expression of a sister I couldn't protect, and the guilt had consumed me.

So I'd made that vow, that if I ever saw her again, I'd kill her.

I wouldn't make the same mistake twice.

This time, I vowed I would kill her, even if my soul was completely destroyed in the process. I'd been cruel to many in my life, because my circumstances had forced me into it. I could be cruel; at the time, I couldn't be to her.

Now, the rules had changed.

She'd threatened Odele, she'd broken Ytgar's heart.

So tomorrow we would ride and meet in battle, and I would finally end her life.

IT WAS THE ICE that hid me from Alexxandria's view as she and her wyvern soared through higher waters and back to Isolde Palace. It was the ice who bore witness to the shock that exploded within me. It was the ice who muffled my cries of fury and heartbreak at what I had just witnessed.

And it was in the ice and silt that I buried myself as my own agony rendered me immobile. My teeth clamped down on the back of my hand as I tried to avoid crying out, but the sob wrenched out of me, torn from the depths of my soul.

The sound of snapping jaws clamping over the body of my queen would forever live within the threads of my nightmares. The sight of her fragile body would be the last memory I ever garnered of my grandmother.

Oh gods.

I pressed my closed eyes into the curve of my tail to keep the tears at bay.

My whole life, I'd pushed the truth so far away from myself, from my mind and my soul, that I hadn't ever stopped to fully register it until this single moment.

She'd been my family; the mother of my father. She hadn't known of my existence, and I'd tried not to think about hers beyond what she was, above all else: my queen.

The intricate truth of what she really was, that some of her blood flowed through my veins, crippled me. She'd died without ever knowing of me and I was alive, knowing that what the self-proclaimed Queen Alexxandria had done would not be forgiven.

I'd make sure of it.

We Iolish were proud mer. As quick to fight one another, but even quicker to band together against a common enemy who dared threaten our rulers. And Alexxandria had killed our queen.

I forced my limbs to cooperate, forced myself to get up from my position of weakness. I let every emotion swirl within me, the tempest of a storm; I let it build and build, let it fester until I was forced into a quiet rage that begged for release.

And I *would* release it.

Iol would release it.

Together, we would fight until there was nothing left of the Uncharted scum that had dared to invade our home.

Together, we would kill them all.

Shadows of Ytgar's fragmented heart followed after us as we led him back to camp. A battle defeated, our hearts heavy with the loss of the Queen of Iol, and hatred threatening to consume our every broken thought.

Ytgar swam into our shared tent, a dejected, far away look on his face, but with his shoulders thrown back and his head held high, as if there was still fight left in him, even after seeing what he'd seen and watching a loved one die before his eyes.

I had no words for comfort, nothing to offer him except for the promise of vengeance that stuck to the roof of my mouth and tasted bitter. Adrian said what I couldn't, promised the future of retribution that we would wreak tomorrow in battle. He squeezed Ytgar's shoulder, though the Iolish Prince did not move, then Adrian turned, and we shared a look of equal parts heartbreak and fury just before he nodded once and exited the tent.

A whole conversation had transpired between us just now. He needed to go prepare his generals for the battle tomorrow, count our losses, and mourn our failed plan. I was to stay here with Ytgar and get through his silence somehow.

Ytgar took slow, steady strokes towards the table that sat in the center of the room, placing his knuckles against the surface. His shoulders lifted and his head hung low, the curtain of silver-white strands of hair hiding his expression, his pain.

My throat tightened.

I hadn't been close to Queen Isadora. To be honest, I hadn't even liked her, but she was Ytgar's grandmother, and while his relationship with her had been strained, he loved her. That was the strange thing about family. They could push you, doubt you, belittle you, or make you feel entirely too small, and yet still you loved them, deep down.

"She died bravely, in the end." My voice was but a mere hoarse whisper that carried over to him with the soft flow of the water.

His shoulders trembled and I wondered if he was crying, sobbing, vowing revenge like I had with the death of my cousins, Silviya and Jessinda.

I dared take a stroke towards him. I wasn't very good at offering comfort, or even good at receiving it. But Ytgar needed me; he needed *something.*

My hand clamped down on his shoulder and squeezed. "She was a warrior through and through."

Ytgar whirled then, the movement so sudden that my arm jostled painful as he yanked his body away from me, leaning away and glaring down at me with rage in his silver-white eyes.

"Shut up," he ground out tightly, furiously.

I blinked, not sure how to respond. "What?"

"I said *shut up*. Don't pretend to know what my grandmother was or wasn't. She wasn't a warrior and she wasn't brave. She was a cruel old mermaid who hated me for what happened to her son. As if it had been my fault that he and my mother died in the orca accident." His chest heaved with the force of his ragged intake off breath. He glared down at me, and everything about him in this moment was unkind and frightening.

Gone was the merman I'd fallen in love with, and in his place was the Iolish bastard who had kept me from swimming away from an unwanted marriage to his prince. He stared at me as if I were a stranger, like we had been strangers so long ago. As if we were strangers now instead of husband and wife.

"The orcas killed my parents, and then the title of prince befell me, and my grandmother despaired because I was the shame of the family. Nothing I ever did was good enough and she was cruel and vicious, so don't float in front of me and tell me how brave she was, because she wasn't brave. She was stupid."

I knew he was only saying these words, digging them out from an infinite well of pain inside. He didn't mean them. Ytgar would never mean something like this.

No matter how many times we argued or fought it had never been like this, and I wouldn't let him close himself away from me like I did him time and time again. Not in this.

I placed my hand against his chest, feeling the erratic pounding of his heart through the tattered furs. The moment my palm touched him, his hand shot out to grasp my wrist so tightly, I cried out in startled pain.

He whirled us, slamming my lower back into the edge of the table. His hands gripped my wrists, keeping them pinned at my sides, while he pressed close to me. So close.

But his eyes held no passion, even when I could feel the hard press of his length beneath his tunic against me, there was no flare of desire. There was nothing but rage.

I knew then what it was he truly needed. The same way I'd needed to feel the push and pull of aggressiveness between our bodies when Silviya had died, he needed this. The reminder; of what, I didn't know. He didn't need the caring princess, the one who would hold him as he cried.

He needed me as I was, and what I could be and offer.

"Let go of me," I hissed through my teeth.

His eyes flared. "No."

I brought my head crashing forward against his arched throat, and he grunted at the sudden impact of pain but held firm.

The flickering rage in the depths of his eyes chilled me more than the Iolish waters ever could. Down to the bone I felt fear; not true fear, but the anticipations of it, and what that gaze could do to someone other than myself. Because I knew Ytgar would never hurt me. Not truly.

"You are starting a game you know you can't win," he said darkly, slowly. His head bent so we were but a fraction apart. His lips hovered dangerously above mine and curled into the smile of a sea viper.

I matched him with one of my own. "I think not."

And then my tail curled around the length of his and I shoved with all my might.

Nothing happened, and I jerked away, my lower back digging into the edge of the table. I foolishly realized that anytime I shoved and he stumbled, he'd been letting me do it to him; he'd been giving me power over him when this merman built of ice could easily overpower me. Logically, I knew that. I'd known that but hadn't given it a thought because I knew, even when I'd hated him, that Ytgar would never harm me. It was still startling to realize that all of my strength wasn't enough to move him even a centimeter.

It only seemed to make him angrier.

He pinned my hands behind me, using one big hand to lock them in place. The other he shoved through my hair, tipping off the crown and tangling out the braids. His fingers curled around the strands and dug into my scalp.

He tipped my head back, and my lips ached with the imaginary feel of him, with the anticipation that he might take my mouth in his and devour me down to the roots of my soul.

His eyes bore into mine, but I couldn't read him beyond the hard, heartbreaking agony that he shuttered behind this; behind the hard press of his body and the fury I knew he needed to unleash.

His hands slipped from my hair and traveled to my waist. I felt his touch like a brand as his palm encircled my hip, but a moment later his touch was gone, and he pulled my wyvern knife from its sheath. The slow sliding of it against leather sent a chill racing down my spine.

He brought it up to my eye level, tapping the tip of the blade against my chin. He slid the edge over my skin softly, so softly so he didn't knick my skin.

I wondered in some wild, crazy part of my mind why I found every single move of his body, even this, sensual rather than terrifying. It should be terrifying, but it wasn't. It was everything I never knew I wanted. Slowly, the knife went down the long length of my neck and with a quick jerk of his wrist, it cut through the strings holding my cloak together. Then the tip got dangerously close to my skin as he began cutting away line after line of embroidered snowflakes and leather and velvet. The rip of the material as he sliced through it rang loud throughout the tent, but all I heard was the erratic pounding of my own heartbeat.

He tore all the way down to the hem, and then lifted to tear through the chemise and corsets underneath. There was a cold, calculated violence about him. He always took his time, was always slow and methodic in all things, even as he tore apart the last of my clothes into tattered ribbons. The material parted to bare me before him, to display the evidence of my arousal.

He tossed the knife to the side and I waited, holding my breath. Every second was a waiting game; he always built the anticipation high. I waited for that, for that slow building pleasure…

A slow build that never came.

Because a tether on him seemed to snap, and it was like unleashing a violent orca from the confines of its cage to watch it buck and wreak havoc.

He lifted his own furs and tunic, and he shoved himself deep inside me.

A gasp tore from my throat, a sound borne of surprise, as the sudden invasion of his body filled me to the hilt. When he began to move, it was in angry, punishing strokes that pushed my body harder against the table until I felt the pain. It was a sensation that mingled in with the quick strokes in and out of my body.

His grunts sounded in my ear, and other than that growling, feral noise, he said nothing else. Words were unnecessary when his body said it all. He was a force to be reckoned with; he was power and the rage of a storm.

His fingers gripped at my skin hard enough to leave bruises and my back cried out with each shove of his body against mine. But the pleasure? It came later, exploding inside me as he hit and hit against that soft place of desire.

This was a punishment, and I took every bit of it as if I deserved it. When he shoved my body down against the table, my hands landing on either side of my head, his member still hard inside me, he moved. His fingers dug into my hips, yanking at the ribbons of material that coated my body.

His mouth opened and threw a string of guttural Iolish at me that my mind fought to understand, but I couldn't think past the shock of pleasure pulsing through the front of my body. I didn't have to understand to know he was degrading me, treating me like little more than a harlot he could take against this table at his pace.

I didn't push back, even as my hands ached to reach up and push against his chest, scrape my nails across his face, or counter with a violence of dark screwed up passion myself. Because this was his moment, and he needed this, and for him I would lay myself bare in a way I'd never done before.

I'd offer up this control like he'd done so for me and take every thrust of him inside me because he was breaking, shattering before my eyes, and I was powerless to stop it except in this. So I closed my eyes and let myself feel both the pleasure and the pain in the movements of his body. I closed my eyes against my own emotions roiling within me like a storm. I closed my eyes and let him find his comfort in me in the only way he knew how, the comfort he could take.

I accepted every single broken bit of him. Wholly. Irrevocably. Just the sight of it was enough to break me too.

So together, we shattered, we screamed, we cried…

…and we were built anew from the crumbling structures of our heartbreak and sorrow.

EVERY THRUST WAS AN angry confession I couldn't admit to aloud. More like, I was too cowardly to admit to aloud.

Coward. Coward. Coward.

I couldn't face the truth of what had happened. My mind couldn't shut it out. The frail image of a once powerful body. The look in her eyes. One moment there, one moment gone. The sound of the beast's jaws snapping closed. Instant death.

Thrust.

Thrust.

Thrust.

All my life since my parents died, I lived in a sense of perpetual obedience fueled only by fear. That I'd never be good enough. That I wasn't what my grandmother wanted me to be, and I hated her for it.

Coward.

Why hadn't I protected her? Why had I *watched?*

The anger I held for myself came out in every agonized thrust of my hips. I couldn't hold back the feeling within my chest as it expanded… expanded…

Odele cried out beneath me.

I knew what I was doing to her, and the more primitive part of me didn't care. Because if I was to suffer, then she very well would, too.

Everything within me snapped. All my carefully constructed control went to ice as I slammed into her again and again and again, throwing my head back to roar.

I fell into the aftermath of what I'd done to Odele, treated her like no more than a common harlot without care, with my heart cracking in my chest. I dropped my forehead to the crook where her neck met her shoulder.

Delicate; she was so delicate, so soft.

I'd always been careful with her. Even when we'd fought, even when she'd forced me to retrieve her every time she swam away, I kept the brute in check, kept my control in place, even when she had a way of making me lose it. And that rough game had become a part of us, a buffer to keep us from feeling what it was we really needed to feel. Even when I was aggressive, even when she unleashed the full hell of her fury, I pushed back but a simple fraction.

Not this time.

I hated myself for this, too.

"I'm sorry," I whispered, my voice breaking against the softness of her skin. "I—I'm *sorry.*"

She should push me away, lift my heavy weight off her body. She didn't, and I couldn't very well find the will to move, either. What she did, though, surprised me.

Her fingers slipped into my hair, and she pulled me closer so we were both angled over the table. "Ssh," she cooed. "It's alright."

It was those words that broke me entirely. I would have preferred her hatred, the sparring of vicious words back and forth so I wouldn't have to feel the gentle touch of her hand and finally accept what had happened.

But she did, and I *broke.*

The tears poured out between the pathetic, rasping sobs. Every emotion clawed its way up my throat, erupting straight from my chest. I gripped Odele tightly, pulling her towards me by the waist. I didn't feel anything else but the infinite well of pain. I was still hard inside her, but there was nothing… only this crippling heartbreak.

"She's dead," I sobbed against her, the sound agonizing and echoing in my ears.

"I know." Her words weren't meant to be either cruel or soothing, but they were gentle. The gentlest, most difficult truth I had to bear.

The next words tumbled out of my mouth in a whispered rush. "Everyone I love dies."

Odele's body tensed, and though I couldn't bear to see the expression on her face, I found enough strength to pull away slightly to look into her eyes. They were searching, tender, and whatever fragmented remnants were left of my heart, she cleaved with that look.

"Is that what you think?" It was a whispered question as her hands slipped to my face, thumbs rubbing against my cheekbones.

"It's what I know, and this just proves it to be true. Everyone I love dies." My throat tightened, but I pushed past my biggest fears, and for the first time in my life shared them with another mer. "Who's next to die? You? Val? Adrian?" I held her tighter, wishing there was somehow a way to mold her into me. "I'm cursed. My lineage is *cursed.*"

"I don't know anything about curses, and I don't know if I have the words…" She cut off, swallowed, and something in her eyes shone. "But I think I understand. My whole life I've felt the same way." Her breath hitched and her eyes closed as if blocking out imaginary pain. "My aunt, my mother, my sister, and I almost lost Odalaea." Her palms pressed tighter against my cheeks as she seemed to pull me closer. "I understand. I have no words, but I understand."

My forehead touched hers. A sense of relief swept through my body just before it rippled away when a cool voice said from behind us, "I understand, too."

My whole body stiffened with shame, though a part of me was too exhausted to even want to muster up anger that Adrian had appeared in my most vulnerable moment, and I hadn't even heard him enter the tent.

Slowly, I lifted my body from Odele's, pulling her up into a sitting position on the edge of the table. I started to leave, to pull away from her, but her tail wrapped around mine and her firm hands kept me in place.

"How long have you been floating there?" Odele asked, a tiny hint of chagrin in her voice.

I threw a look over my shoulder to find him at the entrance of the tent, his arms crossed against his chest. There was no look of amusement over his features, but carved lines of tiredness, of something grave and angry.

He sighed and came deeper into the tent, pulling off his battle leathers as he went.

"I heard all of it," he confessed with no remorse, pulling everything off with deft movements of his fingers until he was in nothing but his tunic. His eyes found mine and they softened. "Come to bed."

Odele's body squeezed mine before she let me go. I pulled away, sweeping her into my arms. I swam us both over to the makeshift bed on the floor of the tent where Adrian was already settling in.

I set Odele down and followed quickly after, keeping my hands on her skin. It was the briefest of contacts that kept me tethered to what, I didn't know, but her touch was what I needed. She calmed my pounding heart if not my tumultuous thoughts.

"I have a confession," Adrian said reluctantly.

I half turned to look at him, but his hands were behind his head, his eyes staring at the tent ceilings. Shadows of the lava globes danced across the material.

"What is it?"

Adrian took a deep breath. "Years ago, I met my sister in battle. I had the chance to end things but—" He broke off, and I could hear his swallow tight in his throat in the dimness. "I let her go." He turned to look at me, and there I saw it; an emotion that matched my own. Infinite sorrow. "I'm sorry," he whispered. "It's my fault. All of it. I helped create the monster she became. If I hadn't brought her to the seven sea kingdoms…"

"It's not your fault," Odele cut in firmly.

But Adrian wasn't looking at her. He was looking at me. As if what his sister had done, that one word she had commanded was a knife that he'd wielded or a weapon he'd forged. But I didn't place the blame on him. How could he have known the monster she would have become? No sooner could he have predicted the outcome of her insanity than I could have the death of my grandmother.

"It's not."

Adrian's eyes flicked to my mouth, as if he could read the words and find a lie in them, but there was none.

He settled back into the cushions, staring up at the ceiling. His hand slipped from behind his head and went to Odele and they grasped hands before he turned and pulled her against his chest.

"Tomorrow," he began, "there will be war."

"Can we not talk about that tonight?" Odele asked.

I pressed closer to her, wrapping my arms around her, and Adrian wrapped his arms around me so that we were tightly cocooned together. A unit, missing a single link.

A tightness gripped my chest. I missed Val. I wished he was here, and wondered how the rebellion had gone from within, and hoped the consequences of our own failure hadn't brought dire consequences for those within.

"Let's just... sleep right now, okay?"

I didn't want to talk about war either, or about what had happened today any longer. I wanted to sleep as if it might be my last night in the ocean, because it very well could be. I didn't want to stay awake contemplating our doom as it hovered over us. So I pressed closer and relished in the feel of their warmth and love as we slowly drifted off to sleep.

HUDDLED IN THE CORNER of my cell, my mind raced and raced for hours. All sound had drifted into a void of nothingness from the outside. Anneli never came back, and neither did any guards. For hours, I tortured myself with thoughts of my own making, with worries and nightmares that had no beginning and certainly no end.

It wasn't until later that the noises roused me from the corner. I darted over to the bars, wrapping my fingers around them and pressing my face against the cold steel.

Guards swam into my vision bearing weapons that they pointed at me. "Take a stroke back," one of them commanded in a guttural voice.

Slowly, I pried my fingers away and obeyed. The guard came forward and opened the gates to my cage slowly, gesturing for me to swim out. I did with my hands in front of me and they reached for me aggressively, twisting my hands behind my back.

A black sack was thrown over my head—as if it were necessary at all, when I already knew the palace inside out. I just wondered if this was a method of torture, but the darkness didn't scare me.

They led me to the throne room.

When they kneeled me on the floor and ripped the sack from my head, I knew what I'd see.

Yet still I was surprised when I saw her. She floated near the open window of the throne room, letting a cool current drift in. Clad in dark velvet and braided hair, she wore the crown of Iol on her head.

Something about her seemed different, less composed. She was speaking to herself in a low, fast, jittery voice that reflected in her twitching movements. Or maybe what was different about her this time was the fact that a black-brown scaled wyvern had its head shoved into the open window and was nudging her with the tip of its nose.

"Your Majesty, we've brought the Iolish scum."

She turned to me, her palm lightly pushing at the nose of the wyvern. It huffed a breath and disappeared out the window. I tried not to stare too long at the spot it had vacated. Instead I turned to her, swallowing at the expression on her face.

The rebellion hadn't worked. That much had been obvious from the moment the guards had gone to fetch me in my cell. Not knowing what happened to Anneli or anyone else… Was Odele alive? Was Ytgar? Adrian?

Fear thrummed a desperate cord in my chest over and over again until I couldn't breathe. I tried to keep my composure as Alexxandria took a few strokes towards me, but I almost doubled over, heaving in gasping breaths.

My shoulders shook, my whole body rattled, and she bent near me so we were face to face. Up close I could see every bump and ridge of that screwed up scar and the sight of it made me want to retch.

"Your friends don't care about you, you know." Her words were both gentle and cruel.

It snapped me out of my fear. I took a deep breath and met her cold gaze with my own but said nothing.

She straightened and took a stroke away from me, half-turning. She appeared to be fueled by madness. Her fingers twitched and her neck kept cocking back and forth.

"They're fools," she whispered, more to herself than to me.

The door behind me banged opened, and a voice drawled angrily, "Why did you do it?" I didn't need to turn. Prime Minister Rollo swam into my line of vision, putting himself dangerously close to Alexxandria.

She didn't flinch or show any visible signs of discomfort besides an impatient sneer and a discreet stroke back.

Rollo pressed closer. "You had the perfect bargaining chip and you wasted it! Why would you kill the queen?"

The blood drained from my face as I absorbed those words. The queen? Queen Isadora? I tried not to move, but I felt my body shifting closer.

"Who are you to question the decisions I make?" Alexxandria demanded.

Rollo's face was wild with fury. "I am the Prime Minister of Iol! I allowed you entry into this kingdom, and you promised me I'd be crowned king if I helped you conquer and sold you secrets. Killing Isadora was never part of the plan!"

Her fingers flittered up to her neck where she stroked them across the velvet languidly. "Plans change. They changed the moment my brother and his ilk decided to march here and try to steal what I've rightfully earned."

"Don't you see what you've done? Once the mer hear about this, they'll retaliate and try to destroy us from the inside like they did today."

So the plan *had* failed. Cosmically. I tried not to let my disappointment show. I tried to show no emotion on my face but listened with rapt attention at anything I could give to Anneli. Anything that might help us be free.

"The mer are no match for my forces. I will execute them if they dare defy me." She waved him off in a dismissive, queenly gesture. I hated her for it. Hated her for wearing the crown that belonged to the queen she'd murdered.

My queen.

Ytgar's grandmother.

Oh, gods of ice…

Ytgar…

"If you start killing the mer, Prince Ytgar will not stop until he has your head on a platter. That mer may be foolish, but he is a Iolish warrior. Do not forget."

So Ytgar was alive. I almost breathed a sigh of relief but caught it in my throat just in time.

Alexxandria narrowed her eyes. "That sounds like a threat, Rollo."

Rollo had the good sense to pale at the deadly, venomous tone in her voice, but he foolishly took another stroke towards her until they were almost touching. "I am your *ally*. You promised me a place at your side if I helped you. I expect you to *listen* to my advice and heed it." He made the foolish mistake of gripping her upper arm until his knuckles went white. "Do you understand?"

"I understand you are trying to lecture me on matters of war when you've fought in none." She didn't pull away, and I felt a slow sliver of trepidation run down my spine at the lethal sound of her voice and look in her eye. Something bad was coming. I felt it down to my bones. "You expect me to listen to a treacherous scum like you who sold out his kingdom for the promise of a crown instead of earning it himself?" A slow curling smile splayed over her lips. "Silly, foolish bastard." I watched as her hand went discreetly to her waist. Rollo didn't notice. He was mesmerized by her voice, the pretty smile, the menacing words. I didn't have time to cry out as she brought the knife swinging upwards and jerked it into his gut.

She barely blinked, as her hand moved up and down up and down. She stabbed Rollo with a rapid, angry force over his gut and his chest, her breathing heavy and a manic look coating her different colored eyes. It lasted so long, and the only sounds were the sliding sound of steel entering flesh and Rollo's pained gasps just before he went silent, his hand slipping from her arm.

Only then did Alexxandria pull away from him and watch as he dropped face first and floated dead in the water.

"You won't *ever* touch me without my permission again," she snarled to his corpse as she pocketed the knife again. She took a breath, turned to the window and said, "Feast."

The next moment happened in a blur. Her wyvern's head snapped into the window like a snake sliding into a hole. Its mouth snapped down on Rollo's body and dragged his corpse away, the echoing sound of bones crunching beneath teeth staying behind to ring loudly in my ears, and I knew without a doubt that I'd dream of that sound for the rest of my life, however long I had left.

Alexxandria smoothed her palms down the front of her dress, as if that could somehow help her smooth composure that she lost so drastically just now. I looked at her. My eyes strayed to those fingers, imagining the way they'd gripped the knife with such surety, how she hadn't even blinked when she'd taken his life, how she hadn't hesitated when she told her wyvern to feast.

I wondered then how she'd killed the queen and decided I wasn't sure I wanted to know.

She turned to me and came closer. I couldn't help myself as I flinched back from her proximity. She didn't seem to mind my reaction as she grabbed me by the front of my fur cloak and pulled me up at eye level easily. "Isadora was a test," she explained softly. "To see what it would take to get Ytgar and Odele to bow before me. They refused, you know."

Good, I wanted to spit out. I was glad they hadn't bowed to her, no matter the cost.

"But I know I can take everything from them, from *Odele.* I'll see her and Thalassar humiliated and all of her mer dead at my fins."

That wouldn't happen. Odele was too smart to be bested by this mer. Deep in my heart, I knew that, and still fear found its way inside of me.

"But you…" Her fingers slipped up to caress my cheek and I jerked away from her touch. "They would give anything for you, even bow to me. I am sure of it."

Dread tightened my stomach. "They won't," I hissed.

She merely smiled. "We will see tomorrow in battle, when you are chained close to me and they refuse to sacrifice your life for mine." And then she brought her hand up with blinding speed I didn't see coming and crashed her fist against my temple.

I fell back to the icy floor, pain blinking in and out of my mind.

Another blow to my head had me seeing the winking lights of two-legger stars.

Another had me giving into the darkness completely.

Odele

My fingers were steady as I methodically tightened my battle leathers against my body. The material was inlaid with leather on the outside and velvet for warmth on the inside. The neck and waist pulled together with belted chains of thin steel that didn't weigh me down. Seal leather belts crisscrossed over my chest and back where I shoved a series of knives through.

Instead of heavy steel shoulder plates, I opted for a lining of fur around my shoulders and the back of my neck, with a velvet cloak stitched onto the back where it flowed down to my waist. Like my warriors, I wore white and gray, but this time no crown adorned my head at all. My hair was braided tightly against my scalp and tucked in so nothing hung loose. So that no one could grab me by the hair.

Today, I was a warrior.

Grim faced yet determined, we mounted our beasts and headed out into battle.

The one plan we had to swiftly save Iol from tyranny had *failed,* so now we had no choice but to meet Alexxandria halfway in the battlewaters. Our forces against hers in the open waters of Iol, away from Aelfrost and without allies.

I could feel the whispered rush of words at Ytgar's, Adrian's, and my backs.

Doomed.

This was a hopeless fight and they knew it. Our forces were nothing compared to hers. I knew that. I should quit, surrender, bow to her like she wanted me to.

But if I did that, then what? She'd kill us anyway, enslave us in a cruel, unjust way; the same way she'd been enslaved and tortured herself. She would push past Iolish borders and conquer the kingdoms at her leisure. I knew I couldn't let that happen. Whether I died today or not in these battlewaters, I would protect what was mine until my last dying breath.

I pulled my mount to a stop. We weren't there yet, but I froze, my breath hitching in my chest.

Adrian and Ytgar, flanking my sides, stopped as well and the armies behind me did too. I could feel eyes on me. I could feel them wondering, questioning. Would I order a surrender? Would I really drag them to a war where we were so outmatched?

I turned my mount around to face them. So many faces looked up at me from behind their helms. Fear coated heavily at their eyes. Fear could get them killed. Determination could help them live.

I took a breath, and I spoke, my voice ringing out across the waters. "I've never been someone to be admired; not for my good deeds, anyway.

You probably look at this battle and think it is hopeless, that we cannot outmatch her. Perhaps you are right.

"I have no words to give you today except for these. I've lost most everyone I ever loved, starting with my mother, and I grieved her in all the wrong possible ways. I threw myself away from the shadow of her memory and into a library in the kingdom of Thalassar with kelps and conches as my only escape.

"Listening to the voices and sounds of battle took me to far away places with generals and captains. I lived it with them, I listened to them die, listened to them win, and listened to them lose. And we might lose today, but I will tell you that there will be no greater honor for me than to die alongside all of you.

"Because one day, they will sing songs of us, of how we made the impossible possible. About how we forged an alliance never seen before and marched into battle with fear, yes, but with determination and bravery in our hearts. One day, conches will be recorded on each and every one of us, and a little mermaid or a merboy will sit in a library listening to it, and our story will give them hope. They will take what we do here today; win or lose, whatever the outcome, they will take it. We will inspire and leave behind the legacy of our bravery for others who are too weak or too scared, and we will give them the push they need to emerge from the shadows and become the warriors they are meant to be." I pulled the sword from my sheath and held it high in the water, determination lining my every feature. "Are you with me? To the end?"

Swords slid through sheathes and lifted in the water, and they responded with shouts and cries that made tears blink behind my eyes. Because I had rallied them together, *me*. I was their queen, and they were willing to follow me into battle.

Till death.

I turned my mount and we barreled forward to meet Alexxandria in the open waters. They were waiting for us, miles of soldiers and wyverns floating at attention. I could feel the eyes taking us in; the sheer size of them was enough to intimidate, but I didn't allow myself to feel it.

Today would determine the fate of our future.

Today would determine the fate of my kingdom.

I lifted my sword higher and let out a battle cry and a command that shook through the waters in the echoing shouts of their own determination. We charged forward at the same time our enemies did.

No fear lived within me as I led my troops straight into the fraying clash of ice, steel, tooth, and claw.

And the battle truly began.

Ytgar

THE CLANG OF WAR was deafening. It was like a violent riptide of a wave that shoved bodies and steel and blood between us. It forced us apart, dragging us deeper into the fray of the war. My eyes didn't scan across the waters, my mind didn't concentrate on where Odele had disappeared to or even Adrian.

I couldn't concentrate on anything.

All I tasted was blood and revenge.

Every time my sword cleaved through the body of an enemy, I was on to the next one before the previous even fell. On and on, I maneuvered my way through armor and flesh. My muscles ached, but I didn't stop. All I saw was the frail body of my grandmother, the snapping of jaws shutting, and the death of my last living blood relative.

My sword of ice tasted foreign blood until the waters all around me were foggy with it, until they blackened with death and I breathed it into my gills, tasting the end of those around me.

And the end tasted sweet.

And I let my sword feast.

My mount tore through the lines in vicious sweeps of claw and teeth. Pushing itself off the snowy silt, it soared to higher waters and attacked the wyverns from above. The cries of these monsters filled my ears like a sweet symphony of the God of Death. Today, my god would reap through these waters and collect the souls of the fallen and relish in this war.

The cruelty emerged within me; the taste of the first moments of battle were infectious, unlocking something I'd wanted to keep hidden but would no longer.

I became what everyone in the Uncharted so feared. I became the King of Cruelty and Death and laughed as my beast ripped through the necks of wyverns. He clung to beasts bigger in size without fear, and this battle was like nothing I'd ever tasted in all its glory.

Scales and flesh flew around me before drifting to the silt below. The legion of my warriors soaring up to intercept our enemies.

For a moment, we seemed equally matched.

But the true battle hadn't even begun. Not for me, at least. No, the true battle would begin when my sister joined, yet I knew without a doubt she was not in these waters. She was biding her time, waiting, watching from afar with a nasty trick up her sleeve that would determine the fate of this war for good.

With an all-consuming rage, I kicked my fin into my mount's side and together we soared. Arrows drawn, I let them fly straight through the throats of the Uncharted who had chosen the wrong side, and I watched them fall into the mouths of creatures that tore them apart.

Again and again, the arrows zoomed through the water.

And each time my enemies were met with death, I laughed alongside the god that guided me to take, to kill.

To conquer.

Anneli

It was time for war.

If the foreign queen thought to intimidate us by publicly executing a few mer for rising against her the day before, she obviously didn't know the Iolish.

Descended from Vikings, the blood of conquerors, of warriors, swam through our veins. She could beat us, imprison us, kill us, but she would not break us.

Our spirits were as strong as our forefathers, and the gods of our mer smiled down at us this day as her armies swam to the battle waters to fight against our prince, our princess, and a new king.

I led the mer because there was no one else to do it, and for a single split second, I felt the blood of my mother coursing through my veins. Like this was what I was meant to do before I shook off the sensation.

Guards had been left behind to watch us. So little guards, and that was Alexxandria's mistake. She thought we'd been broken, were submissive due to fear. But if we had bowed our heads the night before when she had our mer slaughtered, it was only so she wouldn't see the hatred in our eyes and the vicious flash of a plot forming of her death.

We Iolish knew harsh conditions, we knew starvation, and we knew how to bide our time. So we waited until they were gone, the plan a silent thing spoken only between passing stares and hand gestures, nods and low whistles.

So it began.

I unleashed the orcas first, setting them free of their cages and watched them wreak destruction against the guards. Then we moved swiftly, because the best way to end her reign was to catch her by surprise from within.

With whatever tools we could find, anything that hadn't been confiscated, we raised in arms. I slid a small tool into my hand, a shovel with a pointed end, and went after the guards.

I met them among the fray of the orcas' chaos. They were distracted, trying to get them under control. I slid behind the one closest to me, and with all the force I could muster, stabbed the small shovel into his skin. It shocked him into distraction before I ripped his sword from his sheath and slid it across his neck.

Now armed, and capturing the attention of other guards, I faced off against our oppressors. A guard met my blow with his own, the force of it jarring my whole body. I felt the shock down to my teeth and pushed back against his strength. Uncharted circled me, and I thought back to the moment in the dungeon, with three of them surrounding me and how close I'd come to losing.

But I'd had a rake then. Now, I had a sword.

And I wouldn't be bested a second time.

I dodged a blow that stabbed towards me, while thrusting my sword out to another guard. He didn't see the blow coming, and the blade sliced straight through his side. He grunted, bending over and dropping his own weapon.

The fool. I rolled on my shoulder in the silt, picking up his sword as I went. When I straightened, it was with two swords and a thirst for their deaths.

They charged, and with a few expert maneuvers, my sword sliced through the neck of one and into the gut of the other. The third injured one dropped into the cold silt, scrambling away from me as I approached.

"Please," he begged. "Mercy!"

I smiled. "Mercy is for the gods."

Then I slit his throat.

Odele

IF THERE WAS ONE thing I was quick to realize, it was that battles were
nothing like I studied them to be, nothing like the conches portrayed them
to be. No one warned me that the stench of death permeating the waters
would make me want to gag between death blows, or that the waters got
warmer every time a mer fell, or that I'd taste the death of them heavily
on my tongue at such a close proximity.

My limbs were exhausted, my fins from swimming and my arms from
holding shield and sword. I'd been wounded, yet it wasn't a mortal wound
and I pushed on, furious as my sword pierced past armor and flesh.

Pretty soon, everything seemed to become a blur. I no longer saw the faces of my attackers, stopped mourning the deaths that I caused. I stopped looking closely at expressions and focused on the colors that marked friend from foe.

I'd long since stopped looking for Ytgar and Adrian in the chaos, but pushed through the lines of our enemies. I had no way to know who was winning and who was losing; all I knew was the clash of battle and death.

I cried out as my sword thrust through the neck of Uncharted scum and whirled as someone came barreling towards me. I almost cut her through, had it not been for the orca she mounted and the polar bear cloak she wore around her shoulders.

My whole body shuddered with a single wave of relief and I almost dropped to my tail right then at the sight of my friend.

"Anneli." Her name came out a broken word from my mouth, nothing but the bone deep exhaustion I felt pulling at my every limb and nerve.

Her eyes widened. "Look out!"

I acted on instinct, my body dropping to the silt. Something whirled above me, missing me by a hair's breadth. I turned, swiping my sword out at the fins behind me, cleaving through them and rendering the mer useless. He gave a cry of pain and dropped towards me, only to meet the tip of my blade as he impaled himself through the neck.

I got up, unsheathing my sword from his neck with a sickening sound then pushed him away with my fins. His corpse floated away from me and I turned to find Anneli sliding down from her mount.

Amidst the chaos of battle, we met in the middle and embraced.

Her arms wrapped tight around me for the briefest of seconds before she pulled away, her gaze scanning around us. A lump formed in my throat that was too painful to swallow.

"Val?"

Her throat worked as she swallowed, but she held her head high. "He wasn't in his cell."

If he wasn't in a dungeon cell that could only mean one thing.

"Alexxandria has him."

Anneli nodded. "She probably thought he'd been a good shield when you came for her—duck!" She grabbed my head and forced me down into the silt as a wyvern came swooping over where we'd been floating, snapping its jaw closed on empty water.

I gasped into the silt on the verge of having a breakdown. Seriously, war had a weird way of frazzling my nerves like that.

Anneli hauled me up once more. "The Iolish fought back, but all we did was manage to kill some guards and come here to help. Alexxandria is still at the palace; she hasn't come out at all, even when we were taking over. I swear I could see her watching from the window, smiling as if this was all a part of her plan."

A sudden wave of bodies pushed towards us, living bodies charging. I dared a quick glance around to find that all the Uncharted that had been fighting alongside me had been killed. There was no one in sight but Anneli and myself, facing off against hundreds of Alexxandria's mer.

I gripped my sword tighter.

"Not a chance, Princess." Anneli grabbed me and, as if I weighed nothing, threw me on top of her mount, following after me. She kicked it into a rapid swim. Above us, a beast swooped down, barbed tail knocking back the soldiers at our fins.

"Fall back!" Adrian shouted from above us. "There's too many of them! Our soldiers have fallen!"

No, no, *no*. We couldn't lose; we *couldn't*. But we were. We were being shoved back from the lines, and with a sweeping glance around, I noted that every one of our own soldiers was swimming away. We were outnumbered, and those too close to our enemies were swallowed whole into the chaos and didn't emerge again.

My throat tightened and I slammed my eyes shut against the tears that threatened to fall. Since the beginning, I'd known how hopeless this would be, I think deep down I always knew this battle would be lost, even if we lived on in the legacy of others, I knew somewhere in my heart that we would not be leaving these waters alive.

Her armies were just too great, her beasts too many. We were outnumbered, and not even all the intelligence in the world could have saved us from Alexxandria's wrath. I'd wanted so badly to believe we had a chance, that we could save my home and the mer I'd come to love. That I could be someone the mer could look up to. A queen they could be proud of like no one had ever been proud of me before.

"Oh my gods," Anneli breathed.

"What?" I followed her line of vision to the water beyond in the direction we were swimming towards and gaped.

In higher waters, a shadow loomed, a massive thing that was headed straight towards us.

"It's a trap!" Anneli shouted, pulling her mount to a stop. "Stop! They have us surrounded!"

Our soldiers jerked to a screeching halt as they noticed the figure approaching, too far away to make out, but with a speed that was baffling.

Anneli turned her mount from the threat. We were trapped like fish in a net. Threat from behind, and threat from in front. She voiced the words that were in the back of my throat. "We have to fight."

Hundreds of mer came hurtling towards us. We held out our swords.

"To the death," I whispered.

"To the death."

And we charged forward, a twin cry of rage on our lips. This... this was what it was to fight alongside a friend, and perhaps for a moment I'd stopped believing in myself, but as every single soldier followed us to their deaths, I knew that they never stopped believing in me.

Our swords clashed and we found ourselves surrounded from all sides, but we didn't relent. They'd take me to my death, but I'd drag them to the abyss with me.

My sword sliced fins into ribbons, a vulnerable part on the body of my enemies. I cut through them without mercy until I fell off the side of

Anneli's mount. The orca went down, nearly slamming its heavy body on top of Anneli but she rolled her body through the water at the last moment and landed floating up.

Her orca let out a soft cry of distress and just as she went to help it, she was flanked by enemies trying to cut her down.

From my position in the silt, I breathed hard. My sword had clattered from my hand and I scrambled to reach for it; the moment my hand closed around the hilt, a horn blared behind me.

A horn that should have been familiar. A sound my mind swam laps to try and identify. It was the sound of armies, it was the sound of war.

And then the waters darkened, and I knew without a doubt that whatever creature was behind us had caught up and I prayed for the end to be swift.

But that end never came.

Because at that moment, something dropped from the higher waters in a blur of black and red. Not just something, but someone. He moved through the water in lithe movements like he was the sword forged for this exact moment in history.

Where he moved, bodies fell and blood bloomed in savage bursts that darkened the waters nearly black. It was only when they cleared, did I see the dozens of bodies killed as if it had been nothing but a training exercise.

I had heard stories of him in battle, and they didn't call him the Dragon Prince for nothing.

"Kai…"

The Prince of Draconi gave himself a mere moment to smirk in my direction, his blue dragon eyes and elongated features simmering with the thrill of the battle. He whirled, a blur of battle leathers and the shining steel of a katana. Placing his fingers in his lips, he whistled, and the blur above us swooped down low and he jumped onto the back of his dragon and steered the creature into the thick of the battle.

Straight into the body of a wyvern.

The Draconians…

They'd come.

All around me dragons flew and met the wyverns half-way. Screeches filled the water and built a new hope on top of the fear of death. So many Draconian warriors on top of their beasts, and the mere sight of it was enough to bring the sting of fresh tears to my eyes at this history being made.

Iol and Draconi had disliked each other for so long, but now the dragon monarchy was flying into battle to free the orcas from the tyranny.

A smile widened my mouth and I looked up to find Anneli engaged in an epic battle with a skilled Uncharted soldier. They parried back and forth, the clangs of their swords a force rippling through the water. She fought with the fury of all her strength but was still pushed back. She fell into the silt.

My mouth opened to cry out, but a blur dropped from above in front of Anneli, and the Uncharted soldier never saw the katana coming towards him until it was too late, and his head was severed from his body.

The Draconian turned, sheathing his katana in the process. I didn't know how it was possible, but he seemed even bulkier than the last time I'd seen him. His long hair pulled back from his face, the lone strip of white prominent against the inky color of the rest of his hair. He wore black leathers and a simple fur coat, and that single slashing scar across the bridge of his nose looked silver against his beautiful face.

Kane Feng Han reached down and offered a hand to Anneli.

The whale trainer looked at it for a confused moment before she took it and he helped her up, pulling her close to his body, pressing her against his chest. "My lady." His voice was as smooth as candy, his smirk a bit arrogant. He bent and whispered something into her ear, too low for me to hear.

In response, Anneli extricated herself from him and darted past him to where her fallen orca lay.

The pain etched onto her features was too heartbreaking; I had to look away.

Another roar sounded overhead, but this one louder than the rest, and the wing beats the pushed against the water caused a riptide of waves. My nails dug into the silt, but I was pushed back, away, cut up in a tornado of water that spun me round and round again.

Shielding my eyes from flying debris, I stared in fascinating horror at the beast that drove our enemies to retreat, and the figure who sensually slid from the mount and landed beside me in a swirling storm of snow and silt.

Emperor Jiang Li.

He looked down at me, sprawling on the silt with a look that spoke of disinterest, but no judgement. Slowly, he reached out his hand, and I could have sworn I was dreaming, because I took the Dragon Emperor's hand and he helped me up.

"Your enemies have retreated," he said in Dracon. "For now. Gather your remaining troops. We have a battle to plan."

Leagues away from where the battle had been fought, a camp had been erected, mingling with our own. Draconian tents of black and red, with dragons resting outside of them and more soldiers, infinitely more soldiers that could match Alexxandria's completely.

Though weary, I felt a renewed sort of energy, a desperate need for answers. We'd swam here without getting any, as the Draconian had refused to explain. In my mind, I theorized so many things, whispered them with Anneli, Adrian, and Ytgar.

My husbands were covered in injuries, their chests still heaving from the strain, but they kept their heads held high with pride as they swept a look around the new additions to our camp.

I whirled on the emperor and Kai, a single word breaking past my lips. "Why?"

The last time I'd seen them, they'd been adamant that they wouldn't help, that they didn't care about Iol or the Uncharted and that their forces were better spent protecting their own borders from the threat that was Alexxandria.

What had changed their minds?

The question must have been written all over my face, for both Kai and the Emperor smiled. But it was the Eeperor who answered, "Someone was very clever in her persuasions."

"Odele."

I turned at the sound of my name to find Odalaea hovering near the entrance of a tent flap, her Black Moor dragon poking its head out from behind her.

Just the shock of seeing her, and after the day I'd had, caused my tail gave out beneath me and I fell into the silt. Odalaea rushed to me, dropping into the silt and snow in front of me.

I wasn't sure who reached for who first, but one minute there was an infinite amount of space between us and the next we were in one another's arms and we were crying, not caring who circled around us to watch.

"You came." The words tore from somewhere deep in my soul where I thought my family had abandoned me. The place inside me that said I was worthless and unloved, that no one could ever love me the way that I did them, that voice was silenced by this moment here as she gave me everything I'd ever wanted.

"I couldn't leave you, Odele," she whispered, bubbles rising from her eyes. She didn't swipe them away. "You're my cousin and I couldn't leave you."

"Thank you for coming for me."

Her hand cupped my cheek and the look in her eyes was tender. "I didn't come alone."

For a split moment, I thought my eyes were playing tricks on me. That the exhaustion I felt deep into my bones was somehow affecting my mind as well. My gaze strayed over her shoulder and held on the figure behind her, just a few strokes back.

A sob rose up within me and I was powerless as it ripped out.

Odalaea smiled. "*We're* your family," she said firmly, her grip tightening on me.

The doubts within me shattered completely. Every sliver of fear and sense of hopeless abandonment was lost. She'd come back for me. She had cared enough about me to bring not only the Draconian forces, but also the Thalassarin and Kappurin ones.

Because just there, over her shoulder and a few strokes away, floated my father.

And he looked at us with such a tender, caring gaze that the foundations of my chest crumbled, and I held her close and I cried.

Because she brought to me everything I could ever want.

My home.

My family.

My hope.

I AWOKE HOURS AFTER Alexxandria had thoroughly beaten me to find myself chained to the roof of Isolde Palace. As if I were no more than a beast, the bite of cold, steel chains stung the skin around my neck. The chain itself was nailed onto the icy roof, close enough near the edge so I could look down upon Iol from higher waters and see the ensuing battle of Alexxandria's forces and our own.

It was hard to make out details except for the clash of colors, but even from my distance, I could see that it wasn't in our favor.

Thoughts of my wife and my friends meeting their end down there without me pushed me away from the ledge. I huddled in a corner with my palms over my ears, as if that could drown out the distant sounds of the battle leagues away and below, as if the sounds, sights, and my own terrible thoughts weren't imprinted in my soul.

Shadows loomed above me in those terrible moments, and I dared a glance above only to find Alexxandria's black wyvern looming above me. I stilled at the sight of it, not making any sudden movements. If she wanted it to off me, there wouldn't be much I could do against the might of it. But the beast merely looked at me with its yellow eyes before turning its attention back to the Iolish horizon.

With it above me and the battle below, my mind got no rest. My whole body ached, and I shivered from the never-ending cold that sliced through my bones. Hours; it felt like I suffered for hours, trying to keep my sanity intact, trying not to let thoughts, waking nightmares, and my own terror from consuming me alive.

When Alexxandria finally came from whatever hole she'd slithered off to, I could tell by one look at her distorted face that she was enraged.

She paced with wild desperation left and right, looking like an orca trapped within a cage. Then she whirled on me in a single stroke, slamming her fist hard across my face.

My head jerked off to the side and my lip burst open from the force of her blow. I jerked towards her, brought up short by the jerking of the chain, choking me away from her.

I growled, feeling every bit the savage beast she obviously thought me to be.

"I bet you're happy, aren't you?" she snarled.

I wasn't sure what I was supposed to be so happy about, so I kept silent.

"If you think the Draconian army makes any difference, it won't. I *will* get what I want."

The Draconian armies…

My heart soared.

They had come. The Draconians had come, and by the looks of it, had obviously thwarted Alexxandria's plans.

A smile touched my lips, and I didn't even feel the sting of pain.

She growled and punched me across the face again. "Stop smiling!"

I could only smile wider. "No," I answered.

She staggered back a stroke. Ever since she'd taken Jessinda's head, I hadn't dared challenge her again to her face. Not when Scarlet was still alive and in the palace. Where, I wasn't sure, but I'd not risk her murdering another cousin of Odele's.

But now… the Draconians had arrived, and they had ruined her plans and given my wife a fighting chance.

"I said *stop!*"

Laughter erupted from my throat and I doubled over. They had come. They had *come!*

I didn't even feel the next blow to my face when the laughter was so overpowering. She could kill me now and I wouldn't care, because Odele would be safe with the new armies. She'd be protected with the might of the dragon armies at her back.

She punched me again, and this time I fell to the ground and felt the blows in earnest now. But the laughter came out of me still, laced with bits of hysteria and regret. Because I knew there was no way I'd be making out of this alive, and the one thing I would spend my afterlife regretting was that I never got the one moment that mattered.

"I will make them pay," Alexxandria snarled between blows. "They will *all* surrender before I end them."

That one moment that mattered above all others…

"They'll feel what I felt. Because even when I surrendered, they ended me anyway."

That one final moment with Odele.

THE WAR TENT WAS full, and it was a moment for the history conches. Iolish, Uncharted, Thalassarins, Kappurins and Draconians together. While each kingdom had been involved in trade at one point or another throughout the years, there had never been a unity to this scale.

It was the rulers of each nation and their generals who surrounded the war table. It was a sight to see and made me want to gape at them all. Each one more different than the last; each one formidable in their own way.

Emperor Jiang Li floated beside both Kai and Kane. The Draconians were similarly built; or at least, Emperor Jiang and Kane were both bulky, muscular, while Kai was on the lithe side. They wore matching war leathers of black that overlapped like the scales of a dragon, katanas, and dragon shaped helms that they held at their sides.

Beside Kai were Maisie, Captain Saber, and Elias, though the latter kept more behind them and blended into the shadows, content to observe.

Beside Maisie and my former captain was the King of Kappur. With his dark toned skin and short dark hair, he wore the brown, green, and black colors of his kingdom, the insignia of a sea serpent on his breast.

Beside him, my own father floated, like Thalassar and Kappur hadn't just gotten out of a long-floating feud where hundreds of lives had been lost.

Then there was me, Ytgar, Adrian, and Anneli.

"She has wyverns all over the capital," Anneli was explaining, leaning over the map of Iol on the table and pushing figurines into place. "From what I could see, she had beasts even further up north, but the biggest of them is her own." Her palms pressed onto the surface. "She keeps it near the palace at all times, and she doesn't leave it either."

"How many soldiers on the inside?" Kane asked, his piercing near-violet gaze searching intently over her face.

Her eyes narrowed at his attention, but she answered, "About a hundred. It'll be significantly less since the battle started. The Iolish rose up against them, but with them retreating back to Aelfrost, I'm sure they'll execute those who dared to defend themselves." A cold, quiet sort of rage underlay her words. I recognized it for what it was. Murderous.

"Regardless, the odds have now evened out and she knows it." Adrian swept his hand over the board. "My sister knows that the odds are no longer tilting in her favor. She'll hide in the palace and won't come out."

"We can draw her out," Kai said fiercely. His eyes were the still the bright, glowing blue like those of a dragon's; they hadn't receded back to their brown hue yet. It was the thrill of battle thrumming through his veins.

Adrian shook his head. "It won't work. She won't risk herself."

Only I could read the words beneath what he said and what he actually meant. My hands tightened into fists at my side. "Are you saying she'll risk someone else instead?" Like Val. Like Scarlet. Like the helpless Iolish she kept prisoner.

Adrian's single yellow eye found me and the look he gave me was tender. "That's exactly what I'm saying, love."

Over my dead body would she use Val against us. I'd give myself up a thousand times over if I could save him, save Scarlet, even save the Iolish. They were my mer now, and I protected what was mine.

Still, my heart clenched at the thought of death. We'd already suffered such a big loss. To lose more? I swallowed, my eyes finding Maisie's from across the table.

We shared a look of understanding, and suddenly I *knew*. I knew what it was she had felt for so long. The reluctance to send the mer she cared about to war, despite the necessary evil that it was.

Silviya and Jessinda…their deaths weighed heavily on my shoulders, and I hated that their deaths, along with others, was the price of peace.

I nodded at my cousin, sharing that intimate moment of understanding between us. Perhaps the only moment we've had, or ever would.

"We'll meet her soldiers on the battlewaters," the emperor decided, a gleam of something in his eyes, even while his expression remained impassive. "Let them taste their deaths when they behold the might of our forces."

"And if she won't come out…" Kai added.

It was Kane who continued, a smile of complete malice twisting his mouth. "…then we will tear the palace down until she does."

WE WILL TEAR THE palace down until she does.

No one wanted to destroy that palace more than I. But seeing Adrian's reaction… I knew his sister wouldn't hesitate to kill Valmundur like she'd killed my grandmother. He was nothing more than her shield, like the Iolish were nothing more than collateral in her sick and twisted games.

We were close, so close to the end, and I could taste her demise on my mouth like the sweet flavor of a *rakarouris*. But the fear was there as well, coated just in the back of my throat, making it hard to swallow.

Because tomorrow would likely be the last day of this war, and there was a chance that we wouldn't make it out alive. Even with the odds now evened out, I couldn't bring myself to hope. To dare and let myself feel that sensation only to have them crushed if the outcome wasn't what I wanted.

Because if Val died tomorrow, whether we won or not, if my brother was killed by Alexxandria, something within me would die too.

I knew Odele felt the same way when we went to bed and she held us close, when we woke up and she had tears in her eyes. She knew how uncertain today was as I did, as Adrian did.

And when we readied for battle, she helped me strap on my leather and furs with a grim expression. I held her for a moment longer and bent down to press a kiss to her forehead. When I pulled away, she lifted on the tips of her fins and captured my mouth in hers.

We devoured and took, a moment of desperation and a possible goodbye, and my heart couldn't bear it a moment longer. I ripped my mouth away and heaved a breath. "I love you," I whispered, looking into the depths of her eyes for what could very well be the last time. A color of dark copper, with hints of gold sparking through.

Two-legger fire lived within her. It blazed and flared, it melted like molten lava that glared from within its carefully contained glass globe.

"I love you," I repeated just before I pulled away. I didn't give her a chance to reply. I couldn't bear it, so I swam away, hearing the drums of war pulse each fin stroke towards my mount. I hauled myself up on it and kicked it into formation with the rest of the soldiers riding out to battle.

Bodies were lost among so many, and I knew absolutely nothing but the difference in colors and beasts against traitors, enemies. Like an unspoken rule had whispered between the currents between us, we met in the waters. The horns and the drums guided us like a savage battle of old that pushed and pulled, that controlled every clash and clang of our swords, the force of our shields, or the sharpness of our blades.

I could feel the Iolish gods with me in those open waters as bodies clashed and two opposing sides became one, and all that mattered was life and death. In those moments, no one thought of what they were fighting for, but of dodging swords, of staying alive, of seeing tomorrow.

I didn't know if what I was fighting for would even live to see tomorrow. So I fought, arms aching as my sword swung and severed heads and limbs. I dodged blows, felt the pain, but still I pushed on.

Because we had to win today, and I couldn't dare think what would happen otherwise.

With cries on my lips that I felt ripped from the throats of gods of war themselves, I pushed forward, and my enemies pushed back until I was toppled from my mount.

I fought in the sand against an enemy, my shield shoulder screaming as it was dislocated thanks to the force of the blow. But still I blocked the swing of the blade aiming straight towards my face with my own sword. Sparks rained down around my face and I gritted my teeth as I *pushed*.

With a screaming cry of rage, I pushed with my sword and my tail against my opponent, pushing them off of me. They flew back and I shot up. We parried; even while my arm hung limply at my side, we fought. I was favored by the gods for an instant, I knew, because I found an opening against him, slapping the top of his hand, causing his sword to clatter into the silt.

My sword driving through his chest ended him.

I sighed and took a single moment to bend over. My arm was screaming in pain, so I undid the straps on my forearm and upper arm, letting the shield slide from my body and land on the ground, sending a cloud of silt and snow flying upwards.

It was a bad idea to let go of my sword, especially in the midst of battle, but I had to set my arm back into place and quickly.

I took a deep breath and bit the inside of my cheek, my good hand gripping my arm, getting ready to push up, ready for that blinding flash of pain…

But a different pain came instead.

Brunt force against the back of my head sent me sprawling down face to silt. My mind spun and every muscle seemed to scream in pain. I turned on my back, blinking up to stare at the figure looming over me. I barely had time to react before a second blow to my face sent me hurtling towards darkness, but I remained awake long enough to feel a tight grip at my fins before I was dragged through the silt.

Then I fell into unconsciousness.

Adrian

BLOOD ENTERED MY BODY, and I relished in it like the crueler part of me so deeply desired. Laughter didn't trickle out this time, not when I knew deep down this was our last day. Because I vowed to myself I would end it. I would. Even if I had to storm the palace myself, I'd break through the ice windows myself and shove my sword through my sister's heart, even if she took me down with her. I'd kill her.

I would.

This I vowed.

I fought alongside a legion of Draconian warriors. On their dragons, they tore through wyverns and mer alike.

The Draconians were fierce in battle, but none as fearsome as Emperor Jiang Li or his son Kai. They tore through the enemy as if it took little effort and were barely breathing hard from the exertion.

It was that dragon blood coursing through their veins that gave them this higher resistance.

But after hours of fighting, even they could tire out.

I saw it happen, saw their energy waning. I saw the emperor separate from his beast for but a split second. But it was that second all that the enemy needed to sneak up on him from behind.

A single blow to the back of the head sent the emperor sprawling. He would have killed the Draconian ruler, but I was suddenly in front of him, meeting him blade for blade. I wore no shield, but held two swords, one of ice and one of shining obsidian. I'd taught myself to wield in both hands, and with one sword, I disarmed him, and the other I slit through his throat.

Only when he floated away dead, did I turn to look at the emperor, who slowly got up from where he'd been knocked over, a grim expression on his face. I smiled, the biggest 'eat silt' smile I ever mustered in my life.

I was sure he was remembering another time, a time when I'd nearly begged him for help, for his armies, and he'd denied me, and the single promise that had quietly pulsed between us.

That one day, he would need me and would regret not having helped.

That day was today.

I turned away from him and resumed the battle.

Odele

Just as the battle began to thicken, a horn sounded from leagues beyond. A horn that blared across the water, coming straight from the direction of Isolde Palace.

My whole body stilled as, suddenly, every single Uncharted stopped what they were doing. In the midst of battling an opponent, they dodged, jerked back, turned, and swam away. Every beast answered the horn with a shrill call of their own and zipped away from the melee.

We could do little more than float there, dumbstruck, our swords half-raised in preparation to strike empty water. I turned and shared a look with a soldier. Confusion thrummed through me, and for the life of me I couldn't understand…

My gut clenched.

Was this part of her distraction to beat us? Was she calling her soldiers back to the palace because she planned on executing Val unless we surrendered?

My throat caught a tightness I couldn't swallow past. We had to go after them; had to make a plan to sneak into the palace and save Val, had to kill her.

I whirled around just as our own war drums sounded in the distance. Each beat was a language all on its own. Fall back to camp, came the order. Good. I needed to meet with the war generals and leaders. We needed to come up with a plan of attack to end this once and for all.

"She called for a fall back of her troops."

Those were the first words I heard when I burst into the war tent of our camp to find the generals and rulers already there. I did a quick headcount, my heart sinking when I saw neither Adrian nor Ytgar. I tried not to assume the worst, that they'd felled in battle, but my heart was screaming at my mind, even as I tried to keep a cool head.

The generals and rulers looked exhausted, except for the Draconians, who looked as if they'd literally been born in battle.

"Why would she do that?" the Kappurin King asked.

I took a stroke within the tent, heart pounding, a feeling of unease slicing down my every nerve ending.

A deep voice drawled out a reply from behind me. "It's because she has a trick up her sleeve."

I whirled around to find Adrian pushing aside the tent flaps and taking a stroke within. I couldn't help the relief that poured from me and sent me propelling towards him, wrapping my arms around his neck.

His palms encircled my waist as he pressed me closer, one hand going up to cradle my head into his chest. He made soft, reassuring noises that did nothing to calm the storm inside of me.

"I'm alright, love," he whispered.

I pulled away, searching to make sure he was telling the truth. When I saw no visible signs of gaping wounds, I loosed a breath then asked, "Ytgar?"

His hand cupped my cheek, thumb trailing circles against my skin. "Likely on his way now, love."

His words brought no reassurance, but I had to believe them. I nodded and turned back around. The leaders had ceased planning to give me a moment, but when they saw I was now composed, they cleared their throats and Emperor Jiang asked, "What plot could she possibly have?"

Adrian shrugged his shoulders in a gesture that may have seemed careless, but I knew him and could make out the tightness of his posture. He hated the uncertainty as much as we did, probably even more so since the opponent we were facing was his sister.

"Alexxandria is as clever and as vicious as a rockfish. She can lie in wait for a long time and snap when the time is right."

"We cannot allow that to happen," Kane said darkly. His eyes swept around the tent, and I realized he was probably looking for Anneli.

She hadn't come into the tent yet.

I tried not to let that worry me, either.

"I say we attack the palace now," my father said. "Let's finish this."

"That could be playing straight into her plans," Adrian argued.

"It's better than sitting here and letting her and her armies regain their strength. We need to attack hard and fast."

My heart pounded at their words. "What about Val?" My whisper cut through their own arguments and they turned to look at me with varying degrees of expressions. Pity, impatience, annoyance, worry. I tilted my shoulders back in a posture of confidence I didn't really feel at the moment. "Val is still locked in that palace; so is Scarlet. Will we sacrifice them and allow them to be caught in the middle of the war?"

"Whether or not we attack, they'll die anyway." Emperor Jiang's voice was cruel and matter-of-factly. "We cannot sit idly by waiting for the life of one mer, and a whale trainer at that, when thousands are at stake."

I knew that. Logically I knew that. I'd studied for it time and time again in my preparations to become queen. And yet… it was Val. My husband, one of the mer I loved.

"Val is not just a whale trainer," Adrian cut in, his voice low and full of malice. "He's a warrior and a valuable asset to us all and because of it, my sister will use him to get to us."

"Which is why we have to attack *now*. She's going to use him either way; he's your weak spot so she's counting on us not attacking directly because of him. Which means we have to catch her off guard and do it."

My hands tightened into fists. They were speaking about Val like he was just another Iolish citizen, like he was nothing. I understood Maisie now more than ever. One life taken, just one was terrible, but it was even worse when it was someone you loved.

An argument ensued around us, and I barely caught the words past my own pounding heart echoing loudly in my ears. It resonated down to my soul, and I could feel myself starting to hyperventilate, only interrupted by Anneli's sudden, startling appearance into the tent.

I barely registered the look of relief on Kane's face as I turned and watched her swim in with two other guards, tossing into the silt, at our fins, an Uncharted enemy.

We stared down at him, then back up at Anneli, whose face was carved into grave lines. In her hands she held a spear that she pointed at the back of his head and shoved him unkindly. "Tell them what you told us," she demanded, and it was the angriest I'd ever heard her sound, and that instantly worried me.

The Uncharted lifted his face, and I could see the hatred, pure and unbridled, in his eyes as he took me in.

Adrian let out a low growl of warning at the expression and discreetly angled himself a bit closer to me, just in striking distance of the mer.

The mer noted the gesture and smiled cruelly. "Greetings," he said, his voice grating down my spine like rocks rattling together. "I am a messenger sent by Queen Alexxandria. I am here to deliver a message." He looked around the war tent. No one bothered to hide our map from his view, for they knew that he wouldn't be leaving this tent alive.

Anneli jabbed the spear in harder, drawing blood. "Tell them," she snarled. The tightness around her was an eruption waiting to happen.

The mer laughed. "My queen sends her regards to her brother, and welcomes the new armies into the chaos, but even with them here, you will not win. Iol will fall, followed by Thalassar."

A soft snarl of rage erupted from my own throat at the words. Bastard. "Perhaps we'll surprise her and when this battle is done, I'll mount her stuffed head on the wall behind my throne of ice." A cruel smile twisted my own lips.

The mer smirked. "Or perhaps it will end with Prince Ytgar Neves Isolde's head mounted on a pike just outside of the palace."

My blood ran cold.

The mer just cackled. "The war is over," he spat. "My queen has your precious ice prince."

Valmundur

"YOUR MAJESTY, WE HAVE brought a gift for you." A soldier of the Uncharted had appeared on the roof with us, expression absolutely glowing with pride. I didn't like the sight of it; it sent an enormous rip of trepidation down my back.

Anytime the enemy smiled, it was wrong.

I braced myself, my chains rattling as my body tensed.

Alexxandria pushed herself away from the edge of the roof and took a few strokes towards the soldier. Not close enough to put herself in his striking distance, not even close enough to touch. I made note of that, of how little she trusted her own warriors to be near her.

The warrior turned and made a few gestures with his fingers, and from the doors behind him, two soldiers emerged, carrying between them a limp body.

I jerked forward, brought short by the choking of my steel manacles.

No.

No.

His head was lolled, his white hair stiffly frozen against his high, elegant cheekbones. His eyelids fluttered as he drifted in and out of consciousness. He was already chained, his hands manacled behind his back. They deposited Ytgar onto the floor at Alexxandria's fins and he rolled over, his eyes opening and taking in the sight of her.

Without her steel mask covering the marred flesh of her face, she looked even more dangerous somehow. Perhaps it was the manic craze in her eyes as she beheld the Prince of Iol before her at last, or the twisted smile that overpowered her lips.

She had him.

She had what she'd wanted all along.

I jerked relentlessly against my chain.

Ytgar sat up and slid back along the icy ground away from her, startled by the violence of her twisted face.

"No! No!"

He turned and looked at me, chained to the roof of Isolde palace, of his home, and the surprised expression on his face turned into a look of quiet murder that I knew all too well.

"The Prince of Iol, I assume?" Alexxandria mused cruelly.

Ytgar said nothing.

"What a pleasure it is to have you in my home." The Isolde crown glinted on her head, mocking. She was mocking him, baiting him too attack and give her an excuse to stab her hidden knife straight into his chest.

"No, Ytgar! No!" I struggled, but the steel choked off my breaths, made my vision go blurry. I would have died if I could make it to him. I would have gladly given my life for his. "Please, don't hurt him!"

Alexxandria flicked a disinterested gaze in my direction. "Someone silence him."

I felt the blow before I even saw it coming; the hilt of a sword banged against my nose, cracking it. I heard the cartilage break and pain blinded me for an instant.

I gasped. I'd broken my nose before, falling from orcas, but this pain felt infinitely worse. It hurt everywhere, down to the roots of my soul.

"Please," I croaked, blinking my eyes open.

Alexxandria stared between Ytgar and I, as if she could see the thread of friendship that pulsed so strongly between us. Even while Ytgar's expression was a tight mask, he was clenching his jaw, and his gaze kept going to me while his bound hands closed into angry fists.

Slowly, Alexxandria took the knife from the folds of her pockets and brought it out.

"No!" I struggled, despite the blood swarming up to blind me, despite the pain, despite it *all*. This couldn't be happening. I was supposed to protect him, he wasn't supposed to get caught. My prince, my friend, my *brother…*

She snarled in my direction. "Beg me to spare him, whale trainer. Beg me to spare your prince."

I knew what she was asking me, what she wanted me to give up. My Iolish pride. In the very fibers of our blood lived the same pride of our Viking ancestors, who would have rather faced death than to give in to an enemy.

She may as well have asked me to chop off my hand.

But… my gaze when to Ytgar, whose eyes widened. "Val," he whispered, "no."

How could I not?

For Ytgar, I'd give up my pride tenfold. Because if she killed him… if I was forced to go on in this life without him at my side, the merman who had saved my life time and time again, I might as well have lived without arms or fins.

It would be losing a part of myself as essential as breathing.

For him, I'd toss myself into the pits of the ice and meet our ancient gods of death at the doors of their haven. For him, I'd risk it all, even this. For him, I'd take the knife and slit my own wrists if it meant he got to live.

Ytgar must have saw it then, because he jerked towards me. "Val, no!" The guards were on him in a moment, restraining him.

"Beg me to save your prince," Alexxandria purred, delighted at this.

And I hated her, every bit of her, and there's was nothing I regretted in my life more than not killing her when I had the chance. That was my sin to bear, my fault. Every single death was on me.

So I dropped to the curve of my tail, pressing down against the floor of ice. "Please," I whispered.

"Lower," Alexxandria commanded.

I stripped away all emotion from myself. It didn't matter. None of it mattered except for my brother's life. I dropped my forehead to the ground, palms pressing on either side of my head. "Please," I croaked, then louder, "Please, do not kill him."

I could almost feel the terrible smile twisting her mouth and I fought away the urge to grit my teeth together. I hated her. *Hated—*

"I will not kill him." I dared a peek up to find her pocketing her knife again. Relief coursed through me. "I have other plans for him. Bigger plans." She bent down and cradled her palm against his cheek. Ytgar jerked away. "This is a happy turn of events, indeed. With Prince Ytgar in my grasp, I can use him to lure that Thalassarin Princess straight to me."

My throat tightened, and my heart dropped in my chest.

"Straight to her death."

I KNEW I WAS going to kill her the moment she'd taken my kingdom.

I knew I *wanted* to kill her slowly when she'd forced me to watch her wyvern devour my grandmother.

But seeing her force Val to beg for my life made me want to wholly and completely *destroy her.*

And as she threatened my wife with a smile on her face, nothing would have stopped me from reaching for her then and taking that delicate looking throat between my hands, from choking the life right out of her with my own smile against my mouth.

I hated that she looked like Adrian, softer and more feminine, and infinitely more marred, when they were both so very different.

I would have killed her. I would have risked my own life to fight the guards that held me back and reach for her to end her life. But Val…

He was still kneeling, his forehead kissing the floor like a servant, like a slave. Hot rage gripped my chest and I honed it into the quiet sneakiness of frost bite.

I'd kill her slowly like the cold killed unsuspecting travelers for what she did to Val alone.

My best friend's body looked broken, beaten. His nose was broken and still gushing dark plumes of blood, his eyes were swollen, and bruises covered every visible part of his body, from his neck down to his hands. I didn't want to know what the rest of him looked like, because if I knew, I'd foolishly try to kill her right then.

My throat tightened with the force of every emotion I was feeling. I looked the self-proclaimed queen in the eyes. One yellow, one white. I hadn't seen her face; just the teasing hint of scars beneath that mask she'd worn to my grandmother's execution. They were brutal, but I didn't feel sorry for her when she'd wreaked her own havoc upon our waters.

"Odele won't come," I growled.

I prayed she wouldn't, but deep in my heart I knew she *would*. When Odele loved, she did so fiercely, violently, and nothing would stop her from coming after what was hers. And Val and I? We were hers.

I could almost pity Alexxandria for the rage Odele would unleash, but the fear was greater, and I prayed to my gods that Odele had the good sense to stay away, lest she find herself trapped as well.

If I were I to die today, Odele was all Iol had left.

With my grandmother gone, and me dead… there would be no one of Iolish blood to rule the kingdom. But I could think of no one better to rule than her.

Alexxandria smiled. "She will." Her eyes swept over me. "If she loves you, she will." Then she glared at the guards. "Chain him up as well. I must go speak to a messenger. Let him tell her armies that we have her precious prince." And then she was gone.

I allowed myself to be led to the edge of the roof without a fight and watched with rapt attention as they hammered a steel nail onto the roof. They connected chains to it and closed a collar around my throat.

I felt like no more than a wild animal, which they sneered at me for and kicked me with their fins against my ribs before they left.

It was just Val and I… and the looming wyvern above the palace.

With Alexxandria gone, Val slowly sat up and leaned back against the wall. Past the bruises and the pain, I could make out the tortured expression on his face, and I hated her all over again.

"Val." My voice was a sad whisper between us. "Why would you kneel?"

My friend shook his head and let out loud, bitter laughter. "You still don't get it, do you?" His blue eyes pierced me with all the pain of a falling shard of ice. "I love you more than I have ever loved myself. That won't ever change, you idiot. You're my brother, and we're supposed to love our family more than ourselves."

So said the merman who had no family growing up, who only had Anneli and I for years…

"You have a sick idea of what family should be." I leaned against the wall, thumping my head against it and wincing at the pain there. Whoever had brought me here, startling me from behind, had got me good.

"Maybe I have a good idea of it, and you don't have any at all. Besides, who gets to say why you get to be so self-sacrificing and the rest of us don't? No wonder Odele thinks you're such a bastard."

I blinked at him and laughed, a real bout of laughter that I hadn't felt for such a long time. "Fine," I said. "I yield."

Val had the audacity to look smug, even with his face swollen and beaten; how he could manage it, I had no idea. "Damn straight, you do."

I rolled my eyes and a terrible thought set in. "Do you think Odele will come?"

His expression became serious. "Yes." No hesitation, no thought. Yes, she would come.

"I hope she doesn't." I prayed one more time to the gods that she didn't.

Val shrugged. "I hope she doesn't… but I also hope she does."

"And why is that?"

"Because if anyone's smart enough to take down this crazy mer, it's *our* crazy mer."

I chuckled, nodding my agreement. We fell into silence, and we knew without saying what words lay between us like a dark premonition, a worry that wouldn't rest.

We could joke about it all we wanted, but the truth was, we weren't sure what would happen.

And we weren't sure if Odele really would make it out alive or not.

I prayed to the gods she would.

Odele

MY QUEEN HAS YOUR *precious ice prince.*

I gripped for the knife holstered at my waist and before anyone could warn me against it, I shoved the sword straight through the merman's chest.

He died laughing at the expression on my face, and when I pulled the sword from his body, I whirled with it gripped tightly in my hand, my chest panting like a wild animal cornered.

"We have to get him out," I ordered. "Now."

Every single leader took me in, the wild stance, the heavy breathing, and the merman now floating dead within the tent.

Emperor Jiang Li was the first to say, "I think it best if you exit the tent now." Mirrored expressions of agreement reflected on the faces of those around him. Even my father's.

My chest tightened, and I knew what was happening. This had happened before. It always happened, and I had experience with it. With mer retreating from me, abandoning me.

"I am a queen," I stated, head tilting up higher. "And I will not be thrown from my own war tent. We need to plan a rescue. Alexxandria has both Val and Ytgar, and we need to get them back."

"Put the sword down," Kane demanded. He'd somehow angled himself closer towards me with his katana out without me having noticed. He was coming towards me like I was a danger, a menace.

Before he could reach me, Anneli was in front of me, pressing the sharp end of her spear against the Draconian's throat. "Take another stroke towards my queen with that thing," she threatened, "and I'll kill you myself."

His violet-black eyes flashed with violent delight.

"Everyone calm down now," King Dorian commanded. "Put the weapons away. We're not each other's enemy. Can't you see this is what she likely wants?"

Anneli hesitated, but pulled the spear away and pushed me a stroke away from Kane. The Draconian rubbed his throat right over the spot where the spear had touched him and smiled. "The next time you take a weapon to me, my lady, will be the last time…" He shoved his katana back into his sheathe. "That is a promise."

Anneli didn't reply, but I could feel the quiet intensity of the threat shiver through her body.

I sheathed my own sword. "We have to go help them," I urged once more.

Emperor Jiang shook his head. "You are distressed and not thinking clearly." His eyes went to the floating body of the Uncharted messenger as if to say *clearly*. "That rage can harm a war more than help. As of right now, you are banned from this tent and from further war planning. I will not have a mermaid's distress jeopardize this whole mission."

I wanted to scream in his face and pull my sword on him again, but that kind of impulsiveness I would have undoubtedly displayed before would only serve to prove him right.

Val and Ytgar's lives were at stake. Thousands of lives were at stake. I knew it, and I didn't want them dead anymore than these leaders did but…

A sudden idea began to form in my mind, an idea driven by the force of my hopeless rage and desperation. I swallowed and turned to Adrian. He cupped my cheeks in his hands and kissed my lips. "I'll punish him for speaking that way to you," he promised. I could see the own turmoil in his eyes at the news of Ytgar in enemy hands. "But it's been a long battle. Go rest. I'll convince them to save them both. I promise."

But I knew how hopeless it was.

The needs of the many always outweighed the needs of the few, even if one of the few was Iolish royalty. The generals and rulers would not sacrifice so many soldiers to storm the palace. I knew it in the bottom of my heart. And I knew Adrian knew it as well.

So I nodded and forced a smile to my lips. "I'll go rest," I said demurely, as demurely as I could muster, and held my head high as I swam out of the war tent and made my way straight towards another without looking back.

Her tent was in the middle of the camp, protected by guards and her handicapped bulgy eyed dragon. Without announcing myself, I threw aside the tent flaps to Odele's current living space. She was alone with Captain Saber and the Black Blade.

One look at my expression and she turned to the both of them. "Can you give us a moment, please?"

Reluctantly, they left. I knew they were going to float outside the tent and try to listen to every word, so I dropped to my tail and kept my voice low as I begged perhaps the only mer who could understand. "Cousin, I need your help."

THEY WOULDN'T HELP. No matter what I said or demanded, even the life debt the Emperor of Draconi now owed me was not enough to convince them to attack the palace and save Ytgar and Val. I tried, I argued, and they wouldn't listen. I swam out of that war tent a failure to my wife. Had we been in the Uncharted, I would have given up my hands for such an offense.

I was almost prepared for the act when I went searching for her but couldn't find her anywhere. I asked guards, and they said she'd gone to speak with her cousin, so I'd gone back to our shared tent and lay against the mounds of pillows and promptly fell asleep.

The next morning, the side where Odele should lay was empty. Worry nagged my mind as I got up and prepared for the day's battle, for the plan others had chosen. As if this had suddenly become their war, as if they had any right to shove me and Odele aside from our fight, like our ideas mattered less than hers. It was a treatment I prepared myself for and despised.

It was even worse when they'd shoved Odele from the tent.

I'd let her go because I'd wanted her safe from their judgment; and I hadn't wanted her to see me burst into a rage I knew I'd display once she'd gone.

And still I'd been ignored.

I swept my gaze around the tent and found nothing in the room disturbed—as if she hadn't been in the room at all—save for the small change in the position of the chair by our table.

I made my way over to it warily, noting a kelp parchment weighed down with a chunk of rock. On it sat a quill, and scrawled across it, in neat lettering that could be none other than Odele's, lay a single message that made my heart catch in my throat, made me see the red of my own fury.

I read it once, twice, three times, and kept it to memory. With a steady calmness, I bent to pick it up in my hands. Some mer, when they raged, they trembled. I was the opposite. A steady calm settled over me, a murderous intent pushing every single movement.

My heart almost broke, but deep down I knew what Odele had been forced to do, and who had forced her into this. I should have known, *should have known,* that she was prepared to do whatever it took to get Ytgar and Val back, no matter the cost.

Because everyone had turned their backs on her; even me, and she'd gone off on her own.

I knew what I had to do.

And I vowed to my gods that this time, I would not fail my wife.

Valmundur

THOSE HOURS CHAINED TO the roof, exposed to the cold with Ytgar at my side passed in excruciating slowness. We rarely spoke and saw even less of Alexxandria. She didn't reappear that night, or even the next day. It wasn't until the war horns below Isolde Palace sounded that she emerged from whatever cave she lived in.

She swam onto the roof alone, decked in a dark velvet dress with gold trimming, a fur cloak, and her ivory, metal, and obsidian mask covering her face. The light of the ice glinted off that mask, and it gleamed and winked.

She didn't pay attention to us, but she swam close to the edge and looked at the Iolish horizon. I could sense the smile on her mouth, malicious as she took in a deep breath. Like she was a normal mermaid preparing herself for the day ahead.

I hoped she died today.

The wish seized through my body violently.

Ytgar didn't take his eyes off of her as she flittered from one side of the roof to the other. The head of her beast loomed over her, and she slapped it way with an impatient gesture. With a whine, the wyvern lifted above us, ever the vigilant sentinel.

"Today is the day," Alexxandria said, loud enough for the two of us to hear. "She will come. I know she will."

Odele. She was talking about Odele.

She couldn't. A part of me wished, with every fiber, that she'd be the one to end Alexxandria's life, to do what I'd been too cowardly to do. But with that wyvern here... she didn't stand a chance.

Hope was a far-away thing in my chest right now. I tried not to let that hopelessness show, though, as I watched her swim back and forth, back and forth, back and forth.

She stopped just in the middle of the ledge, her palms grazing the icy sides. She wore black gloves that were tight against her hands. I stared at them, at the way she nearly ripped them with the force in which she gripped the ledge...

I knew then I was going to die today.

Because if Odele showed up, I knew Alexxandria would not be lenient with her and because I loved her, I would do all I could to save her. And if I failed, then I'd take my own life.

Because I couldn't live in a world without Ytgar, and I couldn't live in a world without Odele.

A scraping sound caught my attention, causing me to jerk my chained neck off to the side.

My face paled.

My heart stopped.

I couldn't breathe.

"No!" Ytgar screamed, jerking against his own chains. "No!"

Alexxandria slowly peeled the mask from her face and set it down on the ledge before turning to face Odele, every single twisted scar on her face visible in the light of the ice.

Odele swam out onto the roof, looking uncertain and so unlike herself that I looked over her shoulder, hoping Adrian was with her. But when the door to the roof slammed closed, I knew she'd come alone.

"Odele. *No.*" Ytgar yanked against his chains with renewed force and brute strength.

I'd already tried, and he too would fail.

I felt a detached sort of clarity as I took her in. This princess, this *queen*, was willing to put her own life on the line for us.

It was a strange moment to be humbled by it but I was, even while fear viciously clawed its way up every nerve and made my blood swim cold with dread. I couldn't move, I couldn't do much but tremble in place as I took in her steady strokes towards Alexxandria.

She stopped a safe enough distance away.

I took her in, letting my memory take in every single bit of her, every bit I feared I'd forgotten on those dark and lonely nights in the dungeon.

She wore battle leathers in black, shaped like the overlapping scales of a dragon, with white fur around the collar. It was Draconian attire, but I didn't question it. She looked like she had lost weight since I'd last seen her, for the clothes fit her a bit loose around the waist. At her hip, she had a blade of ice and the wyvern dagger Adrian had gifted her on the day of our wedding.

Her hair was braided away from her face, and that expression was carved into grave, fearful lines. Her hand hovered near the hilt of her sword, ready to unleash it at any moment. Around her neck, she wore a chained necklace with Adrian's obsidian ring through it.

Her throat worked up and down as she swallowed. "You wanted me. Here I am."

"No!" Ytgar shouted. "Get back! Swim away!" He fought harder, but Odele didn't even turn to look at him, at *me.*

Alexxandria observed her and bowed, the gesture mocking. "Welcome, Princess of Thalassar. What an honor to finally meet you face to face, in all of our ugly glory." Her fingers grazed over the scarred side of her face.

Odele didn't even blink, her eyes didn't even stray. She cast it a half-second flickering glance before finding Alexxandria's eyes again. I wondered if she'd prepared herself for this meeting. If she had a secret plan up her sleeve.

Odele cocked her head to the side. "Contrary to what you might think, there is absolutely nothing ugly about me." She took a stroke forward, to the side, and forward, so she was passing Alexxandria. She tried to appear confident, but she was swimming… a tad bit oddly… and her voice… I tried to catch a glimpse of her gaze, but she averted it as she swam to the ledge and looked at Iol below.

Alexxandria noted the confidence in her voice, and utter lack of it in her posture. She noted, because I noted. Her gaze narrowed, an expression Odele didn't see with her back turned.

"I've heard many rumors about the ugliness within you," Alexxandria nearly snapped.

At this, Odele turned around, facing her now on the opposite side. She shrugged a shoulder almost carelessly. "Rumors are funny, aren't they? You never know what's true."

A smile curled Alexxandria's lips and her hand went to the folds of her pockets. I tensed. And when she took a stroke towards Odele, I yanked on my chains. "Odele! Careful!"

Odele ignored me.

Alexxandria prowled closer. "Rumors are funny things, but they're so helpful, aren't they? Like, I have heard from many sources that you care for nothing and no one but yourself and yet miraculously… here you are."

"You invited me." Odele seemed to flick those words away with a wave of her hand.

Alexxandria stroked her chin as she prowled even closer, inch by slow inch.

"Odele! Careful!"

She still ignored us.

"I heard from rumors that you tried to flee your betrothal many times."

Odele stiffened as she noted her proximity.

"I also know from rumors that you and your cousin, Maisie Fauna—or Odalaea Malabella Knoll—are *very* similar in appearance."

Odele pressed closer to the ledge. She didn't reply. Why wasn't she saying anything? Why wasn't she reaching for her sword, for her knife?

"I've heard the tricks the two of you have played, and I think you're trying to play one on me right now." She was closer to her now. Close enough to touch. "I know the two of you switch places."

"Odele! Move!"

The next moment happened so fast. Alexxandria's hand was a mere blur as she pulled the knife from her skirts and shoved it upwards, straight into her stomach.

"I know you're not really Odele, because rumor says Odele isn't so self-sacrificing," she whispered cruelly, twisting the knife. "I know you're really Maisie." She pulled the knife out and blood flowed. "Aren't you?"

Gods. No. Gods, no!

I saw it now. It hadn't been Odele…that's why…when she swam in…Maisie had a limp! And Maisie was with *child*!

I gaped in horror at the opened wound near her stomach, blood flowing from the Draconian battle leathers.

Maisie keeled over, gasping for breaths of survival.

"Rumors are such a funny thing," Alexxandria whispered down on Maisie's twisting body. "They tell me so many things. And this was the first thing I'd heard."

No!

I wasn't sure if I thought the word or if it ripped straight from my throat as I watched Maisie keel onto the ground.

Why would she involve herself, knowing the state she was in? Why would she do such a thing?

They'd done it once before, had switched places and fooled us all in the throne room of Thalassar, where we'd witnessed who I thought had been Odele, but was actually Maisie, wed herself to the Prince of Draconi.

I was witnessing something else entirely right now.

Something that drained all the blood from my face and made my heart shatter in my chest. It was like watching Odele die. Logically, I knew she wasn't Odele. It was Maisie… it all made sense, why she wouldn't look us at, why she'd swam in strangely, why she'd seemed so afraid…

And still, to watch her crumple onto the icy ground was too much to bear.

"I'll kill you!" I yanked on my chains, as if I could find the strength within myself to rip them straight off of my skin and lunge for her. "I'll *kill* you!"

Alexxandria ignored me and kicked her fins at Maisie, who grunted in pain.

"Don't you touch her!" Val screamed. "Get away from her!" The despair ripped straight from his soul and fragmented his words entirely. He dropped to the ice, and tears were pouring from his eyes. "Leave her alone! She's pregnant, my gods!"

But the Uncharted witch showed no compassion as she sneered down at Maisie and kicked her one more time. The blood didn't stop flowing, and she didn't stop groaning in desperate pain.

At least I knew she was alive.

But she likely wouldn't be for any longer.

"All you Thalassarins are alike," Alexxandria snapped. "Selfish liars. Bastards. Treacherous." She kicked back her fin, ready to bring it crashing down against Maisie again when a roar sounded from above.

Not the war of her wyvern, but of something else.

A swift dark shadow of a beast blurred through the water in a single instant, heading straight for Alexxandria's wyvern.

The beast never saw it coming.

The small dragon launched itself at the wyvern, clashing against it with a screeching cry as its venomous claws tore through its eyes. The wyvern cried out in rage and pain as blood flowed from its twin wounds. It reached a claw up to smack it off, but the dragon was quicker. It dodged the claw so the wyvern ended up smacking itself instead. The dragon twisted through the water, teeth latching onto the beast's throat. It gnawed and gnashed; blood and flesh floated but the wyvern couldn't dislodge the dragon from its throat before it tore into the sensitive muscles of its throat…

…and killed it entirely.

The wyvern let out a dying screech before its head smacked onto the roof of Isolde Palace, the force rattling the icy building, just before it slid down the side and fell to its death.

"No!" Alexxandria shrieked, swimming over to the ledge and gripping the sides to watch her precious creature fall. She whirled back around in time to see the dragon clearly, to see the bulges of its twin eyes and semi-tattered wings span out.

And then a mermaid slid from the saddle to rapidly float down to where we were.

To where Alexxandria was.

And stab an obsidian blade straight through her chest.

Adrian

ALL IT TOOK TO convince them to storm the palace was show them Odele's note, to read through her plan. A fool's hope of a plan, but a plan nonetheless.

Kai had gripped the kelp parchment tightly in his hands before ripping it right down the middle. I watched with a bit of fascination as his features changed right before my eyes. Every bit of him seemed to elongate, grow. The scales on his orange, white, and black tail hardened, his eyes glowed and his pupils split. It was evidence of the lineage that raced through his veins. Evidence of the dragon entity living inside him.

It was fascinating.

He tore from the war tent, nearly toppling the whole thing down on top of us as he raged through the camp, looking for his wife. For Maisie. I knew already that he wouldn't find her.

Odele and Maisie had slipped from the watchful eyes of their guards somehow and escaped, to switch places and to take down my sister with clever treachery.

Her plan had been simple. *March forward, destroy her armies, and meet me on the roof of Isolde Palace.*

So that's what we did.

We tore through every enemy in our path with renewed vigor. The sounds of blade cutting through flesh and bone filled my ears, to be heard of the roaring of my raging voice and pounding heart.

Odele's note had been very specific. It wouldn't matter if she killed my sister to end it; while her army still floated, there would still be resistance. We were to take them down. As many as we could until we overpowered them at least.

It was easily down now that the Dragon Prince was in a rage, tearing through mer and beast as if he were a born and bred dragon himself. I caught sight of others fighting alongside him as well. Of the one they called Captain Saber, former guard to my wife, and one they called the Black Blade.

Recognition had startled through my body at the sight of him, of a mer from my past. I remembered him, remembered his image through the bars of our prison, the kindness in his eyes and the fear. I remembered the way we'd escaped together, how he'd helped me flee with my sister and other Uncharted.

And my parting gift to him in chunks of pure, rare obsidian that he now wielded in the form of a blade.

To a free world…

Our eyes met and held for a mere second across the battle waters before we dived into the fray. If we survived, there would be time to speak later.

Not now. Not while Odele and Maisie had gone to end this war once and for all…

Kai tore through legions on the back of his lithe, elegant dragon. The creature tore through flesh and bone easily, as if it were connected so intricately to Kai and felt its master's rage.

Behind the Draconian Prince were his soldiers, his father and General Kane carving out a way for Anneli and me to lead our mer through.

I kicked my mount into a fast swim while Kane and the others held open a spot for us. Anneli was behind me on her orca. I dove through first and she followed, but a sudden cry of pain from Kane had us both jerking to a stop.

Anneli whirled to watch as Kane's dragon collided with the massive body of a wyvern. The wyvern lashed out with its barbed tail. It hit Kane's exposed side of his violet tail, and the warrior went crashing to the ground. He fell into a cloud of silt and snow with pain, but his eyes remained open and focused on his mount.

The dragon put up a good fight against the wyvern. Claws raked down scaled flesh, blood clouded, and skin tore open.

Kane got up and immediately winced. A gushing wound was opened at his side where the barbed tail of the wyvern had hit him. The flesh of his scales was opened from his waist, slashing all the way down to his fins on his right side. The fins… They were shredded completely, the wounds bleeding uncontrollably.

"Ryuu!" he shouted up towards his dragon.

The wyvern caught sight of him and made a mad dash, head slamming down, jaws opened wide…

"Ryuu, no!"

The dragon intercepted the blow meant for Kane, leaving herself exposed to the wyvern's teeth.

Kane screamed just as the wyvern bit down and tore off the flesh in Ryuu's neck. Ryuu screeched in dying pain but managed to get in a final blow. With all the strength she had left, Ryuu's claws tore through the wyvern until they died and fell down to the silt with all the speed of crumbling pillars.

Straight towards Kane.

The Draconian tried to dodge but fell over when his shorn fins didn't cooperate.

Anneli cried out, sending her orca into a violent swim towards him. They reached him just in time, yanking him up and on the back of her mount before dodging the falling bodies. When the silt cleared and Anneli's orca slowed, Kane slid off of it and fell into the silt beside the bodies.

"Ryuu…" The word came out a choked sob that I could feel down to my soul. "RYUU!"

My eyes met Anneli's and she mouthed one word to me before she turned her attention to Kane, dropping into the silt next to him. I couldn't make out any words, even while her mouth moved and she spoke to him.

A roaring filled my ears, an echoing of the single word she'd mouthed to me.

Go.

Go.

Go.

I turned my beast and we soared.

To find Odele.

To find my wife.

Odele

Slowly, with every limb shaking, I used the side of the ledge to help steady me back up into a floating position. I gripped it tightly, leaning into it for a mere second before I unsheathed the wyvern blade at my side and the sword of ice.

My wound screamed, but this wound… it was nothing compared to Alexxandria's.

Maisie's obsidian blade shoved straight through her chest as easily as if cutting through a sponge.

It had been a plan quickly hashed out in my own desperation, one I hadn't even been sure would *work*. But if I knew one thing about Alexxandria, it was that she knew us, and because she knew us, she would expect this, the trick we pulled.

Switching places was what we did. It was part of the Thalassarin treachery. She really thought I'd allow Maisie to take my place? That I wasn't self-sacrificing?

That had been her first mistake.

Maisie's face had paled, and her hands gripping tightly at the hilt of the sword shook. I knew, without having to look into Alexxandria's eyes, that the self-proclaimed queen had died. It was the feeling in the water, as if her vile soul had left this world and gone off into another.

Hopefully somewhere awful.

And I knew the moment when Maisie realized this, it would change her life forever.

Shaking, she pulled the obsidian blade from her chest; as she did it, I darted forward. With the blade removed, I took my own and stabbed Alexxandria through the back.

Let my cousin believe that I had delivered the death blow instead of her.

She'd sacrificed enough of her soul for me already.

I pulled the blade out and watched her body sink slowly to the floor before floating back up. I tried not to stare too long at the body. Instead I turned to my cousin.

Maisie's whole body trembled. "I—I killed—" The sword fell from her hand and clattered to the ice.

I reached for her, pulling her into my arms. "You didn't," I lied, and it came so easily. Let them all think me a murderer if I could save Maisie's soul. She'd done it for me like I'd killed for her. "I did."

Her whole body trembled, and her stomach pressed up against mine. I winced at the pain. Better me than her, I reminded myself.

Better me than her.

"I'm sorry," I apologized anyway. Because she hadn't wanted to do this. She hadn't wanted to lie and slip out of her tent unnoticed by her mermen, but she'd done so anyway.

"I did it for you. To protect you."

Opposite sides of the same coin.

I smiled sadly at her and took a breath. "It'll be okay." She'd get through the nightmares.

Eventually.

I had.

I pulled away just as a shadow passed overhead and a figure dropped from it before us. A figure with red hair and a glaring yellow eye that took one look at his dead sister, and I swore I saw something within him crumple.

"Adrian…" I tried to take a stroke towards him, but the wound at my abdomen, right where she'd stabbed me, tugged, and pain shot through my whole body. I grabbed for Maisie, and she tried to keep me upright, but I was heavy. Everything was too heavy.

And I fell into the darkness.

Valmundur

The most terrifying moment of my life was seeing Odele fall a second time and still being absolutely helpless to do anything about it.

She fell to the ground into an unconsciousness before she got up again and looked around a bit dazedly. She saw Ytgar and I fighting against the confines of our manacles and she whirled, daring to go near Alexxandria's floating body and picking her pockets. She procured the keys to our manacles, which Maisie promptly took from her before Adrian held Odele close and helped her onto his hovering mount.

Maisie couldn't free us soon enough. My neck ached where I'd pulled and tugged, but it still didn't compare to the pain of being completely and utterly helpless.

I took a single stroke forward, but Adrian was already urging his mount and they soared away, leaving us there.

I stared after them. Odele… she'd been stabbed. I thought it had been Maisie… This was worse somehow, and I couldn't even explain why that was. I'd been glad for a split second that it hadn't been Odele, and then filled with horror at the thought. I would have preferred neither of them to get hurt.

All because of my cowardice. Because I'd refused to kill her when I had the chance.

"We need to go to her," I gasped. "We need to—"

"We will," Ytgar interrupted. He turned to Maisie and placed his hands on her shoulders. "Thank you." The sound of his voice held eternal gratitude. "For helping."

Her eyes had a haunted look to them, and she opened her mouth to reply but was interrupted by a shout of anger.

"Maisie!"

A dragon swooped down and landed on the roof beside us; from it slid Kai, Captain Saber, and Elias.

Maisie took one look at them, her hand going to her throat to clasp at the ring hanging there, a ring so similar to the one Odele wore that it was no wonder we hadn't been able to tell them apart. She crumpled, breaking apart.

They surrounded her, pulling them each into the circle of their arms and comforting her as she wept into their chests. This moment was too private, too intimate for our eyes.

"Let's go," Ytgar said, his hand clamping down on my shoulder. I tried not to flinch at the pain. But I did. He slowly lowered his hand from me. "We need to see Odele." His silver eyes strayed to the still floating body of Alexxandria. "And then we need to bury her."

Odele didn't stay down for long. She sat in the tent in complete and utter stillness for a few minutes, though that may have been due to the fact that the mage worked his magic on her. It was entrancing. The magic knitted together the worst of the damage before he declared it was in the gods' hands now and he left.

She sighed, smoothed down her dress skirts, and got up. Odele looked at me, no doubt taking in the bruises over every inch of my face, though her expression never softened into one of pity. She looked rather annoyed.

She sniffed haughtily. "Did it hurt?"

I smiled and winced at the pain the action caused my split lip. Adrian hadn't offered up the mage to heal me, and I hadn't asked. It would have damaged my pride—or whatever was left of it—even more. "Yes."

She nodded. "Good. Maybe then you'll think twice about leaving me, you bastard." Then she turned her glare to Ytgar. "I can't believe *you* allowed yourself to get taken. And *you!*" She whirled on Adrian, who merely shoved his hands into his cloak pockets. "Don't ever throw me out of my own war tent again."

"Never," he agreed, a sad smile twisting his mouth.

She nodded once, and while her expression was confident and strong, the next word out of her mouth came out a ragged, broken sound. "Good."

And then she was crying.

She just crumpled to the ground and broke apart. Tears and sobs choked her, her shoulders racked up and down with the heartbroken sound that pierced me down to the last remnants of my own broken soul.

"Odele…" I started forward and she held up a hand to stop me.

When she looked up, the tears swarmed rapidly. "Don't," she ordered. "Don't get close. If you do, I swear to the gods I'll punch you in your stupid face for what you did. *You left me.*" She flung that last accusation out bitterly, angrily.

It cleaved me in two.

"You don't understand. I did it to protect Ytgar—"

She scoffed. "I understand perfectly fine. Who do you think you're talking to? I'm not daft! I'm your wife, and one of the smartest mer in the seven sea kingdoms and *you left me.* Like my opinion didn't matter. Like I didn't need you…" She sobbed and turned her face away like she was trying to hide her expression from me.

I knew that if I made it back to her, we would talk about the fact that I'd left her in the first place. But I hadn't expected her to be so angry, to fling these words straight at my face. Though with Odele, I shouldn't have expected anything less.

Maddeningly, it brought a smile to my lips. I dared a few strokes towards her and bent down, staring at her until she met my gaze angrily. "You want to hit me?" I asked. "Go ahead. Hit me. Punch me. Curse me to the ice and back, I don't care." I reached for her through every screaming protest of my own body, my fingers curling around her upper arms. "When I was locked away in that cell for weeks, when I was beaten—" She sobbed, but I continued, "—there was only one thought that kept me alive, and that was you." My hand went up to cup her cheek. She was warm, solid, in my palm. And nothing had ever felt better. "I thought I'd never see you again."

"Then you didn't have enough faith in my intelligence or my ability to get you out of their alive."

I blinked, opened my mouth, closed it. "No…that's not what I—"

She growled. "Shut up you Iolish bastard and kiss me."

THE HARDEST PART ABOUT war was burying the dead afterwards. It was turning over those floating bodies and seeing the faces of friends or family and feeling your chest cave in two.

Seeing the dead body of my sister for the second time was no exception.

I'd never forget those moments when I dropped onto the roof and saw the blood still freshly dribbling from the gaping hole in her chest.

I hadn't the time to truly process her death though when Odele had fallen and I'd seen the wound on her, inflicted by my monster of a twin.

And yet, despite what she'd done, what she was, something in me still fragmented when my soldiers brought her kelp rolled body to me in preparation for her final moments.

In our culture, we believed the spirits needed safe guidance from their bodies, their vessels, and into the afterlife. It's why songs were sung over the bodies; they helped the God of Death reap them to the underwaters where they belonged, or else their souls would be trapped forever in a dead vessel, in a cage for the rest of their time.

My sister didn't deserve the kindness being given to her, I knew, but I couldn't bring myself to dump her into an unmarked grave like I knew the others wanted to do.

Perhaps only my own mer understood this, the finality in my gesture as I took her body far away from the others and ordered them to dig into the silt. They did so with grim expressions. They would not beseech me this, for they knew, they understood.

When no one else might.

Once the hole was dug deep, I positioned her semi-floating body over the grave. As death progressed, the body slowly sunk to the sea floor to rot and provide sustenance for the coral, the sea life, and even the silt. In the end, we all went back to the ground.

I took a stroke back. She had been wrapped in accordance to our traditions, her whole body in a mummified manner except for her face.

She had been beautiful once, and one half still was, though pale and starting to bloat with death. It was to that beautiful side I looked at now, the curve of her cheekbones, the plump lips…

She always said she wished she hadn't been beautiful because of all the attention she garnered. It was that beauty that caught the attention of those Thalassarin guards, and it was the beauty she blamed for what had happened to her.

She'd become a monster, had let her hatred devour her from the inside out, and she had killed many as she sought her vengeance.

It was a strange thing to watch what vengeance had done to her. I had been with her when it happened, when they'd tortured her, carved up half of her face, and I was there to care for her afterwards as well. I watched as the wound festered, as she purposefully dragged her nails down the sensitive flesh so it would scar. I watched her change before my eyes, and in the process of caring for her, I'd changed too. And then she'd declared her thirst for blood and violence, and I'd developed it right alongside her but for different reasons.

Where she sought to kill and to conquer, I sought peace.

A peace I obtained by becoming a cruel merman.

Eventually our paths had diverged, our goals had become different, and I'd had no choice but to stop the only mermaid I'd ever loved and looked after in my life.

And now she was dead.

Emotion swelled up inside me to choke at my throat. I wanted to open my mouth and sing, to let her soul go to where she belonged and get it over with. But I couldn't find the words, I couldn't find my voice. I was choking… I was drowning in water. I was…

"Adrian."

My head snapped around at the sound of my name and I took in Odele, Ytgar, Val, and to my surprise the Black Blade.

I tried not to look at the Black Blade. He'd been there that day; he'd heard the haunting screams of my sister's pleas, knew my shame, hers.

"What are you doing here?" The words came out sharper than I'd intended.

Odele's expression was soft. Lies. I knew it was all lies. She hated my sister, they all did. They'd wanted her dead as much as…

My breath caught.

As much as I did.

I turned away from her and back to my sister, unable to look my wife in the eye. She came up beside me, Ytgar and Val on my other side.

"You're burying your sister," Odele said. There was no malice in her words that was a question, but not quite. She should have been angry, should have been hateful, but she wasn't.

"I am."

"You didn't tell us."

There was an accusing note that I had to close my eyes against. I swallowed. "I did not think you would care."

Her hand fluttered to my wrist, a soft graze of touch that warmed every nerve in my body. And then she threaded her fingers through mine and gripped me tightly.

"No matter what she did or didn't do… she's still your sister."

It was those words that broke me, the feel of Ytgar's palm sliding into mine, fingers threading through the spaces of my own on my other side, that completely undid me.

I dropped to my tail in the silt, and I wept.

I wept for the mer she had been and the mer she had become. I wept for her broken body, for the scars, for her, and for me.

Between my rasping sobs, I tried to let song come out, but nothing came out of my throat save for tortured sound and heartbreak.

Odele squeezed my hand. "I don't know what to do…"

"Sing," I huffed. "Just…sing…"

So she did.

Her voice rose in a melody that wasn't perfect, yet still beautiful just the same. I listened to the rise and fall of it as my sobbing ebbed. It carried on to my God of Death. I felt his presence as he came to reap the soul of my sister from her body, leaving behind a warmth in his wake.

My whole body shuddered as her body slowly sank down into the grave. Finally, my sister was at rest. I hoped for a moment she was welcomed into the realm of the gods and was not punished, no matter what everyone said she deserved.

She'd already suffered enough.

Silt had been placed on top of her as well as heavy rocks and mounds of ice. One by one, my mer left me. Ytgar and Odele were the last to leave, but I knew I wasn't really alone.

"I hear you go by a new name now," I said with a bit of amusement, my throat raw and aching from crying.

The Black Blade sidled up next to me and sat on the silt at my side, throwing his arm over the curve of his arched tail as he stared at the grave of my sister.

The cold currents ripped at his dark hair, slapping the curly strands against his brown cheeks. A single silver cross dangled from the lobe of his ear; he wore black fur cloaks and an obsidian blade at his waist.

"A namesake I have thanks to you."

My eyes didn't stray from the obsidian blade. Perfectly forged, shaped. "You kept it."

He turned to look at me for the first time, his brown eyes meeting my yellow one. His shoulder came up in a careless shrug, and amusement lined over his every feature. "I sold them, actually."

I blinked my surprise then threw my head back and laughed. He was…different. When I met him, he had been kind, *soft,* terrified of the Thalassarin Selection and what it could bring. He was different now, obviously hardened by life, and with a cold, dark amusement within him that made me smile.

"They're the rarest blades in all of Thalassar. This is the only one I kept." His hand went to pat the hilt of his blade. "Well, this and a ring, but Maisie wears that around her neck. And she coincidentally has the twin blade to this one."

My head shook back and forth. "Odele wears my ring and carries my blade." I leaned back in the silt and eyed him curiously. "How is Maisie?"

I'd heard from Ytgar and Val that she'd been the one to deliver the killing blow, that Odele had tried to spare her from the knowledge by shoving the dagger I'd gifted her into my sister's back.

I'd promised I would be the one to kill her. I supposed in some form, I had.

The Black Blade's eyes narrowed. I supposed that was answer enough. "She was pure. I'm not sure that matters in the grand scheme of things but…she has a soft heart, can't bear to harm anything. What she did…" He trailed off, shaking his head before he side-eyed me with a glare. "Do you hate her for it?"

His tone suggested if I even hinted I did, he'd gut me himself.

I tore my gaze away and looked at my sister's grave. "No." The answer was honest, and he read it, because when I turned to look at him again, he nodded.

"I think about it a lot, you know," he confessed on a whisper. "What happened…how we set each other free."

I snorted. Free? "As free as we could be."

"You're a king now; and, in a sense, family I suppose." He added that almost as an afterthought. "But as king, you can change what needs to be changed. Things we spoke about in whispers between the cages of our prison…"

A free world.

As if reading my thoughts, the Black Blade bumped his shoulder against mine and smirked. "A free world."

Stepping fin back in Isolde Palace had been heartbreaking, in a sense. I felt its emptiness immediately without my grandmother there to fill the spaces of the halls with her commanding, irritating voice.

I'd give anything to hear that voice again. We hadn't had enough time, and what time we did have, we'd wasted. Completely. Because I'd never been the ruler she'd wanted me to be.

I took a stroke into the royal room where her throne of ice sat and halted. Big…it seemed so big, so vast. Like the cushions of it would swallow me whole.

"Intimidating, isn't it?" Odele's voice sounded at my shoulder.

I turned a frozen stare towards her, but she was looking at the throne, not at me.

"Back in Thalassar, when I was younger," she continued, "I used to try on my mother's crowns after she'd died. The crowns of the Queen of Thalassar, before my aunt became my stepmother." A smirk pulled at her lips. "They never fit."

I swallowed. "I did the same," I confessed quietly. "After my father died…I'd sit on the throne. I was older than you were…" I side eyed her. "Bigger too, and it was still too big."

Odele took a stroke towards the throne, unafraid and regal. She still swam slow due to her injury, but she was recovering quickly. It had been days, *days,* and I just now came into the palace to see what had become of my home…

It hadn't been as destroyed as I thought it would be. Servants had been found locked within rooms, and so had Odele's cousin, Scarlet. Nothing was destroyed. But I'd give it all to have my grandmother back. For my last blood relative.

For so long I feared that everyone I loved, everyone I was related to, was meant to die. Now, I was well and truly alone. The last of the Isoldes, Neves, Snows, Frosts… If I died, my lineage ended with me.

Odele drew my grim thoughts away from that and to her as she swam up and sat straight down on my grandmother's throne.

With the wyvern dagger at her hip, the beautiful dress, and fierce expression, all that was left was an ice crown upon her brow.

She smiled at me. "We grow into them, you know," she called out from across the space that separated us. "Into our roles. Into our crown, and our thrones." Her eyes got a far away look to them. "If I were to go back to Thalassar right now and try on my mother's crowns, they'd fit." She lounged back in the seat and kicked up her fins. "It's all about perspective."

I fought back the maddening urge to chuckle. Perspective. Right.

I dared to take a stroke closer. "And will you?" I asked. "Go back to Thalassar to try on those crowns?" It was her birthright. By all means, she never should have even come here. Thalassarin laws stated the heir had to be in the kingdom at all times.

I stopped just at the edge of the throne, our tails touching. She leaned towards me, bracing her hands on the arm rests. "No," she whispered near my lips. "I've outgrown them. Spiritually, I mean." She kissed me, a light peck of her mouth against mine that made me desperately crave more. "Besides…" She sat back down. "I was promised a trip around the seven sea kingdoms, and I want what was promised, Iolish." Her eyes twinkled with a bit of mischief before she pushed herself off the chair and gestured for me to sit down. "I mean, you're the king now, right?"

The word 'king' almost choked the water from my body. I shook my head. "There are others in line before me—"

"You helped save Iol. The mer will remember that and won't give a flying dolphin's tailfin about whoever's in line before you. You are *king,* and you deserve it."

I stared at the empty throne. It beckoned, and I contemplated. Tempting…

I never felt good enough to occupy this seat, because it had been made clear from the beginning that while I had the title of 'prince' this was never mine to inherit. But in those last moments of my grandmother's life, when her eyes had flashed to mine, I'd seen something in the depths of them that she'd never shown me before.

Pride.

Taking a breath, I turned and took a seat upon my throne.

"Even without the crown, you are a true ruler." Odele smiled.

I reached for her and pulled her into my lap. "I don't need a crown."

Her fingers tangled into my hair and she pouted. "Hmm, you sure? You looked very elegant in the one I gave you."

I smiled and pulled her closer so every angle of her body was hard against mine. When I took her mouth, it was a slow, demanding exploration of our tongues, and my teeth scraped over her bottom lip. I pulled away. "I don't need it. I already have everything I want."

THE FOLLOWING DAYS WERE flurry with the activity of the aftermath of war. While heartbreak, sorrow, and loss pressed down upon us, there was also a new sense of hope. Of rebirth.

From the rubble of ice and death, we started to build Iol anew, starting with a change of regime. Due to the treacherous nature of Prime Minister Rollo, we abolished his corrupt form of government and created a new one.

Ytgar had officially been crowned King of Iol as the only last living Neves Isolde—the others had been murdered by Alexxandria, though that hadn't been a surprise when we'd found the remnants of their bodies. There hadn't been a ceremony; just a small coronation where everyone had been present.

Documents had been signed to claim his legitimacy as king, signed and recognized by Thalassar, Kappur, Draconi, and the Uncharted.

I'd never forget the moment when I set the crown of ice atop my husband's head, the pride, the sadness that reflected so deeply in the depths of his silver-white eyes… In turn, he'd crowned me Queen of Iol, and when he'd placed that crown of ice, steel, pink quartz, and black obsidian—crafted in honor of my husbands and my own roots—it didn't weigh heavily at all.

The cheer that went up was a sound borne of such honesty and true excitement that for a moment I could believe that we weren't broken, that we weren't hurting.

The truth was much more complicated than that.

During the day, we kept ourselves busy with reconstruction and everything else; tending to the ill, burying the fallen, diplomatic and political meetings… Ytgar, Val, Adrian, and I barely had time to see one another during the day. But at night…

We used that time to heal our broken bodies as much as our broken souls. We were all caught in the grip of nightmares, taking turns, it seemed, night after night to wake up thrashing and gasping. Adrian would wake up snarling at Thalassarin guards, for the sister he couldn't protect. Ytgar for his grandmother. Val woke up screaming for Jessinda, and though he didn't tell me, I knew he'd been there to witness my cousin's end.

We held each other closer than ever. Perhaps this closeness couldn't banish the dreams entirely, but knowing we were there for one another, that we cared, that we *loved,* well, that was healing in of itself.

Though the Mage had healed the wounds Alexxandria had inflicted upon me as best as he could, the pain had still been there. I had to take it slow because my body and mind were still healing. But after a week and a half, I was feeling renewed. Even Val's face was better, with nothing but a yellow fading color against his cheeks. No permanent physical damage had been done to us, except I'd now forever sport a scar in my abdomen.

Better me than Maisie, who had locked herself away with her own mermen, only occasionally coming out of their shared room within Isolde Palace.

I knew she was hurting for what she'd done, and while it had been a necessary evil, I also knew she would need the time to come to grips with it for herself. Deep down, I knew she would accept it, move on. It would change her, like so much in the past few months had changed me, but she would be fine. She would survive.

We were Malabellas, after all.

I prowled slowly through the halls of the palace, taking in my home. Not everyone had been so lucky in Iol; homes had been destroyed, and we were working quickly to help them rebuild. It wouldn't be the same, and the wound of the violation would always be there, but it was a process…

A servant sped passed me, nearly knocking me down. She let out a startled gasp at what she'd done and bowed her head over the tray of rags, lava globes, and sea herbs she carried. "My apologies, Your Majesty."

I would have yelled at her audacity, screamed at her, but… I didn't. "Who's that for?" I gestured at the tray with a nod.

She looked up. "General Kane Feng Han. Anneli requested it be sent up right away."

My expression went grim. The Draconian general had been in bed for a while now, thrashing with fever. The venom of a wyvern's tail had opened his side entirely, rendering the right side of his fins useless. I knew if he recovered, he'd swim with a limp for the rest of his life, and so his service to the Dragon Emperor would end.

The mage had not helped the wounded beyond healing me. While I wanted to call him selfish, he'd looked me straight in the eye but had seemed to see beyond me as he said, "The gods have a plan for them." I didn't understand it at all, but I respected that he wouldn't help because to use magic required energy. Energy he didn't seem to have.

"I'll take that to her." I held my hands out for the tray.

The servant tried to take a stroke back. "No, Majesty, I—"

"Now."

If anyone knew how to treat Drake venom, it was the Draconians, and the emperor himself had been in to tend to Kane. I knew there was little I could do, but still I took the tray from the servant's hands and swam up to his room. I didn't bother knocking before I went inside.

On the bed, Kane thrashed in pain, delirious with fever. Anneli was alone in the room and at his bedside, swiping a cloth over his forehead. The action calmed him instantly.

I closed the door behind me, and she looked up, startled to find me there instead of a servant.

I came forward and set the tray on the table next to the bed. Anneli didn't say a word, so I did. "You really like him, don't you?"

If she didn't, I wouldn't have offered. But I saw something between them; something had sparked since the moment they'd met.

Anneli didn't acknowledge my comment. "The venom had already been coursing too long in his system. The Draconians say if the fever breaks, he'll live, but he won't be the same." Her gaze went down to the sheets wrapped around his tail, as if she could see through them and at the marred flesh of fins. "He won't be a general anymore. I heard them talking; I think he heard too, and that's why he won't wake." She bent and swiped the rag over his forehead again. "Did you know that dragons to Draconians are like their other half?" She began swiping down his neck, at his bare chest and the muscles that carved his abdomen. "Once your fated dragon chooses you, it chooses you for life?" She swallowed. "His died protecting him."

My throat tightened. I didn't have a dragon, didn't have a pet. But I did have a love for hippocampi, and Anneli for orcas. She bred them, cared for them, *loved* them.

I tried to put myself in her fins, and I could feel the sorrow. She was thinking, wondering, what it would be like to lose your pet, your friend, your fated for life.

"I think he just doesn't want to wake up at all and face a world without his dragon."

I looked at the warrior restless against the cushions. His skin was growing sallow, and I could feel the heat radiating off of his body. He was built as solidly as a rock, though. Taut muscles, broad shoulders and a wide chest, a slim waist with a smattering of scales dotting along his abdomen and where his tail met the V of his hips. His long black hair spilled across the cushions of the bed, the strands like ink or soft sea silk.

I caught Anneli staring before she blinked and started wiping down the fever from his body.

"Do you need anything else?" I asked. There wasn't much I could do here. In fact, there wasn't anything I could do here but offer my friend support, maybe a shoulder to cry on.

But Anneli was strong.

She didn't cry.

She waved me off. "Go back to your queenly things." Her voice held a tinge of sarcasm.

I started for the door, and when I opened it, I could hear Anneli's voice drift over to me, so low I had to strain my ears to hear. "You better wake up, you bastard," she threatened darkly. "You promised to show me that riding dragons was better than riding orcas. All I see is that dragons are whinier."

My mouth twisted into a smile at the insinuation in her words, then dropped open in surprise when I heard a dark answering chuckle, and words that followed in Dracon.

"When I get out of this bed, you'll never touch an orca again in your life…"
I left before I could hear any more from his surprisingly filthy mouth.

Floating by the window of our room, I looked out at the Iolish waters. The reconstruction of our kingdom was in its beginning stages, so it looked like nothing more than a skeletal structure of steel pillars and mounds of ice.

But at least there was laughter, a sound that the currents drifted up to where I floated and brought a smile to my own face.

"That's nice to hear, isn't it?" His voice drifted in from behind me.

I didn't have to turn to know that all three of them were there. I could sense them, like my body was attuned to theirs.

It was Adrian who swam up behind me and wrapped his arms around my stomach and pulled me close to his chest. He pressed a kiss against the soft skin of my neck, tongue trailing a pathway up to my jaw, to my ear, where he bit down on the soft lobe and played with it between his teeth.

"Don't you have things to oversee?" I asked breathlessly, even as I leaned back into his touch, craving more.

I could feel him smile against my skin. "Let's just say we took the day off to be with you."

He turned me within the circle of his arms, and my palms slid up his chest. I glared at him and over his shoulder, where Ytgar and Val were framed. Val looked sheepish, Ytgar just crossed his arms against his chest, looking dominant and infuriating.

And very enticing.

"You took the day off to pleasure me." It came out as an accusation.

"Of course." Adrian nipped my chin with his mouth. "You are our queen, after all."

I smirked, sliding my hands up to wrap them around his neck. "Damn straight I am. So, my loyal subjects, what will you do to please me today?"

Behind Adrian, Ytgar and Val shared a conspiratorial glance before turning that gaze back towards me. Ytgar smiled, and the very sight of it sent a slice of anticipation down my spine.

It held the promise of sensuality.

"First…" Adrian trailed his tongue from the tip of my chin all the way down to my neck. His long, deft fingers went to the ties of my cloak, and the weight slid from my body and pooled at our fins. He pushed down the neckline of my velvet dress to expose my breasts to the cold waters. "I will kiss you here." His breath fanned out across my skin, teeth grazing my collarbone. I arched into his touch as his tongue slid over one nipple, then the other.

"Or perhaps…" Val sidled up to my other side, a gleam of eager mischief in his eyes. "We can start right here…" His thumb went up to my mouth, swiping across my bottom lip. He crowded towards me, his own lips kissing along my jaw before claiming my mouth.

His kiss sent me spiraling. It was an onslaught of sensations to have Val's tongue thrusting in slow, even strokes within my mouth, while Adrian's laved up my nipples with even steadier strokes.

Then solid hands were at my back, steady fingers unbuttoning my dress. Ytgar's warm fingers slid onto my bare skin, pushing the dress down. I dropped my hands from Adrian's neck so he could push the sleeves down my arms. When it pooled around me, I kicked it from my fins.

Then Ytgar's mouth was pressed against my back and I shuddered at the warmth coming off of three of them.

I'd missed this. Their touch, it was healing on its own. I wanted it, needed it, craved it desperately.

Adrian pulled away, sliding down my stomach. "Or maybe, I could start here…" His mouth immediately covered over the slit of my opening. He took the nub of my desire between his teeth and tugged, and my whole body quivered with fragmenting desire. It exploded within me, desire that pierced through my every single nerve ending.

He suckled and slid his tongue into me, his fingers dug into my hips to hold me steady as I rocked against his mouth. Ytgar's fingers gripped my hips from behind, the force of his palms branding me as he pushed my hips into Adrian.

I moaned into Val's mouth, biting down hard against his lip while Adrian slowly slid a finger inside me. I tore my lips from his and gasped as his fingers began their slow thrusts, angling up while his teeth bit and tugged.

Val smiled against my cheek. "Do you like that?" he growled, his hand circling my neck. "Do you like what he does to you?"

"Yes…" My hands gripped through Adrian's strands of hair to keep him pressed close as he dragged me higher and higher… bliss expanded through my body, rising… rising…

Ytgar's hand encircled my neck, craning it so I was looking up into the brightness of his eyes. The pads of his fingers parted my lips, and he shoved his fingers into my mouth. I sucked on them, tongue swirling against him and took him deep into my mouth.

He growled against me, grinding into me from behind. I felt his hardness against me; that's what sent me over the edge. The primal sound of his own desire rippled through me, causing my whole body to shudder completely. My hips jerked against Adrian's mouth, the onslaught of his tongue, fingers, and teeth dragging me deeper and deeper.

I was panting when Adrian slid up my body and let Val take his place. They moved in synchronization with one another and Val…

We hadn't been intimate since we'd found one another again, and the gleam in his eyes told me he wasn't taking this slowly.

I didn't want him to. I wanted him to devour me, body and soul. I wanted every bit of him just like I could see how he wanted every bit of me.

His arm snaked around my hips and pulled me close, while his other hand hiked up his tunic, exposing him to my naked flesh. The tip of him slid warmly across my stomach, and he rubbed his member across my skin, teasing dangerously close to my entrance. "I missed you," he rasped, his voice heady with desire. "So, so much, my love."

I reached for his shoulders. "Then show me." I used him to lever my self up and press myself against him. The tip of his member penetrated my opening, and I gasped as my mouth desperately went to his. "Show me just how much."

He breathed hard, nostrils flaring. "Hold her hard, Ytgar," he ordered, sliding inside me, inch by painful inch. He hissed through his teeth but turned to Adrian, "Keep her mouth busy for me."

I glared and started to protest when both mermen behind me jumped into action. Ytgar pressed his body against mine from behind; Adrian grabbed me by the chin and devoured my mouth with his own, and Val slammed to the hilt inside me. I cried out, tongue slashing against Adrian's.

Every thrust of Val's hips pushed me harder and harder against Ytgar's chest, but he kept me held steady by the hips, his own length grinding into me from behind. It felt *good*, ephemeral, to feel them all so intimately against me.

Adrian's tongue, smooth and warm, tangled with mine in a wild feeling frenzy. He mimicked the eager strokes of Val's hips in a way that made my head spin. I felt so full… so full… and still I wanted *more*. I wanted to feel their skin against me. I wanted them to worship every bit of my body with their hands, teeth, and mouths.

Val slid inside me, deep, the length of him sliding against the nub of my desire. I tore my mouth from Adrian's and gasped aloud, my hands blindly reaching for Val's tunic. With a sharp yank, I tore the material right down the middle. Buttons scattered around the water, but I didn't care. All I cared about was his skin.

My palms met his warmth, sliding over his chest and down the carved ridges of his abdomen and lower still to where our bodies were joined. I watched with fascination at his quick thrusts. They tore gasps out of me, pleasure like I'd never known.

There was something primal and wild about watching his hard member slide in and out of me, watching his length slide against my exposed nub.

Daringly, I slid my hands down between us and touched myself there.

A quick sensation of unbridled desire tightened down my spine.

"Yesss," Val hissed. His movements became rougher, more eager, and I let myself be swept away by it, by *him.* "Do it again," he pleaded. "Touch yourself."

A hand clamped down on top of mine. Ytgar's. He guided me back home, fingers placed gently but firmly over mine like he was an extension of myself, like he was the lord of my every movement. And as he pressed my own finger down over myself, I couldn't do anything but let him take the lead.

My head fell back against the crook where his neck met his shoulder and I gave into the sensation he caused, *we* caused. I turned, my eyelids fluttering open to find Adrian near me.

I gasped. "Do you feel neglected?"

Ytgar pushed my finger and his inside me, timing the movements of Val's thrusts to match with the own movement of our fingers.

He smirked, reaching a thumb out to swipe along my bottom lip. I took the digit in my mouth and sucked it all the way in, flicking my tongue over the pad of his finger. "Not at all, love. I enjoy watching as much as I enjoy the act itself." He slowly pulled his finger from my mouth and took it to his own, the gesture suggestive and erotic.

I groaned, feeling myself get closer and closer to that drop into pure bliss.

"Let me pleasure you." I reached for him one handed. The other was too busy sliding over my nub, tangled with Ytgar's fingers as him and Val both gave me pleasure.

Adrian pulled away with a tsk. "Manners, love. I can wait my turn."

I growled a silent sound of frustration that he swallowed with his mouth in a tangled kiss that left me breathless and sent my thoughts scattering. With his mouth on mine, Ytgar's fingers and my own inside me, and Val's thrusts going harder…harder…harder…

I bit down on Adrian's lip and tasted blood as I spiraled into oblivion, taking Valmundur with me.

He rode the wave out as long as he could, thrusting and thrusting, drawing out my own pleasure as well with each slide of his powerful length. Tremors shot through my body and slowly ebbed. We remained like that. Member, fingers, and tongue inside me while I tried to regain my thoughts, but they were so scattered, I wasn't even sure I wanted them anymore.

"Take me to the bed," I managed to order.

"Your wish is our command." Ytgar's voice rumbled through my back and his fingers slipped out of me. Adrian pulled away and it was Val who wrapped his arms around my waist and lifted me, whirling us around and taking a few strokes towards the bed. We fell atop it, and I closed my eyes at the feeling of falling before I landed against the soft cushions. Val loomed over me and placed his hands on either side of my face so I was caged between his arms. His mouth hovered above mine and the fan of his warm breath sent a tingle through my body.

"Did I tell you how much I missed you?"

I smirked. "You might have mentioned it."

He pressed his hips against mine, his length still hard inside me. I groaned, leaning into him, but he leaned away and slowly, torturously, he pulled out of me and rolled so he was lying on my other side. Ytgar took his place and Adrian plopped himself on my free side, using his hand to cradle his cheek as he watched Ytgar with gleaming eyes.

Ytgar pulled the tunic from his body. His movements were slow and deliberate, and I licked my lips in anticipation as I watched the muscles of his arms flex. He tossed the tunic to the side and looked down at me with a gleam in his eyes.

He was so beautiful, it hurt. My hands went up to run over his smooth brown skin, over his pecs and down to his abdomen. He was solid, reliable, and when I felt that first touch of his member push against my entrance, I arched my hips up to meet him.

"Beautiful," Adrian whispered as he took us in. His eye was glued on Ytgar as he slowly began pushing his way inside me. The single word sent tiny slivers through my bloodstream. I'd just fallen into bliss, and yet my body was ready again. If it was with them, my body wanted it over and over again. I wanted them over and over again.

"Guide him into me," I told Adrian, grasping for his wrist and bringing it between mine and Ytgar's bodies. Ytgar froze, and my eyes narrowed slightly at the action. "Do you want to?" If he didn't, I'd push Adrian's hand away.

But Ytgar met Adrian's stare and their eyes held. A silent sort of conversation seemed to pass between them, though for the life of me I couldn't figure out what they could be saying.

A moment later, Ytgar nodded in consent. "I want to." He gripped my hips, as if preparing himself for the brand of Adrian's touch.

But Adrian was gentle as he leaned forward and wrapped his hand around the hilt of Ytgar's member.

A hiss came out from between his teeth as Adrian pumped long his length once, twice. I watched the workings of that hand against his member. There was dominance in the gesture, strength, and it made my own anticipation rise high.

I wanted him inside me. I felt a quivering there at my entrance, desperate with longing.

But Adrian took his time. The two of them weren't like Val, who was always so eager, so quick. They took their time, they played, they teased. They fought for dominance.

Ytgar's hips jerked in Adrian's hand, and the sight of it had even me gasping, my free hand reaching for Val's. Val said nothing. He didn't watch—I stole a quick peek. He kept his eyes closed, but I knew he was aware of what was happening. I could hear the quickening of his breathing.

The tip of his member was teasing my entrance, so close, and I wanted him home. But Adrian was cruel, mischievous. He sat up, leaned forward, and stroked his tongue down the big length of Ytgar.

Hands fisted at my waist so tightly, the hurt added to the pleasure.

Fascination kept me riveted on the action before me. On Adrian's tongue circling over the tip of Ytgar before sliding up the top of him, all the way up to his waist, his stomach, his chest, his neck… All the way up until he reached his mouth.

And then he took.

He kissed the same way he fought; like a conqueror looking to take down cities and keep them for himself. He shoved his tongue in first, and it was like watching a battle between two dominant mermen trying to best the other. Ytgar kissed him back as fiercely as he would me, and I craved. My own tongue felt heavy with my desire as I watched them, as Adrian's fingers dug into Ytgar's shoulders and slid down his skin, to his chest and lower, just beneath his waist.

I knew he'd grabbed his member by the way Ytgar gasped into his mouth and jerked his hips. And a split second later, I felt and saw Adrian guide Ytgar inside me.

He jerked in to the hilt, and I groaned as the aggressiveness of the action slid me up the bed. I nearly floated up, but Ytgar's heavy body kept me weighed down to the cushions. And when he began to thrust, I knew nothing else but the sensation he was causing me.

My hand gripped tightly to Val's, and he gripped back just as tightly. Fingers dug painfully into my hips, and Adrian laid back to my side, turning my ace so he could claim my mouth for his own.

The taste of Ytgar lingered on Adrian's tongue. I devoured it, sucking him into my mouth. I pillaged and conquered with just as much strength as Adrian, my hips lifting to meet Ytgar thrust for hard thrust.

This wasn't anger, it wasn't desperation. This, what lay between us was a healing, a claiming. It was love. And I felt it with every cry bursting from his mouth as his hips met mine.

Then Adrian's fingers were there, and he was touching me. The warmth of him against me combined with Ytgar's length was all I needed to fall over the edge.

I tried to tear my mouth away to scream, but Adrian swallowed the sounds with his tongue and teeth. He bit down on my tongue. It was pain. It was bliss. It was everything I ever wanted.

Tremors racked through my body, and I convulsed against their bodies. Ytgar roared his own released, pistoning inside me at a new rapid pace that wrung every cry I had left in my lungs from my lips. Sounds that Adrian swallowed with his own mouth and took into his body, his soul. He took bits of me with him, and I let him. Because I belonged to him. I belonged to them all. Just like they belonged to me.

When the aftershocks of my desire started to fade, Adrian pulled away. My limbs had grown weak, I couldn't hold my head, my body up anymore. I didn't feel like I could… not again.

But Adrian, he was a cruel, vicious merman and when Ytgar slid from me, Adrian hiked his tunic up and replaced him and began to move.

"There will be time to rest, my love. *After.*"

My head shook from side to side and I gasped. So sensitive…my every nerve had become overly sensitized and every sensation heightened as Adrian pumped his hips.

He seduced even while inside me, making me his with every stroke. He knew just how to move, what pace to set. What would illicit cries from my lips and just how to bring me balancing on the precipice of that edge. And I wanted every single moment of it, no matter how hard my body protested with its sensitivity, I took him inside me. It didn't matter that my hips couldn't meet up to slam against his, thrust for thrust. He took control. His hand slipped to my lower back and he lifted me, angling himself so he was deep inside me, so deep I could feel him down to the roots of my very soul.

And when he thrust, once, twice, three times, I screamed.

Too easily he dragged me down into that chasm, and still he kept going, again and again until he wrung out another cry from my throat. Until I was exhausted, until he finished with a dark roar of his own and we fell into a heap of exhausted limbs side by side.

Their bodies crowded me, and I welcomed their presence. Because it had been only about a week ago that we hadn't all been together.

And this…I felt as if it had healed us, this closeness, this unity. My heart pounded, confirming it, and I fell to sleep with a smile on my face and my mermen holding me close, knowing that it was done. The war was over, and we were all here with each other.

Safe.

Protected.

Together.

Goodbyes were always bittersweet, laced with sorrow, and just a bit of heartbreak. I felt them all floating before my cousin. They threatened to choke me with emotion, and I should have pushed them away, pretended to be strong for the mer that surrounded us and observed, but I couldn't.

I wrapped my arms around her shoulders and pulled her close, the bump of her stomach pressing tightly against me.

"The next time we see one another," I whispered through my sudden tears, "you'll have children."

Maisie choked on a sob herself and hugged me back, her arms tight. I felt like I hadn't seen her for days and now she, and everyone else who'd helped us win the war, were leaving. "You'll visit often?" She pulled away, swiping away at her tears with annoyance. "Promise?"

"Of course." I crooked my thumb behind me in Ytgar and Val's direction. "Those bastards owe me a sea tour."

Maisie chuckled. "You'll be doing a lot of traveling."

"I certainly hope so. We have a plan to create peace treaties and alliances all around the sea."

"If anyone can do the impossible, it's you."

"I think that's the nicest thing you've ever said to me, cousin."

I turned from her to Prince Kai behind her, my eyes narrowing. "Keep your seed out of my cousin next time, yeah?"

His eyes softened despite my insult, and he grabbed me by the shoulders and pulled me forward into a hug. The gesture surprised me so much, I didn't hug him back. And when I felt his lips near the lobe of my ear, I shuddered. "Switch places with her again, and I'll kill you myself."

He pulled away before I'd even registered the words, a smile in place.

I believed him.

Clearing my throat, I turned to the Black Blade to find him and Adrian face to face, gripping each other by the backs of their necks, foreheads touching. They whispered to one another, words no one could make out. I watched them for a moment. Something similar sparked within the two mermen, like they were cut from the same magical cloth, and it sparked with similar energy.

I turned away from their moment, skipping over Captain Saber entirely after meeting his death glare for a split second—they were going to hold a grudge against me forever for what Maisie was forced to do on my behalf—and I looked at Kane Feng Han.

He'd recovered just enough to make the journey home, though he looked to be rather invigorated now. He was scanning the crowd behind us, the Iolish party who had come to say goodbye to our allies, our friends.

I knew who he was looking for and knew he wouldn't find her. She hadn't come with us to say goodbye, despite having spent every waking moment by his side and assuring herself he broke through his fever. As soon as the Draconian general opened his eyes, she'd left.

I knew because I'd asked the servants.

I skipped over him to the emperor and the King of Kappur. I nodded to them both and then finally, my eyes settled on my father. My throat tightened with emotion. He pushed his way through the mer to get to me until we were face to face.

"Odele," he said, his voice grave and filled with emotion I didn't want to identify.

"Xristo," I replied coolly. I didn't dare call him father, didn't dare open up my heart to that possibility of it breaking. He'd come, yes. Maisie had brought my family to me, yes. I'd been overwhelmed with gratitude when I'd seen him and the Thalassarin armies at the time, but now... I didn't want to let myself hope. Because deep down, a voice told me that he'd come for Maisie, not for me. Because Maisie was more like my mother than I ever was.

Hurt fragmented in the depths of his eyes, but what else had he expected? That I'd stupidly forgive him for all the years of neglect? As if this one action came before all others? As if it ruled out everything else he'd done? I'd called. I'd sent him a message myself and he'd responded, he'd denied.

I couldn't forget that.

Not ever.

My father dropped his voice to a low whisper. "You're different from before, Odele."

"No," I cut in. "I'm the same. You just never bothered to *look*. To *see me*."

He looked ashamed, with good reason. He stroked his fingers down the long length of his dark, jeweled, beard. "After your mother died, I was lost. You have to understand that, Odele."

"Well so was I!" I couldn't help but shout. I didn't care that there were other mer around, that they were likely hearing this exchange. "I was a *child*. She was my mother and she died, and I needed you and you shoved me aside, just like you've shoved me aside every day since." The tears stung behind my eyelids, but I would *not* cry. I wouldn't give him the satisfaction. He didn't deserve another moment of my tears, of my sorrow. *He'd* failed *me*. And I wasn't without my faults, but he couldn't hate me for not trying as I grew, when he'd pushed me away when I was young. You didn't *do* that. You didn't get to push away your child, neglect them for your own grief, and then expect them to come to *you* with words of comfort. Why did I have to try when he hadn't been there for me at all?

"What do you want me to say, Odele? That I'm sorry? Because I am. I failed you…I know I did. I let myself drown in my own grief for far too long, and I wasn't the father to you that I should have been."

"No," I answered coolly, as cool as the ice around us. "You weren't."

And he was still missing the point. He knew what he'd done wrong. I wanted an apology. I wanted him to *try*. For me, for who *I* was, not for who my mother was or who Maisie was. But for *me*. Because he saw something in me, because he believed in me. Because he wanted a proper relationship with his only daughter.

But I feared he'd never give me that.

"I can't get that time back; we both know that."

"I don't want that time back." Nothing could change it; no amount of magic would give me the love I deserved or the father's attention I needed. "It's too late." Those words came out, but my eyes, my brain, my heart and soul, they all screeched.

Fight for me.
Fight for me.
Fight for me.

For once in your life, I need you to fight for me.

If he didn't, he'd be lost to me forever. Because I couldn't keep hanging on to him or the love I'd wished he'd given to me. If I kept wishing for what could never be, my soul would perish.

So fight for me, you bastard, or leave my life forever.

His face fell. "I understand." His hands grasped my shoulders and squeezed, and I knew then that he would not fight for me. "Be happy, Odele."

He pulled away, and I felt my heart break. Again. It didn't matter how many times he swam away from me; it would hurt each time. And I knew without a doubt that if he stayed away, it would destroy me. I could learn to live without him. I'd spent most of my life learning, and I was an adult now. I could do it. I *could.*

He took a stroke away from me and I watched him with a roaring sound filling my ears.

The tears burned and threatened. I wouldn't cry. I *wouldn't.*

So I focused on his face instead. He hadn't taken his eyes off me, his jaw tightened and in the blue depths of his gaze I could see words I desperately wanted to hear. *Don't hope. Don't you dare hope for what isn't there.*

"Odele…" He hesitated. He *hesitated.* But then he took a stroke forward again. "I don't have an excuse," he rushed to say. "For my neglect, for the way I let your stepmother treat you for years. I—you say you don't want that time back. I can't give it to you, but you're my daughter and I—" He broke off and took my hands in his own. "I failed you, Odele. I don't want to fail you anymore."

My throat was sore from holding in everything. It was everything I wanted to hear and yet, "I'm tired of you breaking my heart."

I could see the reflection of his own heart fragmenting in his eyes. "I did it before, but I—I want to be better. I want to be a father to you. I know you might not need me anymore, but I want to be here for you. If you'll let me…" He paused. "*Please* let me."

I took in a shuddering breath. This…this was everything, *everything* I'd ever wanted to hear. "It's not too late," I whispered. "It's not."

His expression crumpled. "Thank the gods." And he pulled me into a fierce hug. The first one in years, and yet it felt right, familiar.

Like this was where we belonged.

After a few more goodbyes, they left, each royal bowing to one another with equal respect and kindness. Even to Adrian, who smirked haughtily at the Emperor of Draconi and winked before bowing. When he rose, he said, "Make sure to have your maps redone because the Uncharted has a new name now."

The emperor's expression didn't change, but I swore I could see respect there. "And what is that?"

"Saavaj'i." His eye strayed to the Black Blade one last time, and he smirked. "It means 'a free world.'"

One year later…

I BOUNCED UP AND down in my saddle, a giddy excitement thrumming through me the closer we made it to the palace. We'd reached warmer waters hours ago, the scent of water lilies drifting through the currents in a welcome greeting.

"You're going to fall off the saddle, idiot." Anneli sneered from atop her orca.

I glared at her and stuck out my tongue. I was queen; I could do whatever I wanted. Something that I didn't need to remind her or even want to because every time the words left my mouth, she sneered down at me and them. It got tiring after a while.

Damn Iolish.

"I'm excited."

The last time I'd seen my cousin had been around six or seven months ago, when she'd sent word with a messenger that her babies had been born. We'd rushed to Draconi to meet our nephews, the cute little things. I hadn't seen them since and couldn't wait to gift them with all the Iolish toys I brought with me.

I side-eyed Anneli. "I thought you'd be excited as well… given that you'll be seeing Kane."

A muscle in her jaw ticked, but she ignored me. It didn't matter how many times I asked, poked, or prodded; she hadn't told me what had happened between them. It was obvious that *something* had transpired between the two, but no one knew what. Not even Val.

"Leave her alone, my love." Adrian came up to my side, riding his own hybrid beast.

Since we'd reached warmer waters, we'd all taken off our warmer cloaks in favor of battle leathers and dresses. Well, I was the only one in a dress. A pretty thing of blue silk with diamonds and sapphires stitched all along the material so that every time I moved, every bit of it from the sleeves to the high neckline, shimmered like ice. Around my neck I wore two necklaces; a ring of carved, black obsidian, and a single conch of ice, carved anew by Val and threaded with science and magic and a message of love from him.

This past year had been evolutionary for our kingdom, for Adrian's as well. In Iol, we had created conches by the thousands and created a library of our own. When messages were sent to us, they did so in carved conches of ice that our kingdom exported across the seas. Homes had been rebuilt, the regime had changed, and the mer were happy, bellies full, and we had alliances in Thalassar, Kappur, Draconi, Saavaj'i, and were slowly working towards the other kingdoms.

Saavaj'i had changed as well. Without the threat of Alexxandria and with the new free movement acts, the mer formerly known as the Uncharted were allowed to roam freely between allied kingdoms and establish homes. It was still a working process, and Adrian's mer were still afraid of the unknown. Because he had decided to stay with me in Iol, he'd separated Saavaj'i into territories and chose a chief to rule over each one for the mer's protection.

The seven sea kingdoms still had a long way to go in accepting the mer into their territories wholly, completely. Adrian was still fighting for their fundamental rights in other kingdoms and searching for those missing immigrants that he believed were locked away in dungeons and camps.

"I can't help it. It's fun to tease her." I winked at Adrian.

He wore black leather gloves and clothes ready for battles in the colors of his kingdom: red, white, and umber. An obsidian and bone crown adorned his head.

"Save the teasing for your cousin," Anneli all but snapped.

I ignored her, putting down her nerves to the fact that she was going to see Kane again for the first time in a year. Either that or she was nervous about something else, like the fact that when our vacation in Draconi was over, she'd be traveling with Adrian down to Ventlair in a new venture of her own. She wanted to adopt lost and broken creatures around the seas and train them, opening up sanctuaries for their salvation and breeding.

I was betting on the former being the reason for her annoyance.

We swam in the tranquility of Draconi before we converged into the city, where there were mer and dragons in abundance and the Draconian palace was in our line of vision.

I picked up the pace until we were practically riding hard towards the doors. They opened for us and I couldn't jump off my mount fast enough. We were greeted by the emperor's guards, who led us into the palace to see Maisie immediately.

The meetings had become an informal thing. There was no going through the throne room to be announced before the emperor and his empress. Not anymore. Not since Maisie delivered her babies. He seemed to loosen the reins on his strict attitude when it came to us.

So they led us straight to my cousin.

They were in the royal playroom—yeah, Draconi had a royal playroom—with the children. It was a massive room with an abundance of bright toys and music for their entertainment.

They were in there now, and I announced our arrival with the loudest squeal I could muster. "Maaaiiiissssiiiiiiieeeeee!"

My cousin whirled around, and her smile brightened. Being a mother suited her. I knew all she'd ever wanted was a family, and now that she had three children, she practically *glowed*.

"Oh my gods! You cut your hair!"

Her long locks had been shorn into a short bob that curled and floated around her cheeks. It made her face look thinner, her cheekbones sharper...

"Why would you do that?" I demanded.

Her fingers went to it a bit self consciously. "You don't like it?"

"I love it, but now I'm going to have to cut mine, too."

Maisie rolled her eyes and Kai suddenly appeared, swimming up from behind Maisie. "That won't be necessary." His voice held a tone of threatening menace in it. I still remembered that last threat to me. To never make Maisie parade around as me again... I wouldn't be surprised if he'd forced her to cut it to avoid us doing that in the future.

The fool.

It would never stop.

Never.

I ignored him and focused on the babies he carried in each arm. They saw me and immediately held out their arms for my attention, screeching, "Aunnttttyyyy!"

"How are my favorite guppies?" I held my arms out, and they bounded out of Kai's to dart towards me. They were young and already strong, intelligent swimmers. I braced myself for the impact of their bodies against mine and wrapped them to my chest in a tight hug. "Odessie."

I kissed the top of the little mergirl on her dark purple head of hair. Big black eyes met mine from beneath dark lashes with absolute trust and the same mischievous expression her criminal father wore. I knew she was going to be trouble one day.

I turned my attention to the little merboy and kissed his dark, silky hair. "Takeshi. How's my favorite little dragon baby?" In response, his slanted brown eyes glowed blue and his features changed completely. Like a little dragon hatchling, he roared. "You've been practicing. Good." I looked around. "Where's Bay?"

"With his father somewhere, probably learning how to hold a sword," a deep voice drawled. Elias Blackfin prowled out from the shadows and greeted Adrian behind me with a nod then came forward and plucked his daughter from my arms. "How are you today, Odessa?" he asked with a smile.

His daughter, named after my aunt and Maisie's birth mother, reached for a dark lock of his hair and cooed.

"I've never seen anything so precious." My heart literally melted in my chest.

Maisie smirked at me knowingly. "When will *you* start having children? I want to be an aunt, too."

I recoiled at the words in horror, bumping into Ytgar behind me. "Gods, Maisie, don't say things like that. Children are cute, but I'm too young for that. I have things to do, places to see first. Besides, I'm fine with being a doting aunt. The best thing about these babies is that when they start crying, I can just toss them back to you." To prove a point, I lifted Takeshi in the water and let him go. Because he was still in his dragon form, he darted expertly straight towards his father, who caught him and twirled him in circles. "When my yearly time comes, I'm going to be locking myself in a closet and I won't be coming out until the week passes." I slashed a glare at my sides, in my husbands' directions. "These mer won't be touching me at all."

Adrian smirked, Ytgar glared, but Val held up his hands in surrender. "Whatever you want, beauty mine."

"Damn straight, whatever I want." My body, my rules. I'd made that clear to them from the beginning. Yes, I was queen, but that didn't mean I had to give in to the ridiculous 'obligation' of giving them heirs immediately. We still had our lives to live, a free world to forge. Children, if they came, would come later.

But looking at them now, I did feel a tug…

No. Stop. Right now.

I shook my head back and forth.

"Aunty Odele!"

I opened my eyes to find Tiberius swimming towards us, holding the hand of his son, Bay. The little merboy had a shock bright of purple hair and the brightest blue eyes I'd ever seen.

"Bay! Come to aunty!" I held my arms opened. Before he swam towards me, he looked to his father for permission. Tiberius nodded and he bounded off into my arms.

He was the more serious of his siblings. He'd been born first of the triplets and had all the personality of his father. In fact, most of the children had inherited their personalities from the three mermen. There were small pieces of Maisie within them. It was in the kindness of their souls. I knew they would be fair and just when they grew into adulthood.

"I brought toys!" I announced. "A whole carriage full!"

The children squealed and squirmed their way out of their parents' arms, even Bay kicked me with his fins to go celebrate with his siblings.

Maisie rolled her eyes. "More toys?" she asked. "They already have a lot."

I shrugged. "Your problem, not mine. I brought *instruments*; drums and a conch recorder that plays infant songs especially made for them!"

Maisie looked like she might strangle me. Kai appeared to be contemplating it. It was Tiberius who muttered, "We are never sleeping again."

"That's the idea." I clapped my hands just as the servants came in with all the toys we'd brought from Iol. "Let's go open them!"

The children swam excitedly over to the coral boxes as they were set down and their fathers accompanied them. Maisie hesitated a second to gift me with a glare and she mouthed the words, *I hate you.*

I mouthed back, *Liar.*

She rolled her eyes and swam to her family.

I started towards them, but strong hands wrapped around my stomach and pulled me to a solidly built chest. Ytgar. Warm breath fanned in one side of my ear. Adrian's. A hand slipped into mine. Val's.

"You're a very cruel mer," Adrian complimented.

"She'll get me back when we have our own children."

"So you *do* want children?" Ytgar nipped my other ear. I shouldered him off me.

"Maybe. Maybe not. Not sure I want to risk them coming out with your brooding Iolish attitude."

Adrian threw his head back and laughed, and I let the joyous sound follow me as I made my way over to my niece and nephews to show them their gifts.

This… this was my life now. I'd been so lonely before, so *alone* with nothing but crowns, silks, gowns, and jewels to keep me company. I had gained many fancy titles these past two years. Princess of Thalassar. Duchess of Frost. Queen of the Uncharted. Queen of Iol. Queen of Saavaj'i.

But none of that mattered as much as *this*, this moment right here as I sat down and surprised the children with their gifts. Nothing mattered to me right now as much as the smiles on their faces and the happiness that pulsated around us like a living, breathing thing.

My life had been perfect before, but I hadn't known the meaning of the word. Not then. But now, now I did. It was defined by the intricate moments in our lives when everything had fallen into place, when our hearts were light, and we knew of nothing and no one but this single moment of joy.

This moment?

This was perfect.

And I prayed to the gods it would always be this way.

Turn the page for an EXCLUSIVE unedited sneak peek at the brand new spin off series from Anneli's point of view

Royal Betrayals coming soon

Anneli

I WASN'T A FAN of Draconi.

It was beautiful, and I'd be the first to admit that it was. With its coral trees and drifting water lilies, bright colors and rich scents, with soaring dragons and delicious food… the place should have been perfect.

But it wasn't.

And it wasn't because of the scenery or the mer population. Rather, there was *one* mer in particular who I didn't want to see, but I was bound to swim into at the palace.

Kane Feng Han.

It had been a year. A long year since the night that shall not be named. The night after the Draconian soldier's fever had broken and I'd found him falling apart near the stables of Isolde Palace. It had been a moment of weakness, of vulnerability… and I didn't want to think about it.

I'd done a pretty good job of shoving things out of my mind. It was a special skill, a talent innately my own. For years I'd hid the fact that Prince—now King—Ytgar Neves Isolde was my half-brother. No one but Val knew that little secret, and he knew how to keep his mouth shut about it.

If I pushed that away, I could push this away as well.

Besides, I had no time to think about that, to think about *him* when I had other things to worry about. Things like this nerve-wracking new venture I'd decided to take on.

I'd grown up with orcas practically my entire life. I knew them, got along with them better than I got along with any mer I'd ever known, save for Valmundur, but honestly, the orphan I grew up with was part beast himself, so he didn't count.

Still, I loved working with animals. If I hadn't been born an orphan, I would have studied to be a veterinarian. But because I had been born to the wrong mother, the wrong father, and shoved into an orphanage like the shameful secret that I was, I hadn't had the opportunity.

Not like that had stopped me. The moment Val had invited me with him to Isolde Palace to be stablemer and help the trainers look after the orcas, I couldn't say no. Together we worked our fins off until we slowly ascended rank. From stablemer to groomsmer, all the way down the line of hierarchy until we became trainers ourselves. To be trainers, we had to learn how to heal the orcas, how to care for them.

Now I just wanted to put my knowledge to good use. I wanted to learn more, how to heal and how to care for broken creatures. To protect them from those who would harm them and to help them from going extinct.

After the war in Iol had ended and everything rebuilt, an empty restlessness had grown inside of me that couldn't be sated. It wasn't until I stayed up tossing and turning night after night in my small cot in the servant's quarters that I realized what that restlessness was.

Boredom.

A fierce desire for more than what I had.

As an orphan, it was a golden rule to always want more than you had, but to never wish for it too hard. That's how it'd been growing up, at least. In a way. When it came to material things, I was always receiving gifts from my father. Gifts and treats; half of them always went to Val. But when it came to his actual love, a family…I longed for it so desperately that it seemed the more I wished, the more far away my dreams became until I stopped wishing altogether.

Things were different now. I wasn't that same little mer from the orphanage who knew hunger, the cold, and beatings. I wasn't anyone's shameful secret to be shoved into a corner with the promise of short, sporadic visits. I'd worked and fought my way up to become the damn good whale trainer that I was, and nothing, *nobody* could ever take that from me.

So for the first time in my life, I planned. I stayed up all night thinking, drawing silty plans on a scrap of kelp parchment until I finally knew what it was I wanted.

A life away from Iol.

A life away from secrets I could never say and mer who would never wholly accept me.

Acceptance came easily to pets. They were trusting, loyal. I needed more of that in my life.

So I was leaving Iol and traveling with King Adrian to Ventlair. I hadn't wanted an escort at all, but Odele, Val, *and* Ytgar had insisted on it. He was traveling that way anyway. He had negotiations to do, and I had a job to find.

I had money saved, but I wasn't sure it would be enough to open up a sanctuary right away, so I'd go and look around for buildings or stables that could be purchased. My goal was to establish a sanctuary in every single sea kingdom.

It was a goal I mulled over as I brushed down our mounts with sponges.

While Odele and the others had swam straight into the palace to go see her cousin, I'd swam straight here. My place wasn't with them, no matter how many times she invited me. Not because they were royalty and because I was a servant, but because I didn't quite feel like there was a place for me there. It wasn't my home.

I was starting to wonder if I'd ever find it.

Shoving that thought aside, I hummed as I brushed through the slick skin of my mount. I took extra care with her because she'd been harmed in the war and was missing an eye. I probably should have left her behind, but just because she was crippled didn't make her less valuable or intelligent than the other mounts.

She was a good girl, desperate to prove herself.

"You and I have that in common, beauty." I slid the sponge over her snout, and she huffed.

"Have what in common?" A slow, prowling sound of a voice purred from the door of the stall.

I froze, sponge gripped tightly in my hand mid-stroke. A muscle in my eye twitched at the sound of the voice. At the *tone*. It was low and seductive, and it reminded me of another night, a year ago, when I'd let myself be swept away by the drawl of that voice and a broken merman who'd had nothing left to lose.

I had vowed to myself that night that I would never see him again. Not because he'd done anything wrong. On the contrary, he'd done everything *right*, but for other reasons entirely.

And now here he was again, his voice a dangerous trepidation that slid down my spine and prompted me to slowly turn to face him.

He floated in the doorway, one shoulder propped up against the edge and his arms crossed against his chest as if he hadn't a care in the world. A far cry better from the last time I'd seen him. His skin had been sallow then, but now it had regained that light brown tinge to it. His hair was a violet-black color like his tail and tied back with a white ribbon.

He wore a loose white tunic that tightened across his muscular chest and did nothing to conceal the curves of his strong arms. He was built as solidly as Ytgar, but more dangerously as well. It was in his dark slanted eyes, the promise of thrill and seduction, and I ignored it completely to take him in.

The tunic he wore swept down his tail so it covered the worst of his scars. Scars that had been inflicted on him during the war, when the barbed tail of a wyvern slashed across his flesh and completely shredded the right side of his fins. I could just make out the jagged tips of the scars but couldn't see his fins at all.

He'd lost his dragon that day, a black beast named Ryuu. That alone had made my heart ache for him.

He looked fine now, though. Renewed. Invigorated. A year could do that to a mer. It could change them for the better, or for the worse.

That sinfully pretty mouth of his curled up into a smile, and he prowled menacingly into the stall. I didn't press back, didn't flinch. I let him stalk forward like a predator until he invaded my personal space and was looming over me.

I felt the heat of his body, his proximity, and I remembered every shudder, every stroke, every breathless gasp...

He bent low so that our lips were but a whisper apart. "It's nice to see you again," he whispered, "my lady."

I swallowed past the lump in my throat, eyes darting down to his mouth before flicking back up to his eyes. "Hello," I replied tightly, almost venomously. "Kane."

Royal Lies

Slave to Ice & Shadows

Princess in Frost Castles

Queen of Frozen War
Origins of the Six series

<u>Academy of Six</u>

<u>Control of Five</u>

<u>Destruction of Two</u>

<u>Wrath of One</u>
A Daughter of Triton series

Triton's Academy

<u>Triton's Prophecy</u>

<u>Triton's Legacy</u>

A Daughter of Triton Box set
Reverse Harem Standalones

Queenie & the Krakens

Lourdes & the Mafia

Paranormal Romance Series

Deep Sea Chronicles

<u>Fall in Deep</u>

<u>Siren Queen</u>
The Blood Novels

<u>Love Bites</u>

<u>Blood Drug</u>

<u>My Master</u>

<u>Last Hope</u>

Young Adult standalone

<u>The Last Mermaid</u>

Aleera Anaya Ceres is the USA Today Bestselling author of several series including the Origins of the Six series and the Daughter of Triton series. Like most introverts, Aleera prefers to curl up with a good book, listen to music, paint, read tarot cards, and snack on the tears and heartbreak of her readers. A proud Mexican-American from the state of Kansas, Aleera currently resides in Tlaxcala, Mexico with her husband and children.

You can find/contact her here:
aleeraanayaceres.com
aleeraceres@aacbooks.com

www.ingramcontent.com/pod-product-compliance
Lightning Source LLC
Chambersburg PA
CBHW030543310726
48979CB00010B/2015/J